PAINT THE WIND

Other books by Cathy Cash Spellman

NOTES TO MY DAUGHTERS
SO MANY PARTINGS
AN EXCESS OF LOVE

PAINT THE WIND

Cathy Cash Spellman

Delacorte Press

Published by
Delacorte Press
Bantam Doubleday Dell Publishing Group, Inc.
666 Fifth Avenue
New York, New York 10103

Copyright © 1989 by Cathy Cash Spellman

All rights reserved. No part of this book may be reproduced or transmitted
in any form or by any means, electronic or mechanical, including
photocopying, recording, or by any information storage and retrieval
system, without the written permission of the Publisher, except
where permitted by law.

The trademark Delacorte Press® is registered in the U.S.
Patent and Trademark Office.

Designed by Richard Oriolo

Manufactured in the United States of America
Published simultaneously in Canada

Quality Printing and Binding by:
Berryville Graphics
P.O. Box 272
Berryville, VA 22611 U.S.A.

This is a work of fiction. Only the people
mentioned below actually lived:

Geronimo
Naiche
General George Crook
General Nelson Miles
H.A.W. Tabor
Baby Doe Tabor
Augusta Tabor
John McCombe
John Arkins
George Fryer
Jerome B. Chaffee
David H. Moffat
Jim Grant

All others lived only in my imagination.

Acknowledgments

The Native Americans say that a story stalks a writer and, if it finds you worthy, comes to live in your heart. The author's responsibility is to give that story voice.

Many generous friends have contributed to the expression of the voice of *Paint the Wind* . . . to them, and to the story that sought me out, I am more grateful than I could ever say.

Carole Baron, my friend and publisher, who wrestled this one out of me with love and intuition . . . and never stopped believing. Whose inspired editing and general all-around genius made Fancy and me the very best we can be.

Donna Boccamazzo, Hart, Chance, and Fancy's greatest friend in the world . . . whose constant loving belief in me and my story and generous hard work on the manuscript did more to bring this book into being than anyone else. No one deserves more credit, praise, and heartfelt thanks.

Tom Brown, Wanda Terhaar, and *Karen Sherwood* of The Tracker School, who provided invaluable information on survival in the Colorado Rockies in winter.

Roe Callahan, who not only read and encouraged, but made certain that Fancy's adventurous journey was architecturally correct.

Forrest Carter, who first introduced me to Geronimo and the Apaches through his extraordinary work, and who made me understand the Way.

Marion Casey, who carefully checked to see that all things happened in their proper historical time.

Professor John Dunkhase, who was kind enough to share his silver-mining expertise and his knowledge of Leadville with me and my story.

Isabel Geffner, who is *always* there for me . . . with the most loving encouragement, the truest talent, and the most constant friendship.

Elbys Hugar, great-granddaughter of the legendary Chiracahua chief, Cochise, who generously shared tribal truths with me, some of which had never been told in the White Man's histories of the Apaches.

Bea Hurwitz, who pursued permission for the quotes I've used, with a dauntless expertise that Wes and Gitalis would be proud of.

Mort Janklow and *Anne Sibbald,* who, as always, believed in me and my work, when it really counted.

Frank Keller, Jr., who gave unstintingly of his vast knowledge of wilderness life, and who shares with me the fantasy of having lived in the West, when it was still its wildest and purest.

Johanna Lee, my dearest pal through the ages, who as always, gets the medal for loving support, good cheer, and sage spiritual advice.

Alexis Megan Palmer, my special friend, who showed me just how smart, resourceful, and beautiful a nine/ten/eleven-year-old can be.

Marilyn Pearlman, my shamanic drumming companion, who provided me just the right expert at the right time.

Dr. John Pirri, Jr., my friend, Doc, the most wonderful expert on firearms in the world, who made me fall in love with guns and their lore, and who shared with me his encyclopedic knowledge of the Old West so that my characters, like Doc, could "ride, shoot straight, and speak the truth." I couldn't have written an authentic tale of the West without him.

Patricia Soliman, magic as Magda, my "Georgian silver ear trumpet" of the spirit, whose astute and tender understanding of my story, and whose brilliant and generous insights made the editing process both joyous and enlightening.

Dr. Warren Steinberg, who very kindly took time from the busiest schedule in North America to make sure Fancy's medical adventures were true to her time.

Ched Vuckovic, my dear friend, and unquenchable creative mentor . . . who is always there to pitch in and make things beautiful.

Eleanore Wrench and *Clifford Bias,* whose extraordinary teachings about metaphysics and magic are reflected throughout my story.

To my adored family, no thanks could possibly suffice . . .

Conny Cash, the best sister on earth, who lovingly read and reread, thinking, suggesting, understanding, and caring . . . who remains, like Mary Poppins, the only "practically perfect person" I know.

Harry Cash, my father, my teacher, my friend . . . so loving, so generous, so wise . . . who fills my world with sunshine and with goodness. How could I ever say thank you enough for all you've given me?

Joe Spellman, my beloved husband . . . whose unwavering faith, tenderness, and love make all the difference. There are no words adequate to express my gratitude for making this, and all my dearest dreams come true. I love you, Joe . . . all there is.

This book is dedicated to my mother

Catherine Cash
1912–1988

Dear Kate,
This one's for you. In love and gratitude.
For all you taught and gave and tried to do.
May you find time in Heaven to read it, when
the Good Lord isn't after you for advice.

From the Journal of
Matthew Hart McAllister

They called her Any Man's Fancy—but it wasn't true, of course. She loved two men in her life and perhaps a third, at least a little. But that's hardly very much in a life like hers, and not near as many as there might have been if she'd been less particular.

Because of her I bankrupted one man, ruined another's reputation, and killed a third, and would again if it needed doing. But that's the end of my tale and not the start, so perhaps we'd best get to the beginning. . . .

Hart McAllister let the pen come to rest and raised his eyes, unseeing, above the paper. It was not the wall of his study that met his unfocused gaze.

He was a man of mammoth proportion. Age had blurred the strong jaw, tarnished the auburn hair with featherings of gray, and dimmed the deep blue of the eyes that had once been keen enough to scout for Geronimo and paint two works that hung side by side in the Louvre. But time had not substantially altered the six-foot-six-inch frame, the buffalo shoulders and head that were carried with the quiet dignity of one meant by fate to rise above other men. He resumed his writing.

My brother, Chance, and I were born in Kansas in the late 1840's fifteen months apart, he being the older. It was a hard land in those days, a place of outlaws and raging prairie winds; a land that asked lifeblood in return for its bounty. That world has long since vanished . . . cities thrive where cattle grazed, corn and wheat fields stretch their golden harvest toward forever, so you could be fooled into thinking that was the way God made it. But back then, it was a life of sunbaked hardship. No tree for a bird to sing in and no reward you hadn't wrestled out of Fate's uncompromising hand.

My brother's christening name was Charles Yancy McAllister, but Chance is all anybody ever called him. And with good reason. He was a daredevil

*when young and a gambler later on. There was deviltry in his nature, but no
meanness.*

*He was the best brother a man ever had in thick or thin. And nothing ever
really came between us . . . not even Fancy. But that's a long story and
maybe not one you'll understand. . . .*

Hart paused and his great head sank toward his chest, in reverent memory. How do I tell their story now? he wondered. How can a generation bred in safety understand what forges characters the likes of Chance and Fancy . . . Fancy and Chance . . . a sound somewhere between a sigh and a groan escaped him.

"Christ!" he whispered to the silent room. "How I loved them both."

Hart McAllister remained unmoving for a while, lost in the long ago. It was the hardship of the times that had tempered them into steel—the hardships, and the longings that had driven them to desperate acts.

History isn't written in history books—it's seared into the hearts of men and women . . . branded deep and washed with their sweat, their toil, their heart's blood.

Resolutely, the old man raised his pen again and let his mind drift back and back and back to what might be called the beginning. There were two beginnings, really. Theirs and Fancy's. She was the center of it all . . . the catalyst and the lodestar. Without Fancy, perhaps none of it ever would have happened. Or, if it did, perhaps it wouldn't have broken his heart. . . .

I

STORMBIRD ON THE WIND

▾▾▾▾▾▾

Fancy and Atticus 1864
Natchitoches, Louisiana

"A homemade friend wears
the longest."

BANDANA McBAIN

Ten-year-old Fancy Deverell woke with a startled cry, roused violently from peaceful dreams. Rough hands muffled her mouth as someone ripped the bedclothes from her small body. Fancy bucked against her captor and fought for breath; terror made the blood pulse painfully in her neck and chest.

"Hush, child!" a familiar voice hissed urgently. "Atticus come to save you!" The hovering form that gripped her straightened to its immense height, and the child recognized Atticus, the plantation blacksmith, conjurer and general factotum.

Shouts and screams and the sharp report of gunfire rent the night outside her bedroom. "Where's Maman?" she gasped, wondering what on earth she needed to be saved from. Life had seemed safe enough a few hours before when Mammy Erline had tucked her in, and opened her windows to the pungent scent of clove on the bayou breeze of Beau Rivage.

"We git your mama if'n we kin," Atticus answered gruffly. Fancy saw flames leap in the yard beyond her window and didn't struggle this time as Atticus yanked the coverlet unceremoniously over her head. Instead, she burrowed into the sheltering arms and pressed her face into Atticus' chest as hard as she could to make the terror go away.

She felt herself bouncing as he ran; heard his breath rasped by smoke, heard shrieks and shouts and gunshots and the curses of laughing men, felt the searing heat of flames.

She sobbed softly into the muffling strength of Atticus' body, but was afraid to cry aloud.

"Dey's gwine to search ever'thin'!" Atticus muttered. His speech had slipped from the language he prided himself on knowing, into the heavy dialect the slaves used with one another. Atticus' wife, a second-generation slave, had taught him better speech than most.

"I want my maman and papa!" the child demanded, trying to shake her head free. "They'll know what to do!"

"Hush, child. Lemme think!" Then, as if the very statement had brought with it the sought-after idea, Atticus whispered triumphantly, "De old cistern!" He yanked the blanket back over her head and started off at a run.

"Dey's killed ever'body dey could find. An' dey's stole everythin' in sight. Dey's not gwine to leave any witnesses to tell on 'em. Dey's jes' white trash in soldiers' uniforms!"

Atticus set the child down abruptly and shook her free of the counterpane. She blinked hard and tried to catch her breath; the word *killed* stuck in her heart, but the haunted look in the old slave's eyes stayed her protest. He knelt for a moment to her level, and some instinct told her it cost him dearly to waste precious seconds, for he glanced right, left, and behind like a fox with the hounds in close pursuit.

"We got to stay alive, Miz Fancy! You understan' dat?"

The child tucked her bottom lip resolutely up under her top teeth and nodded, two large tears reflecting silver in the moonlight. Atticus put his great arms around her so hard, it knocked the breath in a whoosh from her body. He knew she didn't understand at all, but trusted. How could she understand that all life as she'd known it had just ended?

Atticus scooped Fancy up and set her onto his powerful back. The sudden height dizzied her and she clung tightly as he began the treacherous descent into the abandoned cistern. Her arms all but choked off Atticus' labored breath and caused a ringing in his ears that hammered along with the distant sounds of battle.

Damn Yankees! Drunk and leaderless, riding in on horseback waving pistols and sabers, saying they were going to take every last thing they could carry. Or maybe they hadn't been Yankees at all, but renegade Confederates dressed up to give their looting the sanction of wartime.

And the massa, only home from the regiment because of a wounded leg, hobbling out on the verandah to meet them, with the missus in her night wrapper close behind. If Capt'n Deverell hadn't sassed that trash, they might have left him and the missus in peace and settled for looting.

Atticus had known when the shouting started where it would end. Those men were nothing more than dressed-up white riffraff, sneaking around without their captain, looking for a good time and a few spoils. Taking advantage of the fact that since the fall of Vicksburg and Port Hudson there was no law left in Louisiana to punish them.

The Federal Army was in control of the Mississippi, New Orleans, and the Gulf. Winn, Jackson, and many of the other northern parishes had become infested with draft dodgers, deserters, and bands of jayhawkers who roamed the countryside looting and burning. Now the plantation owners needed to fear both the Yankees and the renegade Confederates.

The old stones of the cistern's depths were icy to the touch, despite the steamy night air above, and they were slimy with ancient damp. Atticus repressed a shudder and continued his descent, hoping no water moccasins had made their home in the well.

The child's weight dragged his big frame down, and his breath came hard. Even if you're a strong old boy, he told himself with a grim smile, sixty years is no age for climbing down holes with a ten-year-old child on your back. Thank God she was small for her age and slightly built.

Atticus' feet touched water. He assessed the handhold he had on the cold and crumbling rock surface, trying to judge how long it would be before his fingers could no longer grasp the precarious perch; he spread-eagled his legs, seeking purchase on either side.

"I'm real scared, Atticus," Fancy's tremulous voice whispered into his ear. *Dey's done killed ever'body dey could find* . . . kept ringing in her head, but she couldn't make herself ask, for fear of the answer.

"Me too, honey," he replied softly. "But we cain't talk none 'til we hears 'em go."

He felt her nod. The numbness from the stagnant water was already beginning to creep into his legs; he'd have to dose himself with comfrey and molasses when they got out of the hole, to keep the rheumatism from his bones. Atticus had a little cabin hung with herbs, with strange names like witch's bane and mugwort, that he used in making remedies. Massa Deverell had said more than once that the old slave knew more about healing with nature's remedies than any doctor in New Orleans.

Atticus felt the stifled sobs of the child through his clothes, but could think of no adequate words of comfort. Sometimes it was best to cry things out; sometimes it was the only sane thing to do. He wondered what would be left by morning of what had once been Beau Rivage.

The plantation house that was the envy of the parish sat on the crest of a hill just high enough to provide a splendid view of the rolling green countryside that seemed to reach infinity after crossing over the river tributary that had provided the plantation its name.

The stately Greek Revival mansion, with its sturdy white columns and gracious vine-shaded verandahs, was surrounded on all sides by Louisiana's lush foliage. Succulent magnolias to grace the springtime, elegant elms and beeches to lend stature to the fall. Avenues of sweet olive trailed their silvery veils of Spanish moss like stately dowagers on a traipse to the water's edge . . . crepe myrtle and honeysuckle wafted fragrance sublime as a benediction on the soft bayou afternoons.

The Deverells of Beau Rivage were third-generation planters, long enough on the land to believe it theirs forever. They were a family both God-fearing and well blessed by Him. James Deverell had inherited a plantation of the crop known as The Big Grass, and a considerable fortune to go with it; but he'd worked hard to improve both and was proud in the knowledge that he would leave to his son, Armand, and his daughter, Françoise, the most beautiful and profitable sugar plantation in all Louisiana.

Françoise had the dark hair and eyes of her continental mother, who had christened her thus in a gallant effort to maintain the standards of the French heritage she'd brought with her from Paris and Savannah.

"Dat's a mighty fancy name for sech a tiny child," Atticus had told his master when he heard it, and somehow, Fancy was what she'd been called ever since.

Atticus and Fancy had always been friends. The slave was old, but he was the nicest darkie they owned and the best blacksmith in the parish. Even James Deverell was proud of his slave's accomplishments. The rumor in the quarters was that he knew magic; the child had heard him called "the conjurer" by some of the older slaves who still remembered Africa, but no one would ever tell her what that meant.

Maman, Papa, where are you? Why don't you come for me? Fancy shuddered in the icy dark of the cistern, and clung to Atticus. Her arms hurt from the holding and her back was cramped; her throat felt raw and her head ached. She laid it against the old slave's shoulder for comfort and drifted off to fitful slumber.

Just before dawn the soldiers moved on. Atticus forced his reluctant limbs to move, and with numb and bleeding fingers pulled himself and Fancy to the surface of the cistern.

A thick haze of acrid smoke hung in the air like evil swamp mist. It stung both eyes and lungs and left a silt of black filaments on the wilted grass. The remains of Beau Rivage smoldered dismally on its hilltop; the red sun rising beyond the plantation house grimly echoed the flames that had wrought the ruin. Fancy looked incredulously at the distorted, blackened shell that had been her home.

"Atticus, help me find Maman and Papa!" Fancy saw tears glistening on the old slave's wrinkled cheeks; she reached for his hand and squeezed it hard.

Resolutely they began the walk up the hill toward the ruined house. There was a dreadful and unaccustomed stillness in the air; no bird or insect rent the morning quiet, only the distant crackle of still-smoking embers disturbed the dawn.

The slave quarters were deserted; all who could had fled to the river or the swamp beyond. Atticus felt Fancy's grip tighten as they passed the dead body of Andrews, the overseer; she had never seen death before.

As they reached the hilltop, the remains of the once grandiose portico of Beau Rivage came into clearer focus. "Oh, Lord Jesus!" Atticus breathed in shocked realization. He grabbed for the little girl to shield her eyes, but she'd already seen the shape on the steps.

"Maman! Maman!" Fancy screamed as she tore herself from Atticus' grasp and ran toward the fallen body. "Maman, I'm here!"

Lying like a ravaged doll, her dimity dressing gown pulled up about naked hips, Gabrielle Deverell lay, quite dead. Her pantalets, torn from her body, waited forlorn and damaged several feet away. Fancy lurched to a halt as she reached her mother . . . there was a bullet hole in her chest;

dark red blood had gushed and puddled around her, dried now and darkened to the color of Bordeaux.

Fancy felt the shriek rise up and tear itself free of its own volition. The
sound was everything. It blotted out the truth, the day, the body of her
mother . . . she would never stop screaming. Never! *Never.* Never . . .
She didn't even feel the ground as she fell, nor Atticus' arms as he scooped
her up and pressed her hard against his body. He knew the sound of despair
too well to try to stay its voice—if you didn't let anguish out, it could kill
you.

It was a long time before the screaming died in the child's throat and the
thrashing limbs lay still in the black giant's arms. He crooned a strange
song of soothing into her ear. Fancy heard it vaguely through her sobs; the
words were foreign and rhythmic. Almost against her will she let them seep
into her agony, and in a little while a blackness came and she drifted into it
for comfort.

Atticus laid the unconscious child gently on the ground; she would sleep
awhile, for he had chanted the healing magic into her ear and it would do its
work long enough for him to gather what he must and bury the massa and
the missus.

He scanned the grounds for signs of Massa Deverell and saw the man's
crumpled body on the ravaged verandah. Atticus wondered briefly if the
massa had been forced to watch his house being ransacked, his wife raped
and murdered before he was left to die in the burning house he'd been born
in—the house the Deverells had thought they'd own forever.

▲

Fancy stood at the side of the newly mounded graves; when she awakened, the bodies of her father and mother were gone away somewhere.
Atticus said he'd buried them, but she couldn't think about that now . . .
later she would think about where her maman and papa had gone . . .
later she would find them.

The sickening scent of burning sugar cane filled the air around them. In
her fist Fancy clutched a lock of hair Atticus said had been her mother's.
She stared at the thick brown curl, so pathetic in her hand; it was unlike the
lustrous dark crown of bouncing ringlets her mother had worn so proudly,
and seemed alien, yet she clutched it tightly.

"French women are the most beautiful of all," her papa had told Fancy
once, as he'd watched her mother at the dressing table fixing her elaborate
coiffure. "And men desire them more than any others."

Fancy stuffed the lock of hair into her pocket with the tiny music box she
had salvaged; Atticus said the exquisite musical trinket had been dropped
from a soldier's sack of spoils.

The old man stood stooped by the finished graves, sweat making the muscles of his knotted shoulders and arms gleam. Horrid, ropelike welts crisscrossed his back and glinted in the sun and sweat.

"Poorly as we feelin' right now, child, you and me got to decide what we do next," he said, looking up from the freshly turned earth.

Fancy nodded but didn't try to speak. She saw that Atticus had salvaged certain items from the ruins: a knife, scissors, needles and threads, some slave clothes to replace her own that had burned with the house, and a pair of shoes he must have snatched from her room when he'd rescued her. He'd found his old banjo lying miraculously unharmed near his cabin, and his medicaments had been left undisturbed. Everything else of value had perished or been taken.

"Now, Miz Fancy, we got to git you to somewheres, quick. You could go to your mama's people, if we know'd where dey abide." He cocked his head toward her questioningly. "Y'all know where your mama come from?"

Fancy shook her head. "I only know it's called La Retourne and it's north of Savannah."

"Lot a territory north of Savannah. Don't know rightly how we ever find it wif dis old war goin' on. Y'all could go stay wif Massa Redmond over at Tremayne, I reckon. Less'n, of course, the same thing's happened over dere, and likely it did." Tremayne was their nearest neighboring plantation, but the main house was more than fifteen miles from Beau Rivage. Atticus had seen smoke rising from that direction when he'd emerged from the cistern— that would explain why no help had come.

"I don't like Johnny Redmond, Atticus. He was mean to me at the Fourth of July barbecue, and those Redmond girls are the very limit!"

Atticus chuckled a little; his uneven teeth gleamed against his charcoal skin. "It don't hardly matter if dem girls is de limit or not, honey child, 'cause beggars cain't be choosy."

"I am *not* a beggar!" Fancy replied sharply, stung by the thought. "I'm Françoise Deverell of Beau Rivage and I am not a beggar!" The arrogance of privilege made her eyes defiant.

"Miz Fancy!" Atticus said sharply. "Beau Rivage is *gone.* Your mama and daddy are *gone.* Your brother, Massa Armand, he off God knows where wif his regiment. Dis a serious business, missy, you got to understand!"

"What are *you* going to do, Atticus?" she asked, her voice made small by his distress.

"I expects I'se goin' west, child. To Californy or one of dem places where de sun shine all de time and dere's gold for de takin'. Ain't got no family what needs me now. My wife gone ten years past. All my children sold off long ago . . ." He stopped for a moment and Fancy wondered why Atticus seemed upset by the memory. It was normal for young black bucks to be sold away when they came of age, especially if they were good breeding stock. She knew her daddy'd considered Atticus' eleven sons the best he'd ever bred on Beau Rivage.

"I always thought I'd like to see what all's out west, if I ever git free."

"Are you free, now, Atticus?"

"Guess I am now, Miz Fancy. Leastways dat's what dem soldiers say last night. I heard 'em, when dey run into de quarter. 'Y'all's free,' dey yelled out. 'Pack yo' black asses outa here. Y'all's free.' "

"Then I guess I'd best go with you," Fancy said, trying to sound reasonable. " 'Til we find somebody we know, at least."

Atticus looked at the small miserable child for a long moment; Savannah was as far away as the moon, and with a war on, just as hard to get to. The neighbors would take her, but if he brought her to them, he might be recaptured, and he'd waited too long for freedom to let that happen. He couldn't leave her behind alone. . . .

"I expects you're right about dat, child," the old man replied finally. "I don't rightly know what else to do wif you." He shook his balding head at the strange ways of the Lord and began to gather up what they would need to take along.

They tied what they could carry into bundles, including as many herbs and roots from Atticus' supply as he thought essential. He dosed them both with vile-tasting medicine and they set out in a westerly direction along the riverbank. They would keep to the bayou, away from the main roads, he told her, to avoid any soldiers still in the neighborhood.

"When dis ol' war's over, Miz Fancy, we jest see if we kin find your kinfolk," he said to make her feel better, but he knew in his heart that it would be a very long time before Fancy Deverell would feel better about anything at all.

2 Fancy looked with repugnance at the dark brown paste that Atticus had worked over so laboriously since they'd made camp for the night. Everything about their life so far had been frightening or wearying or both.

She tugged off her soiled shoes and wiggled her toes tentatively. She felt as if they'd tramped a thousand miles, not seven or eight as Atticus said it had been.

Night had fallen around them and the country rang with uncertain sounds. Screeching sounds, and slithering sounds that brought her legs up tight against her body . . . bird sounds and insect sounds and swamp sounds, all scary. Fancy had lived on the bayou all her life, but never before had she been at the mercy of its sounds.

Atticus had built a fire to warm them and had tried to show her how, but she'd been too tired to pay attention.

"What is that smelly stuff?" she asked finally, wrinkling her nose at the concoction the old man had made from roots and leaves.

"Dis here's a stain for yo' white skin, child."

"No!" Fancy's cry of horror was genuine. White skin was a southern belle's most prized possession; she shielded it from the sun with bonnets and gloves and parasols; she coaxed it into perfection with creams and unguents.

Atticus looked up from his work, directly into Fancy's startled eyes.

"Now you listen to me real good, Miz Fancy," he said, his voice as stern as she'd ever heard it. "If we was to be found traveling together like we is, a black man an' a li'l white child, dey'd string me up for kidnappin' before you could blink yo' eye.

"You tol' me you want to travel wif me, child, and I done said awright. But the only least way I kin see dey let you stay wif me, is if dey believe you is a black child. You gotta be my grandbaby, what lost her mama and daddy and is headin' west wif her granddaddy. Otherwise you got to turn yourself around right now and go on over to Massa Redmond and stay wif him."

Fancy considered these facts solemnly . . . there was no doubt Atticus was right. She'd seen what happened to nigras caught messing with white folk, and no one would listen to a child's explanation of the truth.

"If you put that stuff on me, Atticus, will I be black forever?"

"No indeed, Miz Fancy," the old man said quietly, his face unreadable. "Lord knows nobody in his right mind would do *dat* to a person!"

He started to rub the paste onto her arm; Fancy shut her eyes so she wouldn't see it happen.

"What's more, child, I gots to stop calling you Miz Fancy and call you jest plain Fancy from here on in. Ain't no little colored gals called Missy around here."

Digesting the full impact of her sudden demotion, Fancy blinked her eyes open and stared at Atticus. As long as she was white, he was her servant . . . what would he be to her if she became black?

"I don't want to be colored!"

"Ain't nobody *want* to be colored, Fancy—not if dey live in Loosiana!" Atticus' voice held something Fancy hadn't heard there before. Was he becoming what her father called an "uppity nigger?" she wondered. He sounded different than before. Stronger. In charge. Maybe that was better somehow; she just wasn't sure.

"I'll stay with you," she said finally, and her voice, which she had intended to sound imperious, sounded only small and scared.

Miserably, she submitted to Atticus' careful ministrations. Face, scalp, neck, arms, hands, and legs, all smeared with the dismal stain and then washed clean in the chilly creek. Fancy kept her eyes tight shut the whole time and Atticus said nothing of the tear that slid down her cheek. When she opened her eyes to see the damage, she wasn't black, but a dark honey color like a pecan.

Atticus surveyed his work critically. "Thank de Lord you got dark hair and dark eyes, Fancy. But yo' nose and mouth like a white child's, so we cain't make your skin too black or it look suspicious. If anybody ask us about you, we jest tell 'em you is a high yeller."

"What's that?" asked Fancy disdainfully as she strained her neck to look over her shoulder in an effort to view the backs of her darkened legs.

"A high yeller is a child what has a black mama and a white daddy."

"Oh," she replied, her voice choked back because she knew such children were laughed at by both colors. Quadroons, octaroons . . . every plantation had them, although her mother had never allowed her to speak of them. Fancy's eyes were suddenly downcast, and a soft pink flush rose under the darkened skin of her cheeks.

"Atticus' lesson number one, Fancy," he said very gently, bending down to her level as he spoke, so he could coax the downturned eyes to look into his own.

"Who you be is inside you. It ain't got nothin' to do wif de color of your skin or de clothes you wear or who your mama and daddy is. It got to do wif what's in your heart and what's in your head. You hear me, child?" He put his leathery hand under her chin and tipped her face up toward his own. She tried to avoid the intensity of his eyes but could not.

"You jest de same child you was before I put dat old stain on you, 'cause inside you still Fancy Deverell. Jest 'cause Beau Rivage and your mama and daddy gone, you ain't changed none. You still carry dem all inside you, where it count.

"I'se a orphan, too, Fancy. I got took from my mama and daddy way back in Africa so long ago, I cain't hardly count de years, but dey live inside me still. My daddy was a king in my tribe and a great warrior. And de pride of him lives inside dis old blacksmith every day of his life in de white man's world. Every single day!"

Fancy's great teary eyes blinked hard; she'd never thought of Atticus as having a mother and father. Or as being a king's son. Maybe he was still lonesome for his family, as she was for hers. Maybe this horrible empty ache she felt would still pain her when she was as old as Atticus.

"But I *feel* different now," she whispered shyly.

"Sometimes folks git to be different, even though dey stays de same," he replied enigmatically.

"I don't understand."

"What's *different* is de learnin' dat comes of life, Fancy. It changes de way you sees things, 'cause you know more than you did before. De *same* part is what lives inside of you, dat no man can mess wif. Not if dey beat you, or starve you or laugh at you, or try to make you feel ashamed. Dat part, Fancy, is like a holy thing. And dat part never, never changes . . . not even when you gits old like me."

Fancy nodded. She would try to remember the words, for they seemed to come from Atticus' heart . . . and, for the moment, they were all she had to hold on to.

▲

"Atticus!" Fancy's voice was imperious and cranky. "You come back here this minute and pick up my bag. It's too heavy for me!"

Atticus eyed the child speculatively, as if to decide when to begin her education about life.

"First place, Fancy," he said in a dignified voice. "You got no call to take dat tone wif me. I'se a free man now."

She looked astonished and didn't venture a reply.

"Second place, if we is to travel together we got to share de load. 'Cause I'se bigger, I kin carry mos' things. But we got to share and share alike. Dat's jest fair."

"That is *not* fair! You're a darkie and you're supposed to do the work!"

Atticus chuckled.

"You a darkie now, too, Fancy, so I reckon y'all better find out how it feels to have folks expectin' you to work."

"I won't carry it!"

"Then I guess you jest won't have no clothes to change into next time you wants to. All your clothes in dat bundle, ain't dey?"

"It's too heavy."

"Den you best figure out what you kin leave behind, honey. What you need, you got to carry wif you. Dat ain't my law, dat's life." The amused expression on his face made her angrier.

"Then I won't go!"

"Den I guess I jest have to leave you behind." He calmly picked up the huge bundle of all their other belongings and moved toward the edge of the clearing where they'd camped.

The fury of being disregarded made Fancy reckless and mean. "You can't leave me here, you uppity nigger!"

She saw Atticus stop, still as an oak, then straighten himself under the huge pack he shouldered. Without looking back, he walked on.

Fancy stood, defiant hands on hips, watching the retreating figure until she was certain he'd really meant what he said. Then, biting her underlip nervously, she hastily gathered up her small bag, looked around the campsite to make sure she hadn't left any precious belongings behind, and ran after him. She was beginning to learn that every possession was an important one; if you lost a hairpin, there would be no new one to replace it. If you lost a shawl, you'd have no protection from the cold and damp. Instinctively, she pulled her shawl tighter around her as she ran.

She saw Atticus glance over his shoulder at her as she caught up, but he said nothing, simply slowed his long strides to accommodate her shorter steps.

"I'm sorry, Atticus," the child murmured grudgingly. "I shouldn't have called you that."

They walked on in silence for a few minutes, then Atticus spoke, choosing his words carefully.

"Callin' names' a bad business, Fancy. It's real cowardly to sass a man 'cause of somethin' he cain't help, like his skin bein' a different color. I expects y'all be findin' dat out now, soon enough."

Fancy glanced down at the color of her own small hand, and gulped back her pride.

"I accepts your apology," Atticus said with lofty dignity, and he reached for Fancy's hand; she was surprised at the surge of comfort she felt as the great leathery fingers closed around her own.

▲

"Hey you, nigger!" The hostile white voice pierced the air and turned heads in their direction. Instinctively, Fancy moved behind Atticus. The short, scruffy white man with the bushy black beard was pointing at them. "That child don't look like no nigger baby to me."

The man attached to the voice looked at the bedraggled pair with narrowed eyes. "You! Young'un," he called to Fancy. "You come over here, let me get a look-see at you."

"Oh, no, sir, massa," Fancy whispered from behind Atticus in her best nigra voice. "I'se a black child sho 'nuff."

Atticus placed his hand protectively on her shoulder.

"She's a high yeller, mister. Her daddy a white man. She's my grandbaby."

The man smirked a lascivious and knowing grin. "Well, now, that explains it. You must be real proud, boy, that a white man fucked your little girl and give her such a pretty child."

Atticus fought down the blood-red urge to crush this arrogant little man's head between his two great hands. "Oh, yessir. I'se mighty proud," he said.

Atticus shuffled backward obsequiously, shooing Fancy behind him as he went. He knew that such behavior pleased the kind of men who made such statements.

"Shame she ain't a touch older," the man shouted to him as they backed out the door. "Might be I'd fuck the little bastard just like her mama got fucked. She looks right frolicsome."

Out the door at last, Atticus scooped up Fancy in his arms and walked hurriedly away, the ugly sound of the man's laughter ringing in his ears, beneath the rage.

▲

"I hate being poor!" Fancy stamped her small foot against the rock for emphasis.

Fancy picked up her faded blue dress from the small pile of belongings and threw it to the ground.

"I won't wear these stupid rags anymore either. And I won't be laughed at by stupid white trash not fit to shine my boots!"

"You ain't got no boots," Atticus replied with equanimity. He knew the outburst had been occasioned by a trip to town, where Fancy had been teased by the children of a farmer at the general store. She'd been sullen all the way home.

"But I *will* have them. And everything else I want! You mark my words, I'll get back everything I was supposed to have. And more. And I don't care what I have to do to get it, either!"

"You sho got yourself a powerful bad temper, Fancy," he said unbendingly. "You git control of it, or it git control of you. De way you sassed dose children today, you could of got us killed!"

She did not respond, but stood, stubborn and hostile. Atticus, too, held his ground.

"If you think you is mad about us bein' colored, I'se twice as mad about you bein' stupid!

"I don't much care if you throw your clothes on the ground, 'cause you is de one what got to wear 'em. But I sho 'nuff care about you gittin' me lynched." He shook his grizzled head for emphasis. "I sho 'nuff do!"

Then he left her standing alone in the clearing.

Fancy tapped her foot in agitation. She let the angry mask slip from her face as Atticus moved from sight; she knew he was right, but she'd decided not to admit it. Not this time.

▲

"How did you get to be a slave, Atticus?" Fancy asked in her innocence, and Atticus was whirled backward violently through time.

Buy me, massa. I got plenty work left in me. I got gumption. . . .
Here, Mr. Riader. I got you a big buck nigger and a likely wench. She's a
good bearer, too. Three pickaninnies in three years. Ever since she turned ripe
she breeds one a year. . . .
   Open your mouth, nigger! Show this gentleman your teeth. . . .
   The words from the second auction were still seared into the old man's
soul. The first time he'd been sold, he hadn't understood the strident garble
of the auctioneer, unintelligible to a boy who knew only his own Yoruba
tongue. But the brutality had spoken a universal language. The ankle irons
that rasped great chunks of flesh from the bone . . . and left a place for
maggots and rotting infection . . . the whizzing whip that sung like mol-
ten iron as it rent slashes in unwilling hide . . . the caffle of slaves bound
together by chains, heads and shoulders bowed down by the weight of
desperation.
   "What was it like to be a slave?" the child prompted, seeing Atticus'
hesitation.
   How could he tell her of the hold of the ship . . . the vomit and excre-
ment, the anguish and the dying. Thirst, hunger, heat, airlessness. Festered
leg sores. Festered hopelessness.
   "Well, now, honey," he said, drawing each word carefully from within
himself. "Cain't recall too much good about it. . . ."

   Fancy watched Atticus' competent movements as he prepared to settle in for the night. The day had been a hard
one and he looked weary.
   "Tell me about when you were young, Atticus," she
asked, hoping to take his mind off their troubles. "Tell me about Africa."
   Atticus leaned back against the gnarled trunk of a swamp oak as the
shadows from the fire flickered strange leaping shapes on the Spanish moss
above him. He smiled and pulled the child close to him, settling her comfortably in the crook of his arm, against his body. He was thinner now than
he had been; she could feel his ribs when he held her.
   "My daddy was de king of the Yoruba tribe, child," he said, remembering. "Dat's how I come to learn magic, 'cause de sons of the king had to
learn secrets and mysteries de gods passed on to de menfolk long, long ago.
My brothers and me had to go through trials and ordeals before we could
call ourselves men.
   "Had to learn to listen to de gods when dey spoke to me, Fancy. Had to

learn about how to cure things. Learned other things, too, but I cain't talk none about 'em."

"Why not?"

" 'Cause dey'se mysteries and dey'se only for menfolk to know." He smiled at the disappointment on Fancy's face.

"Don't you go pout on me now, child. Ain't nothin' to mess wif, dose old gods! If dey turn on a man, he's a goner, sho 'nuff."

Fancy's head began to creep lower; soon it slipped into Atticus' lap and he reached out to pull the blanket up over the small body nestled in against his own.

"Do you miss your mama and daddy, Atticus?" a sleepy voice asked after a while.

"I misses 'em."

"I miss mine too," she answered wistfully. Then she turned, so she could look up into Atticus' eyes. "I'm real sorry about today, Atticus. If those stupid men had known you were a king's son, they wouldn't have been so mean to you."

"Long's you is black, honey, it don't matter whose son you is. You jest a no-account nigger to folks like dem."

"But that's not fair, Atticus."

"Nothin' much I seen so far 'bout dis life looks fair to me, child."

There didn't seem any more to be said, so Fancy closed her eyes, and snuggling in close as she could to Atticus' warm and sturdy body, she went to sleep.

Atticus sat unmoving, staring into the dwindling fire, surprised by the moisture in his own eyes. He had seen the long ago for a moment, through the child's questions. He had felt once more the breath of what it had been like to be young and free; strong and confident in the swelling pride of your own manhood.

He saw again . . . the glistening shadows of dancers who'd lived only in his memory for decades. Shining naked bodies flickered in the glow of massive bonfires . . . the inexorable beat of drums surrounded him, urging the dancers to wilder frenzies . . . taking over brain and body and soul with their insistent rhythms . . . night sounds, drum sounds, fire sounds. Sounds of sex and life and death all trapped inside him, beating inside him, lost for a lifetime inside him, in the pallid white man's world where respect went to the rich, not the wise . . . where manliness had nothing to do with connection to the earth and nature . . . where even the gods were puny and disinterested in the affairs of men.

Atticus glanced down at the sleeping child and idly brushed her dark hair back from the softly brown skin of her cheek. More than once since he'd started away from Beau Rivage, he had wondered if he'd been right to take

her with him. Right to remove her from the white man's world to endure this life of uncertainty and hardship. At first he'd told himself he'd had no choice, he'd taken her along to keep her from danger. But that wasn't quite true.

Perhaps he'd taken her along because he sensed he had something important to teach her . . . or because he was an old man and lonely, and she gave him a reason to keep on.

Atticus drew the blanket closer about them both and prepared himself for sleep, wondering at the strange ways of the gods. What trick of the Spirit World was this sleeping child beside him? White, female, not even his own. *Why give me knowledge of men's mysteries,* he asked silently, *and then give me a girlchild to teach?*

Atticus lay back beneath the blanket and folded his arms beneath his head; he stared hard at the stars in the ice-blue sky, but there were no answers there.

He should have found a place for her long ago . . . left her behind to the white man's world and whatever fate had in store for her.

Spirit child, he thought as he began to drowse. *Who are you to me?*

▲

"Teach me how to play the banjo, Atticus?" Fancy asked as they finished cleaning up the tin plates from which they'd eaten the scraps of their dinner.

Atticus cocked his head to the side and looked at the child. "Hard to learn the banjo, honey. Got to have a stick-to-it nature to play music."

"I can do it! If you could learn to play, I can, too." She wrinkled her nose at him teasingly, and with an indulgent nod he sent her scampering in the direction of the treasured instrument.

Atticus motioned the child to sit beside the fire facing him and, settling cross-legged on the ground before her, took the old banjo into his grasp. Fancy noticed the size of his hands and the spread of his great fingers on the instrument's neck, and frowned. Her own hands were less than half the size of his.

Atticus sat comfortably, bending his head over the banjo, and Fancy noticed for the first time a sort of reverence in the way he held the instrument. Tenderly, respectfully.

"Each string got a different sound dependin' on where you put your fingers on de frets." He rubbed his thumb over the calibrated ridges on the neck of the banjo and demonstrated a chord, then handed the banjo to Fancy, who tried to make her hands do what she'd seen.

"Got to press real hard on dem strings wif your lef' hand, honey. Got to press so hard it hurts, an' makes red stripes on de tips of your fingers."

Fancy pressed down as hard as she could on the reluctant strings and was surprised to see painful red ridges on the pads of her fingers when she let go.

"That can't be right, Atticus. It hurts too much. You just don't want to teach me is all!"

Atticus chuckled. "After a while you git calluses on your fingers instead of ridges, den your hands is tough enough to play." He showed her the chord again and told her to try it for herself.

She did so, with slightly better success.

"This is too hard for a child to learn, Atticus," she said haughtily, but he only laughed.

"Now, dat jest ain't so, Fancy. My boy Jonah learned when he was younger'n you. But he had a stick-to-it nature."

Fancy stared at the banjo in consternation. He could almost hear her thinking *If some little pickaninny could learn this, so can I!*

"Ain't nothin' worth knowin' dat's easy to come by, honey. Almost as if God makes de good stuff de hardest of all to git, so's we kin appreciate it more, mebbe."

Fancy looked up into Atticus' kindly eyes.

"I'd really like to learn, honest to pete I would, Atticus. If you won't laugh at me, I'll try some more."

"Wouldn't ever laugh at a body who's tryin', sugah. Tryin' what counts mos' wif ol' Atticus." He patted Fancy on the head and smoothed down the little cowlick that had risen from the cornrows he'd plaited to make her look more like a colored child.

"Lemme show you a real good chord to git started wif. . . ."

Later, he watched her sitting quietly by herself, fingering the instrument. Her tongue stuck out a little from the corner of her mouth in concentration. The sounds she made weren't right, but they were better than before.

"Sounds real good, Fancy," he called to her from the edge of the clearing. "Sounds real good to me." But she didn't hear him, she was so engrossed in learning stick-to-it-ivity.

▲

Fancy looked at her shoes in consternation. The soft leather was drenched and muddied, the bedraggled laces clung like lifeless earthworms to the sodden uppers.

Atticus had told her that her shoes were essential tools of travel and that she mustn't risk them by playing on the slippery stones of the swampy stream. But life provided so few pleasures these days that she'd ventured far from the bank, pleased with herself for this little rebellion that made her feel in charge of her own destiny again.

Then her foot had skidded out from under her with a sickening sudden-

ness, and plunged her into icy water, the silty, slimy mud squishing over the tops of her shoes and soaking through to her feet.

Now she'd have to face the music.

Atticus' frown when she reached him said he understood without explanation. He shook his head disapprovingly, but his tone wasn't unkindly.

"Thought I told you to git some water for de canteens and not go playin' around on dem stones."

Fancy shook her head affirmatively, but didn't answer.

"Guess you better change your clothes, 'fore we git on our way."

She nodded again—it didn't seem he was going to reprimand her after all. Quickly she laid down the canteens she'd been carrying and the shoes, which she had rinsed off as best she could in the stream, and began to unpack a change of clothes from her knapsack.

"I guess it's about time you started walkin' barefoot anyways," Atticus said, glancing sideways at her under his gray lashes as she went about the business of breaking camp. "It's best you git your feet toughened up some before de cold weather comes."

Fancy looked up, startled by the absurd notion of walking barefoot. A lady never walked barefoot; never risked so much as a callus.

"I am not going anywhere without my shoes," she said emphatically.

"You got more shoes in that li'l bag you totin'?" Atticus asked, seemingly with interest.

"You know I haven't!"

"Den you got no choice I kin see."

"Oh, yes, I have. We can just sit right here until they dry out."

" 'Fraid we cain't do no sech thing, Fancy. We only got food for breakfas'. Got to find me some work today. We got to keep movin'."

"I won't go barefoot!"

"Then you gits left behind, I expect."

"All I did was play around a little bit," she countered, trying to hold on to her defenses as long as possible.

"Dat's true 'nuff."

"Then why are you being so mean to me?"

"You made your choice dis mornin', honey. You decide you ain't gonna listen to old Atticus, you gonna do's you please. Atticus rule number 603 say you git to choose de way you go, you git to live wif de consequences. De only thing good about it is you learn not to make de same mistake twicet."

Atticus finished organizing for departure; Fancy, dejected, bundled up her clothes again into their small sack. Tying the bedraggled laces together, she slung the soggy shoes over her shoulder and they began to walk.

Atticus smiled just a little to himself at Fancy's progress. A few months ago she'd have pouted all day over such a lesson—now she just took it in hand and did the best she could with it. Life had a funny way of providing all the learning you could stand, if you had the courage to take the teaching in the right spirit.

"Y'all have a good time in that old stream before you fell in?" he asked over his shoulder, after they'd gone a mile or more.

"Sho 'nuff did!" she called back, mimicking his speech.

Atticus laughed aloud at the spirited reply. "Well, den, mebbe it was worth de trouble you got into. You reckon?"

"No," she answered with a rueful small laugh. "It sho 'nuff wasn't!"

Atticus turned with a surprised chuckle and, unexpectedly, swept the child up onto his wide shoulders.

"Den I expects you learned a important lesson dis mornin', honey—so I kin give you a li'l ride, jest 'cause I'se your friend."

Fancy threw her arms around Atticus' thick neck and hugged him tight. As she did so, the bald skin on the top of the man's head and the grizzled gray tonsure of hair around it suddenly reminded her that he was old and it might be a great effort for him to carry her.

She squeezed him hard again and kissed the top of his head lightly. "You kin let me down now," she said, after a minute or two. "So's I kin toughen up my feet before the cold weather comes."

When he did so, Fancy took hold of Atticus' hand and walked at his side, as cheerfully as her unhappy feet would allow.

▲ ▲ ▲

"You 'pear to be a mite peaky," Atticus said, looking up over the pot of stew that simmered on the cookfire. He'd snared a rabbit earlier in the day and had expected Fancy to be waiting impatiently for her favorite dinner, but she was quiet and listless.

"Got somethin' ailin' you, child?"

Fancy was seated on the ground, her knees drawn up to her chest, arms around them, her chin resting despondently on her knee. She shook her head no and said nothing.

Atticus smiled a little to himself; she'd grown to be so much a part of him that it would be nearly impossible to imagine life without her now.

"Got some troubles gnawin' on you, sugah?" He moved in quietly beside her, his body casting its long shadow across her turned-down face.

She nodded yes without looking up at him.

"Want to tell old Atticus about 'em?"

She shook her head no again, and Atticus frowned.

"How's a person to help you, if'n you cain't say what's hurtin'?"

"I was just thinking, Atticus. What if I never get back to Beau Rivage? What if there's no place for me ever to go back to? No way ever to have the things I'm s'posed to have?" She looked up and he could see the tears and worry in her eyes.

"Well, now . . . dat's a powerful lot of what-ifs for one li'l child. No wonder you is feelin' poorly."

Fancy nodded at the affirmation.

"I kin tell you don't want no ordinary cheerin' up, honey. 'Cause dis what-if is real important to you.

"Mebbe what you need is a brand-new dream," he said judiciously. "Jest in case the what-ifs shouldn't work out like you want 'em to. Sometimes they don't, you know.

"Sometimes de Lawd got real mysterious ways, child. Real mysterious. But mostly things work out. I kin tell you dat from my own experience.

"Besides, honey, wif your mama and daddy gone, might be you wouldn't like it none back dere anyways."

"If I didn't dream about going back to Beau Rivage, what would I dream about?" Fancy asked sensibly.

"I been givin' dat considerable thought now, honey. You ain't de onliest one around here got to have dreams, you know."

"You've got to have dreams, too?" she asked, surprised.

"Sho 'nuff do, child! Got to have dreams to keep on keepin' on." He watched her out of the corner of his eye to see if he'd piqued her curiosity.

"I been thinkin' you and me might should head on out to Californy and find us a big old gold mine."

Fancy's eyes widened. "How could we do that?"

"Same as anybody, I expects. We jest git us a pick an' a pan and we dig around some. We got gold mines back in Africa, you know, so I'd know jest how to do it."

"You would? Would we be rich then, Atticus?"

"Lordy, Fancy! We be so rich, we build us a house so big it make Beau Rivage look like a outhouse!" She giggled, but looked unconvinced, so he expanded on the theme.

"We be so rich, we kin buy you ribbons for your hair and silver slippers for your tootsies and everythin' a young lady from a fine place like Beau Rivage ought to have!"

Fancy's eyes lit up at the thought of plenty. "Oh, Atticus, I didn't know you knew how to make us rich again!"

The old man smiled at the relief in the child's face.

"You stick with old Atticus, honey, and we do jest fine." He tried never to lie to Fancy, even in little things; life was hard, no point letting her think otherwise. But this . . . this one time perhaps it wasn't so much a lie as a hope. Everybody needed something to hope for. And besides, Californy was far away and much could happen on the trip. The gold mine would give her something to hope for in the months or years ahead, and by the time they got to Californy she'd be older, better able to understand the need for the fib.

" 'Spect us wealthy gold miners could stand a mite of rabbit stew?" he asked, cheered by her excitement.

"Oh, yes," she said. "We've got to keep up our strength. It's a real long way to Californy." Fancy laughed out loud and Atticus joined in.

 Fancy tried unsuccessfully to close the buttons on the cuff of her dress. Startled, she realized that her arm had grown too long for the frayed sleeve. It was more than a year since Beau Rivage. A year of walking and hitching and catching work where they could. A day here, a week there, sometimes as much as a month in one place if work was plentiful. Fancy looked at her hands with a mixture of disgust and pleasure. They were dirty, work-roughened, and uncared-for, but they had learned to do many things well in their year of wandering.

She could build a fire almost as competently as Atticus—and she didn't need his help any longer to mend what needed mending. She could catch fish with a sharpened stick or cook it over a campfire till it tasted almost like a home-cooked meal. She could follow a trail and keep from getting lost, and she knew the names of half a hundred plants and trees and roots by heart. She even knew the medical properties of most of them. Iris or snake lily for skin rash or deafness. The back of the butternut for griping of the intestines, scabwart for sore throat, angelica for asthma. Horseweed for diarrhea, mistletoe for afflictions of the kidney. In the beginning she'd thought she'd never be able to remember it all without books to learn from or a tablet to write it down, but Atticus had told her that in his tribe, no written records were kept; it was a thing of pride to store great knowledge inside you, in the place where you kept your wisdom. The very fact that she had no copy books as a crutch had sharpened her memory and made it hold more than she'd ever dreamed it could. Her *inside* place was growing fuller every day, she thought with a giggle.

Fancy dashed the cold water from the river onto her face to clear the last vestiges of sleep. As she did so she hummed the lilty song Atticus had played for her the night before on his banjo, as all alone by the side of the stream, they had sung together, laughing and dancing. Soon she, too, would be able to play real tunes on the instrument; Atticus said she had a talent for music. She reached down one last time to scoop a cooling sip of water into her cupped hand.

Fancy felt the fangs of the water moccasin pierce her hand near the wrist, felt the acid shock of poison pumping into her flesh. She shrieked in terror and grabbed her wrist with viselike fingers to keep the evil poison contained in her hand, as the glistening body slithered from its hiding place and continued its unhurried passage downstream. Her face contorted with fear as Atticus tore across the clearing toward the scream; she'd seen more than one slave die from snakebite. He caught her as she sagged precariously on the mossy bank.

"What kind was it, Fancy?" Atticus demanded as he scooped her up into his arms.

"Moccasin," she whispered, terror constricting her throat so she could hardly say the awful word.

The Bowie knife was in his hand so swiftly, she barely saw the move; he scored deep gashes into the soft flesh above the indentations of the fangs. Fancy screamed again, but Atticus held her hand so tightly, she couldn't have escaped if she tried.

Fancy felt the blood and poison sucked from the wound as the world around her ceased to have its proper shape. She was hot and cold; a creeping nausea rose inside her and she ached where Atticus was tying his belt around her arm. Could she be thirsty, too? she wondered dazedly; so many sinking feelings were suffusing her that her sluggish mind couldn't seem to catch hold of them all at once.

Atticus laid her gently on the ground and covered her with his coat. "I got to git my medicines, child," he murmured close to her ear. "You hold on now, you hear me? I git back here 'fore you know it."

Fancy tried to nod her acknowledgment, but the muscles of her neck ached strangely and her body didn't seem to want to do as she told it. "I'm dying, aren't I, Atticus?" she tried to say, but by the time she could make her mouth form the words he was gone.

▲

Atticus held the feverish child in his arms and tortured his brain for something more he could do. He had scarified the wound within minutes of the puncture; he had cut and drawn the venom and packed the gash with chewed tobacco. He had boiled wood betony and valerian for the nerve pains, and root of the ground squirrel pea to ease the muscle spasms, and forced the mixture drop by drop between her tightly clenched lips. Now he must wait.

The crisis would come tonight. The sweating and the nausea would pass and the heartbeat would be shallow and rapid. The headache, bloating, and thirst would reach a crescendo, and then . . . either the fever would break and she would live, or painful paralysis would follow the venom through every cranny of her small frame and she would die.

Wordlessly, Atticus hugged the child's restless body to his own and rocked her like a baby. Fancy groaned softly and her eyes opened for a moment, but he knew she couldn't see him.

There was no point in going over for the thousandth time the *why* of it. Or the countless *ifs. If* he hadn't sent her to the stream for water, *if* he had left her safe at Tremayne, *if* the Yankees hadn't come, *if* there'd been no war . . . the *ifs* were endless and self-defeating.

The ancient secret rose in him inexorably—there was one more thing he could do for her if all else failed. Atticus let the forbidden knowledge once again seep from its burial place in his mind. Powerful forces he had learned of, in his boyhood; forces strong enough to keep even Death at bay. Forces far too powerful to be unleashed except in desperation.

Such magic as could hold back Death was dearly paid for. He would not think the thoughts again unless there was no other way.

▲

With a decisive sigh Atticus laid the desperately ill child on the mossy bank and covered her with both their blankets. He must be quick now that he'd made up his mind; if he hadn't the courage to do what he must, she would die before sunrise. He'd feared the worst from the moment he'd seen the placement of the wound; on top of her hand where the vulnerable veins could carry the poison swiftly through her small body. Her flesh burned as he held her; there were no choices anymore.

Swiftly, Atticus cut a lock of the child's hair and a snippet of her fingernails. He noted the bloodless pallor of the skin beneath the nails, and held her small hand a moment longer than necessary before he let it slip from his fingers.

He rifled his medicine kit for precious herbs, dried and stored laboriously the summer before, against emergency. Stripping off his clothes, he tied a cloth around his loins. The task he was about should be performed naked, as it had been in the jungle. He put his shirt and trousers back on over the breechcloth and prepared to go.

Atticus looked up at the sky and took his bearings. The crescent moon shone meager light. A full moon would have helped his purpose, but he must do what he could with the waxing one. At least they weren't in the moon's dark quarter when all magic was thwarted by nature's laws.

It couldn't be more than a few miles back to the graveyard they'd passed the day before. He tied the packet of herbs to his makeshift wrap, bound his hunting knife with a thong around his waist, and set off at a lope along the riverbank, thanking the gods of his long-gone youth that they were far from town and prying eyes. It amused him in a grim sort of way that he had automatically shifted back to the old gods and abandoned the new one he'd grown so fond of in the white man's world. The old gods were those whose mercy he would beg this night, and in whose keeping he would leave his spirit as hostage for Fancy. The new god, Jesus, he'd learned of in Louisiana was more benevolent but less willing to be bargained with.

When he reached the small churchyard, Atticus stripped off his clothes and cut a strip of turf from the top of one of the mounded graves. He added a handful of grave dirt to the herb bundle, then searched the area for a small flat rock.

Atticus stared for a moment at the fingers of his hand—it seemed to him that he had never seen them clearly before this moment. He laid his left hand on the stone and took a long, deep breath to steady himself. Then, taking his knife from its sheath, he laid its razor edge to the second joint of his pinky, and hacked off his smallest finger.

The unnatural sound of bone and sinew being sawed through made the old man sway, but steeling himself, he let the blood from the wound run freely over the poultice he was concocting; then he packed the injury with chewed leaves, bandaged his hand as best he could, and continued the ritual, according to the old law.

With intense concentration, Atticus pressed the severed finger, the lock of Fancy's hair, and the nail parings into the earth on the grave he'd altered, then replaced the turf above the fetish, pounding it into a semblance of its original form. It would not do to arouse suspicion with an obviously dese-crated grave, lest some unsuspecting person dig up the buried fetish and disturb the magic.

Atticus stood tall, held his arms aloft in an attitude more of salute than of supplication, and called on Death to hear the terms of his bargain: "Fancy's life for mine!" He cried the awesome Yoruba words aloud so fiercely that Death could not mistake his meaning. "I leave you a piece of my own body to seal the bargain," he shouted into the silence of the graveyard. "Come for me at your leisure, Snake God. I will go willingly, if you spare the child."

Atticus felt the intense Power of the magic sucked into his veins from the earth beneath his feet. He heard the wind called up and eerie rustling sounds as the leaves around him began to shimmer and swirl in the dark-ness.

"By the power of all the gods of the Yoruba people," he called out in the language of his young manhood, "my spirit calls upon you, Death!"

The wild wind swirled around him, yet the trees above were frozen into silence as if they, too, were awed by the Power whose forbidden name he dared to speak.

Atticus saw the vision boil up from the scattered leaves, an iridescence at first, that grew and pulsed and coiled like living flesh, brought forth from the putrifying remains of the dead who slept around him.

A swaying serpent face emerged from the luminescence, its lips drawn back in a hideous grin of power.

Alone, to look upon the face of the Snake God would be certain and immediate death; but Atticus was not alone. Spirits rose like phosphorescent mist around him, spirits of his ancestors, wizard beyond wizard back to the dawn of time.

He felt his own soul fortified by their presence, ennobled, enhanced to a thousand times its own immensity by the ancestral spectres.

"I face you, fearsome Snake God," he called out clearly. "I am not some pious beggar asking for a favor—I come here to enter into a bargain with my people's ancient adversary!"

The Snake God's smile died upon its lips, the forked tongue flicked out, nearly touching Atticus' face. The venomous apparition coiled itself around the old slave's legs and rose to envelop the tall dark form, which neither flinched nor fled.

Atticus felt the icy cold of death surge through him then, as the odious reptile curled around his body.

I am dying! his brain shrieked to his pounding heart. This is what death is, this anguished cold, this horrifying aloneness, this eternity of dark . . . *I'm dying,* screamed each bone and muscle, each cell of blood and tissue. He felt his consciousness extinguish, memories blinking off like murdered fireflies. *No!* his soul shrieked madly. *This is too much to ask!*

"Relent!" Death demanded. "Let the child go and all will be as it was before. Choose quickly, your life ebbs."

Atticus felt the last of himself draining, and wanted to live with every fiber of his dying heart. . . .

"No!" he gasped with his last breath. "I give myself for Fancy."

A crooning filled his ears. The figures of the ancestors blended into a single iridescent Being that merged with Atticus, shattering and rebuilding; every cell pulsed with power, every memory returned and with it memories he'd never had . . . ancient knowledge from a thousand brains in a thousand generations suffused his own and he was one with all knowledge in all time. . . .

The Snake God hissed at the unwelcome Light, uncoiled himself reluctantly, and Death withdrew. The soul of Atticus knew the bargain had been sealed.

There would be no easy death for him now; no falling off to sleep in comfortable old age. But it would be an honorable death for he had stood his ground—and the price was not too high to pay.

Atticus completed the ancient ritual with the meticulousness of one who understands only too well the Power he has invoked. He waited for the Ancient Ones to drain themselves from his being, to return to the Eternal Place where they resided. Their departure left him hollowed and bereft.

As soon as he was able, the man who'd fought with Death and won from him reprieve, pulled on his abandoned clothes and hurried back to the child he loved more than his own life.

▲

Atticus removed the poultice from Fancy's wound and brushed the graveyard mixture from all the places on her sleeping body where he'd sprinkled it.

The child stirred uneasily and tried to drag her mind to the surface, from the faraway place where it had wandered.

"Atticus?"

"I'm here, child," he responded gently, tucking the blanket in closer to her body. "You been real sick, sugah, so you best lie still 'til I git you some soup for nourishment."

Gently, the old man spooned a few drops of the warming liquid into Fancy's mouth. He could see that her eyes were clearer and she knew her surroundings.

"You hurt your hand," she whispered sleepily.

" 'T'ain't nothin', honey. Only important thing is you is feelin' better now."

Fancy smiled, or tried to, but sleep again pulled her away to another place. This time, Atticus knew with satisfaction, there need be no fear that she wouldn't return.

 "Now, Fancy honey," Atticus said cheerfully. "What kin you tell me about doctorin' wif tree bark?" He glanced at the girl out of the corner of his eye as they walked along a heavily forested roadway; her confident smile let him know she had an answer to the question that she wouldn't have had a few months before.

"Slippery elm could make a gruel to soothe a stomach inflammation, or it could make a juice to cure a sore throat."

He nodded and she continued.

"Cherry bark could heal catarrh."

"How's about black willow?"

"That's an easy one, Atticus," she responded gaily. "It's a sedative and a tonic."

"You is mighty smart today," he said, shaking his head as if trying to think up a means of stumping her. "You got your tree barks right down pat. But how 'bout roots, now? Dey's real powerful. Got to know what to do wif roots."

He screwed up his face in concentration. "What you do wif comfrey root, if'n you had some?"

"Make a poultice for a wound, I guess," she answered a little slower than before. "I think it's good for chest complaints too. But I'm not sure."

"Right as rain, child! Soon you have so much doctorin' stuffed in your head, it git two sizes bigger."

"You're a real good teacher, Atticus. I never could have learned so much from that old tutor I had at Beau Rivage."

Atticus poked with his walking stick at a plant by the side of the road.

"See dis here red clover? You kin cure whooping cough wif dis flower if you ain't got nothin' better handy."

"How come you know so much?" Fancy asked, mimicking the cadence in Atticus' speech.

He smiled at her. "Learnt some in Africa, long ago. Got to know plants if you plannin' to do magic. Learnt more from my wife, 'cause she was born in the bayous, so she knowed what grows in Loosiana real good."

"What was she like, Atticus?"

"She was purty as a picture," he said easily. "And real kind. Had a great big heart too. Big enough to love everybody."

"But mostly you, right?"

"Mostly me," he replied, pride in his voice. "Yes'm, Beckie love mostly me."

They walked on silently, the only sounds the crunch of stones beneath their feet. Fancy thought she might have made him sad, so she broached another subject.

"I wish I could teach *you* something Atticus, something real good. But you know everything important, seems to me."

Atticus cocked his head to the side to contemplate his small companion; it was nice that she wanted to give something back.

"You could teach me to write my name," he said quietly. "Always thought if I ever git free, I learn to write my name. Case I ever git to own somethin' I could sign my name real good on de bill of sale."

Fancy looked up at Atticus, realization dawning. He was an old man, yet never in his whole life had anything truly belonged to him. Something in the understanding made tears spring up behind her eyes.

"Don't you worry none, Atticus," she said hastily. "When I get rich again I'm going to buy you lots of good things."

"Thank you kindly, honey. But mebbe I jest inten' to buy somethin' for my own self. Sign my own name on dat paper." He smiled down at her to show he wasn't offended. "If you teach me how, dat is."

"I'll teach you to read and write everything, if you want me to," she said magnanimously.

"Dat be right nice, child," he replied. "But I'd be obliged if we jest start wif Atticus."

 The open prairie west of St. Joseph, Missouri, stretched to the far horizon. It had taken them the better part of two years to reach the place where the pamphlets said the wagon trains began. At first they'd headed west almost to the Texican border, then, hearing talk in the towns west of Shreveport, they'd picked up a penny pamphlet that told how to go west with a wagon train and Atticus had decided, on the spot, that they must reach St. Joe.

So they'd headed north through Arkansas, a dangerous place, still ravaged by border raiders and all the riffraff of ex-army men who hated to leave war behind when it ended. Fort Towson, Bogy Depot, Scullyville, Van Buren. Fort Wayne and Neosho, on the outskirts of the Seneca and Shawnee nations. Then on through Mound City and Olathe, where fear of Pawnee raiders still kept people in their cabins . . . to Wyandotte, Atchison, and finally St. Joe.

Atticus kept a map that tracked each place they'd been through; Fancy lettered the names in carefully and sometimes added a little drawing of a cabin or a tepee to remind them of what they'd encountered on the way. Fancy had signed her name at the bottom and Atticus had proudly lettered his in beside it.

The Missouri air was cool and dry. Fancy didn't like the look of the wagon-train master as he shouted orders to the men who were loading the huge Conestoga wagons. He was called Major, as were all such wagon masters, and he seemed to pack enough swagger to make the title believable.

Atticus offered his services to the man for the westward journey, in return for passage for himself and his "gran'child." But the major told him that passage alone was not enough. A wagon would be needed, and supplies, food, bedding, pots, pans . . . the list sounded endless to Fancy, listening from beyond the mountains of boxes, barrels, crates, and livestock that made up the supplies being loaded onto the many wagons of the train.

They'd already heard the prices of such goods from other wagoneers: ninety dollars for a light flatbed wagon, fifty dollars for a yoke of oxen, forty to sixty dollars for a horse. Why, even a fifteen-hand mule cost sixty-five dollars, which might as well have been a king's ransom, it was so far beyond their means. And then there was the incredible list of provisions that each family needed to survive the two-hundred-fifty-day journey west. It had been printed on a St. Joe flyer that she'd read aloud to Atticus, their spirits sinking lower with each item: flour and sugar and coffee and tea. Rice, bacon, hams, lard, vinegar, crackers, raisins, pickles, dried fruit; Fancy had nearly committed them to memory. To say nothing of spices and medicines and so many sundries, it had made her head spin. Even Atticus' optimism had flagged at the hopelessness of such a list. But then he'd hit on the idea of offering services in return for passage, and they had hoped once more.

"I kin cook and hunt," she heard Atticus tell the wagon master with pride in his old voice. "I knows doctorin' an' I'se a powerful good blacksmith. I kin play de banjo, too."

"Wes Jarvis," he said enigmatically. "That's who you want to see."

"He on dis wagon train?"

"No. Not the train. You don't belong on the train, I told you that. You got no provisions. Wes Jarvis got a traveling circus and patent-medicine show. Calls itself some kind of highfalutin theatrical ensemble or some such, but a circus is what it amounts to. If you can do all them things you say you can, Wes might take you on. You and the pickaninny there." The shifting eyes darted past Atticus to Fancy.

"Where we gonna find this Wes Jarvis?"

"He was loading up on grub, same as us this morning," said the major. "Might still be at the general store, might be at the saloon. Might be parked outside of town by the railroad yard," he said, already walking away.

Atticus called a thank-you after him and moved in Fancy's direction, the lightness restored to his step. He leaned down to hug the child in his excitement at the possible reprieve the circus offered. It might not have the substance of a wagon train, but it would have steady meals and maybe even a wagon roof overhead. And there'd be womenfolk too—it wouldn't hurt Fancy any to be around womenfolk at this age.

Atticus took her by the hand and set out to talk his way into Wes Jarvis' theatrical ensemble.

▲

The circus caravan stood restlessly at the edge of town. The canvas tent was half collapsed like a multicolor cake that had fallen in the middle. The wagons, festive from a distance, close up revealed their peeling paint, their rusted wheels and cage bars.

Fancy watched wide-eyed as a huge gray beast, the like of which she'd never seen, stood happily scooping up huge trunkloads of hay and stuffing them into its triangular mouth.

"Oh, Atticus!" she breathed excitedly, pulling at his sleeve and pointing. "What's that?"

"Dat's a elephant, Fancy. Back where I come from we got lots a' elephants, but I never did see one here. . . . Dat's a mighty fine elephant you got yourself, son," Atticus shouted up to a young man on a ladder, who seemed to be scrubbing the elephant's back with a long-handled mop.

The elephant boy grinned back and waved.

"Kin you tell me where I find Wes Jarvis?"

"Lead wagon," the boy shouted from his perch. "He's the one who looks like the *boss*." He emphasized the last word and laughed.

Atticus took Fancy's hand in his own and pulled her away from the elephant. She would happily have stayed.

Calliope music sounded, stopped, sounded, stopped, as if someone were testing the mechanism that produced it. Men shouted to one another and noisily tossed things into wagons. A tall, striking woman walked by, speaking quietly to a pair of tigers on gilded leashes. She seemed occasionally to stop and wait for a responsive growl before continuing the dialogue.

"I love this place!" Fancy breathed aloud as she ran to keep up with Atticus' hurrying strides. "Oh, Atticus, I hope they let us stay."

"So do I, Fancy honey. So do I." The circus was their last hope of going west this year. Everyone knew that if you left Missouri after April, there was no way through the terrible snows of the Sierra Nevada. After the tragedy of the Donner party twenty years before, when the desperate members of a stranded wagon train had resorted to cannibalism to survive, no one at all left St. Joe after April.

Following the sound of the calliope, Atticus and Fancy rounded the corner of the deflated tent and saw a fanciful wagon with curlicue scrollwork on top. It was painted with wide red and white stripes and along the side a gilt-trimmed sign proclaimed:

W.E.S. JARVIS'S
INTERNATIONALLY RENOWNED
CIRCUS, THEATRICAL ENSEMBLE, AND WILD BESTIARY
INCORPORATING THE MUSEUM OF HUMAN CURIOSITIES
AND
MADAME MAGDA
FORTUNE TELLER TO THE
CROWNED HEADS OF EUROPE

Striding back and forth in front of the wagon was a man obviously in command, shouting orders to the tiniest full-grown person Fancy had ever seen. The dwarf stood shy of three feet; his hair was black and was parted in the middle and slicked carefully into identical waves on either side of his head. A child-size monocle dangled from a ribbon attached to a button on his vest, and it bounced as he scurried to stay in front of the pacing Wes Jarvis. For that, without a doubt, thought Atticus, was who the flamboyant white-haired gentleman with the theatrical voice must be.

"We shall do Lear for the Philistines," the voice announced. Suddenly striking the pose of an avenging angel, arms raised menacingly above his head as if to threaten the dwarf, Jarvis boomed unexpectedly, " 'Dost thou call me fool, boy?' "

Falling to one knee, the little man replied undaunted, " 'All thy other titles thou hast given away; that thou wast born with.' "

Jarvis clapped his hands with glee; both men laughed uproariously at their own antics.

" 'Ingratitude, thou marble-hearted fiend!' " Jarvis managed to snap at the dwarf through his laughter. The little man, unperturbed by the rebuke, gestured to Atticus and Fancy to come closer.

"Yes, yes?" Jarvis called to them. "And to what whim of fortune do we owe this unexpected visit?"

Fancy saw Atticus straighten visibly. "We's here lookin' for work, suh," he said in his most dignified tone.

"And a place in your circus!" added Fancy enthusiastically, but a look from Atticus silenced her.

"Indeed?" said Jarvis with a small snort of amusement, and Fancy saw his every gesture was exaggerated. He tossed his head to push back a falling lock of hair, when a simple stroke of the hand would have served the same purpose. "We have no need of more personnel at the moment, Gitalis, have we?"

"No need. And no money to pay, if we had need."

"Alas, a bitter truth," Jarvis agreed. "What do you do, by the way?"

"Anythin' needs doin'. I'se a powerful good blacksmith. Shoe dat elephant a' yours if you want me to. I kin fix anythin' broke. I know doctorin' wif nature's medicines—"

"And he plays the banjo and fiddle and sings like an angel," interrupted Fancy, not about to let this opportunity slip away.

"And you," Jarvis asked Fancy. "Are you similarly gifted?"

"I can work as hard as anybody. . . . At anything you want done. I can sing and I'm learning to play stringed instruments, and—" She broke off, trying to think of some other wonderful accomplishment she could offer.

"You don't speak like a person of the dark races, my dear," Jarvis observed, examining her more closely. In her effort to impress, Fancy had forgotten the "darkie talk" she'd learned so laboriously.

"Her daddy was a white man," Atticus broke in hastily. "Dey let her play wif de li'l white childrun on the plantation an' she git above herself."

"I see," said Jarvis, exchanging a look with Gitalis.

"And what exactly did they call you on this plantation, might I inquire?"

"They called me Fancy."

"Fancy what?"

"Just Fancy."

Jarvis walked closer; he seemed entranced by the child.

"And why do you wish to join the circus, Fancy?"

"We want to go west and we have no money for the wagon train."

"Aha!" said Jarvis, as if he'd made a momentous discovery. "Do you see what we have here, Gitalis? The makings of an honest woman. And of quite a little beauty, too, if I'm any judge. Cleopatra must have had skin your color, Fancy. Did you know that?" He smiled at the exquisite child, whose eyes held so many secrets.

"You may come with us," he announced as if bestowing the crown jewels. "We have little enough, but you may share it, if you are willing to work."

Fancy threw her arms around Atticus and Jarvis saw tears of joy and relief in both their eyes.

"It is a great privilege to be a member of the theatre; never forget that!" The voice was too large for its tiny audience. "We entertain. We entrance them with illusion. We transport them from their grubby little lives to Elysian fields. We educate. We amuse. We set them free! It's a godly calling," he said with a wink at Fancy, then turned on his heel and strode away.

"Teach them, Gitalis," Jarvis tossed over his retreating shoulder. "Teach them!"

Amusement glittering in his eye, Gitalis fixed his monocle in place, propped his clipboard against his hip, and began to rattle off the rules of theatrical life. Another pair of strays, he thought . . . not the first for Wes Jarvis, and surely not the last.

▲ ▲ ▲

The exotic dark-haired woman they had seen earlier walking the leashed cats extended her hand formally to Fancy. The nails were long and well tended, the hand beautiful. Instead of shaking her hand, as Fancy expected, the woman turned up the palm and scrutinized the lines that crisscrossed it in delicate filigree.

"You belong here, for now," Magda said, apparently satisfied with what she'd seen. She had the kind of sultry middle-European accent that rolled its *r*'s and exchanged its *v*'s and *w*'s. "You are of the race that knows Joseph."

"I don't know anyone named Joseph," Fancy replied, not wanting to be mistaken for someone else.

Magda's laugh was throaty and genuine. "You do not understand me, child. It is a saying of the Gypsies . . . it speaks of the special ones. . . . You like my pets?" she asked, seeing Fancy eye the tigers that stalked up and down in their wagon cage. Each time the animals passed by Magda in their prowl, they rubbed themselves sensuously against the cage bars and made a grumbling sound.

"I've never seen anything like them!" Unconsciously, Fancy moved closer and put out her hand toward the cage.

"You must never touch my babies!" Magda snapped forbiddingly. "They are very dangerous. Except with me." She shrugged and smiled. "Perhaps even with me. Jarvis says one day they will eat me up and nothing will be left of poor Magda.

"Come!" her voice commanded. "We will clean you up and find you some costumes to wear. Can you ride? You must learn if you cannot."

"I can ride," Fancy said as she scurried to keep up with Magda's determined stride. The Gypsy was tall and queenlike; her long black hair bounced energetically as she walked. Magda brushed it back from her face absently and Fancy was reminded of the way a high-bred stallion switches its tail to show its superiority and impatience. Fancy was fascinated, for the woman was very beautiful and not in the least like anyone she had ever seen.

The wagon's paint was badly chipped on the outside, but the interior took the child's breath away. Every inch of space was cluttered with exotic debris. Richly patterned fabrics hung in pleated swags from the ceiling, brilliant velvet cushions, some laced with golden threads, were tossed casually about the floor. An exquisite lacquer table from the Orient dominated the wagon's center; on it, in a cushioned nest, stood a giant crystal ball.

Candles in curious metal sconces were everywhere. Mirrors in gilt frames faced each other at angles that bounced back a thousand reflections of the mysterious interior.

"It's so gorgeous here!" Fancy couldn't help the breathless exclamation. Magda smiled approvingly.

"It is nothing!" she snapped, but the child could see the woman was delighted by her enthusiasm.

Magda opened a window that had been hidden by the drape of fabric, and sunlight beamed its way into the small wagon, dust motes dancing in its wake. The light betrayed the fraying of the pillows and the dust piled in corners, the tarnish of the candlesticks and the dents in the antique table, but Fancy could see only the magic of the place.

Magda fished a jangling bunch of keys from her pocket and fitted one into the lock of an old wooden chest. "A gift from a pirate who was my lover," she said as she pulled up the lid and costumes in varied states of disrepair spilled out.

"It is some time since we could afford a wardrobe mistress," Magda said with a sniff of contempt, putting her finger through a hole in the seam of a silvery dress and wiggling it. "But no matter. I suppose you can sew." Fancy nodded her head, but she had already realized Magda did not expect answers to her questions.

"What are you waiting for?" the woman called over her shoulder impatiently. "Take off your clothes."

"I can't," Fancy replied, daunted at thwarting this mysterious creature.

"And why not?"

"I just can't," the girl repeated. To take off her clothes would be to reveal her secret.

"Do not fear, child," Magda said, in a kindlier tone. "I already know that you are not a Negress."

Fancy's eyes widened in surprise.

"About you I know many things," Magda continued. "Life has been difficult. Magda will not betray you." With that she held out the shimmering pile of clothes gathered from the chest.

"In the circus everything is illusion . . . but here, at least, there will be no need for deception."

"I don't understand."

"Magda has seen your hand. Nothing in life is by chance, Fancy. The old man was sent to teach you to be human. Magda will teach you to be a woman. Later, there will be others, with other lessons."

Magda laughed; it was a seductive sound. She reached for Fancy's hand. "It is all written here." She tapped the palm. "And here it can be read." She tapped her own head, lightly.

"Come, my little one. You walk with destiny." With that pronouncement, Magda laughed gaily again and, pointing to the mirrors, said in mock command, "Play! Dress up! Admire yourself in the looking glass. You are very beautiful."

Then she was gone.

Fancy picked up the silver dress and moved doubtfully to the mirror. Could it be true that she was beautiful? It was more than two years since Beau Rivage. Who had she become? I'm almost a woman, she thought, peering at her reflection. Twelve was different from ten. The changes she saw in the revealing glass were subtle but profound. Even the honey-colored skin, which she had so disdained, gave her an exotic quality, the dark curls ringing her face made her seem Gypsylike.

She dropped her homespun dress to the floor and loosed the rough cotton undergarments. Her body shape was new, too; her waist smaller, her hips more curved. The swell of breasts behind small pink nipples had begun. Fancy ran her hand gingerly over her own body. The dark stain ended at throat and thigh and shoulders, the rest of her was white and softly rosy. She smiled at her own reflection and thought she saw her mother's smile echoed in her own.

Glancing at the door to make sure she was still alone, Fancy slipped one after the other of the costumes over her head, reveling in the feel of them. Nothing but scratchy muslin had touched her skin since Beau Rivage. These were tattered, but they were silks and velvets and brocades.

She pirouetted in front of the glass, in conspiracy with her mirrored self in the dazzling garments. She touched everything in Magda's wagon—the golden samovar on the corner shelf, the bewildering deck of cards on the table near the crystal, the books and tea cups and funny beaded curtains that partitioned off the sleeping corner from the rest.

What had the inscrutable woman meant by destiny? Could it be that Fancy's own fate was already written somewhere? What did it matter? They were headed west. At last. They were safe. At last.

This day could be the beginning of everything.

7   Wes Jarvis watched the seductive movement of her body as Magda let the last of her garments slip from her hips to the floor. What a glorious ritual she made of undressing, he thought with appreciation.

She smiled at him enigmatically, then, taking a small bottle of scented oil from the table by her mirror, she began to anoint her own body with it. With absolute concentration she touched her nipples with the oil—first one, then the other—her breasts full enough to sway with the touch. She cupped each of them, tossing back her head, a look of exquisite pleasure on her face. Her waist-length hair, unbraided, fell in dark ripples behind her as she moved her hands in sensuous strokes down her body to her belly, thighs, buttocks. The lamplight in the darkened wagon caught the gleam of her oiled skin and cast flickering shapes on her tawny body.

What age can she be? Jarvis thought as he watched the breathtaking performance. What witchcraft does she use to remain so desirable?

Fancy stood on the top step of Magda's wagon, transfixed by what she glimpsed through the crack in the door. The forbiddenness of the scene unfolding within the candle-lit wagon raced her blood as if she'd been running and stirred something new within her.

She had come to return a script to the Gypsy; now she clutched it close to her pounding heart. She knew she shouldn't watch the naked man and woman, but nothing short of Atticus could have moved her from that spot.

Fancy held her breath and watched.

Magda, sleek as a panther, moved toward Jarvis, where he lay propped up against the cushions of her bed. She pulled back the quilt that covered his loins, and stared at the evidence of what her performance had provoked. Then, reaching out, unhurriedly, she touched the tip of his swollen manhood with skilled fingers.

"So you still care about your Magda?" she said, amusement in her voice, and bent her tongue to the place her fingers had touched. Jarvis groaned with pleasure and, leaning forward, buried his face in her fragrant hair as he allowed the maddening rhythm of her lips and tongue to banish fear and failure and poverty and everything else from the world for a little while at least.

"No!" he said sharply when the insistent mouth was finally more than he could bear. "Not yet, my Magda."

She moved her head from between his thighs, and he felt the sharp loss of her warm mouth as it let him slide reluctantly free. Grasping her shoulders in firm hands, he turned her body, trading places with her.

Fancy strained to see what they were doing; her heart pounded and a peculiar ache pervaded her female parts. She could see only slivers of the drama within, tantalizing her imagination.

Magda lay back, open to him, eyes closed, lips parted with sweet memory of the pleasure she had given.

Jarvis slid his hands over her warm flesh in a proprietary way, as if checking all the places that belonged to him, caressing as he inventoried. He felt the shift of power; he was the giver now. Slowly, teasingly, he sucked each dark nipple in turn, as his hands moved to the places he knew craved touching.

He sensed her desire, felt her struggle with herself not to ask for what she needed, but to let him find his own way.

Kneeling beside her face, Jarvis brushed his penis across her open lips; she reached her tongue for him, but he eluded her.

"He is so big . . . so beautiful," she murmured, her voice husky with wanting. "I love his bigness."

"I know," he said quietly. He was in control. He had always known.

Parting her thighs, he stroked the fragile skin closest to the core of her. Magda moaned with pleasure and longing, arched herself toward his teasing hands. He slid a finger into her openness, slowly, infuriatingly; he stroked the slippery inner folds of her, sensing the swelling he provoked there.

She felt his manhood enter with such exquisite knowledge of its path. Long, languid strokes, each one deeper than the last. Coaxing. Teasing. Tormenting. Strokes of amazing force and confidence.

When the exquisite quivers came, Magda abandoned herself to them, sucking the source of her pleasure into herself hungrily. Desperate, perfect relief and agony combined. It was enough to fulfill. It could never be enough.

Magda felt herself folded close in his enveloping arms as his own fulfillment surged its way into her.

It would be hard to leave Jarvis, the thought crossed her mind idly as they lay in the soft bliss of afterward. She had never meant to stay.

Fancy, weak with confusion and longing, crept down the wagon steps soundlessly and made her way back to her own wagon. Images of what she'd witnessed possessed her. So *this* was what men and women did when they loved . . . this primitive, animal act of lust that was somehow beautiful and holy.

"How come you still got that script?" Atticus asked as she entered the wagon. He peered at her closely; her face was flushed and she seemed feverish. "You feelin' poorly, Fancy?" he asked.

Her heart beat so forcefully she could hardly speak. "No," she managed to say. "Magda wasn't there. I'll give it back to her in the morning. I'm fine, Atticus. I just want to go to bed."

Atticus, wondering at her strange behavior, turned out the lamp and Fancy lay in her bed with forbidden visions tumbling all around her in the dark.

▲

Fancy looked around the circle of faces that had gathered near the circus master's wagon for their final strategy meeting before clattering into the town of their next performance. By now, she and Atticus knew each of the little troupe so well, it seemed they had known them always. Tobey, the clown, the three Marcato brothers who walked the high wire and acted in plays if a Latin lover or *bandito* was called for. Melisande, the equestrienne daredevil who had been born Mary Ellen Quinn in the horse country of County Wicklow. The actors and actresses, the freaks, the artists, and the workers who made up the circus contingent, all were familiar to her now.

The strangest members of the company were Harp and Flute, the Siamese twins, joined somehow at the lower body—a curious garment hid the exact nature of their connection. They were married to twin sisters Lena and Tina, one a singer and one an exotic dancer.

Magda told Fancy the Siamese twins solved their peculiar marital situation by living three days with one sister, then three days with the other. They were perpetually jolly, despite the locomotive difficulties their four scuttling legs caused them. As far as Fancy could tell, they were content with their domestic arrangement. The Siamese twins were the circus's greatest drawing card, Gitalis had assured her—even better than the elephant for getting people to buy tickets.

"When we arrive in Council Bluffs," intoned Jarvis, striding up and down importantly in front of his little audience, "Tobey, you will lead Genghis into the town square, where you will perform your winsome antics to draw the attention of the crowd." Wes' flamboyance and his shock of snowy hair made him seem more messiah than man, Fancy thought as she watched him mesmerize the performers.

"Atticus, you will drive the wagon with our advertisement emblazoned on the side. You will be garbed in your minstrel outfit and will play the banjo to keep the crowd lively." Atticus nodded agreement; he and Fancy were so happy with the circus. He looked into her shining face, no longer stained mahogany but simply tanned by the sun, and felt content.

"The rest of you . . ." Wes waved his expressive hands in benediction over the assorted others: Wu the Chinese cook, Edgar the elephant boy, Donny and Johnny, the grips, Minnie and Horace, the husband and wife who were fine actors on their way to the gold fields of California—eighteen people in all, if you counted Harp and Flute as two.

"You will pitch the tent and tune up the calliope . . ." Jarvis' resonant voice was merry and mischievous. "You will set up the sideshow and hang out the banners, and by nightfall some small patch of land will be not Council Bluffs, but Camelot!"

A babble of excited laughter greeted the speech. There was magic in Wes Jarvis, a hypnotism that lifted everyone, even the circus people who knew his tricks, out of the humdrum.

"He almos' as good a conjurer as Atticus," the old man chuckled, getting to his feet and helping Fancy up too.

"I love the circus, Atticus!" she blurted out. "I love the whole troupe of them and the animals and the plays." She took a deep, satisfied breath, drinking everything in.

"Dey's your family now, child."

"You're my family."

"Dat's true, too. But I'm gittin' on in years, Fancy. One a dese days I be headin' out and you be on your own."

"Not 'til we get to California and find the gold there," she said, as if that were a given.

"No. Not 'til den."

"Tell me again what we'll do when we find the gold, Atticus." She slipped her hand into his and fell into step beside the old giant. She'd spent little time alone with him since joining the theatrical company; there were parts to learn and songs to rehearse and a constant barrage of new information to absorb. But the stories of what they would do when they found the gold, the ones that had sustained her in their travels together, were still their special conspiracy.

"Well, now, let's jest see. . . . First thing, we buy us a real house to live in wif fine furniture and dishes and silverware jest like Beau Rivage." He heard her giggle contentedly, and it made his heart feel light.

"Den we git us a fine old horse and carriage so's we kin see de sights in Californy. Big place, Californy, we gonna need to git around."

"I want matched black stallions," she responded, loving the familiar game.

"Well now, honey, stallions don't seem to be a real good bet for pullin' carriages. How's 'bout we git us a nice li'l pair of geldings, wif real level heads?"

"All right, if we must. But I'll need lots and lots of clothes. Gorgeous clothes, with feathers and lace and fancy buttons. And jewels, Atticus, jewels like my mama had!"

"My, my, child!" The old man chuckled. "We's gonna have to find us a real *big* gold mine to git all dat outta it!"

Fancy laughed and hugged him. Atticus was dearer to her than she could admit even to herself; each time he spoke of "goin' on" without her, terror constricted her heart. He was the lifeline; he was her friend. She kissed him on the cheek, a big stretch on tiptoe, then waved as she veered off toward Magda's wagon. They were performing *Ten Nights in a Barroom* for tonight's audience, and she wanted to check the costumes one more time to make sure they were perfect.

God, how she loved acting. Because of her delicate features, she could play a child as well as an ingenue, and once Wes had heard her sing, she'd been made a regular part of the minstrel shows. She didn't mind being in blackface now, for it was temporary—besides, she told Atticus proudly, she could talk "nigra" better than any white girl alive. She was getting to be a woman, too, with nature and Magda as her guides.

Wes was right about the theatre being a privilege, Fancy thought gaily as she made her way to the wagon. All her dreams were coming back into focus—there were possibilities again.

During their wanderings, Fancy had wondered, when she dared, how she could ever make her way back into the white man's world, the world of plenty. Now she knew the theatre was the answer. She would be a brilliant actress and singer, famous and desirable. Wes said a great performer could cross all boundaries of class and privilege. The magic worked not only for the audience, but for the players as well . . . in the theatre anyone could become someone.

▲ ▲ ▲

"You fill that child's head with dreams," Magda chided, her throaty voice a sensuous purr on the night air.

"Not dreams but hopes, my Magda," Jarvis replied, looking up at the stars. "She has need of them."

"And she is not so much a child anymore, my observant one. Is she?"

Jarvis looked at the woman sharply, a half smile on his lips. "Are you jealous, my wildcat?"

"Youth is to be envied," she replied with a sigh. "I feel old tonight."

"And why is that?"

"I have done the cards." She said it as if the statement explained everything.

"Your magic is greater than mine, Magda," Jarvis said sadly.

"My magic is *nothing*! I know nothing. I am a fraud and my magic is an illusion I conjure for fools!"

Jarvis looked at the Gypsy strangely. It was unlike Magda to deny her powers with him, for he alone knew that they were not fraudulent. She was greatly gifted.

"You are no charlatan, my Magda."

"Ah, my old friend, but tonight I wish I were."

"What did you see that upset you so?"

"The girl will have a strange life. A disturbing life. Her journey has just begun."

"She will not be loved?"

"She will be loved too much. There will be too much of everything. Great riches. Fame. All, too much."

Jarvis laughed mirthlessly. "Such a destiny I could envy."

"No! Great dangers stalk her path."

"And mine?"

Magda looked at the handsome, aging man; her eyes glittered oddly in the moonlight and he could not tell if there were tears in them.

"Your destiny is to make love to me tonight," she said offhandedly, and turned to mount the steps to her wagon, her skirt a paisley swirl. Every gesture is calculated to arouse a man, he thought, knowing better than to press her for information she did not wish to give.

It was a curse to know the future.

▲ ▲ ▲

"How much is in the coffers, my faithful Gitalis?" Jarvis asked, pulling off his costume boots and flexing his toes in the lamplight of the wagon.

"Not enough to make us rich," replied the cynical voice. "But enough to keep our children fed."

The circus master sat down wearily on the bed, but he smiled as he spoke. "Genteel sufficiency, eh, my fine friend. What more can one ask?"

"Superfluity, perhaps."

Jarvis laughed aloud, his laugh a deep, hearty sound in the small space. "We are doing better since those two joined us, though. That you must admit. Magda says they bring good luck with them."

"Magda! Magda predicts what she wants us to believe."

"Ah, but that is merely human nature, Gitalis, and Magda is the most human of women. But do not underestimate her powers. Mark me well, my Sancho Panza, she knows things we do not."

"She seems willing enough to teach you all she knows."

"And you are jealous, little man?" Jarvis asked with a smile and a raised eyebrow. He and Gitalis had been friends for a lifetime, it sometimes seemed.

"She is much woman for a small person like myself, Maestro," the dwarf replied with a lascivious smirk. "But I am lonely. I will try to find someone my own size in the next town."

"There are good things in store for us in the next town, Gitalis."

"Always you think there is something good in the next town. Eternal optimist. Like the Fool in the tarot."

"This time it's true," Jarvis persisted, burrowing beneath the coverlet.

Gitalis smiled and blew out the candle before removing his own clothes and lying down on his small bed.

Jarvis was a remarkable man. A gifted actor and illusionist, possessor of a vast repertoire of Shakespearean plays as well as contemporary ones; a man with the charisma to draw the crowds and the showmanship to send them away satisfied. But he had too soft a heart, and consequently the company always had too many mouths to feed.

They could draw the same crowds with half the players and the money would go farther. But any sob story moved Jarvis to generosity—any freak of nature, out-of-work actor, or oddity unable to work elsewhere had a place with his troupe. And wasn't he, Gitalis, a fine one to quarrel with such largesse? Where else but with Jarvis would an overeducated dwarf with total recall and a desperate love for Shakespeare find employment? He laughed softly at his own foolishness.

Yet this was hard country for touring, too, and it bore watching with more caution than Jarvis knew. Not like the South before the war, where

they'd made their easy way from town to town, and plantation to plantation, through benevolent weather and generous audiences.

The war had come and they had headed west. It was their destiny, Magda
said. "The old witch," he grumbled. Hard as he tried, he could never figure
her out. "Jealous, lustful little man," he chided himself. "You are cranky
only because you lack a woman." He resolved to seek out the acquiescent
Lena the following day. Unlike her sister, Tina, who remained faithful to
her husband, Flute, Lena had no scruples about sharing her favors. "I
already sleep with two," she would say, with some justification. "Why not
more?"

Grumpily, he punched the pillow into submission, and nestling his small
body into a fetal ball, Gitalis went to sleep.

▲

Living space was scarce, so Fancy and Atticus sometimes shared a wagon
with Wu the Chinese cook. Jolly and irascible, one moment slapping his
frying pan against his knee with laughter, the next chasing one or more of
the Marcatos around the campfire with the same weapon, Wu was unlike
anyone Fancy had ever encountered.

He spoke an astonishing pidgin English—Cantonese liberally interspersed
with American curse words.

"Sailor cut off Wu pigtail, fuckin' good!" he had explained when first they
met. "Wu get shanghaied. No pigtail, no go back to China." Then he had
laughed uproariously as if the whole episode was hilarious.

"Wu fix 'em good. Wu make big million dollar in gold mine. Grow new
hair. Go back to China rich like Mandarin. Fucky, fucky!"

Wu made an elaborate ritual of everything he did, from boiling water to
going to bed at night. He was fastidious in all things and prided himself on
being the best cook in the United States.

"But you're not in the United States anymore, Señor Wu," José Marcato
would tease him.

"Then Wu best cook in Nebraska Territory, son of a worm!" he would
shout back, and take out after the young man brandishing a butcher knife.

Wu kept a strongbox in his kitchen wagon and every night he would
unstrap it from its place and count his treasure. Fancy had not seen him
actually do this, but Tobey had done an imitation in mime and Magda had
confirmed that it was so.

▲

Fancy watched Wu bustle around the broad-beamed, sturdily built chuck
wagon that was the hub of his domain. The morning air had sharpened her
appetite.

Wu's wagon was an extraordinary feat of practical engineering, a basic flatbed wagon refurbished to accommodate the needs of the troupe. A huge water barrel was strapped to its side; bulk foods such as beans, sugar, dried apples, grain, potatoes, and onions were stored along its floor. Bentwood bows supported the canvas roof, while a toolbox filled with the essentials of frontier life was attached with iron bands to its side. A coffee grinder decorated the wagon's outer shell, as did the lantern hooks, stake ropes, and pans too big for storage within.

Most ingenious of all, to Fancy's mind, was the hinged rear wooden flap that swung down to form a working table. When the flap was down, supported by its sturdy legs, the interior network of functional cubes was displayed. Shelves for coffeepot, bread bowl, chewing tobacco tin, and vinegar urn became visible. Cubbies stuffed with the Dutch ovens, skillets, molasses and whiskey jars that were the staples of life on the journey. Hanging hooks for the razor strop, and any other items that needed fastening, lined the interior of the largest spaces. There were big drawers filled with salt and lard and baking soda, and smaller ones where tiny phials with Chinese characters on their labels were kept by Wu, with an air of secrecy, next to his precious sewing kit and bandages.

"Tell me about China," Fancy asked Wu when she finally conquered her fear of the strange man with the queer blue dress and the screeching voice that held all but the most intrepid at bay.

"History of China like old man's memory," he replied. "Distant past more vivid than present. Ancestors more important than anything." That was all he would say that day before he shooed her away, but she noticed he said it very clearly.

"Why is it you pretend you can't speak American?" she asked him the next morning, feeling bold. "What you said to me last night sounded just right—not like the pidgin talk you're always scolding at people."

Wu put down the huge tin coffeepot he held, and much to Fancy's delight he bowed from the waist and said, "Woe to the man who tosses pearls before swine." He hadn't smiled exactly, but some inner mirth had shown out through his enigmatic eyes. She had seen it, as he had intended her to.

"I'll keep your secret for you," she told him conspiratorially, "if you'll tell me about China."

Wu had bobbed his head a few times in quick succession and replied, "Fair bargain," before going on about his work.

Since then, Fancy had learned much about the Chinese. He was not at all the caricature he'd invented for the benefit of those he considered his inferiors. He knew many things only a man of education could know, and his philosophy was different from any she'd heard about; he didn't even believe in heaven and hell.

"Learn to live correctly in this life. Not worry about next," he told her, dismissing the whole idea of a Christian hereafter. How like these primitive Americans to have only one all-purpose God, when any fool could see that many were needed to keep the universe in harmony.

"What are you cooking?" Fancy asked, sticking her nose past his shoulder and sniffing at the lumpy mixture in the bowl.

"Cook poison biscuit," Wu replied sourly. "Kill everybody, chop, chop!" Fancy giggled. When Wu talked pidgin to her it meant either that others were within earshot or that he was hopping mad.

"Ay! Mouth and stomach do more harm than good. It was mistake for heaven to endow us with them."

"What exactly happened to make you so mad?"

"Dog-vomit dwarf accuse Wu of stealing food money. I will put dog droppings in his soup and his tiny testicles will wither and fall off!"

Fancy's eyes widened. She was used to Wu's invective—usually his bark was far worse than his bite—so, impulsively, she leaned over and kissed his cheek, then scampered off in the opposite direction.

A small, unobtrusive smile curved the cook's thin lips. Of course he had stolen the food money and tucked it into his strongbox. The food he fed these foreign devils was plenty good enough for their unsophisticated palates. What would they know of the delicacy of a hundred-year egg or the precious flesh of the abalone? What need had they for more than biscuits and venison, rabbit, beef, and trail onions?

Pearls before swine indeed, he thought contentedly as he finished drying the last of the utensils he had used to feed the players, and hung the large slotted spoon on a peg near the door of his wagon.

He had played the fool so long now, the charade was like a cloak he wound about himself in the morning and discarded at night. Wu the unpredictable . . . Wu the fierce-tempered . . . Wu the crazy Chinese cook whose whims must be catered to—these were the roles that served his larger purpose. Wu the shanghaied laborer, no better than a coolie. Without thinking, he touched the amputated pigtail he always used to illustrate the tragedy of his plight. He chuckled as he did so.

"No pigtail," he would say in exquisite mock distress. "No go back to China!" China was the last place on earth he intended to go. China, with its Manchu maniac on the throne and its insidious dangers for one who had flown too high and been shot down. China, with its endless family obligations that could not be met by a patriot on the run. Oh, no. Wu would stay right here in America, where fortunes could be made by any man willing to work for them. Eventually, any of his family left alive would be taken care of and his face restored.

Work and plan. Work and scheme. Work and pretend to be a fool. That was what it would take. As long as no man took him seriously, no man would bother to thwart his efforts. Ten years already had been spent on this circuitous but inexorable route to the future.

Wu had stowed away and worked at the worst jobs a boat could force upon a man. He had jumped overboard in New York harbor and swum to shore. He had starved and then found work in Chinatown where every penny, every fraction of a penny, he had hoarded in his box. Finally, when the time was right and his credentials as a cook were secure, he had begun to work his way west, for west was where the gold was. Even in China there had been stories of men made rich by a single plot of land that held the precious metal—and the anonymity of the new and lawless territory pleased him.

Hadn't he heard in Chinatown of gangs of coolies being herded west to work as navvies on the railroads, or as slaves in the mines? Why would anyone question the motives of one more Chinese in a vast sea of yellow faces heading west? Hadn't the gods been with him in his enterprise so far? They had shown him the way to the circus. Wes Jarvis was a fool where money was concerned, an overgenerous fool, but he was a good boss. The circus was the perfect place for Wu, his eccentricities, and his black box to hide on the way west.

Certain no one was anywhere near, Wu bolted the door to the wagon, lit a joss stick of incense on the little altar he had hidden behind the cookpots, for it would be essential to keep the gods placated on his journey, and unlocked the fastenings of the straps that held the strongbox of his fortune to the floor of the wagon. Opening the lid, he reached within to feel the reassurance of the coins within his grasp.

There were times, of course, when he regretted what had been lost, but that was foolish. He counted the wastefulness of regret to be a Western stupidity. Destiny. No more, no less, had made the revolution of young men fail—the revolution that was to replace the old imperial China with a new reform. So the dreams had died unborn and the intellectuals had scattered. Many had died at the Court of the Son of Heaven; hideous, lengthy deaths. The price of failed revolutions was invariably grotesque.

Why was he alive and so many others dead? Destiny. And because he was smart and subtle and, above all else, patient . . . a day, a month, a year . . . time was of no importance to Wu. Survival was important. And subterfuge. And the gold he amassed, which made it possible for new dreams to take the place of old ruined hopes.

The gods were well aware of his journey and of his great gifts. They had set him on the path and equipped him well for it, but the endurance was his own. That, beyond all else, would build him his empire.

Wu closed and bolted the lid of his box and secured it to the floor.

Satisfied, he pulled the small, precious copy of Lao-tzu from its hidden pocket and settled in to read the philosopher who could be of most help to him in his mighty endeavors.

 Gitalis climbed up onto the three-legged stool so he could reach Fancy's neck with ease; with surprisingly strong, deft fingers he began to knead the fatigue from her aching muscles.

Fancy sensed that he liked the touching, and she welcomed the sensitive fingers. It wouldn't do to have a kinked neck for tonight's performance.

There was far more touching permitted among the circus people than she'd ever remembered seeing in her old life, she thought idly. Men and women embraced. People slapped each other on the rump in passing; sometimes even the men embraced. It was a wilder, looser world than the ordinary, but it was not without its own strict rules, as she was learning from Gitalis, who was the repository of all earthly knowledge.

"In the circus, people help one another," he told her. "What we have, we share; except our privacy. There can be little solitude when people live on top of one another, so we must guard against intrusion in ingenious ways. We create small privacies. . . . We pretend not to know who sleeps with whom, who gambles beyond his pocketbook, who covets another's success. Or wife." He shrugged his shoulders meaningfully and chuckled.

"If someone becomes blatant in his follies, we try to help him—if he will not be helped, we ostracize. It is a strict society, but a just one. And you must remember, Fancy, we in the circus welcome those who would be defenseless misfits in the outside world."

Fancy strained her head backward against the dwarf's probing fingers and found that the kink was miraculously gone.

"Thank you for fixing my neck, Gitalis," she said, touching his shoulder affectionately as she left him, but he knew from the touch that she meant to thank him for the learning. Every time he was with her now, he tried to pass on some knowledge she should possess. She was an eager sponge.

And she had real talent—too much for a tiny traveling show like theirs. Jarvis saw the gifts; he was training her speaking voice and teaching her to act, the old man was tutoring her in the stringed instruments, and already she had mastered the banjo and guitar. He, Gitalis, was coaching her lovely contralto singing voice into an instrument worthy of attention, training her vocal cords with operatic intensity and teaching her to read music with skill and sensitivity. And Magda . . . God alone knew what Magda was teaching the child, but like as not, it, too, was needed. Gitalis shrugged his child-size shoulders and checked his mental file for what needed doing. Go over Wu's accounting of their food supply, to see if that penurious devil was squirreling away a percentage of the food money again. Settle the dispute between Flute and Harp, the two halves were not speaking to each other. He must remember to tell Lena to be less conspicuous about her indiscretions with the three Marcatos. He ducked under the tiger wagon, a favorite shortcut available only to one of his size, and collided with Lena and José Marcato in a surreptitious embrace.

"You have nothing else to do?" he shouted at them in a mixture of Italian, Spanish, and English. "So you stand about trying to provoke Flute into shooting you both! Imbeciles! We do not have enough excitement in our show? Is that it?" The two mumbled startled apologies and rushed off in opposite directions.

"A traveling asylum!" he said aloud, slapping his forehead with the heel of his hand. He watched them go, then, humming one half of the duet in the third act of *Carmen* to himself, he went about the business of getting the circus through another night.

▲ ▲ ▲

"Those three fools are fighting over you again, I see," Magda said with a judicious sniff, as Fancy entered her wagon flushed and breathless.

"They think I'm very pretty," Fancy replied with fifteen-year-old hauteur. "I can't help it if they all want me."

"Most men will want you, Fancy," Magda replied disdainfully. "Are you intelligent enough to make the most of that fact? Or so stupid you'll follow your private parts wherever they lead you?"

"Magda!" said Fancy, crestfallen. "I'm only trying to learn to be a woman."

Magda cocked an eyebrow at her and shook her head. "Come here, child," she ordered in a more congenial voice. "We must discuss."

Fancy sat down carefully, wondering what would come next. "We must discuss" was always the signal that Magda had something significant to say.

"To be a woman is to have great power," she began.

"You're joking, Magda. Women don't have half the rights of men."

"I said nothing of rights, you foolish girl! I speak of *power!*" Magda snapped the words as if speaking to a slow-witted child. "You mark my words: Sex is power as much as money is. Men have both, we have only one. So, we must be smarter than they are. Luckily, this is not hard for us."

Fancy giggled and Magda rewarded her with an amused look.

"You are beautiful, as I am," the older woman said. "In order to use that fact for your own benefit, you must do two things: Bridle your own lust and learn to control theirs."

Fancy felt color rise in her cheeks. She knew Magda spoke freely of forbidden subjects; indeed, all the circus people spoke of topics from which others shied. But she had not believed that words like *lust* were ever spoken among nice people. She looked at Magda, wide-eyed, not knowing how to respond.

"I know these things are not discussed in this land of Puritans. These Americans rut as often as all other men, but they hide the fact behind hypocrisy and pretend to be celibates! They are fools. Mothers tell their daughters nothing and the daughters go to their marriage beds shackled in ignorance. Then they spend their whole lives pregnant and die without ever having understood what I will tell you now."

"What exactly is lust?" breathed Fancy, barely able to speak the word aloud.

"It is what you feel between your legs when that imbecile Marcato caresses you."

Fancy started to protest, but Magda silenced her with a scowl.

"Do you think I haven't seen you flirting and fondling behind the wagons? Do you think I do not know how the blood boils in every man of the troupe when you wiggle your bottom and bat your eyes? Even the dwarf is half in love with you, the little pip-squeak!" Her accent made it sound *peepskwik* and Fancy almost giggled, but stifled the sound.

"Do not protest! This is as it should be. What you must now learn is how to control this power that you have over men, so they will do as you wish. But to do this you must first of all accept your own sexuality. Your own body's cravings, Fancy, are very powerful—you will desire men as much as they desire you. A woman is more often undone by her own lust than by any man's.

"They will seek to own you. This, you must never allow. Such ownership is for peasants, not for us.

"Use your body for your own pleasure, Fancy, when you wish to. Choose the time and the place. Do not be at their disposal. No man, no government, no church must ever dictate the uses of your body, although many will try. It is yours alone, and you alone will answer for its use on the day of judgment. You may use it for your own pleasure or need, but never, under any circumstances, may you place your body's freedom under another's control.

"I will teach you how *not* to have a baby every year, but to do this *you*, not they, must maintain dominion over the urgings of your sexuality."

Fancy hadn't uttered a single sound since Magda had begun to speak.

"You must learn to seduce. And you must learn to turn away the ones you do not desire without making an enemy. Men are more fragile than we —if their pride is hurt, they can be vicious. You must learn to leave them their dignity, even when you reject their advances. You must honor them for caring and honor yourself by maintaining the right to say no.

"Once you have learned to control the power you have over them, you must take care to use it well. All acts in the universe are ruled by the laws of retribution. You will reap what you have sown. You must sow wisely."

"Will you really teach me all I need to know about being a woman?" Fancy asked, her voice little more than an awestruck whisper.

"I will teach you," Magda said, "all but the most essential part."

"And what is that?"

"I cannot teach you courage," Magda said with great seriousness. "That you must learn for yourself."

▲ ▲ ▲

"No, no, no, child!" boomed Jarvis. "From the diaphragm, not the throat! If you persist in speaking from the throat, you will grow nodes as big as turtles on your vocal cords and your instrument will be silenced!"

Fancy put down the script and strove to hold her temper. "That *was* from the diaphragm!" she shouted back.

"That puny sound? Never!"

" 'A truant disposition, good my lord,' " murmured Gitalis from the sidelines.

" 'Give it an understanding,' " Jarvis replied softly, " 'but no tongue.' "

Gitalis nodded, amused, and went back to making his endless list.

Fancy finished the scene, the flush of anger in her tone spicing the lines. Her voice was developing nicely and her memory was formidable. Already she had a dozen roles and a full repertoire of recitations committed to memory. If she applied the correct discipline to developing her acting skills, she could go far.

A tiny knot of people gathered around the performers as Fancy finished her curtain speech; spontaneous applause greeted her closing lines.

" 'Season your admiration for a while,' " her mentor said disdainfully to the impromptu audience, shooing them away.

"Damn you, Jarvis!" Fancy exploded at him. "That was good and you know it."

"What use is *good,* when one is capable of *great*?" he snapped, then deliberately turned his attention to Gitalis and the other matters of the circus, leaving her fuming on the stage.

"She makes progress, Maestro," the dwarf said softly, as both men watched her stamp away.

"Indeed. And the higher her outrage, the better her art. The more I goad her, the harder she strives—if only to prove me wrong."

"You do not wish to break her spirit, of course."

" 'I must be cruel, only to be kind,' as the immortal bard would tell us. Far from breaking her spirit, I hope to teach her to control it. She is a passionate wench, my little man. She simply does not know it yet."

" 'Forbear to judge,' " Gitalis chuckled. " 'For we are sinners all.' "

Jarvis laughed in response and clapped the dwarf on the shoulder.

"Always the perfect quotation at your fingertips, my friend. I envy you your mind."

"As I envy you your body, sire. So we are even.

"What will become of her when she is grown?" the small man asked unexpectedly.

"She has genuine talent and burning ambition," Jarvis answered thoughtfully, "which is why she is worth goading. When the time comes, we must encourage her to leave us and go on to the real theatre. She is sixteen now, I think. Before the year is out she will be ready, don't you agree?"

"And the old man? She will take him with her?"

"Magda says he has not long to live."

"Ah, Magda and her prophecies! A 'tiger's heart wrapped in a woman's hide,' that one!"

"True enough, in some ways. But she cares for the girl and watches her future with misgiving."

" 'Then I shall think nobly of her soul, but in no way approve her opinion,' " responded the little man, pleased with himself for having found an appropriate retort.

Jarvis laughed aloud, tossing back the mane of long white hair from his forehead. Gitalis noticed how much the man had aged in the past year of worries. The lines around his eyes had deepened and his handsome face looked worn. It was good for Jarvis to have taken the girl under his wing; she cheered him and reminded him of his own abilities.

What a tragedy that a man of Jarvis' great talents was relegated to the vagabond life of the circus when he deserved the acclaim of New York or London. It was a blessing, of course, for the circus folk that Jarvis had chosen this particular route to the future, but it was wasteful for such rare gifts to be cast before swine.

▲

"My darling girl, you must sing each aria as if your life depended on it!" Gitalis waved the score in front of Fancy's nose impatiently. "The world does not need one more mediocre mezzo. Do you wish to live your life in poverty or to reach the stars?" He didn't wait for a reply. "The future is in your hands, Fancy. No one else's. You have a *gift*. The stringed instruments are child's play for you, but they cannot give you fame or fortune. The voice can!"

Fancy's head snapped up, anger and frustration evident on her face. "I am working as hard as I can! I study night and day, Gitalis. Between you and Wes and Atticus, I barely have time to sleep."

"If you still sleep you have time to learn more, wasteful girl."

"Damn you, Gitalis! I've had enough of your bullying. In the four years I've been with this troupe I've learned to sing in French and Italian, I've learned so much Shakespeare I recite it in my dreams. I play instruments, I dance, I do comedy. I hawk tickets to the crowd. If I could grow another half, you'd have me doing Harp and Flute's work as well!

"But nothing I ever do is ever enough for you! Nothing is ever good enough or professional enough or anything enough to satisfy you. I'm sick to death of your badgering. You are driving me mad. Why do you hurt me like this, Gitalis? Why?"

"Because I love you," the dwarf answered simply. "And because you will get one chance in this godforsaken world; and if you are not ready, it will pass you by like the midnight train, and you will live forever with your dead dreams and the knowledge of what might have been." His usually resonant voice sounded hollow as he turned to go.

"No chance will pass *me* by, Gitalis," she shouted after him. "You can count on that!"

The small man headed away from her without speaking. Tears came to his eyes and he fought them back relentlessly.

"I love you, too, Gitalis," she called after him, but he knew she meant it in a different way from his confession to her. He did not turn back but kept on walking; he didn't notice Magda until she fell into step beside him.

"Do not worry for her, little man," the fortune-teller said. "She will have more than her share of opportunity. And fame. And love. You have taught her well. You and Jarvis and the old man."

Gitalis wondered at the kind words from Magda and shook his head. When he spoke his voice was gruff.

"The old man will teach her little more. He is failing fast and you know it."

"He is pure in heart and will see God," Magda replied.

"Such bullshit! The pure in heart may see God, but it is only the lonely and desperate who need Him."

He turned abruptly at his own wagon and without saying another word, slammed the door behind him and left the Gypsy standing in the dust, a thoughtful expression on her face.

▲

Atticus raised himself uneasily from his pillow and sniffed the air. It was the third time in a week that he'd dreamt about the snake. The first time the dream had seemed benevolent enough, a small green slithering creature had been seen hanging from a jungle branch. The landscape of his childhood had always lived inside him, and he had not been unduly alarmed by the night image.

The second dream had been of a huge boa constrictor; he'd seen it wrap its insistent coils around a baby goat and consume the struggling, bleating creature. Still, he'd put it down to chance and banished the vision with the morning light.

The third, tonight's dream, had been clear. The eyes of a demon had stared out at him from the serpent's expectant face—a predator come to claim its prey. Atticus felt the clamminess of his skin as he awoke, and shuddered in the darkness. He had seen those eyes before.

It was more than five years since he'd made his bargain with the Snake God for Fancy's life—long enough to forget that the price must eventually be paid.

The old man stood up shakily, forcing his creaking body erect, and moved to the doorway of the wagon. Outside, the stars were glittering pinpricks in the midnight sky, just as they had seemed to him in the Africa he remembered from the long ago. The reach of the gods was long and inexorable. He stood in the opening and watched the darkness for a while, unblinking, unable to return to sleep.

So the time of reckoning was at hand . . . perhaps he would speak of it to Magda, for she was wise in the ways of conjuring and might be able to divine the time and place of his rendezvous.

Eventually, Atticus returned to his bed, but he would not trust himself to sleep until the first faint flush of morning had tinged the horizon.

▲

Fancy laid down the faro hand with a smug laugh. Wes, too, laughed ruefully.

"Quite the little cardsharp you are becoming, Fancy," he said, the lines around his eyes crinkling with repressed merriment. He coughed a bit into a linen handkerchief as he said it. Fancy had a good eye, quick wit, and an astonishing memory for what cards had already been dealt. "We'll teach you 'to drink deep ere you depart,' eh?" he continued, pocketing the hanky. Fancy noted that Gitalis stared concernedly at Jarvis for a moment, then switched his eyes back to the cards in his hand.

"I doubt that *Godey's Lady's Book* would consider faro dealing an element essential to a young lady's education," she countered cheerily. "Now that I know how to deal, can you teach me to cheat?"

Gitalis rolled his eyes heavenward and Jarvis threw back his head and laughed aloud.

" 'Good my mouse of virtue, answer me. Shall we set the child on such a sinful path as she desires?' "

"It seems not so sinful as it is practical," Gitalis murmured with a cynical smirk. "One never knows when a bit of sleight of hand can turn the tide of providence."

"I like gambling," Fancy said. "Cards, dice, I think I have a knack for all of it."

"Will you listen to the child, Gitalis? What will God think of such she-nanigans?"

"He should understand well enough, my liege," Gitalis answered steadily. "The dice of God are always loaded."

Jarvis looked sharply at the little man—the dwarf had reason enough to decry God's arbitrariness. A brilliant mind and sardonic wit entrapped in a body too small to catch the brass ring. Gitalis had been heir to a huge fortune in Europe, but the man's father had been so outraged by his son's "inadequate" stature that he'd banished him and stricken his name from the family Bible despite his wife's entreaties. It was enough to inspire more than cynicism, Wes mused . . . enough to inspire murder.

What would my mother and father think, if they could see me now? Fancy wondered as she left the two men. Was there still such a place as Beau Rivage? When the war was over, had Armand come back to find the ruin of their home and assumed her dead, along with their parents? She'd never felt close to her brother, their age difference had been too great. But he was kin—and he was an unfinished story.

Half of Beau Rivage belonged to her, if any part of the plantation had been salvaged. Her father had told her he would leave the estate equally divided between the two children, as had been her mother's wish.

"A woman must have her own fortune, *ma petite*," her maman had said. "She must not be dependent on any man unless she wishes to be."

Much the same meaning as Magda's words, although Magda knew, as her mother had not, that Fancy would have to fight for every bit of independence. And safety. None of it would be handed her on a silver salver now.

Fancy glanced at the peeling paint on the shabby tiger cage as she passed it. The circus, too, was struggling for subsistence. Wes put on a good front, but business was dwindling. She made up her mind to talk with Atticus about it when she found him; he always knew how to calm her fears. She would speak with Magda, too—surely the Gypsy had noticed that Wes was looking unwell, as if his life force was ebbing. And his cough was too persistent. She made a mental note to see if he'd taken the decoction Atticus had brewed.

Now that she was a full-grown woman, perhaps Magda would take her into her confidence.

9 Magda turned over the fifth tarot card and examined the picture before her. A tower burned against the night sky and bodies cast themselves screaming from its lightning-struck height. Ominous, she thought, but not definitive. A frown formed between her arched brows as she turned up four more cards and placed them one at a time beside the small circle of the tarot lay.

Swords. The ten and four of the suit. Pain, sadness; an exile, a tomb. The Nine of Wands. Strength in adversity. Ability to meet an onslaught boldly. The Last Judgment. An angel calling people from their coffins for resurrection. The card of Eternal Life.

With a gesture of frustration, she swept the cards from the table, shuffled them hastily, then cast the lay a second time.

Drumming the table with agitated fingers, the Gypsy stared for a moment at the result, then pushed the cards aside and rose from the table. She would find Atticus.

Magda made her determined way across the encampment, trying to catch a glimpse of the old man. He was never idle; if he was not performing, he worked with his hands—blacksmithing, coopering, toolmaking. Perhaps she would find him near his makeshift forge.

She caught a glimpse of his gray-fringed head, thirty feet or so beyond the lead wagon. She saw him pit his strength against the windlass—a wooden frame that wound a hemp rope tight enough to pull the staves of a barrel into alignment. Magda stood for a moment watching the competence with which the old man forced the errant staves to his will before slipping the metal hoop around them to form the barrel shape.

"De poor workman quarrels wif his tools," she'd heard him say to Fancy once. "A man kin mos'ly always make somethin' work if he has the will to do it, honey. Don't you never let me hear you say, 'I cain't do dis, 'cause I ain't got de right tools to he'p me.' "

Such good advice . . . such a good, firm heart, she thought. He has given that child more than she knows.

"Afternoon, Miz Magda," Atticus called out when he saw her. "You lookin' for ol' Atticus?" He smiled in pleasure and she waved at him in return.

"You are an artist," she said respectfully.

He looked startled, but pleased. "Jest doin' what I knows to do, Miz Magda. But I do like de sound of dem kind words, all de same." He motioned her to a small stool nearby.

"Want to set a spell? I could stand a li'l company 'bout now."

"I have seen you in the cards, my friend," Magda said carefully. "There is much we could speak of, yes?"

Atticus leaned his weight on the windlass for a moment before replying. "I thank you kindly for askin', Miz Magda, but I don't rightly know if talkin' kin change what you seen in dem cards a' yours."

She noticed he did not doubt her ability to "see," merely her ability to change fate.

"We are realists, we two, eh?" she responded. Magda sat on the stool with her knees apart as a man would do, her skirt wide in front of her. She placed her hands on her knees and stretched her back in the darkening sun.

"The fools do not understand that the curse of our gift is that we know what we must face, before it comes." She laughed joylessly. "When I was a girl, my sisters would say to me 'Magda, Magda find my petticoat . . . Magda, I lost my ring. Look into your crystal and tell me where I put it.' As if the gift of clairvoyance was a mountebank's game for children to play at.

"They would laugh at my seriousness and abuse my 'sight' to find lost trinkets—and I would sit at my window with visions of their deaths in my mind's eye, unable to explain my burden."

Atticus lowered himself to the ground beside her. He was still strong, she saw, but his muscles did not move freely anymore; he lowered himself with care and bent his knees, as if they pained him.

"I learnt to conjure 'cause dat's de way of men in my tribe. My family got wizards, so dey 'spects me to learn wizardin', too. I 'members de first time I seen a vision. Lawd, Lawd, Miz Magda, I thought I was king of de world dat day!"

"So you asked for your gift and I did not, and we are both stuck with it just the same. A good joke Fate plays on us, Atticus. Is it not so?"

"That ol' preacher on Massa Deverell's plantation, he say, 'Man propose, God dispose.' Don't seem to matter which ol' god you got, dey all work de same way."

"You bartered with the gods for the child's life, did you not, my friend?" she asked gently.

"Yes, ma'am, I did jest dat." He didn't question how she knew.

"And you fear the time of payment is near at hand?"

He nodded. "I had some dreams. He comin' for me one day soon. He surely is. I don't regret dat bargain I made wif him, you understan', Miz Magda. Guess I jest not as brave as I thought I be when de time come."

"You are brave enough," she responded with conviction. "I will tell you what I know, yes?" He nodded.

"You will die within the year. She will be with you, but she will be saved. It will not be an easy death, Atticus, but not as dreadful as your God could have decreed—you will be spared the worst because of your unselfishness. I cannot see it clearly.

"You will have taught her all she needs—she will never forget the lessons. Although she fails to live by your rules at times, she will remember them and know she has erred. Your destiny and hers were entwined long ago, my friend. You were sent to be her teacher."

He accepted what the Gypsy said. "I'se had me a good long life, Miz Magda. I had me some freedom. I had me a wife and sons and Fancy. Cain't complain none, I guess."

Magda rose to go, moved by the old man's courage. She put her hand on his arm and squeezed it. "I thought you would wish to know. Forgive me."

"Ain't nothin' to forgive. Always better to know what you is dealin' wif. Don't like surprises so much now I'm old. I would've like to see Californy, all green and gold like dey say. Would've liked to see my sons agin, see how dey turned out. Would've liked to see Fancy git what she needs outta life."

"She will have everything she ever dreamed of."

"It ain't *things* I worry about her havin'. Dat child needs a powerful lot of love."

"Don't we all?" Magda answered with a wry smile, and Atticus laughed a little as she turned to go. He shook his head wonderingly at the visit and, picking up the tools again, prepared to return to his work.

He saw the tall, exotic woman hesitate, then turn back to him for a moment.

"You are a good man, Atticus," she said with emotion. "I admire you very much." Then she turned and made her way toward her own wagon, her long skirt flapping against her legs, her dark braid bouncing. She had not wished to demean his courage with her tears.

▲

Fancy curtsied deeply, her face flushed with the exhilaration of applause. She wanted to shout with glee . . . to dance . . . to hug herself in congratulation. She had sung magnificently in tonight's performance. Even Gitalis had leapt to his feet to applaud her at the end of the aria, and Jarvis' face at the edge of the audience had beamed an impresario's approval.

She searched the animated crowd for a glimpse of Atticus, but he was nowhere to be seen. She felt a small, constricted ache somewhere inside as she realized that these days, the man she looked for was no longer straight and proud as an old oak, but stooped and rounded as a banyan. He'd been acting oddly, too, she thought, not himself at all.

Fancy curtsied again, blew kisses to the audience, and whirled off the improvised stage in a rustle of taffeta skirting. How she loved the feel of the lavish fabric—the sensuous sound of the stiff moiré brought back memories of her mother's ball gowns, of the life that was rightfully hers.

Still flushed with the thrill of applause, Fancy ran to the wagon where Magda was readying herself for the onslaught of those who wished to have their fortunes told.

"Where's Atticus, Magda?" she called out as she set her foot on the lowest step of the Gypsy's wagon. "I want to share my triumph with him. I was *wonderful* tonight!" She laughed, a musical, self-satisfied sound on the crisp night air.

"He's gone," Magda replied abruptly. She did not turn from the mirror to face Fancy.

"Gone where?" asked the girl, puzzled that he would go anywhere with a night's work unfinished.

"To the mountain, child. Your friend seeks communion with his old Gods. He searches for a sign."

"A sign? What sort of sign, and why now? Why not in the daylight?"

"The moon is full tonight—this is necessary for what he seeks."

"Magda, you're frightening me. He shouldn't go off by himself in the dark without telling me."

"He does what he must, girl. He has a debt to pay."

"What debt? What are you talking about, Magda?"

"He has read certain portents in a dream, Fancy. You must let him do as his conscience dictates."

"Well, I'll do no such thing, if it means he goes meandering off into the woods at night like this! Why, he didn't even stay to hear me sing and this was my best performance ever."

Magda's glance was full of contempt. "Selfish child! He grapples with the gods and you speak of songs! Get out of my sight."

Fancy backed away in hurt confusion. She was used to Magda's volatile temper, but this exchange was very strange indeed.

"We must consider the possibilities," Magda said in the quiet of her own wagon.

10 🌿 Wes smiled and reached his arms around her from behind to fondle her breasts, a gesture that could generally soothe her most savage moods.

"No!" she said harshly, breaking away from his encircling embrace. "We must *talk.*"

"There is nothing to talk about," Jarvis replied, annoyed. Why couldn't she leave it alone? No man wants to be reminded of his failures.

"You are sick. Your lungs are filled with phlegm. You are thin as a wisp. Your strength is deteriorating."

"I can't leave the circus."

"The circus is a failure! There is no money anymore. Not since the railroads and Barnum. There is nothing ahead for the circus but disaster . . ."

"No!" he shouted at her, his great voice fierce, angry. "You are wrong. Without the circus there is nothing for me."

"Fool! What is there for you dead? Disband the circus when we reach Denver. The mountain air is healing for lungs like yours! You must stop working for a while. Take what you can get from selling out and give yourself time to get well."

Wes brought his own face close to hers so that she had to stare into his eyes.

"Look at me, Magda!" he demanded. "What do you see? A man who could sell out his friends and leave them at the edge of nowhere without hope? What have they all without the circus? The life of freaks and failures. Where will Harp and Flute go if I disband? To an asylum? And Gitalis with his great brain and tiny body . . . who will see that he is not to be laughed at, but envied? And me, Magda . . . what am I without the illusions and the roles I play? Just another mountebank in a world that cannot afford to believe in magic."

"You have barely the strength to make love to me," she cried in desperation.

Wes stepped back as if struck. "Ah, my Magda, will you not leave me anything?"

Then he left the wagon and she realized she was shaking with the frustration of what was to come. Why would he not listen to her pleas? He would be a dead man in six months if he persisted in this madness. Magda watched the retreating figure from the wagon's doorway; the moonlight reflected on

Wes's white hair and suit, making him seem angelic. The thought pierced her heart and made her angrier still. She slammed the door and locked it vengefully behind her.

Magda flung a pillow violently against the wall. She picked up another to do the same, but in the confined space there was too much risk of breaking something irreplaceable. Another frustration!

"Men!" She spat the word into the unfeeling night. "He thinks he knows so much, he knows nothing! Less than nothing! He is a fool to risk his life. A fool not to listen to me . . ."

Defeated and helpless, Magda threw herself onto the bed and struggled not to cry. She loved him far more than she had ever intended, loved his brilliance and his generous heart, his uncommon insights and his lust that matched her own. She even loved his stubborn pride, despite the fact that it would likely kill him.

Her body felt electric with the fury within, the fight had made her want him desperately. Absentmindedly she moved her hand across her breast and felt the crackle of her own emotion. She realized she was grasping her own breast tightly, as if it could hold the fury at bay.

Tentatively she touched the other breast, taking comfort in its substance, its humanity. They were not Jarvis' hands caressing her, but they were hands, and she needed to be touched tonight. She squeezed the flesh and felt the nipples harden; an almost violent need for release swept through her.

Damn her own body for this betrayal . . . damn it for needing him now, of all nights.

She touched her own belly and felt it tauten. Long tingles of desire pulsed from loin upward; she felt herself swell outward from within. Nerve endings, suddenly exquisitely knowledgeable and needy, flesh welcoming her hand's caress. God! but she was lonely without him . . . how could he risk himself so carelessly? Did he not know what his loss would mean to her?

Samarkand, the great male panther who was her pet, rattled the bars of his bedside cage. He sensed her restlessness, her agitation. She rose from the bed and unlatched the gate. The sensuous black cat stretched himself languidly and emerged from his prison as Magda dropped back upon the bed. Deftly, effortlessly, he sprang up and landed his agile body in beside her. He had been there before.

She stroked the gleaming fur, sensing the iron muscles beneath, feeling his strength, reveling in the danger. Purring softly, the great cat nuzzled her body, pushing her sideways with his careless might. He ran his sandpaper tongue once over her skin and she shuddered at the touch; the animal smell of his breath enveloped her as he narrowed his glittering eyes in communion with her, as if he understood her loneliness and need.

With a stifled cry, Magda wrapped herself around the beast, reckless of the peril. She was a wild thing, caged as he . . . she sobbed her frustration into his hard, muscular body, courting the menace of his caress, wondering if she really cared if she lived until morning.

11 "Atticus! Come quickly!" Magda's request was a demand, her face in the lamplight of the darkened wagon was strained with fear. "Jarvis is very ill."

Fancy sat upright like a puppet whose string has been jerked too tight; Atticus scrambled from his blankets; even Wu was silent in the face of Magda's fear.

"Git my medicine bag, honey," Atticus called softly to Fancy as he pulled up the suspenders that anchored his overalls in place. "I meet you dere." Then he was gone down the wagon's back steps and scurrying into the darkness with Magda's arm through his own.

Fancy glanced at Wu in the semigloom—when the circus had to tighten its belt months before, they had moved back in with Wu. She half expected an outburst from the Chinese, instead she saw a look of genuine compassion on his face.

"Go now!" Wu urged her, shooing her out of the wagon. Fancy lifted the curtain to set her foot on the top step and was surprised to find Gitalis reaching up to help her.

"What's happened, Gitalis?" she whispered as his strong hand eased the carpetbag from her grip.

"He coughs up blood. His head is hot as Hades. He has been keeping the illness from everyone but the witch. Now it has gone beyond her skills."

Fancy started to ask more, thought better of it, and hurried on.

Wes lay on the cushioned bed in Magda's wagon; even in the dim candlelight Fancy could see the fever-stretched face and telltale sweat stains on the bed coverings. His fine white hair plastered to his head made him look like a lost little boy. "Delirium." Fancy heard the word but wasn't sure who had said it.

"Boil dis, child, twicet over. Strain it wif cheesecloth real good, like I showed you. Don't let none boil away. He be needin' ever' drop afore morning.

"We don' break dis heah fever we gwine to lose him," she heard Atticus whisper softly to Magda, as she took the packet and moved away.

"He was a fool!" the woman replied hotly, near to tears. "I have told him a hundred times he gambles with what he cannot afford to lose. He would not listen to Magda."

"He gambled to protect us all, witch!" Gitalis hissed. "Without him where would we be, eh? Stranded on a trail to nowhere. Do not speak ill of him before me or I will cut out your liver and feed it to your cats for breakfast."

"Ain't no time now fo' temper fits!" Atticus said sharply from the sick man's side. "What you been dosin' him wif, Miz Magda? I be needin' to know."

"Asafetida, licorice when I could get it. He was not honest with me about the blood. But I saw in the cards the way it must go, so I gave him cinchona last night . . . and sassafras."

Atticus nodded at each new revelation, then shook his head when the ritual ended.

"Good doctorin', Miz Magda, and plenty bad news. Ain't much else left we kin git our hands on dis time a' year." He frowned in thought for a moment.

"Could be we got to treat de symptoms 'stead a de whole disease fo' a while. Could be we got to git dis fever down first . . . git dis blood coughin' stopped. Den we has time to worry 'bout curin' him."

Magda smiled at his common sense. It wouldn't help to find the perfect remedy for Jarvis' consumption if the patient died of the effects of fever in the meantime; or, worse than that, lived with a damaged brain, as she had seen happen in the wake of intense fevers.

"You are magnificent and I am a fool," she said. Her waist-length hair, unloosed for sleeping, was a rich dark fall that shimmered as she tossed her head. "Cold water, this is what we need. Gitalis, will you help me to help him?"

The dwarf pursed his lips in mock amusement. " 'Her voice was ever soft, gentle, and low, an excellent thing in woman.' " He addressed no one in particular. "For him, anything," he answered, and Magda nodded understanding.

"Tepid water, then, and cloths to bathe him. A tub to put him in." The small man nodded and scurried off—he saw Fancy hunched above a cookpot hung over the campfire as he hurried by.

▲ ▲ ▲

Fancy watched the worried faces gathered outside Magda's wagon. Jarvis had taken Atticus' medicine and been bathed in cooling water; the fever hadn't risen, Atticus said, but it hadn't broken either. Magda and Atticus had moved from the wagon to stretch their cramped limbs and to confer.

" 'Things that love night love not such nights as these,' " Gitalis murmured, and Fancy turned from watching the strained faces.

"Atticus knows what he's doing, Gitalis. He saved my life when I was snakebit. He knows more about healing than you can imagine." She wanted to say, "It will be all right . . . don't worry," but she knew too much of Fate's capriciousness to tempt it by such excessive confidence.

Wu circled the worried group near the campfire and returned to his wagon; it was apparent their medicines were failing. And why should they not, primitive as they were? Not so, his own medicines, the result of three thousand years of medical investigation.

The Three Pure Ones had seen to it that the Flowery Kingdom was blessed with the ancient knowledge of how to cure the ailing body, or the spirit, a subtle differentiation that these fools of white men did not even know existed.

Wu had carefully guarded his healing knowledge and the precious store of Chinese herbal medicines he had hoarded since New York's Chinatown. The bark of dogwood to pacify the ague, the fiery powder applied with a piece of silver to a sprain, which withdrew the soreness and made the swelling subside, and the more complex cures, like the dried herb that, once boiled, could calm the frenzy of the opium addict.

Tiny phials and packets husbanded with the same fierce protectiveness with which he guarded his gold, for he would need the healing preparations to protect his own body and spirit from the ills that plagued the goldfields and, ultimately, to cement his power over lesser men. When a man is dying, he will sell his soul, never mind his gold, for a cure.

Wu Chin had never intended to let anyone on this foolish caravan know of his healing prowess. And yet . . .

▲

Atticus bent his ear to Jarvis' chest and listened to the rattle within; there was seepage in the lungs. A froth of bloody spittle had forced its way to the surface of his lips, the worst sign of all.

The old man raised sorrowful eyes to Magda's and shook his head. Two great tears welled and ran down her high-boned cheeks. She knelt beside the comatose man and wrapped her arms around him protectively.

Atticus straightened his back with difficulty and silently cursed the futility of his efforts. Wes was a good man and many depended on him. Shouts from the campfire startled him. Wu and Gitalis were nearly at blows. You never could tell what shape anxiety would take, he thought. Fear made some people silent and withdrawn; it turned others into animals.

"Son of a motherless maggot! You would turn away the means to cure him! Son of a thousand motherfucking fools . . ."

"Hey, hey! Stop dat, now!" Atticus shouted fiercely as he reached the struggling men. "Y'all should be 'shamed a yo'selfs. A good man dyin' inside dat wagon and you two jackasses scrappin' out heah like chil'run!

Shame on you! Ain't you got no respect? I'se too tired an' too busy to worry 'bout jackasses!"

Gitalis shouted at the huge black man. "He slipped some poisonous potion to the child to give to Jarvis. Who knows what venomous swill is in it?"

Atticus' patience had been pushed beyond endurance by the night's events.

"Ought to knock yo' two thick heads together!" he began, but Wu broke in.

"*Ayeyah!* This ignorant worm dung pisses on the wisdom of a thousand years! I bring good medicine. Fix Jarvis chop chop!"

"What you talkin' 'bout?"

"China medicine! Fixee bleeding lung. Fixee fever!"

"You sure 'bout dat?" Atticus demanded, staring at the phial still clutched in the man's hand.

"Nothing to lose!" Wu hissed, and thrust the phial at Atticus. The old man looked hard at the slanted eyes and read only confidence there.

"Come wif me," he said, turning back toward the wagon. Gitalis made a move to follow, but Fancy grabbed his hand and held him back.

"Nothing to lose," she reiterated softly.

▲

Two hours after Jarvis took Wu's medicine, the fever broke and his lungs stopped bleeding. Atticus pulled the covers up over his patient and tucked them in under his arms.

"Mighty good China medicine," he said to Wu, who nodded acknowledgment.

"Destiny," Wu replied.

▲ ▲ ▲

"Why would you never listen to your Magda?" the woman chided gently. She moved the soup spoon to the man's lips, noting the yellowish skin drawn tight over bone. He had improved greatly in the week since his brush with death.

"I was afraid to lose you," he said, his voice a hollow echo. "I thought you would go if I closed the circus."

"I told you I would stay."

"You are not the only one who can read a heart, my Magda. You cannot tell me you didn't think of leaving."

Magda closed her eyes. How expressive they are, thought the man on the bed who loved her—how intensely animate.

"This is true. I might have gone. Magda, too, has demons." She made a small, rueful shape with her mouth. "I would have returned."

"Perhaps," he said, closing his eyes. She could see that even so small a conversation had drained him.

"Sleep now, Jarvis," she whispered softly as she rose from the bed and picked up the small tray on which she had carried in his food. Magda straightened the cushion she had sat on and headed for the wagon's door. As she reached it, she paused.

"Magda will never leave you now," she murmured to the sleeping man and to no one in particular. Then she straightened her shoulders, walked through the doorway and closed it quietly behind her.

 12   Fancy studied the map that Atticus had husbanded so carefully over the years. She smiled at the childish letters that had eventually neatened into an adult hand. What a circuitous path their time alone together, and their nearly four years with the circus—time enough for her to become a woman and for Atticus to grow old.

Fancy glanced up from the map into the face across the table. It was not only Atticus' hair that was gray now; his skin, too, seemed to have the tinge of ashes beneath the glossy black, and his eyes were rheumy. She reached out her hand to him and clasped his.

"So, my friend, we finally go to Californy." Atticus nodded, as if unconvinced of the wisdom of such an act.

"It would be safer if we stayed here at Fort Laramie, honey."

"Oh, Atticus, I don't want to. I've just got to get to someplace bigger."

He nodded again, knowing better than she what she meant by that.

"Which way you fixin' for us to go, child?"

"Across the North Platte, I think, and down into Colorado. They've got gold in those mountains, Atticus, everybody here's talking about it. The soldiers at the fort say as soon as the word gets back East, the hills will be crawling with prospectors, just like the Comstock and Virginia City. . . . We can get there first and stake us a claim. And if we don't strike it rich enough there, we'll just keep on heading west 'til we hit Californy, like we always planned." Her eyes were animated with the exhilaration of their dream.

"Bein' young a mighty powerful tonic," Atticus said with a smile. "Make you think anythin' possible, don't it?" Fancy wasn't sure if he was chiding her or simply making a statement of fact. Atticus reached out a hand and smoothed back the dark hair from her forehead gently, the way he used to when she was small. He'd invented the dream of finding gold, as a talisman to make a little child believe she could once again have what was lost to her. Now he could see he'd worked his magic all too well; the dream was so real to her, she'd have to follow wherever it led.

"I don't know how many more miles I got left in dese ol' bones, honey," Atticus said honestly.

She squeezed his hand again.

"Don't you worry, Atticus. We're practically there already. See here on the map." She pointed out the distance on the page. "We can't give up now, can we? Not when we're just around the next turn in the road from everything we want."

"No, ma'am!" he said with an indulgent smile. "Not when all dat gold jest over de next hill, we cain't quit. Jes' as long as you remembers one thing: Sometimes ever'thin' we want ain't ever'thin' we need."

"I'll remember, Atticus," she said, not understanding in the least. "I promise." Then she folded up the map and handed it back to him, but he shook his head.

"No, sugah, you keep that now. You de navigator from here on, I 'spects."

Fancy looked at him quizzically, then began to tuck the map into her bag.

"Atticus lesson number three thousand an' sixty-two," he said. "Never let yo' map outta yo' hands. You jest tuck dat li'l ol' piece a oilcloth into yo' bosom, child, and you keep it close to you, jest like I always done. I'se real proud a' dat map, Fancy. Real proud a' all de places we been together."

Fancy tucked the map inside the bosom of her dress carefully. It disturbed her that Atticus would relinquish the precious record.

"Yessir," he continued, half to himself. "Atticus proud a' you, honey— you has growed up real fine. One day soon some young buck gonna come along an' sweep you right off dem li'l feet a' yours, now you is sech a fine young lady."

"No young buck is going to interest me in the least," Fancy said firmly to push away the uneasiness. "Leastways not until I make my fortune, so I can pick out *just* the kind of man I want. And even then I may not marry anyone, Atticus. Not if it means I've got to let him be my master. I couldn't stand that kind of life. Not after all that's happened to me."

"Ain't nothing in dis world as good as a man an' woman what loves each other, Fancy. Don't you remember your mama an' daddy?"

"Of course I remember them, Atticus. But that was different. When you're rich, everything is different. Rich men pamper their wives—poor ones just work them to death."

"Fancy, child, cain't nobody decide where his heart gonna go. One day you meet somebody an' you know he got somethin' you need. 'Til dat day come, you cain't make no rules fo' yourself."

"Oh, yes, I can, Atticus. Because if I don't, I could end up loving a poor man, and never, ever get back what's rightfully mine."

"Onliest thing rightfully belongs to anybody is six feet a earth, Fancy. God don't owe you nothin' more."

"That's exactly my point, Atticus. If God's not going to give me what I want, I damn well better figure out how to get it for myself."

After she'd left the tent, the old man sat quietly for a minute or two. She was tougher than she looked, but with a vulnerable center, angry at Fate and always questioning everything—a displaced person who had to find her way home. He could understand that need. Lately, he, too, had felt a longing to go home.

▲

Fancy and Atticus checked their belongings for the last time and looked at each other above the packhorse's overladen back. They'd been avoiding this awful moment of good-bye.

"Guess we cain't put it off no mo', honey," he said, and she nodded, not trusting her own voice.

Time to say good-bye to the people who had become their family and time to strike out on their own again after nearly five years of comfort, safety, and sharing. The troupe had officially disbanded; the wagons had been sold, the tent struck for the last time, the performers dispersed. Flute and Harp and their wives had been hired by P. T. Barnum, Horace and Minnie had taken the train farther west, the three Marcatos had headed for Texas, Melisande and her horse seemed content to stay in Fort Laramie.

Wes had magnanimously permitted Edgar, the elephant boy, to purchase Genghis for a fraction of his real value and they, too, had found a circus anxious to employ them. Only Wes, Magda, and Gitalis remained behind to face their good-byes.

" 'I have seen better faces in my time than stands on any shoulder that I see before me at this instant,' " she quoted from *Lear* as they stepped into the interior where her three friends waited. The man on the bed raised his upper body with difficulty.

"It is encouraging, is it not, Gitalis, to see that the child has not been totally untouched by our teaching." Fancy leaned over to kiss him, and he could see the tears welling in her eyes.

"No, no, dear child," Wes said, patting her. "You mustn't cry, for a light heart lives longest. We will never forget each other."

"What will I do without you three?" she asked.

"You will remember every word of what we've taught you," Gitalis answered. "You will live a life we would be proud of, and you will follow my advice to the letter."

"And that is?"

"Would you expect less Lear of me than you yourself have offered? 'Keep thy foot out of brothels, thy hand out of plackets, thy pen from lenders' books . . . and defy the Foul Fiend.' " He paused dramatically.

"And one more thing. Be careful of men, my little flower. Remember that 'the Prince of Darkness is a gentleman.' "

"I'll remember, dear Gitalis," Fancy said, kissing him. He clasped her close, tears falling unabashedly down his cheeks.

"And you, Magda? You, who have taught me so much, what have you to say to me before I go?"

"Remember all that the old man has taught you, Fancy, for he is close to God. When your own instincts fail you, listen for his voice within you . . . it will be there."

"And your voice, too?"

"My voice, too."

"I'll miss you more than you could ever know," she said. "You are my family now."

Magda stood outside the wagon, hugging herself for warmth, her wide skirt flapped in the chill wind as she watched the two departing figures and the packhorse they'd purchased fade into the surrounding landscape. Tears stung her eyes, for she knew too much not to fear for the man and girl, and too much to try to hold them back from their fate.

Gitalis stood apart a little, watching, too. The Gypsy heard him mutter something beneath his breath as the little caravan slipped from view.

" 'Maid of Athens, ere we part,' " he said softly. " 'Give, oh give me back my heart.' "

13   Fancy tried not to think about the dead horse at the bottom of the gorge. His dying shrieks still clutched at her stomach and made her fear her own mortality. It must have been a snake hole he'd stepped in, twisting his leg beneath the weight of his body and all their belongings. Poor beast, broken and terrified at the foot of a gorge too deep for them to descend to put him out of his anguish. She shuddered in remembrance of his dying cries; the accident had happened just the night before.

"We'll just do it the way we always did, Atticus," she'd said as they peered over the abyss. But it wasn't at all as it had been before—Atticus was an old man now, not up to the hardships of the trail. They'd both been softened by five years of sleeping warm on a cot, not cold in the woods; by safety and companionship and the communal security of the circus.

Now there was this infernal cold and a threatening sky, to compound their troubles. Fancy gritted her teeth and glanced over her shoulder at Atticus; he looked grim and gray, but they were too far from the last town to turn back. If they kept up a good pace, they would reach safety by nightfall.

The road banked sharply beneath them and fell away to the steep gorge that held the horse's remains and most of their provisions. She put the thought of their predicament from her mind; she could worry about replacements when she got them to safety. The temperature had dropped radically in the last hour and the presence of snow in the lowering sky was unmistakable. Fancy sniffed the frigid air, trying to sense the direction from which the storm would come; she saw Atticus do the same. They must find shelter before the first flakes fell; there were no landmarks to be seen in blizzards.

Fancy saw Atticus falter and thought he'd stumbled. But as she retraced her steps he let his body sink to the ground, listlessly, like a doll whose stuffing had drifted loose.

"Got to rest me a minute, Fancy," he said in a labored voice.

"A storm's coming, Atticus. It won't do to get caught out here in a storm."

"No, suh. Won't do, no way." He tried to smile, but the shadow of something unfamiliar crossed his face. As if a cue had been given, the first white crystals danced past the travelers' eyes. Fancy pulled her red coat nervously around her, and raised her head-shawl for protection.

"Atticus, we've got to move on. This storm is trouble."

"Cain't move nowhere jest now, sugah. You go on ahead and I'll ketch up."

Only severe pain could make him say such a crazy thing—Fancy took a deep breath to calm herself. "We're only a few miles from town, Atticus. I'll help you get there."

"Been havin' pains all day, child. Feels like old Genghis sittin' smack on my chest right now. Cain't hardly breathe at all." Atticus' cheeks, despite the sharpened cold, showed no color.

Terror strangled Fancy's heart. The flakes were no longer scattered specks but a fine white sifting, dry as powder, already starting to cling to the barren landscape around them.

"There's no foxglove here, Atticus," she whispered, struggling to keep her words controlled. It had to be his heart that had faltered; she should have seen it coming. The shortened breath, the flaccid skin, the pallor. Damnation! Why hadn't she stopped to notice . . .

"Ain't no cure for dis, honey . . ."

"Don't be ridiculous!" Fancy snapped. "There's a cure for everything in nature. You told me so yourself."

Atticus knew she was crossest when frightened.

"Ain't no cure for dyin', child," he answered.

Fancy sank to her knees. "But I love you, Atticus," she whispered, "I don't think I could live without you."

"I love you, too, child, but I'se goin' on. . . ."

"I won't let you, Atticus! I love you too much to let you go."

The anguish in Fancy's voice wrenched hard at Atticus, but the pain in his chest made all else insignificant. For a few paralyzed seconds Fancy stayed rooted beside her friend, unable to move or think. If she didn't get Atticus to shelter, he would surely die. She knew what to do to save him, why was the pounding in her head making function impossible? She gulped air into her lungs and rose to her feet, pressing back despair.

"I'm going to save you, Atticus," she said aloud to convince herself. "I'm going to save us both." She glanced resolutely in all directions.

A cave or a tight knot of underbrush could protect them; even a ledge would keep the worst of the storm away until she could build a fire. The wind whistled down the canyon like the lonely voice of God, and the swirling stung her face and blinded her as she searched the terrain for shelter.

To trudge a scant hundred feet in any direction was nearly impossible. She staggered against the thrust of the storm and tried not to cry. What if he died while she was gone, freezing and alone? Fancy carefully retraced her steps; if there was no shelter to be found, she'd build a barrier of boughs and clothing to protect him. "Use what you kin find, honey," Atticus would have said. "Somethin' better'n nothin'!"

The old man's body was already covered with powder by the time she returned to him. His eyelids fluttered open at the touch of her trembling hand and he tried to smile.

"If you leave me alone out here, I'll never forgive you, do you hear me?" Fancy told him with all the grit she could muster. Knowledge surfaced from some all-knowing place within her, at the grayish tinge that suffused his dear face . . . he would not last the night.

She tugged at the bare bones of underbrush to build a baffle for the wind; tears wet her cheeks in freezing rivulets and the wind drove the stinging sleet into eyes and mouth and nose. The frozen branches battled her efforts to bend them into shelter. Her boots and petticoats, stiffened with ice, chafed at her numbing legs; her frozen fingers, clumsy as ice blocks, were useless for the delicate work of saving a life.

There was no sky, no trees, no boulders, no canyon any longer; only the frenzied storm and the body of the dying old man.

Fancy tried to coax the driest twigs to kindle into flame. The tinderbox slipped from her freezing fingers into the snow and she knew, at last, that her struggle was hopeless.

Defeated, she crept beneath the branches and lay down beside the dying Atticus. "Forgive me," she whispered as she covered his body with her own. "I never meant to fail you."

"Goin' home," he murmured as she kissed him.

"Take me with you."

He shook his head and she thought, in anguish, that he looked almost proud.

"Don't leave me, Atticus . . . I'm so afraid . . ."

Fancy sobbed into the shelter of his body; the cold seeped in to stiffen her limbs, but she didn't care anymore, she would lie there beside him and they would go together on one last journey . . .

But she didn't die.

Fancy awoke at first light to find she was still alive. Atticus' great heart no longer beat in the silent chest beneath her, and for one long, vanquished moment she sat beside him, listening to the howling wind that would carry his spirit home. He'd told her once of the stormbird that could breast any tempest and be borne home by the wind. But he has so very far to go to find his way. . . .

Rigid with pain, Fancy forced the burden of snow from her back and shoulders and wondered why she wasn't dead. The wet had trickled beneath her collar and soaked her clothes; the cold had numbed her so she could barely feel her limbs. Why had it not finished the job?

Suddenly, rage pushed all the pain to some dark place within her. "Damn You!" she shrieked at God. "Must You take everything from me?" Only the fir boughs sighed above her in reply.

"I will not die! Do You hear me? *I will not die!*"

Atticus' soul had fled and she was quite alone on the mountain. She forced herself upright and pulled his banjo from his pack; she slipped the frozen cord over her shoulder. Then, clutching her coat and soaking head-shawl round her, Fancy thrust one foot, which she could no longer feel, out in front of her, then she forced the other one to follow.

The snow had drifted while they lay together, so that walking meant wading into the drifts and pushing the encumbering whiteness to right and left ahead of her. Like a tiny plow, Fancy breasted the snow, hands clawing at the murderous white barrier that was trying to kill her.

A boulder moved beneath her tread. A shoulder of snow-covered road gave way beneath her, and Fancy felt herself falling, falling . . .

Cursing all the gods—Atticus' and her own that she had never trusted—she rolled into unconsciousness at the side of the old Indian trail that led to the top of Mosquito Mountain.

II

FIRE
IN THE
WIND
▼▼▼▼▼▼

Hart and Chance
1862, Kansas East of
Grannel Springs

"Good luck is a lazy man's
estimate of a worker's success."
BANDANA MCBAIN

14 Halle McAllister raised her hand to shade her eyes from the harsh prairie sunlight, and scanned the horizon for her sons and husband. The hand was rough and worn from the ruggedness of life in Kansas, but it was a graceful, small-boned hand that looked as if it might have known how to hold a teacup correctly when it wasn't clutching a rugbeater or a rifle.

The dark-haired woman squinted hard and the fine lines at the edge of her blue-violet eyes deepened. There was character in her face, and strength despite a certain delicacy. The Kansas plain stretched flat and yellow-brown in all directions. Halle was about to give up her quest in disappointment, when the figures she sought materialized on the far horizon. As she watched they sorted themselves into a man and two boys. She smiled as the sight of her husband's familiar bigness filled her with the same sense of pride and desire it always had. Large of shoulder, small of hip; red-gold hair and beard glinting in the sunlight, Charles McAllister towered over his two fine sons, who were none too small for their ages of thirteen and fourteen.

Chance, long, lean, and wiry, was on his father's left. He had a shock of jet-black hair that tended to fall in unruly curls over his forehead no matter how hard Halle tried to keep it in trim. His handsome head was turned toward his father and he walked with the jaunty, long-legged grace of a frisky colt. She could guess Chance was laughing and talking, for that was his merry way.

Hart's stocky body was a younger duplication of his father's massiveness. Large head and wide shoulders, in contrast to the muscular leanness of the lower body; the fiery red hair of the father was softened into red chestnut in the son, but even at a distance the resemblance between the two was unmistakable. Just as she could intuit her older son's probable laughter, so Halle could almost sense the shy watchfulness in the younger boy. And the awe-struck adoration of his father, who, as far as Matthew Hart McAllister was concerned, was only one step shy of God Almighty—and not a big step either.

Halle hastily pushed back her flyaway hair toward its neat little bun at the nape of her neck. She stood on tiptoe to wave with one hand as she undid her apron with the other. Not that Charles hadn't seen her a million times in that apron, but she tried always to look pretty for her husband, at least as pretty as the harsh life of Kansas would allow.

Charles and the boys had left the cabin long before sunup; there was a church social planned by the neighbors come Saturday and all members of the family had put extra pains into finishing chores so they'd be free to go. Halle smiled at the euphemism of calling people "neighbors" who lived anywhere from thirty to one hundred and fifty miles away.

"Halle!" The deep voice calling from the distance excited her still, just as it had in the beginning. That it should still be the case after fifteen years of marriage and six babies seemed to her a miraculous gift.

"We did it, Halle!" Charles's voice boomed the news across the intervening landscape. "These boys worked hard as bullocks to get that wheat bundled." She could see her two sons swell with pride.

Charles McAllister smelled of tobacco and hard labor in the punishing sun as he picked his wife up by the waist and swung her around in a big circle under the amused gaze of Chance and Hart, who were used to such exuberant displays of affection between their parents.

The force of the swing knocked the last hairpins from Halle's hair and it fell free as a girl's, a lustrous dark cascade down her back. Something in the way their mother's and father's eyes met made Chance and Hart glance knowingly at each other. They were nearly men themselves now, after all, and they could tell when a man and woman were sweet on each other.

"Come on, bro," Chance called to Hart. "I'll race you to the house so these two can do-si-do together."

Hart looked at his father for signs of disapproval of his brother's flippancy, but he saw only amusement in the craggy face.

He took off after Chance's flying departure and left his parents standing in the dust.

"You three looked so fine striding over the field just now, Charles dear. I'll be the envy of every woman at the social, escorted by three such handsome men."

"You're the one who's a sight for sore eyes, Halle. I swear you looked no older standing there in the sunlight than on the day I first laid eyes on you. And God knows, you're ten times more beautiful now than when you were a girl."

She laughed and touched her husband's lined face with her hands. She'd given up much when she ran off from her Boston Brahmin family with this hardworking, decent man she loved so well, but Halle couldn't remember ever regretting it.

Charles smiled as he draped his arm protectively around her shoulders; he had a proprietary way with those who belonged to him.

"You'd have been real proud of your boys today, Halle," Charles told her, comfortable in the easy banter of a long, loving marriage. He had to duck to enter the small, immaculate house they'd built with their own hands. They'd started out with a sod house that was little better than a cave dug into the landscape, but Charles had seen the need in his wife for a home to cherish and had built her one of wood, a rarity on the Kansas prairie.

"Both of them?" she asked, and Charles looked down with amusement at his wife's expression. He knew she worried equally about Chance's head-strong ebullience and Hart's quiet shyness.

He sat down on the chair by the stone hearth and struggled to tug off the dirt-encrusted boots that felt as if they'd baked into skin and bone.

"Now, Halle, honey, there ain't no such thing as perfect in this world. Boys are boys. They got virtues and they got faults. You know as well as I do, the trick is to help them strengthen the one and overcome the other."

Halle looked into her husband's honest face and saw both wisdom and goodness there.

"With a father like you, my love, to be an example for them, I know they'll be just fine," she said, wrinkling her nose as the second boot fell to the floor and the tang of hardworking feet struck her nostrils. She some-times thought the thing she missed most about her pampered childhood was the chance to bathe as often as she wished.

Her husband chuckled knowingly. "What say I carry in water for the tub tonight so these old feet of mine don't drive you into the arms of some other man at the party tomorrow?"

Halle laughed aloud. If ever there'd been a man born who knew he was loved by his wife and sons, it was Charles McAllister.

▲

"Come on, bro." Chance's sharp whisper roused Hart's head from the straw in the wagon where he'd been dozing. He blinked at the night sky, trying to figure out what time it might be. The afternoon's races and games had finally worn him out enough to crawl into the wagon for forty winks; he wondered how long ago that might have been. Chance seemed wide awake. The cacophony of fiddle music and dancing feet still pounded inside the small building that served as Grange Hall for all the farms from two hun-dred miles in any direction. It wasn't often the far-flung farmers and their wives got together, but when they did, they put a lot of energy into having a humdinger of a time.

Chance tugged on his brother's sleeve.

"You're missing all the fun, bro. There's spooning going on in back of the livery and there's a card game about ready to start, if you'll just wipe the sleep out of your eyes and get a move on."

"How do you know about the spooning?"

Chance laughed.

"Have you ever known me to miss a trick, little brother?"

Hart scrambled out of the wagon.

"Little brother, my eye," he said, picking hay out of his corduroys and tugging his plaid shirt into a slightly less wrinkled condition. Fifteen months younger than Chance, Hart was taller and considerably broader than his elder brother. If there was mischief anywhere in the neighborhood, he knew he could trust Chance to find it and drag him along. And since Chance wasn't above getting into an occasional scrap, it didn't hurt to have Hart's brawn to rely on. Hart thought the arrangement worked out happily for both—if they'd been more alike, they probably wouldn't have gotten on so well.

Mary Ellen McCarthy and Sarah Gentry were giggling just outside the Grange Hall door as the boys walked by. Sarah at twelve was nearing womanhood and she'd had her eye on Chance for as long as she could remember—not unlike a great many of the other young ladies the two boys met at socials or church services.

Mary Ellen smiled shyly at Hart; her brown fingercurls bounced as she dipped her head away from his gaze.

"Evening, Chance," Sarah said, with a boldness that surprised Mary Ellen. "You looked real good in the footraces today."

Chance nudged his brother and turned his best smile on Sarah. The girls he met at Fourth of July picnics or Christmas get-togethers always seemed to remember his laughing blue eyes and confident smile.

"Evening, Sarah. You're looking mighty pretty tonight. Is that a new bonnet you're wearing?"

It beat all how Chance always knew what to say to girls, Hart thought. He always felt tongue-tied when they looked his way.

Sarah giggled flirtatiously.

"Come for a walk with us?" Chance suggested, sounding sure of himself.

Sarah wrinkled up her nose with disappointment.

"We can't move from this spot. It's way past our bedtime, but Mama said if we stayed right here by the door we could watch the dancing inside."

Chance breathed a sigh of relief. The card game where the older boys were gathered was where he really wanted to be; just the texture of a deck of cards in his hand made him feel like the world was his oyster. Only his brother knew he practiced by the hour when his chores were done, fingering the deck, cutting it endlessly to get a sense of each card. Chance had an intuition that if he handled the pasteboards enough, eventually he could make them do exactly as he demanded. Already he could tell the difference between the court cards and the others just by the weight of ink they carried —soon he'd be able to cut to near anything he chose.

Hart indulged his brother in his pursuit of gambling, but he frankly thought all the energy Chance lavished on the cards a waste of time. Given an hour's respite from work, he had more serious business. He would take his charcoal and what scraps of paper were to be found, and sketch trees, skies, fences, birds, cows—whatever there was to see of the prairie life.

Chance winked at Hart knowingly and moved in closer to Sarah; he took the girl's arm confidently in his own.

"Maybe we could sort of wander over there back of the barn for a minute or two, girls, while your folks are dancing. If I'm not mistaken, that reel they're playing is about as long as any ever invented."

The girls giggled conspiratorially and, much to Hart's amazement, agreed to go. The reel was just long enough for a few kisses to be exchanged by Chance and Sarah in the shadows. Hart, too gentlemanly or shy to take advantage of the situation, contented himself with holding Mary Ellen's hand.

"What you don't seem to understand, bro," Chance chided his brother later, on their way to the poker game, "is that girls *like* to be kissed just as much as we like to kiss them. So all that gentlemanly stuff of yours is guaranteed to annoy a girl."

Hart wasn't sure if his brother was right, but it did seem Chance's way was a lot more fun than his own.

▲ ▲ ▲

"Halle, honey, are you feeling poorly?" Charles stood beside his wife's rocking chair and touched her hair with concern. He had watched her hands dawdle over her knitting needles, in the embering firelight. It was unlike her not to work briskly, for there was always a new sock needed or an old one to be mended.

Halle raised her face to her husband's; her eyes were strangely bright and slightly hooded, as if it troubled her to keep them open.

"I think I might be coming down with something, Charles dear. My throat's been scratchy and raw all day and my chest hurts. I didn't want to worry you."

Charles' hands were large and seemed to him too awkward for anything delicate, but he brushed his wife's hair away from her face with so tender a gesture that she smiled up at him, wanting to soothe the worry she read in his face.

"I've always thought the color of your hair was like the wing of a grackle," he said unexpectedly. "Shining black, but with other colors hiding underneath that only show at times."

Halle, flattered and disturbed by the concern she heard in her husband's voice, replied briskly. "Now don't you go all sentimental on me, Charles McAllister! I'll be just fine if I dose myself with sulfur and molasses."

Chance, studying near the oil lamp in the corner, wrinkled up his nose at the thought, and looked over at his brother, who lay with an open book on the cabin floor. His own throat was feeling punk and he'd refrained from mentioning it all day for fear of being dosed with something nasty from his mother's medicine cabinet.

The sound of hoofbeats startled them. A horse whinnied at the hitching rail and hurried footsteps crossed the porch. Charles reached automatically for the Sharps repeater kept always in the chimney corner; both boys were on their feet before the door was opened. The McAllister homestead was miles from its nearest neighbor and travelers didn't wander by so isolated a farm after dark. A dust-covered circuit rider stood silhouetted in the door frame; he'd ridden far and hard, and lather from an overextended horse stained his shirt.

"Miz McAllister . . . Charles," he panted without pause for pleasantries. "Cain't stay more'n a minute; got eight more families to warn tonight."

Charles and Halle exchanged alarmed glances.

"For heaven's sake, Zachary, what are you doing here at this hour of night and whatever are you warning us about?"

"Diphtheria, ma'am. An epidemic. Sarah Gentry's come down with it. And the Sinclairs. Morgans, too. Old man Moriarty and all the Shildkraut kids. Doc Hammer says to tell everybody that was at the social to dose themselves with tonic and swab their throats out with iodine on a feather. He says oncet you get it, cain't nobody do nothin' fer you but pray. There ain't a cure, just some gets well and some don't." Zachary Boggs stopped talking. This was the eleventh house he'd carried the news to—the faces that looked back at him had been all the same—white with fear.

"Surely you can come in for a cup of tea at least, Zachary," Halle persisted. "You look bone weary."

"No, ma'am. Thank you kindly, but I cain't do that. Doc says it's important we all stay away from one another best we can. Nobody knows who's got the sickness inkabatin'. Might be me and I wouldn't like to spread it to you and your family!" He tipped his dust-encrusted hat and was gone.

Charles stepped forward and instinctively took his wife into his arms. The boys saw her sag a little against her husband's ready strength; the fear in their eyes when they pulled away from each other frightened their sons.

Epidemics happened on the prairie—sometimes cholera, sometimes influenza. Near everyone they knew had lost folks to one or the other. All diseases were dreaded, but diphtheria was the worst for it killed quickly and painfully.

Hurriedly, Halle pulled the iodine bottle from the little cabinet Charles had made for her remedies. Her hands trembled slightly as she uncorked the bottle and Hart saw his father place his own large hand around her smaller one to steady it.

"A feather?" she murmured, looking up at him distractedly.

"I'll get one for you, Mama," Chance volunteered, already in motion. He had collected three eagle feathers over time, after his father had told him that the Indians considered eagle feathers signs of manhood.

"You first, Halle," Charles said, his tone brooking no argument. Meekly each of the family members submitted to having the caustic red poison painted gaggingly into their throats. Whatever they could do to save themselves they must do; the hard facts of prairie life meant there would be little chance of outside help if trouble came.

For the following three days, all four McAllisters went about their work, trying not to let the thought of diphtheria dominate them. On the fourth night after Zachary's visit, Hart awoke hours after the family had retired; the acrid stench of the iodine his father had been painting in their throats for days was still in his mouth and nostrils. In the cabin's dim light he could see his father's body outlined against the glow of the fire's last embers; the man was crooning soft words of encouragement to his wife as she lay in their bed.

Hart watched, frightened by the intensity in his father's concentration. He nudged his brother who was lying beside him in the bed and was startled to feel that Chance was sweat-soaked. The older boy merely groaned restlessly at Hart's touch and turned onto his side, but continued sleeping.

Hart carefully hooked his long legs over the side of the bed and stood up. He pulled his pants on hastily, along with a flannel shirt, then moved to his father's side.

"Is Mama sick, Pa?"

Charles looked up at his son and nodded; the boy could see tears glistening on his father's lashes. The woman on the bed tossed feverishly; she coughed a phlegm-filled rattling sound. Even in the darkness, Hart could see that her cheeks were flushed with fever, yet the rest of her face and the hand his father held looked strangely bloodless.

Suddenly, Halle sat bolt upright, her eyes wide and wild. She screamed out something unintelligible and tried to rise from the bed, but Charles restrained her.

"It's all right, love, I'm here," he crooned as to a baby. "I won't leave you for a minute."

Halle's eyes fastened on her husband and Hart was horrified to see she didn't recognize him.

"You'd best ride for Doc Hammer, son," Charles said steadily, his voice hoarse with anxiety, or could his throat, too, be filling up with the gluey death-phlegm of diphtheria? Hart pushed the thought aside roughly; his father was too strong to be stricken.

"I don't want to leave you like this, Pa."

"Do as I say, son. Get your brother up to help me with your mama before you go. I'm afraid if it's the diphtheria she's caught, she's got no chance without the doctor."

"Chance is sick, too, Pa."

Charles lifted his eyes directly to his son's; for the first time in his life Hart saw fear in their dark blue depths. The realization was too much for the boy and he turned his face away hastily. He pulled on his warmest jacket and picked up a handful of yesterday's biscuits from the bread bin; that, plus the jerky that hung by the stove, would serve as food on his long ride.

Hart started for the door, then stopped, hesitant.

"What is it, son?" his father called out to him, sensing the boy's confusion.

It was a moment before Hart replied.

"Could I kiss Mama good-bye, Pa? Before I go?" The father heard the note of controlled terror in his son's voice and understood the shape of the boy's fear, so very like his own.

"I'm sorry, son. It wouldn't be safe," he answered slowly, carefully. "This thing's real catching. But she'll be here when you get back, don't you worry none about that. I'll be making sure of that while you're gone. Just get old Doc Hammer here and don't you take no for an answer. Understand me?"

"Yessir. I understand."

The first bare glimmer of lighter blue tinged the Kansas sky as Hart saddled his horse in the frigid barn and turned his head toward the town eighty-six miles away. Even with luck and finding the doctor immediately, he was two whole days away from bringing help back home with him.

▲

Hart's horse was flagging as he turned into the third house he'd been sent to. Everywhere he'd gone, Doc Hammer had been and left before him; the day was nearly spent and each hour left the boy more anxious about his mother's fate.

His clothes stuck to his hard young body, pasted there by sweat and trail dust. Hart knew his face and hands were filthy but didn't care; there'd be time for washing when his mother was out of danger. To his great relief, the doctor's trap was hitched with the other horses outside this house, but there was a white sheet hung over the door signifying quarantine, so he stood outside and shouted until the silver-haired doctor appeared from beneath the sheet.

"Your family, too, eh?" the man said without waiting for explanation.

"You've got to come, Doc! I think Ma's dying. Maybe Chance too." Hart tried to sound grown up and not as scared as he was.

"I hear you, son," the old man called to him, compassion under steely constraint in his voice. "But you better know right off I can't come with you. Folks are dying here, too, and they're close enough together so's I can see a lot of 'em. If I traipse almost ninety miles out to your pa's place to see one or two McAllisters, twenty folks'll die right here before I get back."

Hart fought down fear and failure—what if his mother died because he had not brought the doctor home?

"But it's my ma!" Hart called out simply, but with such pain in his voice that the old man pursed his lips as if struggling with something and shook his head.

"Wait here, boy," he called, and turned back into the house; a moment later he reappeared with a small bottle in his hand.

"Now you listen real good to me, son, because you'll have to do your own doctorin' and I ain't got time to say this more'n once. This here's quinine. It's not much, but it's better than nothing. This is what you got to know to do with it: you give a dose to anyone you still think you can save. Now, hard as it is to decide, boy, this stuff's precious. Don't you go wasting it on anyone who's bound to die anyway."

Hart swallowed hard and his eyes widened at the doctor's pragmatism.

"Dose 'em twice each day and try to get some kind of food down 'em. Soups, maybe a milk toast. They'll fight you, but you got to try. The disease takes 'em when a membrane grows over their windpipes. Sometimes as a last ditch, you can stick your finger down their throats and tear the phlegm right out of it—sometimes you just choke 'em to death trying. But if you got no choice, well then, you go ahead and chance it, Hart. If you bring anything up, just throw the stuff, rag and all, into the fire and scrub your hands with antiseptic for all you're worth before you eat anything yourself. Understand all I've said to you, son?"

Hart nodded, the true horror of what the doctor was saying squeezing the breath from him. The man wasn't coming because he expected Halle McAllister to die.

"I understand, sir," he said.

"You're a good lad, Hart," the doctor said with great seriousness. "Like your daddy, God help him."

Then he disappeared again behind the sheet and Hart was left in the yellow dust and sun with a tiny bottle in his hand.

▲ ▲ ▲

Lather dripped from Hart's dun gelding as he clattered into the front yard. It was deep night and he felt weak from hunger, thirst, and the adrenaline of danger; a light flickering in the small window heartened him. He slid to the ground and nearly fell, for the strain of riding two hundred miles in two days had turned the muscles of his back and legs to rubber.

Hart pushed the door open and nearly drew back at the overwhelming stench of illness in the cabin. He could see his brother tossing feverishly on the corner bed, and through the door to the small bedroom, he saw that the two figures on his parents' bed were still. Hart moved tentatively toward them, pushing past a stack of soiled linens on the floor. Halle McAllister's slim body was nearly covered by her husband's and they were both asleep. Hart stood undecided for a moment—should he wake his father or let him rest? The sooner the quinine was administered, the sooner his mother would be well.

He drew near the bed and reached out his hand to touch his father, but drew it back as if burned, for he'd seen his mother's waxen face beneath his father's shoulder. Halle McAllister was dead.

Hart had seen death on the farm; in real life, there was no mistaking it. The life force that had animated his mother's body was gone and her blood-less lips and eyes were bluish white with death's unnatural pallor. Could it be that his father didn't know?

Hart stood for a moment, staring unbelievingly. Nausea and vertigo gripped him, so it took all his remaining strength to stay on his feet. Tears spilled down his cheeks; he didn't even try to wipe them away. Tentatively, he reached for his father's shoulder and the man raised a ravaged face to his son's. Charles McAllister tried to speak but a gurgling, choking sound came from his throat instead. A horrible bone-shaking fit of coughing ensued; exhausted by it, he fell back onto the bed into the oblivion of illness.

A terrible knowingness filled Hart's mind; he gulped back tears and pulled the bottle from its place with trembling hands. He took a spoon from the dry sink and forced the liquid between his father's slackened lips. Even as he did so, he felt it was too late, for the gray of the man's skin was very like the color that had frightened him in his mother's face before he'd left—it was the color that had made him want to kiss her good-bye.

He covered both his parents with a blanket; his father's body was hot with fever, his mother's cold in death. He wondered for an anguished moment what in the world to do about his mother's body, it surely couldn't remain where it was . . . Hart was light-headed from fatigue and couldn't think clearly.

Fiercely, he brushed away the tears that blurred the awful scene; he must force himself to do something, anything! He must not stand there seeing what he saw, knowing what he knew.

He made his way back to his brother's side and spooned the quinine between Chance's clenched teeth; then he dosed himself as well with the bitter alum. Mama's gone. *Mama's gone!* The impossible, desperate thought kept trying to hammer its way past the curtain of oblivion that protected him. He wanted to go to his father for help; his strong, all-knowing father who had always stood between him and danger. But he could not force himself to look again into his mother's face.

Fatigue washed over Hart with a numbing finality that he almost welcomed. He sank to the floor against the door frame between the two rooms that held the three who were his world, and putting his throbbing head between his hands, the thirteen-year-old boy sobbed and sobbed until he slept.

▲

Hart smoothed the damp cloth onto his brother's forehead for the hundredth time, and tried to stand up straight. The fever had broken in the night; Chance no longer fought for every breath, but lay in an exhausted trance, more peaceful than he'd seemed in the seven days since this nightmare had begun. Some ancient knowledge told Hart his brother had passed the crisis now—just as it told him his father had not.

More weary than he'd thought a man could be and live, Hart dropped the cloth into the bucket of well water and moved to the bed where his father lay. Charles McAllister no longer looked indestructible; a deadly gray pallor had drained all life from his face and his eyes were sunken into deep slate-tinged hollows.

Hart knelt by his bedside, reached into the bucket automatically, and laid the wet rag gently on his father's sweat-soaked brow. The man stirred and coughed violently, yet even the force of the cough had ebbed, as if the dying man had no strength left to fight the racking spasm.

The man's dozing was unlike Chance's; it was a stupor now. Without wanting to, Hart looked at the angry bruises on his father's arms where he had gripped him during the worst of his delirium. Tears sprang to the boy's eyes at the horrid remembrance of his father fighting to keep his wife with him when Hart had tried to take Halle's body away for burial.

Hart wasn't sure at all that he could have overpowered Charles McAllister, except that a coughing fit had weakened him at the final moment. His father was bigger than Hart, and had the strength of years and wisdom; to fight the man on any level had taken every ounce of courage the boy possessed.

There would be no more battles now, he thought, the sorrow a dull, insidious ache within him. Each breath rattled with a sound that strangled his heart. Almost at the same moment, Charles McAllister opened his eyes and struggled to raise his head from the pillow; he pointed desperately to his throat and gasped for breath like a fish on the bottom of a fisherman's boat. Hart saw that his father was choking and remembered the doctor's awful words. *If you got no other choice, son, go ahead and tear the phlegm from their throats.*

Somehow, Hart had known for days that this awful effort would be required of him. He grabbed the square of cloth he'd placed on the bedpost, and thrust his fingers into his father's mouth, forcing them toward the vile membrane. He felt the rubbery thickness and grappled with it, horrified by its clinging strength. His stomach clutched at the indignity of the task and he forced back rising bile. His father gasped and choked and fought his son's hands madly, but Hart triumphantly pulled the mucus free and flung it hissing into the fire . . . but he saw as he did so that the mass was tinged with bright red blood.

Dark, overpowering despair that he'd fought so hard to keep at bay washed through the boy. All prairie people knew the red of lung-blood, bright and frothy, almost pretty in its effervescence. Unlike that of surface wounds, it was almost always the harbinger of death.

His father lay quiet now; the ghostly rattle no longer sounded, but a terrible stillness had replaced it. Hart knew, deep within himself, that no miracle would save him now.

"Son . . ." The hiss was small and soft, like a whispering wind in summer leaves. Hart leaned his tear-streaked face as close to his father's lips as he could; he was far beyond the fear of contagion, and dying no longer seemed to him the worst that could befall him.

"I tried," he whispered to the dying man. "Oh, Pa, I tried so hard . . ."

Tears ran from his cheeks to his father's and he brushed them tenderly away.

"I'll take care of Chance," he whispered, but he was never certain if his father heard the words. "He's all that's left of us."

Hart, defeated finally, beyond all strength except that of endurance, laid his head on his father's great chest, wrapped his arms around the once stalwart form, and waited patiently for death to end his vigil.

▲ ▲ ▲

The disconsolate boy stood beside the new-made graves, too drained by sorrow even for tears. His father and mother now both lay beneath the fresh-turned ground, beside the four babies they had buried over the years, wrapped only in fragile muslin. Ashes to ashes. Flesh to dust. Strength to nothingness . . .

Hart's mouth was set in the bitter knowledge of life's perfidy. He had not slept, in longer than he could recall; he had feared to sleep, the McAllister farmhouse had become a battleground now for Hart—he would not let Chance go.

His father's immense body had been nearly impossible for the boy to move alone. *You were so big, Pa, so strong,* he'd thought as he dragged the two-hundred-and-seventy-pound man to his final resting place. *How could you die? How could something too small even to be seen have killed you?* The thought had come to him then, that perhaps it wasn't the disease at all that had killed his father, but rather the knowledge of his wife's death. The two were as one life . . . perhaps one simply could not be without the other.

And what of us? some unreasoning desperation within the boy raged at the abandonment. *I need you, Pa! I don't know what to do without you!* But Hart fought the childlike weakness down with his remaining strength. He would bear this like a man, for that was what he must be now. Chance, too. If he lived.

15   "Chance, wait!" Hart called to his brother to be patient, not an easy matter for the older boy.

All salable goods had been sold, all personal belongings rooted through to find what would be worth taking with them. There had been few buyers for the goods and none for the farm itself; the entire area had been decimated by epidemic and nearly every farmer had his own losses to contend with. Now it was time to go, and the knowledge wrenched at Hart with unbearable intensity.

He fingered his mama's Bible reverently and took one last lingering look at the cabin that had held so much of love and life. The sketch he'd made of it would have to do, he thought with a sigh. Why had he never noticed before what an insignificant structure it was, so lonely against the immensity of the Kansas plain? Untenanted it stood, useless as a bird's nest once the birds have taken wing.

Resolutely, Hart tucked the drawing into the Bible and placed it in the saddlebag beneath his leg, trying to keep the tears from flooding embarrassingly down his cheeks.

"I don't like to leave them alone like this, Chance," he said as his brother reined in next to him. The two side-by-side crosses, with the little child-markers next to them, looked forlorn and inconsequential now that the cabin was bare.

How many such wooden crosses dotted the prairie from St. Joe to California? he wondered—monuments to forgotten thousands who had once been loved. His father had told him that when people died on a wagon train, the trainmaster conjured up a name for the spot where he buried them, christening the place right then and there so the folks back home could say their kin was buried in "Tombstone" or "Devil's Crossing," not just some nameless grave in the trackless wilderness. What would the world remember of where his mama and daddy rested? Somewhere between Pawnee and Grannel Springs—somewhere reclaimed by nature, where no one lived anymore.

Chance's voice had a catch in it; he cleared his throat to sound more in control. He was pale from his own ordeal, and the hand he placed on his brother's showed the tracery of bone.

"They're not here, bro," Chance said gently to Hart. "Mama and Daddy are long gone. Don't fret for them. He'll take good care of her."

Hart looked over into his brother's eyes and seeing tears there, couldn't trust himself to speak. He simply nodded, then turned his horse's head toward the open range. It was the strangest thing about Chance—he could seem so frivolous and insubstantial at times, then turn around and say something real important. Hart watched his brother's figure pull ahead of him, mounted on their father's great black horse.

He had been momentarily miffed that Chance had never questioned his right to the animal, never asked if his brother would mind being left with the dun. But Hart had been ashamed of the pettiness of the thought and said a hasty prayer; it wouldn't do to let God think he was ungrateful that Chance had been spared. And, too, he had taken his father's timepiece for his own legacy.

Hart looked back over his shoulder one last time as the horse's motion pulled him toward the future. "I love you, Pa," he murmured in farewell. "I love you, Mama. I'll never forget you . . ."

He was a man now. There was nothing left that he could do for them but be a man they could be proud of.

▲ ▲ ▲

They first headed northward into Nebraska Territory, but it was flat as Kansas and they had a mind to see the mountains, so they followed the Platte into Colorado. They had no clear notion of where they would go or what they would find there, but once the worst of their sorrow had passed, they began to feel the excitement of having no one to answer to but the small voice of conscience. There was no dearth of game or forage and they provided each other all the company needed.

Chance and Hart, bred to miles of golden-brown infinity, saw countryside so mighty, it took their breath away. Rivers emerging from mountain snows, trout streams rampaging out of narrow gorges, cottonwood flats so wide and bright, they made the plains look mystical and rich as a king's ransom.

The beauty of this new world, so far beyond the borders of their childhood, made Chance feel powerful and free. His spirit had never been easily contained; all his life he had sensed an immensity out there, just waiting for him to reach for it. He felt enlarged and immortal.

Hart was roused to a different expansion. This was the West his father had made him long for with his tales—the unspoiled, unfettered territory where a man could be anything he had the strength to be. He would sometimes lie full length on the grass and stare at the immense perfection of the sky and dream of following the Indians to their hunting grounds and chronicling their world before it disappeared forever. Although the pain of what had been lost and what he had suffered alone was still unhealed, he felt the strength inside himself that is called forth by hardships borne in a manly way. Hart felt a special kinship with his brother, too, for he had seen close up how fragile even the strong are when Death lays his hand on their shoulders. Sometimes he would watch Chance surreptitiously and allow himself a sense of pride that his brother lived because he had cared for him through the worst of times.

Hart wanted to be an artist one day; Chance wanted to be rich. But one day seemed a long way off, so for the first few months on their own they simply meandered, getting odd jobs, shooting game for food, enjoying their freedom like forbidden taffy.

Hart sketched everything he laid eyes on; he had a special knack for drawing animals, an ability to capture their wildness in a frozen moment. The screech of the mountain lion still in its throat, the onrush of a wolf in flight, the upward thrust of a bird scared rustling out of its thicket—these were the skills Hart worked on without ever knowing it was work.

Spring had leapt into being in the mountains with a verdancy that the prairie-bred boys found magical. Stately aspens with their silver-green leaves stood up like sentinels in elegant coveys, meadows rife with mariposa and nodding onion spilled color after color into their path. They could not have been more content had they stumbled into Eden, but like Eden, paradise was not as perfect as it seemed.

One night they camped halfway up a mountainside in a friendly-looking hollow. Chance lay dozing near the fire, one hand thrown up over his face to shield the light—Hart's head rested on his saddle, a blanket tucked up under his chin to thwart the dampness.

The click of the Colt's hammer being cocked near his ear jolted Chance into wakefulness; he called his brother's name softly but sharply as he struggled to his feet.

Hart's eyes opened slowly and he looked up into meanness; a man with a black beard on a skeletal face stared down at him from behind a Smith & Wesson revolver. A zigzag white scar pulled the man's right eyebrow askew and there was nothing in his atavistic expression to suggest goodness or mercy.

"You got a poke, boy?" he growled.

Hart looked to his brother for guidance.

"Don't tell him, Hart!" the older boy snapped. "Let him work for it."

A boot snaked out and kicked Chance's legs out from under him. The boy buckled with pain and surprise.

The ugly bearded face looked amused by the interchange and another man, younger and leering, laughed aloud as he ransacked their belongings. Triumphantly he held up the gold pocket watch that had been Charles McAllister's wedding gift from his wife.

"Bastard!" Chance yelled at the robber. "You're not fit to touch my daddy's timepiece."

Without thinking of anything but the possible desecration of his father's watch, Hart lunged out of the grip of the man who held him. A gunshot ripped the ground beside his feet, spitting rocks and dirt, and Hart skidded to a halt before he could attempt a rescue.

"Son of a bitch!" spat the bearded leader with a laugh. "Ain't we got us two feisty pups by the tail. What say we have a little fun with 'em and see how much starch they really got? Get the goddamned rope, Shep."

The youngest robber giggled as he did so, and both boys knew from the foolishness of his slack-mouthed expression that he was feebleminded.

"Shit! Ned," said the third man, "we ain't had a good neck-stretchin' party in a hog's age. That's a damn good idea."

"You don't scare us!" Chance shouted back at them. Hart wished his brother wouldn't sass these men; it was easy to see they fed on violence, and all the firepower was on their side.

"Let's make this hangin' a mite more interestin' for these boys who don't scare so easy," Ned replied amiably. "Stand the cocky one on the redheaded kid's shoulders."

Hart's stomach lurched violently; it wasn't human for any man to do that to another.

The two robbers looked at their leader with sadistic admiration. "Jesus, Ned, that's a damn good idea. Let's see how long the big kid can hold out before his friend swings."

"No, mister!" Hart blurted. "Please. You can't do that. He's my brother."

Ned moved his face so close to Hart's, the boy could smell the man's foul breath. "Well, now, ain't that interestin'," he said with a smirk. "That should make you stand up real tall, boy—for as long as you can, that is." His malicious chuckle was half mad and Hart felt the nausea of despair.

The boys struggled wildly as the three men dragged them beneath a sixty-foot pine. Shep shimmied high up the tree to string the rope and Chance was lifted with great difficulty onto his brother's shoulders; both boys' hands were tied behind them. Hart nearly buckled beneath his brother's weight, but the two younger men steadied him until Chance found his balance. It was obvious from the skill with which they managed the feat that they had played this trick before.

Hart squeezed his eyes closed hard against tears, and fought desperately for equilibrium.

"Hell, you should be grateful to us, son," Ned sneered as the other desperadoes rounded up the boys' belongings and prepared to leave. "We're giving you a sportin' chance here. Why, we could just as leave have scattered your brains where you laid, had we a mind to."

Hart didn't even try to respond, but braced his back and legs against the impossible strain of his brother's weight and struggled against the rope that secured his wrists. He could barely breathe.

Chance, heavy on Hart's shoulders, teetered precariously. The thick cord of rope noosed around his neck tautened against the pull of the great pine, and he had to fight the vertigo that could kill him if he lost his balance.

"Sweet Jesus, Chance!" Hart whispered through teeth clenched with pain and fear. "I can't get my hands loose!" Chance could hear the anguish in his brother's voice and gritted his own teeth against the hopelessness of their plight.

The three robbers rode out up the trail, the boys' horses tied behind their own; only the young, demented one looked back and smiled—pain and death to him were no more than occasional pleasures to be inflicted when time permitted. He waved back merrily before he disappeared into the darkened forest.

"You listen to me, bro," Chance called down, trying to sound brave. "If I go, I go, and that's not your doing, you hear me? I don't want to die and have to worry about your conscience too." He tried to make the words sound flippant, but his voice was hollowed out by fear—his brother knew him too well to mistake the sound.

Hart struggled to stay upright. If he moved, the body above him swayed precariously; if his shoulders gave way before he got his hands free, Chance would die.

Hart forced himself to concentrate on the knots around his wrists, instead of on the agony in his shoulders or the dizzying sway of Chance's body above his own. Or his rage at what had been done to them.

He felt the stickiness of blood spread into his palms from the abraded skin of his wrists. The prickly hemp bit harshly into flesh, but he welcomed the pain, for he hoped the blood would make his hands slippery enough to pull free.

"You still down there, bro?" Chance's voice wavered with anxiety. "If worse comes to worst, Hart, I'm gonna jump off of you, you hear me? So

don't you go thinking it was your fault, whatever happens." Hart squeezed
his eyes tight shut, but the tears fell anyway.

"Jesus, Chance! Shut up, will you? Shut up about dying. I'm gonna get
out of these ropes somehow." Hart's voice came in short, strident bursts—
the strain of staying upright was making breath hard and rapid.

A strange crack sounded under Chance's right foot and he knew Hart's
shoulder had split from the strain of his weight. He'd heard such a sickening sound once, in a horse whose foreleg had splintered when his foot
turned on wet stone. If he shifted his weight to try to lessen the strain on his
brother's broken shoulder, he might lose his balance. He could only imagine
the agony Hart must be enduring, but his brother made no further sound.

"I love you, brother," Chance called down, hoarsely. "I want you to
know whatever happens, you couldn't help it. If I die, I'll just be going on to
meet Mama and Daddy anyway, so you gotta promise me you won't take on
like it was your fault." The sob that shook Hart's body was his only reply.

Hart McAllister closed his mind against the inevitable and fought his
own body for control. His knees trembled dangerously, and twice, as he
worried the knots that secured his wrists, he felt the shift in weight above
nearly overcome his balance. Eventually his own screaming muscle and
bone would be unable to stand the strain and he would buckle beneath the
grotesquely swinging body of his dying brother. How long could he hold
out? He willed himself not to crumple . . . just another hour . . . just
another minute. *Dear God, don't let my brother die like this!*

The crack of a single gunshot rent the darkness. Hart felt the rope jerked
taut, felt Chance lurch, felt his brother tumble from his perch to roll miraculously away into the night. The pain of his broken shoulder exploded into
white-hot agony; the bliss of freedom befuddled his movements and Hart
fell to his knees in the rocky dirt, senses reeling.

Somewhere in the gloom in front of him a man sat on a fine black horse, a
smoking .45 in his hand. Christ Almighty! What a shot that must have been,
to sever the rope with only the light of a dying campfire. What kind of man
had confidence enough to risk another's life on the strength of a single
impossible pistol shot?

The stranger holstered his shooting iron, dismounted and unsheathed a
knife almost in the same movement. Wordlessly he cut the ropes that bound
Chance's wrists, then Hart's. The two dazed boys turned tear-streaked faces
to their savior with a mixture of gratitude and bewilderment.

The stranger was a dark and brooding man with a face of the kind the
ladies think handsome. He wasn't overly tall by McAllister standards, perhaps a hair shy of six feet. He was dressed all in black, his clothes trail-worn
but cared for. You didn't need to see the holster tied down at his thigh to

know what he was, for it was written in his watchful eyes and in the astonishing shot that had freed them.

Hart tried to stand, but his legs wouldn't hold him; the stranger pushed
the boy back to a sitting position and Hart was startled by the strength and
gentleness of the gesture.

"Jesus, mister!" Chance blurted. "That was some kind of shooting, but
what if you'd missed?" Hart marveled that even now his brother could find
words to speak what was on both their minds.

The man's mouth curved into the barest hint of smile, as if to say that
missing shots was not something he ever did.

"Thank you, mister," Hart gasped, finding his tongue with difficulty. "I
don't know how we can ever thank you for what you did for my brother and
me. We were dead for sure without you."

The man nodded acceptance of the thanks; he had noted the *we* and
understood what the death of the dark-haired boy would mean to the other.

Hart saw that the stranger's face beneath his black Stetson was narrow,
and fine-boned. He had great serious eyes with dark lashes long enough to
be a woman's, yet there was nothing womanly in their brown depths—
betraying no stories of the man within, except perhaps that he was cut from
a different cloth and you'd do well to respect him. Hart noted with an
artist's perception that their corners turned down, as if weighted by sorrow.

"My name's Jameson," the stranger said. "Ford Jameson. That was Jerry
Hogan and Ned Putnam you ran a cropper of." He dismissed the third man
as of no consequence. He had a deep voice, low and curiously monotone, as
if each word was dredged from someplace fathomless and sorrowful within
him.

"They don't come meaner," he continued as he motioned Hart near so he
could examine his injured shoulder. "Been tracking them on another matter
all the way from the Dakota Territory, but it seems like you boys got a score
to settle right here and now. If you want to come with me, you can get back
your gear." Simple as that. Ford set Hart's broken shoulder with the skill of
a surgeon and was pleased by the manly way the boy bore the pain of it. It
was obvious to him that Hart cared more about his brother's safety than his
own, and counted a broken shoulder little enough payment for deliverance.

Ford was as good as his word; the following day their horses and goods
were restored to them, and a bit more, too. It was Hart's and Chance's first
experience of killing men, and it wouldn't have sat well except for the
vengeance left in their hearts after the gang's enthusiastic sadism. They
were surprised when Ford said they could ride with him for a while; he
didn't seem the kind of man who craved companionship. Hart's sketching
interested him, though, that and the fact that the boys had been well edu-

cated by their mama. You could tell from Ford's speech that he, too, had come of a decent family.

He taught the boys things about guns their daddy never knew. Never to draw unless you meant to kill; never to kill unless there was no possible alternative. How to shoot with either hand; how to clear leather so fast, it was nearly a blur.

Both McAllisters absorbed all Ford had to teach, for he was a learned man on more subjects than guns. He could track like an Indian and knew enough about the land to live forever on its bounty. He knew books, too, and made the two boys thirst to get hold of some he talked of. But it was the guns they would always remember about him, for they were what Ford was best at.

"Killing is an addiction, like opium," he told them. "If you let the power take hold of you, you'll be a slave to it. One day you'll find you've killed a man and it didn't prick your gut or your conscience. After that, there's no turning back.

"Gain a reputation as a fast gun and every moron with a six-shooter and a thirst for glory will be on your trail. You'll get no peace, and one day, one of them will be faster than you. Or more ruthless. Or luckier. . . . Out here, the way a man handles a gun determines his future," he said, and set them to practicing for hours every day. "If you're better with a pistol than the next man, you've got options. If he's better than you, he'll do all the deciding."

"It's the brain that's your weapon," Ford told Chance as he watched the boy practice. "The gun is only an instrument, like Hart's charcoal. It's the brain behind the instrument that decides how you use any gift." For Ford had seen from the first that Chance had a natural talent with a pistol far beyond the ordinary. By the end of summer the older boy looked nearly as elegant in the way he handled a weapon as Jameson did. He could twirl the heavy .45 around and slip it in and out of its leather with ease and grace. He could draw straight or cross-handed and could put a bullet through the ace on a playing card before it hit the ground.

Hart had a keen eye for straight, fast shooting too—the same trick of nature that coordinated hand and eye for sketching served him well with a gun, but Chance's gift was far beyond his brother's.

And if Chance was handy with a pistol, his prowess with a deck of cards was prodigious. Even Ford, who seldom smiled, laughed out loud a few times over Chance's dexterity. The three travelers played cards at night on the trail and there wasn't much Ford didn't know about gaming, clean or dirty.

"You've got to understand the superstitions, son," he told them. "A gambler's life is chancy, so he wants the odds in his favor. Like tying a bat's heart with a red silk string to your right arm is supposed to make you lucky."

"Does it?"

"Not so's I ever noticed," Ford said, looking Chance in the eye with that disconcerting dark stare.

"Do know you'd best never gamble with a one-eyed man, though. That's bad luck. And never count your chips while you're still at the table, or let any man look over your shoulder—women don't count for that last part, son. A man who draws a pat hand of jacks full or red sevens won't leave the game alive."

He showed Chance how to mark a deck and soon his ability was nothing compared to the boy's, for Chance could deal an ace from the bottom, top, or middle before your eye could blink or your brain could suck it in. Chance was to cards, Hart said, what Ford was to guns.

"By God, Chance," Ford said one night as they bedded down. "With that talent of yours you could be a millionaire or a dead man by the time you're twenty-five."

The time they spent with Ford was growing-up time for both McAllisters. They took on their full height and weight and began to feel the cockiness that comes with being bigger than other men. Chance's extraordinary good looks turned ladies' heads on the streets of the towns they passed through; and although Hart didn't share his brother's startling handsomeness, there was something in his size and ruggedness that drew them as well.

Ford took them to their first sporting house to learn what a man does with a woman. He taught them how to survive such places without succumbing to the special pitfalls that abounded: the chloral hydrate in your drink to knock you out long enough to be relieved of your wallet . . . or the nicotine they spiked the whiskey with, so you'd end up in an alley throwing up your chow while a pair of toughs helped themselves to your cash. Or the girls who lured you to their beds so someone else could pinch your poke.

He shepherded them through enough poker games to keep them all in beans and bacon, and he let them borrow the books he always carried in his saddlebags—books by men like Shakespeare and Milton and Virgil, whose work he liked to read aloud to them by the campfire, late at night.

The two McAllisters spent nearly two years in Ford's company, then one day he said he was moving on—just like that. The brothers were upset at the news, but men don't show such emotions to each other, so they simply thanked Ford for all he'd done and asked him where he was going, but he declined to say.

It was their time with Ford, they always said later, that made them into men as much as anything ever did. There were plenty of tales about the gunfighter that would stand a man's hair on end, but there're two sides to everything, and the teaching side was the one they always chose to remember about Ford Jameson. That, and the fact that he'd saved their lives.

Over the next two years Chance and Hart did a little of everything a man could do—herded cattle, did day labor, worked on a couple of ranches in the Territory, had good times and bad. Eventually something inside a man makes him ache for more, if he's got sand. The McAllister boys grew up and started aching.

They trailherded one last cattle drive, took their wages, and headed for the nearest town big enough to offer a taste of a different kind of living. The town was Denver. Hart had it in his mind to apprentice himself to an engraver, for in those days, when art school was an impossible dream to a boy with his predilections, apprenticeship was the only way to learn to be an artist and every big town had a newspaper with an engraver attached.

Hart was seventeen, and Chance a year older, when they rode into Denver. They had not the slightest notion when they turned their horses' heads onto Larimer Street that one day their names and Denver's would be set down together in the history books.

 16

The man with the unlikely name of Hercules Monroe stood just over five and a half feet, shoes and all. He was a master engraver and an artist, but of more importance to Hart, he was in need, of an apprentice and had advertised in the *Rocky Mountain News* for applicants.

"Taught yourself, son?" he asked Hart, waving the boy's grubby sketches at him in the little shop on Arapahoe Street. Hart had liberated the dog-eared pages from their repository in his saddlebag, and they were the worse for wear.

"Yes, sir," Hart replied, embarrassed that he towered so far above Herc that the man had to look nearly straight up to hold a conversation with him. "My mama studied painting back East, sir, and she showed me most of what I know."

Herc peered up from the level of Hart's belt buckle, never commenting on the boy's size, not in the least put off by it. The man had a fine square head, Hart noted, abundantly covered with unruly dark hair that didn't appear to have felt the benefit of a comb for a while, although he ran his fingers through it often. Herc's eyes were lively and took in the world with the amused and affectionate tolerance of a longtime lover.

"Did she teach you about hard work, too?" he demanded, screwing up his eyes and trying to look fierce and businesslike.

"No, sir," Hart answered him with a quiet smile. "She sort of left that up to my daddy."

"And just what'd he do?"

"He was a farmer in Kansas, Mr. Monroe."

"Well then, go ahead . . ." the man prompted, "tell me what he taught you."

Hart thought hard for a moment. "He taught me to shoot straight, to fish and to farm," he replied slowly, thinking as he spoke. "Other things, too, I guess. To live righteously, to help your neighbor, to protect the ones you love. To get to be good at something you could be proud of . . ." Hart stopped and smiled shyly. "I guess whenever I fail at doing things the right way, it seems to me I've transgressed my daddy's rules more than God's."

Herc tilted back his head to search the boy's face with renewed interest.

"That sketch of the prairie house you're holding is all I've got left of them," Hart finished, his voice low and reverent.

Herc nodded, and rifled the sketches he held for the one described. "There's love here," he said, examining it carefully. "And respect. You draw from the heart, McAllister. No one can teach you that. Not your mama, not Michelangelo nor Leonardo da Vinci. They could alter your sense of line and perfect your draftsmanship, maybe. But the heart . . . that is a country beyond the province of the greatest teacher."

Hart didn't know what to reply to that exactly, or who those fellows were who couldn't teach him anything, so he said nothing. He started working for Herc the following day.

The shop was a revelation to him. Big-time newspapers and magazines like *Harper's Weekly* or *Frank Leslie's Illustrated Newspaper* were always on the lookout for roving artist-reporters who could do pen-and-ink drawings an engraver could convert to wood engravings. As there was special interest back East in the goings-on west of the Mississippi, there was a ready market for on-the-spot drawings of western events. Men like Herc, who were both artists and engravers, were in great demand and earned a fine wage.

"Engraving is painstaking, and if you don't have the guts for hard work, you might as well not even try," Herc told Hart as he showed him through the shop. "Once a drawing has been done by the artist, it's copied line for line in reverse, on wood. In a big shop, where they have apprentices, each one specializes, as they did in the Middle Ages—one lad does foregrounds, one figures, one backgrounds, and so forth. Here I do everything myself, which is why I advertised."

Hart, whose whole life had been starved for access to the work of other artists, was entranced by the clutter of the engraving shop. Sketches lay everywhere—large studies were tacked up on walls and small ones over-flowed every surface. Herc looked with approval at the excitement his work provoked in the boy.

"Engravings are done in small sections," he said, holding one up for scrutiny. "Later they're bolted together. Once the reversed drawing has been completely transferred to wood, the blocks are unbolted and you cut away all the areas between the lines of the drawing. The more exquisite the detail you achieve, the more memorable the engraving. You'll learn the art of the accented line here, lad . . . the nuances of light and shadow . . . the emotional power that can be transmitted by a simple black-and-white drawing."

By the time Hart left the shop, his head was bursting with new terminology and an explosion of hope.

▲

Chance let his eyes grow accustomed to the dim light of the saloon's interior—he had questioned several men on the street as to the most likely watering hole for Denver's elite. He needed a job with prospects and he needed money for a working wardrobe. He looked with distaste at the trail-worn clothes he had spiffed up as best he could for the occasion. It beat all how his brother Hart could be content in trailhand shirts and denims, while he longed for the kind of custom-tailored haberdashery you saw on politicians and businessmen.

There were four tables with games in progress—three seemed populated by ordinary citizens; the fourth was just what he was looking for, a table full of prosperous men. The kind who smoked good cigars and ordered decent whiskey; the kind who could spot a bright young man if he presented his credentials in just the right way.

Chance smiled and sauntered toward the tables. He stretched his dealing hand twice to get the blood circulating; already he could feel the tingle of excitement that always accompanied the prospect of a game. If he could talk himself into the right poker table, he knew how to be noticed. He weighed the feel of the money in his pocket and decided which of the lower-echelon tables he'd use to fatten his bankroll.

By the end of the first hour, Chance had enough money to move on to the table of his choice; by the end of the second, he had made the acquaintance of two lawyers, a banker, the owner of a brewery, and a judge. And by the end of the third, he had the offer of a job interview at Cross, Phipps and MacKenzie, the law firm with the best political connections in Denver.

▲

Hart found that Herc was an artist of real stature and an indefatigable teacher. He browbeat his new apprentice into demanding perfection of himself.

"No!" he would admonish if he disapproved. "This has no life! No blood, no passion! Without passion this work is an exercise in draftsmanship. *With* passion it becomes art."

Herc had three loves in life, Hart soon discovered: his wife, Mercy; his engraving; and a newly invented art form called "photography," which was his obsession.

"Mercy and I have not been blessed with children, so we have been blessed with a camera instead," he told his student proudly, unveiling the amazing contraption. It was a huge brown box with a black cloth covering, under which the little man frequently darted, and under which he could be found whenever a work-free moment presented itself.

"I use the wet-collodion method," Herc explained. "Glass negatives produce prints on paper now, not on metal like the old daguerreotypes did." Hart could see that collodion was a syrupy solution made of gun cotton in ether and alcohol. He watched with fascination as Herc first coated the glass with this vile mixture, then, in total darkness, dipped the plate into a bath of silver nitrate.

"You can't let the solution dry," Herc told him, "or the plate loses its sensitivity. So you must quickly load the wet plate into the camera, take an educated guess about the proper exposure time, then pray that the subject doesn't move and make all your efforts meaningless . . . Then you 'take' your picture!"

Mercy indulged her husband in this other love, photography. She had long ago come to terms with the fact that she could have only the parts of him not consumed by his work, and it seemed to Hart, she felt that part of Herc was better than all of any other man.

Mercy Monroe was a strong-looking woman, a square-jawed, dark-haired Yankee, mighty enough of bosom to have graced the prow of a whaling ship, and long of limb. She was considerably taller than her husband, although neither of them ever seemed to notice that. She had a firm mouth, pepper-and-salt hair parted precisely in the middle and pulled back into a no-nonsense bun. Hart thought this hairdo set the tone for everything about Mercy: symmetrical, practical, scorning unnecessary adornment. Yet she was attractive once you knew her, for she was full of goodness.

It was she who insisted that both McAllisters live with them for the duration of their stay in Denver; she who organized the evenings when all four convened in the Monroe parlor, so the boys could relearn the art of being gentlemen. The parlor was an elaborate Victorian affair, made dark by heavy velvet drapes and prim by a horsehair sofa, yet it seemed to fold its arms cozily around Hart and Chance. The bric-a-brac of Herc's travels and the fruit of his artistic and photographic genius widened the small room's vistas, and the warmth of Herc and Mercy put the boys in mind of their own lost family.

Mercy would pour the tea, and Herc would splash bourbon into the cups when her back was turned. They both talked animatedly of politics and foreign places, of books and art and all the knowledge that helps to civilize a man. Hart and Chance polished up the manners their mama had laboriously taught them, and learned to hold their own in heated discussion.

Mercy would shake her head over Chance's need to gamble and tomcat, but he would bring her little presents bought from his winnings, and she generally forgave him his skylarking.

Because of Herc and Mercy, the four years spent in Denver were among the happiest the McAllister boys had known. They had a family again, they were learning things they needed to know, and they'd grown to full manhood. Yet with growth came restlessness, and a conviction they'd soon need firm plans about getting ahead in the world; without plans, nothing would come of either one.

17   "Ever think of going prospecting?" Chance asked his brother one night after Herc and Mercy had gone to bed. "Never once. Have you?"

"Not 'til lately, bro, but half the clients at the law office made their stake in mining. I've been thinking, prospecting might be just what we've been looking for—a quick way to strike it rich. You know how lucky I am, brother." He added the last with a grin. It was a joke between them that Chance was luckier than any man alive. Hart felt secretly that this particular quality often went hand in hand with a reckless nature, but he'd never thrown that up to his brother, for some sixth sense told him Chance needed to rely on the luck.

"Prospecting might be fine for you, Chance, but I've been giving thought to going back East to art school. Herc says there's a fine new place called Yale that's the best in the country. He thinks I have talent."

"And I suppose this Yale place takes poor boys out of charity," Chance replied cynically. "No, brother, the simple answer to both our ambitions is prospecting."

"How exactly do you figure that?"

"Why, it's clear as the nose on your face, bro. All we have to do is find enough gold to make me rich and to send you east to that fancy school. Two years should do it."

"Two years is a long time."

"Two years and then you're free to go, Hart. I give you my word on it. By then we'll be tired of each other anyway."

Hart tried not to be taken in by his brother's infectious enthusiasm, but he had to admit there was a seductiveness to gold; every second man on the Denver streets had been bitten by the bug.

"I'm game to find out how it all works before I say no," Hart allowed after some deliberation.

Chance chuckled at that—he hadn't doubted for a minute that he could talk Hart into whatever he chose to.

▲

Chance looked up over the tops of his cards to find out if any of the other men at the table had seen what he'd seen. The dealer was a good cheat, but not a great one.

Four of the seven players were oblivious, frowning or deadpan; they examined the hands they held in quiet concentration. One man's glance caught Chance's knowingly across the green felt. He was a prospector, and he, too, had seen the queen slipped from the bottom of the deck. The man twitched a grizzled gray eyebrow and turned his alert eyes disapprovingly in the dealer's direction.

Chance knew the prospector's name was McBain. Folks called him Bandana because of the rolled-up red kerchief he wore wrapped Indian-fashion around his brow. Of scant five feet six inches and slender body, he had the kind of build that looked frail from afar and close up resembled iron springs.

It was apparent that McBain, like Chance, was assessing the wisdom of calling out the dealer. Chance had no intention of brawling; he was wearing a new suit of clothes that he'd saved three months for, and besides, his brother, whom he always relied on for reinforcement, was nowhere to be seen. When last he'd seen Hart, he'd been in heavy consultation with a rosy-cheeked young lady of dubious virtue, and no doubt by now had found his way happily to her bed upstairs.

The play continued two more rounds before the cardsharp double-shuffled and raked in another big pot.

"I didn't much mind, the first two times you did that," McBain drawled lazily. "But I'm beginnin' to feel a mite put upon by the number of aces you got in that deck."

Play stopped, laughter quieted, and the gambler looked up with feral eyes that flashed confidence at McBain.

"You'd best have proof of that remark, old-timer," he replied, unworried. "Or you'd best be a damn good shot."

"The first card you dealt from the wrong spot was an ace of diamonds," Chance said quietly, "the second a queen, the last one an ace of clubs."

The dealer was on his feet in an instant, his gun clearing leather as he rose. Bandana, too, was standing, but Chance's shot rang first, exploding the Colt out of the gambler's hand in a burst of blood and shattered bone.

Men seemed to materialize from every corner of the saloon, swinging fists or chairs, as if the latent urge to break things had been set loose by Chance's gunshot. Hart heard the sound of curses and shattering glass rise from the floor below. He abandoned his pleasure with the lady and grabbed for his trousers; this wasn't the first time Hart had scrambled out of a gambling hall over the years. Chance's particular gifts with the cards had an unhappy side effect of making losers cranky, especially if they were liquored up. Hart was halfway down the stairs by the time he had everything buttoned and his gun belt tightly fastened around his waist.

The fracas was still in full swing when he spotted his brother, a grin on his face and six-guns in both hands, backing out the door real agile, with a man about half his size at his side.

Chance gave Hart the high sign and ducked through the swinging door to disappear into the Denver dark. Within minutes, both McAllisters and the wiry stranger were making tracks on horseback down Main Street, the pianist was once again tickling the ivories, and presumably play had resumed at the poker table. Denver tended to be a wide-open town and nobody paid much mind if a man was shot for cheating, especially if the wound wasn't mortal.

Hart's quick assessment of the situation had turned up no dead bodies. He heard no hoofbeats of a posse on their immediate tail, so he figured nobody had died. A short way out of town, all three horsemen slowed down by mutual consent and eventually stopped.

"McBain's the name," said the little man, sticking his hand out to Hart. "Folks call me Bandana."

Hart saw a man of indeterminate age, his face leathered by a network of spiderweb lines and deep-gouged creases like stretched wire, all tanned to the color and consistency of animal hide. His eyes were sharp and looked to be the kind that could see a lizard move under a creosote bush at fifty paces, and laughed real easy. Hart saw a peck of mischief in McBain, but liked the strength of his handshake and the forthright way he had. Salt-and-pepper hair hung down straight from the knotted kerchief to the man's shoulder; there were waves in it, as if it was accustomed to being plaited. He had a fine straightforward nose, and the kind of toughness to his mouth and jaw that suggested stubbornness or determination.

"Were you getting my brother into devilment, McBain, or did he do the honors for you?" Hart asked with a grin.

"Well, now, I'd say we get equal credit, near as I can figger. No real harm done. That saloon needed redecoratin' and now they'll have an excuse fer doin' it. I got a camp about three miles out of town; if you boys would care to let the dust settle around Mattie's Place before headin' back into Denver, you could bunk with me a day or two. I ain't got but a prospector's tent and some extra bedrolls, but the air seems friendly enough for comfort."

Bandana talked about prospecting long into the night. He'd been on every significant dig from Sutter's Mill to the Comstock, he said; hard-rock or placer, he and Bessie, his mule, had done it all.

"I had me two good strikes," he told them amiably, but without the typical prospector braggadocio. "First time my burro kicked up a piece of rock with ore in it, but my partner jumped the claim and left me near dead on the side of the mountain." He pointed to an old scar that started at his temple and traveled up the scalp. He had to move his bandana askew to show the evidence.

"Second time I was old enough not to get my poke pinched so easy," he said with a small, rueful laugh, "but the lode was too deep to work without capital and I had to sell out or lose it all. I got me three thousand, and they got three million, but there's more where that all come from and the third time's the charm."

Hart could see the excitement building in Chance. Until that moment the idea of mining had been a lark, but here was a man who could show them the ropes, and he'd dropped right out of heaven into their path, just as Chance had expected him to. There were strikes all over Colorado and the Dakotas, Bandana said, and a thousand other likely places where gold was just lying in the Rockies, waiting to be found. South in Silverton, and Telluride, east in the Black Hills and north in Utah, there was no dearth of locales in which to ply your trade. Bandana himself seemed to favor California Gulch, eighty miles southwest of where they sat.

The Gulch had been a boomtown in 1860, he said, when a man named Abe Lee struck gold there in a stream coming down off the Mosquito Mountains. Like all such sites, it had become a rip-roaring rush town in a month, lasted a year or two until the gold ran out and the prospectors followed it, then settled into an ordinary town with nothing much to recommend it. Except maybe Jewel Mack's whorehouse, which Bandana said was a humdinger.

McBain claimed two things that sounded interesting to the boys; the first was that those early gold miners had left too soon, without tracing back upstream to the mother lode. Second, and even more intriguing, was that gold might not be the only thing of value in those untamed hills.

"When I was there in sixty-one, I didn't know carbonate of lead from bicarbonate of soda," said Bandana, "but what I seen on the Comstock was a funny-looking black stuff called lead carbonate that assayed out at two and a half pounds of silver to the ton. I think I seen that selfsame kind of black stuff back in the Gulch when I was there, and I aim to find out if it's silver-bearing."

Long before morning, the decision was inevitable. Bandana knew of a cabin abandoned by a prospector friend when the gold had crapped out back in '65. It wasn't precisely where he wanted to be, but it was close enough to give them a base of operations. Three men could work a dig more efficiently than one, and Bandana's know-how could save the McAllisters months of tenderfoot mistakes.

▲

"You're a fool to go, McAllister," Samuel Phipps told Chance when the young man handed in his resignation. "With that quick wit of yours . . ."

"And that golden tongue," Andrew MacKenzie interjected.

". . . you could go a long way in the profession of the law."

Chance's sober expression let it be known to the two senior partners of the law firm he was leaving that he understood the generosity of their offer.

"I appreciate your wanting me to stay, gentlemen," he replied. "But the truth is, my brother's got a yen for gold that just won't quit, and I feel duty-bound not to let him go off on such a tangent by himself. Like as not, he'll see the folly of it in a few months' time, but he's got his heart set on trying, and you know what gold fever's like once a man gets bit by the bug."

The two older men exchanged knowing glances. From what they'd heard of Hart, and what they knew of Chance, the likelihood was that Chance was the one who was leading this precipitate expedition. Phipps pushed his wire-rimmed spectacles farther up on his nose.

"Well, now, young man," he said with contained amusement, "if this impetuous brother of yours gets the bug out of his system anytime soon, you just hightail it right back here to Cross, Phipps and MacKenzie and get your old desk back. There's more than one kind of gold to be dredged out of Colorado."

Chance left the office whistling. He didn't believe in ever burning a bridge that might one day need to be recrossed, but in his heart he knew that the gold must come first and then the law, and everything else he wanted would follow in its own good time.

▲

"I guess all New England women know how to bid a stoic farewell to their menfolk," Mercy said wryly as Hart and Chance stood in her parlor waiting to take their leave. "It's in our seafaring blood. But I've grown to love you two boys and I don't mind telling you this is a hard day for me." She looked vulnerable, Hart thought, touched by her caring.

"At least, I suppose, there'll be little enough devilment you can get into up in those godforsaken mountains," she continued, trying to lighten the mood of the moment. "From what I hear, any prospector worth his gold pan is so worn out at the end of a day, he's lucky he can find his own feet to take his socks off."

Hart and Chance exchanged amused glances; now they were actually leaving, their excitement was intense. "I don't know about that, Mercy," Chance answered with a grin. "From what I hear, the life of a sourdough is just one long odyssey of sin and dissipation."

"Then you should feel right at home, you young rascal," she shot back good-humoredly. "But what about your brother?"

"Don't you worry your head about us, Mercy," Hart replied amiably. "You know I've got common sense and Chance is immortal."

Mercy couldn't help but laugh at that, just as he'd meant her to.

"You're good men, both of you," she answered. "You've got good hearts, and good brains—and even a modicum of good sense—which is more than can be said for most of your gender, but it never hurts to be reminded of what's important in this life, so I'm taking it on myself to do so.

"I want you to promise me you'll take care of each other and use your heads for something besides a hatrack. Don't gamble too much, don't womanize too much: don't be either saints or fools. Excess of anything is dangerous. Stay truthful, most of all to yourselves. Enjoy life and say thanks if you do." She checked her mental inventory for more, then sighed and opened her arms to take both boys into her embrace; when they pulled away there were tears on her cheeks she didn't try to hide.

"We'll be good, Mercy," Chance promised.

"No, you won't. You'll be human. As long as you're decent, that's good enough."

"If you're ever in trouble and need a friend," Herc said, controlling his emotions with difficulty as they walked down the porch steps, "don't forget where to find us."

It was a very long while before the McAllisters had reason to remember the offer.

18 Bandana's friend's cabin was perched so high on the side of Mosquito Peak, it looked like an eagle's aerie. "Not the kind of place you'd like to come home to drunk," Chance murmured to his brother, when he stared up at the tiny wooden structure seemingly carved into the sheer face of the rocks, so far above the trail, it was nearly invisible.

The cabin was small but adequate; the back was attached to the mountain, the front made of rough-hewn board with a tiny window cut for light. A man didn't expect much of comfort in a prospector's life, Bandana told them; most sourdoughs lived and died in a canvas lean-to despite the Colorado winters. If you made the rough trek into Oro City, the town farther down the Gulch, and if you had fifty cents to spare, you might opt for a six-foot square of straw and floor at the local saloon, but what prospector worth his salt would have enough strength at the end of the day to ride to town? They already knew only the rich could stop at a boardinghouse where, for a dollar, you shared a bed with a stranger or two, and the beds were no great shakes.

Hart watched the landscape change with some misgiving as they left Denver behind them. He admired the mountains soaring up as high as twelve thousand feet, dark green with pine and aspen, gray-brown with rock and boulder; but there was a merciless look to it, too, he thought, an unrelenting quality that somehow let you know right off that anything you'd get from the land would be paid for dear.

Bandana decided early on that the cabin was too far from where he aimed them to be, but it was nearly September and winter would soon be upon them. He said they could stay until the spring thaw and use what time was left before the snows to learn their trade.

Before holing up for the winter, he said they'd best make a trip to Oro City, which is what the gold boomers had named the liveliest spot in the Gulch in '60. For, once the blizzards hit, there'd be no further trips down the mountain for supplies.

▲

For a ghost town, Oro City was surprisingly full of life. The way folks talked of the gold being played out and the miners gone, the McAllisters had expected desolation. But in 1871 when they arrived there, Oro was just another western town of the kind left in the wake of other booms, or railroads, or wagon trails, all over the territory, which is to say there were plenty of people living there and plenty going on.

The main street offered most of the necessaries of frontier life—a post office, a sheriff, a blacksmith, a livery stable, a general store. There were eight saloons, some with dance halls attached, and there was the Crown of Jewel's, a saloon and bawdy house where a man could seek the pleasures of gambling, whiskey, or women, as his needs demanded. There was a newspaper and a hotel of sorts, a clothing store and a slew of cribs, which were repositories of prostitutes on the lowest rung of degradation's ladder.

Although the gold boom had busted, in the hills around town there was still a smattering of prospectors who seemed to think it would come again.

The main thoroughfare was nearly two miles long, following pretty closely the string-bean geography of the Gulch. Construction along the street was simple log structures or rough storefront, some facades with nothing much to mention behind them. No streetlights illuminated the hard-packed dirt street that was deeply rutted by wagon wheels and horses' hooves, but coal lamps in every window provided light and comfort and made the place look festive and sparkly after dark.

As there were more saloons, dance halls, and gambling dens than any other kind of business, and as they seldom closed their doors until dawn, there was the ebb and flow of life in Oro at any hour.

Throughout the day, the streets were rutted by Concord stages, freight vans, prairie schooners, six-horse teams and shouting teamsters. The snap of drivers' whips, the squeak of wagon wheels, the shrill giggles of dance hall girls, the shouted curses of men pushing their vehicles and recalcitrant animals through the throng on the thoroughfare . . . all these sights and sounds may have made Chance's and Bandana's blood run swifter with the certainty of the riches they were expecting to wrest from the mountain, but Hart's blood was racing with a need to put it all down on paper. The tough, lean faces of the drivers, the raunchy looks the dance hall girls cast their way as they wandered by; the palpable excitement of a town that grows up around man's wants as well as his needs. In their first two hours in Oro, Hart had crowded his head with enough fodder to fill a hundred winter nights with sketches.

"You ain't seen Oro if you ain't seen Jewel's place," Bandana told them once they'd left their supply list with the manager of the general store.

▲

"Bandana McBain!" Jewel shouted over the noise of the cowboys and teamsters and gamblers and miners who crowded the bar at the Crown of Jewel's. "By God, you're a sight for sore eyes!" She threw her arms around the small man and nearly engulfed him with her capacious bosom.

Jewel was Bandana's height but seemed taller because of the wild array of carrot-colored curls that ringed her head like a rusty halo. She had wonderful eyes, but she wasn't exactly beautiful—her jaw was too strong and her lips too wide for that—but her body, about which the clinging satin dress left few questions, was astonishing. Flawless white skin with a smattering of freckles, brilliant green eyes, and breasts so large and bouncy no man could look at them without wanting to touch. If her face was less than perfect, it wasn't on record that anybody ever cared after seeing her body.

McBain wrapped his arms around Jewel and twirled her around the floor before letting go.

"You wily old rattlesnake!" she shouted through whoops of laughter. "I see you still know how to show a girl a good time!"

"I should say I do, darlin'. I try to keep my hand in here and there, just so's I don't lose the touch."

"And not only your hand, I'll wager," she responded gleefully as Bandana looked admiringly around the saloon.

"I see you're prosperin', Jewel, even if the boom fizzled," he said.

"Three things a man's got to do come hell or high water, Bandana. Got to drink, got to gamble, got to fornicate. My kind of business tends to be the last to succumb to a change in the economy." Jewel stood facing him, hands on hips, wide grin on her red-painted lips, her formidable breasts pushed up and out by her corset until they seemed to dominate the room.

"You point them damn titties of yours at me like that, honey, and I cain't be expected to talk economics, now can I?" Bandana drawled, with a significant nod in their direction.

"You always were a silver-tongued son of a bitch," Jewel responded with a snort of laughter. "You'd probably just die in the attempt." She was of indeterminate age, somewhere between thirty and eternity.

Bandana raised his glass of whiskey in salute.

"I could think of no happier place to breathe my last," he answered gallantly, and Jewel winked to the bartender conspiratorially as she put her arm through Bandana's and moved off into the crowd like a ship in full sail. Jewel's red-orange hair made it easy to spot her even in the smoky dimness of the crowded saloon. She headed toward the gaming tables.

"How long since we seen each other, Bandana?"

"Winter of sixty-six."

She nodded. "Just about the time the boomers had all cleared out and I thought the end was near. But there were rumors the railroad would be headed this way, and there were men comin' through here real steady, drovers and such. So I played a hunch and stuck it out. I couldn't of sold the place at that point anyway, and I had a lot invested. So I stayed."

"Smart move, it seems."

"So it does. The miners are startin' to drift back in. Don't know why exactly, but they're feelin' their way back to the Gulch. Meanwhile, I got more business than I know what to do with."

She stopped at a faro table.

"The dealer's name is Preacher Bill 'cause he always wears a black suit. Some say he's a defrocked priest, but I ain't so sure." She said it softly so as not to disturb the players.

Faro required a large board with thirteen squares representing the respective values of the cards. The dealer's "case," a small folding box about four inches high, held the deck face up; across the top of the box was a thirteen-string abacus.

"Looks like big business, Jewel," Bandana said approvingly. "What's your bank?"

"We need to keep five thousand or so around most nights, but the limit's twenty-five dollars a card."

"Does the game ever get braced?" he asked, and she smiled with equanimity.

"Last dealer I had brought in a trick box that dealt two cards stuck together, but somebody figured it out and plugged him. Made a real mess on the green felt."

They moved on. "Where there's gamblin' there'll always be some guy trying to put one over on you, McBain. That's just the way men are made, darlin'. You know that."

They both knew the astonishing array of devices invented by the fertile minds of crooked gamblers. Loaded dice and marked cards were only the beginning. "Bags" could be fastened beneath the table from which cards could surreptitiously be drawn. A "hold-out" vest would shoot a needed ace into a gambler's hand by means of a rubber spring.

"Knew a dude out of Dodge," intoned Bandana, "who was known for spilling dark brandy in the neighborhood of his opponents' cards and reading their reflection in the shiny drops. Come to a bad end, as I recall."

Jewel laughed appreciatively; she and McBain went back a long, long way together.

"No nutshell played here, I see," Bandana noted.

"That's a sucker's game," she replied disdainfully.

"They're all sucker's games, Jewel honey," Bandana said, and Jewel rewarded him with a laugh.

"Got some chuck-a-luck for you, though," she volunteered, pointing to one of the most popular dice games, across the floor from where they stood. The smoke in the room was so thick, it was difficult to distinguish specifics at a distance.

"So, tell me, what brings you back to the Gulch, old friend?"

"Got me an idea and a claim to go with it. Got two new friends you might like to meet. Young 'uns, but they got sand."

Jewel's fancy eyebrows shot up.

"Always happy to hear of new men in town," she said amicably. "Good-lookin'?"

"See for yourself, they're bellied up to the bar down t'other end." He pointed to where Chance and Hart stood in conversation with two prospectors, their height and breadth making them easy to spot among the host of smaller men.

"That's a sizable amount of man-flesh, Bandana," Jewel appraised approvingly. "The dark-haired one's handsome as all hell. I ain't personally taken with redheaded men, but the other one's not too bad neither, from where I stand—he's got a real virile look to him."

McBain chuckled. "Oh, they're virile, all right, honey. I'm sure they'll raise a little hell with your ladies of the evening, soon as they get the opportunity. Right now, they're my partners."

"Oh, shit, Bandana!" Jewel said with fervor. "I thought you'd had your fill of partners after the last two times. Don't you *never* learn nothin'?"

He shook his head. "Hell, honey, what's the good of bein' alive if you don't take a few chances? Besides, I like these two, Jewel. You will, too. Come on." He hooked her arm in his own and pointed her toward the end of the bar.

"Ain't they a mite young to be partners, Bandana?" she asked.

"I never worry about a fault a man's sure to overcome," he replied. Jewel smirked and shook her head eloquently; if McBain said they were good men, his word was more than enough for her.

"Hart! Chance!" Bandana shouted over the din around them. "I'd like you to meet up with Miz Jewel Mack, the most bodacious, perspicacious and all-round damn fine woman west of the Divide."

"By God, you're a big one!" Jewel said, appraising Hart's six-foot-six-inch frame and holding out her hand to him in a handshake as firm as a man's. "If you're built proportional all over you could get to be real popular with my girls real quick."

Hart looked embarrassed, but Chance chuckled with delight and slapped his brother on the back before reaching for Jewel's hand and raising it gallantly to his lips.

"It's not size, ma'am," Chance said as he touched her, "but style that counts in this life."

"Mebbe so, honey," Jewel replied, "but you cain't make butter with no toothpick." Which occasioned McBain nearly to choke on his whiskey.

"Welcome to the Crown of Jewel's, boys, any friend of this ornery little critter here is a friend of Jewel Mack. Let me buy you a drink to welcome you to the Gulch."

Rufus, the Negro who tended bar, didn't wait for a further invitation, but set up four glasses. He was nearly as big as Hart, broad and powerful. Like many former slaves, he'd come west looking for freedom after the war and found as much anti-Negro feeling west of the Mississippi as east of it. Jewel had helped him out of a near scrape with the law and given him a job; in return he'd appointed himself her bodyguard. His watchful eyes and ubiquitous ears didn't miss much that went on in Jewel's vicinity. He kept a 12-gauge shotgun under the bar to ensure her continued good health.

"What do you think of my place, boys?" Jewel asked.

"Needs a nude," McBain answered before anyone could squeeze a word in. "A big, buxom, fat-ass nude right up there to soothe the sore eyes of the lonely men who come to share your hospitality. Damned if it don't!"

"I could paint one for you, ma'am," Hart offered, surprised at himself for speaking up. "If one of your girls would pose for it."

"You don't say so!" Jewel responded with unfeigned enthusiasm. "Damned if I wouldn't love a nude hung right up there in front of God and everybody. Might even pose for it myself."

"I think a naked painting of you over the bar wouldn't do much soothing, ma'am," Chance interjected. "In fact, it just might incite those lonely men McBain is talking about to riot."

"Well, ain't you the smoothie?" Jewel replied with a raised brow. "Been hangin' around with Bandana all right, I can see that quick enough.

"I like your friends, Bandana, darlin'," she offered as she turned to go about her business, for Rufus had given her a sign from behind the bar that she was needed at the faro table. "Bring 'em back here to talk to me when life ain't so full of piss 'n' vinegar."

 19   "By God, Chance, that memory of yours is something to behold." Hart sat with his back to the hearth and chuckled at the prodigious feat his brother had performed, calling out in perfect sequence every card each man had played in the poker game the night before.

Chance's answering smile was slow and easy; it was a fluke of nature that he had almost total recall. The books Hart had loved so as a child, he himself had easily committed to memory, although the content had had far less meaning for him than for his bookish brother. The poetry Hart hungered for, Chance could carelessly spew forth by the yard to entertain Hart by the campfire.

"You know, Chance, when you get right down to it, you've been given uncommon gifts by the Almighty," Hart said. "It's real hard sometimes not to be envious."

There was no rancor whatsoever in Hart's honest voice; Chance looked up and caught Hart's eye with his own.

"Don't you remember what Mama told you, bro, when we were real small? 'Son, you haven't got your brother's looks or your brother's memory, but God didn't forget you. Why, you've got more sense in your little finger than he has in his whole body. Chance is likely to risk it all on one throw of the dice, but you'll always figure the odds.' " Chance smiled as he finished the remembered soliloquy, word for word.

Hart leaned forward, stunned by the accuracy of his brother's mimicry. "How in the hell did you ever hear her say that, Chance? You know Mama never would have said a word against you, except I was so down in the mouth because everything came so easy to you."

Chance laughed amiably.

"I know that, brother. I wasn't put out by it, best I can remember. Most likely, I just thought she was right, as usual."

How like Chance, his brother thought—never once had Hart seen him envious of anyone.

"Just so you know, bro," Chance said more seriously. "I do have to work at the cards . . . concentrate on counting down and all. It's concentration and memory combined that makes a gambler—that and an honest game, if you can find one. Even though I can brace a game if I need to, my skills work best with the rules, not against them. Poker, blackjack, you know how I work it . . . most men have a lazy shuffle. Because I remember which way the cards went into the deck before the shuffle, I've got a handle on which way they'll be dealt out, and my trick memory gives me a real edge on most men."

Hart nodded. He'd seen his brother figure out the contents of each man's hand in enough games to know his method worked just fine.

"But I'll tell you something, bro, even after you've whittled down the odds with the skills and the concentration, Lady Luck still has to smile on you, just a little." Chance grinned and poured a cup of coffee from the tin pot, then handed it to Hart.

"The way I look at it, gambling is a means to an end, not an end in itself. Gambling gets us grub when we're low on cash, it can get us a stake for any action we latch on to. And because of my special 'gifts,' as you call them, I'm not really taking risks like most men do . . . I'm generally playing with the odds in my favor."

Hart took a sip of the steaming coffee and chuckled begrudgingly; he knew what his brother said was true. Chance's memory took much of the gamble out of gambling.

"As long as your judgment stays sharp, I guess there's no real harm in it, Chance. You've got to admit, though, you do seem to have a special relationship with Lady Luck."

"Well, of course I do, bro—I've got a gift with all the ladies."

"You great horse's ass. You're going to have to get a new size hat if your head grows any bigger."

Hart stood up and stretched; although Chance was big, Hart was considerably bigger.

"I've been having a fair amount of success with the ladies myself lately, Chance," Hart said, amused as usual by his brother's antics. "I can't decide if it's my size that attracts them, or just my good nature."

Chance looked steadily at Hart for a moment before replying. "It's more than that they see in you, bro. They see that you're good."

Hart glanced sharply at Chance, to see if he was being teased.

"What the hell kind of a thing is that to say to a man?" he chided, embarrassed by the compliment.

"Okay, then." Chance grinned again. "I take it back."

Hart cuffed Chance, as he had when they were boys, nearly knocking him over. Both men undid their blankets and got into bed; Bandana had stayed in town an extra day and they were alone in the cabin. Neither said another word, but each one played the conversation over again in his head and wondered what his brother had really been trying to say.

▲

Bandana began the boys' education about prospecting as soon as their gear was stored in the cabin. Chance and Hart would placer-mine the streambed down the trail from the cabin, he said, and gradually work their way back up from the foothills as the weather got colder, eventually landing in the cabin and staying there, till the spring thaw.

"The name *placer* comes from a Spanish word that means contented or satisfied," Bandana told the boys as they sat around the fire, nights, and soaked up the knowledge he'd spent a lifetime amassing. "That's what you're gonna feel when we strike it rich, you see.

"Long about a million years ago, the earth spewed out pure gold from its fiery depths, and drove it up real violent, along with the rock that created these here mountains. And there it lies, boys, seductive as a scarlet woman, tucked away in tons of worthless rock.

"The richest placers reside in the foothills of mountain ranges, because Mother Nature has pounded those rocky lodes with her winds and weather 'til erosion has crumbled the gangue that holds the gold, first into chunks, then into gravel and sand. After the gold gets set free, by a million years or so of pounding, it's carried by storms to mountain streams and there it lies waitin' for the prospector's pan." He sat back satisfied that he had their full attention. "Any wild mountain stream you find, boys, may have deposited its precious cargo into gravel bars or potholes, ridges or bedrock, where it waits for the man ingenious enough to figger out where to look, hardworkin' enough to wrest it from its rocky repose, and closemouthed enough to keep the news from his neighbors."

Hart and Chance listened, enrapt by the tale. Hart sketched the old prospector in the glow of the fire, and tried to capture in his drawings the eerie thread of hope Bandana was weaving.

"You look for spots where the rivers widen and their currents slow down, and then you set to work, boys. You squat down into that icy stream with the prime tool of your trade in your mitt—a tin gold-pan. Then you shovel sand into that fifteen-inch pie plate for all you're worth. You dunk it in the water and spin it with a slow, flipping motion of the wrist to encourage the sand and silt out over the rim, and then you fan out the drag on the bottom of your pan and, if you're real lucky, little specks of gold, called color, will reward your industry." Bandana took a swallow of coffee and whiskey from his tin cup and continued.

"Fifty or so panfuls is a day's work. If you get ten cents' worth of gold per pan, you can keep your belly full of beans. If your pan yields a nugget, you know you're on the right road. Of course, you could die of old age waiting for that to happen.

"Gold's real stubborn and keeps its own secrets, but by God, when you hold a bit of it in your hand you know you got a tiger by the tail! It's so beautiful and rich-looking it seems too perfect to have sprung from the grubby sand and silt around it.

"And no matter which angle you view it from, gold looks the same. It never wrinkles like pyrites, never rusts nor tarnishes, even after centuries lyin' underwater. Beautiful and incorruptible it is, boys. Unlike the men who grub for it, I might add."

▲

Hart swung the hammer in the morning sun; sweat poured in rivulets down his back and soaked his trousers despite the chill of the day.

The stranger watched silently for a time; Hart saw him out of the corner of his eye but paid him no mind. Chance was somewhere on the other side of the claim with Bandana, but the stranger didn't look dangerous, merely odd. He was stocky as an icebox, although of only average height. His hands were large and callused and he wore the most peculiar getup Hart had yet seen on the goldfields; a bush hat with brim pinned up on one side, a pair of khaki short pants that no one over the age of seven would be caught dead in, a naked chest with a kangaroo-hide vest half covering it.

After a while the man sauntered over. "What yer doin', mate?"

Hart looked up, wiped the sweat from his face, annoyed by the stranger's merry tone.

"Digging a tunnel, obviously."

"And what might you be lookin' for, mate? In that tunnel, I mean." The voice was Australian and thick with amusement.

Hart set down the pick and squinted up at him from the trench.

"Gold. What else would I be looking for?"

"Well, mate. You're not like to find it in that kind of hole." The broad vowels of the bush flattened the words.

"And what business is it of yours?" Hart was too tired to talk to a fool.

"None in this world," the man replied with a grin. "But I hate to watch a man bullock himself into a stupor for no reason. It's a fair treat, mind you, to watch a man your size slag away, as you are. But I hate to see a good man waste honest labor." He grinned again and stuck out a filthy hand.

"The name's Castlemaine. Jonathan Castlemaine, but my friends call me Caz. And around here, sand is what you should be washing through your sieve, mate, forget the hole."

Chagrined, Hart climbed out of the ditch. Bandana had said that friendship or hatred sprang up like toadstools on the goldfields; loneliness could make friends of strangers and animosity could be born of nothing more than a bad night's sleep.

"You're a big one, sure enough," Caz said, squinting up at Hart, the sunlight behind him. Hart laughed good-naturedly.

"Thanks for the tip. I'm new at this, as you've obviously guessed. I could have spent the day in that hole, if you hadn't troubled to keep me from it."

"No bother at all, mate. I heard a rumor there was men workin' the rock over here. You're not alone?"

"My brother, Chance, and our partner, McBain, are around here somewhere. My name's Hart McAllister. They'll be back by suppertime. If you'd care to share our stew, we'd be glad of the company."

▲

Caz arrived with a bottle of whiskey just after sundown. The night had turned mountain-cold and all four men were grateful for the warmth. The only concession the Aussie had made to the dropping temperature was to button up his vest, but he was still bare underneath.

"Where'd you get them scars on your wrists, son?" Bandana asked when the supper had been cleared away.

"Same place as the ones on my ankles and back," Caz replied amiably. "A pesthole called Port Arthur in Van Diemen's Land." He pushed aside his vest and the sickly-white stripes on his back gleamed in the fireglow.

"Nasty place it was, too. Got sent there for stealing food and a bit of whiskey from the bloody bastards who run Australia.

"Stuck me in irons and plopped me in this great stone fortress at the ass end of the continent. Across an isthmus it was, a spit of land attached by a string to the mainland. Trouble is the string's so narrow the guards can see across it, and their dogs can tear a man to shreds if he tries to escape." His voice had lost some of its banter. "Some men figured it was worth the risk."

Chance sat back in the chair, stretched out his long legs, and took a sip of whiskey from the tin cup.

"How'd you get out?"

"That's the rough end of a pineapple, mate. Five years them bastards tried to kill me off. Beatings, starvation, cold . . . and that only the half of it. They was torturers, too, and good at it. . . . Then, of course, there was solitary . . . I spent two years in a black hole trying to stay sane. Men had gone blind from the darkness in less time than I spent there . . . that's when I made my plan to escape or die. Either one was better than what I had, and I figured if I went blind, I'd never get out. So I pretended to be dead. When the guard came to check on me, I throttled him. Best day's work I ever done." Caz's grim expression was mirrored by his listeners.

"I kept to the water by night, made my way up the coast, ducking guards and dogs on patrol. They were so confident that the great whites would get anybody stupid enough to swim that they left this one stretch of water unguarded." He paused.

"Great whites?" Chance asked.

"Sharks, mate. Big as sperm whales, they was. . . . So I swam across by night."

"What about the sharks?" Hart broke in.

"Killed one with a stolen knife. Left the pack in a feedin' frenzy, gobblin' up their mate. Took a nip out of me, too, mind you." Caz pulled up his trouser to display a long-healed wound of mammoth size.

"Jesus, Caz, how the hell did you survive a bite like that?" Chance voiced everyone's question.

"Too ornery to die, mates . . . and too pissed off at them blokes who'd done me dirty. I drug meself to shore, crawled into the woods, and set about the business of survivin'. Didn't make a bad job of it, all things considered. The aboriginals live on grubs and roots, I did the same."

He grinned.

Bandana pushed back the chair he'd been sitting in and stretched himself.

"I'd say you're either the best goddamned liar I ever heard, or you've got guts, boy. Seems a mite excessive to get them scars all over yer body just to tell a tall tale, so I'd vote for believin' you."

Caz grinned. "I can see you're a fine judge of character, mate. This much I'll say for meself . . . I'm a good man to have at your back in a fight, if you're a friend of mine. It's pretty lonely up here on this mountain, so I'm glad to bid you welcome, and I'm grateful for the meal. If I can do you a good turn, I'll do it and expect the same from you. How's that for statin' my terms up front?"

They shook hands all around and parted. The boys and McBain would have ample reason later to count the day lucky when Jonathan Castlemain sauntered into their life.

▲

The weather turned colder and they laid in a wood supply for winter. Bandana said he'd tell them in the spring how to look for silver, too.

"Don't worry if you don't set eyes on me for a goodly while," Bandana said amiably as they made their winter preparation. "If I'm off from here when the blizzards hit, I'll just hole up with a grizzly and hibernate 'til April." They thought it more likely he'd hibernate in town with the buxom blonde he seemed to find uncommonly attractive at Jewel's, but the boys were always most content with each other's company.

The McAllisters watched their mentor ride off with Bessie, on an ice-cold day in mid-September. He was singing at the top of his lungs, the sound echoing all up and down the mountain. He had the kind of been-there-and-back voice both men and women thought winsome, and he'd whip out his banjo at a moment's notice to entertain whoever would listen or himself alone, if no one else cared.

It was early October when Chance and Hart made their last trip into Oro for supplies; they were on their way back up the trail when the snow started. Bandana had warned them that Colorado snowstorms were different from anything they'd experienced before, but they hadn't really heeded the warning, for snow in Kansas had been no casual picnic, and they suffered from the hubris of youth.

"The first flakes are benevolent enough, pretty in fact," Bandana had said before he left. "They sort of dust the white pines and sprinkle the ridges like a layer of confectioner's sugar. Then the winds take over and before you know it the snow's so thick the trail is gone and the footing's so treacherous your horse could make a single misstep that would crash you down a thousand-foot gorge that you cain't even see. One minute there's a trail and the next there's snow so deep your horse is wadin', not walkin'. You cain't read sign, and landmarks disappear. You cain't breathe nor hear nor see worth a damn, and if you're not near home or shelter, chances are your bones will be added to those of the thousands before you who never made it through. More than one man has died within hailin' distance of his own cabin." The boys had listened to what he said, but they hadn't really understood.

It was this first blizzard that changed their lives forever.

III

THE
SNOWBLIND
HEART

▼▼▼▼▼▼

Fancy, Hart, and
Chance Together

"A bachelor is a feller who failed to
embrace his opportunities."
BANDANA McBAIN

20 The snow bit painfully into Hart's face, lacerating his cheeks and forcing him to squint against the frigid assault. His hat was pulled low on his forehead and the collar of his sheepskin coat was turned up protectively, but the swirling, biting whiteness was no longer pretty.

"God damn!" he muttered several times under the wind; they should have set out sooner. Bandana would have skinned them alive if he knew they'd waited until the last moment to lay in supplies. And then, heaping one stupidity on another, Chance had insisted on gambling well into the night, so they'd gotten a later start this morning than need be.

Hart could barely distinguish his brother's shape ahead of him on the trail; the white obscurity danced madly between them, playing tricks with vision.

Chance's long, lean body was hunched forward, driving into the snow. Suddenly he raised his left arm in signal and shouted something to his brother, but the words were drowned by the relentless wind.

Chance halted and Hart was startled to see him slide to the ground. What in God's name could make a man dismount in this weather? he asked himself as he pushed his horse abreast of his brother's and grabbed up the reins from where Chance had dropped them.

"Somebody's out there!" Chance shouted, his voice barely audible over the blizzard. He moved laboriously toward a raised ridge at the roadside; something weird protruded from the drift; it looked like a banjo's neck. Adrenaline pumped Hart's senses to instant alert; anybody under that much snow was either dead or in grave danger of dying.

Chance fought the packed powder as Hart struggled to quiet the spooked horses and pack mule. He bent over the folded form, brushing the snow to right and left.

"Christ Almighty, bro!" he shouted. "It's a girl!" With real difficulty, Chance pulled her free of the freezing white blanket, as Hart edged closer for a clearer view.

Fancy's legs were drawn up tight as a newborn's, her frozen garments were wrapped around her like sculpted swaddling. There was an expression of fierce determination or maybe anger on her face, like that of an avenging angel on a tomb.

Chance leaned in close, hoping to catch the tremor of breath from her nostrils. She was cold as marble, yet he felt the barest hint of warmth escape her and knew she was alive. Chance struggled to keep his own balance as he lifted her body, then plowed his way toward Hart and the horses.

"She's alive!" he shouted triumphantly against the wind, and hoisted her awkwardly into his brother's arms. Hart cradled the frozen girl against his chest, wonderingly. She felt tiny and vulnerable, but even through the thick folds of his sheepskin he could sense that she wasn't dead. Remounting, Chance grabbed the reins of both horses and led the way back up the mountain.

"What in the hell is a girl like this doing out here on foot in a blizzard?" Hart asked as he laid their guest gingerly on the bed in the corner of the cabin, and shrugged himself out of his frozen garments.

"Boil some water, bro," Chance replied authoritatively; he was already beginning to peel away the clothes that were frozen to her skin. Hart remembered that when his mama had nursed anyone, she boiled water, so he scooped snow from outside the door to melt in the iron cookpot. From the corner of his eye he could see the tenderness with which his brother handled the girl, as if she were a doe or a newborn. Chance always had a gentling way with women that Hart really admired. By comparison he himself always felt clumsy and big-footed.

"Got to get these soaking clothes off her, bro, or she's done for," Chance said anxiously, and both men began to undo the fastenings of the girl's dress with difficulty.

"Surprising how hard it is for a man to undress a gal when she's not helping him any," Hart murmured, and Chance just grinned at his brother.

The skin of her face and arms were tanned by the sun, but once she was naked the whiteness of her body was apparent.

"Like the mountain laurel," Hart said quietly, and Chance looked at his brother questioningly.

"I thought she was dark-complected," Hart said quickly, embarrassed that he'd spoken the weird thought aloud, "but her skin's like the laurel flower, snow white, with a tinge of pink beneath."

"Looks more like the blue of frostbite to me," Chance answered, but he, too, had been startled by her uncommon beauty.

She was a tiny thing, almost doll-size next to the two men, yet there was no doubting she was a woman, not a child. She had breasts that were blemishless as alabaster and full for so small a body. Chance and Hart looked at each other over Fancy's naked form, and each could see by the sheepish look in the other's eye he'd had the same urge to touch the quiet perfection. Hart covered her up hastily with the blanket to quell the temptation, and Chance smiled a little at his brother's gesture, understanding it.

"It would take a saint not to be tempted, bro," he said.

"And a real scoundrel to do anything about it," Hart replied shortly.

She appeared to be sixteen or seventeen years old, well past the age when most women married, but she looked so sweet and vulnerable that her innocence seemed all the more in need of protection.

Chance chafed her hands and feet while Hart tried to trickle hot liquid between her lips, but without success. He found himself studying the girl's face intently; an artist can't help but be drawn to a form that moves him, but something in Fancy's still face touched him more than any he had ever seen. It was nearly heart-shaped, with eyes big as a fawn's and lashes that lay upon her cheeks like silken fringe. Her eyebrows were straight across and none too thin; they winged up suddenly at the very end, giving her an elfin look. Her lips, now blue from cold, were sensual and pouty; like her breasts, they seemed fuller than they needed to be, as if nature had been overgenerous.

Hart raised his eyes from the girl to his brother and spoke.

"If we can't warm her faster than this, she doesn't have a chance."

Chance looked sunk in thought for a minute, then stood up suddenly and started to undo his belt.

"Take your clothes off, bro," he said firmly, and Hart wondered if his brother had gone loco.

"I said take your clothes off, Hart!" Chance repeated. "Don't you remember what Pa told us about the Cheyenne and frostbite? We're gonna warm her between the two of us."

The Indians on the northern plains used the trick; two big male bodies can produce a lot of heat in a bed if they've a mind to.

"It seems wrong to do that, Chance. She's so defenseless."

Chance just smiled indulgently at his brother's sensibilities, and stepping out of his trousers, tugged off his shirt.

"Come on, bro—if we can't save her, she'll never know what happened. If we do save her, she may be grateful enough to forgive us."

After a moment, Hart nodded, and pulled his own shirt over his head. He had a hard time taking his eyes off the small naked body that looked lost in the center of the bed. Both McAllisters crowded under the covers, on either side of Fancy, and the homemade bed sagged nearly to the floor beneath their combined weight. Fancy was cold as crystal and almost as fragile; Chance put his arms around her gently, as if it were the most ordinary of acts, and his brother followed suit.

Hart felt the silken cold of Fancy's skin as he laid one big arm carefully across her chest to warm and shield her. He thought he could feel a tiny stirring as he did so, and wondered if she would suddenly awake and finding herself between them, be angry or frightened. "What if she dies, Chance?" he said.

"She might as well have been dead already out there on the trail like that . . . we can't do her anything but good, bro."

The boys tried to think what to talk about, but nothing seemed appropriate, so each was left to his own thoughts.

"Surely would like to feel free to touch her," Chance said once, but Hart was thinking how protective she made him feel, lying there between them; not dividing, exactly, more like connecting.

"I feel like she needs us," he said quietly.

Chance shook his head, amused, as he often was by his brother's turn of mind. "The Lakota say if you save someone from dying, you take responsibility for their lives. Almost like that person belongs to you."

"Then I guess she'll belong to both of us," Hart said, wondering if such a thing could be. Wondering if he would ever forget the feel of her in his arms . . . the soft satin skin, the tender swell of breast and hip, the strangely seductive perfection. He drifted off to sleep, still wondering, and was surprised when he awoke to find Chance standing near the bed.

"She's warmed now, Hart. Maybe you'd best let her be in case she wakes up. We don't want to go scaring her to death, after all the trouble we've taken to save her." Chance chuckled and Hart scrambled out from under the covers. He thought he'd heard an odd note in his brother's voice, just in that moment, and wondered if it might be jealousy. Surely no. Hart put the alien thought from his mind and pulled on his clothes as rapidly as he could.

Later, he had much occasion to think about that day when it all began. There was Fancy, lying between them; she needing help and them providing it. In a way, that's how it always stayed for the three of them, he thought. Fancy wedged in between, creating a special kind of love and a special kind of loneliness.

21   Fancy forced her mind to break the surface of the dark that engulfed her. Like a swimmer pressing upward, she fought a pressured roaring in her ears, as the sunlight drew her.

"She's waking up," Chance whispered, and Hart put the cookpot back on the hearth hook and moved hastily to the bed.

"Atticus?" she murmured, confused by the cold light filtering through the small window above her and by the two tall strangers who stood beside the bed.

Atticus was dead. She knew that, somewhere inside her. Everyone she loved was dead. Fancy blinked hard to focus in an alien world.

The dark-haired stranger sat down beside her on the bed; he was so handsome, she thought she must still be dreaming, but he smiled and spoke and the scent of his body close to hers let her know he was real.

"You've been sick," he said. "My brother and I found you in a drift on the trail. Mightn't have at all if it hadn't been for that banjo of yours sticking up and the red of your scarf."

Fancy shifted her gaze to the large auburn-haired man who stood nearby. He had a kindly, gentle face at odds with his powerful physique; his blue eyes were full of concern.

"Atticus is dead," she repeated softly as two shiny tears welled up and trickled down her cheeks. The two men looked at each other, wondering if her brush with death had turned the girl's mind, but she gathered herself and asked, "Who are you?"

The dark one smiled with relief. "McAllister. I'm Chance, he's my brother, Hart. We and a fellow named McBain prospect these mountains, but McBain's gone off somewhere 'til spring. You're in the Mosquito Range, near Oro City—in our cabin."

"How long?"

"Three days," Hart answered. He thought she had the most exquisite voice he'd ever heard. "Who's Atticus?"

Fancy looked up sharply. "My friend. We were traveling together when the blizzard hit. He was old . . . I think his heart just gave out." It was easy to see she'd loved Atticus; she could barely manage to speak his name. Hart wondered why she would have been traveling the mountains with an old man for a friend.

"What's your name?" he ventured.

"Fancy. Fancy Deverell. I guess I should thank you for saving me. I remember falling . . . it didn't seem possible anyone would ever find me. I was so damn mad at God."

She saw the two men glance at each other and saw the confusion in their expressions, but she was too weak to say anything more, so she closed her eyes and scrunched down into the covers again, and reveling in the blessed warmth, let herself drift off to sleep.

After a week or so, Fancy was well enough to participate in life again. The boys were happy to have her to themselves and hoped Bandana would take his time getting back from wherever he'd gone.

She was an endless revelation; there was joy in her, they found, and terror, way down deep. Joy in being alive, joy in sharing, the kind of joy that makes you live the most you can today, in case tomorrow never comes. Fancy was like someone reborn who hadn't expected a resurrection, but she was more than a little fey, and mourned hard for Atticus, talking about him in endless detail. Death stalked her, she said wistfully, and all those she loved.

There was little to do in the cabin until the thaw, so each man made Fancy the subject of his own study. She was unlike the virtuous wives and mothers, the Sunday-school teachers, whores, or saloon girls who had made up their entire experience of the fairer sex.

Fancy knew right from wrong, but didn't always feel bound by that and she didn't care a fig for convention. She could be hurt as a child by the most unlikely things, and in other ways was strong-minded and more full of opinions than a woman had any business being. She wasn't contrary, Hart said, just willful and wary because she'd been hurt by life. She had a fierce temper, was stoic as a Sioux and uncomplaining—yet she could play the Grand Duchess when it was least expected, and make it clear she demanded to be treated as a lady. She took pains to tell them about her independence; she could take care of herself just fine, she said repeatedly. Maybe she could, Hart thought, but it looked to him like she could use some love to go along with the independence, for she lapped up kindness like a kitten with a saucer of milk and underneath the armor of competency she'd constructed, he thought he glimpsed a soft and frightened girl.

"With that stubborn streak and all those opinions she's got, I'll be damned if I can imagine how any man will ever break her to harness," Chance said one night, after Fancy had fallen asleep.

Hart smiled at his brother in the dark. "But if she decided to ride with you a while, you sure would count yourself the luckiest man alive, wouldn't you?" he answered him.

They all laughed together, planned the future together. Fancy had as much an obsession about striking it rich as Chance did. They would hit the gold fields when the thaw came, they told each other, and make their fortunes. When that happened, Hart would go East to study at a real art college, then he'd head into Indian territory to paint the last true natives of the West before encroaching civilization destroyed the exotic world his father had made live in his dreams; Chance would build the fanciest house in Denver. Fancy would go on the stage and tour the European capitals and marry a man who would lay the world at her feet.

She sang for them every night, or recited from the classics Hart loved so well. He said she had a voice that would put the angels to shame and sometimes she would play a tune from the tiny music box she carried with her and sing to its accompaniment. She'd carried this keepsake from the past with her every day of her life, since leaving home behind. The small blue box with its gilded cherubs played a wistful melody, tinkly as a tiny harp. Fancy would sing along with its haunting sound and the brothers would exchange glances and swell with longing for her. But since neither was free to court her under the other's gaze, they simply longed in silence.

By the time Bandana stomped his way back into the cabin in January, Fancy, Chance, and Hart were friends.

 "I've got a favor to ask of you," Fancy said one night after supper; all three men looked up, interested. The cabin seemed like home since she'd arrived, she'd tidied it and made curtains for the window from scraps of cloth. No one had said as much to the others, but Fancy's presence had woven them into a family.

"Anything short of catching moonbeams, little lady, and I expect we'll give it a try for you." Bandana had taken to Fancy from the first; her sassiness and vulnerability attracted him in equal measure.

"I need to bury Atticus."

Bandana pursed his lips, understanding what must have occasioned the notion. The thaw had started to send its first sparkly rivulets down the gorge. The body would have been preserved by the constant snow until now, but once the snow melted . . .

"You real certain you want to put yourself through that, Fance?" he asked her, getting up from where he'd been strumming idly on his banjo. He walked to where she sat on the side of the swayback bed.

"I have to know he's safe."

"There's no telling what's left to be found, Fancy, or how to go about looking," Hart said. He thought the note in her voice when she spoke of Atticus could have torn the heart from a stone.

"I'll find him," she answered, and no one argued.

The following morning they all equipped themselves as best they could and picked their way out along the precarious and melting trail—they found him where she said he'd be.

The snow had kept away wild animals and delayed corruption, but the thaw had begun its decimating work. Hart moved his body in between Fancy and Atticus to spare her the worst of the sight, but she pushed past him angrily; she felt a need for communion of suffering with Atticus, for she had failed him at the end.

Bandana reached over and pried loose her fingers from each other, then took one little hand in his own; Fancy clung so tightly, she hurt his knuckles, but he said nothing.

The ground was too hard to dig and there was no lumber for a coffin, so the men gathered stones and boulders and piled them into a mounded cairn. Fancy watched them as they worked; she felt riveted to the spot, unable to move, barely able to breathe. She felt the rocks choke off her own air, lie heavy on her own limbs. No! Atticus was courageous . . . he would never fear the darkness. And he was far from here by now, borne home like the stormbird . . .

Fancy steadied herself against memory. She stepped forward, took a deep breath, and spoke her eulogy.

"You were my friend, Atticus. You were strong and full of wisdom. Now I'll never be scared of dying because when my time comes, I know you'll just come for me like you did that awful night at Beau Rivage, and you'll carry me off in your strong arms, and . . ." Her voice faltered and she had to stop a moment to control it.

"We'll go home together."

Hart wanted to reach out for her, but Fancy suddenly leaned forward and picked up two handfuls of snow from the grave in her clenched fists. The onlookers thought she would toss them onto the burial mound, as if they were grave dust, but instead, in some strange ritual, she tilted back her head and rubbed the snow all over her hair and face and hands . . . all three men turned their faces away from the anguished gesture.

No one trusted himself to speak, so Bandana stepped forward and took his place at Fancy's side.

"We shall gather at the river . . ." he began in his rich baritone. Hart and Chance joined in the hymn.

Fancy listened to the three male voices echo down the crystal canyon. *Oh, my dear Atticus, I miss you so,* she thought.

The hymn ended, the last notes seemed to linger for a moment, then faded. Fancy felt Bandana's arm go around her shoulders and unresisting, she let him guide her back along the trail.

 23   "You give me that shovel this minute, Hart McAllister," Fancy demanded. "Just because you're bigger than I am doesn't mean I can't work as hard as you!" Gold fever had propelled them all from the confines of the cabin into the spring day.

McBain watched Hart's confusion and tried hard not to laugh. Fancy was doing her damnedest to pull her own oar and the boys were tripping all over themselves to treat her like a lady.

"Hold on there, Fancy," Hart said with injured pride. "Digging holes in the ground is just not work for a gal. Especially not a little bitty one like you. Now you just leave the shoveling to me and Chance and Bandana."

Fancy's mouth hardened into a line, her eyes narrowed in mute determination. There was no way she could explain how important it was to her to be treated as an equal. They would happily have left her in the cabin to cook and to clean, underestimating her ambition and her temperament. She aimed a defiant look in Hart's direction and went right on digging.

Embarrassed at being ignored, Hart grabbed Fancy's wrist where it held the shovel, without thinking through what he intended to do next. He never got a chance to find out, for Fancy lit into the huge man like a wild thing. If he hadn't been twice her size and young enough to have good reflexes, she might have brained him with the shovel.

Shocked into action by the unexpected attack, Hart held her wriggling like a trapped wildcat at the end of his long arms.

"Damn you, Hart McAllister! Don't you *ever* give me orders like that again, do you hear me? Don't you ever treat me like a child or I'll be out of here so fast, it'll make your head spin! *I* decide what I'll do, not you or anybody else, do you understand? This gold is every bit as important to me as it is to you. Maybe more!"

Her reaction was so disproportionate to what had happened, Hart could see he'd hit a nerve by his well-meaning blunder. So, not knowing what else to do, he held on doggedly to Fancy's arms until, still fuming, she ran out of steam and he let her go. Fancy rubbed her arms where he'd held her, and gave Hart a look that would have cut through steel plate. Wordlessly, she picked up the shovel again and commenced to dig.

"That's a real headstrong little filly," pronounced Bandana, moving in close to Hart's side. "You'd best watch your step with her, young feller."

Hart leaned hard on his shovel, a deep furrow between his thick chestnut brows.

"Did you see that look in her eye while I held her out there in front of me, Bandana? Defiant and terrified all at once? I swear I saw that same expression on a fox with his leg caught in a steel trap, once. There's some powerful big terror inside that little body. I saw it plain as day."

Bandana heard the protective note in Hart's voice and wondered where it would lead.

▲

Hart stretched his eyes along the border of dusk-grayed rocks and scrub pine; the mountain always took on the color of rusted iron after sunset. The land, so lush by day, looked mean-spirited at night; penurious and harsh. He'd lied to Chance and Bandana, said he was checking for a pickax he might have left at the mine site, but he was looking for Fancy. She had the damnedest habit of wandering out alone late in the day and not returning until dark. When he'd chided her, she'd related her tale of living rough on the road with Atticus, as if that automatically ensured her safe passage. But Hart knew experience didn't always equal safety in the wilderness.

Her figure materialized on the hillside far ahead, small and insignificant in the dim silver light. His heart beat faster and he told himself it was relief.

"You shouldn't be out here, babe!" he shouted, startling her. He'd taken to calling her that because it made him feel closer to her, as if she belonged to him. "It'll be full dark before we get back."

"I can take care of myself, Hart. Haven't I told you that a thousand times?" Fancy could be real snappish when she felt criticized, even about some little thing that was unimportant; still, Hart liked to hear her say his name.

"I wasn't trying to pick a fight with you, Fancy," he said, reining up alongside her. "It's just that it's near dark and there're a lot of men in these hills haven't seen a woman in longer than they can remember, never mind one as pretty as you. You could get hurt."

"Horse feathers," she sniffed, but he could tell she was mollified by his saying she was pretty.

"You're not my daddy, Hart McAllister," she said, trying to sound stern, but there was no rancor at all in her voice. She reached up toward him, expecting to be hauled up behind him on the horse, and he obliged. Once there, she snuggled down in back of him and put her arms affectionately around his waist, so he could tell she wasn't mad, just teasing.

"If I were your daddy, I'd teach you more sense than to wander around out here and invite trouble," he said as he nudged the horse into motion. The warmth of her body spread through him like fine brandy.

"What else would you teach me?"

A smile softened Hart's features, but Fancy couldn't see that from where she clung.

"Well, now, that's a real good question, babe. I guess I'd teach you not to be so damned headstrong, always wanting your own way, and I'd teach you that independence doesn't mean you have to be in charge of the world . . . and I'd teach you not to put yourself in danger so often." He stopped a moment, then spoke again.

"Beyond that, I guess I'd think you were pretty near perfect just as is."

Fancy didn't say a word after that, but she did hug Hart tight, all the way back up the Gulch.

▲

Fancy stepped from the icy water and the chill air raised goose bumps all over her body. No one from Louisiana ever gets used to the cold, she thought as she tugged the chemise over her head and let it drop around her hips. God Almighty! but she felt strangled in that cabin. What pleasure it was to stretch out all the kinks of winter confinement. She reached her arms toward heaven, just to revel in the touch of the sun. She wanted to run, to sing, to spread her wings . . .

A twig snapped behind her, dissolving the reverie; Fancy whirled to meet the sound.

Chance stood near enough to touch; an appreciative smile played at the corners of his mouth and his eyes met hers with no hint of embarrassment.

"You've been spying on me!" she said, annoyed and titillated. "How long have you been watching me?" She grabbed for her flannel shirt.

"Don't fret, Fancy. I wasn't spying. I just happened by and you looked so beautiful, I couldn't help but stop." His voice was sincere, disarming. He reached his hand toward her face unexpectedly and touched the soft skin of her cheek with the backs of his fingers. A current radiated from those fingers to Fancy's depths.

"It's sad to cover up something so beautiful with a flannel shirt, sugar. A body like yours was meant for satin and lace." The hand lingered a moment, trailed gently to her throat, and then was gone.

"A man can't help wanting to touch you, Fancy," he said, then turned to go.

Fancy felt the goose bumps rise again; this time they weren't from the cold. She had seen the lust, unmistakable in his eyes.

Fancy watched Chance walk to the top of the rise and fought an urge to call him back. How long had it been since she'd noticed the power he had to make her think forbidden thoughts?

She tucked the hem of the flannel shirt into her pants, wondering just what to do about the knowledge that they wanted each other.

24   Paintbrush and lupine had carpeted the world; summer grasses shimmered in the Colorado meadows, so many colors of green and gold, there was no point in counting.

"Silver huntin's tricky business, gal," Bandana told Fancy, scratching the scalp under his kerchief. "It's a lot different from gold, 'cause you cain't tell for sure if it's silver except with nitric acid or hydrochloric.

"Worse yet, you cain't mine silver by yourself. You need equipment, money, smelters and the like."

"So what do we do when we find it?"

Bandana smiled at her optimism; she hadn't said "if" but "when."

"First off, we keep our samples under our hat—cain't let nobody in on what we got. Jes' keep on sayin' we're poor as church mice, if anybody asks. Curse a lot, too. 'Goddamned stupid-ass mine's not worth the price of the powder to blow it to Kingdom Come!' That kind of thing. Shouldn't be too hard for a thespian like yourself."

"How far down do we have to dig?"

"Far as needs be. Sometimes a few hundred feet, sometimes a few thousand. Cain't say I ever got used to it down there, though. All cold and eerie. Nothin' but the light of a candle to see by, and the smell of dark and damp always in your nostrils." Bandana crinkled up his nose in distaste. "Always had a horror of bein' trapped where the sun don't shine. A grown man don't like to ever admit he's scared of nothin', Fancy, but to tell you God's truth, I'd hate to die in the dark."

Fancy leaned over to kiss his cheek and Bandana brightened.

"If you'll do that more often, I'll tell you all you want to know about minin'," he said affectionately. "Now, the first step to gettin' rich off a mine is to find a real likely-lookin' spot to dig in," he continued, expansive again. "I think that's what we got here. It takes three men to run a site, efficient. One to dig, one to work the windlass that hauls up what you dug out, one to cut timber. That way you can get down three to five feet a day. Then, of course, you need a mule like old Bessie who knows the ropes."

Fancy glanced at Bessie, harnessed to the hoisting system they'd created. A large revolving drum caused the mule to travel round and round in a circle, winding the rope that pulled up the ore bucket onto the drum as she trudged.

"How much will it cost to work the mine once we get to needing equipment?" Bandana noticed she included herself in the *we;* he wondered if she really meant to stay.

"Enough so's a lot of men just find 'em and sell out to somebody with enough capital to make a go. Once we hit pay dirt big, we'll need to cut someone in on our action, Fance. That's when they separate the sheep from the goats. Many's the man's been bilked out of his dreams by the men with the bankers at their backs. 'Course, sometimes it goes the other way, too.

"I once knew a feller had a mine looked pretty good at a hundred and thirty-five feet. He told this investor he could buy the whole shootin' match for ten thousand dollars if he made up his mind before five o'clock that afternoon. Well, the banker held out 'til five-oh-six, but by then this feller had hit a ten-foot vein and the price was up considerable!"

Fancy laughed aloud and stretched her neck in the sun to get the kinks out. Bandana was such an education in useful things. Fancy was long past the point of thinking the knowledge you gained from books was as valuable as what you gained from life. She had been unsafe too long not to value survival skills above all else. Knowledge of things that could get you out of a tight corner . . . knowledge that could make you rich enough to hire men with book-learning to do your bidding.

Bandana saw the calculation that had transformed her expression and wondered. She could hide almost any emotion behind her actress mask, but with him she seldom chose to do so.

He picked up his shovel and squinted up into the sun to judge the time of day.

"One thing about mining that's a lot like other occupations, darlin'—if you don't work your ass off instead of standing around jawin', you don't get nothin' at all!"

Fancy smiled as she left him and started back up the hill. It was an old habit from the days of Atticus—learn from others' skills. Learn everything you could stuff into your brain, because you never could tell when it would be that one tiny piece of information that would make all the difference between living and dying.

▲

"How long do I have to sit still?" Fancy asked Hart, trying to keep her lips from moving significantly. It was flattering to have your portrait sketched, but posing made your back cramp.

"Another two minutes should do it," Hart murmured absentmindedly. He smudged in the black of her hair and looked with some satisfaction on the restlessness he'd captured in the sketch. You didn't find women like Fancy in uppity drawing rooms or schoolhouses or ordinary lives—you found them out West where life was what you grabbed with your own two hands. He was in love with her already, although a young man seldom puts that name to what he feels in his loins.

"Do you think your brother likes me, Hart?"

The artist looked up from his work, crushed by the question. Chance was so often on her lips these days. Did Chance say this? Does Chance like that? How the hell had his brother won her heart right out from under him?

"How could he not like you, Fancy?"

"I don't know, I just can't ever tell for sure what he's thinking."

Hart frowned a little. He had no intention of talking to her about his brother.

"Tell me more about Atticus," he countered. "About how you and he managed on the road. Were you lonely after Beau Rivage?"

Fancy rearranged the muscles of her face and back to a more comfortable discomfort and thought for a moment. It was always good to talk with Hart; when he asked a question it was because he cared about your answer.

"In the beginning I pretended my mama and papa weren't dead. They were just off on holiday somewhere and one day they'd come back to me. I made up elaborate fantasies about their grand travels on the Continent . . . then, after a while, I relied so on Atticus that I couldn't imagine any other way to be. But I felt . . . I don't know exactly, Hart. I guess I still feel . . ." Fancy made a frustrated gesture, not able to put a name to her need.

"Unsafe," Hart filled in the gap. "Vulnerable."

Fancy looked up sharply. It wouldn't do to have him know all her secrets.

"Yes. I guess I've always been on the run."

Hart's eyes were full of kindness for her.

"I think of you as a grasshopper, babe. Always poised and ready to leap away at the slightest hint of danger. Sometimes, just ready to leap to keep in practice."

"And what if I do need to keep moving? That's the only way to get somewhere, isn't it?"

Hart frowned thoughtfully. "Maybe. Maybe not. Maybe a person needs to stand still long enough to figure out what's the best thing to hop toward."

"Well, I know exactly what I'm hopping toward, Hart. Believe you me."

"And that is?"

"Money. Security. A house so big no one can ever harm me in it. Clothes so pretty no one will ever look down on me again. And when I die there'll be a great stone angel over me with wings so wide you can see them a half mile down the road. Not some stupid pile of rocks on a nowhere mountain, without even a cross to mark my passing." She meant to sound defiant, but tears tightened the words.

Hart didn't take his eyes from the page.

"You've no need to worry about Atticus not having a marker," he said quietly.

"And why not?"

"Because I made a cross for him, Fancy. Carved his name on it, too, and put it on his grave."

She was so startled, she lost her pose and turned to face him. "Why in heaven's name did you do a thing like that, Hart? You didn't even know him."

"No. But I know you. I thought it would ease your mind."

Fancy covered her uncertainty by making an elaborate effort to regain her pose. She watched Hart furtively as she did so, for the thought had struck her that he was the most reliable person other than Atticus that she'd ever encountered. How very like him to do an act of kindness and never crow about it.

"Thank you, Hart. That means more to me than I can say."

The artist looked at her over the top of his pad and smiled.

"That's what friends are for, Fancy."

"I never had a friend, but Atticus." Her voice wasn't wistful, just matter-of-fact, but something in the admission touched Hart. He almost said, "You've got Chance and me now," but changed his mind.

"I guess Chance and I were real lucky, Fancy. We always had each other. Life can be pretty hard on you if you don't have a friend to talk things out with."

Fancy wondered if the great empty space she sometimes felt inside might have to do with friends, but she pushed the unwelcome thought away. Money was what she needed; the money to be safe and protected. If you had enough money, you could buy everything you needed for happiness. For all she knew, maybe you could even buy friendship.

"No more for today, Hart," she said, suddenly standing up. "I want to walk up over yonder to the lookout and admire how pretty the world is before we go to work." Hart closed the tablet and got to his feet, amused by her sudden mood shift.

"I can't imagine why you'd want to draw pictures of a girl in clothes like these anyway," she called to him over her shoulder. He knew she longed for pretty things to wear instead of Bandana's old plaid shirt.

Hart watched Fancy's movements ahead of him on the steep climb. The spot she liked best wasn't far off, but the trail to get there was treacherously steep and thick with underbrush. She moved as easily as a jackrabbit. If only she were that surefooted in life, he thought, as he lengthened his stride to catch up with hers.

The world spread out before them at the top of the rise as unspoiled as on the day God made it; mountains stained dark green below the timberline, and above, patches of snow so dazzling white, it hurt their eyes to look on it.

"God does great work when He's got a mind to, doesn't He?" Hart said, and Fancy looked up at him, her expression thoughtful.

"I've never known just what to think about God, to tell you the truth, Hart. Ever since my mama and papa died, it's seemed to me He doesn't pay the slightest bit of attention to us mortals and our prayers."

Hart started to answer, but thought better of it; maybe Fancy had good reason to be doubtful.

She hugged her chest against the nippy air, the cloth of her shirt pulled tight across her breasts. Hart made a mental note to sketch her just that way.

"What do you feel when you draw someone's picture, Hart?" she asked as if she'd heard his thought. "Do you ever feel like you're putting down a little of their soul on paper?" He loved her habit of blurting out to him whatever crossed her mind. Flirtatiousness she saved for Chance, with him she was merely honest.

"Sometimes I feel I can do that."

"My mama once told me darkies don't have souls at all, but I didn't believe her because of Atticus. He had one, sure enough."

Hart regarded the girl beside him with intense interest. Fancy's hair was pulled back with a snippet of rawhide and hung long from the nape of her slender neck, but the wind had loosened willful strands that whipped across her cheeks. He quelled the urge to reach out and touch.

"What made you think of such a question, Fancy?"

"I was thinking about how much I want from this life, Hart, and wondering what I'm going to have to do to get it. If there are souls, then there's probably a heaven and a hell out there somewhere, too, don't you suppose?"

"I can't imagine you doing anything that could land you in hellfire, Fancy. Besides, don't you recall what it says in the Good Book? 'God hath no wrath for the innocent.' "

"Well *I* can imagine it. I can imagine doing 'most anything to get what I want and that doesn't seem very innocent to me. You know, Hart, sometimes I think there's a good Fancy and a bad one, both inside me, waiting to see which one will get the upper hand."

"There's good and bad in all of us, babe." He wondered what it was she feared so in herself—ambition, ruthlessness? or maybe just her own vulnerability.

Fancy tilted her head up so he could see the intensity of her expression. "When you paint that portrait of me you're always talking about, Hart McAllister, you promise me you'll show both the good and the bad parts, because that's who I am, you hear?"

Hart was careful not to smile. "Tell you what, I'll do more than that. I'll paint two portraits of you—two Fancies, the good and the bad. Will that do?"

When Fancy nodded her assent, Hart was startled to see tears glistening in her eyes. She turned abruptly and started back down the trail.

"Wait up, Fancy!" Hart called out. "It's too damned steep to run here— you'll hurt yourself." Damnation, he thought as he started after her, nearly losing his own footing; trying to track the way her mind worked could be a full-time job for a man.

Fancy swiped at her eyes with the back of her hand. She hadn't meant to cry, but the thought of all she longed for and all that might be necessary in order to get it had overwhelmed her. Starting from a cramped little cabin on this godforsaken mountaintop, a thousand miles from nowhere, how could she ever get where she needed to go?

Fancy's foot ensnared itself in a trailing root and she felt herself lurch forward. She grabbed wildly at the air for balance, but Hart's arms caught her as she tumbled. He lifted her nearly off the ground and clasped her hard against his body. She was soft as a rabbit, all curves and cushions—almost without knowing he intended to, he sought her mouth with his own. Fancy lingered in the comfort of the kiss for a moment then pulled away from his lips, yet she clung around his neck and pressed her body into his with a startling ferocity.

"Oh, God, Hart," she whispered in a strange, childlike voice. "You make me feel so safe."

"Those are not exactly the words a man longs to hear from a woman, Fancy."

"Please, don't misunderstand, Hart. I so much need you to understand." But before he could respond, she was off again.

He stood for a moment watching her, and somewhere inside himself he knew that safe was something Fancy had never been, and maybe that was the one thing he could give her that Chance never would.

▲ ▲ ▲

Chance lay stretched out on the summer grass, arms folded behind his head, long legs bent at the knee, relaxed and happy. He smiled at Fancy, who sat cross-legged beside him in the small patch of meadow.

"You look like a little girl, perched there like that, sugar. Like the prettiest little girl ever born." There wasn't much room for respite in their arduous life, but when the opportunity came to relax, Chance took hold of it with both hands.

Fancy rewarded him with one of her most dazzling smiles, her full lips dimpled at the corners, her cheeks rosy from exertion and the sun. Everything about Chance made her heart beat wilder. In some ways it annoyed her that she had to struggle to control herself when he was near, and to control the situation. He had the damnedest way of mocking her when she was uppity and throwing her off guard with his charm when she least expected it. It irked her that Chance, not she, always seemed to be in charge of things when they were together. Hart, she could buffalo with ease, but Chance was always one step ahead of her.

"Tell me about when you were small, sugar—about life on the old plantation," he prompted with a lazy grin. The content of her answer wasn't in the least important to him, but the sound of her voice was earthy and pleasing.

"Why should I tell you stories?"

"So I can get it all straight in my mind for later, of course. When I whisk you off your feet with my newfound riches and shower you with everything a girl could desire." He had a disconcerting way of looking straight into her eyes when he spoke, mesmerizing her with his absolute attention.

"You're teasing me, Chance McAllister."

"I am most definitely not teasing you." He swung his body up into an easy half-sitting half-lying posture very close to hers. Chance leaned near enough to see her blush a little. "I'm going to be a rich man, Fancy." His mouth twitched in amusement as he reached over to brush a strand of her hair back under the kerchief that restrained it. He tugged at the scrap of cloth and let her hair fall loose about her shoulders. The gesture was intimate and sensual.

"You might want to kiss a man who's just promised you the world on a silver platter, sugar," he said, his face nearly touching hers. He encircled her easily with his arm and kissed her full on the mouth before she could protest.

Fancy melted into the sweetness of the kiss and the assurance behind it; her blood pounded and she felt light-headed. She kissed back with more longing than she'd wanted to reveal to him, and only with the greatest reluctance pulled her mouth away from his.

"You could turn a girl's head with a kiss like that," she murmured, trying to cover her own imbalance with nonchalance.

"I have every intention of turning yours," he answered.

Damnation! Fancy thought with annoyance. *He's just teasing me, and I'm the one who's supposed to be doing that!* She half hoped he'd try to kiss her again so she could rebuff him.

But instead, he rose languidly from the ground, brushed the grass and leaves from his clothes and stretched himself in the warm sun. He had the ability to do that—seduce you with his absolute attention, then in an instant, lose interest completely. *He's never serious for more than a minute except while gambling,* Bandana had said. *Elusive as quicksilver.*

"Time to get back to work," Chance said offhandedly, as if the last few minutes had never happened. "Don't forget to miss me while I'm gone."

Fancy watched him saunter toward the stream where the others labored. He walked as if he owned creation, collected as a blooded stallion. Just watching made her long for things she shouldn't.

"A little too much of a good thing, Fance?" Bandana asked with a wry chuckle, from somewhere just behind her shoulder. How long had he been standing there?

"Which one's it gonna be?" he asked. That was part of what she loved about McBain—there was not an ounce of subterfuge in him.

"It can't really be either one of them, can it, Bandana?"

"You've got both them boys turned every which way but loose, little lady. What're you plannin' to do about that?"

"Damned if I know."

Bandana laughed out loud. "You're all right, Fance," he said, giving her shoulder a friendly squeeze. "It's not really your fault you fire up their engines. They're young, you're young . . . nature sees that mistakes are made."

It was Fancy's turn to laugh. "It would be terrible to come between them, Bandana, and being with both of them is damned confusing. Chance makes me feel that everything in the world is possible, all the unlikeliest dreams and farfetched ambitions . . . he wants all the same things I do and he might just be lucky enough to get them for me."

"And what about Hart?"

"Oh, I don't know what I feel about Hart, Bandana . . . he's like a big old furry bear, all warmth and goodness. He'd never let me come to harm, I'm sure of that. But his dreams are so different from mine. He's likely to go off somewhere painting Indians . . . why, just the thought of it makes my blood run cold. I've had enough wandering to last me three lifetimes."

"But the truth is you cain't get all that mixed up with neither one of 'em right now because they ain't rich, and you'll have to go get it all for yourself. Ain't that the real story?"

Fancy looked genuinely startled that he'd seen through to the truth so easily, but she nodded.

"God Almighty, Bandana, I need *such* a lot of things. I can see now I'm just not going to find them on this mountain. That doesn't mean I don't wish I could stay."

"Either one of them boys would give you a powerful lot of lovin', honey. You might find you need that, too, before so long."

"And a baby every year to go with it, and soon I'd look like every other woman in the Gulch, all pruned-up and finished." Fancy's voice was sharp. "And I'd never even have tried to get what I want out of life. Do you really think I could stand that, Bandana?"

"It surely is a sore dilemma," he answered, and she couldn't tell if he was making fun of her or being sincere.

"Just so's you don't flaunt your favors in front of 'em, come between 'em, and then pack your sweet little fanny off and be on your way. Men have been known to do real stupid things over women who looked only half as good as you." He winked at her as he said it and she leaned over impulsively to hug him.

Bandana shook his head in mock distress.

"Now you're tryin' to add my poor old heart to the notches on your garter belt. You should surely be ashamed of your brazenness."

"Don't you wish!"

"Damned right I do!"

Arm in arm they retraced Chance's path down the mountain trail to the claim.

"I will not let my heart or any other part of my anatomy keep me from getting what I want in this life," Fancy told herself as they walked. "No matter what I have to do, or what I have to give up to get what I want, I will get it. By God, I will!"

▲

Chance grinned to himself as he walked the long route back to the cabin. Christ Almighty but she'd looked beautiful shivering there in the sun, all innocence and wantonness combined.

How could any man be expected to live in such close proximity with a girl like that? Had she simply been somebody he'd met in town, he could have charmed her into bed by whatever means were necessary—but because of the strange circumstances in which they lived, there hadn't been the opportunity. And now she was his friend . . . or something like it. Never having had a woman friend before, he wasn't sure just what to do with that fact. But it did change things . . . and it did make the question of seduction thornier. Not less enticing, or impossible, but thornier.

Chance whistled a little as he walked; he felt in high spirits. Hart, hearing the whistle, straightened from his task of chopping kindling.

"Strike gold while you were out walking?"

"Better than gold, bro," Chance replied, with a self-satisfied grin. "There's precious things lurking up on this mountain you could barely dream of."

Hart looked at him suspiciously. Chance seldom drank before sundown and never when there was work to be done, so that couldn't be the answer.

"Well, seeing as how you're in such good shape, maybe you'd care to finish up these chores I've been handling while you were out finding precious things in the hills."

"Can't think of anything I'd rather do, bro," Chance responded generously.

Bandana looked up sharply from mending the water trough. "Must've found a still up there on the mountain. That, or he fell down and hit his head on somethin' sharp."

Chance only grinned as he unbuttoned the sleeves of his flannel shirt and rolled them past the elbow. Not even work could change his mind about what a good day this was turning out to be.

25 🌷 "Tell me more about how rich we're going to be, Chance," Fancy prompted. "Tell me in infinite, delectable detail." She was seated on the floor near the hearth and, except for the long dark hair that was fanned out around her shoulders, she looked like a young boy in the fireglow. She wore Bandana's old breeches and shirt, for the two McAllisters were far too big to be able to offer hand-me-downs. Men's trousers made it possible to sit in all sorts of comfortable positions that would have been unthinkable for a lady in a skirt; Fancy loved the freedom.

Her knees were drawn up and her arms hugged them. Bandana had been playing his banjo, Hart was stretched out beside her, catching the firelight on the page of the copy of William Shakespeare's plays Ford had given him when they parted.

"You mean about how great a lady you'll be, wearing Paris gowns and golden slippers?" Chance teased, stretching himself like a lazy cat before the fire.

Hart looked up from his book and smiled; he knew Chance's imagination tickled Fancy and made her feel confident about the future. You could almost see her expand and blossom with sheer pleasure when Chance spun his gilded web of fantasy.

Hart quenched his own thirst with books instead of tales; in a pinch, he thought he could probably go without food better than without books or charcoal. But he hadn't his brother's imagination.

Hart sometimes wondered if he needed other men's dreams to clarify his own, just as he needed models for his pictures. Once he'd seen a tree or a farmhouse or a horse or a cart, he could reproduce its form and spirit, but first he needed to see . . . needed something tangible to be the catalyst of his creation.

Not so with Chance. Why, he could conjure up the best goddamned dreams you ever heard of, out of whole cloth. And he believed every single one of them would come true, too. No matter how much common sense pointed to the contrary, he knew life would turn out just fine. Even when he'd been perched up there on Hart's shoulders waiting to be hanged, he'd believed it would all turn out all right—or so he'd told his brother afterwards.

Chance had the grit to go along with the dreaming too; he would have walked right on up to God Almighty if he thought God had something good to offer him.

"Let's hear your story, Chance," Hart prompted. "We're all so twitchy with spring fever we could use a good dream or two to get us out of this hole in the wall."

Bandana played a riff on the banjo like the opening of a minstrel show and Chance stood up and straightened his lanky frame.

"Matthew Hart McAllister," he intoned with theatricality, "was today feted by the First Lady of this great nation on the occasion of his newest painting being hung in the drawing room of the White House."

Fancy clapped her hands with glee and Hart grinned appreciatively. You never had the least notion where Chance's imagination would light.

"Mr. McAllister had just returned from abroad, where his paintings of the far western region of the American continent had been purchased by several potentates for their private collections. Mr. McAllister is well known in international art circles for his extraordinarily realistic paintings of Indians in their natural habitat, and of various wild creatures doing various wild things." Chance winked at Fancy and she laughed delightedly.

"The high point of the gala evening, however, was the arrival of the mysterious Fancy Deverell, world-renowned actress and singer, whose name has been linked romantically with several of the richest and most powerful men in the world."

Bandana frowned. "None of that, now, you young jackass; if this was a decent sort of story, she'd be married to one of them rich and powerful characters. 'Linked' ain't good enough for Fancy."

"Give me time, Bandana," Chance answered, with an easy grin. "Don't you know a good fantasy needs to build up a little tension before it comes to a happy end?"

"Oh, Lord, Bandana, do let the man continue . . ." Chance smiled at her, his blue-violet eyes merry; a hint of pleasant male arrogance played around his mouth.

"Informed sources tell us," he continued, coming near enough to Fancy to hold her attention entirely with his gaze, "that Senator McAllister, the artist's elder brother, is the front-runner in the race for Miss Deverell's affections. The senator's great fortune, of course, was made in the gold mines of Colorado and is rumored to be one of the largest ever to come out of that state. The fact that he named his biggest producer 'The Fancy Penny' in honor of Miss Deverell is considered to be proof positive of his intentions."

Bandana saw that the smile had died on Hart's lips and a thoughtful expression replaced it before he returned his attention pointedly to the book in front of him.

Bandana interrupted hastily to move conversation in a different direction from Fancy's affections. " 'The Fancy Penny,' eh, I like the sound of that."

"It's got more of a ring to it than 'The Last Chance' anyway," Hart said, not looking up from his book.

Chance chuckled. "It's hard not to get a kick out of teasing you, little brother, you rise so well to the bait. Guess we'd have to call your mine 'Hart on Your Sleeve,' wouldn't we?"

An uneasy silence followed and Chance, realizing he'd overstepped the bounds of fun, was instantly contrite.

"I was only teasing you, bro," he said softly. "I meant no harm." His eyes sought his brother's with real apology. Hart knew Chance never meant to be hurtful, it was just his unthinking way sometimes to let words slip out that would be best left unsaid.

"That's okay, Chance," Hart said. "It was a damned fine fantasy until you tried to marry off Fancy. Why, any man can see she's meant for better than the likes of us."

"Hear, hear!" hooted McBain as he launched into so spirited a rendition of "My Old Kentucky Home" that everybody in the room joined in.

 26   The wind is so damned mournful on this mountain, Fancy thought as she looked around the dim cabin, grateful for the fire in the hearth and the comforting glow of the candle on the table and the kerosene lamp on the wall. They had to conserve the candles now with winter hard upon them; their tallow supply could give out long before the roads were passable again.

The sounds of the boys chopping kindling outside, mingled with the wind in counterpoint. They talked when they worked, and laughed from time to time, their rhythms in tune with one another. Fancy took great comfort in the male sounds of their work; the thunk of the axes set to new wood, the occasional curses that punctuated the restless wind and somehow held it at bay.

She was becoming too attached to them, too dependent. When the thaw came next spring, she would move on. She had been found in winter, and now it was winter again. A momentary ache tightened her chest at the thought of leaving. On to where? To what? To whom? And what exactly was the value of what she would leave behind? She feared she'd fallen in love with Chance.

Just the thought of him excited her. He knew his place in the world, as she did not. He laughed at life and expected the best from it, while she expected hardship and prepared to fend off danger. How restful it would be to have his turn of mind, and his luck! Why, even Hart and Bandana said Chance carried luck with him as other men did a pocket watch.

Was it his handsomeness that made her want him so? The black hair that fell over his forehead with just the right degree of playfulness, his eyes that queer blue-violet she'd never seen before, his easy carriage that hinted at arrogance and confident strength.

Or was it something more than all his physical attractions that filled her with such relentless longing? Was it some knowingness behind his laughing eyes, some worldliness that curved his mouth into a self-satisfied grin and said, "You can fool the rest of the world, Fancy Deverell, but I know exactly what you're thinking."

It wasn't just that he wanted the same things she did out of life . . . or that he dreamed on a mighty scale to match her own. It was that he wasn't bound by rules and conventions as the others were. He was free in a way they weren't—uninhibited, unrestrained.

Hart provoked no such feelings in her—although she had to admit to herself that his strength and common sense made her feel secure, as Chance did not. Or perhaps it was Hart's staunch adherence to the rules that she liked so much.

Fancy laughed aloud at her own mad contradictions. She was drawn to Chance because he scorned the rules and to Hart because he lived by them! How nonsensical. Yet it pleased her to fantasize about Chance and still have Hart for her friend.

She heard the sounds of chopping end, and Hart's laughter rise above the wind; Chance's echoing response was full of warmth and camaraderie. They were so good for each other, so in tune despite their different temperaments.

The door opened and a frigid gust pushed the two men into the cabin. Fancy struggled to close the door behind them and Hart put his shoulder against it to fight the wind. The men's arms were loaded with firewood, their hats, beards, and bodies sifted with snow. The gladness she felt at the sight of them made her heart beat faster; perhaps she didn't have to think about leaving them just yet.

27 🌷 "What was Christmas like at Beau Rivage?" Hart asked the question as gently as he could; Fancy's growing melancholia troubled him. She'd fussed more than need be over the food that simmered in the hearth; she'd lifted her apron several times to dry her eyes and, once, when she realized he'd caught her crying, she'd blamed the wild onions added to the stew. But Hart knew better.

Deep December drifts had piled up inexorably outside the cabin since sunup, appropriately enough for Christmas Eve. Fancy glanced out the window a hundred times an hour, until the snow obscured the day completely, for Chance and Bandana would have the devil's own time trying to get through to them for the small celebration they'd all planned for this holiday. Why in God's name they had insisted on going out to check the traps two days ago, knowing the dangers of winter travel and the holiday so near at hand, was more than Hart could figure.

Hart felt secret pleasure at having her all to himself and wished he could cheer her. Christmas meant a lot to Fancy, just as it did to him.

She turned from the hearth and tried hard to smile for his sake. "We had a tree near two stories tall that stood in the foyer by the spiral stair," she answered, pride in the memory. "There were ornaments my mama brought home from Europe on her Continental Tour and strings of popcorn my brother and I made for ourselves . . . and beautiful carved angels and Father Christmas in hand-blown crystal. And there were candles on every single branch, so it seemed a thousand fireflies had been captured. . . ." Her voice trailed off with a sigh.

On impulse Hart reached for Fancy's hand and led her to the rocker that was the only comfortable chair; obediently she sat down on the faded rag-cushion seat. Hart sat himself on the floor between her and the fire; he smiled to encourage her to tell more, but when she didn't, he began to speak instead. The cabin had been stilled to a special quiet by the snow, the oil lamp flickered playful shapes on the rough walls. Hart's voice sounded deep and comforting to the wistful girl.

"We used to go as far as we needed to, so we could chop down a tree, Pa, Chance, and me," he said, the pleasure of old memory in his voice. "We'd have to ride damned near forever just to find woods in Kansas, mind you. Then we'd drag it home and Mama would ooh and aah over some spindly little pine like we three had invented trees." He grinned up at Fancy and she couldn't help but smile a little in return.

"We'd grub together any old thing we could find to gussie up that little Christmas tree. Things Mama'd been saving up for the event all year—bits of colored ribbon or snippets of cloth from a quilting bee . . . cookies we could eat afterwards. Even a set of tin cookie-cutters she'd brought with her from back East, hung on hair ribbons. She'd save the whole year's candle ends, Fancy, and we'd cut up bits of pasteboard to make holders for them in the branches. Then, when it was all about as pretty as it could get, my Daddy would read us the story of the Baby being born, from the Good Book. He'd add on tales he'd heard from his folks long ago, of course . . . about how the animals could talk on Christmas Eve, because they'd given up their manger to the Holy Child, and about how it's real important to give food and shelter to any strangers who come calling that time of year, because it might just turn out to be Christ in the stranger's guise."

"I never heard that," Fancy interrupted.

"Once we did have a stranger come by," Hart continued. "An old coot, half starved he was, from losing his pack mule and supplies. He appeared on our doorstep this one Christmas Eve and Chance and I kept tripping all over each other doing things for him, just in case he turned out to be God Almighty in disguise!"

Hart laughed and Fancy said, "I like the way your face crinkles up when you laugh, Hart. You look just wonderful."

Lord, how I love to hear her say my name, he thought, and Fancy saw the fleeting look of longing in his eyes, but it was gone as quickly as it had come.

"My mama and daddy used to have a grand Christmas Ball every year, Hart. My mama'd be busy for a month or more getting the servants to make everything ready—all the seeded raisins and cracked nuts and washed currants and fruitcakes and puddings and such. Mammy'd make benve brittle from sesame seeds she said came all the way from Africa and every single soul on Beau Rivage would have some special part to play in making Christmas perfect.

"There were amazing drinks, I remember, with marvelous names like sangaree and sack posset and syllabub.

"All the women for miles around would come to the fancy-dress ball at Beau Rivage wearing gorgeous gowns, and the men would be fancied up like dandies. I used to watch from between the rails of the big old banister over the entrance hall, as they swirled by down below on the pink-and-white marble floor. Just like dozens of butterflies, they were, Hart. Flitting this way and that, this way and that . . ." Fancy swayed back and forth in the old rocker, eyes tight closed, hugging herself as if she were in someone's arms. "Lord, how I wanted to dance like that when I grew up."

Hart thought the sight of her was inexpressibly poignant. *I love you,*

Fancy, he said somewhere deep inside himself. I'll never forget how you look tonight.

He almost said the words aloud, but some instinct warned him they would not be welcome and he didn't want to break the spell. Hart glanced around the cabin wishing there were some kind of music to be found there, and Fancy's little music box caught his eye. He rose from the floor, took the small keepsake from the shelf, and wound it up until the box's tinkly sounds filled the cabin with harplike music.

"May I have the pleasure of this dance, Miss Deverell?" he asked with great dignity. Halle McAllister had taught both her sons to dance, and neither had passed up opportunities to practice when they'd lived in Denver.

"You most certainly may, Mr. McAllister," Fancy replied, surprised and playful. "Despite my dance card being quite filled up, sir, I shall make room for just one dance with you."

She rose from the chair, curtsied, and moved into Hart's embrace. For the briefest moment the warmth and safety of his arms made her ache with pleasure; had the arms she nestled in been Chance's, she would have been perfectly content. Her head rested low on Hart's chest and her hand was all but lost in his huge callused one. She was startled by the enormity of her own response to the strength she felt in this man, who held her so reverently.

"Why, Hart," she whispered in genuine astonishment, "you're a real good dancer!"

"Any man holding you would be able to dance, Fancy," he replied softly. "Might even be able to fly."

Fancy laughed merrily at the compliment—he really was such a good friend—and Hart felt her relax into his embrace. He wondered if she could hear the heart pounding within him. It was so easy to communicate the moves to her, their bodies seemed no more than one. He felt, as much as heard, the melody rise up in her, a gentle humming formed somewhere behind her breasts, and lifted almost imperceptibly with the rhythm of the moment. The blood rose precariously within him; he longed to press his hard body into hers, but feared to frighten her with the impropriety of such an act.

Fancy sang to the music box's accompaniment, as round and round in the dingy cabin they waltzed to the music of their needs. Maybe he had misread the signs of her love for Chance, he told himself wonderingly. Maybe it wasn't too late to win her heart. He felt the pressure of her pliant body bending, stretching, swaying with the rhythm of the dance. He heard Fancy sigh as if a great burden had been lifted, saw her look up into his eyes—was she seeking something there? Dizzy with reawakened possibilities, Hart bent to kiss her upturned lips with an inevitability that was profound. He had always known that if he once took her in his arms he would never, ever let her go. . . .

Like a judgment from heaven, the door burst open. A frenzy of snow and frigid wind billowed into the room, freezing both Hart and Fancy into startled immobility.

Chance and Bandana stood poised in the doorway for a dumbstruck moment taking in the scene, then Chance laughed a little too heartily and pushed past Bandana, stamping his feet to relieve them of their burden of ice and snow. Bandana walked in quietly behind him. Hart let Fancy slide out of his arms, and tried to regain his self-control.

Fancy's face lit up like a lamp in the darkness. Unembarrassed, she ran to both men, hugging them, helping them out of their jackets, shaking the clinging snow into puddles on the floor. The fire hissed at the wind's intrusion and Hart fought the confusion of pounding blood and loins, and of damnable disappointment.

"I thought you'd never make it through!" Fancy breathed elatedly. "Oh, I'm so glad you're here!" Hart didn't share her glee.

"Take more'n a blizzard to keep us away from you come Christmas Eve, darlin'." Bandana had read more than the scene in Hart's face.

"Got to keep a rarely fine little gal like you happy, don't we?" He bent to pull his feet out of wet boots with the help of a wooden jack, and tried to distract them all with banter.

"Smells like a mighty fine stew you got there, Fance, old girl. Seems we got back here just in the nick of time. Cain't nobody dance right without real music. Cain't get no music 'round here without my old banjo thumpin' out its sound. So if you'll just dish up that rabbit, we'll have us a proper dancin' party later on." He glanced at Hart to make sure his soliloquy had gone on long enough to cover his embarrassment.

"God's whiskers, Bandana," Fancy responded, beaming. "I'd be thrilled to dance to your music." Then, as if she noted Hart's disappointment for the first time, or perhaps even remembered he was there, she added, "Hart's a real fine dancer, Bandana—I'll bet you didn't know that about him."

"But he can't hold a candle to his big brother," Chance said, tossing an amused and speculative look at Hart as he did.

"Wouldn't think I had me a pair of half-ass twinkle toes for partners, to look at 'em, would you?" McBain asked, putting the question mercifully to rest. "Truth is, cain't nobody cut a rug like yours truly, so if you'll just feed the inner man, I will put both these two pups to shame. And a whiskey wouldn't go down too hard neither. It's colder than a witch's tit on that trail out there."

The moment passed, as moments do, and after dinner they gave each other the presents they had made, they sang, danced, laughed, talked, and told Christmas tales. Finally, at midnight, Hart read the story of the Christ child's birth from his mother's Bible. It was well on to morning before all four settled in to rest. The eerie howls of the blizzard only made the tiny cabin seem safer and more secure to Fancy.

"Thank you with all my heart," she murmured softly into the darkness before she drifted off to sleep. "You've given me a memory tonight I won't ever forget."

Bandana, feigning sleep in his bedroll, wondered if each of the brothers thought she meant the words for him alone. "There's gonna be good memories and bad ones them three share before it's through," he said to himself before letting sleep overtake him. "Real good and real bad."

 The four walls of the tiny cabin were pressing in again; Fancy looked toward the window with pinched longing. Winter was endless and the space too tiny to be occupied by four adults. No place to store her meager clothes, but stuffed under the swaybacked bed. No way to cook more than primitive meals, no way to catch even a modicum of privacy, nowhere to stash her bloodied linens from her monthly showing, nowhere to wash, nowhere to live like a civilized human being . . .

Would the memory of Beau Rivage and its gracious, airy pleasures never grant her peace? Fancy punched the pillow she had been plumping and slammed it down on the bed so hard that two feathers flew out and fluttered to the floor.

Sometimes Fancy felt she would burst at the seams, lose control, run screaming out the door and into the endless snow . . . sometimes she felt she would do anything, no matter how grotesque, to escape a future in a place like this . . . sometimes, like now, she would simply endure for one more day.

The tightrope she walked among the men was becoming precarious. Their broodings and their varied loves for her fomented in the cabin's confines, as did the demands of her own need.

She knew now the kind of riches that came from the earth were harder won than she had imagined. Even if the claims paid off eventually, as Bandana insisted they would, three mouths would be enough to feed with the proceeds—and how many years might go by before the payoff came?

She had insisted on sharing in the physical labor, at first to assure herself a part of what they dredged from the mine, later out of friendship, and finally out of a desperate hope that something could be made to yield before she had to move on.

No man would have faulted her industry or her willingness, least of all the three who loved her.

Hart's friendship had ripened into a fierce reliability; he was Fancy's confidant and sounding board. He never tired of talking with her, nor of listening. He'd sketched her so often and in so many poses that the others teased he would never need that stint at art school he so ardently desired, for he had served his sketching apprenticeship with Fancy. She talked endlessly as he drew her, and because she wasn't in love with him, she was honest—no need for subterfuge or flirtation, no efforts at coquettishness or seduction marred the friendship Fancy offered Hart.

Hart had thought long and hard about his love for Fancy; he saw no way to have her for his own. If Chance had been any other man, he could have fought for her love—but such was unthinkable, for his rival was his brother. Besides, when he let the probable futures unfurl in his imagination, there was no way on earth he could offer Fancy what she longed for, needed, and deserved. She was not the girl to follow her husband into the wilderness uncomplaining—she was meant for grander schemes than Hart could ever bring to fruition. Chance could take her where she needed to go.

Hart could see in Fancy's eyes how Chance's dreams sustained her. She was like one from whom all dreams had been drained, who came alive again with their nightly replenishment. If the truth were known, Hart loved those dreams himself. Not that he believed them as Chance and Fancy did, but he wanted to believe, so as not to queer the luck.

So every night the golden future would unfold, then the next day they'd all be back out mucking on the mountain—Fancy with her hair tied up under a scarf like a Gypsy, wearing a pair of boy's breeches and one of Bandana's old shirts, trying to make all they'd conjured up come true.

Soon, something would have to give. Fancy could feel it in her restless bones. It was getting very close to time to move on.

▲ ▲ ▲

"Are you ever afraid, Bandana?" Fancy asked her friend. She'd had the dream again last night, the one she feared most.

"Sometimes," he answered, narrowing his eyes a little to regard her closely. "What are you afraid of?"

Fancy shook her head, she knew and yet she didn't; the formless fear had no edges, only a vast dimension.

"I'm afraid of never getting back to where I'm supposed to be, I think, Bandana. Never having enough, never finding what I'm looking for . . .

maybe never even knowing what it is I need so badly. . . ." She shrugged, unable to explain.

There was such a lost-child quality to Fancy—it touched Bandana's heart. Do lost children ever find their way home? he wondered. What must it be like to have been born to aristocracy and all its promise, then wrenched away to forage for the scraps from others' tables?

"Life's real strange, darlin'," he said, not wishing to stanch her pain with platitudes. "Sometimes we cain't never get hold of what we think we want, sometimes we get it and it turns out to be the wrong thing entirely. Most women take life simple. All they want is a decent man and kids, a home somewhere to take care of. Not too many of them have the talents you do— or the ambitions. You're headstrong, too, Fance. I think most men would have one hell of a time trying to get you to work in double harness."

"But, Bandana, I'd like to just fall in love and hand the whole thing over to some man to take care of like my mama did," she said plaintively, trying to convince herself.

"Bullshit, darlin'!" he said with equanimity. "The kinds of things you want, Fance, ain't ordinary wants for a woman. You've had too much free-dom to knuckle under to authority easy; it just ain't your nature."

"What is my nature?"

"A little wild, a little vulnerable. A lot of got-to-do-it-my-way. If you had money, you could follow your needs and see where they took you. Without it, you may have to compromise . . . learn to play the woman-game. Men still rule this world, Fance, however damn fool they go about it. It looks to me like if you don't marry one and let him do the dirty work, you're gonna have to learn how to do it all for yourself. And you're gonna have to take your licks just like a man does. Once you eat the apple, you cain't live in Paradise no more."

Bandana watched her walk back toward the cabin, the setting sun a red globe silhouetting her against its glory. He was plenty old enough to know what compromises fate could demand in return for giving you what you wanted.

29 "G'day Fancy. You ride that brumbie like you were born in the saddle." Caz reached a hand to steady her as she dismounted; the wind had blown her hair into a wild dark halo, her hat hung down behind her on a rawhide thong. Caz looked her over appreciatively.

"We haven't got a brass razoo, Fancy, old girl, but with you around here, we're rich as Croesus."

"You are the most superlative flatterer in three states, Caz, and don't think for a minute I don't appreciate every outrageous compliment." She laughed, in merry communion with this strange man who worked beside the boys and Bandana, whenever they needed him and whenever his own claim allowed. She had a feeling he'd die for any one of them, if the need arose, for loyalty seemed as integral to his character as laughter.

"Where is everybody?" she asked, straining to untie the cinch and ditch the saddle, so she could brush the dirt and sweat from the "brumbie."

"Gone bush, Fancy, every last one. Bandana's gone to Bullemakanka for all I know, when he goes walkabout there's no telling where he'll turn up. The other two lads let out for town like a Bondi-tram. They'll be back by sundown. I've got you all to myself." He grinned and his amiable face looked almost handsome.

Fancy laughed, she'd grown fond of Caz, his irreverence, his tall tales, and his tough integrity. He didn't let her get away with what the others did, but he was a friend nonetheless.

She picked up the heavy saddle, but Caz pulled it from her grip.

"Now, now, just because you're independent don't mean you have to get a hernia," he said as he set the heavy saddle on its proper peg.

"And just because you're busy doesn't mean you can't stop for a cuppa with a friend," Fancy responded affectionately. She tried to surprise the man, occasionally, with the Aussie slang he was teaching her.

"Cuppa, is it? Never say no to a cuppa."

The two sat companionably on the ground, once they had their tea in hand; the air was crisp, but the midday sun had warmed it just enough for comfort. Fancy leaned back to stretch the sun into her bones. She looked at the square body and leathered face beside her with genuine warmth.

"What do you want out of life, Caz? You're a great puzzle to me."

He chuckled and took a sip of the steaming tea.

"That's because I don't want what you want, Fancy. Nothin' near it. You four all have ambitions that got left outta me. Bandana's got a bee in his bonnet about finding the mother lode, Chance and Hart each got their own needs to goad 'em. Me? I like the day-to-day living just fine. Couldn't care less about tomorrow, long as I got today.

"When I was in that stinking hole of a prison, all I wanted was freedom and the sun. I got both them things right this minute." He squinted at her, smiling. "Got the prettiest sheila in Colorado for company and a cuppa in my hands . . . what could ambition give me I ain't already got? From what I see, ambition just puts you in a kerfuffle and doesn't give you much in return but bigger headaches than the next feller. Maybe give you a bigger house to kark in."

"Kark?"

"You know . . . die. Who needs a big funeral?"

Fancy sighed and shook her head. "I think I do, just not too soon." They both laughed. "Isn't there anything you'd like to have, Caz, that you haven't got?"

The Aussie tilted back his head in thought a moment.

"Like to have a family, Fancy. A couple of nippers and a wife who thinks the sun rises off my big toe. That's about it. Like to start that some time soon, if some pretty little bird would just cooperate."

The laughter in Fancy's eyes made Caz smile; she was a rare one, if entirely too rich for his blood.

"You'd best make a few more trips to town to do your bird hunting, my friend. It seems to me there's a real shortage up here in these woods."

"You just remember that, Fancy, next time you go traipsing off somewhere by yourself. You drive Hart bonkers with your carelessness. He's daft in love with you, in case you haven't noticed. Not that they all aren't twittered over you, it's just the bigger they are the harder they fall." He finished the tea and laid the cup aside, not expecting her to answer. Standing, he gave her a hand up, then brushed the twigs and grass from his pants, to give her time either to pursue the subject or change it.

"You're a good friend to all of us, aren't you, Caz?" she said unexpectedly.

"Damned right I am. What else is life about?" He leaned over and kissed her forehead, a brotherly smack, then sauntered back toward the digs. Fancy cleaned up the cups and thought about how simple life would be if only we could love the one who loved us most, and we weren't plagued by ambition.

"Gimme that sweet li'l hand of yours, honey," Bandana demanded. "Gonna show you somethin' real important."

30 Fancy did as she was told and McBain placed a jagged piece of rock in her palm. The brilliant spring day had lured them out to the mine shaft; a small, timbered doorway led into the dark and musty mountain, where a year of labor had chipped away a tunnel.

"See that? That's what Esmeralda's gonna look like."

"Esmeralda? Who's she?"

"Ain't a she, Fance. Esmeralda's a 'it'! Esmeralda's what I call the mother lode. The one I'm gonna bring in before I die. I think of her as a woman, seductive as homemade sin."

Fancy laughed softly, and Bandana smiled at her. When he smiled, his leathery skin crinkled up like brown parchment, but there was youth and vigor in his eyes.

"Why's she different from the rest?" Fancy stared at the unprepossessing lump in her hand.

" 'Cause she's *Bonanza,* darlin', with a capital *B.*" He drew out the syllables so there was no mistaking the importance of the word. "She's been waitin' here for me ten thousand years . . . settin' and thinkin' about me jes' like I been thinkin' about her. Jes' like a woman. Contrary and hard to git."

Fancy leaned against an outcrop of rock and prepared to listen. She sniffed the air appreciatively and looked around her—spring was happening.

"I'm ready, Bandana. I could use a bonanza right about now."

Bandana nodded and fixed her with a steady gaze. She was a game little thing, all right, but he could sense the desperation that drove her. She wouldn't stay on this mountain much longer and judging by the boys' behavior of late, maybe that was just as well.

"Tell you what, Fance, I'm gonna do somethin' I swore I'd never do. I'm gonna tell you Esmeralda's secret."

"I'm good with secrets."

"I know you are, Fance, old girl. Hell, you're my pal, ain't you? That's why I'm gonna tell you Esmeralda's story." Bandana leaned back and relaxed a little; Fancy, watching, wondered what his age might be.

"Long about fifteen years ago, right around the time they hit it big on the Comstock, I was workin' a dig in Six Mile Canyon, along with a lot of other pick-and-shovel boys. No great shakes it was, but there was enough glitter in them hills to keep a lot of men hopin'.

"Well, this one day, Fance, I'm out hip-deep in the stream, pannin' out my beans money, when this old codger sort of drags hisself up to the edge of the water. He don't say nothin', just sets there lookin' like the last leaf on a November maple. You could see he was down on his luck, real tapped out. Old, too. You know, a lot of men out here look old afore their time, what with the work and the disappointments. But this old geezer was old for true, and since I was just a kid, he looked like Methuselah's older brother to me.

"Any rate, I kept on workin' and somethin' about him kept me watchin' him. Seemed like he was too tired even to drink from the stream. You could see he'd come a long way; clothes all covered in dust and little bits of leaves and needles stuck in 'em, like he'd been sleepin' wild without a bedroll.

"Finally, I couldn't stand it no more, so I calls out to him, 'Hey, gramps, how's it goin'?' I says. 'Not so good, sonny,' he calls back, 'ain't got a pot to piss in.' Well, at that, everybody along the stream started laughin'—but it wasn't a good laugh, if you know what I mean, Fance. They wasn't laughin' with him, but at him. So I says to everybody loud as I could, 'What say we stand this feller to an hour's work?'

"Now what that meant was, whatever you panned in an hour you give it to somebody who was harder up than you. Men did that on the digs from time to time. But 'stead of sayin' okay, they just sort of ignored me. So I says to the old geezer, 'I'll stand you an hour's work, old-timer,' and I did it. Panned out some dust and a small nugget, not a fortune, mind you, but enough to keep him going a few days more. Come to think of it, that nugget was more'n I'd dredged for myself that day, sort of like he had a good angel watchin' out for him.

"So I give him the gold and I shared my stew with him and a blanket, thinkin' I was a damned fine feller for bein' so charitable. Well, now, here comes the interestin' part. While we was whilin' away the night, front of the campfire, he spun me a tale about Esmeralda. Told me he'd found the mother lode. Described it to a fare-thee-well, and I half believed him 'cause he was so sure of all the details, and I half didn't, 'cause he was kind of loco, like a lot of old prospectors get from the lonelies.

"Now, as you well know by now on account of my bein' such a good teacher, gold comes in a lot of different forms out here. It peeks out at you in crystals or wires, in reticulation or leaf or vein. It kin be gold on quartz or gold on galena or any number of other queer ways Nature sees fit to stuff it into these hills. But Esmeralda—she's a bona fide A-number-one vein. So big and gorgeous it'd set a man's heart to thumpin' just to see her twinkle.

"Well, now, next morning I woke up and my blanket, my grub and my burro were all gone. So was the old geezer, of course, but on the ground, pinned under a rock, was a note. It said he was sorry to repay my kindness with thievin' but he was sorta desperate to git home to die. Said in return for me takin' pity on him he was givin' me Esmeralda, on account of he was too old and sick to work her anyways.

"There was a scribbled-out map of Mount Massive, latitude and longitude and a passel of landmarks. Not enough so's I could find her easy, but enough so's I know I'm close."

"And you think the story's true?" Fancy asked, incredulous that Bandana would give credence to a "lost mine" tale. Such legends abounded in the goldfields, and they were all so false as to be a joke to fool a tenderfoot.

"Damned right! I know she's here. Jes' waitin' for me. Not jes' because of what the old coot said, but because I seen it all since then, Fance. Got a sense of it, darlin'; a nose for it. Like some men kin dowse water, I kin find them precious minerals stuck down in these mountains a million years. I done it twicet before. Third time's the charm." He paused to make sure she understood the importance of the gift he was giving her.

"Gonna share her with you, Fance," he said with unmistakable reverence. "I'm gonna find silver for the boys and me and our partnership, but Esmeralda's different. She's solid gold and she's mine alone. Now I'm makin' her yours, too, if you'll agree to my terms."

Fancy looked puzzled.

"You gotta promise me you won't never tell nobody about her and you won't never sell 'er. If I'm alive and either one of us finds her, she's mine to divide up as I please. But if I'm dead, she's yours alone. But not to sell into lesser hands, Fance, 'cause she's my only legacy. I ain't got no kids to keep my name, nor wife to mourn me, nor worldly goods to leave behind. Jes' Esmeralda . . ." He paused and looked her squarely in the eye. "And you."

Fancy knew she mustn't treat his offer with less respect than he did. Bandana was no man's fool.

"I love you, Bandana," she said with finality. "I'll take good care of her if we find her, and I accept your terms."

Whether or not there was truth in the tale didn't matter, Fancy thought when Bandana had left her. There was a bond between them that the secret forged tighter, and that was gold of a different kind.

31 "Got to talk to you about serious subjects, bro," Chance said. The two McAllisters were alone together for the first time in weeks.

Something in Chance's tone made Hart look up from his tin dishful of beans and bacon, senses alert. As long as he could recall, he and his brother had confided in each other; their father always held that blood was thicker than water and brothers' blood, the thickest of them all.

"Been thinking a lot lately about what I want out of life."

Hart chuckled. "Always thought you wanted everything."

"True enough, but it just occurred to me I've got to make a plan for how to get it. A specific plan. There's going to be a lot of money one of these days, bro. I feel it in my gut. What do you mean to do with yours?"

"Same as I always wanted, Chance. Go to school. Learn to draw and paint the kinds of pictures I got in my mind. I'd still like to see if they'll have me at Yale."

"You draw real fine now, bro."

"I got it in me to do better, Chance, but I need to learn things first. Light and shadow. Perspective. There are pictures in my head struggling to get out onto canvas, but I don't have the know-how to do them justice. Look at all I learned from Herc. There's more even he doesn't know."

Chance nodded. Hart knew his brother didn't really understand the urgent need in him to be an artist, but simply wished him well.

Chance stared at the fire as he spoke, his even features looking more rugged in the dark than in daylight.

"I don't want to be a miner. I want to be a mine owner, bro. I want to know what it means to have power, Hart, to hobnob with the men who make things happen . . . maybe try my hand at politics, or go back to the law—I had a knack for that. I don't want to go to school for it, though. I learn better on the job. Don't want to go East either, I intend to make my fortune right here in Colorado."

"While you're making all those mighty plans, maybe you'd better figure out what to do about Fancy, Chance. You two have gotten pretty thick these last months."

Chance looked startled at Hart's boldness and didn't reply.

Hart noted with annoyance that his brother hadn't responded by saying he loved her; of course, that could be because men didn't speak easily of such things. He scanned Chance's eyes for clues to his intent, and finding none, returned his gaze to his plate. He felt his heart do a little flip-flop, like a trout does in a stream when he first finds out you've hooked him. "Just how serious are you about her?"

"Damned if I know, bro. Maybe she won't want any man for the long haul. I'm not all that sure I'd want to stay with one woman forever. I do know we're two of a kind, though, Fancy and me. Both wild cards. And you know how lucky I am, bro—she'd probably have me if I asked her right."

"You know what they say, Chance," Hart replied, quelling his anger. "Lucky in cards, unlucky in love."

"Couldn't be you had a mind to try your hand with her yourself, could it, brother? Because if you do, now's the time to say so, loud and clear."

"You know what I've got in mind for myself," Hart answered, not lying exactly. "Same as I always intended . . . I aim to go off into the Territory and paint me some Indians." Chance looked uncertain; his brother was acting very odd. But then, Hart never had been free and easy where girls were concerned, maybe that was it. It was obvious Hart had a real fondness for Fancy, but outside of that kiss on Christmas Eve, he'd never made the slightest move toward courting her that Chance could see. Besides, it was plain to anyone who looked that she was not the kind of girl for Hart, not by a country mile.

"The life I'm planning isn't the sort she'd ever want," Hart added; this time at least it was the truth. "She's made for the governor's mansion and the likes of you, Chance. Not for a scribbler like me."

"Are you real sure about that?" Chance asked again. He loved Hart; they might be vastly different men, but they were part of a matched set. "No woman would ever be worth interfering with the way things are between us, bro. Not even Fancy."

"I'm sure," Hart answered quietly. In an even contest she would have picked Chance anyway, he thought, and was ashamed of the bitterness that provoked.

Hart poked up the fire with a piece of hickory.

"Are you planning to ask her to marry you, Chance?"

"Good God, bro, don't let's get ahead of ourselves here. I may not be the marrying kind, not like you and Daddy. Might be I've got a ways to go before I know for sure."

Hart looked up from the fireglow, fixed his brother with a steady gaze, and spoke deliberately.

"Don't you hurt her, Chance. She's a real good friend of mine." With that, he tossed the stick he'd been fiddling with into the dying fire, turned and walked away, leaving Chance to ponder his behavior.

Chance had never had the slightest inclination toward approaching life like Hart did, all seriousness and integrity. But that didn't mean he didn't admire his brother for being so upstanding. In fact, he thought that Hart, like their daddy before him, was about the best kind of man you could be.

▲ ▲ ▲

Spring wrought changes in all of them.

"Cain't not feel young in springtime. Not once the sap rises," Bandana told them before he took off to the digs he'd staked out farther up the Gulch. Whether he was off working the second claim, or simply working off his own sap in some mysterious fashion, the three left behind weren't certain. Not that it mattered to them much, for each was infected with the fever in his own way.

The mountain bloomed, the trickles of water became torrents, the creatures with whom they shared their world came out of hibernation and stretched in the sun; the season turned, and the earth became warm and erupted in kaleidoscopic color. Fancy felt reborn.

Chance found there were an amazing number of excuses for being alone with her; and Hart found myriad reasons why he had to be off somewhere that they weren't.

▲

Fancy laughed and the sound carried clear as bells on the brilliant air.

"I feel absolutely wonderful!" she breathed, love making every moment special.

Chance's shaggy head lay in her lap; he was smiling up at her. His dark hair shone in the sunlight and his face, newly shorn of winter whiskers, still was shadowed by the hint of where the beard had been. Fancy thought it a manly face, and handsome enough to take any girl's breath away; she dismissed the fact that it might be almost too pretty for strength.

"What would you do now if you could do anything you wanted, with no worry about propriety?" An indolent smile played at his lips.

"Something wild and reckless . . . like taking off all my clothes and letting the sun warm all the parts of me. Like running naked through that stream over there and letting the wind dry me. Like being lazy and languid and good for absolutely nothing and being waited on hand and foot . . ."

Chance laughed. "The naked part sounded just right to me, why don't we leave it at that?" He raised his head from her lap and brushed her breasts with his lips.

Oh, God, how she wanted him; it was getting harder not to touch as she wished to . . . harder not to be touched in return. If only she had access to any of the devices Magda had told her about to thwart pregnancy, she would have followed her heart and loins, but without such contraceptives she couldn't take the risk.

She'd tried Chance on as a lover in her mind, often enough—in the night-quiet where fantasies could do no harm, where life was what you wanted, not what you got, where people didn't die and houses didn't burn and the worst doubt that ever assailed you was over which new frock would make your husband love you more.

Chance saw the desire in Fancy's dusky eyes; she was growing more wanton, more responsive to his caresses. He knew better than to push her too fast, but any day now . . .

He sought her mouth and finding it willing, pulled her down on top of him, her body covering his on the warm earth. It would be so easy to push her over the boundaries of restraint . . . damn the fact that they were all stuck here together, with no escape. Damn the fact that it didn't seem quite right to do that to a friend.

Fancy pushed herself away from Chance's questing mouth and hands and sat back on the grass, breathless. Her hair was tousled and her shirt buttons were undone. Chance thought she was the most sensual creature he'd ever laid eyes on.

"You have the oddest habit of disappearing right before my eyes," he said quietly, his eyes intent on hers. "Where did you go just then?"

"I don't know. I guess I just never got over growing up rich, Chance. I still want so much."

Chance laughed good-naturedly. "Then I guess you'd have to say I've never gotten over growing up poor, because I want it *all*."

"You're driving me mad . . ."

"We're two of a kind, Fancy—that's not my fault," he said. "And besides, I love you." He hadn't intended to use these words against her defenses as he had from time to time with other women. Could it be that he really meant them this time? he wondered. And how the hell could a man ever tell the difference between lust and love?

"Don't say that," she whispered. "I have to go soon."

He saw she was suddenly fragile and felt a pang of conscience. "Why do you have to go?"

"I don't know why . . . maybe because I'm afraid of what I feel with you. Maybe because I have to go find something . . ."

"Find what?"

"Everything, Chance. Don't you see? I have to find everything!"

Fancy stood up reluctantly and tugged her clothes back into place.

Chance watched her. "I can tell you one thing for certain, sugar," he said. "Whichever man you choose on your way to whatever it is you're looking for, no one will ever understand you like I do."

Touch me now and I'm lost, she thought, half wishing he would do so, just to end the agony of indecision. What would become of her if she let herself love him? Years of hardship and babies and burdens. Dreams were fine, but what if she trusted hers to someone who didn't come through?

And what of her own gifts? Were they to lie fallow forever? Never to sing again for an audience . . . never to act, or to feel the thrill of applause she'd earned with her own initiative and talent. Always to be only an appendage to a husband . . . to his success, his needs, his whims, his dreams.

No. There was no way to say all that to Chance—he wouldn't understand a third of it, even if he wanted to. Hart might understand the conflicts of her soul, but never Chance. That thought startled Fancy, troubled her. So she brushed it aside and kept on walking.

"Get that goddamned jackhammer out of there, bro," Chance shouted irritably. Neither McAllister was irritable by nature, but tensions in the camp were increasing.

Hart squinted up at his brother from the bottom of the trench.

"You got a burr under your saddle this morning?" he asked, taking his own good time to move the hammer to a different position.

Chance straightened up and rested his weight on the pickax in his hands. "And what the hell is that supposed to mean?" Chance had a volatile temper, but he seldom vented it on Hart.

"It means you're being a distinct pain in the ass this morning, and I'll thank you to shape up."

"Me? A pain in the ass? The real truth is you haven't been worth a tinker's dam all week. If you'd been pulling your weight . . ."

Bandana's voice cut in sharp as a new knife; he'd returned to the cabin the day before and been disturbed by the unaccustomed tension he found there.

"The real truth is you two great horses asses ain't worth a tinker's dam between you in this cantankerous mood a' yours, which has more to do with spring and Fancy than with jackhammers."

Both men started to protest, but McBain cut them short.

"It's real hard to put a foot in a shut mouth," he snapped. "So jes' listen up a minute, both of you. Ever since I got back, you two been like a pair of stump-tailed horses tied short in fly time. I ain't sayin' it's easy havin' a gorgeous little filly like Fancy on the premises, but I'm sayin' it's a hell of a lot nicer than not havin' her around. So, if we're gonna get any work done around here, both you boys better get a grip on yerselves." He paused glowering at his partners. "Now, as my dear sainted daddy used to say, 'a wishbone ain't no substitute fer a backbone!' So I suggest you do your wishin' on your own time and your courtin' too. Put your peckers back in your pants and get to work!" With a snort Bandana turned his back on them and stomped off up the hill, his boots crunching gravel as he went.

▲

Chance left for their other camp long before sunup. Bandana had insisted he needed an extra pair of hands, as well as supplies—but Fancy suspected he simply wanted to separate the McAllisters for a few days.

Hart and Fancy rose as usual, ate biscuits and bacon before walking to the mine. The boys had sunk a pit with real promise; already they'd pulled likely-looking shows of color from it, the kind Bandana said were the harbinger of good things to come.

The day was nippier than usual, a pleasant change that made the sweaty work more bearable; Fancy worked alongside Hart through the morning, but by afternoon returned to her chores at the cabin.

Hart found himself working hard and happily until a single mighty pick thrust near sundown splintered the north side of the hole. A torrent of dust and rock shattered over Hart and he stared disgustedly at the huge pile of rubble he'd dislodged. It would take another hour to clean up and he'd wanted to get home to Fancy. An unexpected rumble made the earth tremble around him. Before he had time to wonder what it meant, a wall of water shot out through the hole and knocked him violently against the opposite wall.

Hart cried out as his head struck rock. Fancy, halfway from the cabin, heard the cry and ran toward the sound.

Hart fought for breath against the rushing water that sucked him down. Jagged quartz ripped his shoulder, tearing flesh, but he was too busy staying alive to pay attention to the pain. He pushed his way upward, despite his injured arm and shoulder. His head broke the surface and he gasped air hungrily; Fancy was crouched at the edge of the pit, frantically calling to him.

Fancy grabbed for his shirt collar and dragged him toward her at the pit's edge; he was far too heavy for her to hang on to for long.

She saw Hart fight for consciousness, saw the blood pouring out of the head wound and feared he might go under again. Belly-down on the hard ground, she cursed the water, the stones biting her flesh as she grappled with the nearly unconscious body.

"Hart!" she shouted. "You've got to help me, do you hear me? I don't know how long I can hold you up."

"Too heavy," he gasped.

"No, you're not, Hart! You just have to help me!"

She could see him gather what strength he had left for the effort to hoist himself out of the pit. Fancy grasped an outcrop of slippery rock with one hand and prayed it would hold against both their weights, as she let him use her body as a rope for the upward climb. She thought she would be rent in half, but clung nonetheless, as Hart drew himself up inch by inch, grasping rock or dirt or root along the way.

The two sprawled, breathless, on the earth above the hole in a stupor of exhaustion. Fancy was too weak to do anything about the blood flowing from his wounds; still she searched his body with her eyes and saw that none were life-threatening. When she was able to move again, she helped him stagger to his feet and managed to lead him home to safety.

▲

When Hart awakened, he felt Fancy's presence in the cabin so intensely, it seemed to him the dimensions of the place had grown smaller and shaped themselves around her. She'd saved his life; she'd cried when she thought him doomed . . . the memory of her hands and face and tears filled him with an unlikely hope.

Fancy made him sit in the small rocker while she tended to his head and shoulder wounds. "God Almighty, Hart, you scared me silly." She was talking as she worked on his shoulder, he had no idea at all what about. His head, still unsteady from its bout with the rocks, was filled with her.

Hart felt dizzy and disoriented. He'd seen it unmistakably in her eyes, in her desperation. He should never have abandoned his love for her. He could give her everything she needed for happiness; somewhere deep down inside her she must have always known that. He'd been a fool to let Chance take the initiative, a fool not to let her know how much he loved her. No matter what she believed she wanted out of life, he alone knew what she needed. He could make her feel so loved, she would forget the foolish, unrealistic dreams that had seduced her. . . .

Hart reached his one good arm around Fancy, so forcefully that he nearly knocked her off her feet. He stood up suddenly, carrying her upward in his arms . . . she fit so perfectly against his body. All the passion he'd poured out into paper portraits burst like the first flash of lightning from a gathering storm. Hart wanted her, wanted everything they could be together, more than he'd ever wanted anything in his life. He lifted her easily, ignoring the pain in his head and shoulder, and crushed her mouth to his own.

Fancy, shocked by the unexpected assault, was equally shocked by her own response. Her mutinous mouth wanted Hart's . . . she wanted his arms around her, his huge, hard body . . . No. That was crazy! She didn't love Hart. Or did she, at least a little? If she didn't, what was it she was feeling, had been feeling ever since she'd nearly lost him?

"I love you, Fancy." Hart breathed the words as he kissed her. She knew he was carrying her toward the bed. How could she stop this without hurting him? Loving, kindly, generous Hart, don't you know that I would never want to cause you pain?

"Hart, no, please!" Fancy's voice pierced the man's passion like stinging nettle. "I love you, but not this way. Please don't make me hurt you!"

There wasn't nearly enough conviction in the sound to have stopped him, Hart thought later. Had he laid her down on the bed, torn away her clothes, and taken her body in his hands as he longed to do . . . had he kissed her just one more time, he could have overcome every one of her doubts.

But not his own.

He saw the stricken look in Fancy's eyes and let her slide from his arms to the floor. His hands fell away from her impossible softness, and reality crashed in on him, like the pounding in his head. Stunned at how close he'd come to taking advantage of her innocence, and betraying his brother's trust, he stood for a long moment trying to figure out how the fractured boundaries between them could ever be put right again.

Hart's head throbbed so, he couldn't think.

Fancy, horrified by the pain she read in his dear face, reached out to touch him. "Hart, I'm so desperately sorry . . . I love you both, in my own way. Truly I do."

He forced himself to move, grabbed his shirt and jacket from the chair where Fancy had placed them, and lunged from the house.

"Hart!" Fancy called after him, frightened by the look on his face. "Hart. Please come back!"

The injured man mounted his horse with difficulty and turned the dun toward the trail. This is the moment you get hold of yourself, Hart McAllister, or you get the hell away from both of them, he told himself as he kicked the horse into motion. Whatever relationship there could ever be between him and Fancy, it couldn't be behind his brother's back and it couldn't bring her to harm.

Hart gritted his teeth against the jarring of his injuries and felt the blood begin to flow afresh as the horse made tracks across the rocky terrain. He would get control of himself or he'd never go back to that goddamned star-crossed cabin. He gouged his heels into the dun's flanks and the startled horse lengthened his stride wildly, kicking up a cloud of dust and gravel in his thundering path.

▲

Fancy spent the day in a state of agitation. Hart was in no condition to ride around alone; both the shoulder and the head injury could turn mean if they weren't cared for.

She'd handled his advances so stupidly—but what else could she have done? She knew he loved her. Why, in her own desire for Chance, had she so neglected him? And what could she have done for him that wouldn't have made things ten times worse?

She brooded through the day, took up one task after another, then abandoned them. She even saddled up a horse toward noon, with the intention of riding after Bandana to ask his help, but Chance was with him. It was her own fault for having stayed too long where she didn't belong. She must leave this place before she destroyed the men's love for each other, and whatever they felt for her, in the bargain.

Chance had never asked her to marry him—even if he had, she couldn't say yes. There was nothing left to happen among them all that wouldn't bring somebody to injury. Fancy cried until she thought she had no tears left, and she wasn't in the least sure which of the three of them she cried for most.

A hundred times she thought she heard the sound of distant hoofbeats; running to the doorway, she would scan the horizon to see if Hart had come back. Each time she was uncertain if she felt relief or sorrow that there was no sign of an approaching rider.

▲

Hart didn't return that night. Instead, it was Chance who walked into the cabin and found Fancy sitting by the fire, wrapped Indian-like in an old blanket.

"Hart's gone," she said.

"Gone? What do you mean gone?"

"We had a quarrel," she said hopelessly, not knowing what else to say. "I'm so sorry, Chance, I don't know what to do to fix it. I've just messed everything up so badly for all of us . . .."

Chance crossed the room in a single stride. He knelt beside Fancy and scooped her into his arms. She looked so sweet and vulnerable, so in need of being loved. And they were alone at last.

Fancy laid her head on Chance's chest and cried. He understood her need to be comforted, she could see it in his eyes, feel it in the strength of his caress. He was kissing her as she talked and sobbed, he was whispering words she couldn't quite understand. All the longing rebelled against, reveled in, welled up in a torrent. Chance's strength was touching, awakening —and she was too tired to struggle any longer. Chance kissed her with all the exquisite passion of a man who has what he wants at last within his grasp.

His hand slipped inside her shirt and she felt the careful intimacy of strong hands on tender places, and the touch was gentle. There was no roughness to the urgency in Chance . . . no clamorous, breathless, palpitating madness as there'd been in Hart. There was something else entirely . . . a wildness held in check, a power so defined, so confident, it had no need for recklessness.

What did it matter, in this one glorious moment, that Chance was unpredictable? He would be lucky instead—lucky enough for both of them.

"It's all right, Fancy," he whispered, his lips caressing her ear as he spoke. "I'll make everything all right. Don't worry . . ."

"We shouldn't, Chance . . ." she murmured.

"But you want to . . ." he answered, and with practiced gestures, far stronger than before, he spread her body open like a flower. He was not like his brother. Chance would take what he wanted without thought of consequence. The knowledge both repelled and excited her.

Was it arrogance or knowingness, or simple lust she saw in the violet eyes poised above hers on the bed? There was nothing left in the universe except Chance's mouth and Chance's hands and Chance's probing body. She felt hard chest and belly against her own, the thrusting strength of manhood and nothing else mattered in all the world. For the first time in her life she belonged to someone . . . someone wilder, freer, infinitely more knowledgeable. She was sucked up into darkness and blinding light. There was no thought or sound or world or understanding. *This* was being a woman. There was pain, but it didn't matter. Chance was everything she wanted and there was no past or future, only now. She was stifled against his hard body and couldn't breathe. She screamed and he muffled the scream with his kisses. Fancy twisted and turned beneath his thrusting body but he pinioned her with the all-knowing strength of manhood and she was lost in velvet darkness, wetness, fierceness, light. A swirling, endless light that enveloped them in ecstasy before the brilliance faded.

Neither of the lovers on the bed heard the hoofbeats near the cabin at a walk, or saw Hart's stricken face turn from the window, streaked with tears.

▲ ▲ ▲

Fancy wondered ever after about the exigencies of fate that had caused things to happen exactly as they did. Had Hart's accident and its aftermath never occurred, would she have been so vulnerable to Chance that night, or would she perhaps, instead, have found the courage to leave both brothers behind her forever?

The weeks after her seduction passed as a blur. Hart returned, but nothing was ever the same among them. "Once you eat the apple, you cain't live in Paradise no more," Bandana had said, and he was right.

The easy camaraderie they'd all shared had vanished, replaced by embarrassment, awkwardness, bitterness, and regret. Uncomfortable silences replaced their stories of the future . . . Hart and Chance brooded separately, but Fancy could see that the rift between them was eating into each man's soul. Chance never spoke of marriage, and if he had, she would have said no.

Even before she realized that her monthly showing would not come, Fancy knew she would have to leave the mountain.

She hadn't thought of pregnancy until the morning after. Sometimes, she felt glad of the defiant bliss that had been consuming enough to blot out even fear, for one glorious moment of communion. Sometimes she thought she had been a fool.

Bandana tried to speak of what troubled her, but she couldn't find the courage to tell him, so eventually he abandoned trying and left the camp entirely to go back to the claim on the other side of the Gulch.

Fancy had used the age-old dandelion test of pregnancy, when first she'd suspected her condition. With trembling hands she'd dropped the fresh-picked dandelion stem and leaves into a puddle of her urine; she'd watched the telltale red color suffuse the leaves and had felt so faint, she had to sit on the ground until the weakness passed.

She had knowledge of how to end a pregnancy; all herbalists knew that goldenseal or quinine could cause abortion in the early stages. But she also knew how deadly such ministrations could be; if they were performed incorrectly, she could die an agonizing death.

She had thought of telling Chance about the baby, but his behavior since their lovemaking had been in no way reassuring—and besides, once she told him, her fate was sealed; no longer would decision making be in her own hands.

She had awakened this morning to acid nausea that ate into her body, just as remorse now etched her mind. The thought of Magda came to her as she retched behind a bush on the outer edge of camp. Magda would know what to do.

Fancy made her preparations for leaving the cabin with a troubled heart. She tried to imagine how to say good-bye, but no words seemed right, so she decided to consign her good-byes to paper. It would be best if the men had no inkling of the trouble she was in, best if they could remember her as she'd been in the flower of their friendship. She hadn't lied to Hart at the end of it, she thought; in her own way, she did love them both.

Fancy wrote as resolutely as her heart would allow:

"Dear Both of You,
Time to go, I'm sad to say. I guess I don't have to tell you how grateful I am to you—not just for saving my life, but for giving me back my dreams.

Now that I remember them, I've got to go after them. I guess all those years on the road left me restless so—it wouldn't be fair for me to wait around for you two to give me what I long for.

I've got to make my own fortune and judging from the way lightning tends to strike my life, I'd best get at it as quickly as possible.

I love you both. There, I've said it right out loud. It's clear to me now that I'd come between you if I stayed. I'd hate myself for that and you'd hate me for doing it and then all the good we've done each other would be forgotten. I love the memories we've shared more than you know—I intend to keep them tucked away inside me, always.

The unintended irony of the statement stabbed at her, for there was more within her of their sharing than simple memories.

Some day, Hart, you'll be a famous artist and you'll paint my portraits. Both of them.

Some day, Chance, when I'm rich and renowned, I'll come sing for you at the governor's mansion.

Take care of yourselves. I'm little but I'm tough, so you needn't worry about me.

I'm not tough enough to face saying good-bye, though, so you'll just have to forgive me for sneaking out while you were gone.

I'll never forget all we were together.

I'm sending all the love I have to you and to Bandana. Tell him for me that if I had only one friend left in this sorry world, I'd want it to be him.

Fancy

IV

DRIVEN BY THE WIND

▼▼▼▼▼▼

Fancy Moves On

"You never know your luck 'til
the wheel stops."

BANDANA McBAIN

33 🌿 Fancy forced herself to pay attention to the steep trail through the mountains. There was no use looking back. She pulled her jacket tighter, trying to quell the loneliness. She didn't like to be alone—alone was full of fears and history.

A wolf howled somewhere ahead; the eerie sound bounced back and forth through endless canyons before it faded. She wasn't afraid; she'd faced worse than wolves with Atticus, but it was a desolate sound.

Fancy knew the woods, what to eat and what to stay shy of, what to use for fire, what for bedding, yet she must not be careless. She was distracted, and accidents happened to anyone heedless in the woods; she forced herself to pay attention to the road before her.

She would go to Denver. Magda and Wes had been headed there when the circus folded. She would find them and Magda would know what to do. Perhaps her tarot cards would disclose if this child she carried would ever see the light of this world.

Eighty miles across the mountains could be done in six days walking, if she put her back into it. There was little enough to carry; only Atticus' banjo, her music box, the herbs she'd put up last summer and the clothes the men had given her, all stuffed into an old carpetbag.

She'd tried not to let herself think about the baby, but it dwelled in her consciousness, just as clingingly as it did in her womb. She'd expected pregnancy to make her feel entrapment and despair, but there was a strange sense of kinship with this flicker of life within.

▲

She pulled the blanket close around her and settled in to sleep. There were so many memories in the woods . . . and it was far better to think of Atticus and the long ago, than to worry about the future. She hoped, as she dozed off, that in sleep there would be no dreams.

Something brushed Fancy's face, rousing her; a rough leather glove closed around her wrist and all vestige of sleep was banished by adrenaline. Three men loomed over her in the clearing. Their hands were already unfastening their belts.

Fancy fought at the bulk that pinned her, but she was small and the man was strong. The ground that had seemed so benevolent a moment ago now scraped blood from her shoulder, arms, and buttocks through the fabric of her clothes. The man tore at her shirt and breeches; filthy hands and ragged fingernails raked her skin. Leather chaps and trousers were pulled halfway down the man's legs to reveal his malevolent organ. Fancy felt her stomach lurch and she nearly vomited.

He lunged forward onto her body and she glimpsed the world in fragments; a patch of pale slate sky beyond his shoulder, a leering mouth questing for her own, a smothering weight of flannel and buckskin cutting off breath and escape, the rank smell of unwashed skin and teeth and clothes.

With a mighty wrench her thighs were pried apart; a searing white-hot poker of flesh was thrust shockingly between her legs. Fancy felt her inner folds assaulted, torn; pain ripped secret places. Fancy squeezed her eyes tight shut and thought of dying.

"I'm next, Harve! Leave some for me." There was laughter somewhere.

His rutting done, the grunting man lay still on top of her for a moment and the desperate girl gathered herself, waiting for him to lurch to his feet. The instant he rose, she scrambled out from under him and ran toward the trees at the edge of the clearing.

"Lookit her run, Jake!" a voice behind her shouted. "Jes' like a rabbit, ain't she?"

Fancy heard the pursuers' laughter as she struggled through the undergrowth. Her heart raced uncontrollably; she couldn't breathe to run. Brambles cut her knees and fingers; she slipped on something slimy and flailing out with her arms for a nonexistent handhold, she slid backward down the grade.

Rough fingers clasped her ankles and yanked her, screaming, into the arms of one of the men. He forced her back against a tree, while another passed a rope around her waist and the trunk. Isolated feelings of pain scraped in and out of sharp focus; cold wet bark raked naked skin, a broken tree branch drew blood from her pinned arm; goose bumps tightened the flesh of her breasts.

"Pert little nipples she's got there, ain't they, Elmore?" the short man said. He'd pulled down his trousers and his manhood had risen threateningly from its nest of dark hair.

"If'n you hold 'er laigs up fer me, I kin get me a piece of this sweet thing," he called out, and Fancy felt her legs jerked out from under her. *They're going to kill my baby,* she thought suddenly, and a wave of new fury strengthened her. She wrenched against the rope, a dying creature in a snare; she kicked out ferociously and connected with the man's belly, heard him grunt and double over in pain.

"No!" she screamed in outrage as another man took the first one's place and tried to wrestle her legs apart.

A gunshot shattered the air like a sign from God. All motion ceased. The man wrenched himself free of Fancy, as a whiskey voice broke the unnatural stillness.

"When you get to hell, you filthy son of a bitch, you tell 'em Jewel sent you!" A second gunshot flung the rapist reeling past the tree before he crumpled to the ground.

One of the other two had nearly cleared leather with his six-gun before a bullet sent him sprawling backward. The third made the mistake of diving for his saddle scabbard, but his hand never closed on the Winchester.

Fancy, sobbing, sucked in great gulps of air in an effort to stay alive; she couldn't see her savior clearly through her tears. Atop a prancing palomino gelding sat a woman, neither old nor young, her face set in a vengeful expression. Her body was too voluptuous for the man's shirt and riding breeches that contained it, and too young somehow for her face, which was worldly-wise. A holster was tied low on her thigh and the gun that had emerged from it was obviously an intimate part of her apparel.

Jewel dismounted, the Colt still unholstered, and walked to each of the three bodies in turn, nudging them sharply with a booted toe . . . none were alive. She gave a grunt of satisfaction and kicked the last one for good measure.

She pulled a skinning knife from its sheath at her belt and sawed straight through the hemp that bound Fancy, and the girl slid to the ground, her legs too rubbery to hold her.

"Did you know 'em?" Jewel asked, her voice husky with anger and concern.

Fancy shook her head no, and tried to get up onto her feet; as she took a step forward, the ugly pain between her legs buckled her again and Jewel's hand shot forward to support her.

"You sit, kid," she said authoritatively, and Fancy sank to the ground as the woman collected her torn clothing.

Fancy clutched the shirt protectively to her body and stood up; Jewel saw a trickle of blood wend its way along her thigh. She pulled off the neckerchief she wore and soaked it in the stream before handing it to Fancy.

Her face aflame, Fancy swiped at the sticky blood—don't let it be my baby, she prayed, still in shock. She pulled on her shirt and resolutely made her way to the water's edge to clean away what had been done to her. Jewel watched the fierce determination and pride that made the injured girl fight so hard for control.

"You need a place to stay, kid?" she asked gently. She pulled up the hat slung from a rawhide thong about her neck, pushed it down firmly on her head, and waited for a reply.

Fancy, weak and disoriented, hesitated. "I can't think right now. I was going to Denver."

Jewel grunted. "Long way, Denver. You ain't in shape to go there today, that's for damn sure. You look like you could use a good stiff whiskey. Besides, there's woman things you got to do now to fix what them bastards did to you."

Fancy looked wistfully at the trail and nodded.

Jewel looked at Fancy's bedraggled condition, then at the three dead bodies.

"It might be we should move on outta here, kid. The sheriff's a real pain in the arse about dead bodies, even if they deserve to be that way. A woman in my profession cain't be too careful of stayin' clear of the law."

Fancy still said nothing.

"Got a name?" Jewel asked, and the girl replied in a voice that sounded nothing like her own.

"Fancy, eh? Great name, kid. Got any friends in the Gulch?"

Fancy shook her head no, emphatically. "I was going to Denver to look for work. I'm an actress and a singer, and I've been out here prospecting for gold and silver."

"Oh, shit! Another half-assed tenderfoot lookin' for easy money. Just what the Gulch needs."

"No! I'm not like that. I've paid my dues . . . I'm not afraid of hard work. I'm not afraid of anything."

Jewel put one foot in the near stirrup and turned to look at the ravaged stranger. Her laugh sounded more like a man's than a woman's.

"Then it's a good thing I found you, honey. 'Cause you ain't got the sense God gave a chicken. I'm the only woman I know tough enough not to be afraid of man nor beast." She hoisted herself into the saddle and checked the movement of the frisky horse.

"Hate to ask you to ride, kid, the way you must be feelin', but there ain't no other way. My horse can carry us both, and your belongings. A little bitty thing like you won't even make him breathe hard."

Fancy looked at the three dead men with revulsion.

"Do we just leave them here?"

"From what I seen of 'em, they sure as hell don't deserve buryin'. They'll give the wolves a good dinner—probably be the only charitable act any of 'em ever done."

Jewel gave Fancy a hand up behind her. Fresh pain shot upward from her injured parts; she straddled the horse, but she bit her lip to keep from crying and clung to Jewel. She felt the warmth of blood between her legs and wondered if she was miscarrying. She felt oddly protective of the baby now.

"Not a word of what's gone on to any of my girls, ya hear?" Jewel said once, and Fancy nodded, too depressed and heartsick to care where she was going or what would happen once she got there.

▲

Fancy sat gingerly on the edge of the bed and struggled for control. She felt ill and irreparably injured—bruises and cuts stung all over her body and the searing pain within her woman-parts throbbed constant memories.

Jewel had been kind and efficient. She'd made Fancy bathe and douche with pearlash and then vinegar; she'd put hypericum on her cuts and arnica on her bruises. After that, she'd left her guest to grapple with her own demons. Fancy had made no mention of her pregnancy, but Jewel had eyed the swollen, darkened nipples with an expert's understanding and said nothing. The bleeding had stopped after a few hours, and Fancy was surprised at her own relief.

Rape. How could such savagery be called by such a simple name? No one word could explain the terror . . . the helplessness and the mad agony of responsibility, as if she had somehow caused it to happen, or at least had failed to stop them. Fancy fought down the sense of despair she always experienced when anything slipped through her guard; a darkling terror beyond all reason.

She stood up shakily. There was no point at all in trying to sleep—the possibility of dreaming was too awful to contemplate. She looked at the galvanized tub that stood by the fireplace—she'd left it only minutes before, but she still felt unclean.

Perhaps if she bathed again, it would make a difference . . .

▲

Jewel knocked softly before entering; when there was no response she peeked inside. Her eyes ran swiftly over the empty bed and rested on the tub. Fancy's head had fallen to the side as she lay in the soothing water, sound asleep.

"I know how you feel, kid," Jewel whispered into the room's stillness. "Dirty and ruined." She shook her head at the unfairness of life and walked to the side of the tub.

She touched Fancy gently on the shoulder, but the girl jumped, startled and afraid.

"It's all right, kid. You're safe now. You just cain't stay in this tub all night. The water's gone cold."

Fancy nodded and rose, obedient as a child. Jewel walked to the foot of the bed where an afghan lay folded, and picking up the heavy woolen coverlet, she spread it over the exhausted girl. She stood for a moment watching Fancy's body settle into a semblance of repose, a thoughtful expression on her own face, then she turned down the kerosene lamp on the table and tiptoed out of the room.

▲

It was nearly nine o'clock when Jewel pushed open the door to Fancy's room again; she was no longer clad in trail clothes. Her lurid red hair was coiffed into elaborate fluffiness and she was corseted and gowned in a way that made her spectacular bosom seem even more so. It was hard not to stare at those breasts, Fancy thought, embarrassed.

"Great tits, ain't they?" asked Jewel with a hint of some emotion in her voice that Fancy couldn't name. Aggression? Pride? She nodded assent.

"These titties were my downfall and they damn well been my resurrection." Her voice was throaty, companionable. "This place is a saloon and a whorehouse, case you been wonderin'. I'm the head whore. Jewel Mack by name. The miner's friend from here to the Comstock." She waited for that piece of information to be digested, and Fancy studied her face with curiosity.

It was square-jawed and determined. The nose was straight, the mouth sensuously wide and full, the eyes were large and intelligent with fashionably curved eyebrows, and a pasted-on beauty mark adorned the right cheek. Jewel's face was artfully painted, arresting and memorable, but it was her body that everyone would remember, for it was simply breathtaking.

"I don't know how to thank you for what you did to help me out there."

"Men outnumber women hereabouts five hundred to one. A woman traveling alone in these hills has to watch her step."

Fancy nodded, not trying to explain. She remembered Hart's endless warnings and the memory made her want to cry.

"Been thinkin' about you, kid. Thinkin' maybe we better talk some about what happened to you—it looked pretty dicey from where I sat and it's best not to hold bad memories inside if you can help it. I got about an hour to spare right now before the sourdoughs start to raise the roof downstairs, so if you'd care to commence tellin' me your story, I'm all ears."

Jewel studied the beautiful young girl with the intensity of intuition that had made her a successful survivor. Ideas had begun to percolate the moment she'd rescued Fancy. It wasn't every day a female of quality landed in the Gulch, much less a female of quality who needed a helping hand from the likes of Jewel. It wouldn't do to push the kid just yet, she had some getting-over to do. But after that . . .

Fancy talked, haltingly at first, but Jewel was an old hand at listening to woman-troubles. She probed gently, carefully, letting Fancy get the horror out of her system, onto the table where the hurt could be stared down. The kid had spirit, but no woman was tough enough to withstand rape without grave injury. Unless Jewel missed her bet, the kid had been vulnerable, way down deep, long before those three bastards had come into her life; and there was more to the story than she was letting on. A man, a pregnancy . . . whatever it was, she had heard it all before.

Jewel shook her head sagely as she let herself out into the hallway. The kid might have real possibilities once she healed.

Fancy, drained of everything but profound sorrow, fell back into an exhausted slumber. She dreamed about her baby and knew that it was safe. When had the spark within her changed from a problem that entrapped her to a life she could love and protect? A baby . . . her baby . . . Fancy thought the thought or dreamed the dream, she wasn't sure which . . . but in the vision, her baby was safe and it was hers alone, to love forever.

Jewel Mack, born Julia McClosky in Pittsford, Pennsylvania, drew the stink of the coal mines into her lungs from the moment of birth. The sky darkened by coal dust into perpetual twilight, the slag heaps that inexorably consigned all life and greenery to destruction, the brain-numbing sound of machinery pounding the earth into disgorging its black and noxious produce—these were the sights and sounds of her early years that passed for childhood.

Jewel Mack, madam of the most prosperous whorehouse in California Gulch, sat in the small rocking chair by the upstairs window of the Crown, facing Main Street. She held her mother's diary in her hands. As always, when she turned back the scarred cover of her mother's book, a still-sharp pang of sorrow and a host of images arose in her, called forth by the stained and tattered pages, traversed by the spidery cursives of her mother's script. Old-fashioned, simple words were there; God-fearing and steadfast in the face of all hopelessness. From the moment of her mother's death, Jewel had read and reread the woman's diary a thousand times. No matter what Fate had taken from her, it had left her this small book as consolation.

June 24, 1852. Mr. McClosky says we are going West to the Oregon Territories or to California. I begged him not to make us go so far from home and family, but to no good end. Those who have gone on the wagon trains are lost forever to their loved ones. God grant me strength to do my Christian duty. I struggle with the devil daily. The hatred wells up in me at my husband's touch. God has set him above me as my spouse and I must do my best to be obedient.

"My days are swifter than a weaver's shuttle and are spent without hope." Job 7:6

July 18, 1852. My heart is jubilant. Mr. McClosky has found that the cost of a wagon and foodstuffs needed for the trip west is more than $800. Cornelia Swift and her husband have been saving two years to amass only half this extravagant number. Maybe God will grant me a year or two longer with my sweet mother and father and all those I love before I am sent into cruel exile.

"Many waters cannot quench love, neither can the floods drown it." Song of Solomon 8:7

April 18, 1854. God grant me strength to bear with this awful sorrow. My heart is a stone within me. Today I kissed good-bye my sisters and my brothers and their dear children. I saw my parents for the last time on this earth. All that I have in this world, save my Julia, Ezekial, Hachaliah, and little Daniel, has been shorn from me. All my life is in this horrid wagon where I write and pray for guidance. I am a wayward soul and question God's plan.

"If thou faint in the day of adversity, thy strength is small." Proverbs 24:10

Jewel felt the tears, and the anger, well in her as they always did when she read this book. How different were the diaries of the women like her mother, on the wagon trains headed west, from those written by the men. The women wrote of anguish at leaving home and kin, despair at the prospect of the hardships they would encounter along the way. Most of them would be pregnant on the six-month journey, or nursing the newly born, as they jounced away their lifeblood and strength in the springless flatbed wagons that carried them farther and farther from their homes and families.

Mrs. Healy's baby died today [her mother's diary read]. *Mrs. Fuller's little boy fell from the wagon and the wheel ran over his poor body crushing the life from his tiny bones.*

Tragedy made matter-of-fact by its frequency.

Stopped to bury Cora Jensen and her three youngest last night. Bad water was the cause of the bowel flux that took them from us.

For the men, there was the spirit of adventure, the camaraderie of hunting, fishing, Indian fighting, the possibility of riches and opportunities unheard of in the East. But for the women in exile, life held immeasurable misery. They bore the endless stream of babies that came, they nursed the relentless bouts of illness that plagued the doctorless trails, they bathed the

bodies of the dead, if there was water for it, and sewed the shrouds to clothe
them for their eternal sleep.

The litany of Mrs. McClosky's life was echoed by all the other women on
all the other wagon trains: give the baby suck, in its knotted sling that frees
your hands to gather buffalo chips as you trudge behind the wagon . . . tie
the remaining children by a rope to your waist as you ford the swollen
stream. Unload everything inside the wagon—sometimes two thousand
pounds of it—and load it all onto rafts to cross the rivers. Repack the lot on
the other side. Cook what there is, on a fire of dried buffalo dung beside the
wagon; avoid the rattlesnakes, if you can. Relieve yourself behind a wall of
other women extending their homespun skirts to afford you some measure
of privacy. Pray that your monthly "showing" comes at a time when there
is a stream nearby to wash your bloody cloths, or else carry the fouled
fabric patches with you until laundering is possible. Most women wore red
flannel petticoats, so their monthly bloodstains would be less embarrassing.

In truth, the diary was superfluous, for Jewel had every detail of her
mother's life etched eternally in her soul. Every anguished step, from the
moment they'd left Pittsford, their pitiful wagon loaded with less than
enough to see them through, lived within her. To the grave, she would carry
the look she'd seen on her mother's stoic face on the day they'd left their
home behind forever. Staring straight ahead, eyes dulled by desperation,
Mrs. McClosky had never once looked back as they'd pulled out of the
rutted street where her home had been. But Jewel had.

She'd seen the men smiling and waving their exuberant good-byes. This
terminal wrenching from all their wives held dear was no more to them
than a chance for riches or adventure—she could see it in their laughing
eyes and dancing horses, and in their haste to be under way. For Jewel had
always, by some quirk of fate, understood the workings of men's minds.

Jewel Mack, at her window in Oro City, let her body become one with
the rocker's rhythm as she let her mind drift back, back, back in time to
when she had been Julia . . .

Twelve-year-old Julia McClosky was used to men staring at her with lust on their
faces. Ever since her breasts had begun to develop the previous year, even before it
had become apparent that they would continue to expand long past the point where
it would have been seemly to stop, she had felt their glances and the change in the
way they treated her.

Boys from school, who had in the past made fun of her plain face and freckles,
began to eye her with a furtive interest. Miners walking past her house with swinging
lunch pails in their hands seemed to linger as they made their way toward the

colliery. She was embarrassed by the magnitude of the changes in her body. Not that she didn't want to grow up, for with adulthood would come the chance of freedom, but the alterations in her form were not subtle ones like those of the other girls.

Julia's rebellious breasts, which had begun sensibly as tender swelling places, had, in the space of one year's time, exploded into huge ripe melons that seemed to precede her indecently, no matter how hard she struggled to contain them. The other girls, too, had noticed her burgeoning womanhood and greeted it with envy and derision.

But it wasn't the girls' attentions that troubled Julia most, or even that of the boys and men. It was the terrible new look she saw in her father's eyes whenever he was near, and the seemingly accidental touches she somehow knew weren't accidents at all. The bumping together in doorways where there was ample room not to; the prolonged hugs that hadn't happened before, the nightly tucking in that was a dreadful development.

Long before the time when her father had first crept to her bed and forced her to submit to his gropings and fondlings, Julia had known that danger and perversion lurked behind his new awareness of her body.

She could smell his whiskey breath, feel his scratching whiskers abrade her face, sense the nauseating danger. . . . She had never told her overburdened mother what she endured at his hands. She had endured alone. As long as she could remember, Julia had known and accepted her mother's frailty, and done the best she could to help her. As each successive baby had been born, she herself had taken on its rearing. Washing, diapering, clothing, and minding them, each new burden easing the ones her mother shouldered. She had done it gladly to save her mother's waning strength.

So there was no way in hell she would ever have told her mother of the stinking, groping man who had ended her childhood so brutally. In fact, Julia had told no living soul of her shame in the two decades since then. Not even Ford Jameson—he had found out for himself.

The quiet young man from the neighboring wagon had watched her, too, like so many other men on the wagon train, but not in the same way. Julia had felt Ford's shy eyes follow her as she left the wagon each morning, to begin her predawn chores. Several times he had even helped her carry water in huge crockery jugs, or taken heavy firewood and buffalo chips from her arms as she struggled to balance them. Once he had killed a rattlesnake that lay in her path.

Too shy to know what to say to a girl, Ford had never said much of anything at all to Julia. Unlike the lascivious glances of the other men that had made her blush at first, and then become defiant, Ford's watching made her feel protected, cherished. As if he cared about what happened to her.

He was fifteen or sixteen and near as big as he would get in height at the time the train set out from St. Joe, but he was lean to the point of scrawniness and although the width of his shoulders promised future strength, he was nowhere near full growth. He traveled with his uncle and aunt to Oregon, and it was known about the train that he was a penniless orphan who had been taken in by them and none too gladly.

Jewel blinked away the Colorado street outside her window and saw again, in her mind's eye, the stars gleam bright against the indigo sky beyond the McClosky wagon. . . .

Her mother's death from fever two weeks previously had left the girl both numb and agonized. Like a wound that has sliced through nerve endings and dulled them at the surface, but left a deeper unreachable agony sealed within, her mother's passing had left young Julia in mourning and despair. It had also left her with the full burden of her brothers and sisters to care for, and the full brunt of her father's attentions.

Julia had taken to sleeping on the ground beneath the wagon. Fear of rattlesnakes held less terror for her than fear of her father's caresses.

Thirteen-year-old Julia McClosky lay on the hard-packed earth and stared at the imperturbable heavens above her head, while she prayed to God for deliverance. Her mother's presence had stood between her father and her, in some intangible way. If things became too hideous, Mrs. McClosky could be told, Julia had fantasized in the worst of times. Now even that small protection had been taken away from her and terror had possession of her every waking hour. Julia looked up at the immense expanse of open land and sky and felt entrapped as she never had before; she could barely breathe for the tightening noose of danger.

She could run away . . . but where, in this ocean of sand and hostile landscape? She could tell someone . . . but who would believe her story? And if they did, would they then not also know her shame?

Shame. She felt it in every pore. Disgust and revulsion at the things she had submitted to. Probings and fingerings of a more and more intimate nature, only held back at all by the knowledge of the mother sleeping ignorant in the next room. Now her mother slept forever and there would be no stopping her father's sweating, ugly lust that had insinuated itself into her consciousness, so that all hope of happiness and goodness had been blotted out.

Jewel sighed away the ugly memory, closed the tattered cloth cover of the precious diary, and let her gaze take in the scene on the street below. This was the here and now, she reminded herself—all that plagued her so grievously had been *then*. It was Fancy's plight that had called it all up so vividly in her mind . . .

How long ago was it, when she had decided never to live the life of the women on that train? So long had the need *not* to live her mother's life been with Jewel that she seemed to have been born with it. Anyone hearing her life story would have concluded that the tragedy on the wagon train had set her course, but Jewel knew this was not so. Long before that, she had vowed no man would ever own her as her mother had been owned. The tragedy on the trail had only proved that Fate agreed with her.

Ford Jameson could shoot a good deal better than most farm boys. He could tell a good gun from a bad by the sense of it in his hand, could hunt as well as the older men on the wagons whose job it was to keep the train supplied with jackrabbits, coyotes, and any other creatures God chose to set near to the wagons.

The type of shooting Ford was practicing every chance he got, out of sight of the others, was a different kind entirely. His father's old Smith & Wesson pistol and a Henry rifle were the only legacy from his long-dead parents. He wasn't sure when he'd realized he had a knack for guns. Long, long ago, he supposed; time out of mind.

He could clear the holster with the S&W as quick as you could blink your eye. It would've been quicker, too, if he could have tied the leather to his leg as he'd heard the professional shootists did. It was not that Ford wanted to be a pistoleer or anything lawless, rather that he had always been an outcast, unwanted and alone, and outcasts had the need to protect themselves.

There was no excess ammunition on the train, where every item counted as the possible difference between life and death, so he couldn't practice shooting much, except when he hunted. But every minute that was free he could practice the *feel* of things. The feel of the weapon in the cup of his hand, the way the handle seemed to fit his palm as if born there, the fluid grace of the draw that was swift as God's own retribution. The sense of the cold blue-black steel barrel as an extension of his hand and arm, an extension as natural as the pointing of a finger.

No one knew, of course. If there was one thing you could say about Ford Jameson, it was that he kept his own counsel.

"Unnaturally quiet" his mother had called him when he was a toddler who didn't cry when he bumped his head and who asked for little in a household that had not enough of anything. But he had always known he wouldn't get what he asked for, so it had seemed pointless to him to ask.

He was a quiet boy and self-contained. He had, in the absence of teachers, taught himself a code of conduct. He was kind to hurt things and vulnerable ones, who were not as strong as he, for he had a firm belief that he had been blessed with inordinate strength to make up for all he had not been given. He knew his Bible well, for his uncle spouted it night and noon, but while Ford loved the rhythm of the words and the power of the thoughts they conveyed, he felt only contempt for the man who prattled goodness endlessly, but was not good.

Ford Jameson watched life, assessing it. He had an analytical mind without benefit of the schooling that might have honed his considerable gifts into brilliance. He read voraciously, a book always tucked inside the buttons of his shirt as he worked. How often had he wrapped a borrowed book carefully in cloth before tucking it in close to his skin? It wouldn't do to let sweat stains make him an undesirable borrower.

He analyzed people, too. When you're quiet, people tend to pay you little mind, he'd found, so he had ample time for observation. And observe he did. The hypocrisies of the Sunday-school Christians who had none of Christ's charity in their souls; the pretensions of those who dismissed his worth, because he was an orphan with no prospects. And the kind ones like Auntie Mae, who looked for the good in a man and then blew on the drowsy spark of it to make a flame: *"The Lord weighs the sins of the warm-hearted and those of the cold-blooded in different measures,"* she had told him, and the words had become his standard.

Auntie Mae had been the one lodestar of Ford Jameson's life. Soft, gentle, plump, giving with no thought of getting, she had taken the unnaturally quiet child to her heart and understood why he did not speak . . . so she had spoken. Endlessly, she had chatted to him of life and love and goodness; of how kindness is the single greatest good and meanness of spirit the single greatest sin. She had filled up the empty places in his soul and her simple faith had become his code. When she, too, died, he had been cast upon the charity of the uncharitable aunt and uncle with whom he now traveled.

Ford Jameson had watched the young girl named Julia, with the large breasts, the sweet plain face, and the haunted eyes, from the first day the wagons had assembled at St. Joe. He had seen her herd the younger McClosky children efficiently and with long practice, seen the gentleness with which she treated her pregnant mother. He had seen, too, the fear that crossed the girl's face when her father was near. Did the man beat her? he wondered. Ford saw no evidence of it on her person, but that meant little, for it could be disguised.

Something about the girl touched him. Not merely the quickening that her ripe body produced in him: it had become a fanaticism with him that he could ignore the weaknesses of the flesh. Go without water, food, rest. Go without love, kindness, speech. Only when you could conquer these needs could you be fully in control of your destiny. But something deeper, hidden, some subterranean vulnerability beneath the more obvious ones drew his attention to Julia. She became his silent study as much as the copy of Virgil he had borrowed from the Hendersons.

He would watch and wait and somehow, sometime before the wagons reached Oregon, he would know her secret sorrow.

If water hadn't been so scarce and tempers so short, maybe none of it would ever have happened—or at least not the worst of it.

Three days into the Humboldt, the clothing hung in sweat-damp folds about the frightened travelers, the endless sand that filled their lives stuck in the creases of clothes and bodies; it rubbed their skin to blisters nearly as big as the ones raised by the sun. Water became an obsession, for there was not near enough of it and things would be worse before they got better.

Julia seldom wandered far from the wagons in the darkness of night camp, but something in her father's manner had made her wary on this particular evening. She wrapped her shawl tightly around herself and shuddered. The desert air, so viciously hot by day, was icy at night. She picked her way carefully among the sagebrush clumps; it wouldn't pay to disturb a sleeping rattler curled for his night's comfort beneath a bush.

The immensity of the night sky made her feel freer and the cold seemed a blessing on her sun-scorched skin. She tried to pick out formations in the pinprick expanse of stars above her head. She heard him before she saw him—heard the crunch of stone on sand behind her. When she turned and saw her father, a small frightened scream gasped out of her before she knew she'd made a sound. He whirled her around to face him and she could see in his flushed face that he had been drinking.

"No, Pa!" she pleaded, her voice a hoarse and childlike whisper as he pushed her down on the ground and wrestled her clothing from her shoulders, ripping hand-sewn buttons in his haste to free her breasts. Julia struggled against his hard, insistent strength. She should have screamed louder in the beginning, she thought later, but the horror of people running to help and finding out her shame had stopped her. And then it was too late. A hot hard thing was pushing at her, tearing at her private places. His hands, dirty with sand and gravel from the ground, were pulling her legs apart as his sweating body pinned her to the earth.

Julia fought against the sickening intrusion with all her strength. "No, Pa, please, no!" she sobbed. "Don't do this to me." But he silenced her pleas with his hand on her mouth and then it was too late to scream. She felt him enter her—a searing, battering, tearing hurt that seemed to rend her in a way that could never be repaired.

She shrieked into his hand and felt him pulled backward off her body with a grunting sound of surprise.

Behind and above them stood Ford Jameson, taller than her father but nowhere near as broad. Julia saw her father jolted to his feet, hitching up his trousers as he went.

"This ain't no affair of yours, boy!" McClosky said threateningly as he backed off far enough to hike up his pants and gauge his opponent.

Ford stood, fists clenched at his sides, the corded muscles of his neck and jaw working, a savage strength in him that Julia hadn't seen before. He said nothing, but the look of contempt on his face was easy enough to read.

Dazed, ashamed, terrified, Julia pulled her torn clothes up over her body and tried to stand. She saw her father reach for his gun belt, saw Ford wrestle him to the ground . . . heard the shot that killed the older man.

Ford said he hadn't meant things to end as they did, McClosky shot through the heart and dead before the powder cleared. But the men who hurried from the wagon train didn't believe his story.

Julia was a slut, they said, and Ford had had his way with her. Hadn't everyone on the train seen the way she flaunted her body in front of the men? Hadn't they seen with their own eyes the way young Jameson watched her late and early? Her father had done the righteous thing following them out there into the desert to break up their love tryst . . . protecting his daughter's virtue with his life. The little bastard deserved to be hanged for it, they said.

Ford said nothing in his own defense and Julia could see in his eyes that never from him would they hear one single word with which to shame her.

She didn't tell them, either, what had really happened. How could she? But she did slip her father's gun to the boy in the wagon, where they kept him tied while they sat around the fire and decided where to hang him at sunup. And she did cut him free to use it.

Ford Jameson used that gun to make his escape on a horse she held as he mounted and fled into the desert. The fine Christian people of the train had shunned her after that—they had dumped her, with only the clothes on her back, at the first hole-in-the-wall outpost they'd hit after the desert. They'd taken her brothers and sisters and all her worldly goods and left her at the edge of the Humboldt Sink to die. But she hadn't obliged them.

Ford, too, had made his way in a less than perfect world. There was no way back, he told her later. No way back once you had the law on your tail and the reputation of a murderer.

Later, he'd lived up to his gunslinger name, but maybe that was necessity, too.

Once you were a fast gun on the wrong side of the law, every maniac in the Territories tried to beat you to the draw to enhance his own reputation.

He'd be coming back now soon, Jewel told herself. It was near time for Ford to come riding back into her life like he'd always done over the years. She never knew exactly when it would be, but it was getting so she could feel when the time was coming.

She pushed her chair back from the window, replaced the diary reverently in her lockbox, and forced herself from reverie to motion.

People said whores didn't have the heart to really love a man—deep-down undying love of the kind the poets used to write about. Jewel knew better.

35　"Well, now," Jewel said emphatically to Fancy. "There's the question of what we're gonna do with you, ain't there, kid?"

Fancy was seated on a small rush chair by the window; the madam remained standing, an elbow propped against the cheap highboy that occupied one wall.

Fancy felt stronger than the night before. *You kin live through near anythin', honey,* Atticus would have told her, *one day at a time.* Tomorrow she would give herself grieving time, but today she must find a way to survive.

There was appraisal in Jewel's glance. "I've given you a lot of thought, since last night, kid. . . . You say you need a grubstake and I know a way you could get one real fast, but you might not like the price you gotta pay for it."

"I'm willing to hear what you have to say, Jewel. I'm grateful to you for saving my life."

Jewel nodded, satisfied by the reply. The girl had spunk and that could take her a long way.

"There's a lot of men in this town, kid, and almost no women. What women are here, are sportin' gals like me and mine. Sometimes men get a hankerin' for somethin' a little more . . . exotic, you might say, than your basic whore." She paused and Fancy frowned, uncertain of her meaning.

"Like what?"

"Like a virgin. There's men out here'd pay a year's poker winnin's for a shot at a bona fide virgin. Maybe more." She watched for the girl's response with careful calculation.

Fancy smiled, bitterly. "I'm not a virgin, Jewel."

"Close as any of them buggers'll ever get to one. You're green enough so's they'll never know the difference."

"What exactly would I have to do?"

"Same thing we all do, honey. Let him fuck his brains out and tell him he's wonderful doin' it!"

Fancy pushed back her loathing; before yesterday she would never have considered such a preposterous proposition.

"You give it some thought, kid," Jewel was saying, "I'll come back later on and we'll talk some. I know better'n you think how you're hurtin', but I know somethin' else too. Life's real tough, but long as you're alive you kin still give it a run for its money. And if you ain't got no choice, you might as well be brave."

Jewel hesitated. "I can tell you somethin' else, kid . . . if you gotta climb a hill, waitin' won't make it any smaller—and self-pity'll kill you faster'n anything I can think of."

Fancy tried hard to think clearly. If Jewel's proposition could give her enough money to reach Magda, maybe she shouldn't reject it out of hand. She had no way of knowing how long her search would take and no money to sustain her until then. The brothers and McBain were high up in the mountains, far from town; they came into Oro only once every few months or so for supplies. Long before their next town visit, she could have her money and be gone to Denver; once there, Magda would help her sort out the future.

"I'll hold an auction," Jewel was saying, aware that Fancy was listening with renewed attention. "Get the biddin' up real high. Make sure you don't get pawned off on somebody who goes in for rough stuff. I'd split the take with you, of course. Twenty-five percent to you, seventy-five to me—seeing as how it's my reputation and overhead, and my customers we're talkin' about. Then you can stay here and work for me, if you want to. The working girls get ten percent plus room and board, so you can see I'm bein' real generous about the twenty-five percent." She paused for effect.

"Sixty-forty," Fancy said, looking Jewel in the eye. "And I get the sixty."

Jewel sat down with an exaggerated shrug. "Well, I'll be damned! You must be feelin' a mite better."

"Look, Jewel . . . if I do this, it's got to give me what I need. I owe you for what you did, but I've got to get to Denver for a time to sort out some troubles. Then I might need a place to stay and a means of earning a living, but there's no way in this world I'd ever be one of your girls. I'm an actress and a singer. I can do Shakespeare or musical comedy or dance hall . . .

or just about any other entertainment you can think of. I mean to make something of myself, something big. What happened out there may have slowed me down, but it sure as hell hasn't stopped me."

"What's in Denver that ain't here, too, kid?"

"Survival."

Jewel's painted eyebrow twitched upward. The kid was real interesting; she wondered what kind of trouble was driving her so hard.

"Have it your own way, kid. Just give me an answer about the auction soon as you can—I could start the ball rollin' tomorrow and you could have the whole thing behind you in forty-eight hours." She headed for the door, stopped, and turned back toward Fancy.

"Tell you what. How about you come have dinner with me tonight? I promise I won't press you none about the auction. I don't get women visitors hereabouts too often and, well, I'd take it real neighborly if you'd come to dinner. I know you ain't got nothin' better to do . . ." She smiled almost shyly at her guest.

"I'd like that," Fancy answered, wondering what on earth she and Jewel could possibly find to talk about, but grateful at the thought of not being left alone with her own dark thoughts.

▲

"Whorin's a decent enough business," Jewel said matter-of-factly over the roast chicken. Fancy noticed that while the woman's table manners weren't elegant, neither were they coarse. Someone had taught her . . . but who? Fancy watched the madam with the shrewd eye of an actress assessing character traits for future reference. Jewel was full of contradictions; although she was uneducated, she was smart and canny. She was fun to be with, too. Fancy's spirits had improved considerably since arriving in the little sitting room off the bedroom, where Jewel took her meals.

"Oh, there's bad parts, too, don't misunderstand me," she continued, warming to her subject. Her face was animated in the glow of the fire and she seemed anxious to make a good impression. "And there's a lot you got to know. Like how to skin a man back to see if he's got the clap, and how to tell if a girl's really got her monthlies or if she's just malingerin'. And if she don't get her monthlies at all, you got to know what to do that won't kill her in the bargain." Jewel sat back from the meal with satisfaction.

"Got to know men, inside out. How to hustle 'em, how to fuck 'em, how to comfort 'em—dependin' on the circumstances. All told, it ain't the worst life, I guess. It's done all right by me, so I cain't complain none.

"It's a real shame you won't consider bein' a whore. A looker like you could fetch a pretty penny in a place like San Francisco or New York City. Even Denver . . ."

Fancy took a sip of the wine Jewel had put out for their dinner and shook her head emphatically.

"Not me. That's not how I plan to get rich." Jewel heard the defiance and ambition in the girl's words.

"It don't look to me like you're too far along on the path to riches yet, kid. You expectin' to find a gold mine like the rest of them suckers out there?"

"I *am* a gold mine, Jewel. I just haven't found a way yet to make that fact pay off."

Jewel threw back her head and laughed appreciatively. "I like you, Fancy. You got what it takes. I've got a hunch you and me have more in common than you think."

Fancy smiled a little. "How'd you get into this business, Jewel?" she asked to change the subject.

"Just lucky, I guess," Jewel said, bitterness beneath the words. "I was hungry. I had no place to sleep. A man offered me a meal and a bed and I took it."

"He took advantage of you?"

"Or me of him, I guess. I mean, I didn't love him or nothin'. Like I said, I just needed somebody to help me stay alive. There was a lot of others after that. In a lot of towns."

"How old were you?"

"Thirteen or so, near as I can recall. Got took in by a House when I was fourteen or thereabouts. It seemed a real good deal to me by then. I mean, stayin' in one place, not havin' to pack up my belongin's every mornin'. I had this little knapsack made from a bandana . . ." Jewel made a descriptive gesture with her hands as if folding a knapsack, and Fancy was moved by the poignancy of it.

"Not having to worry about gettin' them stole from me was good. Eatin' regular, you know? That was real nice." Jewel smiled, a soft smile of remembrance and regret.

"I understand," Fancy whispered, recalling only too well what safety the circus had provided in her own nomadic life.

"Did you ever have a friend? I had one named Atticus. I guess he made all the difference."

"Yeah, kid, I had me a real good friend. I just don't talk about him none."

"Sometimes it's awfully hard not to be scared, isn't it?" Fancy said, not sure exactly why she did.

"Scared? Hell, honey, I been scared every day of my life since I was twelve. Scared is what keeps you movin'. Scared is just another word for bein' alive."

The two women looked at each other in the candlelight and something intangible passed between them. Fancy went back to her room later with a sense that to be a woman alone in the world took far more than independence. It took guts.

 Fancy knocked at Jewel's door and was startled by the gruff response from within. "Go away!" Jewel's voice growled, 36 without asking who was there.

"Jewel! It's me, Fancy." She was surprised by the rebuff; the friendship she'd sensed in the woman the previous night couldn't have vanished so quickly.

"Ain't got no time now for visitors, Fancy."

"Jewel! Are you all right in there? Something's going on around here— everybody's hanging crepe, I can't get a word out of anyone . . ."

The door squeaked open a crack and Jewel's worried face peered out at her from the opening. "Ain't got no time for you now, for Christ's sake!" Hurt by the rejection, Fancy almost turned to go when she noticed blood splatters on the front of Jewel's gown.

"God Almighty, Jewel. Are you hurt?"

Jewel grabbed Fancy's arm and yanked her through the opening, then slammed the door behind her.

"It ain't me. It's Nellie. The damn fool was in the family way and let some quack have at her with a piece of wire."

Fancy's stomach lurched at the words; she'd given considerable thought lately to all the ghastly tales she'd ever heard in the circus about abortion. She looked in the direction Jewel had indicated and saw a thin, fragile girl tossing feverishly on the bed. Jewel seemed to have wrapped her lower body in rags, but the state of the bed said she'd bled through them several times over.

Fancy swiftly crossed the room. She put a practiced hand to the sick girl's brow, then held her wrist and cocked her own head, listening. Nellie's forehead burned with fever; she was sweat-covered and nearly gray from blood loss. She whimpered with pain, like a frightened animal.

"My God, Jewel! This girl's in a real bad way. What'd the doctor say?"

"The doc? He's the old fool who *did* this to her." Fancy's throat constricted.

"What have you given her?" She pulled back Nellie's eyelids and looked into her glazed pupils in a practiced fashion.

"Laudanum," Jewel replied, curious at the competency of Fancy's ministrations. "Thought to ease her passin'."

"In my room," Fancy said hurriedly, "there's a carpetbag. Under the bed. Have someone fetch it. Quick!" She turned to look Jewel full in the face. "I mean it, Jewel. If we're going to try to save her, we haven't much time. I know what I'm doing; please trust me."

Uncertainly, Jewel moved into action—Fancy heard her shout orders to someone outside the door before she returned to the bedside.

"Get me boiling water, Jewel, a lot of it. And soap—any kind of disinfectant you can lay your hands on." She began to undo the reeking bandages.

"Hemorrhage, infection, fever, shock . . ." Fancy ticked off the symptoms to be dealt with, rifling her mental pharmacopoeia for knowledge. *Cure de symptoms,* Atticus would have said. *Give you time to cure de disease.*

"There's only so much we can do, Jewel," Fancy called over her shoulder, without looking up. "After that, it'll depend on whether it's the infection that's real bad, or just the bleeding. How strong she is will make a difference, and how much she wants to live."

"What can I do?"

"Get a pillow under her legs. She's in shock from hemorrhage. If we lift up her legs and cover her with plenty of blankets we may buy enough time to save her." Jewel did as she was told.

Fancy was scribbling something on a sheet of paper at the desk. "I'll need these things for a draught, if you can find them. Bayberry, ginger, white pine, cloves, and cayenne. Most of it should be in your kitchen, Jewel. Get someone to take the proportions I've written here and put them through a fine sieve twice, then steep one teaspoonful in a cup of boiling water for fifteen minutes. If we can get Nellie to drink this remedy, it may cool the fever."

Jewel nodded as a knock sounded at the door. Mary Ellen was visible at the opening, white-faced and carrying Fancy's bag. Jewel snatched the satchel from her hand, gave the girl the herbal recipe, and packed her off to the kitchen. Fancy could see in Mary Ellen's face the empathetic fear of what had befallen Nellie. Some said pregnancy was the reason why one out of every five parlor girls committed suicide.

"I need leopard's-bane and monkshood for the bleeding," Fancy told Jewel as the woman carried both the bag and a basin of soapy water to the bedside. "God! I wish I had some sabrina." She'd managed to strip the bloodied rags away from Nellie's body and reached for the sponge in the bowl to cleanse her patient.

"I can do that part, honey. You go find what you need in your bag here while I get her cleaned up." Fancy nodded, and rose from her kneeling position beside the bed. She rooted through the carpetbag, found what she wanted, and headed toward the door.

"Fancy!" Jewel called after her, and the girl turned, her hand still on the knob, to look back questioningly.

"I just wanted to tell you . . . thanks. I really mean it."

"She's not saved yet, Jewel."

"But you're tryin'. You're tryin' real hard and that's what counts. Most people don't care much what happens to the likes of us."

Fancy saw the gleam of tears in Jewel's eyes; she nodded, then slipped quietly from the room to make her decoction. It seemed the woman had meant to say more.

Jewel bathed Nellie's shivering body and covered her over with her own blankets; she brushed the sweat-matted hair back from her pale face and sighed. More than once over the years she'd buried the remnants of such butchery as this child had suffered—septic abortion was a real crummy way to die.

Fancy administered her potion and settled in beside the bed to watch, as Jewel sat down in the rocking chair near the window. It was night outside, and the boisterous sounds of Oro's seamier side wafted into the room on the evening air. Kerosene lamps were being lighted all up and down the street, like fireflies.

Jewel spoke, after a while. "I wouldn't have figured you to get mixed up in such as this. How'd you learn doctorin'?"

Fancy took a deep breath; it would be a long night, and she felt a camaraderie with the other two women in the room. The battle they fought was a woman's war, no man could ever suffer it, or fully understand.

"My friend Atticus taught me. He knew a whole lot about a lot of things, doctoring was only part of it . . ."

Jewel and Fancy kept their vigil as the night wore on. Every hour Fancy checked the girl's bandages, poured a little of her medicaments into Nellie's unresisting mouth, watched and waited.

"I cain't help thinkin'," Jewel said once. "That poor kid on the bed coulda been me."

"Or me," Fancy replied.

"No. I mean really. I know a lot about not gettin' pregnant . . . bein' in this business and all. I know about eelskin tents that you put inside you, and French secrets that a man can wear. I know all the recipes for douches— alum, pearlash, sulfate of zinc, you name it. Even know the natural remedies, like oak bark and red rose leaves and nutgalls, not that I ever put a store of faith in 'em. But once, a real long time ago, I got caught like Nellie."

"You were pregnant?" asked Fancy, surprised by the revelation and the display of friendship that prompted it.

Jewel sighed. "Yeah. I surely was. Lookin' back, I think I wanted it to happen. Wanted a kid, you know? Way down deep. Somebody to belong to me. I was in love real bad . . ." She paused, remembering.

"Anyways, when I realized the daddy couldn't marry me, 'cause he had troubles of his own just then, I decided I didn't have no choice but to get rid of the baby—but by that time, I'd waited too long. Near five months it was, so none of the remedies I knew were worth a damn, except to make me so sick I wanted to die.

"So I found me a quack who did a big business with the crib girls in the back alleys."

Fancy noted that Jewel had leaned forward in her chair, her arms folded protectively across her belly as if safeguarding something inside. She was sure the woman didn't realize she was doing so and Fancy tucked the eloquent gesture away inside herself.

"I was scared shitless, kid, believe you me. I walked around in torment for a week before I got my courage up. Cried all night before I went in there to that quack. Cried 'cause I'd grown to love that baby . . . and 'cause I was real alone. I hadn't even told Ford about it, 'cause the law was after him and he was on the run."

She took a breath before continuing. "This abortionist had a dirty old table where he did his butchery. Christ, I can still see that filthy gray sheet he laid over me. . . ." Fancy could feel the woman's anxiety all the way across the room.

"I was naked down there and quiverin'; and this quack was just about to start in on me with a long wire of some kind, when Ford come bustin' down the door and grabbed me. How he even knew what I was up to, I ain't sure. Damn near put that old geezer through a wall he did, hangin' on to me half naked as I was with one hand, punchin' the doctor with the other. He drug me outta there and saved my life most likely."

"Great God, Jewel! What happened to the baby?"

Jewel was silent for a moment, lips tight shut, eyes distant—finally she smiled. "I give her birth a few months later, of course. I got a real fine daughter back East, Fancy . . . her daddy even sees her from time to time." Jewel said the last with shy pride.

Fancy stared at the woman and bit back the questions she longed to ask.

"Her name's Dakota," Jewel volunteered. " 'Cause that's where we was when it all happened. Her father got 'em to put his last name on the birth certificate. Jameson, it says. All real official and everythin'. I mean, nobody would ever know to see it that him and me wasn't really married when she got born."

So Ford Jameson was Jewel's lover . . . Hart and Chance had told her of their time with the gunfighter.

"Why in God's name didn't you get married?"

"How could we?" Jewel snapped at the stupidity of the question. "We couldn't very well go before no judge with Ford wanted by the law in damn near every state west of the Mississippi, could we? It wouldn't be much of a christenin' present for Dakota to get her daddy hung, now, would it?"

Fancy wanted to cry. Why was life so full of questions without answers, unfairness with no hope of redress? Babies without fathers . . .

"I'm glad you've got a daughter, Jewel. No matter what, you've got someone to love you."

"She don't know nothin' about my real life, of course. I sent her East when she was just a little tyke. I figured that way, maybe someday we could all be together, her and us, I mean, if things changed and all."

"That would be lovely, Jewel. I hope it works out for you."

Nellie groaned just then, and Fancy checked her patient. The pulse was less erratic, the skin less fiery—if Nellie lived until morning, there was a real chance of saving her.

Standing up to face the woman seated in the rocker, Fancy said, "I've got something I'd like to tell you, Jewel, but you've got to promise me you'll keep my secret."

"I'm real good at secrets, Fancy."

"I'm in the family way, Jewel. I fell in love with someone I shouldn't have."

"Hell, kid, we all do that, that's just part of bein' a woman."

"He doesn't know about the baby, and I don't want him to. It's all terribly complicated . . ." Fancy faltered. "I have this friend in Denver . . . if I can get to her, I know I can stay there until after the baby's born. She's very wise and she'll help me figure out what to do, I know she will."

"Listen, Fancy, you can stay right here with me. We'll work out something. Plenty of kids get born in whorehouses. Not as many as get conceived there, of course—"

"No! Not my child. Not here." Then, realizing she might have hurt Jewel's feelings, she started to speak again but the older woman cut her off.

"It's okay, Fancy. I understand. I got my kid out, too. I was just tryin' to help."

"I know that, Jewel, and I appreciate your generosity—truly I do. Fact is, I've been thinking ever since we talked about the auction . . . Maybe there's a way we could help each other. Afterward, I mean.

"What if I took part of the money the auction brings in and invested it with you in a partnership? I won't need much to live on until the baby comes, not if I can get to Magda and Wes. You've got a saloon downstairs—

I could show you how to make it into a real theatre. Later, after the baby comes, maybe I could show you how to bring in customers like you've never seen before."

"I don't need no more customers. I got all I know what to do with now."

"There are lots of saloons in the Gulch, Jewel, but nobody else in this town has a theatre. It'd give you a legitimate business too—one where you could hold your head high."

"Son of a bitch! Ain't you the little sweet-talker?"

"What do you say?"

"I'd say you got real possibilities as a salesman, honey, but I'd have to think this through careful. This saloon's all I got . . . I need to be right smart about what I do with my money. How do I know you can do what you say you can?"

"Just get me a banjo, or bring in a piano player, and I'll give you a performance tonight that these miners will never forget. You'll have to show off the merchandise you plan to auction off anyway, won't you?"

Jewel rose and walked toward the bureau, her back to Fancy. She mistrusted partnerships but she liked the kid.

"I'll consider it, Fancy. If you decide to come back to Oro after the baby . . . and *if* I like what I hear tonight. But the split would be fifty-fifty."

Fancy smiled for the first time in forty-eight hours; any circus performer worth her salt knew when she had a fish on the line. *Always know when to quit,* cara mia, Gitalis would say. *Always leave them wanting more.*

"We'll talk about the split," Fancy said quietly. "After you hear me sing."

Fancy walked to the bed to check Nellie's dressing and to hide the small smile that played on her own lips. Maybe there was hope after all.

You don't know it, Nellie, Fancy thought as she touched the girl's forehead. But if I save you, we'll be even. I'll have given you back your future and maybe you'll have done the same for me.

▲

Fancy checked her music for the last time and breathed in the exhilaration of working once again before an audience. God Almighty, was there anything so seductive as applause? The miners out front in the Crown might be grubby and bereft of social graces, but they were an audience nonetheless, and she longed to touch them with her spirit.

That's what performance is, she thought, excited by the laughter and anticipatory applause, the ability for my soul to speak to theirs, directly—no barriers of class or style or education between us, only the strength of talent to bind us together. If a performer projected truth, be it song or dance or recitation, the audience would hear the honesty and respond. Fancy longed for the grace of that response to wash her spirit clean.

What incredible power it was—the power to create a new world, better than the real one, softer, safer, more compassionate. More everything, in fact, than poor reality provided.

Who shall I be for them tonight? she asked herself. What fantasy shall I fulfill? She stepped out onto the makeshift stage determined to be every dream they'd ever dreamed. She would make them want her and in so doing, their love would free her for the future.

Fancy danced to the tinkly off-key music of the nearly toothless piano player, then she sang. The men cheered the bawdy ballads, as she knew they would. They pounded their feet and stomped their gun butts on the tables. When she knew she had them where she wanted them, she recited stirring poems of battles victorious, of honor and of love.

Finally, late in the evening, she sang the songs that reminded them of their lost youth, the haunting melodies that stir men's blood and make them dream again, despite the odds. She sang softly, tenderly, as if the lyrics were whispered to each listener alone.

Jewel and Rufus watched the girl's act wonderingly. Where had she learned so much about human frailty? Where had she learned that hearts break more often than they are fulfilled, and that life's long highway has many turnings that only the strong survive?

The final note of the last song lingered over the hushed room, over the rugged faces, now softened by their memories. The audience was so enrapt, it took a moment to collect its wits enough even to applaud, then wild, uncontrollable clapping and stamping and shouting thundered through the Crown.

Fancy smiled and blew kisses of promise to the men who crowded around her so closely, they took her breath away. It took Jewel and Rufus quite some time to extricate her from the crush of cheering, lusting men.

37   Fancy paced agitatedly back and forth in the room Jewel had given her above the saloon. She looked hard at her reflection in the mirror to see if her fear about the auction taking place in the floor below showed. It would not do at all to face this night with red-rimmed eyes and a sniffling nose. She'd said yes to this auction for a purpose, she had paraded herself before the lascivious eyes of potential "buyers" through three shows a night, for three nights running, and this was not the moment to lose courage.

Your body is your own, Fancy, Magda had said, years before. *No church, no laws, no God, no man can own it. Use it for pleasure or for profit, as you*

*will. All the other resources of the world belong to men. You must use what
resources you have been given to make your own way.*

Fancy touched the lace edges of the borrowed peignoir and wondered, if
life had been different, whether this was how she might have looked on her
wedding night.

She took a deep breath and forced the fear back—an act of will, like
Magda's domination of the great dangerous cats in the ring.

She might not have made this bed by choice, she thought, but by God,
she'd lie in it without sniveling.

▲

"What the hell's going on here, Jewel?" McBain grabbed the madam's
arm as she whirled past him in the frenzied crowd of revelers. The Crown
was filled to the roofbeams with more men than McBain had seen in one
place since he'd gotten back to California Gulch. "You givin' away money
here tonight, darlin'?"

Jewel's laugh could barely be distinguished above the noise of the rowdy
miners, cowboys, businessmen, and drifters.

"Hell, no, sweetie. Got somethin' better 'n that. We're gonna auction off a
goddamned bona fide A-number-one-type virgin here tonight."

"Holy Jehoshaphat, Jewel! Where in the hell did you find one of them
critters out here? They're scarcer'n five-pound gold nuggets."

"Just sorta stumbled in here one day, you might say, Bandana. Got a
body on her that'd make an old man young again."

"Then what in the Sam Hill is she doin' auctionin' herself off like a prize
heifer?"

"The kid's got no money and no friends and she needs a grubstake real
bad, Bandana, so I made her a proposition that'd get her some fast money.
Anyways, she's smart and I like her, so I'm givin' her a piece of the take
tonight, along with two-thirds of the purse from the auction."

Bandana rubbed his chin with his hand in wonderment at Jewel's exuberance. She wasn't known for her willingness to share profits, unless you were
down-and-out, or a friend. Then you knew you'd find an open hand at the
Crown.

"How much do you think you kin raise with this little auction of yours?"

"Oh, anywheres from a hundred bucks to a thousand, I'd say, dependin'
on the mood of the crowd, of course. Last time we did this, the girl brought
in three hundred and sixty, but she wasn't near the looker this one is."

"What time's the biddin' start, honey?"

"Nine p.m. Come back to see the fun, Bandana," she said, slapping the
wiry miner on the shoulder. "Believe me, old Jewel wouldn't steer you

wrong. Any man who gets to spend the night with Fancy's gonna carry a real sweet memory out with him tomorrow mornin'."

Bandana laid down the whiskey he'd been holding. "Shee-it!" he said aloud. Fancy. Poor kid. Then he swung into motion.

How in the hell had she got herself into a fix like this one? And where in God's acre had Chance got to anyway? Good thing Hart wasn't with them, there'd be no telling how he'd react to such news as this. Why, it was only happenstance that they were in town at all. If the Long Tom hadn't broken and the winch along with it, they'd be high up on Mosquito Mountain for another two months.

Bandana did some rapid calculations; the gold in his poke might be worth a thousand, in a pinch. He hadn't planned to check in at the bank office until morning. He did some hasty mental gymnastics to assess how much he'd need to get the repairs made and keep the work going at the claims. Hell! What difference did any of that make? Fancy was in trouble and that's all that counted.

The night air on the street nipped at him as he passed the swinging doors and loped onto North Street—there were at least a dozen places Chance could have got to. God damn! He only hoped McAllister was at a nice visible poker table somewhere and not in some lady's boudoir with his pants around his ankles.

The Gold Coast Saloon on East Second Street was the next to last place Bandana thought of, but that's where he found Chance emerging into the darkened street, a disgruntled look on his face. Bandana called out, "Where the hell you been, McAllister? I been all over this godforsaken town at a dead run scoutin' you!"

"Looking for a friendly little card game, Bandana," Chance replied good-humoredly, "but the only action in town seems to be over at Jewel's place. Thought I'd give it the once-over."

"That's why I been huntin' you, boy." The exasperation in McBain's voice made Chance look sharply at the little man. "It's Fancy they're auctionin' off, for chrissake!"

Chance grabbed Bandana's arm so forcefully, it rocked the smaller man. "You sure about that?"

"Damnation, McAllister! Why the hell else do you think I been runnin' all over hell's half acre to find you? We gotta do somethin'."

"First she up and disappears without a by-your-leave, then she pulls a damn fool stunt like this," Chance said harshly. "What kind of idiot is she?" He still smarted from Fancy's sudden departure and from the guilt he felt over his own relief that she was no longer a problem.

McBain looked up disgustedly into Chance's face. "I'd say the kind that's in a peck a' trouble, wouldn't you?" Without waiting for a response, he turned and made tracks for the Crown of Jewel's with Chance in his wake.

▲

"Okay, boys!" Jewel shouted above the din of the packed saloon. "You know the rules well as I do. The biddin' starts at one hundred dollars and goes up from there to God knows where." A whistle of appreciation for the large sum, and envy from those who couldn't afford to bid, rose in the room.

"Men, you all saw the little lady perform here last night, so you know she's prime merchandise. Pretty as a picture and innocent as a newborn." Murmurs of approval greeted this part of the speech; there was undisputed agreement about Fancy's desirability.

"Now I'll tolerate no bad treatment, as part of the deal. I don't want this one ruined right off the bat by some sadistic horse's ass who don't know how to treat a lady. So no matter who bids the highest, old Jewel here reserves the right to say no to any man who ain't worthy of this singular privilege."

"Any man with a hundred dollars to spend on one night seems purty special to me!" shouted a nearly toothless miner in the front row, and everyone, including Jewel, howled with enjoyment.

"This little lady's too good to be wasted on a piker, Louie," she called back jovially.

"Even a piker could give her a good poke," he returned, and the laughter was twice as loud.

"By God, I'll bet you could, too," Jewel agreed with a hearty laugh, and the audience roared and pounded on the tables with hands and pistol butts. "But now it's time to start the festivities. So what exactly am I bid for the sweetest little piece of virgin woman-flesh this side of Fort Laramie?"

"It can't be Fancy," Chance whispered to Bandana. "She's not a virgin."

"I sure as hell don't want to hear how you happen to know that, you young jackass," Bandana hissed back at him.

The two stood at the rear of the crowded room, to the right of the swinging doors. The smoke was so thick in the yellow light from candles and kerosene lamps, it was hard to see anything clearly, but it appeared from where they stood that every male in town, from age sixteen to eighty-six, was jammed into the saloon. Sitting, standing, leaning, the would-be bidders and the simply curious were all at as high a pitch of excitement as if a new Sutter's Creek had been discovered.

Bandana and Chance assessed the leering faces in the audience with rising apprehension. Whatever fluke of fate had brought Fancy to this predicament, neither wanted to see her spend the night with any of the rough, lecherous crowd that filled the barroom.

Chance kept his poker winnings in a soft-skin money belt beneath his shirt. He wondered briefly what his brother's reaction would be to his spending all their cash on Fancy, then dismissed the concern . . . Hart would understand he couldn't possibly stand by and let some fool win Fancy out from under their noses. He had more than four hundred dollars in his money belt—Bandana had more. In a pinch, he'd win the rest by whatever means were necessary.

"One hundred and fifty," he heard the deep voice of John Henderson, the town banker, boom.

"One hundred and seventy-five," Chance called out in retaliation.

"What you fixin' to do with her if you're the high bidder?" Bandana asked, tugging at Chance's elbow. The miner's voice sounded husky, troubled.

"What do you think I'll do with her?" Chance responded, without looking down.

Bandana searched Chance's face, then turned his gaze back onto the boisterous crowd.

"Two hundred is the bid, gentlemen," Jewel shouted above the din.

"Two-fifty," called an elegant-looking business-suited man at Chance's right.

"Three hundred dollars," Chance countered. A murmur ran through the room and a number of heads shook negatively. There would be fewer bidders in the running from this point on.

"Three hundred dollars for this gorgeous little missy," Jewel called out over the hushed crowd. "Gentlemen, just think of the indescribable pleasures awaiting you this very night if you are the lucky man to be the first to taste the nectar of this sweet virgin flower. Just think of all you could teach this little lady . . ."

"Three-fifty!" shouted Henderson, throwing a significant look in Chance's direction.

"Four hundred," Chance responded, returning Henderson's appraising stare.

"Five hundred dollars," said a scruffy-looking miner near the front of the room.

"Five-fifty," Henderson shouted hastily.

"Six hundred," called Chance, wondering how much money Bandana might be willing to contribute to the kitty.

The bid bounced back and forth across the room, tension rising with each escalation. At eight hundred dollars Henderson hesitated, then turned away from the bidding with a rueful smile.

"I hope you enjoy your investment," he said to Chance as he passed by him on his way to the door.

"Well, now," called Jewel, appraising the hesitancy on the faces of the other bidders and delighted by the prospect of Chance's being the winner. "It looks to me as if this handsome young gentleman has just bought hisself a virgin."

A murmur of excitement rose in the audience as she raised the gavel to strike it on the bar.

"Going once . . ." she called mirthfully. "Going twice . . ."

"One thousand dollars!" McBain yelled out in a rock-hard voice.

Chance turned an astonished look on the little man at his side.

"What in the hell are you doing?"

"Savin' you from doin' somethin' we'd all live to regret, you young fool," McBain snapped back.

Jewel dropped her hammer, yelled, "Sold! And the next drink is on the house!"

"Just a goddamned minute there!" Bandana shouted, in a tone that cut through the pandemonium. Faces all over the room followed him as he elbowed his way to the bar. Bandana pulled the leather poke from inside his shirt and laid the gold dust on the bar next to Jewel's hand with a flourish.

"Kindly convey my money and my good wishes to the young lady in question, Miz Jewel," he said in a voice loud enough to be heard by all, even if the room hadn't stilled so you could hear a heartbeat. "And tell her for me that her virtue is worth one hell of a lot more than a thousand dollars, and that an old pal of hers sends his love."

"If you could get it up, you could give her yer love yerself," called out a drunken voice at a front table.

"You shut your filthy mouth!" Jewel spat. She turned to say something to Bandana, but he and Chance were already halfway through the swinging doors.

Rufus slid a whiskey into Jewel's hand and poured one for himself with elaborate dignity.

"Mighty classy little bastard," said the black man before he downed his drink in a swallow.

Jewel nodded, too startled to speak. No matter how long she stayed in this business, every once in a while a man could still do something that surprised her.

Bandana had thought of asking to see Fancy—trying to find out the nature of her predicament. But she'd chosen to leave them and to keep her troubles to herself. He would respect her need for both privacy and escape; if she'd only asked him, he would have given her the money anyway.

He heard Chance hurrying after him, but Bandana had no desire to trade speculation with him just now—no desire to talk to anyone at all. A good stiff whiskey and a bed in the stable, alone with old Bessie, were all he wanted in the world tonight.

Bandana waved Chance away and kept on walking.

V

INTO THE HURRICANE

▾▾▾▾▾▾

Fancy's Journey

"Nature is a mother."
BANDANA MCBAIN

38 🌿 Magda strode across the yard from where the wagon had deposited her, the supplies from town slung over her shoulder in a string-mesh bag she'd made for this purpose. The sunlight glinted off the distant mountains in a dazzling silver-white radiance that seemed to her the light of heaven. Never in Romania had she experienced this precise brilliance that could injure your eyes if you stared at it too long. She found it cleansing, healing, intensely spiritual.

Wes was better—infinitely better than might have been expected considering the extent of the consumption that had damaged his lungs. Only Magda knew how close to the Angel of Death Jarvis had come, for she had seen it in the cards, that desperate configuration that presages doom, unless a miracle intervenes.

Now the second crisis would have to be faced—that of a man who has lost his livelihood. Already, with his returning strength had come the irritability and the discontent.

The circus was done, the animals gone except for her pet panther, which she refused to abandon in his old age, the people scattered to their individual destinies. Only Gitalis remained, faithful, cranky, dissatisfied genius that he was. He and she had come to terms with each other, through Wes' two years of illness, but by unspoken decree neither let on that anything had changed. She would have missed the verbal sparring and occasional sting— and without the little man, Jarvis would be in worse mental and emotional condition than he was.

As long as the dwarf lived with them, Jarvis had an entourage—he was still an impresario, never mind one temporarily without company. Minus Gitalis, he would be just another unemployed middle-aged actor, used up and with no certain future.

Magda welcomed the hour away from the sickroom; she needed time to think and to formulate a plan to galvanize Jarvis into action. There was nothing as debilitating for a man as unemployment, and he was not a creature to be kept caged and idle long. Within the month, Jarvis would be strong enough to be pushed from the nest, but first she must decide what to push him toward.

Theatrical life was physically depleting. Even with the Rocky Mountain air to heal them, Jarvis' lungs would never again be whole. But what else could a man of his special and copious gifts turn his hand to in these primitive mountains? There was no part he could not play, but it would be important to find one worthy of him, for a man employed beneath his level was an emasculated man, and her own future and Gitalis' were inextricably intertwined with his.

The crystal was blank about their future, and the cards mute. It happened sometimes, usually with her own physical depletion. All would change once April brought its life-renewing energies.

Magda straightened her body in an imitation of her usual litheness and sniffed the tingling air. Soon it would be spring.

▲

Jarvis brooded, sitting in the small back bedroom, and pulling on his boots. "No one understands my suffering," he told Gitalis with exaggerated disgruntlement. "Everyone thinks my lot is easy."

"We all have enough strength to bear with the misfortunes of others," Gitalis replied.

Wes smiled, his bent-over position hiding his expression.

"I have been deserted by Destiny, my friend."

"You were born deserted, as were we all," said the dwarf with no sympathy whatsoever. "We make our own destiny."

"Magda would quarrel with that premise."

"Perhaps not," Gitalis responded enigmatically. Wes' mouth twitched into a secret smile—he knew the little man had come to like Magda more than he could let on and still save face.

" 'O God!' " Wes cried suddenly, standing and addressing the dwarf as if he were an audience. " 'I could be bounded in a nut-shell, and count myself a king of infinite space, were it not that I have bad dreams.' "

"They were not bad dreams, my liege," replied Gitalis with a derisive snort. "They were your life."

Jarvis laughed heartily at that, slapped his friend on the shoulder, and moved toward the door of the bedroom.

"I vote we show this tiny prison room a fair pair of heels, my friend. I feel the need of fresh air and sunshine and the company of others."

"You 'dare the vile contagion of the day'?"

"I do, and with unfeigned enthusiasm. It's time we go abroad, good sir, and try to set our sights on some gainful employment. I fear the treasury could bear some restocking."

"Nothing new in that," Gitalis said, but it was obvious, as he scurried about the room gathering his hat, coat, and walking stick, that he was elated at the prospect of going out.

▲ ▲ ▲

Finding Magda was far more difficult than Fancy had imagined. She left Jewel and Oro behind the morning after the auction, with a tentative promise to come back in six months, although the fact that Bandana had learned of her predicament made her doubt she would ever return to the Gulch. At least not until she could do so in style and repay him his kindness.

Denver was a wild, open town in the early 1870s. Saloons and bawdy houses filled rutted streets. Cowboys, drovers, railroadmen shared the dusty thoroughfares with millionaires, made newly rich by railroads, commerce, gold or silver.

The iron tracks had reached the mile-high city in '70, and ever since then the town had burst into the extraordinary bustle of a boom in the making. Railroads had reconstructed everything to their own convenience—shops, houses, plants, breweries, and flour mills followed the tracks that provided for the business being brought into the newly constructed city.

A streetcar line had been laid, with tracks branching off in every direction to transport a potpourri of immigrants speaking languages as diverse as Babel: Slovaks, Serbs, Croats, Poles, and Russians in one neighborhood, Germans in the next. The inevitable Irish, left over from the railroad gangs; even Chinese seeking a place of refuge from the persecution that had pursued them ever since they'd been imported as railroad workers and deposited willy-nilly wherever the work stopped. Of course, there were those who felt the exclusion of the Chinese was justified, for they had brought with them the curse of the poppy flower, opium. The temptation to experience its raptures had wrought havoc among miners whose lonely, desperate lives made them easy prey to opium's oblivion.

Fancy had scoured the theatre district and the offices of impresarios looking for her friends, for three weeks, to no avail. She had been to the newspaper offices and pored over back issues, in hopes of finding one of them mentioned in a players' notice. It was growing harder not to feel despair.

The small boardinghouse in which she'd secured a tiny room, inexpensive though it was, would eat up her money quickly if she didn't find them soon. She loathed sharing a bed with the toothless old granny who was the only other female boarder, but she could endure anything if only there was hope of finding Magda.

Fancy was walking dejectedly down Blake Street, after another futile effort in the theatre district, when she spotted the dwarf, a small, stalwart shape in court jester's motley, hawking tickets on a street corner.

"Donovan's Burlesque!" Gitalis shouted in a diction meant for Shakespeare. "Gaudy girls and minstrel melodies. The last of the red-hot, wide-open burlesque palaces, where real-life pleasures and voluptuous ladies fascinate the heart as well as other parts of the anatomy. Where beauty, song, and dance combine to scintillate and educate. All for two bits, ladies and gentlemen. A paltry price to pay for such enticement." Then he began it all again.

Oh, my poor dear Gitalis, what ill fortune can have brought you to this? she wondered. Fancy forced the joy of finding him to push all lesser thoughts away. "Gitalis!" she shouted, and the dwarf whirled toward the sound. Then, without moving from the spot he stood in, he opened his arms wide to her and she saw as she ran toward him the tears running down his painted cheeks.

Fancy and Gitalis hugged and danced each other around in a circle. Where have you been? You look wonderful! You're so thin! Where is Wes? Where is my Magda? I thought I'd never find you all!

Gitalis shrugged off the painted sandwich board that imprisoned him.

"I'll take you home this instant! Jarvis and Magda will be beside themselves that you are found."

"But don't you work all day?"

"They expect me to prostitute myself until dark, my blossom, or until the tickets are gone, whichever delightful happenstance comes first, but they must learn that life is sometimes filled with disappointment."

Fancy laughed at his irreverence.

"But then they won't pay you."

"A depressing truth, but a truth nonetheless."

"Then we mustn't leave, Gitalis. Give me a handful of tickets and I'll take them to another corner. How can they object to having two salesmen instead of one?"

Gitalis considered the offer gravely.

"A woman wise as she is fair," he said at last, and taking off his ribboned hat with a flourish, he bowed elaborately, but peeked up at her, challenge in his eye.

"What poem do I call to mind, my pretty?"

Fancy thought a moment, then responded, gleeful that she'd remembered.

"The jester doffed his cap and bells," she said in her best theatre voice,

> "And stood the mocking court before;
> They could not see the bitter smile
> Beneath the painted grin he wore."

Gitalis, proud of his pupil, supplied the next verse:

> "Earth bears no balsam for mistakes;
> Men crown the knave, and scourge the tool

That did his will; but Thou, O Lord.
Be merciful to me, a fool!"

Passersby, who had ignored the dwarf or laughed at him, now paused to wonder if perhaps Donovan's Burlesque had more to offer than they'd imagined. Before the hour was out, Fancy and Gitalis had performed a one-act play, seven soliloquies, and countless poetry recitations. The tickets were gone and they were walking arm in arm toward the wagon that would take them to the little house where Wes and Magda waited supper, unsuspecting that there would soon be another mouth to feed.

39 Fancy didn't prosper in her pregnancy despite Magda's ministrations. The baby felt cranky and restless; Fancy wondered if, in its unborn state, the child knew of its own doubtful origin and fought against its fate.

Nausea persisted long into the sixth month, and a debilitating fatigue dogged her heavy footsteps. Magda watched and doctored—when Fancy awoke with swollen fingers and ankles, she mixed a diuretic of herbs and fed her dried pears and asparagus that she'd put up months before. When Fancy's melancholia sent her teetering into bed, to sob out her loneliness and fears, Magda sat and rubbed the girl's aching back and crooned to her strange lullabies in foreign tongues or told her fairy tales she could someday tell her child.

When she wasn't sick, Fancy was more than content with her life with her circus friends, for she felt loved and safe despite their poverty. She laughed with Gitalis and read aloud to Wes; she reveled in learning again, and in having a chance to use her knowledge. But it was Magda who kept her sane.

"The child will be a female," the Gypsy pronounced with satisfaction. Fancy lay on her back on the floor. Despite her thinness, the girl's belly was so mountainous, she couldn't see her own feet. Magda stood above her, a crystal pendulum swinging counter clockwise in her hand. She had sung an incantation, prayed, and waited until the small glittering piece of quartz had begun to quiver and finally swing in a rhythmic circle over the protruding belly.

"I'll probably never be able to get up off the floor to find out if you're right," Fancy said, struggling upward.

"Of course Magda is right. Such things as this are child's play."

"If it's such child's play, why won't you ever tell me anything about my baby?" she asked, delighted Magda had finally relented and told her the gender of the child she carried. The ache in her heart for Chance would be worsened by a son, but a girl could be her friend and companion.

Magda watched Fancy closely before replying. The girl was taking her plight bravely enough, more cheerful than not in the face of a hard pregnancy, no father for the child and no certain plan for the future. Magda had plumbed her own heart for answers; she'd consulted the cards and the stars and the crystals, for Magda knew the means to return the small life that Fancy carried to the Universal Life-force whence it had sprung. But she also knew the karmic consequences of such an act, and would not presume to advise Fancy about her course of action, for that choice, and its consequences for many lifetimes, must be Fancy's own.

"Some knowledge is best left to the future to unravel," Magda said, not ungently. "I wish to place no psychic bees in your bonnet, child." She smiled at Fancy and, seeing her consternation, relented a little.

"I will give you the gift of her name if you wish, now that you know her sex."

"Her name? How can you possibly know her name when I haven't yet had a moment to think of what I want to call her?"

"Foolish child. Your daughter's name was written long ago in the Akashic Record. Have I not told you that the future and the past go on, even as we speak—and all has been written for aeons in the mind of God?"

"Tell me, then. What will she be called?"

"Aurora. She will be named for gold and most aptly, for she will make many choices because of her need for wealth. She will bear four surnames in this lifetime."

Fancy felt her throat constrict. Did that mean that Aurora would one day bear her father's name, or did it mean she would marry more than once? Magda's knowledge could be terrifying as well as useful.

"And will she be . . . loved?"

Magda looked long and hard into Fancy's eyes before she finally spoke, her voice oddly flat and enigmatic.

"She will be loved . . . far more than she deserves."

"But Magda . . ." Fancy began, the strange prophecy unnerving her.

"No more."

"Magda!"

"No more!" Magda snapped, and turned away. "Only the gods can bear to know the future, child. We would burn and plummet like Icarus were we forced to know our fate."

"But *you* know . . ." Fancy persisted. The look of anguish Magda turned on her stayed her words. What agonies did Magda bear in payment for her great gifts? Fancy wondered suddenly. And what in God's name had she bargained for them in payment?

▲

"I don't see why God lets sickness happen to people, Magda. It's downright sadistic for Him to let people suffer so much." Fancy tried to rise from the chair, but her belly imbalanced her and she sank back with a sigh. Magda knew the girl's condition had made her fretful. She sat back and let her sewing come to rest in her lap.

"Illness can be a hero's journey, Fancy," Magda answered.

"What does that mean?"

"Sometimes illness offers us a roadblock with a signpost, child. The sign tells us what purpose the roadblock serves . . . how we struggle to clear the path can be heroic and full of dignity."

"But why on earth would anyone create illness as a roadblock?"

Magda's hands again ceased their motion and the needle came to rest. "There are many, many reasons one might do so, Fancy . . . to cry for help or love, perhaps. Or to prove that one has been hurt by life . . . even to design a lesson for oneself that must be learned."

Fancy looked unconvinced. "What causes us to get sick, then?" she asked.

"Many, many things can be the catalyst, Fancy. There are poisons and impurities all around us. And the mind is a powerful creator too—our thoughts can injure us, as surely as a runaway train. Too much attachment to the material and not enough to the spiritual . . . greed, envy, fantacism. Fear of life, surrender to discouragement, frustration from unfulfilled goals . . ." Magda smiled. "Do you wish to know more?" Fancy nodded uncertainly and the Gypsy set her sewing aside.

"You believe that you are made of solid matter, Fancy, but in truth, you are made of the same energy as the stars. Trillions of tiny particles of energy . . . all brilliantly colored and all in ceaseless motion. Your physical body is merely the densest matter, the slowest-moving energy, if you will. As you sit before me, child, I see your energy bodies glimmering all around you. There are four to connect you to the earth and four to connect you to the Unseen. If these energy bodies of yours were to become imbalanced, the physical entity that is Fancy would become ill."

Magda saw that her pupil now listened carefully. "There is also karma to consider when illness strikes. We bring in debts from other incarnations, and we fall heir to the group karma of the times in which we live. There are inherited diseases of humanity, as well as those of individuals—you know them as epidemics, blights, wars. . . . The individual entity can be harmed by the karma of the group, as well as by his or her own.

"And, of course, Fancy, your soul's own desire to grow may cause it to choose illness as a testing ground. One may incarnate into any number of trials for the express purpose of learning from them."

"Are you saying I might have gotten born into my family, knowing Beau Rivage would burn and I would have to go through all that I've survived? That's monstrous, Magda."

"Not if you understand that the harder one's life, the more lessons one can learn from it—and the farther along one may progress on the path to spiritual enlightenment."

"That sounds to me like precious little to get in return for suffering," Fancy said indignantly, and Magda nearly smiled.

"Perhaps you had debts to pay back, Fancy . . . we pay the piper in eternity for what we escape in time. Have you not wondered why despots are allowed to live, or torturers are permitted to ply their evil trade? They may escape punishment in one lifetime, but they will not escape the wheel of karma. They will pay the price of their choices before they are done. It is the Law."

"All this sounds farfetched to me, Magda. And I don't see what any of it has to do with me."

Magda frowned at Fancy's resistance. "Have you not seen how your resentment and your unfulfilled love have affected your health?" she asked.

"Oh, Magda, don't be ridiculous—I'm just sick because I'm pregnant."

"You are sick because you are unhappy, child, and if you do not change your attitude, your milk will make your baby sick, too."

"Well, I simply don't believe any of this."

"Whether you believe the sun will rise tomorrow morning or you do not, Fancy my child, will have no affect whatsoever on the sunrise, I assure you."

▲

"I've been thinking about what you told me last night, Magda," Fancy said tentatively as she watched the Gypsy studying a tarot lay, the following morning. "There's so much you know. I want to ask if you would teach me magic." Magda's ebony eyes rose above the cards to meet Fancy's, shadowed by intense emotion.

"You would learn what could destroy you, Fancy? Pandora's box held no more evil than this knowledge you seek."

"Don't tease me, Magda. I'd really like to learn, and life is so dull for me now. This would be the perfect time."

Magda folded up the deck with a practiced gesture. "To learn true magic, child, the road you must follow is arduous. A misstep can be more dangerous than you dream . . . even fatal. Few travel the Path without mishaps."

"Then how did you learn?" Fancy asked, hoping for a lengthy answer. The days were winter-long now, shut in and chafing.

The Gypsy faced the girl, studied her, deciding. Finally she sighed, her eyes veiled, as if she looked backward into darkness.

"I was born into this world with a caul covering my face . . . the gift or curse of second sight was mine from lifetimes past. In this incarnation my soul's purpose was clearly written, Fancy. My family saw the way I must go, from the beginning. . . .

"When I was six years old, fate set my feet on a lonely road, for an old Gypsy appeared at the gates of my father's estate. She said she had been waiting for a child with my gifts to be sent as her apprentice, and that she had come to claim me. I was frightened and did not wish to go with her, but she was famous in our land for her prophecies, and my father was superstitious. I was born to a great house, you see—one with dark and ancient roots. My father feared the woman's magic."

"You weren't born a Gypsy?" Fancy asked, startled.

Magda smiled at her naiveté. "I was born a countess . . . I was apprenticed to a Gypsy. Destiny, as our friend Wu would say." She shook her head at Fancy's surprise and laughed, quite mirthlessly.

"Tatiana trained me in herb craft and in divination. She taught me to read the runes and the tarot, showed me the future in the dark crystal. By night, with the old crone at my side, I would escape my earth body and fly to the astral plane, held only by the silver cord that binds us to the material world. I met the dead, who were mired between the worlds. I saw the past and a thousand probable futures. I conversed with angels." She laughed again, a hollow sound. "And devils. Oh, yes, child, demons are as real as angels, as real as you or me. The lower astral teems with them, reeks of their sulphur stench. It was hard to learn not to be afraid. For three years, when I was near puberty, it was my karma to rescue the ones who cried for help from the lower astral realms. By the Goddess, the terror of that time assails me still! Hideous demons, thought forms of the criminally insane, ancient devils assigned the duty of snaring souls too weak to flee—these were the monsters I battled nightly, while by day I was only a child."

Fancy shuddered. There was no mistaking Magda's sincerity, or her pain. "But why, Magda? Why you?"

"Of those to whom much is given, much is expected, Fancy. It is the Law. My soul is old and full of arcane knowledge . . . the more one knows of the universe, the more complex the riddles one is set." She paused, and shook her head ruefully.

"And I was arrogant," she breathed, as if it hurt to speak. "Sweet Jesus, I was arrogant." Magda stared at Fancy to see if the girl could understand.

"But Magda, how could you not be proud of such amazing accomplishments?"

"But that is the test, of course, Fancy! To know greatness and to keep humility. Tatiana told me of the Right-Hand Path, which leads to Light and to Goodness, and of the Left-Hand Path, which leads to Darkness and to Evil, but in my vanity, I saw only the power that comes of knowing more than others know." Magda clutched herself tightly and rocked back and forth.

"I could talk to the animals in their own tongues . . . I could traverse the universe in a heartbeat . . . I could *change* things, Fancy, can you conceive of it? If I could heal, I could also make ill. If I could see the future, why not change it to my own design? If I could bind things to me on the Inner Planes, why not money, jewels, nations, men? Oh, child, can you even dream of the temptation that attends such power? I was a sorceress, not a mere woman! I could harness nature with my spells, for I had been initiated in my thirteenth year and was consecrated to the Goddess as her priestess."

"Not to God?" Fancy asked, appalled.

Magda waved her hand dismissively. "God is the male force in the universe. He has dominion over worlds, but Isis is nature, and the Earth Mother . . . what good is one without the other?"

Fancy blinked at the reply. What tiger's cage had she opened with her unwitting questions?

Magda continued patiently, her throaty voice low and clear. "I went to Paris. I became a disciple of a certain Hermetic Order, which I must not name. The Magus of that order was powerful beyond even my wild ambitions, and he was beautiful, as only the few who can transcend nature are beautiful. His face was legendary . . . you would recognize it, if I were to show you his picture.

"I took the sacred oaths of the Order that bind me still upon the Inner Planes . . . and I accepted willingly the awesome penalty for betrayal, a penalty so odious it cannot be described in mortal terms. I rose through the grades of mastership with ease: Neophyte, Zelator, Theoreticus, Practicus, Philosophus . . . Christ! Even the names of the degrees still fill me with passion. I sucked up the knowledge greedily, and then, when I was seventeen, I passed the final portal . . . I crossed the Great Abyss, as had the ancient Egyptian pharaohs, in the King's Chamber of the Great Pyramid. I died and was reborn, Fancy! It is a mystery few survive.

"And my arrogance swelled like a festering wound, poisoning my reason —for between me and absolutely unlimited power lay only three degrees of mastership, and only a handful of humans down all the ages had ever journeyed so far without disaster." Magda's eyes glittered in the dim light like a panther's, she licked her lips, an animal gesture that made Fancy's flesh tighten. This was a Magda she had never seen.

"I've relived my folly ten thousand times in search of redemption," the Gypsy said wearily. "I will do so one time more, so that you may know the price of jousting with the gods." She ran her long fingers through her hair, straightened her spine, and sighed.

"I was in love and lust with the Hierophant of that Order. I saw myself as Isis to his Osiris; I knew he traveled Right and Left Paths freely, Light and Darkness, as he willed. For this I did not condemn him, but merely admired his virtuosity.

" *'Do what thou wilt shall be the whole of the Law,'* he told me, and I believed. *'We* are beyond the constraints of mortals, my Magda. The road to enlightenment must lead us down dark highways. How can we understand good, if we have not tried evil?' Intellectual seductions, physical seductions . . . can you even guess at what a priestess knows of sexuality, Fancy? He seduced, and I seduced, and each of us had mastered sensual arts of unspeakable power. We made love, and our passions shook the earth! I wanted him for myself alone." She hung her head before speaking again and her dark hair fanned out around her shoulders like a nun's coif. Her voice was anguished.

"I bound him to me by rituals forbidden since the dawn of time. In doing so, I interfered with his karma and with my own. I failed the test of my initiation, by the sins of pride and lust combined. The Law will not be mocked, even by a Mage, Fancy. It has taken me a lifetime to loose the bonds I fastened with my great and arrogant will.

"He was evil, while I was merely a fool. He was the instigator, but it was I who forged the instrument of my own undoing." Fancy could barely breathe for the intensity of emotion in the small room.

"One night, I sought my beloved, in an obscure corner of the Astral Plane. He had warned me not to follow . . . when I found him it was apparent why he had forbidden me. Oh, Fancy! The unutterable *evil* of what I found shrieks inside me still!" Magda took a long deep breath before going on. "The little demons climbed upon his lap for comfort, and hideous serpents wound themselves about his cloven feet. He bore the Jackal's visage, and a funnel-shaped cone of blackness entered his body at the crown chakra and suffused his entire being. What arts he had used to conceal the consummate evil of his nature from me, I could but guess. He was a black magician of the highest degree attainable, not a seeker after truth as he had purported to be. He had lied, because lies are the logic of the Left-Hand Path, and I had bound myself to my own destruction.

"I cried out in my anguish and gave away my presence. He set his creatures of the night upon me and I had to do battle for my very soul! I would have lost the fight and been plunged into eternal slavery, for my own skills were meager next to his—but in my extremity I called upon the Goddess—called the sacred, never-spoken names and she appeared before me, her sullied priestess. The bearers of her fiery sword surrounded me, and led me to safety, through the Crack Between the Worlds."

Magda sat, still as a stone statue, legs wide and palms flat upon her knees, strong and fierce.

"My punishment was exquisite . . . I would remain a Priestess, in this world and in the next. All rituals to be due the Goddess, all payments to be exacted of me, just as if I had not failed the test of Eden. My gifts would remain, but only sporadically, and not entirely at my own command, so I could never again suffer pride. I, who had sought power, was doomed to exile, poverty, and the life of a wanderer. I, who could seduce any man living, was doomed to love one for whom power had no meaning.

"There were compensations, I suppose. I was not damned, as I might easily have been—my Priestesshood was not rescinded. I am quite mortal now, but age does not trouble me as it does the rest of humanity. You would be shocked and repelled, Fancy, if you knew how very old I am. If you knew of the men I have loved in successive generations, only to watch them wither and grow old and die. It would seem the Goddess will not let me easily off the hook of this incarnation. And how wry is Her humor that I keep my seductiveness, despite the years! Perhaps, She would remind me thus, of my great folly. The earth is the Mother's, sex is the Mother's, fecundity is the Mother's. I was allowed no child of my body, although I longed in my exile for one to comfort my loneliness. But it seems that now She has relented in sending you to me. I am grateful, and I count myself deserving of this boon, for I have followed Her dictates and accepted Her punishment without rancor. I still wrestle with the sin of Pride, you see."

Magda laughed a little to shake herself loose from the dreadful history, then she sighed.

"And I am left with my staggering remorse, for I have passions to regret that other mortals do not even know exist." She paused, breathing deeply, as if coming out of a trance.

"So, child. Do you still seek to learn magic?"

"My God, Magda! I don't know what to say to you. What a wonderful, terrible story."

Magda stood up, unflinching as a gladiator.

"Learn from my life, Fancy! Learning is all there is." Then she was gone and the girl sat unmoving on the cushion, with visions of angels and demons battling in her head.

Magda shut the door gratefully on the last client of the day. Quite a number of women now made their way from town to seek her counsel and their money was more than welcome, but this one had drained her psychically. She made a mental note to cleanse her crystals carefully with the sound from a Tibetan bell before using them again, for the woman's illness was of the spirit and contaminating.

Moonlight on the new-fallen snow caught Magda's eye as she passed the small window that looked out toward Denver, several miles away. She stopped to admire the pristine blanket that had coated the hillside; the same moonlight that silvered and blued the woods would be turning Denver's buildings into palaces, shanties into fairyland. *Thus are you able to clothe the soul in glory, Mother,* she thought reverently, *despite the grime of life.* The thought made her smile.

"Why do you grin like the Cheshire feline?" Gitalis asked sharply, seeing the Gypsy outlined in the moonlit window, shadowed by the glow of the hearth.

"Because I have gone soft in the head," she replied. "And because I have been admiring God's handiwork."

"We have handiwork of our own to show you," Gitalis said, pointing to the next room where Wes sat at the table working. Fancy looked up from the knitting in her lap, and stifled an amused smile.

Magda winked at Fancy as she passed, and followed Gitalis into their small bedroom. She reached her arms around Jarvis from behind and pressed the back of his head to her bosom as she peered over his shoulder.

Pleased by the caress, Jarvis laid down his pen and leaned back into the cradling arms.

" 'Cassius from bondage will deliver Cassius,' " he announced, his voice affectionate, intimate.

"How so?"

"It has occurred to me that I may not tread the boards again, my wildcat, yet must I earn my keep." Magda released him from her embrace and sat down on the chair across from his to listen.

"Denver is a young place, Magda, full of exuberance and energy . . . and no wisdom whatsoever. I have begun to write observations, commentaries if you will. And the perspicacious editors of the august *Rocky Mountain News* have this very day shown the good taste to buy three of them." He was elated as a child and attempting to appear calm.

"You are magnificent! And the men at the Rocky Mountain newspaper are brilliant to recognize such genius." The relief of it made Magda feel light-headed—she looked at Fancy and saw her grinning. The Gypsy had watched Jarvis chew on the knowledge of his infirmity, brooding, all through the endless months of recovery. Nearly two years had gone by while she and the dwarf struggled to support the entourage.

Gitalis had finally settled for the vaudeville job that paid the bills, while Magda established a reputation among the wealthy matrons of Denver. Table rappings and seances had become popular as parlor games among the rich, and Magda's presence had added flavor to enough gatherings so that she too had been able to swell the coffers. Only Wes had not found employment.

Magda could see her own relief mirrored in the dwarf's eyes. "We will celebrate," she said, rising. "Fancy, we must prepare a feast worthy of such a triumph." Fancy put aside her work and rose from the rocking chair with the clumsiness of late pregnancy.

Magda glanced at Gitalis and saw the smile of satisfaction curve his lips. "And they say miracles are past," he murmured, preceding her and Fancy into the kitchen. " 'The man shall have his mare again, and all shall be well.' "

Magda turned toward the dwarf and spoke quietly. "You have been a good friend to him, Gitalis. And to me, in time of trouble. I am grateful and will not forget."

Gitalis looked startled by the compliment, but said nothing.

"I'm of a mind to cook your favorite meal tonight," Magda told him.

" 'O day and night,' " he replied, " 'but this is wondrous strange!' "

Magda, her face turned away from him, smiled. The energy generated by their animosity had been useful through the years. What energy might be produced by friendship?

 41   Fancy's time drew near and Magda worried about the isolation of the cabin. This would be a winter baby and snow could make movement nearly impossible in an emergency. Their cabin was five miles outside the city and dirt cheap because of that, but five miles in a Colorado winter could be infinity.

The child was ill placed and the pregnancy had drained Fancy's strength. No one who saw her at this moment—dark circles beneath her eyes, swollen ankles, waiflike thinness, except for the huge belly that proclaimed a life of its own—would guess at her former beauty. Even her hair had lost its luster and her eyes were full of sorrow and longing.

Fancy seldom spoke of Chance, but Magda knew he possessed the girl's thoughts night and day. Like a spar in a hostile sea, she clung to the memory of the brief happiness they'd shared. Chance was, Magda suspected, not so much a man as an embodiment of the girl's own longings. What man of flesh and blood and bone could measure up to such a need? Even if he loved and married her, how could any mortal not be doomed to failure by the standards Fancy's fantasy had set?

There was a wealthy woman in Denver for whom Magda did readings; she was due for another—the woman's money could pay for a medical doctor's opinion, in the city. Magda set little store by doctors; she knew as much as they did of medicaments. Nonetheless, Fancy should have every possible opportunity for this birth to go well—if a doctor with a diploma on the wall could ease the girl's mind even a trifle, the trip would be worth the effort. Besides, Fancy had barely left the cabin since winter had set in; a sleigh ride down the mountainside, snugly bundled against the chill air, might put roses back in the girl's wan cheeks. The Colorado countryside was never more beautiful than when it glistened in its snowy garments.

Wes heartily concurred, as did Gitalis, who had been brooding for weeks over Fancy's malaise. Neither his antics nor his massages had roused her from her deepening depression, and he knew that self-pity was itself a disease that could cause a person to waste away.

"We'll accompany you to town, my Magda," Jarvis told the Gypsy when she broached the plan. "I have three new columns to present to the august editors of Denver, and Gitalis has his tickets to cast before swine. We'll make a day of it."

Fancy watched the preparations for the trip with a heavy heart; the snow brought with it such bittersweet memories. Little more than a year ago she'd laughed and sung and danced away Christmas Eve in the company of those she loved . . . where were they now? Did Chance ever stop for a moment to remember her, as she did him? Did he sometimes hear a sound, or catch a glimpse of some elusive shape just out of focus, and think that he had seen her, as she looked for him in every passing shadow? And what if they were to meet? What could she tell him of this child who grew beneath her heart?

She fantasized sometimes that one day, she and Aurora would be walking down the street and Chance would see them. In that one moment, all that he'd lost would crash in on him and she would have her revenge for what she'd suffered alone. Sometimes in the fantasy, Aurora was a child, sometimes she was a woman, but always the recognition was instantaneous and the vengeance was the same.

"Then why not tell him now, *cara mia*?" Gitalis had asked when she'd described to him the imagined scenario. "Why not let him come to you and help you with your burdens?"

"No! That isn't what I want, Gitalis. When that day comes, I must be rich and famous and Aurora must be accomplished and beautiful."

"But why, Fancy? So this Chance of yours can eat his own heart out at what he has lost?" he'd asked, disturbed at the passionate love and hatred beneath the words.

But she'd never answered the question, and had turned again inside herself to the place where her sorrow dwelled.

▲

Fancy and Magda stood on the street corner outside the doctor's office and waited for Jarvis. The examination had been brief; the man had told them nothing more than that he concurred with Magda's assessment of the child's breech position. Fancy must be in the lying-in hospital, he said. By no means should she give birth at home, for surgery might be called for if the baby remained ill placed. Magda thought the most therapeutic part of the entire visit had been Fancy's outburst of temper at the man. "Magda will deliver my baby," she told him emphatically. "And without surgery."

Frost clouds puffed about their reddened faces as the two women breathed the frigid air of Denver. There was snow in the slate-colored sky by the time Wes collected them outside the doctor's office.

"Gitalis has tickets to the burlesque for us all," he told the women, in high spirits at having sold two of his three articles. "Would it not cheer you to stay in Denver tonight and celebrate, my Magda? Gitalis and I could sleep at the theatre overnight, and we could surely find a boardinghouse that would provide you ladies snug harbor." Both Magda and Fancy could see his excitement at the prospect of being inside a theatre again.

"You stay, Wes," Fancy volunteered, looking to Magda for confirmation. "I'm afraid the doctor made me feel quite unwell and I think I need to be home in my own bed tonight."

"Stop here overnight with your little friend, Jarvis," Magda pronounced good-naturedly, "but not longer than tomorrow—I fear the weather gathers itself for a blizzard. If you and Gitalis can get home on horseback, then stay and play together. Fancy and I will take the sleigh."

Fancy saw a look of old understanding pass between them; even burlesque would bring with it the heady smell of greasepaint and scenery, of dust-laden theatre curtains and dirty plush seats, the roar of applause— ambrosia to an actor that can never be explained to one who hasn't tasted its seduction.

Magda mounted the sleigh, tucked the robes around Fancy, and took the double reins in her strong hands. What arcane power was it the Gypsy had over animals that they did her bidding, as if she were Mother Nature in disguise?

Fancy nestled back beneath the covers and closed her eyes. She'd wanted to see Denver and had felt invigorated by the trip to town, but now the elation was gone. In fact, she felt a strange new back pain, low and girdling, and a griping in her belly. She was glad Magda was heading the team out of town.

The first few flakes of snow were wet and insignificant, but within minutes they turned to driving sleet. Fancy hid her face from the stinging needles and tried to wish her increasing pain away.

Magda gritted her teeth against the weather that obscured her vision and fought for control of the sleigh. It was skittish as ice skates and she was unfamiliar with its idiosyncrasies; Jarvis had borrowed it from a local farmer, and he or Gitalis had always driven the sleigh on their infrequent outings.

A mournful howling brought Fancy's head out from under the covers. "Why do the wolves howl so?" she called to Magda, who sat hunched forward on the driver's seat. There were always wolf packs in the hills, sometimes in large numbers, but they kept to themselves and foraged on animals too winter-frail to elude the pack, or on rodents nosed from their snowy burrows. So familiar were their cries to Fancy's ears that it had taken her a while to realize there was something more urgent in the sounds she heard rising on the wind. The howlings seemed as if the beasts were communicating back and forth to each other in an escalating frenzy.

Magda muttered under her breath, "They speak of hunger—the winter has been hard and they have less to feed on than they need. They suffer gravely."

Fancy didn't ask how Magda knew. It wouldn't have surprised her to learn that Magda spoke the wolves' tongue; she was already certain Magda knew the language of the great cats, for she had often seen the woman when she was alone with Samarkand cease to command him as animal trainers do, and simply converse with him in low and purring tones, which he always answered.

"Would the wolves come after us?" Fancy asked, alarmed by the concern in Magda's voice.

"They would not wish to harm us, Fancy, but hunger is every creature's goad. They would kill us to save their own children."

They sped on over the snow, the only sounds the jingling bells and the creak of the old sleigh as it strained against the upward climb. The sleet changed to snow and a blanket of white soon obscured the trail. Fancy burrowed farther down into her nest of blankets and tried to quiet her fear.

A violent impact hurtled her forward and upward like a ragdoll. The sleigh teetered sideways, then crashed with a thunderous cracking sound. Fancy screamed as her body hurtled through the air, then crumpled into the drifted snow. The helpless horses shrieked as they were thrown to the ground. Magda, nearly buried by the upended cutter, cursed the gods in every language she knew. Ignoring her own injuries, the Gypsy struggled toward Fancy and, with great effort, pulled the injured girl to her feet.

They surveyed the damage; a great jagged rock that had lain across the snow-obscured trail had been their undoing. One runner of the Portland cutter was splintered, its iron reinforcement bent grotesquely.

The driving snow pelted the women's faces and numbed their hands as they strove to free the struggling horses and pull them to their feet. Pain gripped Fancy's belly and forced her to stand upright for a moment—the spasm was dizzying and she nearly fell. She fought hard for control, for she knew that all Magda's efforts must be bent on righting the sleigh and saving the pain-crazed animals.

In vain, the Gypsy tried to push the cutter to an upright position, while Fancy fought to still the terrified beasts, shivering in the whipping wind, her feet near frozen by the soaking ice beneath. Magda didn't try to shout against the storm but saved her strength for the struggle. The sky had darkened, although it was barely dusk, and the sound of the wolves drew nearer. A chorus of howls brought both women's gaze up sharply to the horizon. On foot, they were easy prey.

On the far mountain behind them, a huge wolf pack stood rigid in the wind. A giant gray shape lifted its head toward heaven and loosed one long, eerie cry.

"The leader," Magda said, straightening to listen attentively. "He knows we are in distress." She ceased to grapple with the broken sleigh.

"Can you ride, child?" she asked urgently. Fancy, not in the least sure she could, nodded yes. Magda pulled a knife from her belt sheath, stripped the half-mad horses from their double harness, and clinging to their bridles with all her strength, she split the reins, so each could be ridden separately. The animals had no saddles, so she led the better horse to the side of the wreck, to enable Fancy to mount; it took every ounce of concentration to force the horse to her will. A groan escaped the girl despite her determination to be brave for Magda's sake; a line of sweat broke out on her forehead and she thought she might faint from the agony in her loins. Steeling herself against the shocking pain that ripped her when she tried to get her leg over the horse's back, Fancy forced herself to do it.

"The baby comes?" Magda asked. Fancy nodded and tried to keep from fainting. Magda took a deep breath, as if assessing the best way to help her.

"The wolves come, too," she said without pity. "Do you understand?" The wet wind whipped Magda's black hair out behind her.

Fancy gulped back pain and fear, and nodded resolutely.

Magda mounted the second horse like a Magyar chieftain, looped the remaining thong of leather through the throatlatch of Fancy's horse so she could lead both beasts if the girl fainted or dropped the reins.

"Our lives depend upon our horsemanship. Connect your spirit to your mount's, or you die!" She slapped Fancy's animal with her reins, then kicked her own into motion and started up the trail.

Fancy looked back over her shoulder and saw the wolf pack lope into motion behind them.

"How many are there?" she gasped to Magda.

"Enough!"

Magda leaned close to her horse's ear, talking to it intently, pushing it forward by force of will—the answering whinny sounded wild and dangerously high-strung. Fancy clung to the mane with intense concentration. She had ridden bareback since childhood—if only her leg muscles were in better shape, if her balance were normal, if her belly didn't spasm, twist, and burn, she could have sat the horse despite the storm—now she clung on doggedly and prayed for courage.

Fancy felt something burst free between her legs and hot wet liquid dribbled down her thighs to the horse's laboring flanks. "My God! Magda," she cried. "My water . . ."

But Magda was leaning low over the horse's neck whispering urgently into his ears, and Fancy couldn't tell if she'd heard the words above the deafening storm.

The gray-black wolf shadows were gaining ground, but the cabin was less than half a mile away. Fancy clamped her legs around the horse's flank and prayed with all her heart for deliverance.

▲ ▲ ▲

Fancy lay exhausted and sweat-soaked on the bed inside the house. The fire Magda had started in the hearth was blazing, but the girl felt no warmth from it; the ride through the storm had sapped whatever reserves she'd had to draw on and she was cold as ice.

Magda placed her hands on either side of Fancy's belly and held firm until the contraction subsided. The child lay sideways in the womb, the worst of all possible positions. She must not communicate her fear to Fancy, so Magda forced herself to smile.

"First babies are notoriously thoughtless," she said briskly to cover her own anxiety, for Fancy's labor was becoming rapidly more intense. Too intense for the safe delivery of a breech. . . .

The wolf leader cried somewhere outside the cabin and a chorus of answering howls raised the hairs on Magda's arms. She liked wolves—the wolf deva had once been her ally—but tonight they were nothing but hungry predators. If they were starving, the pack would be gathering courage for an assault. Magda glanced uneasily at the size of the small windows to gauge the danger of intrusion. In Romania it was not unheard of for the brutes to crash through doors or windows to molest a family; how she wished Jarvis and Gitalis were with them, if only for moral support.

Fancy moaned softly as the next contraction tensed her belly and arched her back. The girl was so narrow in the hips, so tiny overall, not built for breeding. *Damn the fool who had gotten her into this fix!* Magda set about preparing the small room as best she could for what would come and sent a silent entreaty to Wes and Gitalis to beware the wolves. It would not be the first time that a message from her had reached Jarvis telepathically.

She set out what herbs she had and a pile of clean cloths; she hung a cauldron of water on to boil and placed the blankets Fancy had knitted in the small cradle Gitalis had built. It was an act of affirmation that before morning a living child would occupy its own bed. Magda undressed Fancy with gentle hands and covered her with the ancient patchwork quilt she herself had made as a child. She folded the cover tenderly around the suffering girl and thought how long a road she herself had traveled since plying those childish stitches and dreaming of greatness.

Sweat soaked Fancy's hair into flattened ringlets and pain tinted circles beneath her eyes, so that when she dozed, exhausted between pains, she looked corpselike. Magda made the sign against evil at the thought, and breathed deeply to force herself to calm. The baby would have to be turned before morning, that was certain.

She tied an apron around herself with a resolute sigh, wound her braided hair atop her head and covered it with a clean kerchief, rolled up the sleeves of her dress, and began to scrub her hands in the bowl of soapy water she had placed on the counter. Those fools of doctors delivered babies with hands filthy from surgery or autopsy; no wonder so many died of puerperal fever. No midwife worth her hire would make the same mistake. She looked at her own hands in the firelight; they were large and strong, too large for the task at hand. If only the dwarf were here. . . .

Magda stared at the boiling kettle for a moment, considering which of the herbs she'd brought would have most efficacy. Had the birth been progressing normally, she could easily have hurried the labor, but that wouldn't do until she'd turned the child from its unnatural position. She selected an herb that would dull the pain without stopping the contractions, and another to impart strength. That she would take herself.

Fancy whimpered again and struggled as the spasm convulsed her. "Help me, Magda," she whispered hoarsely. "Please help me!" Fancy moved her lips and writhed as the next wave hit. Her mouth was bruised and swollen from biting her lips to keep from crying out. Her hands twisted the covers as each new wave of pain engulfed her.

Magda hardened her heart against the hurt she must inflict and turned Fancy onto her side; she probed the rock-hard belly for the baby's head and feet, then gently but firmly pushed to manipulate the child into a head-downward position. Fancy groaned with the pain of it, and Magda waited for the contraction to pass to try again and again. But the baby clung to its transverse placement and Magda, despairing, ceased her efforts.

The wolf pack howled again, this time considerably closer—Magda moved to the window. She swirled away the frost from the pane and was shocked to see a huge number of ghostly presences circling the small house. The wolves must be starved indeed to venture so near a dwelling.

"Sweet Jesus, not now!" she said aloud, as if admonishing a recalcitrant child. Then she took the strained herbal brew from the pot at the hearth and tried to spoon some into Fancy's mouth.

Fancy meant to cooperate, but her agony made concentration impossible. She looked up with fever-wild eyes that begged for mercy. Her lower back was being torn by an agony that sent shooting daggers into her loins to meet the spasms that clutched her belly. It was impossible to have such pain and think, to have such pain and live. The whole world had turned red with it; her belly extended from her brain to her feet; there was nothing left of her but the baby and the impossible, unrelenting torture. Every trace of beauty was gone from her swollen face, her cracked lips opened and closed, gasping for breath. She moaned with the same relentless rhythm as the wind.

Magda knotted towels, tied them to the footboard of the bed, and placed the ends in Fancy's hands for leverage. The pains were coming faster now.

"Scream, Fancy!" Magda commanded her. "You must shriek your head off if that will help you." But Fancy shook her head wildly and strangled the sound. Her cries are like the baby, Magda thought, tears running down her own face at the girl's suffering; they try to free themselves but are trapped inside.

She would attempt again to turn the baby from the outside—if she could not, there would soon be no choice but one . . . to reach inside the womb itself and pull the head toward safety. But the danger . . . Magda forced her own heart to stillness. One child in a thousand delivered under such conditions would live. And the mother could be torn to shreds and bleed to death in anguish, or could survive the first ordeal only to die of fever from infection. She could survive both, and go mad from the pain and the indignity of having a child torn from her body against nature's will.

Fancy drifted on clouds of fire, even Magda's hands caused anguish now.

She would willingly have died if it would end the pain. She chewed her lips to bleeding, and tore at the towels until the bed groaned with the strain. Her mind drifted in and out of reality. Once she even saw Chance standing at the foot of the bed and she begged him to hold her, but he dissolved before the onslaught of another contraction and Hart took his place.

She felt Magda smooth the matted hair from her forehead and croon strange words into her ear, but nothing mattered anymore. She thought she heard herself scream, but she had fought so long not to that she wasn't certain.

Magda pulled the purifying tincture from her bag and prepared to try to turn the child. Fancy's strength was ebbing fast; it was increasingly obvious that if the baby couldn't escape the body that entrapped it soon, both would die. Why in God's name were the other two not here with her! They could hold the girl at least in loving arms—without them there would be no choice but to tie her to the bed against the torture she must endure. Curse the storm! Curse the wolves! Curse the fool who made her pregnant and hadn't the wit even to know!

The howling outside ceased abruptly—only the wind keened, as if alive. The silence was far more ominous than the sound had been and Magda knew in her soul that the wolves were coming. Soundless paw pads in the snow . . . Every sense alert, hair standing out on arms and neck, Magda whirled to face invasion just as the window splintered and a hurtling gray body crashed past her into the cabin. The leader stood poised to spring, his eyes glowing red as the fire coals, his fangs bared for battle.

Fancy, on the bed, opened wild unbelieving eyes. The wolf-leader crouched to pounce and Magda seemed to grow in stature before Fancy's incredulous gaze. The Gypsy's arms were raised above her head in some ritual too primeval to name; a guttural sound escaped Magda's throat, a growl, a moan, a she-wolf howl so piercing that the crouching animal slicked back its ears and whimpered, its own growl dying on back-turned lips.

Magda's wolf cry crescendoed, then died slowly in her throat and a weird chanting replaced it. Her upraised arms crackled with a rainbow fire that riveted the wolf's gaze. Slowly, deliberately, Magda lowered her arm to her side as her chant grew louder; she pointed her glowing index finger at the cringing beast and he began to whimper. The wolves outside the cabin cried, yelped, howled for their leader, but the leader could no longer control his body or his brain.

Magda spoke again, her voice so commanding it seemed to fill the cabin and the mountain and the world. Fancy saw the power that emanated from Magda's body, a crackling glow that made her seem twice her normal size. She ordered him, and the wolf rose trembling from its crouch, subdued, whimpering pitifully as a beaten dog—then, as if released from a spell, it turned and leapt again through the window to the pack beyond.

This isn't happening! I'm delirious. I'm dying. Fancy's mind whirled. Wolves are not turned back by humans . . . Magda cannot change her shape, cannot glow with iridescent colors. No! This is all madness from the pain. Another contraction dragged Fancy's mind away from the mystery of Magda's magic. She shrieked aloud in wildest terror, as if the hallucination of the wolf had finally broken all control.

"Dying, Magda," she whispered. "We're dying. . . ."

Magda drew near the bed and stood like a stone sentinel. She centered her breathing . . . left nostril to empower rationality, right to free her intuition. Calm. She must be very, very calm and strong for Fancy's sake. Two lives hung in the balance; if she lost her courage, she would forfeit them both.

Breathe deeply, Magda. Breathe from all the seven centers of Universal Energy. Feel the colors of the chakras enliven you. Trust the Old Knowledge of a thousand lifetimes that you carry in every cell. She touched the crystal amulet around her neck, and entered the silence of her own soul.

The acrid smell of whatever Magda had bathed her hands in made Fancy want to retch, but she was beyond even that. She felt her hands being tied behind her head to the bedboard. No! Magda would never do such a thing to her! She felt her legs pulled apart and something thrust into her most intimate parts. Sweet Jesus, what was happening? Something so much worse than all before it that it had no words. Magda's hand was burrowing inside her, pulling, probing, tearing something primal from her. Fancy shrieked for mercy. She wrenched herself away from the terrible invasion, the betrayal . . .

"The head, Fancy!" Magda screamed above her cries. "Courage, child! The head is through. Push for all you're worth!"

A great slithering something passed through Fancy into the world. She heard a shout of triumph from Magda, then the tiny angry voice of protest from a living throat.

"A daughter, Fancy! You have a daughter!"

Magda held a bloodied rag doll that moved of its own accord. Fancy saw the Gypsy wipe its eyes and siphon something from its tiny nose, then swaddle it in a scrap of cloth and lay it wriggling on her breast.

A daughter. If only she had the strength to care, Fancy thought through the stupor of exhaustion. She would truly love to have a daughter. . . .

Fancy and Magda sat on the billowing grass, the baby lay on a square of blanket between them. Aurora had grown well, considering her brutal entry into life; the beautiful child gurgled contentedly in the soft spring sunshine.

"The devas are playful today," Magda said absently, fondling the newborn grass beside her skirt. "How they love the spring."

"And what exactly are devas that they should be so merry?"

"They are the Shining Ones, child. A Sanskrit word. You would call them angels. The Indians know them—this is why they give thanks when they borrow from nature."

"Do people have angels, too, Magda? Do I have an angel?"

Magda laughed aloud.

"You, child? Of all humans, how could you doubt your celestial guardian? I assure you that your particular angel works harder than most."

"Now you're teasing me."

"Only a little," Magda replied. "The time has come for you to go, has it not?" She asked the question carefully. Fancy nodded.

"I'm going to try the stage, Magda. I can't go back to Oro—not yet. I'll write Jewel to tell her. Wes says New York's the place for me. I still have some money from the auction, the part I left with Jewel. I think there's enough for a train ticket and a boardinghouse, at least for a while. I'll try to find someone to care for Aurora while I work. . . ."

The Gypsy nodded. Fancy was still young enough to believe everything possible.

"Show me your hand," she commanded, and Fancy held out her palm to Magda.

"When the road is steep and the path obscure, remember this: There are no excuses for anything, Fancy . . . we change things or we do not. Excuses rob you of power and weaken your resolve. All is justice in the universe. If your ambition is immense, so are the obstacles you must overcome to achieve it. But you may find that what you want, and what you need for happiness, are two entirely different matters."

Fancy frowned, unsatisfied by Magda's words. "There's so much I don't know yet, Magda. Sometimes I'm afraid."

Magda looked thoughtful for a moment. "Remove your clothes, child, and I will teach you something you should know," she said suddenly.

"Why do I have to take off my clothes?"

"Do you know nothing of obedience, Fancy? A practitioner of metaphysical disciplines must comply with her teacher's instruction, not ask questions!"

"Is metaphysics another name for magic, Magda?"

"No, no, not at all," the Gypsy replied, amused. "Metaphysics is merely the study of Universal Law . . . of God and Goddess, if you will, and the way in which this, and all the other unseen worlds, function. Magic is a willful act that uses Universal Law to accomplish some human end. You are too willful already, you need no more temptations of that sort."

Fancy laughed. "But you are teaching me some things that most of the world doesn't know."

"I teach you what is useful, and will prove to you there is more to life than what your physical senses perceive. I would never teach you magic."

Fancy pulled her shirt off over her head and let her skirt drop to the ground, so she was clad only in her shimmy.

"Lie down," Magda instructed, and Fancy complied. She saw that the Gypsy had a pouch full of glittering crystals that she was emptying onto the lap of her skirt.

"There is no point in *telling* you about the power of the crystals, Fancy. You must *feel* the energy yourself, or you will doubt."

Fancy lay back in the sunlight; the clear, sweet air raised goose bumps on her body.

"Pay heed to what I say, child. It will be hard to concentrate, once the power of the stones is on you."

Magda took several deep breaths to center her consciousness. "We do not merely breathe air, Fancy, we exchange energy with the universe. There are seven great exchange points on your body, through which you receive energy from the vast universal ebb and flow around you. They are called chakras."

Magda laid a blood-red stone on Fancy's pubic bone. "This is your root chakra, mark it well. The root defines your material form . . . in your case, it seems to work conscientiously, for you are beautiful. This root controls the physical part of your sexuality. Its color is the red of blood, and of the earth. If it becomes blocked by injury or wrong thinking, you will lose your power to give or receive pleasure." She laid four small crystal points around the red stone, and Fancy felt a curious swirling tingle, as if a path had been opened through her body and a cool breeze blew through it. Magda moved her concentration up to an inch and a half below Fancy's navel, and laid a bright orange citrine there, to glitter in the sun.

"Your belly chakra vibrates to a bright orange frequency, child. This is the seat of all your creativity, and your ability to generate life, Fancy. If it falters, you will be barren in mind and in body." She surrounded the citrine with a circlet of soft orange stones that Fancy thought might be amber;

again, the whoosh of cooling air ran through the girl's body, making her feel transparent. Magda moved her hand to a place at Fancy's waist.

"Your solar plexus is the seat of your belief systems—all you *think* you know of reality. It is the place where your ideas are stored. Its brilliant yellow energy has the capacity to transmute realities." Magda stopped, senses alert. "There is a blockage here."

"What does that mean?" Fancy asked, raising her head in curiosity. Magda pushed her down again.

"Breathe deeply, child! Breathe in through your solar plexus . . . *think* yourself into your body's consciousness. . . ."

Fancy felt two crystals laid upon her eyelids and breathed as she'd been told, feeling stranger with each breath.

"Oh, Magda," she whispered. "I'm seeing the oddest visions in my head."

"What do you see?"

"A dusty storeroom . . . filled with boxes that have been sealed and resealed, endlessly. There's a door that's boarded over, and I'm standing with my arms pressed against it, frantically trying to keep the door closed."

"And what is behind the door, child? Tell me!"

"Memories, Magda . . . terrible memories that must never, ever come out of their hiding place!" The vision shocked her and surprising tears ran down her cheeks.

"You have blocked the energy of this chakra, child, to protect yourself. You've stored your sorrows in those boxes, and you've blocked your own life flow. If you persist, the organs around this center will wither and you will become ill."

"What can I do?"

"Let the memories go, Fancy. Open the door and the boxes, place the sorrows in the sunlight . . . sweep the shadows out of your world. The crystal's energy will help you free yourself."

Magda held a wand of clear quartz in her hand; she passed it clockwise over the girl's solar plexus and waited. A vortex of energy whirled around Fancy. The door blew open and the boxes shattered against the walls of her vision. Ghost-shapes fled the boxes, sucked up by the whirling tornado— when the winds subsided she saw herself standing alone in the sunlight. "Are my memories gone now, Magda?" she asked, stricken.

"Only the shadow forms . . . the memories remain. It is quite possible that in your ignorance, you will re-create these thought forms, for they are at least familiar."

Magda laid a large green emerald between Fancy's breasts, with six small rose quartz points around it.

"Breathe the green of the emerald into your heart chakra, Fancy, and tell me what you see."

"I can't."

"You can. You must! What do you see?"

Fancy's face contorted. "It's torn in half . . . my heart is broken on the floor like a child's toy. I snatch it up and try to glue it back together, but I'm crying too hard and I can't see what I'm doing."

Magda's voice was a command. "Focus green light on the broken heart, Fancy. Surround yourself in the healing green light and watch the mending restore your heart."

The sobs that had shaken Fancy subsided and she found that the vision had changed to a tranquil pastoral scene. Green grass stretched endlessly to the horizon, she and her ravaged heart were nowhere to be found.

"The heart is the center of your entire energy system, Fancy, the transformer of your spirit. All chakras below it have to do with matter, all above, with spirit. You must find the balance between the two in order to know happiness.

"Imbalance causes illness . . . stricture causes illness . . . fear causes illness. Balance is the reward of our learning process, the prize we must seek for wellness. If we were truly in balance, we would never die, never age, never suffer illness . . . but neither would we be human, or learn humanity's lessons."

Magda placed a cool blue-lace agate on Fancy's throat and the girl saw herself on a lavish theatre stage singing the final notes of a poignant love ballad. The audience seemed overcome with emotion, dabbing at their eyes and struggling for control. The heightened state of consciousness let Fancy see clearly the power she had over them, the magnitude of her sorrows were the secret of her success.

"They love me, Magda," she whispered. "They feel my sadness and they cry with me."

"You will transmute your suffering into art and the audience will hear the truth in your voice. Karma, Fancy! The throat is the seat of your life's gift, your soul's purpose. Tread carefully on the freedoms it provides you . . . all your challenges reside there."

Magda placed a midnight-blue azurite between Fancy's brows.

"I see swirling colors in a midnight sky . . . I don't know what they mean."

"You are seeing with your Third Eye, Fancy . . . the eye of the spirit. Never doubt that there is more to the universe than what your physical eyes can see. Today, you have looked on Infinity."

She placed a final clear quartz cluster at the crown of Fancy's head and a flood of cool, unearthly sunlight washed through her, so powerful she could barely hear Magda's reverent words.

"The crown is the place of transformation. When you die, your soul will exit through this doorway, taking with it the seed atoms of your being. For now, breathe in the Light of God and Goddess through this portal . . . breathe deeply of the Universal Life-force that it may strengthen you for your journey."

The stones were lifted one by one from Fancy's body and the energy subsided until she was only herself again.

"What happened to me, Magda? I've never felt anything like it." She was giddy and exhilarated; there was an unbearable ache in returning to the mundane.

"Man's soul is like a tidal pool, child . . . connected to the sea by a submerged channel. To the casual observer it appears landlocked, yet the water rises and falls with the universal currents. Your soul is connected to the world soul; your energy to the Universal Energy; thus do we all rise and fall with the cosmic tides, even those who never know such tides exist."

"Could you heal any ailment with these crystals, Magda? Even the hopeless ones?"

"Crystals are merely energy generators, Fancy. Each different stone supplements the energy of the human it contacts in a special way. There is no magic to it, only an enhancement of life-force. Crystals can help open a chakra to reveal the problems hidden there . . . but then the true 'healing' rests in the hands of the seeker. What will he do with the new knowledge of his own ailment? Will he believe what he has seen, and modify his life? Will he let go of the fear that constricts, or the greed that imbalances, or the lust that endangers? Will he pay the price of health, which is unflinching self-knowledge? Will he choose to live in harmony with Universal Law? Or will he blunder on just as before?"

Fancy shook her head. "What else can the crystals do?" She tried very hard to reattach herself to reality, but her sense of that had been altered and she felt disoriented.

"Some crystals are star seed, Fancy. They were programmed with information only the Initiate can read. Some were programmed by the high priests in Atlantis, before the last inundation, so that all arcane knowledge would not be lost. The same priests placed this knowledge in the brains of dolphins, too, but it cannot yet be retrieved, except by skilled shamans. Some crystals were programmed on far distant stars."

"How do you read the future in your crystal ball?" Fancy's voice was hushed; she could no longer disbelieve.

"That is a complex matter, child, even I do not know precisely how it empowers me," she said. "The crystal is a focusing point for the clairvoyance of the mind . . . but it is something more. A doorway through the Crack Between the Worlds, where all realities meet, all time, all space. The power of the scrying crystal is sacred—were I to misuse it, not even the

Goddess could save me from my doom. And, too, the crystal ball I carry with me has been used by priestesses down the corridors of time, since the Dawning. It vibrates to their energy as well as mine, and thus it amplifies my powers. When I die, a priestess will be sent to retrieve it."

Fancy sat up, blinking in the sun, and Magda watched her nearly naked body, perfect as only youth is perfect, full-breasted, narrow of waist, flat-bellied, and long-limbed, all in exquisite proportion to her size.

"You will need no magic to bind a man to you, Fancy," she said solemnly, "the Goddess has given you other enchantments." Then she rose from her kneeling place and hooked the bag of crystals onto her belt again. "Come. I must cleanse the crystals now."

"How do you do that, Magda?" Fancy asked, tugging on her shirt. "How do you bind a man so he desires only you?"

"Foolish girl! Would you repeat Magda's stupidity and pay the same price?"

Fancy put her hand on Magda's arm. "I want to know, Magda. I really want to know."

Magda's eyes flashed malevolently. "I am not ready to give you the gift of the sword that could cut your throat. And you are not ready to receive it." She turned and strode off down the hillside and Fancy, feeling stronger than she had in months, watched her go.

43 Fancy had kept in touch with Jewel, throughout her pregnancy; she felt kinship for the woman who'd saved her life. She'd decided to write her of the decision she'd made, and hoped Jewel would understand.

Dear Jewel,

I have a baby daughter—she is so beautiful I sometimes think she can't be real. Her hair is black as a raven's wing and her eyes the most gorgeous blue-violet you've ever seen. She looks entirely too exquisite for this imperfect world.

She has changed me, I think, into a woman. I feel unselfish as I never have before and find myself wanting things, not simply for ambition's sake, or because I feel I deserve them, but in order to make a life for my child—to keep her safe, as I never was myself. Now I can fully understand how much you love Dakota.

I have decided not to return to Oro just yet, but to head for New York City to try my hand on the stage—so I'm afraid I'll need the money I left in your keeping. I hope you'll forgive me and understand that I must try to make something of myself—I don't want to grow old wondering if I might have won the pot of gold at the end of the rainbow, if only I'd tried harder and made the right sacrifices. Does that make any sense to you?

I want you to know that I haven't forgotten the notion of starting a theatre in the Crown, so after I've learned my trade, I may be back on your doorstep. Meanwhile, I'll try to keep in touch. I'm excited at the prospect of finally being on my own and scared to death too—I'll let you know how New York treats me and my precious Aurora.

Give my love to the girls and to Bandana when you see him. Tell him I miss him more than I can say.

Your loving friend,
Fancy

Jewel put down the letter, a thoughtful expression on her face. The only person she'd ever met with black hair and violet eyes was Chance McAllister. My, my, my! So *that* was why Bandana had bid so high at the auction. She wondered if he knew about the baby or if she should tell him. Probably not . . . Fancy's secret was her own business. She shook her head and walked toward the bar where Rufus stood guard over the money she would send today.

Jewel knew as she did so that she had not seen the last of Fancy Deverell.

▲

Magda stood quietly in the doorway of the tiny room, watching Fancy. She moved stealthily as one of her great cats, and frequently surprised the girl with her presence.

"Fancy," she said softly. "I have decided to give you the gift of strengthening before you go. Come . . . we will go outdoors and I will show you."

Fancy followed, grateful for the respite from packing. Magda planted her feet wide and bent her knees slightly; she looked like an athlete in training.

"Do as I do," she commanded. "Remove your shoes and ground yourself by greeting the earth barefoot.

"Straighten your spine and drop your hips . . . let the flesh and muscle hang gently from your bones . . . draw energy from the earth below and from the sky above as if you were a tree . . . center this energy in your spine."

Fancy attempted to emulate Magda's stance.

As she had with the crystals, Magda directed Fancy's concentration up the body, chakra by chakra, color by color. An electrifying energy swirled through the girl, enlivening every cell. Her arms began to tingle and swell, as if all the heightened energy was collecting there.

"My hands, Magda. My hands are on fire!"

"Wonderful, Fancy! Bravo. The power is collecting in your hands . . . you could use it to heal. Were you to touch someone now, he would be filled with your energy."

"My God, Magda! I've never felt anything remotely like this . . . it's a kind of ecstasy."

They began the walk back to the cabin and Fancy had to restrain the urge to run, leap, frolic; she felt free in an unaccustomed way.

"Magda, you are absolutely incredible! You know everything . . . more than everything. Oh, Magda, tell me how to bind a man. I want to know what you know."

"You are drunk on unaccustomed energy, you ninny. You have touched the life flow, that is all. Now you think your wings are grown great enough to fly! You are a baby girl, first learn to walk." She laughed as she left Fancy to finish her packing, but the girl was so filled with rapture that nothing could mar the day.

▲

Gitalis and Wes were silent in their sorrow, Magda hid hers in movement. Tomorrow Fancy would go, and the baby with her. The little cabin that had rung with their laughter and tears would be still again. Magda had been brooding through the night . . . what had she left undone, untaught, unprepared? The rock-strewn path of Fancy's life had spread before her in her dreams, and she had awakened sick with anxiety. What a curse it was to know so much.

She threw back the covers and arose. She pulled the ancient grimoire from its Chinese chest, and thumbed the pages of the magical book of spells nervously, for what she sought. *The Binding Spell.* Anguish flooded over her, unleashed by those potent words. . . . Fancy had begged again to be taught, but how could the girl withstand the temptation of the snaring spell, if she herself had been undone by it?

> In the west I stand,
> at the Hierophant's station.
> By the virtues of the Cup,
> I seek the aid of the Elder Ones.
> Lend me Thine hand, ye Great Ones
> beyond and behind my being . . .

The words and their intonation reverberated in her soul, thrusting her back into the abyss, sucking her down to her own doom.

This trap I set, this snare I lay
to bind his heart to me this day . . .

Tighten the magic girdle, circumambulate deosil to the west, place the object-link to the man upon the altar. The ritual lived in her, as it always had. She swayed with the memory thick as incense, seductive as sin itself.

You are my quarry,
You, the unwary . . .

Her head throbbed with the ancient music of the spheres . . .

Evohe! Evohe! Evohe!

Magda snapped the book shut. No! Fancy would be destroyed by knowing, Magda would not be the instrument. She yanked open the drawer and buried the grimoire under a mound of clothing. It was hidden knowledge that should damned well stay that way.

▲

Fancy looked about her nervously before she pulled the grimoire from the drawer. Her heart pounded as she opened the magical journal and she ceased to breathe. She'd known for years of the book, seen Magda pore over it, been forbidden ever to read it. . . .

The bold scrawl on the pages was Magda's; Fancy thought the spidery scratching must be Tatiana's. It looked ancient, mysterious, the pages smelled with the must of ages.

Nervously, Fancy copied down the binding spell . . . she hated doing it behind Magda's back but the idea of the spell had obsessed her ever since she'd heard it could be done.

If it was true . . . if you could truly influence a man to love you, or even to be captivated by you, perhaps you could use the same magic to seduce an impresario or an audience . . . or a man who was uncertain of his love for you. Hastily, Fancy scribbled down what she could understand. The old woman's scrawl was in a foreign tongue, but Magda seemed to have recopied it in English later on. She wrote furiously, glancing nervously out the window. Who knew how long they'd be away on their shopping mission?

What in heaven's name did *deosil* mean, or *widdershins*? What was the

"Opening Exercise of the Temple Rite" that was called for . . . it was easy enough to find the proper phase of the moon, as the instructions said to do, but there were other instructions that made no sense at all and half the Names of Power were unpronounceable.

Fancy thrust the book back into its cubby and pushed the drawer shut, relieved. Even if she never used the spell, or if it really had no magic, she was reassured by having it. Practical information had always appealed to her most of all.

▲

Magda sniffed the air of her room and let her senses snake out in all directions. The force-field has been disturbed—there was a ripple in the protective shield that warned of an intruder. She sighed. So Fancy had taken matters into her own hands. So be it. One cannot keep another from her destiny. Magda would not mention the deception unless Fancy did; if the girl asked for an explanation of the grimoire's instructions, she would teach her, but to do so Fancy would have to own up to the theft. How subtly the universe lets us weave our own noose. Magda shook her head at the stupidity of the girl's deception.

Without instruction Fancy could never work the spell properly anyway. There was nothing to do for now but let the whole incident pass by.

VI

HEADING TOWARD SUNRISE

▼ ▼ ▼ ▼ ▼ ▼

Fancy Goes East

"You better go armed against
the Philistines."

BANDANA MCBAIN

44 "Get them off the stage!" The jeers outshouted the theatre company's Hamlet. "Give us burlesque or give us our money back!" After the kidney-jostling ride in an overnight stagecoach, the derision of the audience was infuriating.

"Cretins!" Hamlet hissed under his breath to Ophelia. "We give them the Bard and all they want is slapstick."

"It's better than the apathy in the last town," Fancy murmured through clenched teeth. "At least we know they're alive out there."

Life since leaving Magda, Wes, and Gitalis had been a bitter, backbreaking experience. She'd found quickly enough that before an actress conquered Broadway, a great many other obstacles had to be mastered, most of them in backwaters like this one. Three years of hardship already separated her from Denver. Three years of the almost impossible task of motherhood, under the particular constraints the theatre imposed. Three years of rattrap hotels and hunger, of numbing cold in unheated railroad cars, of the hostility of boorish audiences like this one, who demanded burlesque instead of Shakespeare.

At least this repertory company meant steady work for thirty weeks, even if it also meant dragging from town to town, all over Christendom. The bad news was that each "jump" seemed to take her farther from her dream of New York; the good news was that the years of practice had made her a professional again. Shakespeare, variety, burlesque, music hall, comedy, tragedy . . . there wasn't any role she couldn't tackle now.

Having Aurora to provide for made life harder, but it also gave Fancy's ambition both impetus and sanction. No effort was too overwhelming, no sacrifice too great, no obstacle too impossible, because she strove not only for herself but for her daughter. Eventually the struggle, the ambition, would pay off, she told herself doggedly when life was its bleakest; when the right opportunity came along, she would have suffered more than enough to know how to grab hold of it with both hands.

Fancy sighed and tried to remember her next cue. When you performed a different play every other day, you sometimes found yourself substituting Lady Macbeth for Ophelia, not that it would matter to those farmers beyond the footlights.

▲

Fancy stared in loathing at the rapidly moving black spots on the gray sheet in the boardinghouse bedroom. Bedbugs! Roaming the sheets in frenzied squadrons. She yanked the little girl back from the bedside and crushed her dark head against her thigh to hide the sight.

"Bugs, Mommy," the words came through the muffling. "I hate bugs!"

"I hate them, too, darling," Fancy whispered. And I hate the cold and the hunger and the poverty, she thought savagely, but she couldn't frighten the child by saying any of that aloud.

"Make them give us another room, Mommy. Please!"

Fancy steadied herself to say no to her daughter—this room was all she could afford, maybe all there was in this fleabag town. And she was too exhausted to drag her trunk downstairs again, to look for another place to stay.

"Mommy will fix the bed, Aurora," she said, steady as she could. She picked up the bar of soap from the washstand and wet it into stickiness with the water in the bedside jug; she would do what the burlesque dancer in the last town had taught her. Taking a deep breath for courage, Fancy Deverell, of Beau Rivage, slammed the soap bar down onto the dirty sheet a dozen times in rapid tattoo to capture as many little black specks as possible so she and Aurora could find some fitful sleep before the light of morning.

▲

The nightmare sweated Fancy into wakefulness. Terror, stark and un-abated, filled the nooks between her bones. It was forever the same dream. Torn, ravaged. Images of rape and violence. Then the running. Until her breath was sucked from her lungs and her legs could carry her no more, and she would fall down screaming. Down, down to the Predatory Dark Thing that laughed as it pursued her. Down, down to that horrific place where there was no justice or even mercy. *Hell.* That's what it must be, she always thought, as she fought for breath and turned up the lights and changed her soaking nightclothes and peered into all the dark corners of the room to be absolutely certain it had been a dream.

When had the nightmare come to stay? After her mother's death, or with Atticus on the road, or after she'd been raped? Sometime, so long ago that the Predatory Dark Thing seemed always to have lurked there on the fringes of her sanity.

Aurora heard her mother scream herself awake and peered at her, con-fused and angry. Mothers were not supposed to be afraid of anything. Fancy tucked the little girl in with soothing words.

She pulled a dry nightgown on over her shaking body and got back into bed, avoiding the sweat-soaked sheets as best she could. She reached out for the lamp on the bedstand and turned down the flame to a tiny glow. But she didn't turn it out.

45

"Ever notice how we don't seem to talk about our dreams for the future since Fancy's gone, bro? Like we used to, I mean?" Chance asked, riding next to his brother up the gorge. The overgrown bracken to right and left, and the loose stones underfoot, made the passage with pack mules arduous.

"Ever notice how saddle sore you can get after three days riding like this?" Hart replied.

Chance laughed and Hart found it hard not to respond to his mirth for it always seemed as genuine and free as an act of nature.

"Why don't you like to talk about her, bro? We three had a lot of good times together."

"That we did." There weren't many weeks that went by when Hart didn't ache with remembrance of those times. Try as he would to forget, Fancy was always there inside him, tucked into some sacrosanct place that time did not erode.

"I've still got those dreams, you know, bro. There's a feeling inside me that I was meant for something special—rich and maybe famous, too. I never really felt like I'd been born in the right place. Even when I was a kid I was sure I was destined for fame and fortune." He glanced over at his brother to see if Hart understood.

"I still dream a few dreams, too, you know, Chance. In my fantasies I see myself as the greatest painter ever to render the West on canvas. I see my name as the one on everybody's lips when they think of Indians. But here I am with a string of pack mules, living on beans and sourdough. I seem to remember you telling me when we started prospecting, it would take two years at the most to get me to art school." Hart smiled good-naturedly. "Just how long ago was that, now?"

"Don't you worry, bro. We're both going places, you'll see. I'm never wrong when I get a hunch and I'm always lucky."

"You weren't so lucky last night in that poker game."

Chance winced a little, then chuckled. "That little bastard must have sold his soul to the devil for those last three aces—they had no business being where he could get his hands on them." Like all true gamblers, he was affable in losing as well as winning. "I got luckier later."

Hart had seen his brother leave the gaming tables with a girl named Jane, whose athletic prowess and enthusiasm for the male anatomy were legendary in the Gulch.

"You're lucky all right, lucky you can still ride a horse this morning."

Chance laughed outright. "You're just trying to distract me from my fantasies. But I'm feeling too full of piss and vinegar to be dissuaded today." He nudged his horse forward with a light touch of spur.

"You'll see, bro," he called to Hart over his shoulder as he pushed the horse into a heartier lope, for the ground had finally leveled. "I intend to have it all!"

It wasn't long after that they hit it big and Hart had reason to remember his brother's prophetic words.

 "I'm cold, Mommy," Aurora said hoarsely. Her throat sounded scratchy again, and Fancy reached automatically to feel her daughter's head. Then she pulled the little girl onto her lap and cradled her against the chill of the unheated railroad car. The train seats were agonizingly uncomfortable; Fancy tried to adjust her back to less of a cramp, but the child's added weight made it impossible. She sighed resolutely and patted Aurora's back, wrapping her with the folds of her own coat. Sleep would have to wait a little longer.

"Don't get sick, baby," she whispered, squeezing Aurora close. "I just don't know what I'll do if you get sick again."

"I'm cold, Mommy," the child repeated listlessly.

The train clickety-clicked in the endless, icy dark and Fancy stared hopelessly out the window. Pittsburgh, Cleveland, Philadelphia . . . and all those wretched nonentities in between. All those freezing trains by night, after an exhausting day of rehearsal, plus two performances, all those boardinghouse keepers she paid extra to mind Aurora while she worked—if she didn't get a break soon, she didn't know how much more either one of them could bear. The life of a prospector was no harder or less rewarding than the life of an actress. Christalmighty, by the time she made it big she'd have paid her dues in blood.

▲

"Miss Deverell's performance was honed in the provinces, and it shows," the review in Cincinnati said brutally. What the hell did the critic think Cincinnati was, if not provincial? Fancy's belly tightened, hurt and anger sizzled in her gut; she threw the newspaper into the basket. Criticism hurt, God damn it . . . it undermined creativity and put the skids to confidence. And what were critics anyway, but fringe people, living on other people's sweat and talent, hovering at the edges of an actor's soul, picking it to death

like carrion birds. If you can't fly, kill the ones who do. She glimpsed her face in the makeup mirror and saw there nothing but rage. That was good . . . more useful than hurt. She dabbed the last of the greasepaint onto her cheeks and headed out to face the audience. She'd just have to work harder, learn more, that was all.

Fancy tipped up her chin defiantly and decided not to hear the catcalls as she walked onstage. If you let an audience smell blood, they'd tear your heart out.

▲ ▲ ▲

I am so afraid, Fancy thought, staring out the boardinghouse window into the darkness, forlorn and weary. *What if this is all there ever is for us?* She glanced at the small sleeping Aurora in the swaybacked bed and rubbed her own arms against the bitter cold.

Nights were the worst times . . . fear grew fierce and vengeful in the dark. Hopelessness swelled and festered, nothing ever found its solution until morning streaked across the sky. But sometimes by then, a bone-chilling fear of the future had already undermined her. How do you go on believing in yourself when no one else does? There were actors with the repertory company who were in their sixties, still grateful for a few weeks steady work. She'd slit her wrists before she'd face a lifetime of this misery and degradation—she would make it big or die in the attempt, there could be no middle ground for Fancy.

She pushed the hunger down, down beneath her fear. There'd been money enough to pay for only one supper tonight, so she'd told Aurora she wasn't hungry enough to eat. Now the pangs of emptiness gnawed at her like an echo of all the other emptiness in her life.

Fancy took the tiny music box from its hiding place in her trunk and wound it up, letting the harplike music fill the empty dark with solace. She cried silently and softly, hugging the box to her breast, so as not to wake Aurora. After a very long time, she crept back into bed and fell into a troubled slumber.

▲

The theatre manager leered at the beautiful young actress behind his wet cigar and Fancy's stomach lurched. He never came near without brushing her breast or rump, putting his arm around her, his ugly breath close enough to nauseate. She pulled back hastily; she'd grown used to fending off men with more hands than brains.

"What're you saving it for, little lady?" Harvey laughed. "I'm as good as the likes of you can get."

"In your dreams, you troll!" she replied spitefully; this kind of living was beginning to fray her nerves and make her fight back. There was little room on the road for civility.

"I could help you if you'd just get off that high horse, Deverell. Make life nicer for you and that kid of yours, while you're here in town." Fancy snapped her head in his direction.

"I'm a married woman, Mr. Armstrong. That should be made apparent by the fact that I have both a child and a wedding ring."

"Rings can be bought at the corner store, and as for that little by-blow of yours—"

Fancy slapped his face with enough force to make her fingers numb.

"You bastard, don't you dare speak that way about my daughter . . . you're nothing but a petty tyrant, trading on your tiny speck of power to make everyone's life miserable." There were too many men like Harvey Armstrong in the theatre; it attracted them like flies to honey. She said a few other things too.

When Fancy finished the performance, a pink slip was in the envelope along with her pay. She dropped it onto the dressing table as if it were dirty, and tucked the needed money into the bosom of her corset. Armstrong could only keep her from performing for the two days she'd be in Chicago, then the company would move on and she would work again. This wasn't the first time she'd encountered the likes of him.

"Harvey's a mean son of a bitch, honey," Maisie called out as Fancy passed by her dressing room. The blowsy blonde always played ladies of easy virtue and Fancy suspected it was typecasting; she stuck her head out the door and caught hold of Fancy's arm. "You know, honey, it might be near time for you to stop bein' so uppity with these guys, just so life won't be so hard on you. This is the third time you've gotten docked because you wouldn't play footsie with some bum like Harvey. And you know it ain't gonna stop, Fancy. Men are men, rich or poor they all want the same thing from us. Maybe your life would get easier if you'd start puttin' out."

Fancy shook her head wearily. "I'd willingly starve before I'd consort with the likes of Harvey, by God I would, Maisie. But I'm sure as hell beginning to see why a woman needs a protector. You can bet your last dollar it wouldn't be worth my while to put out for anybody who couldn't do me a lot more good than that nobody!"

Maisie inclined her head for a closer look at Fancy; her untidy blond curls had dark roots, but she was a sweet person, beneath the warpaint. She'd baby-sat with Aurora on more than one occasion.

"You're probably right about that, doll. It's too late for me by now, I'm used merchandise, but you still look brand-new. With a little help from somebody rich and powerful, you might just be able to make the big time."

"I think I've got to do it soon, Maisie," Fancy replied, sounding discouraged. "I'm afraid my strength is petering out."

She kissed Maisie on the cheek and went back to the boardinghouse, thinking hard about the conversation. If you have to sell your soul, you'd best get one hell of a good price for it.

▲

"You're not paying attention!" four-year-old Aurora scolded.

"Yes, I am, darling. Mommy's just a little tired tonight."

"I've been waiting for you all day, Mommy, just so you could play with me." The child was growing more and more possessive.

"And I've been playing with you ever since I got home, sweetheart. We've played cards and I've read you stories and now we're playing dolls . . ."

"But you aren't paying attention, and you didn't play with me at all while you ate dinner."

"For heaven's sake, Aurora! All I ate was some cheese and crackers. It couldn't have taken me more than four minutes, start to finish." Oh, what was the use of arguing with the child, the truth was that with children you could stand on your head or hang from a hook and it was never, ever enough for them.

Fancy's head hurt and her throat was raw from too many performances without respite. Methodically, she picked up the doll again and started to undo its homemade dress. Her tired fingers fumbled the task and a button popped off.

"Oh, Mommy, *now* look what you've done!" Aurora wailed. "You've spoiled my dolly."

Fancy threw the doll to the floor distractedly, fighting tears of frustration and fatigue.

"For God's sake, Aurora, I haven't ruined anything! I'm the one who made that dress for your dolly and I can damn well fix the button." She bit her underlip to keep from saying more; it wasn't Aurora's fault that she was tired and they were poor and Fancy was damned near the end of her rope. She forced herself to pick up the doll and begin again.

"Why are you crying, Mommy?" the child asked accusingly, as if her mother had no right to frailty.

"I'm not crying, darling, I just have something in my eye." Aurora deserved only the best that life could offer, and if it killed Fancy, that was exactly what she'd give the child.

▲ ▲ ▲

The actress clutched the flyer she'd been handed:

Notice to Performers
You are hereby warned that your act must be free of vulgarity and coarseness.
Such words as Liar, Slob, Son of a Gun, Devil, Sucker, Damn, and all others unfit for the ears of ladies and children, will provoke discharge, if used.

Ladies' and children's ears heard plenty worse than those words in life, Fancy thought, but she knew that a man named Tony Pastor in New York was behind this move to clean up vaudeville. He had the right idea, too, for his reforms were beginning to move variety shows into legitimate theatres. Maybe he could be the answer to her prayers.

They were "breaking the jump" from St. Paul to Cleveland with a week of night-stands in tiny towns best left unnamed. Room too dark, too cold, too warm, too small . . . the steam rattles, the chambermaid sings or weeps, the bed sags, the bugs bite. Slobbering drunks, noisy musicians, snoring neighbors, tasteless food, steamer trunks lugged up three flights of stairs . . . she hoped this one would be an "easy jump." She was tired, and the current role she played was grueling. The last two theatres had had no drawing room sets, only farmhouse kitchens, so her role had had to be hastily rewritten and rememorized.

It was time to show the hinterlands a clean pair of heels; she was ready as she'd ever be to try to make her mark where it counted, and if she didn't try soon, she was liable to become used up and bitter, like so many of the has-beens or never-beens she'd met on the road.

What she needed was Broadway, that was clear as crystal. Big-time booking agents, big-time impresarios, roles that did justice to her gifts, could change this never-ending drudgery into hope again. She still loved the theatre passionately, even if the theatre didn't currently reciprocate. It would. When she got to New York at the end of this tour, she would stay there and make her stand. It felt like a lifetime since she and Aurora had left Denver; there'd been more than enough hardship and plenty of practice.

Tony Pastor was the man of the moment, according to all the actors' scuttlebutt along the jumps. He was the one she'd see when she got to New York, if she had to take all her clothes off and audition naked to get his attention.

Fancy looked in the mirror and grimaced. She'd be better off naked than in these hand-me-downs—she'd have to have one good audition dress, at least. Maybe there'd be enough money to buy some decent fabric in the next town; working on the dress would fill the long, lonely nights between here and New York with tangible evidence of the future. She picked up *Harper's Weekly* from the dressing table and began to search for news of what the prosperous were wearing these days, and hoped that it wouldn't be too complicated for her meager dressmaking skills to duplicate.

47 Mr. Pastor was Italian, there was no mistaking that. His elegant black mustache and hair made him look foreign as an opera star; his bearing was almost military and he had the look of a man who knew exactly what he wanted.

Everyone in the New York booking agencies said he was a showman par excellence, and that his effort to raise vaudeville to the level of legitimate theatre was making him rich. He'd priced the seats in his spanking new 14th Street theatre at a dollar and a half, and he'd banished the crude or vulgar from his performances, so that women, for whom variety had always been considered too daring, could see his shows. Fine artists with well-known names were appearing at Tony Pastor's, and Fancy breathed a sigh of pleasure when she saw how scrupulously clean, even pretty, the premises were. If she could get a job at Pastor's, she might be noticed by those who counted. She hoped her dress could bear scrutiny, without looking too homemade; she'd copied a Paris original that sported the newest modified bustle.

"What can you do, kid?" Tony Pastor demanded as he looked her over with a skilled eye.

"I sing and dance, Mr. Pastor, and I have an excellent Shakespearean repertoire. I've done repertory, and have two dozen roles at my fingertips."

"Sure, sure, kid, just like everybody else in New York. But what do you do that's special? Just yours, you know? Like nobody else in the whole frigging world could do it as good as you."

The question rocked Fancy, for in that split second she understood why she hadn't yet succeeded—she had copied others, never once breaking ground of her own. Thunderstruck, she cast about in her mind frantically for something she understood better than anyone else. Anxiety pounded in her ears, she could not let this chance escape her; there was only enough money in her purse for one week's rent. *You will transmute pain into art and they will hear the truth in your voice,* Magda's words broke through her agitation.

"I've suffered gravely, Mr. Pastor," Fancy answered, and the dignity of the reply caught the showman off guard. "I understand heartache. I can make people cry."

He looked at her with renewed interest, and more than a little amusement.

"You think that's a good thing to be able to do, kid? Make people cry? Convince me."

"Life's hard, Mr. Pastor, I don't think anyone escapes unscathed. My sorrow is like a tuning fork for other people's sorrow. When I sing or recite or act, they vibrate . . . because I know the truth and so do they."

Tony Pastor settled back in his newly purchased red plush seat. This one didn't sound like the others, didn't look like them either.

"So make me cry, kid," he said, settling deeply into the chair and steepling his hands in front of his lips.

Fancy pulled off her gloves and set her hat aside, diversions to provide time to think . . . she would sing first, then recite.

"Do you know 'Father, Dear Father, Come Home with Me Now'?" she asked the piano player, and he nodded. "In the key of G, please." And then she sang . . . or rather, Tony Pastor told his wife that night, she became the brokenhearted child who begged her father to return from the bar to her dying mother's side. Her great dark eyes filled with courageous, desperate tears, she became every lost child who has ever begged for what she needs for salvation, only to be denied. Tony Pastor was startled to find, as the haunting notes died in Fancy's throat, that there was genuine moisture in his own eyes. He saw the piano player wipe his face surreptitiously with his handkerchief, and he knew in his heart that he had found a potential winner.

Fancy recited then, and the impresario tried to fathom what it was she did that set her apart. She was a waif, of course . . . a fragile, exquisite waif who could break your heart with a glance of those expressive eyes—but she was more than that, for there was bravery and defiance in her desperation. She was young as the frailest orphan, and old, in knowledge of the wicked ways in which the world can rob you of your dreams. She was frail and mighty; like a willow the storm might bend but not break, or the sparrow who outlives the winter. She was enduring, and oh, the painful knowledge in that face, in the subtle gestures of her hands and the language of her small body. How could one so young know so much of loss? he wondered. How could she communicate it so intensely?

Fancy, on the other side of the footlights, knew she was home at last, for she had finally grown into her gift—her rare and special talent that was like no other. Could this be what Magda had meant by her soul's purpose? She didn't even have to see the tears in the men's eyes, or notice that the cleaning woman was standing propped against her mop, tears streaming down her weathered face, to know she had the job.

48 Fancy was happy at Tony Pastor's, but it was only the first step on the ladder. At least she was finally in New York, where she could learn how the climb could be accomplished. You needed a manager or impresario to break into Broadway, everybody said so. You could do variety or burlesque or road shows without one, but to make it to the Big Time you needed a manager who had access to the theatre owners and the "angels" who backed the new plays. The trouble was that the best managers chose their own clients from the endless stream of hopefuls, and in order to reach the important producers you had to be represented by one of a tiny handful of men, who wielded unconscionable power.

The theatrical manager named Sidney Glick was the man the two show biz bibles, *The New York Dramatic Mirror* and *The Theatre Magazine,* claimed had unearthed more great female talent than any ten others; he'd seen Fancy three nights running at Tony Pastor's, before leaving the scribbled note she now held in her hand. The top half of the door to his office was of frosted glass, behind its fuzzy distortion she could see a bustle of activity. Fancy took a deep breath, straightened her audition dress, and walked inside.

A small dog in a clown collar leapt up at her, yelping, a pair of twins in identical striped suits blinked their identical blue eyes, a small child with a bow in her ringlets and the kind of stage mother Fancy had learned to detest, all sat on hard wooden chairs before a Cerberus of a secretary, who guarded the manager's door.

Warily, Fancy introduced herself and sat down to wait her turn to see the man who could change her life.

"Fancy," Sidney Glick intoned. "Fancy Deverell." He drew out each syllable. "The name has class, kid. I like it." He sat behind a shabby desk, a sour-smelling cigar clenched in his teeth, his feet occupying the top of a pile of disheveled papers. Fancy thought he looked like a toad.

"I received your note, Mr. Glick," she began. There was something unhealthy about his face, as if he'd lived under a rock for long periods, far from sunlight.

"Yeah, yeah. I caught your act at Tony's. Thought you had something . . . sex appeal, pathos, you know. You had those suckers crying in their beer. That orphan routine is a great gimmick, kid. I gotta hand it to you, that's a new one on me and I thought I'd seen 'em all."

"I've never had a manager, Mr. Glick."

"That's why your career is in the crapper, kid. You get *bubkes* in this town without a manager."

"I like Mr. Pastor," Fancy said defensively, feeling soiled by being near the man.

"So you'd like to stay in vaudeville 'til you're old and baggy, right? You wanna be *meshugge,* I got no time for you."

Fancy held her temper. "Why did you ask me to come here, Mr. Glick?"

He removed his feet from the desk and leaned forward intently. "You ever heard of Augustin Daly, the big producer?"

"Of course I've heard of him, Mr. Glick. He puts on the most lavish productions in New York. I'm not naive."

"Maybe yes, maybe no—that we don't know yet. But Daly's got a new play, just finishing auditions. He's got great plans for this play, Fancy Deverell, and it just so happens there's a role in it would fit you like a sausage skin. *If* I happened to be your agent, that is . . . which, as of this moment, I'm not." He leaned back in the swivel chair, then rose and walked up close to where she sat; she could smell his rank breath as he leaned near to her.

"It could be, I would want to become your agent," he said provocatively, reaching out to touch her. Fancy recoiled. He reached again for her hair, and she sat very still as he played with a long, dark ringlet. "If I did that, it could be I could get Daly to audition just one more actress for this role and I could put some muscle behind getting him to like you a lot. . . .

"You suit yourself about this, Fancy Deverell, but you consider real good before you get uppity with Sidney Glick. There's nothing you get in this world without you give something back, understand? I'm a real simple kinda guy. I get you a shot at a role that could make you a star—you, a nobody from Hicksville, Vaudeville, U.S.A. —and what I get in return is I get to fuck you. It's real simple." He dropped her hair and walked to the door.

"Now you go home and think about it real hard. Ask around. See if your pals at Tony Pastor's don't think Sidney Glick can open doors for you. Then you come back here and we play a little hide-the-salami and everybody wins."

He opened the door, dismissing her with a curt nod. As Fancy rose to leave, her teeth clenched in impotent rage, another ingenue was already walking into his office.

▲

The fury that knotted Fancy's belly propelled her along the busy streets with an overpowering urgency. Revulsion, nausea . . . not even the auction had made her feel so soiled. Tears of outrage streaked her face as she made her way to the park bench, too angry and agitated to go home.

That loathsome son of a bitch stood between her and everything she'd ever wanted. She didn't have to ask anyone whether he could get her the audition, everybody in New York knew Glick pulled the strings that opened the doors to major Broadway shows. He not only got you the audition, he pressured the producers; if you came to an audition with his imprimatur, you were damn near assured of the job. She shuddered inwardly at the thought of his crassness, the physical ugliness that had made her want to run as far as she could. The idea of his touching her intimately was unthinkable. . . .

But so was the life that stretched before her if she didn't do as he asked. She'd feared she might have to sell her soul to get what she wanted; now she knew it would be her body that was forfeit.

Fancy put her head down in her hands and cried until the dark had fallen all around her. She barely made it back to Pastor's in time to cover her red-ringed eyes and nose with makeup for the eight o'clock show.

She'd have to make a fast decision; how many tailor-made roles would there be on Broadway in a single season, and waiting out another wasted year was more than she could bear.

▲

"How do I know you can deliver what you say, Mr. Glick?" Fancy stood in his office with her back to the door.

The man's expression was contemptuous and lustful, simultaneously. Fancy saw it with a kind of studied detachment; she would go inside herself to stay away from him. Only her body would be dirtied and that could be washed clean.

"You wouldn't be here if you didn't know I could get you what you want." He walked around the desk and leaned against it.

"You really think you're something special, don't you, Fancy Deverell . . . better than me, it's right there on your arrogant kisser."

Fancy watched him with the intense fascination of a mongoose in the cobra's lair. *Your body is your own,* Magda had said eons ago . . . but that wasn't true today, she had come here to sell it to this revolting little man in return for a future that was bearable.

"I've accepted your terms, Mr. Glick. I don't have to like them."

He laughed, an ugly, callous sound. "You don't have to like it at all, Fancy Deverell . . . but you better make damned certain *I* like it." He locked the door behind her and unfastened his belt and trousers.

He moved to the couch and sat back, reaching inside his pants to liberate an organ far too large for his puny body. He laughed at the revulsion on

Fancy's face and beckoned her toward him. Like a sleepwalker, she moved in his direction . . . he reached out and pulled her roughly to her knees in front of him. She let herself be pulled.

"Make me want to do you a favor, kid," he said as he grabbed a fistful of her hair and pushed her face toward the pole of flesh that protruded from his pants.

Fancy Deverell of Beau Rivage quelled her urge to throw up, and bent her dark head to the revolting task, with all the skill she could muster. Her only revenge would be in making sure the bastard would never forget.

Sidney Glick looked up from his sexual stupor when the act was complete.

"Holy shit, you got real talent, kid, you could—"

Fancy, already on her feet, cut him off.

"That's my part of the bargain, Mr. Glick. Now you fulfill yours."

"Or what?"

The beautiful young woman locked his eyes with her own.

"Or I'll cut your heart out," she said deliberately.

Sidney Glick tucked himself back in his trousers. This one was very interesting. He could make a lot of money from the career of an interesting woman, and the only thing he liked better than sex was money.

"Four o'clock, Friday at 237 West Forty-fifth. My secretary has the script on her desk. Learn the role of Laura and meet me there."

Fancy nodded and headed for the door. She'd done what she had to do and she hadn't let him see what it cost her.

She hurried home. Inside her room she tore at her clothes and threw them from her body, grateful that Aurora was out with the boardinghouse owner's daughter, so she was alone. She felt dirty, injured . . . the water from the old pipes clanged and hissed into the porcelain tub. Fancy vomited into the commode, then sank to the floor beside it, a broken child whose limits of endurance had been reached. What lower act than this could Fate demand of her? What would Atticus say if he knew the price she was willing to pay to win?

▲ ▲ ▲

THE WAIF OF WINCHESTER IS A WINNER

She's a waif, this tempest-tossed Miss Deverell. A waif with eyes that hold fathomless sorrow, a mouth just tremulous enough to make us long to save her, just brave enough to make us applaud her heroism. No man could fail to be moved by the nuances of this performance. The tiniest gesture does not escape her unerring eye . . . the prostitute's arms folded protectively over her belly, when the wicked madam speaks of her unborn child . . . the pathetic mime of the homeless girl folding her worldly goods into a knapsack to move on, once again to nowhere. One cannot forget such perfection of detail, one cannot help but be moved by the sensitivity of one who looks like an exquisite child, but seems to know more of suffering than a single lifetime could provide.

Nor can one avoid alluding to Miss Deverell's beauty, for this poignant soul of a broken sparrow resides in the body of a bird of brilliant plumage. This tiny Circe, with the mane of shining ringlets and the body of Diana, will set many a heart a-flutter among the stage-door Johnnies before this season ends.

And season it is, for *The Waif of Winchester* will run a good long time, if I'm any judge. Audiences love nothing so much as a good hard cry.

Fancy put down the newspaper, tears of triumph blurring her vision. Her sacrifice had been worth it after all—she pushed the thought of Sidney Glick's naked body down, down deep into the place of horrors that must never be remembered. She had a terror of reviews, those terse cruel words that could dash your hopes to pieces and strangle your muse for the next performance. What if she'd done what she had to do to get this role, and then the newspapers had hated her? It had taken courage to read what the critic for the *New York Sun* had said about her . . . but oh, how the generous words soothed her soul and poured balm on the wounds of years of desperation and the memory of Sidney Glick.

Sorrow was her metier . . . how ironic and appropriate. If audiences liked to cry, then, by God, she would give them a sea of tears to match her own. And in return, they would give her salvation.

 49 Fancy curtsied to the crowd with all the dignity of a grand duchess and blew kisses to the eager men in the gilded boxes. She breathed the full essence of adulation in; it coursed through her blood, warm as cognac. Because of her spectacular reviews, people had been lined up all around the block waiting for tickets to *The Waif of Winchester.* She'd hidden outside the theatre door to watch the scalpers charge outrageous fees for the chance to see Fancy Deverell perform and tried to make herself believe that the price she'd paid for this had been acceptable. Success was the best revenge.

Fancy scrubbed the greasepaint off her face and fingered the small white card that lay on her dressing table. *Jason Madigan,* it read simply, but the substance conveyed by the creamy stock and lustrous engraving was another matter. It wasn't unusual for an actress to be invited out to dine by a stranger who'd seen her perform, but only the great actresses and great beauties garnered the attentions of the rich. Fancy had learned not to spurn the attention of the rich men who liked to be seen with beautiful actresses on their arms. There'd been more nights than one when she wouldn't have eaten at all had it not been for the dinner invitations of such men as this Jason Madigan; nights when she'd been grateful Aurora was fed at the boardinghouse as part of their room fee.

Fancy hummed as she applied her lip and cheek rouge with care, and fluffed her abundant hair into the latest coif. The patronage of the powerful could cut ten years of struggle off her climb to the top. The world was what it was and she could lose no more time waiting and hoping.

▲

Fancy lifted the skirts of her gown above her ankles and looked with distaste at the mud beyond the curb. Great God! Would she never be able to forget what it felt like to have just one pair of shoes to her name?

"Are we going far, Mr. Madigan?"

"Just across the street to my carriage, Mrs. Deverell. But there's no reason you should have to ruin your slippers, just because my driver can't get closer in this crowd. If you'll allow me the liberty . . . ?" Jason lifted Fancy off her feet and carried her across the rutted roadway to his brougham with ease. He wasn't a tall man, but he was powerfully built.

"How very gallant of you, Mr. Madigan," Fancy said, startled by the gesture; it was lovely and unexpected to be taken care of.

Jason smiled acknowledgment; gallantry came easily when he was in a good mood. He'd seen her play on opening night and been won over by her unusually perceptive performance.

"I thought we'd dine at the new Delmonico's, Mrs. Deverell. It's very pleasant and private." The deep voice was manly, Fancy thought, stealing a glance at him as he stepped into the carriage beside her. He wasn't handsome; his square jaw and matching body precluded that. His gray eyes were sharp as flint and watched the world with unwavering appraisal; his lips were thin enough to make it clear they'd brook no interference, and his jaw was tough as an anvil. No, it wasn't a handsome face, despite its sculpted silver brows that matched his lustrous crop of silver hair and the fine down-turned mustache, of a darker gray, that gave it stature, but it was the face of a man used to money and power. The fact that his behavior was decorous and courtly was welcome relief—Fancy hadn't been feeling kindly toward men, of late.

The restaurant's opulent interior spoke of wealth and extravagance; she found that comforting and smiled at Jason. It pleased him to see that he'd delighted her with his choice.

"May I ask you what business you're in, Mr. Madigan?" she began as the waiter poured their wine.

Jason settled back in his chair to answer. "I'm in many businesses, Mrs. Deverell. Banking, for one thing. Mining, another."

"Mining? What sort of mining?"

"Whatever kind there is to be done, I suppose. Silver is where I made my first money. Then gold. Now I dabble in a number of such enterprises. Are you interested in mining?"

Fancy laughed and shook her head. "Would you believe that you're dining with a sourdough, Mr. Madigan? I've done more mining than I like to recall. In Colorado—California Gulch, to be exact. I can't say it brought me anything more than experience and blisters."

"Is that where you met Mr. Deverell? Aurora's father?"

Fancy's face clouded. "How exactly do you know about my daughter?"

"My dear Mrs. Deverell, I was enchanted enough by your performance last evening to make it my business to learn everything I could about you."

"And what precisely did you learn?"

"That you are obviously well-bred and probably from the South, but no one knows exactly where. That you have a small daughter so beautiful that theatrical agents would give you anything you asked if you'd put her on the stage, but you refuse to do so. That the whereabouts of your former husband is shrouded in impenetrable mystery, by your own design." He watched her shrewdly for signs of response or anger, but Fancy kept her face impassive, except for the barest hint of mirth at the corner of her mouth.

"A little mystery is essential in a woman's past. Wouldn't you agree, Mr. Madigan?"

"When a woman is as lovely as you, Mrs. Deverell, a little mystery can only enhance her charm. That doesn't preclude my trying to satisfy my curiosity, of course."

"Perhaps we should talk about your own mysteries, Mr. Madigan. How exactly did you get into the mining business?"

"I worked my way through metallurgical college and engineering school when other men headed out to the hills with a tin plate in their hands. After Sutter's Creek, any fool could tell there was going to be more gold and silver found in the Rockies.

"I made my way to Virginia City and the Comstock. Did day labor in the Ophir and Homestake. Learned to dig and to double-jack and all the rest of a miner's dirty jobs, just to learn the business from the inside out." Fancy examined the man more closely and he watched her do so. He was of slightly more than medium height and stocky, but not an ounce of fat displaced the muscle of a body used to the tyranny of hard work and exercise. His success was not a fluke; she admired that.

"Philip Deidesheimer, the country's leading authority on mining technology, took a liking to me. Deidesheimer was a graduate of the Freiburg School of Mines in Germany and had practiced his profession in California before coming to Colorado. It was he who developed the system of timbering in 'square-sets' that made mining the Rockies feasible. You do know about square-sets?"

"Only by reputation, not personal experience, Mr. Madigan. The mine I worked was just a hole in the ground."

"Square-sets are short, massive timbers, fourteen inches square and six feet long, mortised and tensioned at the end. They're assembled inside mine shafts to form interlocking cubes of immense strength to hold up the rock walls and ceiling. The resulting system is a honeycomb of uplifting timbers that can deal with the crumbling recesses of the Rockies. Square-sets are what made it possible to open the Comstock to extraordinary depths."

Fancy took a sip of her wine and looked properly impressed.

"Of course, you know that gold and silver are not the only wealth to be made around a strike, Mrs. Deverell. Once minerals are found, other needs mushroom . . . carts to carry ore, timber for square-sets, flumes to carry timber down from the mountaintops. Cartage, smelting, labor. . . . A man's got to be prepared to cash in on a boom, of course. And to be ready, he's got to have cash and he's got to believe it's going to happen. I'm a believer, Mrs. Deverell. I believe we walk into our own vision of the future, and my vision holds nothing but abundance."

After Jason had brought her home, Fancy lay on her bed without undressing and savored every word.

Men were the answer to everything—showgirls with half her brains and beauty and none of her theatrical gifts were taken under the patronage of powerful men and suddenly became stars. Men had money, men had power, men controlled critics and newspapers, men owned theatres. It was their world and she had to make her way in it—she just wished she didn't find the thought so disturbing. If men were the gatekeepers to the future, she'd damn well be better off with the likes of Jason Madigan than the likes of Sidney Glick.

The phantom of Chance had no business complicating this . . . he was merely a girlish folly of racing blood and romantic yearnings, not a man to make life bearable and full of possibilities. Fancy would have to banish Chance's memory and move on to someone with whom she could build a future. At the very least, it wouldn't hurt to have the friendship of a man like Jason Madigan.

Fancy got up from the bed and walked to Aurora's room to kiss her sleeping child good night. Sometimes it was hard to know clearly what she did for herself and what for Aurora. The two of them seemed a matched set pitted against a hostile world—who could blame her for wanting help with the struggle?

Fancy sighed a second time as she pulled off her shoes and stockings and wriggled her toes in freedom. She'd handled Jason just the right way for now; he'd be back.

She pulled a nightgown over her head and buttoned it; then, feeling fettered by its confines, she yanked it off again and went to bed naked and restless.

She dreamed of Chance McAllister.

▲

Great God, but that woman could make a man's knees weak, Jason thought as he made his way home. Those dark velvet eyes dancing promise in the face of an angel—or rather, a face that would put an angel to shame, for there was more imp than angel in Fancy Deverell, if he read her right. More spunk, in fact, than he'd ever encountered in any woman of quality. A most arresting combination. She might even have the makings of every man's fantasy—lady in the drawing room, whore in the bedroom. In fact, he thought with a degree of satisfaction that pleased him enormously, she had many of the makings of a potential consort.

Tildy, the wife of his youthful poverty, had never lived to see him prosper. She'd dragged behind him dutifully from mining camp to mining camp, but her strength had not been as fierce as his own and she had perished in some nameless backwater, their spindly infant son along with her. After her, there had been many women, but never a potential partner.

Until now.

 50 "The little princess' hair was black as ebony, her lips red as roses, her eyes were the color of two star sapphires . . ." Fancy always began the story the same way, for she knew Aurora identified with the princess of the story—and with good reason, for the child's extraordinary beauty was such that she seemed far too lovely for ordinary life. Whenever Fancy and Aurora walked together, people stared at them and whispered as they passed by; both knew it was because they were beautiful.

Fancy took her daughter walking every day, rain or shine. The small house in which she'd taken rooms was near a little park, and a few blocks beyond that were the houses of the rich. Each morning, no matter how tired she was from the previous night's performance, Fancy would rise to breakfast with Aurora. There was no money for a governess and while Mrs. Donaher, who minded the child in Fancy's absence, was kind and loving, she had no knowledge of decorum; so, daily, Fancy taught her daughter the graces of her own lost childhood—graces Aurora would need when they were rich.

"Porridge is always spooned away from you, darling . . . a well-bred little girl always curtsies respectfully when introduced to an older person . . ." A great many of the lessons were lost on the restless Aurora, who paid little heed to lessons of any sort, but she adored receiving her mother's attention and therefore made enough progress so that Fancy felt she'd done her part.

Aurora loved their morning outings, when hand in hand, she and Fancy walked along the footpaths of the city to see the houses of the rich. Fancy would spin stories in her thrilling voice, and Aurora would see the splendid palaces of stone and marble, and dream that she lived there instead of in the dingy boardinghouse where everything was brown or gray for serviceability.

Fancy would tell her daughter fairy tales of handsome kings and princes, who whisked their ladyloves off from their sculleries to the castle on the hill, and somehow the stories would all blend into one satisfying and amorphous cloud of hope and promise for the little girl. She already knew she was beautiful as a princess, and that her mother looked like a queen. Aurora had even watched Fancy on the stage, dressed in regal trappings and wearing a golden crown, and that memory, too, was somehow woven firmly into the tapestry of her imagination. Stories, truth; fantasy, reality; theatre, real life . . . there were no clear-cut delineations for Aurora. Only the certain knowledge that her mother was the center of a universe of beauty and that the shabby surroundings in which they currently dwelled were a mistake and temporary . . . for they both belonged somewhere else . . . just where she wasn't certain. But her mother knew, and she would set it right.

"Do you see those funny stone creatures on the side of that house, Aurora? Do you remember what they're called?"

"Gargoyles, Mommy. And they have them on castles too."

"That's exactly right, my darling. And can you tell me how many footmen it would be proper to have serving a banquet at such a castle?" The little girl thought for a moment.

"One footman for every two guests," she answered finally, in her baby voice.

"And which fork would you use to eat the oysters at that banquet?"

Aurora laughed, musically. "Oh, Mommy, that's a silly question. The oyster fork, of course!"

Fancy thought her daughter brilliant. She recognized, of course, that the little girl was petulant and that it was impossible to teach her anything that didn't interest her, but Fancy assumed this was simply because there wasn't money for a real tutor. Later, when Aurora went to school, everything would work out well enough.

She worried about Aurora's not having a father, but, as she didn't know precisely what to tell her about her father, she told her very little, except to say that Captain Deverell had been handsome and brave, and had died before the child was born. Someday she would have to cope with Aurora's questions, but perhaps by then she would be safely married and Aurora would have a father of her own.

Fancy loved her daughter, savored the precious moments they spent together; but the rest of life was hard and enervating. Even theatrical success did not guarantee an actress' salary being adequate to support a household that included a child and housekeeper. Salaries, even for stars, were not nearly as extravagant as she'd hoped.

But she was being noticed by the right people, and success added new confidence in her own ability to wrest from Fate what she demanded. Besides, she always thought when overwhelmed by the problems of life, what was the point in worrying about things you couldn't change?

▲

"You look as if you're carrying the weight of the world on those lovely shoulders tonight, Fancy," Jason said as he sat down beside her at his dining club.

Fancy smiled ruefully. "I'm afraid Aurora isn't feeling well again and my play will be closing soon and life always seems to cost more than I earn. . . ." She shrugged her fashionably bare shoulders enough so that her bosom rose and fell enticingly within the black velvet bodice, and sighed.

Jason relaxed visibly . . . these were simple logistical problems, easily solved. He'd been fearful that Fancy didn't find him attractive.

"Perhaps I could say a few words to Daly or Wallock about your salary and your next assignment. They're the most influential producers at the moment, I believe."

"Is it really as simple as all that?"

"They're both members here, Fancy. We've done a bit of business together, from time to time. I'm certain they'd want to be helpful."

"You have no idea how furious that makes me!"

"That I should try to help?"

"No! That I should kill myself to be the best actress in New York and struggle for years to get recognized and damned near starve to death in the process, and all you have to do is say two words to the right person over your goddamned port and cigars!"

Jason laughed with no compassion whatsoever. "Don't be a fool, Fancy. Life is what it is. The world turns on power. Those who have it, have everything."

The simple logic stopped Fancy's gathering soliloquy. She took a deep breath and started over.

"I've had to fight for every scrap, Jason. You can't possibly understand how brutal life is for a woman who must make her own way."

Madigan leaned back in his chair, hooking his thumbs into his pants pockets as he did so; it was a gesture full of confidence.

"I expect that's only part of the truth, Fancy. My bet is that you love being in charge of your own destiny, but that your ambition is so monumental you just haven't yet been able to achieve all you want out of life—and that's what makes you angriest of all. You'd be damned good in business, Fancy. So few women understand the intrinsic power of business. It's an instinct. A gift. Like your ability to sing and dance." His voice was soft and insolent. In a way it was a relief that he wasn't just another besotted lothario.

"You're right, of course, Jason. But success isn't as simple for a woman as it is for a man. We're expected to be stupid about money . . . and endlessly selfless, something I don't excel at. We're taught that the last thing on earth a man wants in a woman is a brain that registers more than home and babies and what to do about diaper rash and the croup."

When Jason smiled this time, he wasn't taunting her, he was simply amused. "No man wants to compete with the woman in his life for business supremacy, Fancy." He reached into his breast pocket for his cigar case. "We get more than our share of rough-and-tumble from other men. What we crave from a woman is comfort and a certain healthy amount of adoration. We're selfish bastards for the most part. . . . We want what we want and we can afford to pay for it. On the other hand, unlike some of my colleagues, I rather like the idea of a woman with a brain and business acumen and a certain healthy ruthlessness. It might make a man's love life all the more interesting.

"May I smoke?" he asked, and she saw he was enjoying himself enormously.

Fancy reached for his cigar case instead of replying, and extracted an elegant Havana. She took the silver nipper from the vest pocket where she'd seen him store it earlier, rolled the cigar expertly near her ear, and, satisfied by the sound and feel, she clipped it deftly and lit the end. The fragrance of the perfectly aged leaves reminded her of other times. She handed the cigar back to Jason with a self-satisfied smile and he laughed appreciatively.

"So you know about comfort, too, do you, young lady? Now, where in God's name did you learn to put on such a performance with a Havana? In another one of your theatrical productions?"

Fancy lifted her seductive eyes to his. "Long ago, in another world . . . my mother did this for my father."

"You are a most mysterious creature, Fancy. A man would never be bored with you." He made a mental note to set a Pinkerton to the task of tracing the more elusive elements of her past.

"I'm a mystery even to myself, Jason . . . I sometimes think no one understands me less well than I do." *No man will ever understand you like I do, sugar,* Chance had said, long ago. Fancy felt a tug of hurtful memory. What was wrong with her tonight that she was so vulnerable?

Jason watched her mood shift.

"Will you see me again?"

"Of course I will—but I can't promise you more than that."

"Fair enough. There's nothing more intriguing for a man than a challenge. If there isn't anyone else you've set your heart on, Fancy, my chances are as good as the next man's, I expect."

Fancy tossed her head to free it from unwanted remembrance. It didn't make the least sense that no one had ever touched her heart the way the brothers had; a true friend and a lost love. Hart and Chance were history, Jason and she were now. She tilted her glass toward the man who had so much to offer and wondered if a touch more champagne would make him seem any more romantic.

51   Bandana had led the McAllisters to a new spot on the side of Mount Massive that he said his "nose" assured him had real promise. It wasn't that the boys' hopes had dwindled, but after more than six years of digging, they knew for sure there was no such thing as easy riches. Gold or silver, Bandana always said magnanimously . . . we'll be willing to take whichever one finds us first.

When they hit the vein of silver, they decided to stake the claim as "The Fancy Penny," for old times' sake.

"Got to write up a sign on a pine board," Bandana told his partners expansively. "Got to do it proper, so no sidewinder who comes along after us can git away with tellin' the law we never staked out right."

He took a stubby lead pencil and scratched the following on the wood:

THE FANCY PENNY

Notice is hereby given, that we, the undersigned citizens of the United States, having complied with Chapter 36, Title 32, Revised Statutes of the United States, and the local regulations of this here district claim by right of discovery fifteen hundred feet in length and six hundred feet in width, along the mineral-bearing vein to be known henceforward as The Fancy Penny beginning at center of discovery shaft and running seven hundred feet in a northerly direction.

"Always say northerly and southerly and such. It gives you a chance to swing your stakes around every which way between here and the North Pole! Ain't no way to tell exactly what *northerly* means, and so long as no other claim gets in the way you got what you might call latitude. Let's see, now, where were we? Oh, yes . . ."

Eight hundred feet in a southerly direction and seven hundred feet easterly and westerly. Located this 22nd day of May, 1877.

Locators: Otis Bandana McBain
Charles Yancy McAllister
Matthew Hart McAllister

"Otis?" the McAllisters chorused in unison, but Bandana threw them a look that said he'd ditched his given name with malice aforethought.

So nearly seven years after they'd ridden into California Gulch with Bandana McBain as their mentor, Hart and Chance McAllister struck it rich. The year was 1877, and they weren't the only lucky ones.

▲

A frenzy of activity agitated California Gulch as big-paying mines began to be registered faster than the assay office could process what they found.

George Fryer brought in the New Discovery and Haw Tabor the Matchless and Chrysolite. Broken Nose Scotty struck pay dirt on Breece Hill, while Chaffee and Moffat's Little Pittsburgh in Evan's Gulch, John McCombe's Crescent and Evening Star on Carbonate Hill, and a dozen more were all major silver strikes brought in within a single year.

A sort of madness set in as the population spread along California Gulch like prairie grass. Jewel's bet had paid off in spades; once again she had a boomtown by the short hairs.

A bonanza of new buildings sprouted—saloons, gambling dens, parlor houses on the one hand, and the ritzy Saddle Rock Café on the other, where the newly rich could dine in style. The sawmill had men standing in line to grab the wood as it came off the buzz saw, stores opened up between dusk of one day and dawn the next. Even a church was raised, although what need there was of that, few miners could fathom, though rumor had it that mail-order brides could be brought in more readily if a community had a church.

A newspaper office opened its doors when John Arkins left his job at the *Denver Tribune* and started the *Chronicle* in a clapboard shanty with nothing in it but the printing press he'd spent his life savings to buy.

In fact, the town of Oro grew so rapidly it needed a new name. Leadville was chosen because carbonate of lead was making Oro into a treasure city, rich as Xanadu.

"Dumb name for a city in the clouds," Chance said when he heard the choice.

"Don't matter what they call it," Bandana answered. "Bonanza is what she is while she's makin' men rich, and Borosca when she's all played out."

Some men made money because they were smart, others because they were so lucky they couldn't lose even through stupidity . . . like Haw Tabor, who bought a worthless mine that had been conspicuously seeded with nuggets to fool a tenderfoot. Haw hadn't dug five feet farther in the "worthless" shaft when he uncovered one of the biggest producers of all time, the Chrysolite.

In the space of a single year, three stage lines were bringing in twelve coaches a day. Two thousand men were engaged in freighting in the food and fur, diamonds and drilling equipment, wine and women, that were to change Oro from a mining camp into a city.

Chance became an emissary to this growing pandemonium of commerce; he took to the business of making friendships as if he'd been born to glad-handing. Before long there wasn't a banker or businessman, railroad tycoon or local merchant, with whom he wasn't on a first-name basis. The money from the Fancy Penny gave him the wherewithal to hobnob, his own personal powers of persuasion gave him the chance to make those acquaintanceships pay off.

You couldn't say the money changed Chance, exactly—he was flamboyant and headstrong with or without it. What it did do was open up possibilities for him that would never have existed otherwise.

Chance had soaked up a fair amount of knowledge of the law while working in Denver. His trick memory made learning easy, so he'd been able to pick up the jargon of anything he set his mind to, as if he'd been born knowing it. The fact that he cut such a handsome figure tended to make folks forget that he didn't know it all. He looked and acted like a man destined for great things, and most people tend to be swayed by a man's opinion of himself.

Credentials didn't count all that much west of the Arkansas in the 1870s; few men in the West were educated for the jobs they tackled. Even the doctor in Leadville had started out life as a carpenter, but after sawing off a few legs in the War Between the States, he'd decided to make surgery his trade because it paid better than carpentry. If you struck it rich, no one ever questioned your right to rule the world.

And there was no denying Chance's natural talents, sometimes the best credentials of all: He was blessed with a golden tongue and a gambler's instinct for which issue to latch on to. When it came to speechifying, he could put Daniel Webster in the shade, or so they said in Leadville.

It didn't take Chance long to figure out where the power was going to be in the Gulch, and which of the men who'd gathered quick riches would have the sand to make a career out of what Lady Luck had given them. The mines were a stepping stone to power and influence; with his new clothes and old ambitions it wouldn't take Chance long to make his mark in the mushrooming world of silver.

▲

With bonanza came a whole new set of responsibilities for the three owners of the Fancy Penny. Silver mining demanded vastly different skills from prospecting. Shafts had to be dug deep into the mountain, men had to be stratified into bosses and laborers, records must be kept, banking contacts established.

One of the partners would have to learn to be a businessman on a grand scale, that was certain. Bandana understood hard-rock mining, but had a horror of life below ground. Chance was the obvious choice for liaison with the powerful men whose friendship was needed for prosperity. Hart worked easily with people, he was organized, he could draft the drawings needed for the work, but nothing could have depressed him more than being stuck with running a mining operation.

"One year, damn it!" he told Chance and Bandana when they made him the proposition. "As God is my witness, I'll run this place for one year and not a day more. Then I go to Yale!" Hart hated the world beneath the earth; no artist belongs where the sun never shines and nothing of beauty grows, he said. He also hired Caz Castlemaine to be his second-in-command.

The shafts were dug straight down toward hell, hundreds of feet straight into rock and blackness. It was always bone-cold at the top, and hot as Hades as you descended into territory nature never meant man to see. The temperature in a drift could reach 130 degrees and if you worked near an underground hot river, you were in distinct danger of breaking through to water that could parboil a man in the blink of an eye.

The air below the ground was unfit for human consumption; it was too far from the top for any hint of freshness, and too loaded with noxious gases and fractured rock particles to be safely breathable.

Hart learned from the Cousin Jacks, experienced Cornish miners imported to work some of the other shafts, the age-old trick of taking canary birds down into the hole to test the air quality. If the bird keeled over, the air was poisoned and the men had warning to escape. Hart sketched the poignant picture of burly, dirt-encrusted miners ascending from the depths with wispy little filigree cages of songbirds in their toughened hands.

In order to get below, the miners rode a conveyance attached to a cable made of braided steel wire. In the early days, a platform was hung from this cable, then a simple iron "cage" replaced that, but the precariousness of riding either one did not diminish. If a man stuck an elbow or toe out of the cage, his flesh exploded into bloody fragments, smashed on rock and timber as the car descended at impossible speeds.

In the Fancy Penny, the cable halted at a thousand feet, where the main drift, or tunnel, ran east to west along the lode line. All along this drift were cross-cuts, going north to south, and winzes, or short shafts, that connected up to other levels. Narrow-gauge railroad tracks stretched along the floor to carry out the ore once it was dug. There was also an iron pipe that carried water, which was constantly being forced upward from the shaft bottom by a monumental pump in a seemingly fruitless effort to keep ahead of nature's endless seepage.

At the thousand-foot level, rock was painfully hot to the touch. The men were forced to work in breechcloths, with resin-hardened hats on their heads to catch the rockfall, and heavy shoes on their feet to protect them from the jagged floor. Hart installed massive air blowers to force surface air down the shaft to the men, but even that couldn't make the climate bearable. Ice was passed from the mountainside to the miners and the scramble for a handful whenever it arrived was a testament to the infernal heat below ground.

Men sometimes fainted coming out of the depths into the cooler air of the up-shaft—if that happened and they toppled from the cage, their bodies were broken by the rocks and retrieved with grappling hooks. If a man fell into a sump of boiling water, the flesh was flayed from the bone.

Black powder had been replaced in the early seventies by dynamite. A blasting cap, containing fulminate of mercury, could be set off by a spark or by a jolt, causing the dynamite sticks to explode. Sometimes it did the same for the miners, who had a habit of carrying caps loose in their breeches, mixed in with their tobacco.

The men drilled holes for the dynamite and fired them in an orderly sequence; sometimes one of the holes would not go off with the others, and a man needed to show great care in both counting the holes that did go off and in hunting for the "missed shot," as more than one miner died in pieces after finding such a missed shot, by accident, with his sledge.

"An artist was never meant for life below ground, dammit!" Hart told Bandana on more than one occasion.

"I'm not all that sure any man is," McBain replied.

Finding a bonanza and running the empire it builds are two different kettles of fish, some men are born to one, some to the other. The trouble is, Hart realized early on, you never know till you get there, which one you are.

 52   "What do you really want out of life, Fancy? And spare me the glib answer and fluttering eyelids that satisfy other men." Jason asked the question in the easy camaraderie that had developed between them during the past months.

The performance had been a good one, and Fancy had gone back to Jason's house, looking forward to the scrunch of fine carpet beneath bare toes, and the psyche-soothing champagne that would help her unwind from the performance. She sat on a chaise, feet curled beneath her, contented as a pet cat.

Trying to decide when to be seduced had given Fancy quite a bit of trouble; she couldn't keep Jason dangling forever. They'd been together a great deal and he'd been patient, but she didn't want to lose him through reticence. She decided to be honest in replying, not coquettish.

"I want to be a great actress, great enough to be remembered. I want to be rich enough never to be fearful. To have absolute power over my own fate . . . and to have a hell of a lot of fun, before I die."

"Fair enough and entirely achievable." Jason had taken off his jacket and loosened his tie, and was seated with his arms spread out across the back of the couch. He looked expansive, in control, and Fancy envied him.

"And what do you want, Jason? You who appear to have it all. And spare me the vague answers and the manly withdrawal that satisfies other women."

Jason chuckled. Occasionally she got underneath his guard; it was curiously pleasant to be honest once in a while.

"Something more than I have, Fancy. Always something more. I'm greedier for life than other men, that's why I succeed."

"What is the 'something more' of the moment?"

"Would it startle you if I said I am sometimes lonely?" He drew the words out carefully, surprised at his own candor. "My son died, you know. I never told anyone how that devastated me. It's an odd man who doesn't want to found a dynasty."

Fancy didn't answer and after a moment he spoke again. "I would have liked to marry a woman who understands me."

"Surely there have been many applicants for that job."

"I'm a complex man, Fancy. Few women could satisfy my needs."

"What were you like as a little boy, Jason? It's hard to imagine you as other than you are now."

"I don't know, my dear . . . serious, studious, driven, I suppose. I was a worrier, too. I admired my father, although he was a cold man. I spent my boyhood longing for his approval . . . pushing myself to greater and greater feats to please him."

"Didn't you want his love, as well as his approval?"

"I suppose I would have wanted that, too, had there been the slightest chance of attaining it. He wasn't the affectionate sort . . . never held me or kissed me that I recall. Even on his deathbed, I remember, I tried to kiss my father good-bye, but he wouldn't have it." The man's voice was husky and Fancy paid closer attention.

"Was your mother loving?"

Jason stared past Fancy into memory. "She would have been more so, perhaps, if it hadn't been for my father's coldness. He didn't approve of coddling a boy, you see. He intended that I be strong and independent. Did me a good turn in that, I suspect."

"Didn't anyone ever just love you?" Fancy asked, disturbed by the revelation.

Jason blinked back into the present and looked at his companion. "Perhaps you will, Fancy," he said with a smile that was almost shy.

"What about Tildy?"

"She was too afraid of me to love me. I was a hard man, when I was young."

And not much different now, Fancy thought, but perhaps you have good reason. Impulsively, she left the chaise and moved to his side to kiss his cheek.

"What was that for, my dear?"

"That was just because you've never let me glimpse inside before."

But Jason knew the kiss had been to replace the others he'd never had, and that letting someone inside was the greatest danger of all.

"What do you long for, Jason," she asked suddenly. "Something that money can't buy."

He smiled at her.

"The same thing everyone wants, even you, my dear . . . to be happy, to feel fulfillment, perhaps even to be loved."

Fancy set down her champagne glass and looked into Jason's eyes searchingly.

"I never knew until this moment that you were vulnerable, too, Jason. What an endearing revelation." He took her into his arms and this time she didn't resist. He'd been very good to her and she was grateful . . . grateful enough and lonely enough to let whatever would happen, happen.

"You are infinitely more attractive when you're human, Jason," she said, trying hard to want him as she knew he wanted her. "It's very hard to love a man of iron."

Jason made an oddly strangled sound as he folded her close; could it be he'd never let any woman in before? she wondered as she returned his caresses. And what might she encounter beyond the facade? Fancy wound the fingers of one hand in his hair and with the other, she methodically unbuttoned his shirt.

▲

Why had he let Fancy wander into vulnerable places? Jason asked himself the next day. Why did it feel so pleasurable to have let her through his guard? Her responsiveness had been remarkable—for months he'd tried to seduce her, only to be deftly sidestepped again and again. Then, one or two small revelations of weakness had burst the floodgates . . . how curious that vulnerability should be more seductive than power. How could any man ever understand the workings of a woman's mind?

Christ! she was good in bed. She'd actually undressed him, egged him on, begged for more and matched his lust, desire for desire. She'd opened that perfect body wantonly, yet with exquisite delicacy . . . touching him, panting to be touched in turn, swollen lips attesting to her fervor, pouting nipples longing to be kissed, pinched, sucked. By God, it had been a night to remember.

Jason handed the florist the hand-scribbled note that would accompany the three dozen roses, and walked to his carriage whistling a tune from Fancy's show. Maybe he'd produce her next show himself, find a vehicle to showcase her particular talents . . . he certainly didn't intend to leave her in the clutches of that amateur Glick. There was no reason for her to need a manager, when he could simply open whatever doors there were that needed opening. A few well-placed introductions and the knowledge that she was under Jason Madigan's protection would be all that was required.

53 Chance thought it best to stay on cozy terms with all five of Leadville's prosperous banks, as it would remain to be seen which one would take the most liberal view of his real estate aspirations. Now that the Fancy Penny was starting to pay off big, land seemed as good a place as any to start an empire. Haw Tabor was president of the Bank of Leadville and a major voice in most of what happened in the town.

Chance checked his new timepiece and watched the doorway of the Clarendon Hotel from his place in its lobby. Most of the important business in Leadville was consummated in the Clarendon's large reception rooms, or at its red-plush bar.

Tabor shook the hands of three or four prosperous-looking men as he made his way across the lobby to the overstuffed armchair Chance occupied. He, too, had his eye on a political future. He pumped Chance's arm firmly before sitting, high-signed to a waiter, and pulled out a cigar before settling in to business.

"Damnedest mess out there you ever saw," he began jovially. "So much building going on you can't stand five minutes on the street corner for fear somebody'll put a roof over your head."

Chance smiled and ordered a drink of his own. He had an agenda in mind for this meeting.

"What do you hear about the Bland-Allison Act, Haw?" he asked casually. Tabor was reputed to have powerful friends in Washington who funneled him information.

"The word is Congress will pass the act whether or not President Hayes vetoes."

Chance raised an eyebrow. The Bland-Allison Act was a compromise, designed to pacify western silver interests by allowing two to four million dollars of silver to be coined each month. The eastern establishment fought for gold; the western financiers fought for silver, but at least this legislation would mean about half of the silver mined each year could be moved from commercial use to government, which would probably result in rising silver prices.

Haw leaned back in his chair as he spoke. "The good old boys on Wall Street are still pushing to keep the gold standard and give silver the boot, but we've got some firepower in our camp too."

"I've been thinking, Haw," Chance replied quietly. "It wouldn't hurt if we considered organizing some sort of 'Silver Alliance' to keep an eye on things."

Tabor's ears perked up. McAllister had a good head on his shoulders and he was making a name for himself in the Republican party locally. He was unschooled in finance, of course, but then who among them wasn't?

"You mean a kind of club for the big silver boys?"

"I mean an organization to watch whatever needs watching. To keep silver interests in the newspapers, maybe to lobby for us in Washington. It might help us keep a consensus among our own, as well. You know miners are an independent lot—they don't work easily in double yoke, just because they suddenly get wealthy. The backers of the gold standard are rich and well organized. We're just rich."

Tabor smiled at Chance's shrewdness. "Good point, McAllister. Maybe a group of similarly minded men could watch out for our best interests better than individuals. You willing to spend some time getting such a project off the ground?"

"If that's the way to get it done, I am." Chance wondered, as he said it, how his taking more time away from the mine office would sit with Hart, then dismissed the thought, certain his brother would understand.

Haw Tabor left the meeting with a cautious interest in Chance McAllister. He'd been watching the young man at town meetings and mine owner gatherings for some time now. He himself intended to be senator of this new state, so he viewed Chance's political ambitions with a keen sense of appraisal. McAllister was young and most likely reckless; yet any man who'd ever played poker with him knew he was a contender. He was damned plausible too—handsome as hell, with a manner that could charm the birds from the bushes. He'd bear considerable watching.

▲

Hart listened to Chance's recounting of his conversation with Tabor with amusement.

"How much do you really know about this silver-versus-gold controversy you're getting mixed up in?" Hart asked, with his feet propped up on the mine manager's rolltop desk. The shift was over and his own day had ended a few minutes before; he was tired and had been gladder than usual to hear the shift whistle blow.

Chance grinned. "Not a whole hell of a lot, to tell the truth, bro. But I figure I can learn real quick if it'll get me in tight with the power boys."

Hart shook his head. "And you just assume you're supposed to swim with the big fish."

Chance sat forward in his chair and looked earnest. "Listen, bro. We're going to be up to our asses in silver pretty soon now. If the pro-gold men have their way, all U.S. currency will be backed by gold, and silver won't be worth piss-all.

"I'd be the first to tell you that banking isn't my long suit. But dealing with gamblers—and that's all they are, Hart, heavy hitters—why, that's right up my alley. It's plain as the nose on your face, there's no faster way to make a name for yourself than getting in tight with the power brokers. There's a lot of land out there in the Mosquitoes that's got silver in it, and there's a lot more real estate right here in Leadville that can be turned into money if we just get in on the ground floor. The choice of who gets access to that real estate is going to be in the hands of just a few men, and my chance is as good as any to be one of them."

Hart shook his head again, and chuckled. "I guess you've got to aim high if you're ever going to get off the ground. Just don't get so big for your breeches Bandana and I will have to make an appointment with your secretary to see you."

Chance grinned again and Hart laughed aloud. "You sure do have the right smile for politicking. Damned if you couldn't sell corn to Kiowas."

Chance was relieved by his brother's approval. "And that's the very least of my assets, bro. You just wait and see."

"It doesn't appear I've got any choice in the matter, whatsoever." Hart pushed some papers into a drawer and locked the rolltop before getting out of his chair. "Care for some dinner, Chance? Bandana says the steaks at Bauer's place are the only ones in town didn't die of old age."

Chance put his hand on his brother's shoulder, a warm gesture. "I'd like that fine. About the only thing wrong with being rich that I can see, is you and I seem never to see each other anymore."

Hart nodded, wondering if that loss seemed as great to Chance as it did to him.

The older brother followed the younger through the door and waited while he locked it.

"You know, bro, I expect it seems to you that I'm always dreaming up impossible schemes and shooting the moon—and I guess you're just too damned practical to approve of all that I get into. But I've been thinking lately that I'd like to explain a couple of things to you, best I can."

Hart looked up, surprised by the serious turn in the conversation.

"I know it looks to you like I go off half-cocked on these wild schemes of mine, doing things I've got no business doing. But to tell you the truth, bro, I don't have a whole hell of a lot of choice in how I go about things. What I mean is, I don't have a God-given talent like you do, or a backbone like Daddy's, that can slave away a lifetime on moral principle and be satisfied with nothing to show at the end of it but righteousness.

"What talent I got is in my way with people, and in my dreams, which is just another word for ambitions, when you get right down to it. You've got to work with what you've been given in this life, Hart—if you've got big wants, you've got to try for them or else you'll die wanting. I don't intend to grow old feeling maybe if I'd tried for the moon and stars, at least I'd have had one hell of a ride. Does that make any sense to you, at all?"

"A short life but a glorious one . . ." Hart replied quietly, touched by his brother's need to be honest with him. "That's what Alexander the Great asked of the gods, Chance. I guess I do understand what you're telling me."

Chance looked squarely at his brother and Hart saw the caring in his eyes as he spoke again.

"The second thing I want you to know, bro, is that even if I don't always take your advice, or do the things you think I should, I value what you tell me. It's just that sometimes, I don't know how to do things your way, so I've got to do them mine. But that doesn't mean I don't know yours is the right way." His voice was low and earnest. "You've got a lot of Daddy in you, Hart. I admire that more than you know."

Hart heard the catch in his brother's voice; sensed that what he'd said had been long brooded over. It was hard for men to show strong emotions to each other—was it fear of vulnerability that stopped them? Was it unmanly to care so much? Their daddy had cared, and he had been a man.

Hart's voice was husky when he replied, "I understand, Chance . . . better than you think." He paused a moment, casting about for the right way to say what he needed to. "I love you too."

Slightly embarrassed, slightly relieved, each man mounted his horse and headed toward town.

▲

Chance's Silver Alliance was a huge success and secured him a foot in the door of the elite. His total recall made it easy for him to play back, word for word, conversations in which important things were said; and he had a natural gift for knowing what to say, when.

His gambling and womanizing were looked on askance by the men in the party whose job it was to keep on the lookout for potential candidates, but "What the hell," they said among themselves . . . at least they were both manly pursuits, and any red-blooded American boy who looked like McAllister could hardly be faulted for taking advantage of the women who threw themselves into his path.

Fancy felt Aurora's head for the dozenth time; the child was feverish again. She'd tried a score of herbal remedies, but nothing worked for long.

54 🌿

She checked her purse to see if there was money for another doctor's visit and was relieved to see there was. The special foods she'd purchased to try to tempt Aurora's finicky appetite had depleted her budget, as had the milk bought from a special herd of cows, and all the other tricks she'd tried to strengthen the little girl. But there was Mrs. Donaher's salary to contend with, and the fact that she'd left the boarding-house and rented a tiny place of their own.

She didn't mind sacrificing for Aurora, but this new play was grueling and had sapped her own strength, and it made no sense at all to her that Aurora did not respond to her own vast knowledge of remedies.

"I don't feel well, Mommy," the child whispered hoarsely—Aurora's throat was always the source of her problems. Tonsillitis, the doctor had called it last winter, then quinsy throat, now it just seemed to be a chronic weakness. *The throat is the seat of your soul's purpose,* Magda had said. . . .

Fancy glanced at the clock and saw it was nearly time to leave for the theatre. Aurora watched her mother's agitation and leapt on it, her big eyes fever-bright.

"Don't go, Mommy. I feel really sick this time."

"I don't have any choice, sweetheart. I can't leave all those people at the theatre with no leading lady, can I?"

Aurora pushed out her bottom lip. "You have an understudy."

"Oh, if you only knew how dangerous that is, my darling," Fancy said, as she stood up with a sigh and prepared, reluctantly, to go.

Mrs. Donaher was standing in the doorway, tying on her apron; the small plump woman feared for both mother and child. "Don't worry, missus. I'll take good care of the little one while you're gone."

"Give her this medicine one more time, before she goes to sleep, please, Mrs. Donaher. I'll be back just as soon as the show is over."

"Why don't you love me, Mommy?" Aurora asked, tears welling in the corners of her great eyes.

"Not love you, darling? Of course I love you!"

"If you loved me, you wouldn't go away and leave me when I'm sick."

"If I don't work, Aurora, how will we eat and pay our rent and Mrs. Donaher?"

"I don't want Mrs. Donaher! I want my mommy!" Aurora began to sob and the sobs provoked a coughing fit. Fancy worried about coughing; so many children died of consumption that any cough was suspect. Aurora knew it was an excellent way to get her mother's attention.

Mrs. Donaher saw the frightened look on Fancy's face and stepped forward. This little one had her mother wrapped around her finger, and poor Mrs. Deverell tried so hard to make up for the time she spent away from the girl.

"Don't you worry now, dear, I'll watch her like she was me own. There's not much I haven't seen of little ones—what with the seven God gave me, and the three I raised for me poor sister, God rest her. Now you just go about your business and we'll be right as rain here."

Aurora turned her back on her mother deliberately, and facing the wall, began to sob. Fancy took a step toward her, then realizing that sympathy would only provoke more weeping, she turned and fled the room.

Fancy had the niggling feeling that Aurora's constant illness was somehow connected with the child's inordinate need for attention, but she didn't know what to do about it. She spent every minute she could with Aurora, playing, reading, teaching, talking. But the little girl was a bottomless pit of need; no matter how much she gave, it was never enough. Sometimes Fancy felt she was drowning in Aurora's need . . . and in her own, to boot. But she couldn't think all that through just now—in half an hour she would have to give a creditable performance. There were important backers in the audience tonight and to perform well she must gather all her resources and concentrate . . . concentrate . . .

▲

The doctor looked up into Fancy's troubled face and removed his spectacles. "I'm afraid your daughter has pneumonia, Mrs. Deverell," he said gravely. "It can be very serious in a child her age. Life-threatening, in fact. She'll have to go to the hospital; there really isn't any choice."

People died in hospitals, Fancy thought, frightened—people she loved died before their time. Could it be she'd forgotten some important maternal task and this was to be her punishment?

"I'll see to having her admitted to the ward, Mrs. Deverell. You must take her round to the clinic immediately."

Fancy looked up distractedly. "Ward? Clinic? I won't have my little girl in a clinic, Doctor. Private care is what I want."

The doctor eyed the shabby surroundings.

"Can you really afford that, Mrs. Deverell? Private care is costly, and I assure you, the patients on the ward get excellent treatment."

Fancy straightened her spine. "Thank you for your concern, Doctor, but

I wouldn't consider putting my child into the hospital without the best of private care."

The doctor shook his head as if to say there's no dealing rationally with the mother of a sick child. "As you wish then, Mrs. Deverell. Just remember that speed is essential now . . . your daughter's condition could turn critical at any moment."

Fancy shut the door behind the doctor and leaned her head against it, trying to breathe. People died of pneumonia . . . she shut out the hateful thought, swiped at the tears on her cheeks, and gathered her courage.

She scribbled a hasty note to Jason asking help; it would tip the balance of leverage irrevocably in his favor, but there was no time to worry about that now. He'd asked her repeatedly, during the last months, to live with him, and she'd managed to hold him off without offending, for much as she took comfort in his company, she didn't love him. Now she thanked God silently that she hadn't broken with him, as she had sometimes considered when he pushed her. What on earth would she do in this crisis without him? Fancy sealed the envelope and hastened to the bedroom.

"I'll take her, Mrs. Donaher," she said as steadily as she could. "If you'll call us a cab, I'll get her to the hospital. Just take this letter round to Mr. Madigan for me. Please be certain it goes to him directly. Don't leave it in anyone else's hands."

Mrs. Donaher read the terror in Fancy's eyes and responded. She'd lost only one of her seven, but there wasn't a day of her life when that little lost boy didn't live in her heart.

▲

The hospital room was whitewashed to a bluish tinge; the smell of disinfectant permeated the woolen blanket on which Fancy had laid her head next to Aurora. She listened absently to the hospital sounds—the occasional moans of a patient in the ward farther down the hall, the soft footfalls of the nursing nuns in the corridors, the clickety sound of their rosary beads.

An aged nun entered the room to check on the child's condition. She took her pulse, which was rapid and irregular, and changed the sweat-soaked bed linen.

"I've asked God to spare your child, Mrs. Deverell," she said softly to the young woman who hadn't left her daughter for three endless days and nights.

"A lot of good that will do, Sister," Fancy replied.

The nun stood very still, hands folded beneath her capelet. "You seem so very angry when you speak of God, Mrs. Deverell. May I ask why?"

"Because God has taken everyone I've ever loved from me, Sister, and I *am* very, very angry."

"It takes immense faith in God to rail at Him, child. Only those who believe deeply take the trouble to be angry. Surely He knows what's in your heart."

"If there is a God, Sister, why does He never answer my prayers?"

The nun pursed her lips in contemplation, then replied in a compassionate voice. "Sometimes, my dear, He answers and says no."

For a long time after the nun had pattered down the hall, Fancy thought about what she'd said with terrible misgiving.

▲

"Can't breathe, Mommy." Aurora's voice was a whisper. Her rattling breath sounded ragged in the small bony chest and every effort to pull air into her diseased lungs made the child suffer.

"I love you, baby," Fancy whispered, stroking the fevered forehead. The doctor had done all he could, but the infection still filled the child's lungs with fluid and the fever still hovered far too high for safety. Fancy put her arms around her daughter and felt that the sheets were again damp from the fever sweat. On impulse, she pulled the clean blanket from the foot of the bed and wrapping the little girl in its fold, she lifted her out of bed and onto her lap.

So frail, she thought, clutching Aurora close to her heart. I cannot bear to lose you. . . . The crisis would come tonight, the doctor said; the fever would peak and then dissipate, or the infection would outdistance all that medicine could do and would rampage its way through the little body that had no strength left to fight back. Fancy rocked the child, racking her brain for some effort left untried. Magda could save her, but Magda was far away. . . .

"I wanted to live in a big house, Mommy," the child whispered. "Mr. Madigan said he'd take care of us . . ." A fit of uncontrollable coughing wracked her. Spasms convulsed the small limbs and left the fragile body fighting for breath.

Fancy held her daughter so close that the rattle in her chest reverberated against the mother's heart. An unutterable sense of failure welled in Fancy; all she'd ever wanted for Aurora was safety and plenty . . . but what had she provided her? Bedbugs and poverty, dragged from pillar to post, weakened so this insidious illness could destroy her.

"Stay alive, baby," she whispered into the girl's dark hair as she rocked her. "If you just stay alive, Mommy will get you what you need, I swear it. I'll let Mr. Madigan take care of us and bring us to his big house and you can feel safe, sweetheart, truly safe and warm. And you won't have to be afraid of anything ever again. I promise you, darling. Just stay alive, Aurora . . . please, sweetheart. You just have to stay alive."

Fancy tried desperately to remember what Magda had taught her of healing, so long ago. Why hadn't she paid more attention? She remembered the healing energy she'd once felt fill her hands . . . how in God's name had she gathered it? She moved to the door, and glancing once, up the corridor, closed and locked it behind her.

Fancy tried to recall the colors of the chakras, and how to get her spine into proper alignment. Damn it all, there had to be a way to remember! She lowered her hips and tried to imagine the flesh hanging from her bones as Magda had taught. Red, orange, yellow, green, sky blue, indigo, white-gold . . . that was it! It was worth a try. With every ounce of energy she could muster, Fancy sent her own chakras spinning and eventually she felt the tingling fire seep into her arms and hands, as if filling twin cups. *Magda, help me!* she cried out in her heart. Trying to breathe in the strength she needed, Fancy laid her fiery hands on her daughter's chest and prayed to a god she barely believed in, with all the fervor of a zealot.

When the doctor returned to check on Aurora at 11:00 p.m., he found her lying in the rocker in her mother's arms. Much to his amazement both mother and child were sleeping peacefully.

▲

Aurora's illness was the turning point for Fancy in many ways, for it made her feel vulnerable again, and made clear the virtue of not having to cope with adversity alone. Jason's money paid the bills, Jason's presence made the staff snap to, Jason's kindness made life easier. For all she knew, it may have been Jason's power that saved her daughter's life, not God's.

If only I could love him, she thought moodily. He's strong and smart, tough enough to protect me and Aurora—he's even generous enough to want to. And he's lovable in small ways, like the constant barrage of flowers, candy and toys for Aurora, the countless indulgences . . .

But he isn't Chance. Maybe love like that only strikes once in a lifetime and, lightning-like, is gone forever. Maybe no one could bear that intensity on a day-to-day basis anyway. . . .

It was time to make some decisions; Jason had asked her to be his mistress. He hadn't asked her to be his wife, as she'd expected. He'd been angry at her refusal, just as she'd been angry at his proposing the wrong thing. Damn it to hell! They'd had a terrible row and he'd said he intended to see other women and she could go to the devil for all he cared. She had waited three days for him to call and apologize, but there'd been no word at all.

Fancy drummed her fingers nervously on the chest of drawers before deciding that she mustn't lose him now, not when Aurora still needed care and she had made a promise to her child. Goose bumps rose on her arms as she unfolded the wrinkled sheet of paper, then refolded it and finally flattened it out on the desk. She hadn't even looked at it since that day in Magda's bedroom, years before.

The hairs rose at the nape of her neck as she began to assemble the items the paper said she would need. . . . What if the spell didn't work. . . . What if it did?

Fancy pushed her hair back hurriedly from her forehead, there wasn't much time before the housekeeper returned.

If only she knew what *deosil* meant. . . .

▲

"You seem defeated rather than elated in accepting my offer of a home and all that any woman could wish for, Fancy," Jason said astutely, standing next to Aurora's bed at St. Vincent's Infirmary. "Many women would jump at the chance to share my world." He'd decided to feel pleased at her acquiescence, rather than hurt by her lack of enthusiasm, but it was difficult.

Fancy took a breath before replying. "You must forgive me, Jason, if becoming your mistress is not the apex of all I had in mind for myself."

Jason threw back his head and roared with laughter. At least she was honest—he would have seen through self-serving subterfuge in an instant.

"Then become my wife instead."

Fancy's eyes darted to his; never once before this had he mentioned marriage.

"Let's not spoil a good thing, Jason," she said carefully. "I'm too tired to get married." The smile that accompanied the rebuff was weary enough to make it believable.

Jason pursed his lips, deciding whether to be angry or relieved. Marriage could always come later. Fancy was doing this for the child's sake, and for expediency, not out of adoration. No matter. All life was leverage and how you used it. He would get a good return on his investment in Fancy and Aurora, and so would they. The three days he'd spent waiting for her to call had been unnervingly empty.

Jason bent down to Aurora's bedside and lifted the little girl into his arms. He'd gone out of his way to be good to the child and she'd responded in kind. How starved for a father's love this bird-thin daughter of Fancy's was, and how exquisitely beautiful. Even drained by her illness, Aurora's beauty had caused nurses and doctors to look in on her more frequently than was strictly necessary. That, and the fact that Jason Madigan was paying her bills.

Jason smiled a little—life was so very predictable. The thought made him pause. That's what made Fancy special—she was not predictable at all. Just when he thought he had her where he wanted her, she flitted away; the fun of the chase made Jason feel young again. He hugged Aurora, picked up her small valise, and led Fancy down the corridor toward his waiting carriage.

"Are you all ready to come home to my house, Aurora? It's awfully big, you know; we may have to give you a road map, so you won't get lost finding your new room." He smiled benevolently.

"I like big houses, Mr. Madigan. I always wanted to live in one."

"Well, then, now that your dream has come true, we can't have you calling me Mr. Madigan, can we? How does Uncle Jason suit you?"

Aurora hugged the man who held her. "Uncle Jason sounds wonderful," she said contentedly, relaxing into his strong arms.

"At least one of the women in the Deverell family is glad to be coming home with me," Jason chuckled, casting a sidelong glance at Fancy. He would have given quite a lot to know what she was thinking.

55   The year after Aurora's illness was the most magical of the child's life. Every dream she'd dreamed while poor, every happiness imagined on her daily walks through the streets of the rich, was now reality.

Hardly a week went by when Jason didn't present her with a trinket of some kind; when he traveled, he sent home parcels of goodies. He engaged a proper nanny, and a tutor, so that Fancy was able to see her daughter's education seriously under way. He bought the child a pony with fine blood lines, so she might ride with them at their summer house in Tuxedo Park. Aurora had taken to riding like an eaglet to flight.

The child was not the only one for whom life had improved; Fancy had to admit Jason's money and influence had changed the complexion of everything. She learned the jargon of business, and the uses of power by powerful men. Her theatrical career skyrocketed, not simply because of Jason's importance in New York—she was, after all, immensely talented—but he opened the doors and her gifts allowed her to walk through them, so that Fancy Deverell was soon a household name spoken with envy. The very fact that Aurora was so happy and well cared for allowed Fancy the freedom to stretch and expand and succeed.

She hobnobbed with the greats and the merely self-important . . . she wore Paris gowns and furs and jewels. The press followed the gilded couple on their glittering social rounds, and Fancy reveled in the attention. In fact, she had so many of the things she'd always coveted that it troubled her deeply that she wasn't happy.

But Fancy didn't love Jason Madigan.

What you want and what you need may be two very different matters,
Magda had said, and Fancy had never understood her meaning, until now.

▲

"You didn't need Dinero's company did you, Jason?" Fancy asked the
question over dinner. She'd begun to pay close attention to Jason's business
machinations. The attention flattered him, and he allowed her freer access
to his dealings; he liked acting the role of tutor.

"I didn't need it financially, no. That's astute of you to observe, my dear.
But I did need it to teach that pup a lesson about who's in charge. Power
is a funny game, Fancy. Even after you win it, you only get to keep it if
you know how to wield the thunderbolts. Some men lack decisiveness,
some lack the balls for the dirty work, some simply don't see the big picture clearly enough to want it all. Power demands showmanship. Nailing
Dinero to the wall will deter others from making the same mistake he
made."

"Which was?"

"Thinking he could play in my league."

Fancy rang the bell to signal the servants to clear the table for dessert.

"What would you have done in my place, my dear?" he asked. "You
know this scenario, how would you have played it?"

"Slapped his wrist, I suppose, which would only have made him angrier.
I can see that breaking the wrist is far more effective as a deterrent, I just
don't think I'd have the stomach for it."

Jason laughed heartily. "I told you you had the instincts for business,
Fancy. All you lack is the ruthlessness. But give me time, my dear, and you
may even develop that."

Fancy smiled without meaning it, as she rose to take coffee and dessert
before the drawing room fire. She had no intention of staying with Jason
nearly long enough to learn ruthlessness. She was happy, now, that she
hadn't married him, for it was clear to her that the life she led was not
enough. She didn't want to be merely an appendage to any man; much as
she liked the comfort and safety Jason provided, she felt fettered by their
relationship. A songbird in a gilded cage is still a captive, and there were
things she was learning about him that were disturbing.

Fancy didn't yet know exactly how or when she would escape—and she
intended to learn everything possible before going—but she definitely intended to go.

▲ ▲ ▲

"Damn it! I thought I told you to stop those union organizers."

"I tried, Mr. Madigan, but they're real determined, sir. Their lives are on the line here—if we break the strike, their families will starve."

"That is not my concern, Goretti, I gave you specific orders that you failed to carry out and your failure is costing me money."

Fancy stood outside the half-opened door and listened, her horror genuine. She'd read about the dock strike in the papers, her sympathy with the unionizers. She hadn't known Jason owned stock in Amalgamated Shipping. God Almighty, was there anything he *didn't* own stock in?

"Jeez, Mr. Madigan. I don't think there's any way to stop them unless we kill the bastards."

"How you stop them is not my concern."

"If we kill them, Mr. Madigan, can my men count on your friends at City Hall to cover for us? I don't want to end up in jail or nothin'."

"You do as you see fit, Goretti. I assure you there will be no repercussions over your efficiency. The men at City Hall are as tired of these infernal dockers as I am."

The man let himself out of the study and Jason resumed his work at the desk. Fancy stepped into the room, shaking with indignation. Jason frowned at the realization that she'd overheard the discussion.

"You would actually *kill* those poor men on the docks just to break this strike, Jason? I can't believe I heard you say that."

Jason looked annoyed, shuffled his papers, then sat back and stared at her.

"I will kill no one. And you had best learn not to eavesdrop, if you can't handle what you hear. Survival goes to the fittest, Fancy. Read Mr. Darwin. When it comes to paying for your jewels and furs and caviar, you're not so squeamish about asking where the money comes from. Business is hard and dirty. The losers can get hurt if they're in the way. I don't make the rules, Fancy. I just live by them."

"Is murder one of the rules?"

"Just one of the occasional hazards."

"That makes me ill."

"See that you're over it by six. The governor is stopping by for drinks and I'm taking him to see you perform."

Fancy nodded perfunctorily, sick at heart. How naive she'd been to think there was any line he would stop at, if something he wanted was on the other side. And he was right that she'd never questioned the origins of the money that pampered her.

At least she hadn't married him. Money and power were one thing . . . murder was something else entirely.

▲

The bed creaked with Fancy's restless movement. The nightmare had awakened her and she'd lain there, with visions of Leadville vivid in her mind.

With each day she resented her entrapment increasingly, but now she feared Jason, too, and knew escape might not be easy. He didn't like to lose and didn't take rejection gently. It was in bed with Jason that she most often thought of leaving.

Almost as if he'd heard her thoughts, Madigan turned to take Fancy into his arms. She groaned inwardly; they'd already made love once tonight and she didn't relish the thought of another session. She felt the hardened flesh press against her buttocks and knew there was no evasion.

Jason crushed Fancy's lips hard against his own and rammed his body into hers. She'd noticed that the quality of his business day markedly affected the nature of his lovemaking. He was angry and frustrated tonight, and it showed in the savagery of his assault. She was repelled but unresisting, resigned to the return she must make on all he provided her. The longer she stayed, the more she felt like a prostitute, paying for everything with her flesh.

Not that he wasn't capable of being a tender lover, too; he was often a fine technician, who played her body to perfection. But he could be brutal . . . or careless . . . or callous, as he was tonight. But his moods and motivations no longer mattered to her; she felt repelled by the violence she sensed in him now, and by the unthinkable acts of power he committed entirely without conscience. Ever since the Amalgamated incident, she'd made it her business to learn as much about his business as she could.

She'd seen firsthand how power games are played, how money buys not merely comfort, but everything and everybody. For a year she'd lived in Jason's considerable shadow, with everything anyone could wish for, except freedom and self-determination and the love of the right man. And she had to admit that in the beginning, none of that had mattered enough to offset the rewards and Aurora's love for him.

She felt guilty for not loving this man who had given her so much of what she wanted. It wasn't his fault that she'd misunderstood her own rebellious needs—but it wasn't hers that he'd turned out to be a murderer.

Jason climaxed, rolled over in the bed, and was asleep in minutes. Fancy, wide-eyed, and unsatisfied, waited until he was asleep to get away. Gingerly, she pulled back the covers and tiptoed to the marble bathroom where she sponged herself clean of him with quiet determination, before going through the adjoining door to Aurora's bedroom.

Aurora's hair spread out around her on the pillow like a dark and silken cloud. Fancy stood for a moment taking in the lovely picture, barely breathing. I love you so much, she thought. How can I hurt you by leaving here? Will you ever forgive me if I do?

As if she'd heard the thought's echo, Aurora stirred uneasily in her sleep and drew her legs up into a fetal ball beneath the covers. Fancy leaned down and brushed her daughter's velvety cheek with her lips.

Silently she turned and made her way back to the bedroom. She would read Jewel's letter one more time, and see if it still made her heart beat faster . . . see if she really had found the escape route.

> Jewel Mack, Proprietress
> The Crown of Jewel's
> Leadville, Colorado
> June 1, 1878

Dear Fancy,
You've sounded way off your feed in your last three letters, kid. Damned if I don't think New York disagrees with you. Each time you write you seem less happy and who could blame you, stuck out there with all them concrete buildings and having to ride your horse on a path in a park, instead of out in God's country. Even if you are the best damned actress in New York and everybody knows your name, what fun does that give you?

So I've got a proposition for you, and I want you to think real hard before you turn me down. There's a boom on here in Leadville, the likes of Sutter's Creek! Every second bozo on the street has struck it rich enough to have gold hanging out of his ears—including Bandana and your friends the McAllisters, who, by the way, named their mine the Fancy Penny, in your honor, I'd guess if I had to.

That theatre we talked about once could rake in dough by the sackful, if we do it right now and don't let some other saloon get the drop on us.

Come home, Fancy! Do yourself and Aurora a favor. Cities are no place for a kid to grow up. Just let me know real quick if you're game, because if you say no, I'll have to find someone else to be my partner.

> Your friend,
> Jewel

Fancy folded the letter and stared at the cream-colored stock; she'd re-read it so often during the last week, the paper was dog-eared. Jewel's proposal could give her exactly what she'd need to make a life independent of Jason, and just the mention of Chance McAllister's bonanza made Colorado seem seductive all over again. If he had all the money he'd ever dreamed of, would he still remember what they'd once planned together? They'd named the mine the Fancy Penny, they couldn't have forgotten.

There was no way on earth to leave Jason and remain in New York City; he would pursue her with the same single-mindedness he reserved for anything he wanted. But Leadville was far enough away for safety, and the one place on earth where she could finally put her unfinished business with Chance to rest.

Fancy tucked the note back in the dresser drawer; she hadn't felt this excited about anything since she'd gotten her first good reviews.

I've done what I set out to do, she thought. Three hit plays in a row and my name in all the best newspapers, my posters on every other tree trunk and construction site in the city . . . even if nothing else ever works out, I can always look back on that success.

She sighed and pulled her peignoir tight around her against the midnight chill; she'd act on Jewel's letter immediately—a telegram, tomorrow morning. With what she now knew of theatrical productions and of business, she and Jewel would have a land-office enterprise going in six months. Nobody liked a good time better than a miner whose lonely life had finally paid off big. Fancy had ideas for other businesses, too, the kind that sprang up in boom times in boomtowns—she hadn't lived so long with Jason Madigan without learning a thing or two.

She would be an entrepreneur with money in her pocket and no man to answer to, in a clean, new place where there were trees and rivers and horses and . . . Chance McAllister.

"Fancy!" Jason's voice cut through her reverie. "Where are you?" Oh, God. She'd have to find a way to tell him she was leaving. It was hard not to be a little afraid of Jason.

"I'm coming back to bed in a minute, Jason," she called out. "I have a headache and need a bit of air."

Tomorrow she'd find a way to break the news to him.

▲

"You can't be serious, Fancy. You can't possibly mean that you intend to leave me." Jason tried to regain his equilibrium but this blow had come out of nowhere. Most of the world scrambled to be in his charmed circle. No one ever tried to get away.

Fancy steadied herself to brave the storm.

"It isn't that I don't care for you, Jason, please understand that . . . no one could have been better to us than you."

"Why, then?"

"Because I'm only an appendage to your life, and that's not enough for me. We do what you want, when you want. We make love when you want to, eat when you want to, travel when you want to . . ." She faltered, unable to express her need. Why did it sound so selfish and so mundane to demand her own life back?

"Is that such a hardship, Fancy? Isn't that just the way the world is for women who are loved?" His voice was incredulous, hurt.

"Yes. That's exactly how the world is, Jason, and it's not your fault that it's not enough for me. I need to make my own future and Aurora's somewhere far from here. I don't want to raise her in the city."

"You'd leave the theatre, too? It's inconceivable. I think you've lost your mind."

"I have another kind of theatre in mind, Jason. Far from New York."

Jason's fists clenched and unclenched at his side. "And another kind of man? Is that what this is really all about, Fancy? Is that son of a bitch in Leadville suddenly available?"

Fancy started, like a fawn in the thicket. "What do you mean by that?"

"Do you think I'm such a fool I haven't had the Pinkertons on your trail since day one? There isn't anything I don't know about you, Fancy."

Her eyes widened with shock. "Why, you self-serving bastard! That's just the kind of high-handed horseshit that's making me leave you, Jason. I will not be owned—not by you—not by anyone." Fancy turned away angrily and stormed toward the staircase. At the first landing, she called out to him.

"You can have your Pinkertons follow me to the edge of doom, Jason, for all I care . . . but I'm the one thing on this earth you will never own."

Jason heard the reverberation of the slammed door and felt rooted where he stood. Didn't she know how much he loved her? Never had he let another woman into the secret places of his heart . . . never had he let himself be vulnerable with anyone. Oh, God . . . there'd never be another. Jason wiped his handkerchief swiftly across his face, then he swallowed his pride and climbed the stairs after her.

He stood in the doorway of her room and saw she'd had the servants carry her theatre trunk up from storage. "I love you, Fancy. You must know I do. And I love Aurora. Be my wife . . . don't throw away a life like ours for a worthless dream and a scoundrel who wouldn't even marry you. . . ."

Fancy snapped the trunklid back. "It wasn't like that," she said, wounded that he knew her secret. "I never gave him a chance to keep us."

"You're doing the same thing over again, can't you see that? You have a man who loves you, and you're running away again. Think what this will do to your daughter."

"That's a low blow, Jason. This is between you and me, isn't it?"

"But I've given you everything—"

"Yes. You've given me everything, including love, and I'll always be grateful. But you didn't do it out of charity for the famous lost waif of Broadway. I paid my dues, Jason! I gave you what you wanted every day of our life together, in exchange for what you gave me, and God knows I tried to *be* what you wanted, but I just can't be that anymore. Let me go, Jason, in God's name. I don't want to have to hate you."

Jason heard the finality in her words; he reached out toward her, but she didn't reach back. He'd never begged for anything since the day he was born; he let his hand drop to his side and stared at her for a long, silent moment.

Jason walked shakily down the spiral stair and locked the door to his study behind him. He sat for a time without moving, the tears rolling down his square face.

There were things he'd have to do to protect himself . . . have her followed, make sure she meant him no harm with all the secrets she possessed . . . but not today. If she were a man, he'd have her killed, but he hurt too much to be practical. Was this what losers felt, this abysmal desolation? Or was this agony reserved for lovers?

He glanced at the stocky, square body reflected in the gilt mirror beside his desk. He saw middle age . . . gray hair, face lined with experience, a grim expression born of power. How could a woman like Fancy love a man who looked like this? Wouldn't she always long for youth and handsomeness, for the ephemeral perfect lust of the young that nothing, not even money and power, can compensate? He took the photograph of Chance McAllister out of the Pinkerton folder on his desk and stared at it with hatred.

Jason Madigan put his silver head down on the desk where deals were consummated daily that made men tremble, and he cried.

▲

Fancy stood with her back against the door, a pain like a toothache in her head. What if he was right and what she planned was insane . . . she'd have to leave quickly before his logic or his love undermined her resolve.

"I'm so sorry, Jason," she whispered into the silence. "I never meant to harm you. I didn't even know you could be harmed . . ." What if the Binding Ritual was responsible for his obsessive passion. No! That was absolutely ridiculous. This was 1878 and the ritual was just some stupid Gypsy superstition, and besides, she hadn't even done it right.

Fancy, guilty and nervous, moved to the closet and began to yank her clothes off the hangers, wondering why on earth she could never stay where it was safe.

▲

Jason didn't thunder at her as she walked out the door the following day. In truth, he seemed more injured than vindictive. He would miss her, he said, and he would miss Aurora, who clung crying to his waist.

Jason reminded Fancy of all she was leaving behind in her career and her life-style, but never once pleaded for her to stay. His dignity surprised her.

Truth was, he had no frame of reference for the emotions he was feeling, that threatened to unman him. He wanted to beg her to stay . . . he wanted to weep for his loss . . . He wanted to kill her. He would force the unfamiliar emotions into insignificance . . . he would obliterate her unworthy memory . . . he would forget the love and the longing . . .

He would hire a detective from the Pinkerton Agency to follow her to Leadville.

VII

THUNDER ON THE MOUNTAIN

▾▾▾▾▾▾

Fancy, Her Friends, and Her Enemies The Late 1870s

"You kin strengthen the soul
with sweat faster'n
with prayin'."

BANDANA MCBAIN

56 When Fancy stepped off the stage from Denver with her daughter by the hand, she thought Leadville was like a patch of recent bean sprouts, one day nothing but a seed, the next a thousand stalks of green life bursting out.

The Kansas Pacific Railroad was raising money to run the Denver and Rio Grande along the rim of the mountains she'd mucked in seven years before. The Atchison, Topeka and Santa Fe was edging along the Arkansas valley; once the railroads were complete there'd be no stopping the boom times, for trains could bring in the hard-rock machinery and take away the ore. They could also provide the brocade and ebony, the European silver and crystal, the antiques and the reserve-stock wine and brandy, the cigars and the diamonds for the big winners.

Fancy could feel the rhythm of expansion all around her. Every intuitive bone responded to the possibilities; she'd made the right choice in leaving New York. Back East, there were cities with conveniences and culture and history, but they were bound into their own ways and those ways belonged exclusively to men. In the West, she sensed a newness, as if the world had been born this morning and you could do anything you wanted with it.

Women were scarce here—scarce enough so men tended to give them the latitude to be entrepreneurial. Many's the woman who supported her husband's prospecting efforts by baking pies and cookies or taking in laundry, and nobody batted an eye at that. In Leadville, nobody would care if Fancy tried her hand at empire building. For all she knew, they might even give her a hand.

▲ ▲ ▲

JEWEL'S RULES

Gentlemen are expected to wash out of doors and find their own water. Lodgers must furnish their own straw. Beds on barroom floor reserved for regular customers. Persons sleeping in the bar are requested not to take their boots off. Lodgers inside rise at 5 a.m., in the barn at 6 a.m. Each man sweeps up his own bed. No quartz taken at the bar.

No fighting allowed at the tables.

Anyone violating the above rules will be shot.

Jewel stood back to admire the new sign that adorned the bar at the Crown. She smiled with satisfaction and the smile made her face beautiful and young. The artist had achieved exactly what she wanted, small gold curlicues at the corners and a heavily embellished crest at the top. Other than that, the lettering was big and simple.

"Got to be able to read it with a bellyful of Taos Towse," she'd told the sign painter, whose own belly was full of the stuff so frequently, she knew he'd understand.

It was tough enough, Jewel thought, to handle the tired, lonely, uneducated, frustrated, and otherwise desperate men who came there in droves, as she had been doing for years in one brothel or another, but to handle them when they were likkered up was another matter entirely.

Part of the problem was that a saloon wasn't just a place to drink. It was a hotel, an eatery, a gambling den, a livery stable, a social club, a political arena, a dance hall, a trading post, and sometimes even a mortuary. Old Dan Kelleher had been laid out real nice in front of the bar before they'd planted him, which had seemed only fitting as he'd breathed his last right here at the Crown of Jewel's anyway. Of course, all of that was the good news, because it meant the revenue was always steady from one part or another of the options of the Crown's hospitality, and business was seldom slowed by changes in the economy.

"Pour me a whiskey, will you, Rufus?" she called to the bartender, who raised an eloquent eyebrow at her. Jewel seldom drank before sundown.

"And make it the good stuff. Not any of that cow piss the miners live on." She noted the disapproving eyebrow. "And no comments to go with it neither, *if* you don't mind."

The man smiled enough to show he understood, not what she said but what she meant. He placed the shot glass and the bottle on the bar with a practiced *thunk* and wordlessly returned to shining up the bottles. A good barkeep made a hundred dollars a month, vastly more than a miner's wage, and as far as Jewel was concerned, Rufus was worth his pay times ten.

"Might be I'm gonna like bein' an impresario," Jewel said with an expansive wave of the hand to Rufus, or the air and nobody in particular. She'd already outlined for him what would be involved in creating a theatre for Fancy.

"Better like it," Rufus replied laconically. "Gonna cost you money, sweet thing."

Jewel looked at the big colored man in the lamplight. "Or it might just make me some," she replied. Then she threw back the whiskey neat without a grimace. Rufus shook his head and grinned; even smiling, he looked like a man you wouldn't want to mess with. He was huge and powerful; his bald head gleamed in the light from the chandelier.

"When God give you dat hollow laig, you s'pose He knowed what yo' profession gonna be? It come in mighty handy."

Jewel laughed, but didn't answer. She thought of Rufus as a friend. In her kind of business, it paid to have someone trustworthy to watch your back— especially if he handled Remington's new double-barrel shotgun like he'd been born with it in his hand. She plunked the shot glass down and headed for the second floor.

▲ ▲ ▲

Fancy curtsied for the last time and threw kisses to the wildly cheering audience. The lonely men loved her when she sang the ballads they remembered from their lost childhoods . . . they loved her when she sang the bawdy lyrics of the cabaret . . . and when she danced, or recited poetry. Truth was, thought Jewel, watching the rapt audience of ragged, bearded, dirty, hard-drinking men, they loved the kid, period.

Fancy's little music hall had doubled Jewel's business in two months. Despite Rufus' dire predictions about the time that would be taken out from serious gambling and drinking, just the opposite had occurred. The miners drank steadily while Fancy performed, the "beer jugger" girls scurried back and forth from the bar to the tables, and the gamblers either gambled through the performance or came earlier and stayed later to compensate for the time their pigeons spent listening.

Fancy swept from the platform amid a chorus of cheers, whistles, and stamping feet. It fascinated Jewel that such a little bitty thing could look so grand as she entered and exited; no one ever missed the moment of Fancy's arrival or departure.

Ten minutes later, Fancy reappeared, out of costume and dressed in a robin's-egg-blue gown that showed off her bosom in its youthful perfection; her eyes, lips, and cheeks were enhanced with subtle color, or perhaps just flushed by the adulation of the crowd.

"Evening, Jewel. Nobody looks as good in red as you do." Fancy smiled engagingly as she reached the larger woman's side. Jewel was dressed in a tightly corseted red taffeta dress with black lace on the stays and decolletage. Rumor had it that the sturdy supports needed to prop up Jewel's monumental bosom were made of steel; that once a crooked gambler had tried to shoot her and the bullet had ricocheted off a stay and given her time to wing the man with a tiny Derringer kept in her garter for such emergencies.

"Scarlet as sin itself, kid. What could be more appropriate? You could have heard a poker chip fall into the sawdust tonight while you were singin'. Could've swore I was in church."

Fancy smiled graciously at the compliment; she knew it was entirely true.

"Have you got a minute to talk about an idea I've had about making extra money, Jewel?"

"Always got a minute for that, I guess. You sure don't let any grass grow under you, do you, kid? The cabaret's only open two months and now you got another business percolatin'."

Fancy was ambitious in ways Jewel hadn't even imagined a woman could be. Jewel knew her way around a buck, but Fancy's need was voracious . . . unsatisfied by success, unsatisfied by whatever money she put in her poke, maybe insatiable. She was headstrong, too; Jewel was keeping a close eye on that particular failing.

"I've been hearing things and I've been thinking, Jewel . . . when I was working the digs with the boys, it seemed to me there were two things the men needed more than anything. A safe place for their money and someone to do their laundry."

Jewel laughed uproariously. "There's sure as hell a third thing I can think of, Fancy—that's where the bulk of my business comes from! Besides, by the look of most of them men, you wouldn't think that laundry was a big priority."

"I mean it, Jewel. They trust you, and they like me. I'm telling you we could do it. They don't trust bankers and they don't want their money where they can't lay hands on it. As it is, I'll bet there are plenty of men who'd rather have their pokes in your vault than under their cots. What if we started a little sideline offering to bank it for them? We could learn about investing—I lived with a man who started out a miner and ended up a banker—"

"Hold your horses, kid! I keep their gold as a favor. Rather have it safe in my vault with Rufus and his twelve-gauge to keep an eye on it than see 'em bury it under a rock in the Mosquitoes and get their throats slit guardin' it. But I don't know a damn thing about investin'."

"But *I* do, Jewel, and what I don't know we can learn."

"And what's this fol-de-rol about laundry? That's a pretty far cry from bankin' or sellin' booze or nightbirds or entertainin' for that matter." Fancy realized for all Jewel's protests she hadn't said no.

"It's just another opportunity, Jewel, and a damned good one. If we open a laundry, we'll have men lined up in a queue that'll reach to Denver."

Jewel scratched the underside of her chin, thinking. "Need a Chinaman for laundry, Fancy. Had 'em on the Comstock. They know more about laundry than any men alive. But I ain't seen one since."

"The railroad's coming through here, Jewel. When they hook up the Union Pacific to these mountains there'll be all the Chinamen we could ever want. Besides, I know one who'd be sensational. His name's Wu. I'm not sure exactly where to find him, but if I can, he'd be the perfect man to run our laundry business and maybe a few other things I've got in mind. He's as ambitious as we are and smart as paint. We'd make money, Jewel. Lots of money."

Fancy's voice had risen enough to attract the notice of the men around her.

"Anybody looks like you, sweet thing," said a drawling man in a sweat-stained ten-gallon hat, "shouldn't have to worry about makin' money."

Fancy smiled warmly; she remembered Magda's tactics for keeping men at arm's length without offending them. "If I had a man like you at home, Bent, I wouldn't have to worry, now, would I?" she replied with just the right hint of coquettishness, then she returned her attention to Jewel who was watching her appraisingly.

The kid was no fool—banking was a tricky proposition, although not one Jewel hadn't dabbled in, in her own way. She didn't keep the men's gold entirely as a favor, she was paid for her services; it was an easy and lucrative sideline she'd learned about in other mining camps. Every camp needed a woman who was the "trusted repository"—sacrosanct, untouchable by un-written law. After all, on a mountain a thousand miles from nowhere, some-body had to be declared neutral territory or no one's poke was safe; and she was a damned good shot with pistol or rifle. And then there was Rufus and his shotgun. "Buckshot makes a mean and oozy corpse," he would have said to anyone stupid enough to trouble him or the gold.

Fancy was smart all right, and quick to spot an opportunity, but Jewel would be damned if she'd cut the kid in on everything—at least not right away. Laundry, on the other hand, that was a whole new area of enter-prise. . . .

"Why don't you see if you can find this Wu feller. See if you can get him in here for a little chitchat. If I think he can do it, I suppose we've got enough money in the kitty to bankroll some soap and a clothesline, just for the hell of it."

Fancy smiled her delight at the answer; now all she had to do was find Wu.

▲

Fancy Deverell
The Crown of Jewel's
Leadville, Colorado
September 18, 1878

Dear Wu,
I have no way of knowing if this letter will ever reach you. If it does I want to offer you a business proposition.

I now live in Leadville in the Mosquito Range about seventy miles from Denver. Destiny has given me a part interest in a music hall and a saloon. While it is not yet the success I once dreamed of, it is at least situated in the goldfields and so I still believe firmly that all we once wished for can be ours.

The proposition I offer you is this: The town of Leadville is growing daily. The miners need laundry done and I propose to start a business to do it for them, but I am busy with other enterprises. If you wish to participate with me in this venture, please (and I truly hope you will, Wu) contact me at the Crown of Jewel's, in Leadville, Colorado. I will make you a partnership arrangement that is certain to please you.

I send my hopes that this letter finds you well and prosperous and that I may see you soon again.

With love,
Fancy

She tucked the letter to Wu inside the one to Magda and Wes—she thought she remembered the Gypsy saying she knew where to reach him. She also arranged to have an ad run in the Chinese newspapers in New York and San Francisco. If Wu Chin was alive, she'd find him, she was sure of it.

Fancy had invited her three circus friends to come to Leadville to be part of her little theatre, but to her surprise, they'd declined. Denver was their home now, they said. Jarvis was a respected newspaper columnist and Magda had many prosperous clients who depended on her advice. Even Gitalis now managed the burlesque, and they were content to remain where they were.

Fancy sealed the envelope with a sigh. She could hear Aurora's high-pitched voice outside the window; thank heavens the child seemed to be making friends at last.

The first few weeks after New York had been a nightmare of anger and surliness. Aurora had so adored Jason, his "castle," and the fairy-tale life he'd provided. She'd cried for a month after leaving and hated every minute of the trip west. Fancy'd outdone herself on the train and stagecoach trip to divert her, but when Aurora was displeased with life she made certain everyone in her vicinity shared her misery. Fancy had sung to her, held her, told her stories; she'd pointed out the passing prairie and woven tales about every inch of desert or mountain as they passed it by, but Aurora had made it very plain that none of this was of the slightest interest to her.

"She's the strangest child, Magda," Fancy told her Gypsy friend when they stopped by Denver on their way to Leadville. "Sometimes I think she loves me as I love her, and other times I think she hardly cares if I live or die. She has no interest in any of the things that excited me when I was little. She learns only what she wants to learn and not one jot more. Why, at her age, I was a sponge that soaked up every drop of knowledge."

"Did you think she would come to you a clean white sheet of paper, Fancy, on which you could write what you wished to see? Her soul is as old as yours is, child, only the body it inhabits is young. You and she may not be friends at all, you know. Mothers and daughters seldom are."

"But that's absolute nonsense, Magda. I adore my daughter—I've slaved for her and gone hungry so she could eat. I've worked myself into a stupor and then gone home to play dolls, so she wouldn't feel different from the children whose mothers didn't have to work. There isn't anything I wouldn't do for her—I love her more than anything."

Magda's eyes, when Fancy looked into them, were utterly uncompromising. "What difference how much you love her, Fancy, if she loves you not?"

Fancy drew back as if slapped. "How could she not love me? Are you telling me that my daughter doesn't love me?"

"I do not say it is true, Fancy—only that it is possible. We do not come unbound into this life."

The words rumbled uncomfortably in Fancy's subconscious, as she heard her daughter's laughter. The child was happier now, everything would be just fine.

▲

The tall, handsome figure at the back of the saloon leaned casually against the wall with arms crossed in front of his chest. Beyond the glare of the improvised footlights, Fancy recognized Chance and felt her heart constrict. This was the third time she'd glimpsed him watching the show, a strange expression on his face that she couldn't put a name to. He never stayed to speak with her, just watched for a while, then left before the show was done.

She forced herself to ignore her racing pulse and pay attention to her next cue. One of these days the confrontation would come . . . the moment of looking into each other's eyes and finding what lay hidden there. She was almost grateful that the moment wasn't now.

57 "Miss Fancy!" Lem's voice carried over the din in the saloon. "Trouble, Miss Fancy." Lem Cleary, the sheriff's deputy, was a nice boy, not bright but big and well-meaning. "Got a Chinaman in the jailhouse says he knows you. Name of Woochy or somethin' like that."

Fancy grabbed the boy's arm and squeezed it elatedly. It had been two months since Magda had said she'd try to contact Wu; she'd all but given up on finding him. "Oh, you gorgeous man, for bringing me such good news!"

Hurrying over the uneven boards that served as sidewalk, Fancy heard Wu's high-pitched shrieking even before she reached the jailhouse.

"May the gods pour boiling oil on your genitals! May the worms eat out your stinking entrails! May your manhood be consumed by maggots!" Lordy, he's in rare form, she thought as she burst through the jailhouse door.

Wu cowered in the corner of the only cell, his hands shielding his head from assault. Embarrassed, the sheriff stopped his upraised arm in mid-arc. The Chinaman had been beaten; his skin was discolored, his eye blackened; a bloody gash ran from scalp top to temple, and blood splotched his familiar dark garments.

"You really know this feller, Miz Fancy?" the sheriff asked.

"I most certainly do, Sheriff. Whyever is he in jail?"

"Ran a cropper of a couple of Jack Benedict's boys on the street. Sassed 'em good in American and Chinee. Goddamnedest mouth on 'im you ever heard! Screamin' things about people's gentiles . . . if you'll forgive my language, Miz Fancy. Cain't believe he's a friend a' yours." The Chinese were often hated and feared in mining towns; some said it was because they took jobs from white men, others said it was because wherever they went, opium went too.

"Is there a charge, Sheriff?" Fancy asked, trying not to laugh. She'd found her woman-in-distress act was generally the most effective when faced with men in authority.

The sheriff stood easier and scratched at his head. He had a thick thatch of steel-gray hair with a tendency to curl at the ends. It gave him a dandyish air, at odds with his rough clothes, massive shoulders, and paunch.

"Well, now, young lady, I don't rightly know about that. Sassin' a peace officer, I s'pose for starters. Disturbin' the peace, somethin' of that nature. Usin' obscene lingo . . ."

Fancy mustered up an injured look. "Oh, dear, and I need him so badly, too, Sheriff. You see I've hired the man to work in a new business Jewel and I are starting, and I need his special expertise."

"Hope you're plannin' a cursin' business, then, missy. 'Cause I cain't say I ever heard a better expert than this ol' boy."

Sheriff Harley nudged the Chinese with his toe. "He's all yours, such as he is."

Wu rose with surprising agility. He opened his mouth to speak, but Fancy silenced him with a fierce look that faded instantaneously as she turned her gaze back to the sheriff.

"I must say, Sheriff, that's most gentlemanly of you. I give you my word of honor I'll keep Wu out of mischief."

"Sort of thought you and Jewel were more in the business of getting people into mischief than keeping them out of it," Sheriff Harley said as he opened the creaky door and stepped back for her to pass through. No one in town was really certain if Fancy's interest in Jewel's business included the whorehouse part of it, but it occasioned enough speculation so that the righteous housewives of Leadville gave her a wide berth.

"I'm branching out, Sheriff. You just watch me."

"Damned if I won't, Miz Fancy," he agreed as she waved good-bye. "That's one fine-lookin' woman," he murmured to the deputy when she was out of earshot. "There ain't a man in Leadville wouldn't like to get hisself a little piece of that."

"Son of a poxed pig!" Wu hissed at the same moment. Fancy fought back an urge to throw her arms around him right there on the dirty street and kiss his welcome cheek for all she was worth.

▲

Wu Chin bowed to Jewel, his face a mask. He wore a dark blue cotton dress; his hands were tucked out of sight within the wide sleeves.

Jewel waved him and Fancy to a seat. The Crown was nearly empty, for it was morning; Rufus was sweeping up the debris of broken glass and bedstraw from in front of the bar. A thin beam of pallid sunshine filtered sleepily through the windows.

"So you're the one Fancy's been tellin' me about," Jewel began, obviously in charge. "What exactly do you know about runnin' a laundry?"

"All Chinamen know about laundry," Wu said. Was it irony or bitterness beneath the words?

"Must be a real clean country, China." Jewel thought she might as well put him on notice right away she wasn't to be messed with.

"Look," Fancy interrupted hastily, "there's money out there waiting to be made. I want to grab it before anyone else does. Wu's hardworking and smart. He'll do a good job for us."

Jewel looked unconvinced. She tilted her chin at Wu. "What've you got to say for yourself?"

Wu pursed his thin lips but said nothing.

"Whose money we plannin' to use for this business anyway?" Jewel pursued.

"Mine and Wu's. Yours, too, if you want in on it."

Jewel breathed in a significant breath, which caused her bosom to rise and fall so that it seemed she had made a statement of some important kind. Then she leaned forward in the chair.

"I'm in. But you and me will own it, and the Chinaman works for us."

Wu spoke before Fancy could answer.

"Money, one-third, one-third, one-third." He indicated the women and himself with surprisingly well-cared-for hands. The nails were longer than Fancy remembered. "Work hundred percent Wu. Business belong to Wu!"

"Son of a bitch! No little yellow bastard's gonna use *my* money to fund a business *he* owns. You're nothin' but a Chinaman!"

"You nothing but whore. Wu not hold that against you." His audacity caught Jewel off guard. "Chinaman, whore, what difference if we make money together? Money good deodorant!"

Fancy saw Rufus' jaw unclench and Jewel fight to control laughter. "Son of a bitch," she said again.

"Daughter of motherless dung heap," Wu replied. A small twitch of the mouth, which might have been a smile, accompanied the words.

Jewel laughed out loud. "Money, one-third, one-third, one-third," she said, controlling herself with effort. "Ownership, one-third, one-third, one-third."

Wu narrowed his upturned eyes in calculation as apparent as if he'd pulled out his abacus. "One-third, one-third, one-third. Wu get paid salary for work."

"Fair enough."

"*Big* salary."

"Don't push your luck!" Jewel rose from her chair, but she winked at Fancy as she turned. The deal was exactly what she'd intended it to be when she'd begun the negotiation; perhaps the same could be said of Wu. But I'm the biggest winner here, Fancy thought contentedly. The cabaret was only the beginning, a way to get capital to invest in other businesses—businesses that wouldn't depend on youth and beauty, as acting did. All you needed to succeed in business was intuition, ambition, and avarice, all of which she possessed in plentiful amounts—plus the courage to strike while the iron was hot. Other people might think she was headstrong, but her ability to leap while others hesitated was going to make her a fortune. If Jason had taught her anything, it was how to cash in on a boom-in-progress.

▲ ▲ ▲

"Well, I'll be dipped!" Jewel slapped her knee for emphasis. "How the hell d'ya do that?"

Wu smiled and tapped his abacus.

"Wu count money, fucky, fucky! Wu not make mistakes."

"Mistakes? You slant-eyed machine! You not only don't make mistakes, you do sums so fast it makes my head hurt."

Wu grinned and Rufus, standing behind the bar, winked at Fancy.

Jewel and Wu, whose relationship had gotten off to a rocky start, had developed a grudging friendship, although the level of swear words rose in decibels and inventiveness when they were together.

"Tell me about this bathhouse idea of yours, one more time," Jewel prompted. "I never heard tell of the like."

Wu bowed in acquiescence. "Wu build house, big tub inside. Fit many men, many women."

"That's real democratic," Jewel said, obviously taken with the idea.

"Miners filthy disgusting pigs."

"You won't get no argument from me on that."

"Plumed Birds wait in tub for miners . . ."

"He means the girls," Jewel called over her shoulder to Fancy and Rufus. "He talks real colorful, don't he?" She was teasing Wu, but he accepted the words with good humor now. He'd made his own assessment of Jewel's character and was content to be her partner.

"Plumed Birds introduce them to delights of cleanliness!"

"Delights of nakedness more likely. I like the sound of it. What'll we charge 'em for the delights?"

"Wu charge fifty cents for bath, dollar twenty-five, if Painted Bird is required for further delights."

"Just a doggoned minute there, Wu. What the Sam Hill do you mean *Wu charge*? This here's a partnership, ain't it? And my girls get a dollar fifty for any 'delights' they provide."

"Birds of Jewel get dollar fifty. Birds of Wu get dollar twenty-five."

Fancy and Rufus exchanged a glance that said, "Better run for cover."

"Birds of Wu! What goddamned Birds of Wu?"

"Wu import pleasure girls from China for fucky, fucky!"

"You cut that pidgin crap with me, you yellow cocksucker." Jewel was obviously astonished at Wu's boldness in moving in on her territory. "Who'd want a yellow whore anyway?"

"Some men like steak, some chop suey," Wu replied, unimpressed by Jewel's explosion. "Pleasure Birds of China know things Jewel's Birds cannot imagine."

"Oh, they do, do they? Like what?"

"Like how to make old cock young and young one like bull. How to make pleasure last beyond man's wildest dreams. Besides," Wu continued loftily, seeing that he had her full attention, "Wu consider to share profits with his partners." He bowed toward Fancy and Jewel. "Wu is civilized businessman." He tapped his abacus. "Eighty percent Wu, twenty percent Fancy and Jewel."

"One-third, one-third, one-third!" Jewel and Fancy chorused simultaneously. The Chinaman nearly smiled as he spoke.

"Wu get paid salary for his honorable labor. Very high salary."

"Break out the good stuff, Rufus," Jewel called to the bartender, benevolently. "We got to celebrate this little yellow bastard puttin' one over on us." No one in the room was happier than Fancy; three businesses were considerably better than one.

 58 Fancy finished the show and started the obstacle course toward her dressing room behind the bar. The passage of thirty feet could take ten minutes because of the men who surged forward to flirt with her after each performance.

She'd nearly reached the door that led to a few moments of quiet, when she saw the stranger. He was dressed all in black and even from a distance was arresting. The newness had long since faded from his shirt and trousers, and his black serge coat was covered with the dust of many trails, yet he seemed fastidiously groomed and carried himself with dignity.

The black Stetson hat he wore showed silver on the band, and the brim worn low across his forehead gave his face an air of mystery. Something distinguished him from the milling crowd of men—a sense of stillness that was unexpected . . . a steadiness and confidence that girded him like a mantle.

Endurance was written in his somber eyes and his movements were so graceful, they seemed effortless, yet beneath the easiness, an eerie alertness quickened. The quiet eyes watched, the quiet body was poised to spring—the man's contradictions breathed tension into the air around him.

His face was clean-shaved, but the shadow at his chin was that of a heavy-bearded man who must take pains to appear shaven. He had a straight nose and a mouth, neither too full nor too narrow, and a dark mustache. He wasn't handsome, but he was undeniably sensual. Fancy felt a tingle in the blood.

You could never forget those eyes, she thought, puzzled and mesmerized.

They were vaguely hooded, beneath the hat's wide brim, full of knowledge and of sorrow—not of the self-pitying kind, just world-weary and beyond illusion.

Fancy realized she was holding her breath, and wondered how the stranger had done that to her from across the floor. She could see his gaze was taking in the room and it seemed to her every man it touched on must have felt seared by the glance.

The dark eyes met Fancy's in their passage; he didn't smile, yet there was a minute tightening of the small lines around his eyes and mouth that might have passed for acknowledgment.

Fancy was about to make her way to the bar to ask Rufus if he knew the man, when two things happened simultaneously.

The men in the room appeared to have taken the stranger's measure just as she had. Like the parting of the Red Sea, a pathway cleared before him—men moved backward or sideways to provide him passage, as tamer beasts part ranks for a predator.

As the space around him opened, Fancy focused on the elegant black cartridge belt from which hung a set of holsters, tooled in the Spanish fashion and tilted slightly forward. The plain ivory butts that protruded were the only white in the blackness of his garb. She couldn't see from where she stood if there were carvings on the handles, but the ivory gleamed yellow from long use. The pistols were so much part of the man's anatomy that it had taken a while for her to focus on their separate existence.

As the power of the stranger's presence communicated itself by some mysterious osmosis to the room, the second surprise took place.

Jewel had been leaning over the crap table, when her eyes rose from the game and met those of the stranger. She ceased to laugh; she straightened visibly, then moved toward him as if drawn by magnetic force.

The man's face softened in some way Fancy couldn't name, showing profound relief, although no perceptible change had taken place there. How Gitalis would have envied this man's ability to show emotion without overtly changing expression. Jewel and the stranger walked toward each other slowly. Fancy felt she was watching some fabulous drama unfold, for the electricity in the air between the two was nearly visible to the naked eye. Finally, they stood face-to-face. Neither said a word; they didn't touch and yet their touching on some intimate level reached Fancy all the way across the room. She raised her eyes to Rufus, who had come to the end of the bar where she stood.

"Who in the hell . . . ?" she whispered, then realized with confusion that Rufus' eyes were bright with unshed moisture.

"Ford Jameson." His reply was low and final, as if the name explained everything. As he said it, Ford and Jewel by unspoken agreement turned toward the stairway that led to the second floor where Jewel lived.

▲

As the door closed behind them, Jewel turned to the man she'd loved so long and walked into the arms he held out to her. He was not a large man, but there was intense power in the sinewy body. She let this strength flow from him into her; he let the comfort of her welcoming breasts fill his life, for however brief a moment.

"I knew you were coming," she whispered.

"It's been a long time, Julia." He held her tightly to his heart and rested his head wearily on her shoulder. His voice was curiously husky, as if it had been injured and repaired, yet it was gentle and at odds with the danger that lurked within him. He was the only one in the world who called her Julia now.

"How long can you stay?" she asked, leading him to the chair beside her bed and bending to pull off his boots. They were tooled black leather like the gun belt, old and trail-worn.

Ford watched her as she tugged off the boots and caressed his tired feet with love. He unhitched his gun belt and handed it to her; she placed it carefully on the table beside the bed. Jewel saw Ford automatically judge the distance from table to door; she had turned the bedside chair to face the door with the same unconscious understanding of his need. She crossed the room and checked the bolt, then knelt again beside his chair and saw he had undone the buttons of his shirt and trousers.

"I can't say how long, Julia," he told her gently, touching both hands to her face and tipping it upward, searching her eyes for understanding.

He saw the tears mist them, but she nodded unprotesting.

"Whatever time we've got . . ."

"As long as I can, you know . . ."

"I know."

Undoing the buttons of her gown, Jewel raised herself toward him; her breasts swung free of their covering. The man filled his hands with her pliant flesh and with what seemed like a groan torn from the deepest part of his soul, he pulled her to him. She was all he'd ever known of belonging.

Ford buried his head in her abundance, his mouth sought her nipple like a dying man finding water in the desert. He sucked hungrily, longingly, yet with infinite care.

Jewel moaned with her own need and reached for his risen organ with skilled hands—just the feel of him, the weight of him, the reality of his flesh incited her.

"I've missed you, needed you . . ."

"Oh, please do that, just like that . . ."

She had never wanted anyone as she wanted Ford. He ached for the release that her silken wetness could provide, but forced himself to give before taking, for he loved this woman, had always loved this woman. Ford slid his muscular body down her belly and buried his mouth in the most secret source of her. Jewel cried out with the exquisite pleasure of his lips and tongue; she opened herself as she never did with other men. Tongue, lips, fingers, touches so tender and knowledgeable, they drove all else from her world. Swollen pleasure so intense, she felt faint with its perfection.

"Oh, please," she managed to whisper, "I need you inside me . . . I've needed you so long . . ."

Ford raised his body above her own and slid his aching manhood into the hot and welcoming folds of Julia. Even then he controlled his movements, tantalizing, tensing, slowly inching his way within and slowly drawing back, again and again and again, until she thought she would die of desperation.

"Now, Julia . . . ?" he whispered.

"Now. Oh, Christ, please, now . . ." as he plunged wildly into her, bursting into her, exploding into her as all the pent-up frenzied longing of each one flooded the other with fulfillment.

Ford Jameson slept for hours after they'd made love. Jewel sat in the chair beside him and watched the door. She knew the only hours of his life he ever slept in peace were the ones he spent with her.

▲ ▲ ▲

Fancy waited impatiently for Rufus to finish with the customers who had inconveniently chosen this, of all moments, to order.

"Rufus!" she called out exasperatedly. "You come back here this minute and tell me who he is!"

The big man smiled a slow, knowing smile at her impatience.

"Ol' friend of Jewel's," he said in his usual abbreviated fashion. "Gun-fighter. Best I ever seen. Mebbe the best there is."

Fancy digested this fact with widening eyes. "But what was it I just saw happening between them? It seemed as if all motion in this place stopped to give them room."

"Queer, ain't it? Always like dat wif dem two. Ford come by, Jewel ain't got eyes nor ears for nothin' else. Thinks he hung de moon. Mebbe he did." He nodded at the thought. "Damn fine feller."

"But I thought you said he was a gunfighter."

"You walk a mile in dem moccasins, 'fore you go judgin' de man, missy. Fast gun like dat, ev'y crazy in de Territory come after you. Never turn yo' back. Never sleep nights. Never trust no one. Never rest. Jest keep movin'. Keep stayin' alive. 'Til one day, some crazy kid is faster 'n you. Lessen you kin git a job marshalin' somewheres, your life jest one dead body after 'nother.'' He stopped a moment, then added, "Dey been together a long time.''

"Together?" Fancy said incredulously. "Rufus, I've been here for months and this is the first I've ever laid eyes on the man! How can you call that together?"

"Dey together all right, missy. Don't you make no mistake 'bout dat, now. In dere heads dey together all de time . . . an' in dere hearts. Lotta folks live in de same house every day, ain't together like dem two is. He come when he kin. She knows when he be comin', too. Git all twitchy and quiet-like. He come in dat door soon after.''

"How long will he stay? Will I get a chance to meet him?"

Rufus picked up an empty and put it into the tray with the other dirty glasses. "If'n somebody on his tail, he be movin' on right quick. If not, he stay long's he kin. Man like dat got a feel for danger . . . knows when it's a-comin'. Mostly moves on outta its way. One day, he won't move quick enough.''

Fancy shook her head in wonder and walked slowly past the bar to her dressing room door, but her eyes almost involuntarily stole up the stairs in hopes of one more glimpse of the mysterious stranger whose arm had encircled Jewel Mack on the stair, as if he owned her.

▲ ▲ ▲

"Saw Dakota, Julia," Ford said as he sat on the bed and pulled on first his socks and then his boots. The woman seated at the dressing table mirror gave an involuntary start.

"She's grown real beautiful," he said, stamping his heels down firmly to get the boot's fit friendly to his feet.

Jewel turned toward him on the little bench, her eyes suddenly full. "How is she? What's she like?"

Jameson smiled a fraction, or rather his eyes softened from their usual vigilant wariness, and he walked toward the window and looked out as he answered.

"She's taller than you and real slim, Julia. I heard one of the other girls call her 'elegant.' She has my dark hair, I guess, and eyes. She's halfway between little girl and young lady. A little gangly like a newborn filly, but graceful too. She's doing well at school they told me. Another few years and she'll be all grown up and graduating.''

Jewel nodded.

"She asked for you, Julia, and I told her you loved her. She said she loves you, too, and waits for your letters. Wants to come home to visit once she finishes her schooling.''

"How'd you come to see her?" Jewel asked, her throat so dry, she could barely speak.

"I was riding with the Earps in Kansas, a while back. Wyatt and Virgil needed a hand with some trouble and cattle. Then a little rough stuff happened at the Lady Gay in Dodge and I got laid up on account of a bullet in the brisket." He almost smiled. "Seemed a good excuse to take the stage into St. Louis for a spell. Seems like as I get older, I take to thinking more about mortality."

"What're we gonna tell her, when she's full-growed?" Jewel asked, as if the question hadn't come up a thousand times before.

"Same as we always told her, Julia," he said steadily, the quiet surety of his voice reassuring, calming her. "That her mama lives in the mountains for her lungs and her daddy's business keeps him traveling most of the time. Been thinking, maybe Europe is the place to send her next. I hear a lot of girls from good families travel a year or so in Europe when their schooling's done . . ."

Jewel looked at Ford strangely for a moment, as if she hadn't heard him correctly. Then she laughed aloud.

"Good families, hmm? The kid's got a gunslinger for a father and a whore for a mother—that's what you call a good family?"

"Yeah," he said, with a slight gentling of the lines at the corners of his eyes and mouth. "You can tell just by looking at her she comes from real sturdy stock."

▲

"Been a long time, Otis," Ford said, stretching out a firm hand toward McBain as he drew up alongside him on the street.

Bandana grinned. "Ain't but two men in the world I'd get a kick outta seein' today, Jameson, and the other one's dead!" He grasped Ford's hand and pumped it hard.

"I baptized my spirit with a mite too much Taos Towse last evenin'," Bandana explained as he motioned Ford to walk along with him. "The top of my cranium has rebelled a bit since my eyes pried open this morning."

"Must be getting old, Otis," Ford said amiably. "Never knew you to feel your whiskey before."

"I fear I'm gettin' worse than old, Ford. I'm scairt I might be gettin' wise as well."

"And rich, I hear."

"Damned if I ain't! Rich enough to see you to a steak at the hotel if you'd care to indulge yourself with an old friend." Bandana noticed several new lines and a scar that hadn't been on Jameson's face when last they'd met.

"I'd like that real fine, Otis." Bandana saw that his eyes were searching the road that stretched behind him. "Can't stay long, so we'll have to make it soon. At our age, it's best to see old friends when we can."

"Posse or bounty hunter, this time?"

"One or the other or both. Wouldn't like them to catch me here. Be hard on Julia if that happened."

"Ever think of marshalin' or sheriffin'?

Ford nodded. "Rode with the Earp boys a while back in Dodge. Heard from Virgil there's room in Montana for a man good with a gun—if he's willing to clean up some range trouble for them, there'll be no questions asked. That's where I'm headed."

"What about Jewel and Dakota?"

"Jewel understands. Dakota doesn't know."

Bandana nodded. "Well, there ain't no sign of a hangin' party jest yet this afternoon. What say we ride up into the mountains and I show you where the strike is. Like you to meet the two young fellers I got for partners, too."

Ford looked hesitant.

"Might be a real good hidey-hole should any of them bounty fellers happen to ride this way. Might be you could use a couple or three good men at your back if that happened."

"I fight my own wars, Otis."

"Cain't no man stand alone forever, Ford."

"I thought you swore off partners after the last one," Jameson said, avoiding a response to McBain's statement.

"I did for a while. But Hart and Chance happened along and partnership just came natural."

"Hart and Chance? Not McAllister?"

Bandana shook his head, pleased with the response. "I knew from them you knowed each other . . . I thought to surprise you."

"Damned if that's not the best news I've heard lately. I always wondered what became of those two boys."

"May have been boys when you knowed 'em," Bandana said with a chuckle. "They're men now."

The two old friends moved off toward the livery stable with Ford still watching the late afternoon sky in the special way of the hunted.

▲ ▲ ▲

Ford and Bandana climbed the steep trail toward the Fancy Penny with the sun an orange ball headed for the horizon. The clatter of their horses' hooves on loose stone caught Hart's attention as he stood outside the mine manager's office, deep in conversation with Caz. He stopped and stared, disbelieving, at Bandana's companion.

Ford had changed so little with the years; the coiled-spring body, the sorrowing eyes, were the same as he remembered.

"Ford!" he yelled. "Ford Jameson!" Hart covered the ground between them and grabbed the gunfighter in a bear hug that startled Bandana with its exuberance. There were damned few men who could touch Ford Jameson and live to tell the tale.

"Bandana told us you two knew each other, but I never thought to see you here in Leadville."

"How long has it been, Hart? Ten years?"

"Nearer fifteen. We were just kids when you saved us."

He still thinks of his brother and himself as a pair, thought Ford. It wasn't often you found that kind of loyalty in this sorry world.

"Is Chance still as handy with a deck of cards as he was back then?"

"Better, I expect. He's pretty good at a lot of things these days—politics, silver, wine, and women high up on the list. He'll be pleased as punch to see you, Ford."

Jameson smiled inwardly at the pride he sensed beneath the words. Hart had grown to be a man much like the boy he remembered—honorable, loyal, and God Almighty big. Six-foot-five or -six, he'd judge, and broad as a Missouri ox. Ford, studying Hart's eyes, saw no sign of weakness there; he wondered what he'd find in Chance's.

▲

"By God, it's you!" Chance shouted over the din at the gambling tables, the pleasure in his voice unmistakable. He stood up and pushed back his chair. "Deal me out, boys," he said to the other men at the table, and moved toward where Bandana and Hart stood grinning, next to Ford.

"I never thought to see you again," Chance said as he pumped Ford's hand and clapped him heartily on the back.

"Never thought to see you so prosperous," Ford replied.

The four men traded stories over dinner, of all that had happened to them in the years since they'd parted company.

"Julia invited us to see the show at the Crown tonight," Ford said over coffee, and Chance and Hart exchanged uncomfortable glances. Neither one knew how to cope with the fact that Fancy was back in Leadville.

"Damned good idea," Bandana responded before either McAllister could decline. "Got somebody there I'd like to introduce you to, Ford. She's a real old pal of mine and I'd like for you to meet her."

▲

"So Fate has decided to take it out of my hands," Fancy thought nervously when Jewel told her the boys were out front and wanted her to join them after the show. She'd so hoped that Chance, at least, would seek her out after she returned, but only Bandana'd had the courage for that.

She'd intended to end tonight's show with a can-can, flaunting plenty of ruffled bloomers, but instead, before the last number, she signaled the piano player there'd be a change in the repertoire.

"There are some very dear old friends of mine in the audience this evening," she said to the assemblage, and the listeners quieted to a few muffled coughs. "If you'll indulge me, I'd like to sing a song to them I think they may remember."

Fancy walked upstage center and began to sing, her voice a clear crystal bell that encapsulated all the sadness of a sorrowful world. The song from the music box, they used to call it, as if it had no other name . . . the song of Beau Rivage and Christmas Eve and a thousand lonely nights of longing.

The other men in the bar arched to see the fortunate ones she was singing to. They were surprised to see Bandana McBain and the McAllisters enrapt by the haunting refrain.

Rufus handed Fancy a glass of water as she left the stage, and a towel. "You best dry your eyes, girl, before you go on over dere." She did so gratefully, pretending she was blotting the sweat of the performance from her face as she composed herself.

Hart jumped to his feet, followed by the other three as she drew near, and then, somehow, it was all easier than she could have imagined, for there were introductions and hugs and laughter and drinks all around and somehow the years had melted away and they were simply together again.

The physical reality of Chance's face and form, which had haunted her dreams and nightmares, quickened Fancy's loins and heart with bittersweet memory. *I remember . . . Oh, Lord, I remember everything,* but her face showed only the sweet smile of friendship. Hart lifted her off the ground with his hug, and Bandana held her close for longer than need be.

I love you now as I did then, she thought later, lying on her bed, her heart beating like a triphammer . . . and you're just as capable of throwing me into a tailspin now as then . . . just as handsome as in my fantasies . . . just as seductive and smart and desirable. And now you're very, very rich . . .

Oh, Chance, you are just what I want in this world, just as I feared you'd be. Now all I'll have to do is figure out what I intend to do about that.

59

Fancy reined her horse in lightly; the gelding had a soft mouth and responded easily. She loved to ride "à la clothespin" as Bandana called it, astride in a split leather skirt she'd had specially made; on horseback, she was reckless and utterly without fear. *All wild creatures recognize one of their own,* Bandana had told her when first he'd seen her on a horse. *I'm free when I ride, Bandana,* she'd replied. *It's the only time I'm ever truly free.*

The swinging door to the Crown creaked open just as she dismounted and Ford Jameson emerged, tipping his hat to her as he neared the hitching rail. Fancy peeled off her dirty riding gloves, and put a hand on the man's arm to detain him.

"I was hoping you'd be here," she said, breathless from the exercise. Ford stopped, and Fancy felt enveloped in his mysterious stillness; he had a disconcerting habit of looking down at the ground as he spoke to you, as if he didn't wish to burn you with the power in his gaze.

"Ford, I've been wanting to ask a favor of you—I need to learn to handle a gun." There was no trace in her manner of the coquettishness she used on other men. "I should have learned long ago . . . My daddy would have taught me, I'm sure. But Atticus didn't want me touching guns—it was the only thing he wouldn't teach me. Jewel said I should ask you. She told me you taught her . . ." She trailed off uncertainly, for an odd expression had changed Ford's eyes, as if he were remembering something painful.

His gravelly voice was gentle when he spoke. "I'll teach you, Fancy. Go borrow a pistol and gunleather from Julia, while I get my horse from the livery. I know a place."

Fancy felt a clamminess in her palms. What was it she always sensed in him that was dangerous? He'd been nothing but tender and courtly toward her; not since the southern gentlemen of her childhood had she seen such innate grace in a man. In another, better world Ford would have been someone important.

Ford reined in near a small stand of trees and signaled her to dismount. He lifted the Comanche-length split reins over his horse's head and left the mare ground-tied, reins dangling.

"Won't she spook from the gunfire?" Fancy asked, hitching her own mount to a tree.

"Cavalry horse. Trained to lie down in battle so you can fire over her belly."

Fancy raised her eyebrows in surprise, but Ford was already walking to a place thirty or forty feet away. He set up a row of tin cans on a tree stump and then returned to Fancy's side.

She strapped the gun belt around her middle, clumsily pulling it closed to the smallest notch; the gun rode high at her waist and made her feel uncomfortable. She feared the heavy weapon now she was so close to it.

"Lower the leather a mite," Ford said, studying her. "Halfway between wrist and elbow is just right. Some wear it low on the hip, but you don't want to have to lift the gun too high once it's drawn."

Ford demonstrated with his own weapon: his right hand moved, strong and effortless, to grip the butt of his Colt. The draw was so swift and sure, it seemed not to have happened at all, yet there was the revolver in his palm, and the shot had knocked the first can down before Fancy was even certain Ford had pulled the trigger. She looked at the man wonderingly. "Mebbe he's de best dere is," Rufus had said.

Ford replaced the gun in its holster so tenderly, it barely touched the surrounding leather; the fluid move was perfect, organic. With intense curiosity, Fancy saw Ford flex his right hand once above the grip, as if to release an energy that had built up within him and no longer had a place to go. Fancy stared at the hand, seeing it clearly for the first time. It was long and lean; the veins stood out in bluish lines above the strength of lean muscle. They were intelligent hands, doing what they were born to do.

"There are fancy rigs," he said softly. "You needn't know about them, except to know they exist so you won't be taken by surprise." A sadness flickered in his eyes before he lowered them again. "Some men cut away the leather from the trigger guard for access . . . some carry in their waistband, but that's a dangerous thing to do, lest you geld yourself.

"Some men keep a twenty-dollar bill folded in one empty chamber to protect themselves. They call it burying money.

"There's a rig that swivels on the belt so you never have to clear leather at all. Only a coward resorts to such."

Fancy saw a change had come over Ford—his movements had altered, legs slightly bent, arms loose, hands poised in perfect control. A power that hadn't been evident a moment before emanated from the man; he was lighter, freer, and infinitely more dangerous.

"Take the gun in your hand, Fancy. Treat it with respect. A gun is as good or bad as the one who holds it—just a tool, like a scythe or hoe or hammer. A gun wasn't meant for killing people; it was meant for hunting game to feed a family . . . or killing rattlesnakes to keep your loved ones safe." He moved his body toward the target, not facing it head-on, but turned a little to the left.

"You stand your ground, like you were part of the earth. There's a sight on the end of the barrel so you can line up with the target . . . after a while you'll just remember to point the barrel like it was your finger." Ford raised the heavy pistol as he spoke.

"You pull back the hammer with your thumb as you draw, Fancy, then all that's left to do is pull the trigger." He showed her it was the first pad of her finger that was to work the trigger action.

"All one motion, Fancy. Grip, cock, raise, aim, fire. All one swift simplicity." He said it as if it were easy to accomplish.

"You move like the gun is part of you, Ford," she said, awestruck.

The dark eyes raised slowly to her face—were they filled with bitterness, or endurance? The unreadable expression unnerved her so she had to look away.

Fancy tried to emulate Ford's easy stance. She closed her hand on the pistol grip and was surprised to feel how agreeable its solidity seemed; the gun was heavy, yet it nestled comfortably in her hand. She felt Ford move behind her, to help lift her arm to the proper position.

"Men's arms are stronger, Fancy. This pistol weighs near five pounds." She wondered for a fleeting moment if he would put his other arm around her, taking liberties, as most men longed to do. But he simply steadied her grip and then moved away to let her fire. When she did, the shock wave traveled up her arm and the muzzle rolled skyward.

"Hold the pistol looser in your hand, to give the butt ease to roll back a little, when you fire. If you take the recoil in the palm, it protects your arm."

Fancy raised the pistol a second time. She held it looser and it rolled back smoothly; she hit the last can cleanly.

"That's fine, Fancy, that's just the way." His husky voice was strangely gentle. I wonder what he's like to make love to, she thought fleetingly, there was such strength and tenderness in the man.

Fancy let the pistol hand fall to her side, grateful for the praise, and turned to look at her teacher, but he was staring out over the meadow to the mountains beyond, his gaze on something Fancy could not see.

She raised the muzzle of the gun and, aiming carefully, fired again and again and again. She had the oddest sense that this was something she was going to be very good at.

▲

"How does a man learn to be a gunfighter?" Fancy asked Ford, after watching him execute a Border Shift for her, cross-tossing the guns in the air and catching them effortlessly. He'd been in the Gulch over a month now and she'd grown fond of him.

"You can't learn it, Fancy. You just get born with the gift and Fate does the rest."

Fancy took her target stance, raised her Colt, and fired; she'd grown more than proficient under his tutelage, and easily shattered the empty bottle twenty-five yards away. Ford didn't smile exactly, but she could see he was pleased with her progress.

Fancy released the cylinder latch and pushed out each spent cartridge from the chamber with the ejector rod, carefully hoarding the spent brass casings so they could be reloaded with powder and lead later. She handled the weapon competently now, confidently; she liked the feel of it in her hand. She glanced up at the shootist as she pulled new cartridges from her belt and inserted them expertly into the empty chambers.

"How did you and Jewel get to know each other, Ford?"

"We were kids together once . . . on a wagon train, about a thousand years ago. Known each other 'most all our lives, I guess."

"You more than know each other—you're like a matched set of tinder-boxes when you're together. Sparks fly—everybody notices them." She smiled to see that he was already setting up another set of targets—this time, considerably farther away. She had a hunch he enjoyed the time he spent teaching her.

Ford shrugged, his dark eyes fastened on the ground. "Julia and I share history, Fancy. We've come a long way together."

"Why can't you stay with her, then? So you can both be happy." Fancy took aim and fired, making the tins jump as she hit them neatly; she wanted, needed, to earn his respect with her shooting.

When he spoke again, she sensed he wanted to tell her something of consequence. "Sometimes you think you can stay. People say love loosens its ties with time but that's not true, Fancy, the bonds grow tighter with the years. The history you share only binds you closer.

"Trouble is, if you settle in, you lose the edge. Happiness does that. It tames you." He turned toward her and fastened Fancy with his eyes to make sure she understood. "It's the edge that keeps you alive."

"I'm so sorry, Ford." Her voice was full of caring.

"Don't fret for Jewel and me, Fancy. We have more than some." He actually smiled when he said it.

"I'd like to teach you something you might need to know one day," he said suddenly, as if he'd made an important decision. "Take my guns from me."

He withdrew both Colts from their leather and grasped them by the barrel, as if to surrender them. Fancy reached out to take the pistols from the man, but in a gesture so swift it seemed a blur, the guns were whisked from her startled grasp, twirled magically around in Ford's hands and she found herself staring down the business end of both six-shooters.

"God Almighty, Ford! How'd you do that?"

He grinned at her surprise; it rendered his face boyish.

"They call that the Roadagent's Spin, Fancy. It's a real good trick to know if you're ever in a tight spot." So he is having a good time teaching me, she told herself with satisfaction. I knew it.

Ford performed the trick again, and this time she saw that his trigger finger remained locked inside the trigger guard like an axle, so he could spin the gun around completely, grasping the grip in his palm as it twirled into firing position.

Fancy laughed gleefully. What a shock *that* maneuver would be to an assailant who tried to disarm you. It was just the kind of self-protective knowledge that was truly valuable.

"Show me again. Slowly this time, if you please, professor."

Ford did so indulgently, for Fancy was a talented pupil; she could imitate nearly anything she saw. She tried again and again until she'd gained a semblance of proficiency; he knew that until she perfected the difficult maneuver she'd keep on practicing; he liked that trait in her.

Fancy beamed at her friend with unfeigned admiration. "You are absolutely astonishing, Ford. It's hard to believe anyone could ever shade you with a gun."

Jameson never answered her, just slipped the revolvers soundlessly back into their holsters and walked away on the pretext of setting up another target; but Fancy knew in her heart that his thoughts had slipped away again to the dark, unapproachable place where he really lived.

I'm going to learn the Roadagent's Spin, she told herself with conviction, if I have to get up two hours early every morning from now on to do it. Just so I can make him proud of me.

▲ ▲ ▲

Fancy tried to concentrate on the script, but the words kept fading into reverie. She was lonely, and all because Chance hadn't come to call as she'd expected he would. It had given her time to brood about what she really wanted from him. Even if he did come courting now, she wondered, could it ever be the same as before? She was so different from the girl who had fallen in love on a mountaintop, long ago. Her needs were so voracious now, her sense of her own abilities so strong—could she really live at the whim of any man . . . even Chance?

She'd spoken to Ford about her odd turn of mind during their morning practice, sensing he would understand her ambivalence.

"We've been homeless, Fancy, you and I," he said. "Outcasts don't think like other people. We sense danger before it comes—we protect ourselves, or we die. Ambition is part of it. If we're not better at what we do than the others—we're done for." He'd hesitated, then raised his eyes to hers.

"It's harder for a woman, Fancy. You're supposed to let a man take care of you. People like us can't do that."

"Oh, but I wish I could! I wish I could ever just feel . . . satisfied. Content, like other women seem to be."

Ford smiled at her self-deception. He knew she didn't want to be like the others; truth was, she held most women in contempt.

"You aren't like other women, Fancy. Once you live by your own resourcefulness you can't ever let that competency go. Shouldn't ever. They'll kill you if you do."

"But I could make mistakes if I do it all myself, Ford. All those other women don't have to fear that."

"Nothing for nothing in this world, Fancy. If you never dare anything, you never fail. Could you live a life where you never dared?" She saw there was amusement and kindliness in his stare. There was a graze of bullet scar on his chin, and an unevenness of texture that might have been from a burn or even a pox; the imperfection made the face stronger, more memorable. The long black lashes rested on his cheek when he looked down again; there was something boyish in that, but the permanent furrows between his brows were old and world-weary. If he didn't belong to Jewel . . . she pushed the heretic thought away.

"Fancy."

"Yes?"

"Worst thing can happen to folks like us is we lose the edge. Get lazy. Or complacent. Or satisfied. They can go from being at your feet to being at your throat real fast, if you lose the edge."

"But I don't want to have to live on the edge forever."

"No choice, Fancy. That's what you give up in return for doing it all your own way."

Fancy sighed at the remembered conversation. Ford was right, of course. But that didn't mean she couldn't try to prove him wrong and get to be content like other women.

▲ ▲ ▲

The big man wore a canvas raincoat tied up over his horse's flanks, exposing both the Sharps he carried in the saddle scabbard and the Winchester that spanned the blanket roll behind him.

He rode easy for so big a man, easy but wary, as if he searched incessantly under the wide-brimmed Stetson that shaded his darting eyes. Marshal or bounty hunter, the men in Leadville who noticed his arrival, catalogued him mentally as one or the other, even before he took out the tattered poster with Ford's picture on it and showed it around.

Ford had been tracked down often enough before so that what happened next had been well choreographed in advance by those who cared about him. Jewel packed his things wordlessly as Rufus kept the stranger at the bar in earnest conversation. Fancy saddled two horses, stowed Ford's gear and held his mount, while he dropped down from the half-roof over the rear porch to the waiting animal's back.

"Did you do what they want you for?" she asked the man who had become her friend.

"Yes. But not the way they say, or for the reasons they think."

"Will they hang you if they catch you?"

"Never get the chance to hang me, Fancy. It says 'dead or alive' on that poster he's carrying."

Her eyes widened. "You mean that man'll kill you instead of taking you in?"

"Only if he can, Fancy," Ford said, but the hollow sound of running was in his tone, the sound of a man who was, once again, alone.

60

"You get any time to see that kid of yours lately or to have any fun?" Jewel closed the ledgers; business was spectacular but Fancy was not.

"What do you mean by that?" Fancy snapped. She'd been performing every night, and by day overseeing the other enterprises, and the strain was beginning to show.

Jewel cocked her head and pushed the last of the ledgers across the table. "I ain't never seen a woman work like you, Fancy. It's all you think about. How much money's coming in, how to invest it, what new business to start next. Between that and your shows at the Crown, you're burning the candle at both ends. Don't you believe in fun anymore?"

Fancy took a deep breath and tried not to be angry, for there was truth in what Jewel said.

"I'm so afraid of being poor, Jewel. I've been without, and I hated every minute—now that I know how to make money, I feel as if I have to tuck away every penny I can, fast as I can, like the devil's on my tail."

Jewel pursed her lips deciding whether or not to argue.

"I think there's more to what's wrong with you than that, kid. I think you're still carrying a torch for Chance McAllister and you damned well better put it out or do something about it, because he is gettin' to be a major fact of life around Leadville." She'd seen the longing in Fancy the night the boys and Ford had come to the Crown, and the disappointment that followed when he didn't return.

"Look, kid, McAllister is going places. Now they've struck it rich, that boy is makin' a name for himself six ways from Sunday. Some little gal is gonna up and grab him, and if you don't want that to happen 'til you get your licks in, I think you'd best get your head out of the sand and start movin'."

Fancy looked at Jewel, all the confusion she felt about Chance clear in her eyes.

"I don't know what to do about him, Jewel. I ran away from him because I was afraid he wouldn't ever have anything—now he's got it all and I still don't know what to do. I can't tell him about Aurora—"

"Why the hell not?"

"Because I don't want him marrying me out of obligation, that's why. You've got to swear to me you'll never tell him. That's my secret and no one else's."

"For God's sake, kid, I won't give him the time of day if you don't want me to, but I think you're a damned fool not to get this straightened out one way or the other. And it's not just your secret, either."

"What do you mean by that?"

"What about Aurora? Don't she have any rights in this? She might like to know who her daddy is one of these days."

"Her daddy's dead. How can I suddenly resurrect him?"

"Damned if I know, honey. I'd just hate to see somebody else snap him up, before you figure whether or not you're through with him. Not that I think he's such a great prize, by the way . . . I ain't once met a gambler who was a passable husband."

Jewel gathered up the ledgers and rose to go.

"Whatever you decide, kid, have a little fun for yourself. All work and no play makes a woman flat-chested and squinty."

Jewel was right that you only get what you want by going after it. The trouble was, Fancy wanted Chance to be the one to make the first move.

▲

Jewel rode up into the mountains for the express purpose of meddling. It wasn't in the least like her, but Fancy needed help and maybe the McAllisters would know how to give it. Hart was the steadier of the two, she'd start by getting to know him better. Bandana had been her friend a lot of years, and not all of them plump with good fortune; if he liked the McAllisters well enough to be their partner, there had to be substance to them.

She hailed Hart from the distance and eased her palomino to a walk in his direction. He reached out a hand to help her dismount and Jewel, charmed by the courtly gesture, tossed her leg up over the saddle and slid down into waiting arms.

She tilted back her Stetson and Hart noted the straggles of bright orange ringlets, stuck to her skin by sweat from the band. She looked sketchable standing there, easy beside her horse, womanly and full of vigor.

"I come with a business proposition for you, Hart," she said. "I want me that big bold nude to go over the bar at the Crown—just like we talked about years ago. Somethin' real fancy with a curlicue gilt frame that'll be the talk of the Gulch. Fancy says you're the man for it. Are you still game to paint me a masterpiece?"

"Fancy said that?"

"She did and more."

"I'd really like to help you out, Jewel, but Chance and Bandana'd raise hell at losing their mine manager to portrait painting."

"Bandana owes me more'n one favor and Caz can handle things around here for a week or two. Besides, I've set my heart on this picture and I don't give up easy. I come to tell you I'll do whatever you say, so's we can get it done. If you want me to come up here to pose for it, I'll even do that. Now, I know you're rich and all, so you don't have to do this kind of thing, Hart, but I'm hoping you'll do it out of friendship and a desire to see good art in Leadville."

Hart regarded the woman for a moment, with considerable amusement; the idea of Jewel's body unfurled on a mountain filled with woman-desperate men was almost too much for his funny bone. Of course, most men knew she could outshoot them six times running, but even that might not deter them at the prospect of seeing that body in its natural state. The idea of being near Fancy was seductive as hell, even if he was a damned fool to consider it.

"Tell you what, if you can talk my brother and McBain into giving me a two-week dispensation from this hole in the ground, and you can give me a place to work undisturbed, and you won't hold it against me if it isn't the masterpiece you deserve . . . I'll give the painting a try for you."

Jewel eyed the huge man with amusement of her own, deciding he had one of the nicest faces she'd ever seen, all strength and amiability.

"I'll answer for Bandana and Chance, Hart. You can work at the Crown and I'll shoot the kneecaps off'n anybody that disturbs you." She paused. "One thing I know about in this life, Hart, it's men. Rich or poor, you'll never do less than your best, is my bet. And with me for your model, how could you go wrong?"

What a pity it was that Fancy had her heart set on the lesser of the two men, Jewel thought, as she hugged Hart on impulse, in farewell.

Hugging Jewel Mack was one of the nicer things could happen to a man, Hart mused as he boosted her into the saddle; then he watched her ride away, wondering what had really prompted her visit. Could it be that Fancy wanted to renew old friendships after all, but didn't quite know how, any more than he did?

▲

At first, Hart thought he'd paint Jewel with the Rockies for a backdrop, prospectors and all. But once he saw her stretched out on the fancy settee in her bedroom, it was plain that no man's eye would ever get to the background while that sumptuous body occupied the foreground.

Fancy was more Hart's personal style of feminine pulchritude—small and fine-boned, elegantly rounded to a less voluptuous measure—but there was no denying the effect Jewel's overabundance had on a man.

The artist stood at the easel he'd constructed out of timber from the local mortuary, and tried to decide how to handle the blatancy of Jewel. There was so much more to her besides a body; pride and sadness, side-by-next the bravado, lust, and jollity everyone knew so well. She was his first commission and he meant to live up to her trust.

The madam dozed comfortably on the chaise wearing nothing but goose bumps and a lusty smile; she had no more compunction about being seen naked than other women felt fully dressed, which seemed only reasonable to Hart, because of the flawlessness of what he saw.

Unaccustomed to working in oils, or on anything bigger than a sketchbook, he was trying to cope with the tricky medium when he felt a small hand on his arm and turned to find Fancy standing behind him. Her presence took his breath away, as it always had. She'd filled out since her time on the mountain and she had the bearing of a woman, not a girl, but her eyes were Fancy's and her voice was the one that rang in his dreams.

"I missed you," she said, as if he'd been a train she was to take an hour ago.

"I missed you, too. I'm glad to see you, babe." There, it was out, the old endearment; she smiled at it and he was glad.

"You're trying to see past her warpaint, aren't you, Hart?"

He nodded, surprised she understood his dilemma.

"She's afraid, you know. Afraid the world will take back everything she's struggled for. Afraid it's a desperately hard place out there and she may wake up one morning and be at its mercy."

Hart wondered if Fancy might not be describing herself as well.

"What do you think she'd like to see in this portrait, Fancy? It seems to mean a lot to her."

A medley of emotions crossed Fancy's face before she replied. "Paint her as if the worst had been the best."

"Make her a courtesan, instead of a whore?"

"That's it exactly, Hart. Paint her as she might have been if life hadn't

played such dirty tricks. And be good to her like you always were to me."
Then she was gone.

"Paint her as if the worst had been the best," he repeated under his breath, after she left. And that's just what he did.

▲

"How'd she seem to you, bro?" Chance asked, when Hart had finished the painting and returned home.

"More beautiful, if anything. More mature, I suppose you'd call it, Chance. A little chastened by life, like the rest of us. She's got quite a business head on her shoulders, too, it seems. Jewel told me a man would have to get up pretty early in the morning to outwit her in a deal. . . ." He stopped, wondering what Chance really wanted to know.

"Did you know Bandana sees her all the time, since she's come back?" Chance said enigmatically.

"No, I'd no idea of that."

Chance looked his brother straight in the eye as he said, "She's not a woman a man forgets easy, is she, bro?

Hart shook his head no but couldn't find exactly the right words for a reply.

"What do you really think about men, Jewel?" Fancy asked the question as she gingerly lowered her naked body into the steamy depths of the galvanized tub in their new bathhouse, and settled under the water with a sigh of unmitigated pleasure. There wasn't anything in life a hot bath couldn't cure, or at least improve considerably.

Jewel snorted a laugh from the other side of the great tub, which was, for once, free of grubby miners and "fallen angels"; only hot, clean water with some sort of flowery scent that Jewel had contributed. Her wiry hair was pushed up on top of her head in an unruly mop of red, tied with a ribbon.

"Most selfish critters God ever made. But I love 'em. Most of 'em anyways. Always have."

Fancy stretched out under the water, letting the warmth dissuade her muscles from the tensions of the night before.

"Me too. But why do you?"

Jewel knitted her penciled brows a moment in thought, then smiled. "They're kinda simple. . . . Simple needs. Simple pleasures. They think simple, too. Kind of in a straight line. Not stupid, mind you. Just less complicated than we are. Course, life's easier for 'em than for us. They don't get babies when they fornicate, don't have bodies that fall apart easy." She paused to take inventory. "Near all they have to worry about is fol- lowin' their peckers around and makin' money." Both women giggled at this assessment.

"Maybe I like 'em 'cause it's easy to figure what they want and what they're thinkin'. Why?"

"Because the whole subject of men is making me miserable at the mo- ment." Fancy made idle patterns in the water with her hand; she looked young and ingenuous to Jewel as she spoke, like a precocious child puzzling out the mysteries of the universe. "I think I really want one of my own."

"One that heats up your engine, you mean?" Jewel asked, and Fancy laughed ruefully.

"My engine's always heated up, Jewel. It's my head and my heart that aren't so easy to satisfy!"

Jewel snorted merrily at that and ducked her head once, under the water. When she came up, she heard Fancy say, "Every man I meet falls in love with me . . . except Chance."

"Don't matter who loves you, kid," Jewel broke in, running her hands over her hair and face to push back the water. "Matters who you love. A man could love you 'til hell freezes over, and if you don't love him back it don't matter more'n a tick on a buffalo."

"So what happens when you fall in love with the wrong one?"

"Hell, honey! *Everybody* falls in love with the wrong one. Women are real jerks where men are concerned. Even the smart ones. Besides, there ain't nobody perfect out there. Some got millions in the bank and tally-wackers so small you can barely see 'em. Some're good-hearted but dumb, or smart and mean. It all depends what sets your heart aflutter. Most women ain't got the choices you do. You might say you got more chances to choose wrong than the rest of 'em." She chuckled at her own humor and sank down lower in the tub. "You're so headstrong, kid, you were almost bound to pick wrong. But then some of the wrongest men I know could give you the best damned memories. Seems to me, Chance McAllister falls right into that very category."

Fancy laughed and let her mind drift for a while. She never really under- stood why everyone thought her headstrong—she only did what needed doing to survive. If you don't have an easy life and there's nobody to take care of you, how can you be anything other than headstrong? Wasn't that just another name for having the courage of your own convictions?

▲

Fancy shook the bolt of dimity to unfold its pretty pink flounces to the floor of the Tabor General Store.

The deep voice behind her was a shock.

"You were born for brighter colors, sugar. Red satins and purples, I think. And black lace. Don't you ever forget the black lace." The voice of a thousand desperate dreams sounding pleased to see her. Fancy turned toward Chance, trying not to remember how long she'd loved and hated him.

He stood beside her, confident and smiling, in the Levi pants and muddy boots of a digger, and a buckskin jacket that had seen better days.

"You haven't changed one bit, have you, Chance?" she said. He saw the moisture in her eyes and was touched that she'd missed him so.

"Well, you've changed, Fancy." He held her out at arm's length, his touch lingering too long for propriety and too short for her needs.

"What are you doing in town in those work clothes?" she asked, lowering her voice to thwart the disapproving stares of Augusta Tabor and several of her female customers. "You're such a dandy these days, hobnobbing with the rich and cutting a wide swath through all the ladies' hearts."

Chance laughed easily at the flattery. "Hart makes me work for a living from time to time, just to keep in practice. He says neither the law nor politics is a decent profession for a man. I've been to the mine."

It all sounded so natural on his lips; Hart, the law, the mine.

"There's so much that's happened in all our lives, Chance, isn't there?" she said wistfully. "There just wasn't near enough time the other night to talk about it."

Chance smiled and she felt bathed in sunlight.

"If you'll have dinner with me tonight, we can fill in all the blanks for each other. I've missed you, Fancy. How about the Clarendon Hotel at eight?"

"The Clarendon?" she said to cover her agition. "How grand you are these days. Seems to me the last meal we had together was possum and beans."

"They were good times, weren't they?"

"They were good times."

"Have dinner with me tonight, sugar. You won't regret it."

"You know I can't meet you at eight, Chance. That's the time of my show."

"After the show, then. And wear something red. I'm in the mood to celebrate."

He didn't wait for a reply, but turned a dazzling smile on Mrs. Tabor and her customers, ignoring their disapproving glares. "Good morning, ladies," he said as he passed them by. "I trust you're having a lovely day."

Fancy suppressed a laugh. Stupid old biddies . . . imagine what they'd say if they knew the truth. She watched the retreat of tight muscles and broad shoulders and felt all the old longings. Chance had cut a dazzling figure in town since striking it rich; she wasn't the only woman who'd felt the lure of those eyes that undressed you so knowingly, you didn't care what they saw.

She fingered the bolt of red silk that occupied the place of honor on the shelf above the practical chintzes and muslins and broadcloths. She couldn't have a dress made by tonight even if she wanted to, and who the hell was he to tell her to wear red . . . but perhaps a scarlet scarf or sash wouldn't hurt.

Chance whistled softly as he walked down Harrison. He was glad he'd finally made the move. How many times had he thought about Fancy over the years, playing and replaying the moments of their brief love affair and longer friendship? Sometimes angry, always lusty, often glad she'd disappeared and removed all need for decision making. He'd felt guilty, too, sometimes, that he'd taken her innocence too lightly, but he'd always dismissed the guilt as unnecessary. They'd been no more than kids playing at life; now they were adults capable of making choices. It troubled him not in the least that she had a child; being a mother had settled her down, made her less elusive, more human.

Why did it all seem so natural and inevitable, as if so many years hadn't passed them by? Maybe because he'd always believed they'd find their way back together. Perhaps that had made him sanguine, or even rebellious— he'd never been one to be pushed into choices. Yet the memory of Fancy's tempestuous nature had stayed with him through dozens of encounters, lingering insistently. The cool hauteur, the fire banked beneath . . . the intelligence, too keen for a woman, and the femininity too pervasive to be thrown off course by intellect. On such a woman as Fancy, men had been known to stake kingdoms in times past—but only such men as could handle the challenge.

▲

"If I weren't so gallant, I might even say she's more beautiful than her mother." Chance pronounced the words easily as he met Aurora, and Fancy breathed again. Was it relief or anger that was foremost in the sigh? Chance had met his own daughter, but he had not known her . . . and that wasn't exactly what she'd wanted to have happen.

Chance bent his knees to bring his face closer to the little girl's. "I've looked forward to meeting you, sweetheart," he said with a smile. Aurora responded warily. This friend of her mother's wasn't Jason, but he was handsome and seemed nice enough.

"I'm very pleased to meet you," the child replied with an elaborate curtsy, and Fancy beamed approval.

"You may run along now, darling," she prompted. The lies she'd told him about Aurora's father had come easily enough to her lips after all the years of practice, but why hadn't Chance known they were lies?

"I don't want to go, Mommy. I want to stay and play with Mr. McAllister." The voice was firm. Chance chuckled at the flattering response.

"See there, I told you, Fancy. It's a simple matter of irresistibility. Let her stay. It isn't every day I have a chance to be seen with two such beautiful ladies."

Aurora thought perhaps Mr. McAllister had possibilities after all.

▲

Chance lounged on the steps behind the Crown, while Fancy sat contentedly beside him. The day was warm and the flies swarmed thick around the two horses tethered to the hitching post. The roan whinnied softly in annoyance and tossed his head in an effort to avoid the distracting insects.

Fancy wore her split-skirted buckskin and a plaid shirt open at the neck; a red bandana was tied beneath the collar. "Cain't live west of St. Louis without a bandana, honey," McBain had told her years before. "Use it to wash your face, plug up a bullet hole, keep the sweat out'n your eyes. Sling up a broken arm, help you breathe in a sandstorm. Goddamnedest invention anybody ever thunk up!" She smiled at the memory as she tugged at the knotted bandana and used it to flick at the horseflies as Chance spoke.

"There's money to burn, sugar. Money now for everything we ever dreamed up there in that cabin. Of course, Hart keeps reminding me it'll take a minute or two to get it all out of the mountain to where we can spend it."

Fancy laughed softly, noting that he'd lately begun to say "we" about most things. "How like you, Chance. You think it all happens magically with no work attached. No wonder Hart has to crack the whip to keep you in line."

He squinted at her in the bright morning sun. "I recall a time when you wanted to believe in my magic."

"I still do. It's just that I've lived long enough to know that life doesn't work that way. Atticus always said, 'Anythin' you git for nothin' is likely worth jes' that.' Mostly, Atticus was always right."

"Far be it from me to dispute such a source, but in this case it's not 'something for nothing' at all. We worked our asses off for the money in that hole in the ground, Fancy. All of us. And the odds are we'll work harder still before it's all out and spendable."

"I suppose you're right. You just have a way of making everything sound possible . . . I guess I'm afraid of believing too hard."

Chance's expression softened at her vulnerability. He liked the instincts he was feeling lately, the desire to take care of her and make her happy.

"Then why not let me do the believing for both of us, sugar? You just sit back and let me make the dreams come true."

Fancy smiled her answer and tried to remember she was supposed to play hard to get; it was such a bother to remember all the rules of the game on a lazy morning when you were in love.

Chance had that teasing look in his eye that she knew so well. "If I were to ask you to have dinner with me tonight, do you suppose you'd say yes, or would you feel forced by propriety to play hard to get and turn me down like you did last Thursday?"

"As a matter of fact, it would be quite unseemly to accept such a last-minute invitation. . . ."

"But the truth is, you don't care a hoot in hell for seemliness. Not deep down underneath. You've got too much goddamned spirit for that, Fancy. And ninety-nine times out of the hundred you think people who pay attention to proprieties are damned fools."

"I care very much about doing things the right way!"

"Except where it interferes with your doing what you want to do?"

"Are you suggesting I'd like to throw propriety to the winds because I'm just dying to have dinner with you tonight?"

"Exactly that."

Fancy laughed, low and throaty. "Well, you'd be quite right. Just don't tell anybody."

Chance's chuckle sounded heartily irreverent.

"You are one in a million, Fancy, my girl, and my magic is plenty strong enough for both of us, you can count on it. I've got meetings all over town today, but I'll come collect you after the last show tonight and we'll teach this town something new about style."

He rose to his feet, then leaned down close enough so she could feel his breath on her cheek.

"Stick with me, Fancy. I'll give you everything you ever wanted and some things you never even imagined."

She studied his face without knowing she was doing so. The broad intelligent forehead and fine straight nose; something about it called to mind the head of a stallion—high-strung and restless. The eyes were restless, too, seeking something big and elusive—just like her own. Something others didn't even know existed.

He kissed her lingeringly, provocatively, on the lips. "No more *no*'s between us, Fancy," he said quietly as he pulled away. "I intend to make love to you tonight. Think about that today, sugar."

He mounted the dark horse and turned its head effortlessly toward the mountains. Startled and titillated, she let him go without saying a word.

▲

Fancy spent the day in a state of agitation. She wanted Chance so desperately, and yet she feared him, too, for to want him so completely gave him power over her again. She changed her clothes twice and her lingerie four times before there wasn't any time left for changing.

It seemed to Fancy that Chance's eyes hadn't let hers go for an instant, since he'd picked her up for dinner. She felt mesmerized by them, lost in her own desire and confusion. Anticipation hovered at the edges of her hard-won composure; just the thought of lying in his arms again was nearly overwhelming.

"Do you remember what I told you this morning, Fancy?" he asked quietly, as the supper she had barely touched was cleared away.

"You know I do."

"I've never forgotten . . ."

"Nor I."

"There've been other men for you since me?"

"A few. And women for you?"

"More than a few. But none like you."

Tears welled up in Fancy quite against her will; she'd lived a lifetime since leaving him. Chance saw the tears and reaching for her hand, pressed her fingers to his lips, still watching her carefully, as if she were a fawn who might be frightened away by a sharp sound.

"I'm sorry I was such a fool back then, Fancy. I was too young and stupid to know how to handle things. I was confused by the way you acted . . . and I knew Hart loved you, too. I didn't know what to do about any of it. Can you ever forgive me for letting you go?"

Fancy closed her eyes to shut out the hurt his words called up; two tears spilled over and ran down her cheeks in silent reproach.

Chance signaled the waiter and stood up abruptly. "You're coming home with me, Fancy. We'll change the past as well as the future."

Her heart pounded as insistently as the ache in her loins; she'd wanted him since time began, but she was so afraid and didn't know exactly why.

Neither said a word on the short carriage ride to Chance's house. He could feel her fragility, sense the fiddle-string tension . . . he wondered what on earth could be going on behind those stricken eyes. He helped her alight from the carriage and she clasped his hand tighter than need be.

Chance unlocked the front door and led Fancy into the parlor. He could see, as he turned up the gas lamp on the table, that she was trembling.

What was it she longed to say, but couldn't? It wasn't lack of passion that deterred her, he was sure of that . . . and of the fact that he loved her. The haunted expression on her face confounded him.

"Oh, Fancy, love . . . I must have hurt you more than I knew," he whispered as he unhooked her cloak and let it fall to the floor at her feet. The tension in Fancy was so great, he thought the wrong move might shatter her like crystal.

"Do you want me to do this, sweetheart?" he asked softly. "Tell me." She nodded yes.

Wonderingly, he unfastened the buttons of her gown and let it puddle around her feet. The corset beneath was of soft cream eyelet; her nipples above it were hard from cold, or passion. Fancy let him untie the laces without a single word; he touched the flesh above the eyelet reverently and saw a shudder run through her, but still she didn't make a sound.

"Don't torment me, Fancy," he said, wondering what strange game she played with her silence.

"What do you know of torment?" she whispered harshly, reaching for him . . . the sound she made as he lifted her into his arms was somewhere between a sigh and a sob. He carried her to his bed as confused as he'd ever been, wanting her beyond anything on earth.

He knew he must be gentle . . . must seek out her secrets carefully. . . . He traced her lips with his fingers, loving the fragile skin, wanting to protect it from hurt. His lips sought hers and found her mouth as questing as his own.

"I love you, Fancy . . . don't be frightened. I'll never let anyone hurt you again." Didn't he know he was the one who'd hurt her most of all?

His knowing hands caressed each part of Fancy, as if she were the first woman he'd ever explored. He held himself in check to intuit her pleasure, trailing his fingers down her body to the places he remembered. He caressed her with tongue and lips, heard her moan softly, touched and sucked and licked each private place that had dreamed of him through years of loneliness.

Fancy stirred in his arms, as if brought to life by his kisses; her body became pliant in its quest for him.

"Lie still, Fancy," he whispered. "Let me do it all."

He wanted more than anything to give her exquisite, endless, aching pleasure, the kind that would bind her to him. "I've wanted you for such a long time. . . ."

He rubbed his flattened hand across the dark curls between her legs, and she quivered. "I'm going to tell you a story . . ." he said softly, his voice husky with intimacy, and memories tumbled around her with his whispering words. He wanted to do something that would remind her of the past . . . something that wouldn't frighten her.

"There was once a beautiful Chinese princess, who was to be the concubine of the Sultan of Persia . . ." he began, his voice as intimate as his wandering hands. He ran his fingertips along the inside of Fancy's thighs and felt her quiver in response. "She was renowned for her beauty, but she was so innocent that the Sultan knew he must initiate her carefully into the arts of love."

Fancy nestled in closer and Chance knew she was listening as well as feeling; as his hands caressed her so did the sensual rhythm of his voice.

"The Sultan came to her bedchamber on the first night and lay beside her, wondering how to win her heart, not merely her body. The princess trembled as the Sultan drew his hand down the silken length of her . . ." Chance's hand brushed Fancy's skin with such delicacy that shudders of desire followed his fingers' touch.

"On the second night, he kissed her breasts . . . he took the tender nipples in his mouth and sucked them softly, insistently, until she was faint with longing . . ." His mouth caught Fancy's nipple and lingered there until she arched against the feelings flooding her; she whimpered a little and he insinuated his hand between her legs, parting them with exquisite care.

"On the third night, he touched the place between her thighs so tenderly, so lovingly, that she opened herself to his caress . . . he kissed her inner lips as gently as if they were the petals of a flower. His tongue touched places so tender, she moaned and called his name . . ."

Fancy heard the sensual words and remembered every story he had ever told her . . . and then his tongue was teasing, circling softly as a butterfly's wings, the rhythm driving her mad, and there was nothing in the world but his insistent mouth and her aching need. Making love was an art form for Chance, his special virtuosity of pleasure.

"I want you," she begged, uncaring about anything but release. "Oh, Christ, I need you, Chance . . . I've always needed you."

He complied, almost lazily, moving within her to a rhythm that made her weak. He wasn't the only man who'd ever made love to her, but he meant to be the only one she'd never forget.

Gently, inexorably, Chance sought out every nerve ending of desire, as he wove an erotic tale only he would ever think to tell. Seduced by the story, and the memories and the man, she tried to pull away, the pleasure too intense, too close to pain, but he held her in his arms and pinned her to the bed with control so passionate and knowledgeable, there could be no escape.

He knew her now, had trailed her through each tremulous expansion; he could tease or torment, thrust or withdraw, give or withhold, as he was doing now, until her desperation and his own would explode them both into one blazing moment of fulfillment. The slick wet intensity of Fancy forced Chance to relent and, calling out her name, he plunged her into ecstasy.

▲ ▲ ▲

The mine office had long since closed for the day and Hart had stayed late to catch up on the paperwork that seemed to be reproducing at an alarming rate. Chance's visit surprised him, gladdened him; they talked awhile of unimportant matters, but it was apparent Chance had something major on his mind. It took awhile for him to get around to it.

"Do you think Fancy really was ever married to that little girl's father?" he asked finally, and Hart fumbled the key in the drawer he was locking, to give himself time to formulate a reply before turning to face his brother.

"What the hell made you ask that question?" he responded irritably.

"I think I'm in love with her, bro. The child bears Fancy's maiden name and the stories she tells about the daddy just don't have the ring of truth in them. I don't give a damn if she had an affair with some guy or not, it's just that I don't know if I should push for the real story. God alone knows what happened to her after that stinking auction."

"Ever think you might be the daddy?" Hart's voice was too serious for Chance to imagine he was joking.

He was shocked that his brother knew he and Fancy had made love; he hadn't thought anyone knew. "No. I never did," he answered.

Hart lifted his honest eyes to Chance's; he'd obviously given this considerable thought. "The timing's about right . . . and her eyes are the same queer blue yours are. Like Mama's eyes."

Chance let out an eloquent breath. "You don't miss much, little brother, do you?"

Hart smiled, but there was no joy whatsoever in the expression.

"I would've been real willing to miss this conversation, Chance. But you did ask me."

"Why wouldn't she tell me if Aurora's mine, for Christ's sake? Especially now?"

"I don't know. Maybe pride. Maybe she's lied to the little girl and can't figure her way out of it. Maybe she thinks it's best to let history be history. Fancy doesn't think like the rest of the world of womenfolk, in case you haven't noticed."

Chance heard the bitterness in his brother's voice.

"You know, I never meant to hurt you, bro, by loving Fancy. It wasn't anything I planned at all, it just seemed to happen. We're so much alike, Hart, she and me. Mavericks, both of us. Wild cards. Still, I'm sorrier than

I can say if I hurt you by loving her." He cleared his throat, embarrassed, uncertain what to add, hoping Hart would understand.

"If what we're thinking's true, Chance, I'd say Fancy's the one who's been hurt, wouldn't you?"

Chance nodded, seemed about to speak, then changed his mind. He stood up abruptly and walked from the room, leaving Hart to wonder at the curious fact that Chance had never seen Halle Hart McAllister in Aurora Deverell's eyes.

 62 "You could be governor of this state, McAllister, if you learn to play your cards right and keep your pecker in your pants." The man who spoke was Elmore Trask and he carried more than enough weight in the Republican party to open or close the doors to the Colorado statehouse.

Chance had been cultivating acquaintanceship with party kingpins in a variety of ways; being seen in the right meetings, spending money on the right party-backed causes, contributing ideas that were innovative and noticeable. Trask was a formidable but necessary rung on the ladder he intended to ascend.

Chance held his temper in check.

"That's mighty interesting, Elmore. But as it happens, I have more interest in seeing silver get a fair shake in Washington than in my own political aspirations."

Elmore Trask snorted; it was a sound of extreme world-weariness. "Cut the bull crap, McAllister. It's no secret you're ambitious. It's also no secret we've decided to make Haw Tabor senator instead of governor, so that leaves a clearer track for you. I've been watching you awhile now and I like a lot of what I see. But you got two flaws that could mean trouble—gambling and tomcatting. And while they're fine manly pursuits, either one can make you real vulnerable in an election. You hear what I'm saying, boy?"

The man moved his ponderous belly backward in the armchair, seeking to ease some unspecified discomfort.

Chance hunched forward in his own chair and fixed Trask's porcine eyes with his own.

"I hear you. And the fact that I'm willing to believe you have the good of the party in mind makes me inclined to overlook your singularly offensive way with words. As it happens, I intend to propose marriage to someone before the week is out, so my tomcatting days are about to end. But I'm not a boy, Elmore, and I'll take it real personal if you ever call me one again."

Trask smiled. It put Chance in mind of something Bandana once said about a rattlesnake. "Just 'cause he don't rattle at you don't mean his fangs fell out."

"Make no mistake, McAllister. The party can make you and it can break you just as quick."

"And you make no mistake, Elmore. I'm willing to work for the party because its interests and my interests are one and the same. I'm a rich man and I intend to get richer. Now, I don't mind sharing some of those riches with a party that means to keep silver healthy, and if running for office is in the cards, I'm game for that, too. What I'm not game for is cringing in the corner every time you rattle your chains."

Elmore pursed his fat lips contentedly. So far McAllister seemed to have passed all the tests with flying colors.

▲

"Oh, Jewel. I'm so happy!" Fancy said, exuberant as a child. She was sitting at the enameled table in the parlour house kitchen with a mug of steaming coffee in her hand.

"I can't tell you what a gorgeous time Chance and I had together last night. And what plans we made! I don't think I've ever been this happy in my whole life."

Jewel bent down to pick up a dropped hairpin and Fancy almost giggled at the sight. Frowzy hair all this way and that, loose dressing gown flapping open as she bent, the movement exposed an enormity of bosom beneath.

"God's nightgown, Jewel. I don't see how you stand upright carrying those things around with you."

Jewel stretched herself lazily, hands on hips, back arched so her chest thrust forward. "Gotta make the best of what God give you to work with, kid. Many's the man has volunteered to help me hold 'em up." She pulled a mug from the cabinet with an exaggerated yawn and motioned for Tillie, the cook, to pour her a cup of coffee. Then she sat down with the thud of one to whom morning was an unnecessary distraction.

"Best-lookin' man in Leadville, all right," she pronounced. "And a hell of a lot of fun, I'll grant you that." Fancy cocked her head to one side questioningly; she'd heard the unspoken disapproval in the reply.

"But?"

"Gambling men are great for business and lousy for life. So . . . much as I'm happy to see you in love, I just hope you know what you're gettin' into."

"But he's not only a gambler, Jewel. He's got a high-grade mine and everybody knows he has political prospects . . ."

"Don't ever trust a dreamer, Fancy. Dreamin' men'll sell you heaven on a plate, but they ain't got substance. When I started monkeyin' around tryin' to get you two together again, I was hopin' you'd see Chance for what he is and stop carryin' that torch that was burning a hole in your gut. I thought he was more dangerous to you as a phantom than as a real man, with real live faults. Now I see I might've made a big mistake buttin' in. Take my advice, kid. Have some fun with Chance, maybe even let him scratch that itch of yours, provided you take precautions, but don't start seein' moonbeams and marriage licenses. Dreamers can break your heart real easy."

"Jewel! I thought you *liked* Chance McAllister."

"Do like him, honey. I hear he's hung like a bull, too, and knows what to do with it. And I've heard it from enough sources to know he don't like keepin' it in his trousers too long." She took a sip of coffee and waited to swallow it. "I just wouldn't want to give him houseroom is all."

"You're wrong Jewel. Chance's going places, you'll see. He's going all the places I want to go."

"Yeah? Well my experience is that gamblin' men make you pay real dear for the ticket to ride." With that Jewel hoisted herself out of the chair and flounced from the kitchen. Fancy felt her elation dampened by her friend's words, for there was part of her that knew they were true.

Then the memory of their times together surfaced. She'd made love to other men; in truth, she knew a good deal more of sex than any nice woman should. Yet, never with anyone else had she felt one iota of the ecstasy she felt with Chance, and that kind of fulfillment wasn't something a woman would walk away from a second time.

Not that everything was perfect, exactly. Chance was hard to fathom sometimes; his moods were mercurial and he acted always on whim or instinct. But he always did seem to win, so perhaps he knew best. It would have been easier to figure him out if he ever let her take control of anything, but just when she thought she had him in the palm of her hand, he was off on some tangent that had nothing to do with what she'd had in mind.

And how he did love to have fun—he was a spectacular dancer and he never seemed to let work interfere with pleasure. Other men always wanted to talk about how brilliant they were in business, but Chance had other, more interesting stories on the tip of his tongue. And it didn't seem to hamper his ability to succeed; everything he touched turned to money.

Why, then, did she seem to see Atticus' old face frowning disapproval in her dreams? *Flashy man,* he would have said. *Steer clear o' de flashy ones, child, dey ketch yo' eye but dey don' take good care a' what belongs to 'em.*

But you don't get the flamboyance, the excitement, and the dreams from the slow and steady ones, she wanted to argue back. The ones who husband their possessions with care and probity don't make a girl's heart beat faster and her loins yearn for something exquisite and reachable.

Fancy put the troublesome arguments away—she could do that with things. Tuck them away, far down inside a drawer within her, close it up, and turn the key . . . sometimes for good. Occasionally the thoughts crept out again in the fearsome time of night to haunt her, but mostly she could push them back where they belonged.

She would get Chance to ask her to marry him and that would solve everything once and for all. Then, finally, maybe she and Aurora would find a home.

63   The day was perfect, crisp and sunlit, breezes carried the scent of pine and wildflowers over the top of the mountain. Chance had taken Fancy for an outing in his new phaeton carriage. They'd driven to Silver Plume to see the newly built railroad that circled the peaks there.

Fancy's spirits were high, the eleven-thousand-foot altitude was heady, and she was in love. Chance watched her with a proprietary eye—she was everything he wanted in a woman, and everything he needed to complete the dream. Wife, lover, mother for the dynasty he intended would come after them.

"Sugar," he said, taking her hand in his own and pressing it to his lips. "I have a present for you." He pulled the velvet ring box from his pocket and she took it, questioningly.

"I'm hoping you'll marry me, Fancy. You'll make me the happiest man on earth if you say yes."

She searched his eyes and found nothing there but love, then opened the box and gasped at the size of the emerald ring glowing regally on its velvet cushion.

"Good God, Chance, that's the most spectacular ring I've ever seen." Jason had bought her jewels, but nothing like this one.

He chuckled. "I asked you a question, Fancy. You're supposed to give me an answer."

She pulled her gaze from the astonishing gem.

"Of course I'll marry you. I'm mad about you. I thought you knew."

Chance took her in his arms and kissed her. Fancy nestled contentedly there and thought nothing in the world could touch them now. It had been so easy to repair the past. . . .

"There is one thing I need to know, Fancy," he said gently. "I didn't want to ask until I knew you'd marry me. Aurora, sugar . . . is she mine? Hart says she looks like Mama."

Hart says! Why don't *you* say? . . . Fancy forced herself to answer calmly. "I always thought you'd know her as soon as you laid eyes on her, Chance. My heart nearly stopped beating when you met her and didn't realize she was yours."

Chance tried to digest the knowledge—it was one thing to speculate, another to know for certain.

"How you must have hated me, Fancy. To keep that secret for so many years must have tormented you."

"Sometimes I wanted to make you suffer, too," she answered honestly, pulling away from his embrace.

"Why the hell didn't you tell me when you came back?"

"I'd learned to live without you by then. I wasn't sure I wanted to be vulnerable again. And . . . I didn't know how."

"But if I'd known, Fancy . . . you must believe I would have done the right thing."

"Married me to make an honest woman out of me?" she said derisively. "Don't you know I'd never settle for that, Chance? I'll marry you because I love you, and because I want to spend my life with you, but don't delude yourself for one single minute that I'd ever marry you because of Aurora. I'm worth more than that, damn you! If you don't know that by now, then you can just take your ring back and forget the whole thing."

She pulled away from his grasp and reached for the door handle, the suppressed anger of years making her suddenly want to run. Chance's hand shot out to stop her, but she pushed past and jumped from the carriage to the ground, agile as a doe.

Chance was on his feet beside her in a stride; his hands were on her shoulders turning her to him. She struggled angrily to break free, but his hands were in her hair and around her waist; strong impatient hands that made struggle pointless.

"You ran away from me once, Fancy, but by God, I won't let you do it a second time!"

He swung her up into his arms and crushed her to his chest so tightly, she could hear the thunderous beat of his heart. He kissed her, until she no longer wanted to protest but let her mouth accept the invasion of this man she'd always wanted. What did it matter about the past when the future spread before them? She let him lay her down on the new grass and cover her body with his own. She ceased to think, or wonder or worry as anger transmuted into passion; there was no room in her for anything but lust. Time was theirs to do with as they wanted, he was her phantom lover, real at last, and there was no history at all.

▲

"I've got something big to tell you, bro," Chance said, standing in the doorway of Hart's room, barely able to contain his elation.

Puzzled, Hart motioned his brother in; Chance looked handsome as a matinee idol in his dove-gray coat and trousers, carefully stitched by the finest tailor in Leadville. Hart smiled a little—clothes like the ones Chance was wearing would have made him look like a trained bear in a circus.

"I did it, bro. I got her to say she'd marry me."

"Fancy?" Hart managed over the lump in his throat.

"Just like you to play dumb," Chance said with all the goodwill in the world. Hart thought it an understatement, but tragically accurate.

"Of course, Fancy, you big jerk. Who else am I in love with?"

How can I be so glad for him and so damned sad for me? Hart thought. Oh, Fancy, my Fancy, how can you let this happen? Don't you know you'll be like two moths flying into the flame and no one there to save either one of you?

"Are you happy for me, bro?" Chance asked, needing his brother's approval more than he could admit. "We'll be good for each other, you'll see. I'll take the best care of her. I give you my word on that."

Hart heard the love in his brother's voice and could have wept for the pain of it. *Blood is thicker than water and brother's blood the thickest of them all. . . .*

Hart answered his brother's need the only way he could. "Are you crazy? Fancy's the greatest gal ever lived and no man could make her happier than you. How could I not be happy for you?" The relief on Chance's face was eloquent. Hart felt a rage at himself building up inside. What a prize fool he'd been for never lifting a finger to make things turn out differently. He wouldn't let his brother feel the brunt of it, for he didn't deserve to . . . if any man was at fault in this stupid mess, it was he himself.

"I'm real glad you two finally made the big decision, because otherwise I might've missed the festivities," he said on impulse.

Chance face clouded over. "What do you mean, bro?"

"I'm heading east, Chance. Now there's money enough, and I've put in the time I promised, I'm going to Yale just like I always planned. I'm going to the best art college in the country."

"That's terrific news, Hart. Wait 'til we tell Fancy. My brother's going to be the greatest artist in America, and with a college degree to prove it. God Almighty, bro, wouldn't Mama and Daddy be proud of you?"

Hart could see the pride and love in his brother's eyes and it defeated him. The spark of rage went out, leaving only loneliness. Hart put his arms around his brother and hugged him, so he wouldn't see the tears that filled his eyes.

For the weeks before the wedding, Hart tried his damnedest to be happy for them. They took such joy from each other . . . and he loved them both.

▲

"By God, Fance," Bandana said, looking at her appraisingly in the dim light of the Crown's front room. "When them boys found you, there wasn't enough on you to pad a crutch and look at you now."

Fancy put her arms around Bandana, laughing. He always made her feel like a beloved little girl.

He stood back to get as good a look as possible. "I swear a woman can go further out here with a rouge pot than a man with a horse and a side of bacon."

"What are you doing in town anyway, Bandana? It seems to me you've shown this place a clean pair of heels since you struck it rich. Still out there trailing Esmeralda for us?"

Bandana winked conspiratorially. "I've arrived in Leadville to loiter and to dissipate, Fance, old girl. And to share boughten dalliance of fallen women."

Fancy laughed outright and Bandana saw the saucy dimples in her cheeks and remembered how much he loved her. He hoped life would treat her gently for a while, although he didn't think it likely.

"May I see you to a whiskey, my friend? Just to get the dalliance off to a good start?"

Rufus poured the brown liquid into the glass and smiled at Bandana; he liked the little man.

Bandana tipped the shot glass toward Fancy and downed the liquor with a practiced toss. He set the glass back down on the bar resoundingly, and shook his head.

"If a man had enough of this whiskey, you couldn't drown him. You could shoot him through the brain or heart and he wouldn't die until he sobered up." His humor always made Fancy feel merry; she took his hand and led him through the thicket of revelers.

"What exactly are you doing with all your money, Bandana? Truth is, you haven't changed a single thing in your life to make it easier. Doesn't it make any difference to you at all that you've struck it rich?" She noticed he wore the same clothes as before the strike, except for a new pair of boots.

"Well, now, darlin', that's the question, ain't it? You know I struck pay dirt twicet before, but I never kept none of it, so I didn't have the problem of disposal, you might say. Then I went seriously broke and that didn't appeal to me none. Now I've got money to throw at the birds and I find I'm plumb depressed by it 'cause my pals are gone."

He looked up at her soberly and she could see his wistfulness.

"I had friends when I had nothin' else, Fance. Good friends. Now you're a woman of substance, Hart is chompin' at the bit to head East to that artsy place, and Chance is all dandied up and talkin' to the hoity-toity . . . I ain't got but me and my money. Tell you the truth, darlin', the money don't mean a damn thing to Bessie and me."

Fancy reached over and laid her hand on top of Bandana's gnarled and callused one.

"I used to say I wasn't afraid of nothin' but a decent woman and bein' on foot; but by God, Fance, I think I'm afraid of stayin' in town and bein' rich, and livin' a closed-in life like what I see around here. Got to be pertected from the glares of the saintly, I expect. Too old a dog for new tricks. Don't feel at home in store-boughten clothes. Even these new boots pinch my big toe so bad I wisht I'd of kept my old ones."

"So what are you going to do, Bandana?" Fancy asked softly. How sad it was that his dream had come true but hadn't made him happy.

He let out a long breath. "Soooo, after your weddin', old Bessie and me are headin' out."

"You *will* wait for the wedding?" she asked anxiously. "I couldn't get married if you didn't give me away."

"Yes, ma'am, that much I'll do." He squinted up his eyes at Fancy and squeezed her hand.

"You almighty sure you're marryin' the right McAllister?" he asked, his voice no longer teasing.

"What an awful question, Bandana. Exactly what do you mean by that?"

"Mean to say, sometimes the thing that glitters don't have the value of the thing that don't. I love them boys, Fance. Don't get me wrong—but I love you more. It'd grieve me real bad for you to git hurt."

Fancy sat straighter in her chair and bit back the quick reply that had sprung to her lips. She'd never known him to give her any advice that wasn't sound and it upset her to think he disapproved of Chance.

"I love them both, too, Bandana. But it's different for me with Chance; it always has been, you know that . . . he's wild, like me. He wants the same things I do, and he's going all the places I want to go. You act like I could have them both." She stopped a minute, deciding if she should say more, then spoke again. "You know I couldn't say this to anybody in the world but you, but crazy as it sounds, sometimes I wish I could. I know Chance could use a little of Hart's common sense."

Bandana laughed out loud and shook his head emphatically. "One good man's plenty, Fance—one bad one's more'n enough. No, darlin', I think you got to pick one or t'other, that's fer damned sure."

"Don't you see, Bandana, Hart's following a different drummer. Can you really see me wandering around Indian camps while he paints his pictures? I've had enough of living like a Gypsy to last me two lifetimes.

"Oh, Bandana, I want to be rich! I want a big house and servants and . . . and . . ."

"To be took care of?"

"Exactly. Is that such a bad ambition?"

"No, darlin'. It ain't bad at all. Seems to me a woman should be took care of. It's just that men with Chance's particular bent ain't the take-carin'-est kind, generally speakin'."

"But Chance loves me, Bandana. You know he does. And he's not as frivolous as everybody makes out—every single investment he's made has been a good one. Besides, I'll still have Wu and Jewel and you. And you know there's more money than God has, in that mine up there."

"Just as long as you're sure you know your own mind, darlin'. That way I'll be able to go off with a clear conscience."

"Bandana, I've loved Chance since I was a girl. You know how he's haunted my heart damned near forever. I'm finally going to get what I've wanted so long, and it seems almost too good to be true. I'm really scared it will all just disappear out from under me, so please don't frighten me any more than I already am."

Bandana's expression softened. "Don't mistake my meanin', darlin'. Chance is a dandy feller. Got a heart as big as Montana. Got the purtiest dreams I ever heard tell of, too. Mebbe he's got the sand to make 'em all come true for you, little lady. I'd be the last man alive to throw a monkey wrench into the machinery."

He pushed back his chair and planted a scratchy kiss on Fancy's cheek; there didn't seem much left to say that would be valuable. "Got to be about a little raucous ballyhoo now, Fance. I'm headed over to Mary Jane Conroy's. Her parlour house is famous for its iniquity."

Fancy reached out impulsively, wrapped her arms around Bandana's waist, and clung there for a long moment.

"I love you, Bandana."

"Course you do, darlin'," he replied, more touched by the gesture than he could let on. "If you had only one friend left in this sorry world, you'd want it to be me . . . I ain't never forgot what you said in that letter."

▲ ▲ ▲

Jason Madigan sat at his ornate desk and brooded. He'd been doing quite a lot of that since Fancy'd gone.

It bothered him that he missed her so continuously; he'd never given a second thought to any of the other women who'd populated his bed over the years. No woman was irreplaceable . . . but it was hard to be convinced of that when no replacement for Fancy ever made him happy.

He'd been so angry at first that the fury had overpowered the hurt, but the pain was real and palpable and damnably enduring. It galled his spirit that he'd lost what he wanted to another man. Jason wasn't used to losing.

He stared out over the desktop to the lavish room beyond. He had everything a man could dream of . . . except a confidante, except a lover who truly understood him. Christ! Why had he ever shared his vulnerabilities, his fears, his weakness with her? Why had he let her wander deep inside his soul. Why did he miss her so goddamned much it hurt—in the ego, in the mind, in the heart. Jason swiped at his eyes, which had misted over for some stupid reason.

The report on his desk said she had plans to marry Chance McAllister. Of course, he was the one man she still craved—women like Fancy never get over rejection.

Ever since her departure, he'd tried to replicate her in someone new. Beauties were a dime a dozen in his world, but even among them there were superior and inferior gifts. He'd analyzed Fancy's fatal attraction endlessly. She was smart and quick-witted, with an uncanny knack for getting to the core of matters. He'd taken keen pleasure in her business acumen that saw with special clarity . . . even her avarice was enticing, and she was so eminently teachable. But she was more than just the sum of her parts . . . there was that damnable waiflike quality that made a man want to save her from some unknown peril . . . the lost-child terror staring out for a heartbeat from the courageous facade. Some women were good and men loved them because of it, others were bad and were loved for that alone. But Fancy was both, and that made her utterly unique. Maybe he was just getting old and softheaded.

Christ! I'm obsessed with her, he thought, as a savage anger swept through him yet again, at her stupidity in choosing McAllister. Damn her, that he couldn't forget what she felt like in his arms, craving so wantonly what he knew how to give. Jason thundered for his secretary. The young man threw open the door and scurried nervously in, notepad in hand.

"Get the railroad car ready, Horton, I'm going to Leadville. Tomorrow morning, for an indefinite stay. Have Carter pack enough for a month, cold-weather gear, business suits, dinner jacket, the works."

"Leadville, sir? Colorado?"

"Of course Leadville, Colorado, Horton. Haven't you heard it's the new silver capital of the world? Or haven't you been reading all the mining reports that have crossed your desk in the past months."

"Oh, yes, sir, I've read them, sir. I just didn't know you had a special interest in Leadville. It represents such a small part of your holdings, sir."

"Well, now you know, Horton, so make the arrangements. And quickly."

The tall, gangly young man closed his notebook and retreated fast. Of course he'd read every word that came into his periphery, just to protect himself from his employer's wrath. There'd been too many occasions, over the three years he'd worked for the man, when he'd witnessed the power Mr. Madigan wielded to let Edgar Horton ever feel either safe or secure in his employ.

It was a good job, better than any he'd ever had, but he knew of two instances, at least, in which Jason Madigan had had men killed, a dozen in which he'd smashed reputations, and a handful in which he'd forced men into bankruptcy, so Horton had no illusions whatsoever about the kind of man he worked for.

The boy wiped the sweat from behind his round rimless eyeglasses, slicked back his lank dark hair, and made a list of all the chores necessary to get Mr. Madigan to Leadville expeditiously. The private railroad car was always ready for travel, but he'd have to alert the staff.

He allowed himself a tiny smirk, for he'd read the confidential report from the Pinkerton Agency, too. Silver wasn't the reason Mr. Madigan was going to Leadville, Miss Deverell was. The only wonder was that it had taken him so long to get moving. He'd never known Mr. Madigan to let go of anything he truly wanted.

 Fancy tried to calm herself enough to greet the unwelcome visitor who'd arrived out of nowhere. Jason looked surprisingly at home in the Crown of Jewel's, against the tawdry backdrop of miners and whores, she thought; he'd been a miner, long ago, of course, but that was in another life.

Jason reached for her hand and lifted it to his lips in a proprietary way. "You're looking more beautiful than ever, Fancy. I've missed you."

His presence scared her to the bone; the fear made her rude.

"Why are you here, Jason?"

"Now, now, Fancy. That's an entirely inappropriate way to greet an old and intimate friend." He lingered on the word *intimate* and she bristled despite the fact that he seemed more injured than snide.

"Why are you here, Jason?" she repeated.

"To do business, Fancy. And to see old friends. You needn't be concerned that I've followed you out of malice. If that had been my intention I wouldn't have let so much time elapse. You are entirely safe from me . . . if you wish to be."

Fancy exhaled the breath she'd been holding. "Forgive me, Jason. You're right to chide me for my manners. But you must know it's a shock to see you here . . . my life is very different now." Her heart beat against the stays of her corset like a caged bird in the presence of a condor.

Madigan smiled. "I understand you're quite the entrepreneur now, Fancy, and damned good at it. I always maintained you had the best business brain I ever encountered in a woman."

Fancy tried to relax. Jason didn't seem predatory, merely friendly.

"I've also heard of your impending nuptials, my dear, and while I can't say I'm glad about it, I am most anxious to meet the young man who's won your heart. He must be someone special."

"You always did do your homework, Jason. Can I really trust you not to interfere in my life now that it's finally getting settled?"

She tried to read the look in Jason's eyes as he replied, but it was too complex.

"You may trust me to have only your best interests at heart, Fancy."

"What brings you here, Jason? Leadville is hardly the center of the business world."

"The silver, of course. Wherever there's a mineral boom, there's plenty to interest me. I once told you there's as much money to be made around a boom as there is from the metal itself. Flumes, timber, smelters . . . I've been in this game too long to pass up an opportunity like Leadville."

"If you're going to be in Leadville for a time, Jason, perhaps you'll come to the wedding," she said, trying to behave as if his visit hadn't thrown her off-balance.

"Oh, I expect to be here off and on for quite some time, as it happens, Fancy. I'm even considering taking a house in the area, to make my stay more palatable . . . perhaps you recall that I do like my comforts. I daresay I'll meet this young man of yours in the course of business, but I think I'll forego the wedding invitation. My heart isn't quite that forgiving, I fear."

"You wouldn't do anything to harm him?" she said, disturbed by his icy tone.

Jason chuckled. "Now, now, Fancy. I'm sure your young man would be quite put out that you have so little confidence in his ability to take care of himself. As you well know, there's no room for sentiment in business and no man worth his salt would expect quarter from another because of a woman. I'm afraid your Mr. McAllister will simply have to do his best in his dealings with me as I will with him, and you must evaluate the two of us based on the outcome. That's no more than fair, now, is it?"

Damn him! He's playing cat-and-mouse with me. Fancy's eyes narrowed. "You just go do your damnedest Jason, and play whatever machismo games you feel you must—but don't for one moment make the mistake of thinking that I'm a prize to be won by the highest bidder. I am not a poker chip to be played for in any man's game—yours or Chance's."

She turned and walked away with that imperial hauteur he'd always admired. Jason watched Fancy's retreat, a slight smile on his lips. She always did have spunk and style . . . it would be interesting to see what this McAllister pup had to recommend him.

▲ ▲ ▲

Bandana made a face at his reflection in the looking glass. His usually tangled salt-and-pepper hair was neatly combed, a clean bandana occupied its expected place on his forehead, and a suit of somber color covered a starched white shirt. He twisted his head uneasily within the high stiff collar and tugged at the black string tie.

"God damn! Looks like a layin'-out suit, don't it?"

Hart laughed at his friend's discomfort; it was the first time all day he'd felt like laughing.

"You're not likely to have a burying suit, Bandana. When you go, they'll just lay you out with Bessie and your pickax and put a claim stake over your old bones."

"Never been part of an official weddin' before, givin' away the bride and all." He eyed Hart's formal finery, which looked absurd on his enormous muscular body. "How's it feel to be a best man?"

Hart stared at this friend steadily for a silent moment before he answered in a voice that was hollow and resigned.

"Damned lonely."

Bandana nodded understanding.

"Never been without my brother before, Bandana. Not really, that is. We never went our separate ways before." He lowered his eyes to the carpet as if inspecting his boots for some unsuspected dust. "Today, I guess I'm losing both of them."

"You got guts, boy, to be takin' this so gentle."

"Not guts, Bandana. Common sense and no choice at all. It's him she wants, and he wants her. I just hope I'm man enough to wish them well, and hope to God they'll be happy together."

"Sure as pigs got wings!" said Bandana with a derisive snort. "You no more think that's gonna happen than I do. We both know your brother ain't the marryin' kind. To say nothin' of his bein' too big for his britches since he struck it rich. And Fance . . . well, when it comes to men, old Fance ain't got the sense God gave a chicken."

The two somber men took one last look at themselves in the mirror. "Here we stand, in store-bought clothes, looking like we're on our way to a hangin', not a weddin'. We'd best turn up the corners of our mouths a mite, son. Got to make the bride happy today. She's a rarely fine girl, even if she did pick the wrong McAllister."

Hart smiled at Bandana's appraisal. "She's a rarely fine girl, all right. And Chance is a damned good man and he loves her and he'll do his best by her."

"If he don't, boy, he's gonna answer to me for it. He may be young and strong, but I'm old and wily. I could give him a right lively time."

"Maybe you ought to mention that to him, Bandana," Hart said wryly.

"I might jes' do that. Might jes' make me feel one hell of a lot better. Might jes' go out and get drunker'n I ever been tonight after this here shindig's over and I might jes' take you along to do it."

Bandana clapped Hart on the shoulder and they walked from the hotel room with as much spring in their step as they could muster.

▲ ▲ ▲

Chance ran his hands over Fancy's naked back with proprietary appreciation. She was finally his. He felt buoyed by the knowledge that everything in life was turning out just the way he wanted. Now he and Fancy could have fun together all the time.

There was a radiance to her skin, he noted, feeling expansive as only one who has won a great prize can be. How she loved the exotic tales he spun for her in bed . . . how she loved to be loved. He smiled at remembrance of her exuberant joy. "Nice" women were supposed to be shy of their bodies, reticent about sharing them with their husbands. He'd heard other men speak of their wives' modesty in the marriage bed, with a queer mixture of annoyance and pride at their wives' reluctance.

That was sure as hell not Fancy's way. Her lust matched his own, and then some. Chance chuckled softly as he saw her stir happily beneath his roving fingers. Oh, yes, indeed, there were good times ahead. Languidly, she moved beneath his touch and with a soft moan of pleasure turned her body up to meet his willing one.

"Fancy," he breathed into her hair as he buried his face in the dark cascade that fell over her shoulder. "I love you . . . I love you more than I've ever loved anybody."

There didn't seem much doubt from the enthusiasm of her response that she returned the emotion.

Hart assessed the mining operation that had been his domain for so long, with an eye toward leaving it behind. The Fancy Penny had grown large and efficient under his aegis, he thought with satisfaction. The mine manager's office where he hung his hat was a wood-frame affair, fifteen by twenty feet big, which housed a rolltop desk with cubbies full of files, assay reports, payroll chits, and all the other paperwork required to run a mine. There was a fine potbellied wood stove, two straight-back chairs for visitors, and the walls were hung with maps and shaft charts. Though he wouldn't call it homey, he thought it a decent enough place to work, and a damned sight better than down below—but all that notwithstanding, he'd be thrilled to turn it over to Caz Castlemaine and walk away.

He closed the office door behind him and squinted into the sun. To the left of where he stood was the dry room—a rickety wood structure with a stove, where the men changed their wet clothes and warmed up after each shift. It was also there so the foremen could keep an eye out for high-grading, the practice of tucking away the choicest nuggets into pants pockets. Hart smiled a little as his gaze lit on the dry room; the miner's lot was so grim that Caz and he both turned a blind eye toward high-grading more often than not. A pilfered nugget could mean the chance to get a doctor for a sick child or to put bread on a man's table. At three dollars for a ten-hour day, not too many men were able to keep their families' heads above water, since prices in Leadville had skyrocketed.

Caz was definitely the ablest successor to his job, Hart thought as he watched the man talking animatedly to another miner. It was a blessing the Aussie had accepted working for them when they'd struck it rich, with no rancor over their having hit bonanza while he had not. As far as Hart could see, Caz bore them only goodwill and loyalty. He was grateful Caz existed. It was long past time for him to go.

Hart swung his gaze past the men and took in the bustling camp. Sounds rang from the toolshed where the blacksmith plied his ceaseless trade, sharpening steel drill bits, fixing sledgehammers, and making sure all equipment for the narrow-gauge track and ore cars was kept in trim.

Everywhere Hart turned his gaze, the view was bleak. The hillsides had been stripped for timbering—what once had been lush and green was brown and scarred. Slag heaps, called tailing dumps, dribbled down the hillsides like nasty gashes in nature's plan. Even the stream that rumbled nearby had been sullied by processing the milled ore into slurry for the smelter.

Hart let his eyes rest on the mine entrance that marked the tunnel they'd wrested from the rock with their own hands. It seemed forbidding now, a portal to a cold, damp world of impenetrable darkness. Hart knew the interior honeycomb like the veins on his own hand, for the charts were his to guard and understand and make decisions about. *Oh, Lord, I never wanted any of this,* he thought with annoyance. He was annoyed a lot of the time now, it seemed—ever since the wedding, all life had darkened.

He didn't like the idea of hanging around and begrudging Chance and Fancy their happiness. They seemed so suited to each other, and so much in love. Yet, Hart found himself getting angry at his brother over little things that had never bothered him before. It was time to move on . . . a fresh start and an old ambition would heal the parts of him that needed healing. He would put the past behind and begin again at Yale.

▲ ▲ ▲

The excitement Hart had felt dissipated on the long stage and train ride east. He tried to buoy his spirits with common sense—Chance and Fancy had made their choices, at Yale he, too, could begin a new life. But common sense was cold comfort and the fact that he'd been fool enough to let it happen rankled.

The train chugged endlessly through open prairie and the wide golden vistas brought back childhood memories. His father's words whispered back to him, over the familiar landscape. *Don't you ever let anyone tell you being an artist ain't a manly calling, son,* his father had said. *Integrity is manly. Truth is manly. You keep that in mind and you'll do just fine.* Hart remembered the words now, and they sustained him.

He unpacked his bags in New Haven and settled into the rooms that would be his for the next few years. He could see the Gothic-spired buildings from his boardinghouse window; the campus was lusher and gentler than any landscape he'd yet seen.

Hart shrugged his six-foot-six-inch body into the proper tweeds he'd bought for the occasion, but they made him feel imprisoned, and he set off for his first class feeling like a country bumpkin awkwardly attired for the city.

▲

The large, airy studio had a raised platform in the center, much like the makeshift stage Jewel had set up for Fancy in the Crown. Hart looked uncomfortably at the other students who were seated on high stools before their easels—he was out of place as a bull in an ox yoke.

Soft faces unweathered by hardship, bodies bred to citified self-indulgence met his inquiring glance. Each student was seated comfortably behind an easel, busily working with charcoal or crayon, his hands unroughened by day labor. Hart looked at his great callused hands, and shifted uncomfortably on a stool absurdly small for his size.

Every easel pad was covered by sketches of female nudes. Most of the naked female bodies Hart had ever seen had been in whorehouses, and even then they were generally partially clad in some frilly red or black fol-de-rol. The door opened at the rear of the hall and a small, irritable-looking man in a blue smock entered, along with a young girl in a loose, flowing garment. The man led the model to the posing platform; she pulled the robe off over her head, to reveal a body naked as a brook trout and just as unselfconscious.

The professor positioned the girl in a reclining pose on a floor mat, with no more thought than if he were arranging a bowl of apples. "You may commence your work," he announced, in some foreign accent Hart thought might be French.

Quick, deft strokes to right and left of Hart began to sketch in the basic form of the reclining nude. He felt clumsy and inept, so he simply stared at the girl's body, wondering how in the world to begin. Her skin was softly tawny and, at the moment, covered by goose bumps from the chill of the floor. Hart examined the full curve of her breasts; the dark nipples were puckered from the cold, the soft heaviness caused the one nearest the floor to drop slightly downward; he thought he'd like to sketch just that portion of her anatomy, it seemed so oddly eloquent.

"You are not here to indulge your lustful fantasies, Mr. McAllister," the biting voice of the professor snapped, from somewhere over Hart's right shoulder. "Do you plan to ogle the young lady, or do you intend to draw her?"

Hart felt like a kid caught with his hand in the cookie jar.

"No, sir. I intend to try to draw the young lady." He saw several wellbred mouths around the room twitch with amusement.

"And what do you wait for, may I ask? A personal invitation, perhaps? Or is it that such immense hands, which appear to be those of a common laborer, are incapable of holding charcoal, other than to shovel it into a furnace?"

Hart suppressed an urge to pick the cranky little man up by the scruff of the neck; he picked up the charcoal instead and began to sketch in the outline of the nude. It was apparent that his lines were not like those of the other students; their pads were filled with delicate swirling strokes, accented by lights and darks that gave them dimension—Hart's were bold, dark, different. The professor looked scornfully at the pad. "As I suspected! Your work is as primitive as you are." A ripple of uncomfortable mirth swept the room.

Hart's eyebrows came together in a frown; letting a bully think you're cowed was always dangerous.

"Well, now, Professor, if there wasn't room for improvement, I wouldn't need you to teach me, would I?"

Mireau met Hart's eyes for the first time. "We have not yet ascertained that a farmer is capable of learning what I have to teach," he said disdainfully.

"I was born a farmer, Professor. But more recently I've been a miner. Been a ditchdigger, too, and an engraver. Cowhand . . . you name it. Point is, I came to Yale to learn to be an artist. I was sort of under the impression that's why people went to art school."

Laughter disrupted the class again, this time it was aimed at Mireau; the man's venom had stung each of them in some way before.

The professor stood his ground. "And with whom, might I inquire, have you studied? Who has taught you such an undisciplined and stubborn line?"

Hart held his temper carefully in check; a man his size learns early on to keep a tight rein. "My mama, God rest her, taught me what little I know . . . and a fine man, name of Hercules Monroe, taught me engraving. I wouldn't take kindly to anyone speaking ill of either one."

An easel stool was pushed aside and Hart heard an educated southern voice speak out from behind him.

"If you'll forgive me, sir, for interrupting, I think perhaps I might be able to be of assistance to Mr. McAllister in disciplining his line. After all, Professor, he has not yet had the distinct privilege of studyin' under your skilled tutelage as we have, sir." The self-possessed southerner turned to Hart. "I'd be delighted to act as your tutor for a bit, if you'd be so inclined, Mr. McAllister."

Without waiting for either Hart or Mireau to respond, the man extended his hand. "Rutledge Canfield at your service, sir," he said with a conviction that left no one in doubt about his good intentions. Hart, too, stood for the first time, towering ludicrously over the diminutive professor. He put out his hand gratefully to Canfield, pleased to feel the strength in the man's handshake. The southerner was fair-haired and handsome, three or four inches shorter than Hart, but by no means a small man. He moved with the studied athletic grace of a fencer or polo player, and had about him the easy aura of privilege. His features were regular and aristocratic.

Canfield laughed good-humoredly at the obvious disparity between Hart's size and that of every other man in the room.

"If I may be so bold as to say so, sir, I think it would behoove us all to withhold judgment about this gentleman's work, in deference to the fact that it appears he might be able to lick us all in a fair fight." This time the amused laughter was distinctly benevolent. It was easy to see by the response of both students and professor to Canfield's intervention that he held an honored place in the class.

Hart grinned in relief, warmed by the gesture of friendship. "I sincerely doubt that would be the case," he said. "But I do appreciate the generosity of your offer, Mr. Canfield. I can see by looking at everybody else's work how much I need it."

"Graciously said, sir," Canfield answered. "Perhaps we should work out the details of our tutorial after class so the professor can continue giving us all the benefit of his pithy observations." The sudden twitch at the corner of Canfield's eye that might have been a wink made Hart grin.

The professor turned with a disgruntled harumphing sound to the next student, and Canfield nodded at Hart as if to say "Everything's all right now." He returned to his own easel and continued work, as if nothing unusual had happened.

▲

"Seems as though you about saved my hide in there, Mr. Canfield," Hart said when they'd left the classroom behind. The man laughed amicably.

"Not at all, Mr. McAllister. Not at all. It appears to me that you could well handle considerably more than the evil-tempered little Mireau. And my friends call me Rut, much to the embarrassment of my sister, I might add."

"Seems like you've got the professor buffaloed."

"The simple fact is, the man's a genius. If there's one ounce of talent inside you he'll beat it out. He's a sadistic little brute. I suspect it comes from his diminutive size, but his bedside manner has a tendency to paralyze newcomers, who have no way of knowing what a brilliant little bully he is."

"He doesn't seem to bully you."

"No. He's not enough of a fool for that. My granddaddy, you see, had the foresight to marry into an illustrious Yankee family that used a large part of its fortune to keep this fine university solvent. And my daddy and my favorite aunt are the reason there's an art school at Yale."

Hart raised his eyebrow in acknowledgment of the way of the world, and Rut laughed.

"Your own story I suspect, sir, may be far more colorful than mine. If you would care to accompany me to the Old Heidelberg, perhaps you'd tell me a bit about it over lunch."

Hart learned more about how the other half lives in that afternoon than a lifetime in Colorado could have taught him. Rut knew everything and everybody; he accepted all that was good in life as his due. He'd never been poor and never been desperate, as a consequence of which he'd spent his life pursuing perfection of mind and body by the hardest routes he could find.

"If you're born to excess, you have two choices: relax and grow soft on the available pleasures, or use your resources to hone yourself into a man other men will respect. That's what I'm attempting," he said.

To that end Hart discovered Rut spoke three European languages, played every sport you could name, most of them well, and had taken honors in history and politics at William and Mary. He'd come to Yale to learn about Yankees firsthand, and to make use of what his relatives' endowment had purchased. He was a fine artist, but as is often the case with men who have too many talents, he had never committed himself to the undeviating pursuit of any one of them. Hart later came to think that Mireau's respect for Rut was as much a function of his recognition of Canfield's genuine artistic gifts as of his pedigree.

▲

Yale University
New Haven, Connecticut
October 16

Dear Chance,

I know you'll be wondering what has become of your wandering brother, so I've decided to keep you posted on everything I experience in this amazing new life. You know how I've always loved to hear the tales you spin—now it's my turn.

First, the school itself. Yale is a venerable old institution and has a high opinion of itself—well deserved, I expect. The College of Fine Arts is new since '69 and was made possible by a grant from the aunt of my new friend, Rutledge Canfield. It seems she and her husband lived for years in Europe and were appalled by the "artistic illiteracy" of Americans, so she provided money to Yale so they could incorporate a college of fine arts into their curriculum. (That's a fancy word for the subjects they offer for study.)

The buildings are something to behold, a lot like the cities in Europe must be. The architecture is full of spires and stained-glass windows—they call it Venetian Gothic—and believe you me, nothing like it has ever been seen west of Arkansas.

We are an experiment. Never before has anyone in this country deemed art as important a pursuit as the older professions of law, medicine, and theology.

Chance, I love this place. All those dreams I've harbored damn near forever can be fulfilled here, and then some. I had to really hustle to catch up with the academic studies that are mandatory; my education was woeful compared to my classmates. Thank God Mama and Ford Jameson instilled in me such a love of books—it has carried me through.

Some of my professors say I have real promise—we shall see. There's so much to know, Chance, and I'm so lucky to have this opportunity to learn. What would Mama and Daddy say if they could see me now?

Give my love to Bandana and Fancy. I miss them, but most of all I miss you. Hope all goes well at the mine. Write if you can.

Your errant brother,
Hart

 Being married to Chance was better than Christmas and the Fourth of July. Fancy hadn't been poor for a while, but not since childhood had she felt rich as she did with Chance, for he knew money was meant to be enjoyed.

He had her frocks made by the fanciest couturier in Denver; extravagant dresses with flower-strewn bustles and lace by the profligate yard. Assortments of petticoats, peignoirs, and shimmies were shipped in from Paris—lingerie with delicate embroidery on the finest linens, silks, and voiles, lace that must have blinded scores of tatting nuns, even a satin robe with a collar of maribou that made her look sensuous and regal—all were gifts from the generous hands of Fancy's new and adoring husband. What Chance didn't give, he encouraged her to buy—high-heeled silver slippers, silk stockings, a fur coat—there was no single dream they'd fantasized on their destitute mountaintop that Chance didn't remember and realize.

He even supervised the architecture of their grand new house, and left Fancy to order the furnishings, wall coverings, and carpets from catalogs provided by his railroad cronies.

"I swear I don't know how you have time for work at all, you spend so much time on me," she told Chance contentedly, as they sat in the newly completed master bedroom suite.

"I told you to stick with me, Fancy, and I'd give you everything you ever wanted." Chance's reply had become a ritual response. He smiled at his beautiful wife, as he stood in front of the Jacobean armoire from which he'd just pulled a freshly starched shirt.

"Well, I certainly can't say you reneged on that promise, even if you are a bit smug about it," Fancy answered him, amused and benevolent.

Chance didn't bother to reply, but crossed to where she was seated at her boudoir table and kissed her, the kind of kiss that led to other things.

"I have this story I've been wanting to tell you . . ." he murmured as he let his hands stray down her back. She pushed him away playfully.

"I don't know why I even bother to dress up in all these gorgeous clothes you buy for me. All you ever want to do is get me out of them!"

They made love an uncommon amount, she thought delightedly. She wondered if those prune-faced biddies, who still turned up their noses at her on the street, were sought out by their husbands so constantly and so deliciously—surely not, or they'd be less surly.

It had come as no surprise whatsoever to Fancy when she found that she was pregnant again; not even Jewel's contraceptive measures could withstand such constant assault. She had mixed feelings about the pregnancy— thrilled to be carrying a wanted child, conceived in love and luxury—but the horror of Aurora's birth was still stark within her. Fancy didn't want to die, now that all her dreams were coming true. Chance would dote on the new baby, for he'd turned out to be a loving parent to Aurora, even if the little girl made it obvious in a thousand ways that she'd wanted Fancy to marry Jason instead. They'd decided she was too young to be told that Chance was her true father; later, when she was older, the right time would come.

▲ ▲ ▲

It was after midnight when Fancy heard Chance come in the front entrance; instead of climbing the stairs to their bedroom, he walked to the study and shut the door behind him. His tread sounded oddly reluctant. Fancy slipped from bed, wrapped her dressing gown about her, and ran downstairs.

Chance was sitting by the study fire staring idly at the burning logs; he looked up, but didn't rise to embrace her.

"We've got to talk, sugar," he said with an unaccustomed brusqueness. Fancy sat down in the leather wing chair beside the hearth, apprehension replacing her curiosity.

"Things can't go on like this, Fancy."

"Things? What things? What on earth are you talking about?" Her mind raced toward scattered possibilities . . . everything had been so perfect a moment ago, now the old fear of something catching her off guard tightened her belly. "Whatever's wrong, love? Did something happen at Chaffee's that upset you?"

"You can't go on working, Fancy," Chance said, not looking her in the eye. "I've asked you nicely about it ever since we got married—now I'm telling you. It's made me a laughingstock to have an actress and a saloon owner for a wife."

Fancy stared at her husband. She'd thought for certain the question of her work could wait until after the baby was born.

"I thought you wanted me to stop working so I'd have more time for us, Chance, and because I'm pregnant . . . it never occurred to me you were ashamed of me. I was under the misapprehension that you loved me."

"I *do* love you, Fancy, don't you see, that's the whole point. I don't want other men staring at you, lusting after you . . . and I sure as hell don't want a wife who makes a spectacle of herself doing work better left to men."

Color rose in Fancy's cheeks; she'd forgotten he could be cruel.

"You knew exactly who I was before you married me, Chance. I didn't keep any secrets from you about my profession. You never said a word about my businesses."

"It never occurred to me you'd want to keep on working after we were married, Fancy. I thought you'd just settle down like other women. . . ."

"I'm *not* like other women, Chance. I'm a damned good actress, and a damned good businesswoman—and I intend to remain both."

"And how the hell do you think it makes me feel having my wife run a bathhouse and be part owner in a whorehouse-saloon and God knows what else in Chinatown? Don't you think men snicker about it behind my back? It's bad for my political future, Fancy, and to be honest with you, it brings up rotten memories."

Fancy's voice quieted to a dangerous monotone. "Exactly what memories do you refer to?"

"That stinking auction, if you must know. Just tonight somebody made a snide remark about it. I would have decked the bastard if Tabor hadn't intervened."

"You of all people should know why I was in *that* particular fix, Chance McAllister. I wouldn't think you'd have the gall to shame me with it."

"Damn it, Fancy! I don't want to hurt you, you must know that . . . it just isn't any good this way. I love you so much I want everyone to respect you because you're my wife."

Cold fury settled around Fancy, like an ice-mantle. "I don't want to be respected because I'm your wife, Chance. I want to be respected because I'm *me*."

Chance looked at her in consternation. "How the hell could I have known you'd want to keep on working after we were married? It isn't as if I can't afford to keep you in style. And, damn it, you're going to have our baby—you must see that what I'm saying makes sense."

Fancy, hurt beyond words, just stared at her husband; what could she possibly say that wouldn't demean them both? Maybe it was embarrassing for a candidate's wife to be so flamboyant, but flamboyance was part of who she was . . . part of what he loved about her, wasn't it?

Chance tried to put his arms around her to soothe the hurt so clearly written in her face; their tempers were quick to kindle as their lust, but usually the latter healed the former. Fancy pulled away from his grasp.

"So I'm good enough to make love to, but not good enough to defend against your cronies?"

"It wasn't like that, Fancy. You're twisting my words."

"I'm twisting things? What exactly do you think this little scene has done to my feelings? Throwing the auction in my face after all these years! I have no intention whatsoever of giving up my businesses—Jewel and Wu were there for me when you weren't. I'll stop performing until after our baby's born, but you have absolutely no right to ask for more than that."

"You're overwrought, Fancy. Maybe it's the pregnancy."

"And what do you know about pregnancies, Chance? You were conspicuously missing from the last one."

"That's low, Fancy. Whose fault was it that I didn't know?" Chance stood, fists clenched, his eyes like a winter storm.

Fancy turned soundlessly and walked up the stairs, tears on her cheeks. She heard the slamming of the front door, but she didn't care where he went as long as it was nowhere near her tonight.

Chance stood outside his own house and replayed the conversation, angrily. He'd been right and she'd been wrong—what he'd asked was no more than any man would. Damn her that she was headstrong as a mustang, and just about as unpredictable. He didn't want there to be anything wrong between them, he'd been happier since their marriage than ever in his life. He glanced up at their bedroom window just as the lamp was extinguished. Damn his hasty temper . . . now he'd have to find a place to sleep tonight and a way back into Fancy's good graces tomorrow.

Tired and frustrated, Chance McAllister headed into town.

▲ ▲ ▲

Chance squinted with the assault of morning sunlight. His head ached and he felt foolish; he should never have let her goad him into spending the night with Maddy. Not that he didn't have a right to do what he wanted, now that Fancy was pregnant and the doctor had cautioned sexual restraint. But he hadn't wanted Maddy at all, it was merely injured pride that had put him in her bed last night.

Chance told himself that bedding the occasional floozy didn't change what a man felt for his wife. He intended to found a dynasty with Fancy. He squared his shoulders and headed for home to make things right with his wife.

Fancy looked lost in the big bed, her legs curled up in a fetal position, her arms hugging herself like a child's. Her posture tugged at Chance's heart; she'd looked the same that far-off time when he'd found her in the snow. He sat beside the sleeping figure and rested his hand on the familiar curve of her body.

Fancy stirred; the night had been fitful and sleepless until nearly morning. She'd cried herself to sleep feeling lost and hopeless, no longer angry, merely bereft. Chance leaned close and brushed his lips against her cheek.

"I'm real sorry, sugar. I was a damned fool last night. I guess my pride hurt over anybody faulting you. You mean more to me than anything in this world and I want everybody to know how perfect you are."

Fancy sighed and reached her arms around his neck, grateful for a way back into their love.

"I'm sorry, too, Chance," she murmured. "I guess the old wounds run deeper than I thought. My head hurts so much from trying to puzzle it out, I just can't fight anymore."

She tried to rise, but he folded her into his arms instead.

"I know how to make you feel better, sugar. I'll tell you a story and make the pain go away."

Grateful for his touch, Fancy turned and slipped her chemise off over her head. She saw in his eyes that her body was beautiful and felt redeemed by the acknowledgment.

Chance's hands, strong and knowing, began to knead the tension from her flesh, the sound of his storytelling voice was both soothing and inflammatory. She turned her head from side to side, soaking in the luxury of his strength, reveling in the trail of sensitive fingers down her spine from neck to buttocks. Long, firm strokes that melted her anxiety into contentment, tender exploratory fingers that moved her legs apart and reached between to search out her deeper pleasure.

Fancy moaned a little as she felt his hot hard strength insinuate itself between her thighs, seeking welcome. She stretched herself to take him in, loving the long, pulsing perfection that she'd feared through the night would never be theirs again. To lose Chance a second time would be unthinkable.

He lifted Fancy's body and drew her in with maddening patience until she was once again completely in his power. She let the spasms fall in rings around her, through her, in her—like the widening circles from a pebble in a pool. The intensity of feeling left her breathless, as she felt him pull away and sink to the bed beside her, still cradling her in his love.

For an instant, last night's hurt tried to surface, but she pushed it back and listened only to the voice of her body. Could it be, she wondered as she drifted off to sleep, that their bodies were perfectly mated and not their souls?

▲ ▲ ▲

Fancy waved to Chance over the heads of the other people in the audience at the political rally. His speech had been so well received; there was cheering and clapping and congratulating going on. What a fine actor he would have made, she thought, filled with love and pride; politics and acting had so much in common. Ever since their fight, Fancy'd made a concerted effort to pay more attention to her husband's career and less to her own. She'd had to stop performing because of the baby; it made good sense to put pride aside and let Chance think he'd gotten his way. The other businesses were a handful she didn't want to deal with just now, and she did so want to be a perfect wife.

Chance caught Fancy's eye and smiled; he looked so grand up there, beguiling the crowds with his talk of the future—so much the way he used to spin dreams for us in the cabin, she thought. Now everybody in Leadville was caught up in Chance's dreams; even the state politicians had turned up to hear what he had to say about expansion, and everyone knew Elmore Trask didn't waste his energies on undeserving contenders.

All those people who'd been so sure she was marrying wrong . . . all those who thought Chance didn't have any substance, could just eat their hearts out now. As could all the nasty churchgoing harpies who'd put it about that Chance was marrying a whore. Anyone could see he was going places, and she and Aurora and the new baby were going with him, the world and all its petty snipers be damned!

Jason stood at the edge of the crowd assessing what he'd seen, staying clear of Fancy's line of sight. McAllister was good. Very good. He had friends, oratorical skill, and the kind of charm that took a man to high places. It was easy enough to see why Fancy was enchanted by him; Chance had the kind of physical sensuality that mesmerized women. But there were other qualities a man should have, that were equally seductive and far more substantial over the long haul—and Jason suspected Chance lacked these. Nonetheless, he would be an intriguing adversary.

It was obvious McAllister would have to be gotten out of the way before he could woo Fancy. Madigan sighed as he thought it; he was not a patient man by nature, but Fancy was worth it. Besides, there were few real pleasures left he hadn't already mastered; removing McAllister from Fancy's path could be a chess game of the spirit, and a challenging and entertaining one. Now that the railroad went straight through to New York and he had a private car of his own, there was no reason why he couldn't spend as much time in Leadville as pleased him. He'd already started construction on a hunting lodge and established business and banking connections, so what-ever happened with Fancy in the future, his time in Leadville would be valuable. Jason knew precisely which deals to make and with whom, where to curry favor and where to carry a big stick. He'd already spotted John Henderson at the Fiduciary Bank as a useful ally, and Judge Krasky struck him as eminently manipulable. Fancy might have been the catalyst that had brought him here so willingly, but she wouldn't be the only treasure to be plucked from Leadville.

It was fortuitous that Hart McAllister had moved back East and that McBain had disappeared again into the mountains. Whatever plans he had for dealing with Fancy's husband would be far easier to accomplish if Chance McAllister was left to his own devices.

Jason smiled at Chance as he drew himself into the crowd of well-wishers around the platform. Perhaps it would be best to become McAllister's friend.

▲

Dear Bro,

Thought I'd best let you know what I've been up to with your money and mine. There's opportunity on every street corner now and I'm trying not to let any fruitful possibility escape us.

Real estate seems to be the fastest, surest bet. The more silver, the more people arrive—they all need housing, stores, gambling halls, cafés and every other item you can think of. I'm buying claims, too. Some have panned out, some haven't, but before long every square inch of the Mosquitoes will be taken and I'd kick myself from here to Albu-querque if I hadn't grabbed what I could for us.

The Silver Alliance is working even better than I planned. The big boys like to be members of exclusive clubs and silver's the most rarefied of them all. We've sent lobbyists to Washington and we're tight with the men who pull the strings.

Sometimes I look around and say, "What the hell are you doing, McAllister? What makes you think you can pull this off? You're noth-ing but a Kansas farm boy." Other days I've got more confidence than God Almighty. So far, I've added a tidy bundle to our assets and I've made powerful friends—but I suspect you know I walk a tightrope, bro, and it's important when you do that, never to look down.

Your letters convince me Yale is everything you hoped and then some. I like the sound of Canfield—seems as though we're both headed up a rung or two on society's ladder. Rut sounds decent and solid, which is two points more than I can say for any of the men I'm hanging out with, most of whom would cut your throat for the practice.

Fancy said to send her love. I guess I don't have to tell you I send mine, too.

Your entrepreneurial brother,
Chance

67 Chance watched the men around the poker table with a practiced eye. You could tell a great deal about a man by how he played the game. Mean-spiritedness showed, and avarice, intellect, conscience, integrity—all were there to be deciphered by the initiate. His own long suits were memory and optimism, or maybe they were just different names for the instincts of a born gambler.

"I'm afraid those jacks of yours have a way to go to beat my flush, Monty." Chance laid down his cards face up, with the flourish of the showman, and gauged the responses around the green-felt battlefield.

Harvey grunted disgustedly as he tossed in his cards, Haw laughed out loud, Monty slapped his hand down on the table and left the group without a word.

"How'd you know what he was holding?" Fancy asked from behind Chance's shoulder as the men dispersed. She loved cards and wasn't without talent, but Chance's gifts were awesome.

"I'd been counting down, that narrowed the choices considerably. And old Monty has a 'tell.' "

"A tell? What's that?"

"Gamblers and con men watch for them in a pigeon, sugar. A quirk of some kind, an idiosyncrasy. Like playing with a pinky ring when you're on a roll, or twitching your nose when things are tough. Monty pats his bald head when he's got a borderline hand, and he plays with his chips when he knows he's got it won. If he'd had a royal flush or four aces he would have had his hand on his chips all through that last hand."

Fancy laughed delightedly at the secret, it was so much like her own technique, always watching for the nuances in everyone's behavior . . . tucking away each new piece of reference material for when she'd need it.

The two walked arm in arm out into the raucous Leadville night. The stars seemed near enough to touch in the crystal air and Fancy felt Chance's exhilaration. He'd been showing off for her at the poker table, it made him seem young and ingenuous, despite the sophistication of the game.

"What were you and Hart like when you were small?" she asked, wanting to know everything about him.

"I don't know, sugar. I was restless, I guess. And happy. Hart always was the serious one, who knew just where he was going and how to do things right. All I knew was what I wanted.

"Hart was my little brother, Fancy, but in a lot of ways I looked up to him, relied on him, because he was so solid."

"Did you envy him, or want to be like him?"

Chance chuckled good-naturedly. "You can't be what you're not, sugar. I never thought I was supposed to be anyone but me. But I admired Hart just the same. Still do."

He guided her deftly over a puddle, a protective gesture; she held fast to his arm, savoring the moment.

"My daddy was a man you would have loved, Fancy. Big as an oak, red-haired like Hart. The kind of man who takes real good care of his own. My mama made our world gentle, even elegant, despite the hardships of prairie life . . . despite the poverty. She remembered the graces she'd learned in her girlhood . . . it must have been hard on her to have left such a soft, pretty world behind to follow my daddy. In some ways, maybe you and she have a lot in common."

"Except that she left her world willingly, and she had your daddy to lean on."

"Well, you have me now, sugar. You don't have to be afraid anymore."

Fancy heard the pride in her husband's voice and wished with all her heart that she could trust his ability to keep her safe as much as she did his intent.

▲ ▲ ▲

Fancy looked radiant sitting in Jewel's parlor; the lethargy of the first few months of pregnancy had passed and she'd begun to glow.

"Chance has been so wonderful to me lately, Jewel," she said exuberantly. "He sends me flowers for no occasion whatsoever, and he's so happy about the baby he could burst."

"I'm real glad to see you so shiny, kid. You look about as happy in your marriage as anybody I've ever seen." She refrained from saying that she and Rufus had both caught Chance casting appreciative glances over her girls, and they'd heard stories from other houses. Of course, he was a man and no more than human, but Jewel's instincts told her it was mighty near the beginning of marriage for a wandering eye or any other part of the male anatomy and didn't bode well for the future.

"I hear that husband of yours bought up some more property day before yesterday, honey. He seems hell-bent on owning all of Colorado."

Fancy frowned a little. "I do hope he knows what he's doing, Jewel. It seems to me he doesn't pay very much attention to the mine now that Hart's gone, and I'm not sure he really listens to Caz, or does his homework on any part of the business, before he acts. It's about the only thing about him that makes me nervous."

"Even if you're right, honey, men don't much like their wives mixin' into their business dealin's. Better watch your step on how you handle your doubt in his ability—he might start bein' a little less wonderful, if he thinks you're a better businessman than he is."

"I try not to interfere, honestly I do, Jewel. It's just that you know how hard it is for me to trust anybody . . . and then I see Chance trusting absolutely everybody with our money, and it simply sets my teeth on edge."

Jewel laughed and shook her head.

"It never ceases to amaze me how the same qualities that attract men and women to each other when they're single, make 'em mad as hornets at each other once they get hitched."

"I was never attracted to Chance's trusting everybody!"

"No, ma'am, but you sure as hell was attracted to the fact that he did as he damn well pleased and didn't ask nobody's by-yer-leave. Now you're pissy 'cause he ain't askin' you for advice."

"What are you telling me, Jewel?"

"I guess I'm advisin' you to take what joy you can, whilst you can, honey. I'm sayin' you got money and a husband, and a baby on the way—maybe you should just go ahead and enjoy the bejeezus out of them good things you got on your plate . . . and quit worryin' about what you cain't change anyway."

About the best they could hope for would be if the two of them piled up some real good times together, she supposed. Some real bona fide A-one type happiness to be a bulwark against their own inevitable follies . . .

"How are you feeling physically these days, kid?" Jewel asked, to brighten her own mood.

"Oh, I'm just fine now, Jewel, much better than when I had Aurora. But Lord, this belly is heavy to carry around all day. God help the poor cows who have to do this all their lives—I can't fathom how they stand it."

Jewel laughed good-naturedly. "Nothin' much comes easy to the female of any species, I guess. I'm glad you're not doing the shows now, Fancy. There's plenty of acts we can book in here 'til the baby comes and you might just get a kick out of simply bein' a great lady for a change."

"Maybe it *will* be nice to sit around all day and be pampered," Fancy said. "Maybe now I'll have the chance to do all those things other women occupy their time with. I wonder what they are."

Jewel laughed out loud.

"I mean it, Jewel. I don't have a clue what other women do all day. I've been a field hand, a prospector, an actress, and a business owner, but I've never once been idle. Well, maybe it's time to find out. There surely isn't any business in the world worth losing Chance over."

Fancy hugged her friend and waved to Rufus on her way out the downstairs door. It always made her feel so much better to talk to Jewel; she managed somehow to just take life as it came without getting lost in endless speculation as Fancy did.

From her window, Jewel watched Fancy step into her elegant rig and disappear down Harrison. She hoped Chance would at least let the kid deliver this baby in peace; Lord knows, she'd suffered enough carrying the last one alone. She said a silent prayer that Fancy would be spared the knowledge, for a little while at least, that she was still alone.

 Visions of the Christmas he, Chance, Bandana, and Fancy had spent together at the cabin began to plague Hart as the semester drew to a close. "I'm homesick for a threadbare log cabin perched on a rock," he chided himself. "Now that's pretty damned stupid." But "home" has mostly to do with the people in it, so try as he would, the vision of the long-ago Christmas haunted him as the holiday neared.

Rut was packing for his trip home to Savannah when Hart entered his room.

"I don't suppose I could lure you into coming home to Eden with me," the southerner said. He hadn't missed Hart's mopiness as the holiday approached. "My family tends to be boisterous and a bit hard to take around holidays, but all things considered, they're a civilized bunch, and we'd like you to sample a taste of southern hospitality."

Hart's eyes lit up for the first time in weeks. "I'd be so grateful for the chance to share a family this Christmas, Rut, that they could all sit up and howl at the moon for all I care. Are you certain there'll be room for me?"

The merriment the question provoked in Rutledge Canfield was inexplicable to Hart until he arrived at Eden, the Canfield plantation north of Savannah.

An avenue of stately oaks led from the road to the house; they overhung the carriage path so lushly that the temperature beneath their shady canopy must have been a full fifteen degrees less than in the surrounding meadowland.

Near the residence, long avenues of hothouses bathed in the Georgia winter sun. "My father fancies himself a horticulturalist," Rut explained as they passed by. "He has imported exotic flora from all over the tropics, I'm afraid. You'll have a steady diet of pineapples and bananas and breadfruit at every meal if you make the mistake of complimenting him on his prowess."

The graceful architecture of the plantation house spoke of generations of privilege. An immense rosewood piano and a harpsichord both graced the Aubusson carpet in the music room; cherry desks, mahogany liquor cabinets, satinwood armoires, enhanced every corner. There were Dresden vases in one room, Sèvres in the next; exotic Oriental porcelains brimmed with flowers in such profusion, Hart's eye didn't know where to light first. Pervading all were the mingled scents of sweet-olive, magnolia, honeysuckle. Eden indeed, thought the man who'd been born in a prairie farmhouse and graduated to a miner's cabin.

Into Hart's astonished hand a servant planted a frosty glass of brandy, sugar, and peppermint. "Julep," explained Rut with an offhand chuckle. "It's the obligatory panacea for all ills of our climate." Rut's southern drawl had become more pronounced as they'd traveled southward.

"If you're wondering how this plantation managed to escape the wrath of Sherman on his way to the sea," he offered, noting Hart's discomfort, "our money didn't come from slaves—at least not for some generations. Half of it is northern factory money, the other half comes from farming and commerce, shipping and such in New England and Savannah . . . banking, too, and just about any enterprise you can name that makes money. We have powerful friends in the North, who proved immensely helpful during the war. The hostilities caused us some problems, of course, but nothing at all compared with what our neighboring farms endured."

"You call this a farm?" Hart asked, thinking of his daddy, and the plot of bare dirt and rocks the man made to bloom in Kansas. Rut didn't answer, but took his friend's arm and propelled him up the satinwood staircase.

"No need to meet anyone until dinner," he said genially. "That'll give us time to freshen up. Nobody moves around here during the middle of the day, but after you've rested, I'd be pleased to take you on a tour. You ride, of course?"

"That's one thing I can do," Hart replied, grateful for this small inch of common ground.

"Fine then, fine. I'd offer you boots and breeches, but I'm the largest male in my family and I doubt you'd get more than one leg into my size.

"Tell you what. We'll both just wear our dungarees and be done with it." Rut seemed delighted by this solution to a problem Hart couldn't fathom, until after he'd seen the elegant shirt and jacket Rut wore for their outing.

Hart chuckled when he drew near the pristine paddock. "People don't live this good where I come from, Rut, never mind horses."

The stable boys—Rut called them grooms—smirked when they saw Hart, but a frown from Canfield silenced them.

Rut put one slickly booted foot into the stirrup of the horse the groom held for him, and sprang onto its back with the kind of effortless grace Hart associated with generations of aristocracy. The former farm boy mounted easily and they trotted off together.

"Someday," Hart said, looking out across the most spectacular piece of real estate he had ever imagined, "I'm going to have me a farm . . . a place where I can hold the warm earth in my hands, and watch things grow from it. A place with a studio that lets in God's sunlight to bathe a man's soul in inspiration."

"You've a long way to go before then, my friend," Rut replied.

"Before I have the money for it, you mean?"

"Not at all. I mean you'll have to satisfy all the wanderlust in your soul first, Hart. You'll have to paint those Indians you're always fantasizing about. You'll have to see Europe. Be seen by the critics. The world of the artist is no longer as solitary as it once was. You'll need to meet the right people of influence."

Hart laughed. "What I want is painting, not politics, Rut. You make it sound like I'm running for office."

Rut smiled at his friend—he had sensed at university that Hart had no notion at all of how attractive his craggy features and powerful body were to women.

"I'm afraid that's the way the world works, Hart. But don't you worry—I've got a few tricks up my sleeve for you that may help a bit. As a matter of fact, I've asked Mother to invite René Dusseault here to Eden this weekend. He's probably the most influential dealer New York or Paris has to offer. It's important that you get to know such people." Hart looked skeptical.

"You're good, Hart," Rut said, reading the uncertainty in his friend's face. "Very good. Your work is bold and strong. Sensual, too, and robust. You've got something new to say and one day people like Dusseault will want to hear it."

Hart thought a moment, troubled by the inequity in their stations. "And just what can I do for you in return, Rut? All this . . ." He gestured with his hand toward the endless beauty of Eden. "Your hospitality. Your help. I'm in your debt already and don't know how to repay it. Why are you doing all this?"

"You're my friend, Hart . . . and you have something that a great artist must, and I can never, have."

"And that is . . . ?"

"Hunger," Rut replied. "All this precludes it . . . I have gifts, you see, but I have been blessed with too much of life's comforts ever to feel the hunger you feel.

"I could go to the Indians as you intend to . . . I could paint them skillfully. But I could never understand the starvation in their bellies . . . or the deprivation, or the frustration of rejection. Or the fear of annihilation. These emotions are denied me by the plenty you see around you. Like Cassandra, doomed always to tell the truth and never to be believed, I am doomed always to understand the mechanics of genius, but never to achieve it."

"And you think that I can?" Hart asked, stunned by Rut's candor and the generosity with which he viewed his work.

"I do. So I have appointed myself your Svengali."

"I don't know what to say, Rut. You seem to have far higher hopes for me than I do for myself."

"Ah, the shortsightedness of genius," Rut said with an unreadable expression on his handsome face; then he laughed aloud, at what, Hart wasn't certain, put spurs to his gelding, and ran Hart a race back across the meadows to the stable, just as dusk was beginning to tint the sky mauve. He took a fence so high, it nearly spooked the roan, but Hart could see it was a show of pride and skill, defiance and manliness. Rut was a strong man, for all his sissified upbringing.

▲

If Rut was the apple of his mother's eye, it was plain to see that the apple of his father's was Rut's sister, Pallas. Tall, dignified, more arresting than beautiful, Pallas was unlike the other southern ladies Hart met in Savannah; she was as straightforward as her brother—as smart and capable, too, from what he could observe.

She didn't flutter and fuss over men, as seemed to be the custom there. Pallas was cool and collected as the goddess she'd been named for; she handled life with an aplomb that would have done justice to a general. But what intrigued Hart most about her was the knowledge she had of the history of art, and the books she owned on the subject . . . books printed in Europe with colored plates so exquisite, they took his breath away.

Like her brother, Pallas seemed good at everything she attempted; but at twenty-five she was already considered an old maid by the standards of the ladies of Savannah—and, therefore, a failure. Southern men, Rut told Hart very seriously, looked for docility and flirtatiousness in prospective brides and Pallas was an unlikely candidate on both counts.

She was tall, lean, and long-boned like her brother, with strong, sinewy muscles, more like a man's than a woman's for all her slenderness. What seemed almost prettiness in him verged on handsomeness in her, and the planes of her face were too sharply drawn to be thought pretty. She had a squarish jaw that hinted determination and intense brows too straight to be coquettish, yet Hart thought her a fine figure of a woman. It was apparent she was a tree in a garden of hothouse flowers, and as such would never be accepted.

It was Pallas whom Hart escorted to the Christmas Ball, and Pallas who introduced him to René Dusseault. She'd lived in Paris and studied art at the École des Beaux-Arts. Hart had a sense that perhaps she and René had been lovers, but that seemed so implausible an idea, in the strait-laced setting of Eden, he would never have suggested it to Rut for fear of being challenged to a duel over his sister's honor.

Dusseault was shorter than Pallas and slightly built, yet there was unmistakable muscle to the man's litheness. He had a black mustache and a shapely goatee on a pointed chin; indeed, all the planes of the man's face were angular, his nose long, thin, and arrogant. He had flaring nostrils like a jungle beast and there was about him the aura of a predator held under tight rein by civilization. His clothes were elegantly European in cut; he exuded both education and breeding, yet there was a barely bridled sensuality Hart had never encountered in an American man. Rut tolerated the man because of his credentials, but Hart could see he didn't like him. Pallas, on the other hand, was an entirely different person when she was with René—less constrained, less the ice-goddess, more the woman. Hart watched them together, observing the language of their bodies; there was a clear intimacy between the two. He wondered if Rut saw it, too.

"My dear René," Pallas said in her breathy low voice that Hart found the most enchanting part of her. "I have someone very special for you to meet." She tugged on Hart's arm to extricate him from the circle of men with whom he'd been talking.

Dusseault appraised the big westerner intently. He clicked his heels gracefully and bowed a little when the inspection was done. Hart inclined his head and reached out a hand to shake Rene's manicured one, and found the handshake surprisingly strong for one who looked so effete.

"My pleasure, monsieur," Dusseault said in a voice designed, Hart thought, to beguile women. "I understand from Mademoiselle Canfield that you are a major new talent."

"Not a bit of that, I'm afraid, Mr. Dusseault. Somebody's been pulling your leg."

The dealer smiled, smoothly in control. "Do not be modest, Monsieur McAllister. Both Mademoiselle and Monsieur Canfield have said otherwise and I have not yet known them to be mistaken about talent."

"I'm just a beginner."

"If the gift is genuine, beginnings and endings are the same—merely necessary parts of the process. Cézanne considered his own early work so far inferior to that of Delacroix that he destroyed many of his first pieces." Dusseault seemed genuinely distressed by this, but as Hart had never seen the work of either Cézanne or Delacroix, he couldn't comment. Pallas, sensing his ignorance, squeezed his arm and insinuated herself into the conversation.

"My brother assures me that even the great Mireau has conceded Mr. McAllister's superior gifts."

Hart laughed aloud at that. "Mireau has conceded me nothing at all but a begrudging place in his life class, I'm afraid." He felt shy and ill at ease in this heady company. What would Chance and Bandana and Fancy think if they could see him now?

"He is charmingly modest, René, but I've seen his drawings—Rut brought some home with him. There's a primitive dynamism in them, and a raw sensuality that is really quite heroic. You'll want to keep your eye on Mr. McAllister." She chose her descriptive words with care and Hart saw that Dusseault listened respectfully to what she had to say. The Frenchman reached inside his coat when she was done and extracted a calling card.

"My card, Mr. McAllister. One day I feel certain we shall meet again—perhaps in Europe? I will remember what I have heard." Pallas smiled like the proud mama. Dusseault reached for her hand and kissed it, but he lingered longer than was strictly necessary and Hart saw the knowing look that passed between them before the man clicked his heels and moved off into the festive crowd.

▲ ▲ ▲

Pallas opened the verandah door to Hart and motioned the servant with the breakfast tray to place it on the white wrought-iron curlicue table. "I'll come right to the point, Hart," she said. "I like you and I like your work." She waited for Hart to respond. He didn't, simply waited to see where she was headed. The corners of her fine but determined mouth twitched a bit in amusement at his restraint.

"You may have noticed that I don't plan to lead my life like others of my gender," she said with the pugnacity of one who expects to be rebuffed. Hart's smile was gentle.

"My mother manages to cope with my oddity mainly because my father and brother are enlightened men. They knew early on that I lacked the docility of temperament necessary for the life expected of a woman. And," she continued, smiling so that the frosty set of her face melted just enough, "I believe they rather like me."

"So do I," Hart said, and Pallas, caught off guard, leaned forward and clasped her hands on the little table. It was a gesture for a boardroom. "I shall not marry. At least not here. Not now. Frankly, I don't give a damn if I ever reproduce. Rut will carry on the family name and Mama and Papa will be satisfied. I fear my maternal instincts are limited and I shouldn't like to inflict a careless motherhood on some poor unsuspecting child." Pallas was trying to sound callous, but Hart saw uncertainty in her eyes. She'd chosen her path, but she wasn't as sure as she'd have him believe of where it would leave her at the end.

"I am more European in my soul than American," she said, softening a little. "I've had lovers, I intend to have more. I've seen and done things that would give the nice ladies of Savannah the vapors. I like life, Hart. All of it. And I have a talent for art. Not like yours, of course. Just an instinct for what's good. I can differentiate the merely fashionable and showy from the timeless. I know what will endure."

Pallas took a breath, poured coffee into both their cups. Her hands were beautifully cared for and beringed, but they were not the hands of a dilettante. They were vibrant with energy and competence; if they wouldn't cosset babies, they would most assuredly accomplish something equally worthwhile.

Hart watched Pallas carefully as she spoke; he wasn't sure where the conversation was headed, but one thing he intuited with certainty—she wanted him for a friend and perhaps something more. Not a lover, he thought, that unheard-of word she used so casually.

"Where I come from, Pallas, competent women are respected, admired. On a farm, in a mining town, a woman works beside her husband dawn to dusk, maybe beyond. Division of labor is all it is—the men I respect wouldn't know what to do with some of the useless decorations I've seen in Savannah." Hart took a gulp of his coffee and looked at her over the rim of the cup, his eyes warm and merry.

"Whatever you're capable of being, Pallas, I'd say you should just go ahead and be it. Be the best you can be, and for God's sake, don't let any code of conduct that demands uselessness of its women stand in your way."

Pallas looked at Hart, really looked at him with her strange pale eyes. The glacial facade dissolved. Could it be that her coldness was a means of protecting herself from a world she knew must disapprove of who she was?

"I'm going to be an important power in the art world, Hart," she said finally. "Not here. I can't do it here. In Paris or London maybe. When that happens . . . when you're ready, I want you to come to me. I'll make certain the world has a chance to see Hart McAllister's work." Her eyes were shining and Hart wondered if she held back tears, or if it was simple relief at being understood.

"I'll try to be ready for you," he told her with a good-natured smile.

She looked to see if he might be laughing at her, but he wasn't. He was just thinking it was real nice to dream big dreams.

VIII

DUST IN THE WIND

▼▼▼▼▼▼

The Legacy...The 1880s, Leadville and Denver

"Friends come and go . . . but
enemies accumulate."

BANDANA McBAIN

69 Fancy was only eight months pregnant when her labor started; she timed the pains, trying to keep her fears submerged. Magda was nowhere near and she had never known a baby born so early to survive. She'd lulled herself that the pregnancy had gone so well, the delivery would, too, but it was hard to be optimistic as the pain clawed at her belly and undermined her confidence.

Why had Chance gone to Washington knowing she was so close to term? Even if he couldn't do anything to help, just knowing his luck was near at hand would have soothed her. She felt the disappointment of his absence viscerally . . . it brought back bad memories.

She gripped the banister and made her painful way upstairs. She'd best call a servant to make preparations, just in case this was not false labor. Antiseptic, water, scissors, bandages, twine for the cord. Another wave hit her, low and encircling, and she barely made it to the bed; there was no longer any doubt in her mind about whether or not her time had come.

Fancy pulled the bell cord sharply and wondered if she'd best call the doctor or the midwife; the real work tonight would be her own, as it had been for all women, in all time, but if there were complications because of prematurity, perhaps the doctor would be best.

Fancy drove the memory of Aurora's birth back—she needed courage tonight, not memories. She struggled to change into the nightdress she would wear for her ordeal. The water that trickled down her leg was hot as tears.

Fancy's daughter entered the world five miserable hours later, just as Chance's train pulled into the Leadville station.

He was shaken by Fancy's appearance when he entered their bedroom. She looked ravaged, frail and gray, her eyes as sunken as her belly, and she took his hand listlessly. "I needed you tonight, Chance," she whispered when he bent to kiss her clammy cheek. "Where do you go, each time I need you?" She drifted off to sleep before he could reply.

Dear Bro,
Fancy and I have a brand new daughter. We've named her Françoise after her Mama, but I think I'll call her Fan. She came a month early and she's just a little bitty wisp of a girl because of it—you could hold her in the palm of your hand. The name Fan seems ethereal enough to suit her—I sure do hope she's stronger than she looks, not that I have

much experience of babies, but she seems so damned fragile to me. I guess I'll need to take real special care of her.

I failed Fancy, I'm afraid, bro, by not being there when her time came, but the baby arrived early and I was off on a business trip. In some ways, I confess, I was relieved not to be there; I'm not sure I would have had the courage to see her suffer for all the pleasures we've had together.

Hart put down his brother's letter, and rested his chin on his hands as he stared off into space; he wasn't sure why the words disturbed him so. Chance's letters were always straight from the heart; he seemed able to express on paper a vulnerability he would never have voiced aloud.

Fancy's strong, but she's fragile, too, bro, and I had this awful premonition about losing her because of our love. I guess I feel guilty about a lot of things where Fancy's concerned, although I try hard not to show it. And, truth be known, she's a real handful. Fancy's not a woman like Mama, satisfied to help her husband build a life, and take good care of her kids. Fancy wants the world at her feet, and she has the goddamnedest willingness to go right on out there and try to get it for herself. Maybe the best bet is for me to grab it first and just hand it over to her . . . whatever it takes to make her happy, I'm sure as hell planning to try.

I've bought more property and I'm cultivating a relationship with the powers-that-be—there've been three trips to Washington so far, this year, for the Silver Alliance. Sometimes I'm sorry I started the damned thing, it eats up time like a pocket watch that's wound too tight.

Hart noted there was again no mention of the mines; he made a mental note to write Caz.

Come home one of these days, bro. I'm real lonely sometimes.

Your loving brother,
Chance

▲ ▲ ▲

Françoise McAllister was never called anything but Fan—the airy name seemed a perfect metaphor for her wispiness. Her hair was the platinum of fairy wings, despite the dark hair of both parents, and her delicacy frightened Fancy from the first moments of life.

"She's nearly see-through, Chance," Fancy said worriedly, as she held her tiny daughter to her breast. "And she scares me to death when I nurse her. She just stares up at me with those elfin eyes that are older than I am and I swear she doesn't suck enough for a mouse."

"She's delicate, sugar. Just because you and Aurora are so robust, you can't think every female is. She's cut from silk instead of velvet, that's all." Chance found he couldn't let himself think that Fan might be endangered.

He adored his daughter and displayed inordinate patience with her when he was at home, playing with her, cosseting, talking with the tiny doll-like child as if she understood each word. He'd tried so hard to reach Aurora, but her cold, hard knot of resentment was tied too tight for him to loose it, and his failure as a father hurt and puzzled him. He'd never before known a female of any age he couldn't get around, and his own memories of childhood were of a family of intense love and loyalty.

But this newborn baby was a clean white blotter ready to soak up all the love he sought to give. Her fragility made her all the more precious. He found he liked protecting what was his.

Fancy marveled at Chance's devotion to Fan and sometimes even felt irritated by it for some reason she didn't quite understand. She wondered, later, if she let herself get pregnant only three months after her daughter's birth because she resented losing Chance's attentions to the baby, or because it delayed, for yet another year, the question of what to do about his opposition to her working.

She said it was because she was so happy as a wife and mother, and because she wished to get all childbearing over with quickly, so she could resume life and get her figure back. But Magda merely raised a disbelieving eyebrow at that explanation and Fancy saw in the Gypsy's relentless mirror her own self-delusion.

There was only one reason Fancy became pregnant so soon after Fan's birth . . . it was to erect a bulwark of life, against the mortality she read in her daughter's fragile countenance.

70 ❦ Fancy watched her newborn son in his cradle with pride and satisfaction. Tiny perfect toes and fingers, arms and legs in constant motion, unfocused blue eyes with a fringe of lashes like her own, shining dark hair like Chance's. There were no signs of frailty in this robust nine-pound boy, born only a year after his sister Fan. She'd tried to fight the feeling down, but Fan's frailty made her feel guilty, as if she'd failed some great unspoken test of motherhood.

John Charles McAllister's arrival had been as easy for Fancy as both his sisters' had been difficult. The new mother couldn't help but think that from the start, boys were easier and probably more fun than girls.

"Blackjack," Chance named his son, standing proudly over the cradle, looking at the mass of gleaming black hair that framed the perfect baby face.

"Blackjack McAllister, that's what we'll call him. He'll have my luck and your looks," he said, turning to Fancy still in her lying-in bed, and she'd laughed contentedly. "Better that, than the other way around," she replied.

"With that combination, Fancy, and the money from the mines, my son will rule the world."

Chance had made their home the finest in Leadville, he'd made it clear to everyone that Fancy was the queen of his empire, Aurora and little Fan, the princesses—now there was a prince to complete the tableau. Safe, secure, rich beyond fear, Fancy told herself—as it had been at Beau Rivage a thousand years ago. . . .

A twinge of sadness moved through her, as it always did when she thought of her childhood; how she wished her mother could be here to see her fine new son and growing daughters. She fingered the golden locket at her throat; Chance had had it commissioned by Louis Comfort Tiffany, to house the preciously hoarded strands of hair that were her mother's, for he knew that they, and the salvaged music box and banjo, were Fancy's icons. Someday Aurora or Fan would wear the locket; meantime, all three of her brood would have the childhood she'd been robbed of, a childhood full of the safety of "having."

▲ ▲ ▲

Fan McAllister failed to prosper. From the baby's infancy, Fancy knew she was damaged in some subtle way, for even at the breast Fan suckled barely enough to stay alive. Eight months was just not enough time for a baby to stay in the womb; she was incomplete and some of the component parts she lacked were essential ones for life. She had an extraordinarily joyous disposition, far too good-natured for humanity and that, too, filled Fancy with foreboding, for she thought Fan entirely too angelic for this world.

It frightened her to think her daughter might be slow-witted; she'd seen such children over the years, never able to dress themselves or achieve even the most rudimentary skills. Survival was the paramount need in Fancy's mind, so the fear that her daughter might never be able to fend for herself was more terrifying than she could admit to anyone, even Chance. It wrenched her heart to see Fan's struggles to complete the most ordinary of acts. She thought the baby somehow sensed her own deficiencies and tried so hard, just to reassure her doting father.

Chance would hear no word of complaint about her progress. "Why the hell should every child born have to do everything exactly the same," he'd thunder every time Fancy tried to broach the subject. Fan was so delicate, how could anybody expect her to do the things bigger, stronger children could? Didn't Fancy see how unfair such expectations were?

"She's slow, Chance. Truly slow . . . I'm afraid we'll have to deal with the fact that she may never catch up with other children her age. She'll need special help . . . we'll have to find someone who knows what to do about her needs . . ."

Chance's wrath could be kindled easier by the subject of Fan than by anything else. "How can you say such a thing about your own child, Fancy? That's a mean-spirited thing for a mother to say."

Fancy bit her lip at the fear in Chance's eyes.

"But she can't do anywhere near what other children her age can, Chance. You've got to listen to reason about this. Blackjack is a year younger and far more capable and agile."

"God damn it, Fancy, Blackjack's a *boy.* You just can't compare them. That's not fair to Fan. Besides, even if she's not as strong as he is, she talks better than any little child I ever heard of."

Fancy shook her head despairingly, for even the girl's precocious speech was inappropriate for her age. It seemed to Fancy that the gods, seeing how shortchanged the child was in other ways, had tried to compensate with this strange linguistic largesse.

Chance lifted his daughter from her crib and hugged her protectively; her eyes glowed at his touch, no one loved her like her daddy did. Agitatedly Chance walked up and down the Chinese carpet, the wobbly blond head cradled on his shoulders, which were set in the granite stance that told his distraught wife he would not be moved.

All during the first two years of Fan's life, Fancy marveled at the endless

patience Chance showed the child. When she teethed, he was the first one at
her cribside to lift her into comforting arms . . . when the croup kept her
and the household sleepless for three nights and days, it was Chance who
left his bed to keep watch in the nursery, much to the annoyance of the
nursemaid.

"When she cries, I want her to be picked up, do you understand me?" he
told the nanny.

"That only encourages a child to cry more, Mr. McAllister," she said
quite reasonably. "A baby learns very quickly what gains attention and this
child is coddled far too much."

"I want my daughter to learn that the world is a warm, safe place, Mrs.
McArdle," he replied in a tone that brooked no argument. "I want her to
learn that she's loved so much that when she cries, she'll always be comforted, when she's sick, she'll always be cared for, when she's hurting,
there's one of her kin right there to protect her. If you can't handle teaching
my daughter those very simple principles of life in this household, then I
suggest you find other employment."

Even Mrs. McArdle had to admit she'd never met a child with a sweeter
disposition. When Fan was two, she finally learned to crawl; it strained her
body to a pale purple color to do so, but her determined and ceaseless effort
eventually moved her across the nursery floor. When she got where she was
going, she would stop to catch her labored breath and smile a secret smile of
infinite achievement. Her asthma kept her from making major forays, but
she loved the warmth of the fireplace and would drag herself, panting with
the effort, as close to the hearth as she could manage. Chance had an extra
fireplace installed in the nursery, so his daughter would never need fear the
cold, for it had a tendency to tinge her skin a spectral blue.

The doctor said her heart was weak as a sparrow's, and that it wouldn't
do to become too attached to a child who wasn't likely to see school age, but
Chance told Fancy the man was never to set foot in their house again, and
she had to find another doctor.

▲ ▲ ▲

Fancy sensed a deep, unspoken sorrow in Chance whenever he'd been
with Fan, but for some unfathomable reason he was reluctant to share it
with her.

"I love her, too, Chance, but I see how hard life is going to be for her and
I think we have to face the fact that Fan may never be right-minded."

"How can you even think such a thing about your own child, Fancy? If
she's slow, we just have to find better ways to teach her. By the time she
goes to school, she'll be all caught up."

"Will you never listen to reason about that child, Chance?" Fancy said with exasperation. "I love her just as much as you do, but you're spoiling her to death with your constant attention. We can't let her grow up thinking everybody's going to kowtow to her forever just because she's sick. That won't do anything but give her an incentive to stay that way."

"For chrissakes, Fancy, you can't think that baby is pretending illness just so she can get extra coddling?"

"No, of course not. But we've got to find a way to help her stretch her own wings, Chance. Her life is going to be hard enough without our spoiling her into immobility."

"What are you trying to say?"

"That you're so wrapped up in her the rest of us are lonely . . . and I'm so afraid for you, Chance. Afraid you'll love her so much you won't survive if something happens to her." There. She'd said it aloud. The worst fear. Chance's expression softened, the vulnerability peeked out from beyond the mask of confidence he'd constructed.

"I know it's hard for you to understand how I feel, Fancy," he said wearily. "Sometimes I don't understand all of it myself. But Fan's my first child, my baby . . . I know, I know, there's Aurora—but you can see how she's kept me at arm's length, never given me a minute's chance to be her daddy. But Fan . . . she's all mine to take care of. Sometimes I try to think how my daddy would be with her, if he were here. He was a strong man, Fancy, strong and rough-hewn in some ways, but you've never seen anybody capable of tenderness like my daddy was. He could nurse a broken bird like it was the most important creature in this world . . . if he loved you, you knew nothing on this earth could ever harm you, because it'd have to get through him first."

Fancy heard the love and respect in her husband's remembrance and the unspoken fear for his child.

"Hart always said what killed him wasn't the diphtheria . . . it was the knowledge that he hadn't saved my mama. God Almighty, Fancy, but he loved my mama." Chance hesitated, as if afraid to voice the rest aloud.

"I'm so afraid for my baby, Fancy. So afraid I won't be able to save her when the time comes . . . you know, sometimes I think she's just like you, without all your competencies, just a frail little girl who needs a powerful lot of taking care of, and in return, she loves me all there is. She lets me in, Fancy . . . in ways neither you nor Aurora ever have."

The fire crackled beside Fancy, the sounds of sap-sparks bursting like firecrackers into the pained silence between them. Not knowing what in the world to say, she crossed to Chance's armchair and took him in her arms and the two frightened parents of a damaged child simply held each other to fend off what they feared.

▲

Blackjack toddled into his sister's nursery and smiled at her through the bars in her crib. He could do so many interesting things that Fan could only long for. She reached her nearly translucent fingers out of the crib bars and Blackjack closed his sturdy hand around hers and squeezed it tight. He liked to touch this living dolly, to get things for her that she couldn't reach. He knew Daddy loved to talk to Fan and hold her; sometimes, he would let Blackjack hold his sister, too, just as if he were grown up.

"A man takes care of the women in his life, son," Daddy would say. "They're not strong like we are, so we have to be real gentle with them and keep them safe from harm. The kinder you are to your sisters, the better sort of man you'll grow up to be." Blackjack worshiped his father; whatever Chance said was gospel to the little boy who looked like a small mirror image of the man and who loved him with absolute devotion.

Blackjack wished his sister could get out of her crib more to play. She was awfully old to still be sleeping in a crib and there were plenty of games he knew she'd be good at if only she were stronger. On impulse, he handed her a playing card from the precious deck his father had given him. Fan held it in her hands, staring at it with interested eyes, then she said "Pretty," and bit off the corner to see if it tasted good too.

Blackjack grabbed the card back from Fan's mouth hastily. Even if he loved his sick sister, she wasn't allowed to eat the cards Daddy had given him.

 71   Chance lay back against the tree and watched the two little children play at the edge of the stream. Fancy had admonished him not to let Fan play in the chilly water, but they were having such a happy time splashing around. Blackjack held his sister's hand so she wouldn't go too far; his little-boy laughter pierced the sharp spring air like a bell-peal, and Fan's sweet giggle sounded to Chance like a benediction. She'd managed to get to be three years of age, against everyone's predictions. Her asthma seemed better than it had, and she could walk now, even if it was with difficulty.

"Come on over here," the father called lazily. He preferred taking these two out without their nanny, who hovered too close for his taste, and who didn't offer the slightest bit of whimsy. "It's time to make up stories." Both children squealed their delight, nobody in the world told stories like their daddy. Chance saw his son start forward, then reach back for his sister's hand; even though he was just a toddler, Blackjack seemed inordinately protective of his sister. Fan looked at her brother, adoration in her fey eyes. The little boy slowed his own steps patiently while she made her awkward way, one foot dragging, as it always did. Seeing that both children were barefoot, Chance felt a momentary pang of conscience about Fancy's admonition, so he rose and retrieved their shoes from the bank of the stream. Hastily he pulled the little stockings up over his daughter's feet, they were cold as icicles and slightly blue; he chafed them to get the blood circulating, then laced up the high-buttons and helped Blackjack on with his boots.

Leaning back against the tree, Chance took one child into the crook of each arm and let them nestle against him. He felt Fan shiver and shifted to shelter her.

"Come on over to this side, son. Your sister's cold and it's up to us men to keep her warm." For an instant the memory of Fancy lying between him and Hart came vividly to Chance . . . was there ever a way for a man to shield the women he loved from all that life doled out? He brushed the unwanted thought aside and formed a circle around the two children with his own body.

"Tell me a 'once a time . . .' Fan lisped. She had a remarkable facility for language, far beyond her years, but her speech had idiosyncrasies, short-cuts only Chance and Blackjack seemed intuitively to understand.

"Once upon a time," Chance began, casting about in his mind for the perfect tale. "There was a little girl named Dewdrop . . ." Blackjack tugged at his sleeve to remind his father to include him. . . . "And she had a brother named Beau. Beau loved his sister so much that he would do anything she asked him, and one day in January, when the snow was high as the tops of the pine trees, Beau saw his sister crying. 'Why are you crying?' he asked her and she said, 'Because I'm very sick and there are no flowers left in the world. If I had a flower, I could get well.'

"So Beau put on his golden armor and set out to find the flowers. Now, he glittered so brightly that the snow melted in the garden and the sunflowers thought spring had come, so they poked their sleepy heads up through the frozen ground to see the shining little boy.

" 'My sister needs you,' Beau told the sunflowers.

" 'But if you pick me now, before my time, I'll die,' the sunflower whispered.

" 'But you'll be loved so much it will be worth it,' Beau said. 'To give your life to do a good deed is the noblest death of all.'

"So the sunflower agreed to go with Beau to save his sister."

"But Dewdrop died," Fan completed the story unexpectedly. "And they buried her with the flower. And Beau stayed by her grave forever and ever." Chance was struck to the heart by the strangeness of this little child, whom he loved so much. Maybe being bedridden so long had given her a macabre turn of mind.

Both children looked immensely satisfied with her depressing finale.

"I'd say that turned out to be a pretty sad story, wouldn't you?" Chance said, hugging his children against the chill wind that had arisen. "In my rendition I was planning to have everyone live happily ever after."

"When she died, Dewdrop went to live with the eagles, Daddy, and she learn to fly," Fan persisted.

"She did, darlin'? How do you know that?"

Fan fixed her pale blue eyes on her father's, it seemed to him for a moment that he could see straight through her to the sky.

"Remember when I couldn't walk, Daddy? I think then . . . if never I can walk, maybe learn to fly. So I watch the birds, and the eagles do it best. Everybody has wings in my dreams."

Chance was terribly disturbed by what Fan said, so he scooped up both children and held them close. The day was growing colder and he suddenly needed to go home and get Fan to the warmth of a fire.

▲

Fancy always said it was the day Chance let them go wading, when Fan caught the cold that became pneumonia, but no one knew for sure. All they did know was that her breathing grew labored, and the cold that would have been minor for another child deepened into lung inflammation. Fever brightened Fan's eyes until they looked like pale blue stained glass; her tiny lungs were so filled with phlegm, every breath became an agony. Chance would have breathed for his daughter if he could, would have died in her place, but the gods don't give that latitude to parents.

Fancy struggled day and night for weeks to save her child, after the doctor had long since shrugged his shoulders at the futility of the effort. She begged Magda's help, then railed at her for failing, and looked accusingly at Wu whose medicaments had not made any difference. Both the Gypsy and the Chinese knew the little girl had passed beyond the power of mortals, so they simply endured the fury of the frenzied mother and the anguish of the guilt-ridden father. They stayed close because they feared to leave Chance and Fancy alone with the dying child.

Fancy's desperation drove her to meanness. "You've killed her," she accused her husband. "Why couldn't you listen to me when I asked you not to let her go near the water? Why can you *never* listen when I ask anything of you?"

Chance answered out of grief and terror. "What do you care, anyway? You never loved her the way I did. You would have packed her off someplace where people put their slow-witted children, if I hadn't shamed you into keeping her."

"How could you even *think* such a thing? I never once considered such a terrible thing. If you'd left her to me and Mrs. McArdle none of this would have happened."

They flayed each other over the child's sickbed until Magda finally lost patience and growled, "Fools! Would you kill her with your petty war? Look at her eyes, she is begging you to love each other. Her pain is greater than yours . . . can you not be unselfish long enough to let her die in peace?" The Gypsy strode from the room, Wu followed wordlessly, and Fancy and Chance, defeated by the truth, knelt down beside Fan's bed too numbed by sorrow to fight each other, or death, any longer.

"Sad, Daddy . . ." the little girl murmured once, a dreadful wheezing sound; the phlegm rattled ominously behind her small words and neither parent knew if she spoke of their sorrow or her own. She said no words at all to Fancy.

Chance saw his father's death in the child's struggle to breathe, and thought his heart would burst with grief. Fancy, white-faced in the knowledge of her failure to save her baby, unrelenting in her blame for Chance, never spoke a word of comfort to her husband, for the wrath that filled her could have murdered the world.

It was Chance who held his daughter in his arms as her breath whispered out to find Death, a small sound, like the cry of the wind. Fancy, despairing, reached out to close the eyes death had glazed, but Chance snatched Fan away from her grasp, and clutching her to his heart, he carried her from the room to sob out his anguish, leaving Fancy to face her grief alone.

Her heart was a stone in the breast that still remembered the baby lips that had sucked so softly, so short a time ago. "I will never forgive you for this," she called after him, the words chilling everyone who heard them. "You took her away from me in life, and now you've claimed her in death, and I will never, ever forgive you."

▲

Dear Bro,

We buried our little Fan, day before yesterday, God rest her sweet soul. Fancy wanted to send you a wire, so you could try to get home for the funeral, but I didn't want to do that. No one should come home to sorrow . . . home should be where love and happiness wait for you. I guess I'll never really get over the feeling of comfort there always was for us when Mama and Daddy were alive. Remember, Hart? I've been remembering so much, these last terrible days.

You never knew my little girl—I'm real sad about that, bro. She was never long for this world—I guess I always knew it—and that's why I fought so hard against anybody who tried to make me see . . . especially Fancy. Something happens to you when you have a child, I can't explain. You grow bigger and wider, so you can care for it—you feel older, wiser, more responsible, less selfish. You remember kindnesses your own parents did you and you want to do everything right.

I failed in a lot of ways, I expect, bro, but not in the way Fancy thinks. I never meant to endanger my baby, it didn't seem possible that letting her dip her little feet in that stream could take her from us like it did. She loved the water so . . . I'll carry it with me to the grave, bro, that I didn't protect her when it counted. There was this story Fan told me about a little girl who died and afterwards she went flying with the eagles up in heaven. I guess I'll never see an eagle that I won't see my little girl in its flight. Pray for me, will you, bro?

> Your grieving brother,
> Chance

72 "It doesn't make the least sense to buy anything from Jacob Braintree," Fancy sniped at Chance across the breakfast table. "He's a scoundrel of the first water and he's never had a real claim in his life."

Chance put down the morning paper with annoyance and took a studied sip of coffee before replying. How the hell she even knew about Jake was beyond him; she'd been impossible to live with since Fan's death.

"Jacob Braintree is none of your affair, Fancy. I think that claim will pay off eventually, and it was a bargain, one way or the other."

"You've bought four other claims in the last two months and none of them looks promising to me."

"Five," Chance answered wearily. "And they're not any of your business either." He put his napkin on the table and stood up to leave. "You never used to be like this, Fancy. Picking at every bone. You've got to forgive me for Fan, sometime . . . you must know how much I loved her."

"I used to have more to occupy my mind when my child was still alive," she said, made cruel by her pain and guilt. "I'm thinking of going back to work."

Chance took a deep breath before replying. "You know I don't want you to do that, Fancy."

Her head came up defiantly. "If what you do is none of my business, I can't see why what I do is any of yours."

Chance left without another word and Fancy lingered over her coffee, feeling miserable and alone. Nothing in life was bearable since Fan's death. She missed the happiness and the laughter of their life before; missed the sense of being loved absolutely. For a moment she felt a pang of guilt about the way she was treating him, but her own grief was inextricably tangled in responsibility. Only blaming Chance prevented her from blaming herself . . . and she simply didn't have the strength to fight that battle now.

▲

Chance stood at the faro table beside Haw Tabor—the gambling club was a private one set up for the likes of the two of them. He knew he shouldn't be here this evening; but it was hard to be around Fancy since Fan. He sometimes thought all life was divided—before Fan, after Fan. . . .

Marriage had changed Fancy, changed them both, he thought with an ache of rebellion. He'd never expected it to be peaches and cream, but neither had he anticipated her fierce commitment to motherhood, her endless insecurities, or her unreasonableness about business. How could she expect him to be home every night of the week, when she'd been so damned distant since their daughter's death, her every glance full of accusation.

Why the hell couldn't she just trust to his dreams and visions as she had before marriage, like everybody else in Leadville did? Weren't those dreams part of what she loved about him? It seemed to him a lifetime since he'd felt loved by Fancy.

Chance glanced at his watch; he had to make a decision within the next few minutes. He'd made a halfhearted date to see Jennie before the night was out—there wouldn't be much time, of course, if he was to get back early enough to say he'd been with the boys at the club all evening. There was respite and replenishment with Jen; her kind of bolstering was just what he needed after the hard days he put in. Politics was tough, running an empire made demands never even imagined in the days of youthful dreams; always being on your guard was tiring, always being where you could be seen and talked about was more pain-in-the-ass than pleasure. And the day-to-day chores of business were not his long suit, yet he couldn't let the facade crack for an instant. He missed the good times with Fancy, when she was a sounding board and friend as well as a lover. Before Fan, there'd been a different Fancy. Before Fan, he'd been immortal and all dreams still had the potential to come true.

Chance put his watch back in his pocket and picked up the cards. Maybe there'd be time for just a quick visit to Jen's before heading home.

73 🌿 The enormous steamer trunk arrived from the East and Fancy struggled to pry open the lid, hoping the new clothes would cheer her. She'd ordered a king's ransom in Paris fashions for herself, Aurora, and Blackjack, because their social obligations demanded it and because her sagging spirits did, too. She knew it was time to come out of mourning and try to live again. Too much black in a house was bad for the children.

She pulled out the mousseline de laine dress first and the piqué cloak and cashmere hood in softest peach for Aurora. Even a nanny's uniform, with proper stitched and ribboned cap, was folded neatly beside the children's clothes.

Reaching down into the lower portion of the giant box, she fished for her own acquisitions: an elaborate flower garniture for her hair and a chignon of curls. She'd sent a strand to the wigmaker for matching, and the resultant curls would enhance her own so that not even her cattiest neighbors would know the difference.

A damasse silk and satin toiletter, for full-dress occasions, was beneath the tissue. There were so many obligatory occasions now that the business of being rich kept them on the dinner circuit. Fancy held the dress out before her at the mirror, surprised at her own relief that it wasn't black; the basque and flowing train were of brocaded aqua satin with silver laid-in plaits.

Nobody in Leadville or Denver will be able to hold a candle to this, she thought, surprised at her own excitement. She'd been numb so long, feeling lively was an unexpected pleasure. She'd decided to make amends with Chance, maybe that was what was making her feel hopeful. Her own loss had obscured the pain of his . . . she'd been crueler to him about Fan's death than she'd known she was capable of being. He'd loved that baby so, she could only imagine how Fan's suffering and death must live inside him, an anguished guilty secret. Fancy grimaced at remembrance of how she'd punished him with her coldness and disdain. And through it all he had been kind to her and oddly gentle, as if their daughter's death had taught him humility. Magda and Jewel had both berated her for her behavior, but the relentless chilling numbness, like a sleet storm of the heart, had kept her mean. Christ, if Chance was as lonely as she, she'd done a dreadful thing.

Fancy laid all the finery out on the bed and decided to do something splendid for her husband, something kind, that would show how much she still loved him.

He enjoyed clothes nearly as much as she did, but he didn't have the time to fuss over them, these days. She would take one of his suits for measurement, and send it back East to have a splendid new jacket and trousers made for him in the very latest style. It wasn't all she would do, but it was a beginning. Fancy entered Chance's dressing room, a place she seldom visited, for the valet handled the picking-up, pressing, and cleaning of her husband's wardrobe.

Humming softly to herself, feeling better than she had in months, Fancy chose a jacket and patted it down to make sure nothing had been left in the pockets. There was no money there, but the rustle of paper revealed a scrap caught in the torn lining of the right-hand pocket. Fancy fished it out and glanced at it absently as she laid it on the dresser.

Then she blinked hard, in a useless effort to erase what she'd seen . . . the handwriting was so obviously a woman's.

Lunch on Thursday, Chance darling, it read. *I can't wait to feel your strong arms around me.* It was signed *Jen.*

Fancy tried to make the topsy-turvy world turn right again; there'd been some terrible mistake, he was with her every night he wasn't working. But not every lunch . . . or every hour, some knowing part of her argued back, and maybe all those nights of business weren't what they'd seemed. She saw him suddenly in another woman's arms, naked, lustful, playing that alien body as he did her own, telling her stories . . . she felt an urgent desire to retch.

She sat a long, long while staring out the window, emptied of all but heartache and remorse. Then she dressed, not in black, left the house, and headed for the Crown.

▲

"What am I going to do, Jewel?" Fancy asked when she'd finished crying. Jewel handed her another hanky and waited until Fancy had obediently blown her nose.

"You'd be a fool to do anything. He is what he is, and you're far from blameless in this."

"But this other woman . . ."

Jewel snorted contemptuously. "You find me a man who don't have more'n one and I'll eat Rufus' twelve-gauge for lunch."

"But I never knew it would be like this . . ."

"And why the hell not? Don't you know nothin' about men, kid? They love you to death when they're courtin' you, but once you're married they cool down faster'n snow on a stovepipe. And what the hell made you think you could treat him like a leper and not have him find somebody who wouldn't?"

"Why didn't you tell me, Jewel?"

"Because for the last few months nobody could tell you a damned thing without gettin' ankle-bit."

Fancy shook her head miserably. "All I know is I still love Chance and all my hopes are tied up in him . . . and right now I'd like to cut his heart out."

Jewel chuckled. "That's more like the Fancy I know. You got two kids and a lot of responsibilities now; why not just reel him back in. You still got your figure and your brain. How about using 'em both for a change."

"But how can I face him, knowing what I know? How can I let him make love to me without hating him and always wondering . . ."

"Honey, that's a question damn near every woman who ever lived has had to answer for herself . . . cain't nobody tell you what to do or what to feel. All I can tell you is this, Fancy, you've got a hell of a lot to lose now, and you better consider real careful whether or not you want to lose it."

Jewel stood with her hands on the sink, staring out the back window and thinking about Fancy, after the girl had left. Poor kid, she'd been so happy for a minute or two . . . was there any feeling in this whole frigging world like that first mad flush of love? When he's perfect and you're perfect and the whole damned world is perfect . . . just for those few glorious moments before reality sets in. She sighed and shook her head—there were times when she was glad she and Ford couldn't be together all the time. Maybe it had spared them a hell of a lot of heartache.

74

"The men want more money," Tabor said disgustedly. "Those damned fool miners are going to price themselves and us right out of business."

John Henderson cleared his throat ponderously. "How much more?"

"They're making three-fifty a day and want four. I say we knock them down to three and show them what this kind of union crap gets them."

Chance stood, his shoulders resting against the library wall, and watched the portly, self-satisfied men with whom he had so long curried favor. If he didn't back them on this important issue, his political future could be on the line, but dammit, he'd worked those mines, and so had they. Didn't these fat cats remember the intolerable double shifts to make ends meet, the heat and the cold, the rock dust in your nostrils and lungs, the consumption and the desperation . . .

"Three-fifty a day doesn't buy all that much in Leadville, since the boom," he said aloud, and all eyes turned toward him incredulously. "You can pay as much now for an egg as you used to for a night on the town."

"What are you saying, McAllister?" Tabor frowned; the boy had a fine career ahead of him if he didn't get stupid.

"I'm saying we can afford the raise they're asking for, and that they deserve it," Chance said, unflinching. "You've been down below, Haw, you know we're rich and they're desperate."

Shocked, silent eyes met each other around the room, a number of throats were cleared. McAllister must have lost his marbles, was clear in every face.

Tabor didn't even bother to dignify Chance's statement with acknowledgment.

"I've formed a militia, gentlemen," he said, turning back to the group around the fire. "A light cavalry company that I think we can put to good use in this little brouhaha. If we march our soldiers up and down a few times in full regalia, I think those miners will get our point and reconsider their walkout."

"Unless your light cavalry knows how to double-jack, muck, and set powder, they're not likely to do you much good after the men walk." Chance's voice was hard. Being ignored didn't sit well on his temper, and there was something unholy about these overstuffed men in their overstuffed chairs, deciding the fate of the likes of Caz.

"Don't you worry about working the pits," Haw said harshly. "Them boys got to feed their families—they can't hurt anybody but their women and children by walking out on us. And if they do, the railroad can have a load of scabs in here in twenty-four hours."

"I'm thinking of raising the wages at the Fancy Penny and the Last Chance," Chance said evenly. Jason Madigan watched with fascination; maybe McAllister would end the chess game earlier than he'd imagined. He himself had taken to spending a week or two in Leadville every few months; there was ample money to be made here and gossip suggested the McAllister household was none too stable.

Elmore Trask leaned forward in his chair. "You do that, boy, and you can kiss your political ass good-bye." The use of the word *boy* wasn't lost on Chance, but neither was the sense of loathing he felt for the selfish bastards he'd chosen as political bedfellows. He wished Hart or Bandana were here to talk it all out, but in his heart he knew they'd agree with his stand.

No one spoke after McAllister left the room; it didn't seem there was much left to be said.

75 ❧ The train and stage ride across the country was arduous, but Hart's excitement at homecoming made up for the physical discomfort. His years at Yale had been the most fulfilling of his life; he had real talent, and now the knowledge to give it wings. He understood the human form with surgical precision; hadn't he stood at the autopsy table beside Mireau and learned anatomy from muscle and bone outward? Even without the degree that was still a few credits away, he was well equipped for the job he'd coveted. It was time to go home and share life again with those he loved. Chance's letters, always open and loving, had been guarded lately, shadowed by something more than just his sorrow over the death of the little niece Hart had never known.

He watched the prairie click by outside the train window; the wheatfields stretched beyond the horizon into memory. He saw again his father's massive shape against the vast expanse and heard the much loved voice, in a distant echo. "By the time you're grown, son, this land on which we stand will all be history. I've seen the East, Hart—cities cover the earth where trees once grew. Cobblestones and dirt and poverty have all grown together into something unnatural.

"Here and farther west, the earth is still as God meant it to be . . . trees and rocks and streams as clean and pure as on the morning of Creation. The Indians understand the balance . . . they live with the land, not off it. They give back when they take, and say 'thank you' to Grandmother Stream or Grandfather Rock if they borrow from their bounty." The deep, comforting baritone and the soft chuckle lived in Hart and always would. What had it cost that strong, good man to sanction his son's thirst for art, when he must have longed for a farmer to follow in his footsteps, to love the land he'd watered with his life's blood and sweat.

"It used to be I worried about you, son," Charles McAllister had said. "That you'd get caught up in dreaming and leave the land we've fought so hard for here. But I was wrong. I think maybe God means for you to paint what He created, so it won't be forgot. All this beauty will soon be changed by what men like to call civilization . . . the Indians will be pushed back and destroyed, and with them the last true Keepers of the Land will vanish from the face of this earth. Maybe you can be the one who bears witness to the greatness of what the Good Lord gave us, and that's a mighty calling, son."

A mighty calling . . . The words were still as powerful as on the day they'd first been spoken. How is it that certain moments stay intact inside your soul forever, while others blur and fade like the tattered fabric of a dream?

Pallas had tried to persuade him to join her in Paris, to continue his studies there, but Hart was lonely for the West and needed to see Chance and Fancy one more time before going away, perhaps for years.

He alighted from the Denver stage and made his way toward the three people he loved most in all the world. Bandana was the first to greet his return.

"By God, you look like some city feller, wouldn't know a cactus if he sat on one," McBain said, eyeing Hart's store-bought clothes with amusement, and the man in them with affection. "Fancy sent me word you was headin' in, so I come to town to see if the East has corrupted you."

"How'd she know where to find you?"

"Oh, she's got her ways, Fance has. Her and me got us a claim up yonder. It's a perfect partnership—I own it and work it, she comes to visit once in a while. Not much dust, but a powerful lot of fine scenery to feast yer eyes on."

Hart laughed. Bandana acted as if he'd left only yesterday, not years before.

"How are they, Bandana? My brother and Fancy?"

McBain squinted his eyes and tilted his head up toward Hart before replying.

"There's more'n one answer to that question, young feller. You want the one fer the newspapers, or the one fer family?"

"What do you think?"

McBain nodded. "Near as I kin figger it, the death of that little fairy child of theirs hit 'em real hard and they ain't got over it yet. Fancy and Chance spend enough money between 'em to keep a small country in beans and bacon. Maybe not so small. Got a dandy house about the size of a hotel. The kids are sproutin', as kids will do, without a whole lot of discipline, but more love than you could shake a stick at. Of course, they got governesses and servants up the wazoo, so I suppose they manage.

"Them two, who used to be regular folks, are now the toast of Colorado, according to the newspapers in which I wrap my fish on occasion, but nothin' is ever glittery as it looks, far as I kin tell. Seems to me you don't get rich and famous in this world without workin' yer fingers to the bone, and you don't get to know every important Tom and Dick without spendin' damn near all yer wakin' hours entertainin' or bein' entertained. And you sure as hell don't get to the statehouse—which, by the way, is where they say yer brother's headed—without compromisin' a goodly portion of yer convictions to the will of the power brokers and the party. And that, in a nutshell, is how they are." He hesitated, looking at Hart, his eyes squinty from the sun, then continued. "To say nothing of the fact that Chance has taken to sharing his favors with the fallen angels of Leadville. And Fancy ain't done nothin' I can see to prevent it." He stopped for breath, then spoke again. "Besides all that, there's big trouble at the mine . . . and old Bessie seen fit to up and die on me."

Hart digested the soliloquy in silence and was unable to answer, for the sadness it provoked in him. Bandana never gossiped; he obviously thought these were things Hart ought to know.

"Like I always said," Bandana finished up as he pointed Hart toward Chance's new house on the hill, "the higher you climb, the more rocks you gotta dodge along the way."

▲

Hart decided to check out the mine first. It was chilling to see how damaged the area around Leadville had already become. Trees stripped, ground gray with tailing dumps . . . he wondered how anything good could come from a process so destructive.

"Chance has gone mad as a meat-ax," Caz said when Hart had settled in at the Fancy Penny. "He's told me to put a sock in it everytime I complain about what's going on. And who the hell can find him when you need him? He follows everybody's advice except mine about how to spend the mine tucker. You know he's always been as game as Ned Kelly when it comes to spending—the Fancy Penny and the Last Chance have been expanded radically, but Chance has leveraged everything to buy up more and more properties—and on some of them I think he's got a raw deal. Now there's so much squawking among the men and so much strike talk that I've sent for Bandana to ask his advice. You know McBain, mate, he's gone bush again, and you damned near need a net to pull him into town."

It seemed to Hart that none of what Chance was doing was wrong in itself. In the hands of a brilliant speculator or even a decent businessman, what his brother was up to might work just fine, but Hart had a hunch Chance was operating out of his depth, or that somebody else was pulling his strings. It could be Chance's ego had gotten the better of him; it wasn't easy to keep your equilibrium, in the face of overwhelming riches.

He saw the worried expression in Caz's eyes, the dark circles around them, and the deep frown lines that hadn't been there when he left. Whatever was wrong at the Fancy Penny was serious, and it wasn't new.

"What's the real beef with the men, Caz?" he asked, knowing he would hear the truth. Caz fancified and embroidered only when storytelling, never in answer to a straight question.

Caz rubbed his chin, collecting a huge store of facts into an orderly progression. "The arrival of the new railroad last summer brought in a shitload of cheap labor, Hart. You know how it is, mate; miners are itinerant workers, they go where the work is. Easier transportation meant a flamin' flood of men from all over the state willing to work for tuppence ha'penny. Our boys here in Leadville were cut off at the knees.

"Owners is owners. A glut of new laborers means only one thing to them, laddie buck. Lower wages. Now Tabor has invented this half-ass militia to put down a strike over how much the men get paid. He's a cheap bastard, if you ask me—rich as Croesus and not about to put a bob in a beggar's cup."

"And where does Chance stand in all this?" Hart asked, incredulous that so much in his brother's life could have gone awry in the same few years when everything in his own had fallen so perfectly into place.

Caz shrugged. "Chance's heart is with the men, mate, I'll give him that—and a rum time he's had fighting the politicos over that, let me tell you. Chance knows the pit, knows what the men are up against down there. You've got to give him credit, he's held the line and refused to lower wages even though the big boys have threatened to pull out their support for his political aspirations. I'd say your brother's made some real bad enemies among the other owners by siding with the men.

"Trouble is, at the end of it, in the men's eyes, Chance is still one of the blokes in the big houses, while they live in shanties and feed their families on salt pork and sourdough. The kettle's about to boil over, mate, you mark my words it is." Caz took a breath as if deciding whether or not to say the last of it, then he shook his head and said, "About Fancy, Hart. She's feeling real crook. She blamed your brother for the tyke's death—unfairly, too. Never saw a man so ga-ga for a child. The little one was damaged, you know—she was slow-minded, but loving as a kitten. Chance needed the love she gave him, is my call. Fancy loves him, but she's a prickly pear—soft on the inside and covered with thorns. My guess is they've torn each other up pretty damn good. Ain't love sublime, mate?"

Hart tried to digest all he'd heard. The trip's exhaustion had made him irritable, and every piece of news was lousier than the last. Before leaving the mine office, he asked to look through the ledgers and came away more puzzled than ever. Chance had moved all their money into paper assets, leveraging himself up to his new Stetson. If anything happened to tip the scales . . . didn't his brother see how precarious things were?

Hart went back to town feeling sobered and uncertain. The mine was bringing in vast sums of money, but without him or Bandana to keep an eye on it, where would it all go? And how soon? If other rich strikes could run out of ore, so could theirs; and if nothing had been put away for safety, they'd all be back out on that bare-ass mountain scraping for supper money.

▲

The McAllister house stood on the top of a small, well-manicured hill, a commanding Victorian presence that dwarfed the lesser structures of the town below. Hart rang the doorbell like any other visitor and waited while a servant summoned Fancy.

He settled uneasily into a gentleman's chair near the corner window and looked around with curiosity. The parlor—or was it called a drawing room in so ostentatious an establishment?—was ornate and filled with patterns. An Oriental rug covered the parquet, antimacassars perched decorously on the arms of chairs and horsehair sofas, a piano occupied a place of honor between the large windows. He was pleased to see, among the many framed lithographs and photos on the walls, a sketch he'd made of Fancy long ago; it occupied a place of honor above the mantel. He could read the love in it so clearly, he wondered if Fancy, too, could see its transparent emotion.

Her footfall on the stair brought Hart back to attention; she stood silhouetted in the doorway and her beauty struck him forcibly as ever—a tightening of the solar plexus, a pounding of the pulse, a self-admonition to get control—and then they were hugging and crying and talking all over each other's sentences, and the feel of her in his arms made question marks superfluous.

"Oh, Hart, you look so grand! Why, you seem positively elegant in your city clothes and you're twice as big as I remember."

Hart smiled at her exuberance; the overpowering life-force that engulfed a man when she was near was part of her magic. It was so easy to be lost in her. . . .

"You look more beautiful than ever, Fancy. Marriage and motherhood must agree with you." A cloud passed over her expression and she answered honestly, as he knew she would.

"Chance and I have made a terrible mess of marriage, Hart." She took his hand and led him to the solarium, a room blessedly free of velvet.

A sunbeam fell across Fancy's shoulder where she sat, spilling yellow light onto her organza dress and ringing her in an aura of golden radiance.

With annoyance, Hart felt his pulse quicken. "What's happened, Fancy? When I left, you two couldn't breathe for happiness."

Fancy bit her bottom lip as she always did when nervous.

"It isn't just one thing, Hart, it's so many big mistakes. Chance is gambling hard and tossing money into dubious places. He's got troubles at the mine, too. Strike talk . . . of course, to give the devil his due, he has stood up against the other owners quite courageously and he's the only one who has. But the whole thing's a terrible disgrace, really . . ." She stopped and dropped her eyes to her fidgeting hands.

"Oh, Hart, that isn't it at all! I'm just babbling to cover up what I can't bear to say to you. I was too hard on him after my baby died and I turned him away with my coldness. He has other women, Hart, and that made me so scared and so mad I went back to work, and now we've fought so much I don't see how we can ever fix things up between us."

"Do you still love him, Fancy?" Hart asked quietly, fearing his own response to her pain.

"Yes, I love him! But that doesn't matter a damn, because he's shamed me, and I've gone and got independent again." Hart could hear the hurt pride clearly.

"But that isn't what you want, is it, Fancy? Not really."

"No, but it's all I've got, Hart. And I'll be damned if I'm going to eat crow and tell Chance it's perfectly all right for him to sleep with every nightbird in Leadville."

"Didn't you know the kind of man he was when you married him, Fancy? Didn't you see the wanderlust and the wildness?"

"Yes, I saw it, Hart, but I thought we'd be wild together. Now here I am, stuck at home with two children and all the responsibilities in the world, and he's out exercising his wanderlust and his wildness with other women and with money that belongs to all of us."

"Other women have forgiven their husbands for infidelities."

"Damn it, Hart, I'm *not* other women! I've fought too hard for life to let any man take me for granted. I'm not afraid of being alone and doing it all myself—I've done it before, and by God, I can do it again, if I have to."

Hart's voice was husky when he answered her. "There's nothing good about being alone, Fancy. We all need somebody to love, even if that somebody fails us, sometimes. Take it from me, babe, we all need somebody to love."

Fancy wondered if he was still in love with her . . . it seemed unlikely after all these years.

"I'll go find Chance and see if between us, Bandana and I can talk some sense into him, but dammit all, Fancy, you're the one who married the man. Even if he's done you wrong, maybe you just have to be big enough to forgive and forget and move on from your hurt. You've got children to think of . . . and you've got a commitment."

Hart left Fancy sitting in her parlor, hands in her lap and a chorus of thoughts clamoring in her head.

Hart walked out into the light of late afternoon, unsettled and angry. You're a damned fool, Hart McAllister, he told himself. You've just done everything you could to send her right back into his arms, when all you really wanted was to take her in your own.

"There isn't any question in my mind," Madigan said, pushing the map across the table toward Henderson, "the main body of ore runs into the Fancy Penny. I've been down there half a dozen times consulting on one thing or another." The map of the Mosquito Range was crisscrossed with hundreds of claim lines, all looking like so much chicken-scratch to the banker. "The McAllisters and McBain are going to be very rich for a very long time.

"I've staked out every piece of property around there that they don't own and I've set up a number of dummy companies to accommodate the income."

Henderson nodded; his friends in the East had told him everything he needed to know about Madigan when first he'd come to Leadville. By now their dealings were many and all lucrative.

"I've purchased the Little Nell, the claim just above theirs that was abandoned by Hopkins, years ago," Jason continued. "Not in my own name, of course. You never know . . . in a pinch there are other measures one could consider. . . ."

Henderson frowned. "I think we should try to get what we want the easy way first, Jason."

"If I'm right, and the lode line is under their part of the mountain, you may be very pleased to do it any way that will force them out."

Henderson looked up from the map and nodded; it was easy to see how Madigan had amassed his empire. Besting a man who's both smart and ruthless was damned near impossible.

"What exactly is it you're suggesting here, Jason? Hypothetically, of course."

" 'Hypothetically,' it wouldn't take more than a few judiciously placed charges of dynamite to flood their mine enough to keep them from working it. With labor conditions as they are, and the fact that McAllister has made enemies by siding with the men in this labor dispute, I don't imagine the other owners would rush to his aid."

"To what end?"

"Force them to sell."

"They won't."

"Then we buy whatever outstanding shares there are and short the stock fortuitously just at the moment the unfortunate 'accident' takes place. Our people in the East could sell short at the proper time and we could make a bundle."

"All anonymously?"

"All anonymously, or through any of the blinds I've set up. Chance has other mines; if he had to, he could abandon the Fancy Penny altogether and still stay solvent with the Last Chance."

"We at the bank can make more money if Chance McAllister stays very, very rich, Jason, and I have no personal ax to grind in this, while I suspect you do." He'd seen Madigan chatting with Mrs. McAllister on the street more than once; how much of this scheme was based on money and how much on lust?

Madigan snorted a laugh. "Let's understand each other, John. Every man has a right to take what he can by being a better businessman than his neighbor, or a tougher one."

Henderson nodded. "In principle I concur completely, but for practicality's sake, let's just play this hypothetical notion of yours out, Jason. Wouldn't it be damned dangerous? What if you accidentally loose some hot underground river into the shaft and kill somebody? I saw a man pulled from such an accident once—they got him out, but the flesh fell off his bones like a chicken in a stewpot. Besides which, you run the risk of rendering the richest strike in the Gulch unusable. Could be you're letting your personal feelings toward McAllister interfere with your business judgment."

"You don't get anything in this world by being reticent, John."

"Nor by being greedy, Jason. You know my father used to say to me, 'John, the bulls make money and the bears make money, but the pigs never make money.' I think I may have to pass, on this hypothetical what-if of yours."

"As you wish," Madigan replied with equanimity; he had no need of accessories.

"It would not be in the bank's best interest to have you mention any of this to McAllister, of course," Jason said evenly, gauging his companion correctly.

Henderson looked directly into the man's face with a slow smile. "No, I don't suppose it would be."

▲

Jason made his way out of the Little Nell's broken-down entrance and looked to right, left, and behind. He'd set the charges close enough to the wall separating the two claims so no one would ever be able to tell it hadn't been a missed shot in the Fancy Penny that caused the explosion. It had taken weeks of careful investigation to assess the correct placement, and to make sure dynamiting was being done in the Fancy Penny, near enough so a missed shot could obfuscate the cause. Making certain Chance McAllister would be below ground at the proper moment had been the difficult part—

the man spent precious little time at his own mine for an owner, and Jason considered it a stroke of great good fortune that he'd overheard Chance tell McBain he intended to visit the men on the morning shift.

Jason wiped his hands on his denim workpants and mounted up. If he'd set the timing device correctly, he'd catch the morning shift around their break, thereby giving himself plenty of time to get back home and provide a reasonable alibi, should he ever need one.

▲

Hart clapped the resin-hardened hat onto his head with distaste and nodded to Bandana, who had just done the same. He'd talked McBain into accompanying him on the first shift, as a means of testing the temper of the men below. Chance had intended to question the men himself, but Hart had argued that he and Bandana had a better shot at getting honest answers, and Chance had reluctantly agreed to stay behind.

Hart and Bandana clung to the thick wire cable of the cage on the sickening descent, remembering to keep their limbs away from the rushing rock. Best thing I ever did was to leave this stinking hole behind me, Hart thought grimly, as the world above was lost in eerie darkness.

The two owners made their way among the sullen men, but even those who were usually open and talkative eyed them with suspicion. Finally, they headed for the lunchroom in search of men in a more communicative mood.

The hollowed-out space next to Stope 18 was euphemistically called "the lunchroom." The cavelike opening in the rock face was ringed by primitive wooden benches; it was the spot where, once each shift, the men took a break and ate whatever they'd carried down with them in tin buckets.

Johnson and McNamara were seated along the left wall of the lunchroom as Bandana and Hart arrived; Jakes, Kittery, O'Brien, Kowalski, and Schmidt straggled in, giving the two owners a wary once-over. At least the visitors weren't dandied up like that other McAllister, who always looked like an ad for a custom-tailor shop.

"How's it goin', Mick?" Bandana began; he'd known the stocky Irishman long enough to expect a civil reply, but the square-bodied man merely shrugged.

"Thought you had a reputation as a jawsmith, McNamara—you ought to know Hart and me ain't here to stir up trouble. We cain't help you none if we don't know the score."

The man shrugged again but said nothing.

Bandana turned toward Jakes. "How about you, Augie? Near as I kin recall you always have a hand, voice, or foot in anythin' lively. You willin' to talk about what's troublin' you?"

"You're all right, McBain, you ain't never done any man wrong I know about. I'll talk to you. We're thinkin' about walkin' out because we're dirt poor, us and our families. A lot of men are gettin' rich off our sweat, includin' yourself, even if nobody'd know it to look at you." All the men smirked at that, including Bandana. "That's okay, mind you—that's just the way the world is, some's luckier than others. But men like us are paid more for our labor some other places in this state, and we want a fair shake here in Leadville. Prices are damned high and our kids gotta eat."

Bandana nodded. "Cain't fault yer logic, Augie, but the way I hear it, Chance McAllister's been on yer side in this thing agin' the other owners. Ain't that so?"

Augie Jakes never got a chance to reply. Explosion thundered through the shaft. Sudden darkness engulfed the men; bodies crashed in all directions under a hail of rock and splintered timber. The explosion doused their oil lamps and candles, but they didn't need light to know the mine had caved in around them.

Hart strained his massive body against the entombment of fragmented rock, and found, with intense relief, that he could pull himself free. Dust and rock particles sucked up into his lungs, and he fought to speak above the painful pounding in his ears.

"McBain!" he shouted, shocked by the unaccustomed reverberation of his voice in the filthy space. "Johnson! McNamara! Jakes!" Grunts or hoarse responses, or ominous silences, greeted Hart's roll call. "Kittery, O'Brien, Schmidt, Kowalski!" Coughs and gasping breaths or cries of pain punctuated the names as Hart ticked off what men he could recall were on this shift. All but O'Brien responded. Kittery moaned and those who could walk, moved toward the sound to help him.

The dark and musty smell of rock that had lain undisturbed in nature's bosom for a million years filled the space with a sickening density. What was left of the air was barely breathable. Water seeped and dripped. Hot water.

Someone struck a match and a tiny candle flame cast flickering illumination on the garish tableau. Seven or eight fear-sick faces materialized; Hart could read in each that this was a moment every man had prepared himself for from the first time he'd ever gone hard-rock—a contained terror that was always in the gut, eating at it like a tenacious maggot—fear of being buried alive.

"You're hurt, Bandana," Hart said sharply. A patch of dark blood fouled the shoulder of McBain's shirt in the candle's quivering light. "There's filth all over that cut—you'd better let me try to clean it up a little so it doesn't get infected."

"Infected!" Bandana snorted back. "Hell, meat don't never spoil up here in these mountains. What water we got we'll need for drinkin', not cleanin'."

"If we're all buried alive, infection won't matter much," McNamara volunteered.

"Let's inventory what we got that's useful," Schmidt called out. The men groped in the ruins for the lunch pails they'd been holding before the explosion; most had been spilled or buried; three remained intact.

"Count the candles," someone said—fear of dying in the dark was even worse than starvation.

The men checked their injuries and their small group of supplies in an orderly fashion. One was hurt besides Bandana, but not gravely. O'Brien was dead and Kittery was nowhere to be found. Two half-spilled oil lamps and eighteen candles—thank God the next shift's candles had been stored beneath the lunchroom's bench; it was enough to keep one light going for three to four days, lighting the new from the last of the old, if the air held out. Each miner understood that the candles used oxygen too precious to waste, but the alternative darkness could drive a man mad. They'd all heard stories. . . .

"We've got bits and drills and picks," Hart said. "Maybe we can dig our way out."

"We're six hundred feet down," Bandana answered quietly. "And this seepage don't look good to me. Out there, they know where the water's comin' in from, down here, we don't. If we weaken the wrong wall we could get parboiled."

Hart weighed the danger of digging against sitting and waiting to die. "We could sound out the walls, and get a sense of where the water's coming from. I've a hunch it's the direction of the Little Nell—but you can't dig with that bad arm."

"What beef I got is in the shoulder," Bandana said shortly. "I kin dig like the next man."

Hart didn't argue.

Both owners eyed the walls warily in the flickering shadows. It was damned hard to hold back the primal fear of burial.

"If that water breaks through, we'll be drowned, boiled, or steamed long before starvation, thirst, or madness kills us," Bandana whispered to Hart.

"Always good to have choices," Hart replied grimly, his eyes meeting Bandana's in the darkness.

Each of the trapped men tried to clear a patch big enough to sit or lie— their cramped ruin was jagged with crushed rock and only the splintered square-sets gave them space to stay alive.

Hart knew the tunnel charts better than the others; he asked if anyone had paper and pencil, and Kowalski sheepishly proffered a scrap, the reverse side of which held a love note from the man's wife. Hart carefully avoided reading it; with Bandana's help he rendered an approximate map of the interior.

"Here's where I put us—at least two hundred feet from the most logical direction for help to come from." Bandana nodded agreement and glanced once again around the black hole.

The men had settled into two small groups, the owners on one side, the rest of the survivors on the other; one man seemed intent on examining the rock wall, another was fashioning something out of a broken powder case and a piece of fractured pipe. Bandana shook his head at the resiliency of the human spirit, and turned his attention back to Hart—it struck him that if you had to be stuck in a tight spot with somebody, Hart was a good bet. Bandana kept his voice low for privacy.

"How the hell d'ya think that water got through? Far as I know, there was a million tons of quartz between us and it."

"Who cares how it got in," Hart replied. "The real question is how the bloody hell are we going to get ourselves out of here?"

"Got somethin' for you, McBain," Jeremy Johnson interrupted, handing Bandana the box he'd been busy on for the previous hour. McBain glanced up to see what the boy held in his hand and was startled to see that out of the fractured powder case, he had fashioned a crude musical instrument; four tightly drawn rawhide shoelaces had been stretched into strings. In his other hand he held the pipe length, one end was plugged up and the other had been made into a mouthpiece so that, given the crack in the pipe and its drill holes, a flute of sorts had been fashioned.

Bandana fingered the thudding strings of the unimaginable instrument. "Let me see that, young feller," he said as he and Hart exchanged glances at this attempt to whistle past the graveyard. Anything to help keep spirits up would be worthwhile, their own as well as the men's.

"That's a damned fine invention you got there, son," Bandana said with considerably more enthusiasm than he felt. "I just might be moved to a chorus or two." Johnson pulled a penny whistle from his pocket and the huddled men made as much noise as possible with the improvised orchestra.

▲

Cave-in! Damn it to bloody hell, was there anything else in his life that could come crashing down at this moment? Chance didn't wait to hear the end of what was being said by the mine foreman who'd pounded on his door.

He felt the air shut off from his own lungs at the thought of his brother trapped in the mine shaft. Dead or injured . . . suffocated by a mountain of rock. Hart, who hated the world beneath the ground. . . . No! He couldn't let himself think such thoughts—not now, not when he had to think clearly to save them.

A steady gray rain beat down as he made his way toward the mine works; funerals and disasters always happen in the rain, he thought grimly as he neared the entrance. Men, women, and children were already gathered in tight murmuring knots, crying out for information about their men.

Chance shouldered his way gently through the crowd. Inside, Caz and several shift foremen were already gathered over a shaft chart. Lanterns swayed in the gloomy morning light, throwing yellow shadows over the oilcloth.

Caz clapped him hard on the shoulder, a gesture of compassion.

"What the hell happened?" Chance demanded.

The color rose in Caz's already ruddy face, then drained again. "Explosion. Somewhere around Stope 18. The whole front end is caved in. It's flooding, Chance. I can hardly bring myself to say it out loud to you, mate. Underground river. Hot as blazes. We'll have to get them out of there fast, or . . ." He let the thought trail off.

"Could be six, mebbe eight days dig," a man named Flynn piped up. "Might not be worth it, considering the odds a' gettin' them out."

The ferocity in Chance's eyes stopped Flynn short.

"Get every man you can lay your hands on and start them digging! Sound the alarm to every mine around for volunteers. Pay them anything they want. Get a survey team in there, now, to find out the extent of the damage. I want to know exactly where those men are and how to get them out."

"We're doing that already, mate," Caz said low and evenly.

"Then do it faster, Caz. I'm going after the other owners to enlist their help. When I come back here, you sure as hell better have more to tell me than that you can't get them out of there in less than eight days!" Caz bit his underlip; he knew, better than most, the love the two McAllister brothers bore each other.

Chance turned abruptly and strode from the building; the men behind him shook their heads and murmured among themselves.

"Gonna be some hell of a time gettin' men to go down into boiling water," Santori, the cage man, said to no one in particular.

Caz cut him off; it never paid to let bad news get started. "Somebody hightail it over to Mr. Madigan's office. He's in town from New York this week, and he's got more mine-engineering experience than the rest of us." Someone nodded and headed for the door.

▲

Madigan, having ditched his gear and tethered his roan inside his own stable, was warming himself before the fire with a cup of coffee and the morning paper when the foreman from the Fancy Penny pounded on the door and asked him to come quickly, his help was needed.

▲

Chance left the last mine owner's office, swearing under his breath. Four in a row had said no. His stand on the strike had made him enemies; he hadn't realized how many or how vindictive. It was all done gracefully, of course. "Sorry, McAllister, I can't spare the men." "Too dangerous down there; you can't expect me to risk men's lives on a hopeless cause. Your men are dead already." A half-dozen other excuses, equally lame.

Chance hoisted himself into the saddle and turned the great black in the direction of the mine; if no one else would help, he'd have to get the men out himself. He was startled to see Jason Madigan dismounting from his horse just outside the entrance to the manager's office.

"What are you doing here, Madigan? Gloating like everybody else?" Chance asked, curtly. There was no way to avoid Madigan now that he'd become a fact of life in Leadville, but after Fancy had owned up to her affair with the man, it had been damned hard to be civil to him.

Jason held his temper; his voice gave evidence of the tight control that reined it.

"I can't blame you for holding my former relationship with your wife against me, McAllister, but I understand there are men below ground who need all the expertise you can muster. I'm a damned good mining engineer and I'm here to offer my help. After we get those men out, we'll have ample time to settle any personal grievances there may be between us."

Chance searched Madigan's face for other motives, but there appeared to be only sincerity in the man's sharp slate eyes.

"I accept your offer," he said.

Together they pushed past the crowds and walked into the mine office amid the cries of the townspeople who milled restlessly in the rain.

▲

Madigan, McAllister, and Castlemaine bent over the chart table, oblivious to the escalating pandemonium outside the small wooden structure. Women carrying infants, children waiting for their fathers and older brothers. Friends. Rubberneckers. All creating a hubbub of weeping voices interspersed by curses and shouted demands for information; the only louder sounds were the thunder and lightning that echoed down the mountains and the constant tattoo of the rain on the tin roof.

Madigan made one last calculation on the pad before him and straightened his back.

"According to Mr. Castlemaine's reconnaissance crew, McAllister and

McBain—assuming they remained together—are somewhere in the main drift, but probably quite a distance from the central shaft. The other crew, I'm afraid, was working on the seam nearest the Little Nell. It would be almost impossible to assume, judging from the inclination of the tunnels and the rapidity with which the water appears to be rising, that they could have survived. My vote would be to abandon work in the latter area and to concentrate all efforts on the former."

Caz looked up; he sounded hesitant. "If it weren't for that wall of boiling water down there, there might be a closer route."

Heads snapped up, all eyes alert. Caz shifted a little as if unwilling to explain what he meant to say.

"The old shaft, you know the one, Chance . . . Hart moved the drifts away from there when the square-sets went in. He said the rock was unstable because of the width of the lode. If that shaft's intact, it can't be more than twenty feet east of them."

Recognition dawned in Chance's face. "What are the odds it's flooded?"

Madigan moved the chart toward Caz. "Show me exactly where it is," he said, and the Australian drew a pencil line through the chart.

Jason answered carefully. "It certainly looks like a possibility. Damned close to the fault, though, and possibly blocked by the water."

"It's worth the gamble." Chance spoke decisively. He turned from the table and saw that Jewel and Fancy, trailing rain from their cloaks, had both entered the shed; how long they'd been standing there he couldn't tell.

Fancy reached for his hand with her own; whatever troubles were between them, a disaster of this proportion surely took precedence.

"Hart and Bandana are down there," he said.

"Oh, Chance, not both of them . . ." Jewel, standing behind Fancy, said, "Shit!" and gripped her hard enough to steady the younger woman on her feet, as Chance moved toward the door.

"I need volunteers!" he shouted into the crowd. "There's a possibility we can get to some of the men through the original shaft. McAllister and McBain dug that hole themselves—odds are they'll remember it's there and head that way if they can."

"That shaft was abandoned years ago because it was unsafe!" someone shouted. "It ain't even timbered like the rest!"

"There's scalding water down there," another voice shouted. "Those men are dead already."

"You lily-livered sons o' bitches!" Jewel snapped from the doorway. "Ain't any one of you man enough to keep a fellow human from bein' buried alive? I'm ashamed of the lot of you."

No answer greeted her question, and she curled her lip in contempt. "If none of you are man enough to go in after them boys, I sure as hell am!"

She moved her sturdy body in beside Chance's. "I got friends down that hole," she said. "You can count me in."

"That won't be necessary, Miss Mack . . . it's a gallant offer, but I'm afraid ladies aren't fitted for this particular task—except perhaps by courage. I'll go with Mr. McAllister in your place."

Jewel looked up, surprised to find it was Jason Madigan who had spoken.

A boyish miner from the crowd came forward. "I'll go! Me da's down there."

"I'm in," said a huge man with a shaggy red beard and a thick brogue. "The lads down there are me friends."

"Count me in!" said a wiry Scotsman who stood in the big man's shadow. "I'd not sleep nights knowing I left men livin' below ground without trying to get them out."

"I'm in, as well you know," Caz said.

"No." Chance's answer was definitive. "I need someone up top I can trust."

Chance turned toward his wife one last time; he saw the tears that filled her eyes, and sensed her love for him in her terrified expression. He touched her cheek gently with his hand; the remembered softness nearly made him wince.

"Don't let them die in the dark," she whispered, barely able to form the words. He nodded, understanding. Fancy stepped back beside Jewel and let the men file past them through the doorway that led to the accessway to the old mine.

▲

Hart uncramped his long legs and stretched as well as he could in the suffocating confines of the hole. Never thought I'd die down here, he said to himself as he strained to unkink the crick in his back that had happened when he fell.

"Bandana," he said, coughing in the foul air, "aren't we somewhere in the neighborhood of the first shaft we ever dug?"

"You thinkin' we're one hell of a lot closer to the first shaft than to the main cage?"

Hart nodded vigorously.

"Been thinkin' the same thing myself."

"How close would you say we are? Ten feet, maybe? Twenty, tops?"

"If it's still there and not full of rock and water. Odds are Chance or Caz'll remember it, same as us. You, me, and them dug damn near all of it ourselves."

"I think we should get the men digging in that direction," Hart said.

Bandana shook his head. "It's more unstable over there, and we're not sure about the water."

"But if we're right, it's a damned sight more of a possibility than the main shaft."

"Been watchin' the water. It's rising outside us. You can tell by the sweat and trickle."

"True enough. But mostly on the western side of the hole—the old shaft's to the east. I say we chance it." In the dismal darkness the pocket compass he held glinted dully.

"Notice how loud the sounds from your watch get in the dark?" Bandana asked cryptically, and Hart knew he meant the men would be better off working than sitting. Tomorrow there would be no food, the day after that, even the small swallows of water they'd allowed themselves would be gone.

Their sodden clothing already chafed their skin and left it raw or blistered; the men had stripped themselves of all but essentials in the first few hours. Bandana stood up in the dark, ducking to keep from hitting his head on a jutting timber, and lit the new candle from the last flickering spark of the old one.

"Men," he said, his voice bouncing against the imprisoning walls. "There's a chance we can get out of here, but to do it you're each gonna have to know the odds."

"There are no odds," Johnson responded. "We all know they can't get to us by blasting because of the water and we're in too far to dig. We're dead men."

"You think that way and you're dead already!" McBain shot back. "Other men have got out of this particular suburb of hell. As for me, I'd rather die of diggin' than of bellyachin'. "

"He's right," said Kowalski. "We ain't got much to lose, let's hear him out."

"The first shaft we ever dug wasn't fifteen feet from here. A couple of pick-and-shovel men worth their salt could get that far in a few days. We got four teams here by my count. I say we burrow our way outta this mole hole."

"Workin's better'n thinkin', " Johnson agreed, picking up a sledge and motioning to his partner to grab a drill. They had extricated what tools they could from the rubble right after the explosion and there were at least enough to make an attempt. Long into the afternoon, which was neither night nor day to them in their tomb, the eight trapped men worked the rock.

▲

The sluicing rain had changed to a relentless drizzle when Chance, Jason, and the others reached the original shaft, but the water still ran off their slickers as they loaded themselves and their equipment onto the old platform that was lowered by windlass into the pit below.

"We'll head for the winze above their drift," Chance instructed without hesitation, knowing the value of appearing confident. "Get close enough to find out the depth of the water in their direction. If it's too deep to blast our way in, we'll tunnel in from above them." Madigan nodded agreement.

"How well-timbered was this section?" he asked.

"Badly. But they wouldn't have been working in the old drift . . . the newer areas were square-set."

The small team made its way gingerly to the winze, then unfurled the rope ladder carried by Monahan, and lowered it into the tunnel below.

"I'll check it out, sir," offered the smaller Irishman, named Shaughnessy. "I'm the size you need for this job."

Chance nodded and the little man scrambled down the ladder and was back within fifteen minutes. Dripping wet and grimy, he stood panting before them, sweat pouring from his face, water draining from his clothes.

"Hot as the hammers of hell, sir," he said panting. "And wet as the Boyne. Hot and cold water must be mixing somewheres in there. You can stand in it, if you ignore the blisters, but if we burst the seam to that hot spring with a blast, we'll boil 'em like spuds."

"And us."

"We don't even know if they're alive," said Madigan reasonably.

"Oh, they're alive, all right," said the little man, looking up with startled eyes, as if to say "didn't I tell you?" "I heard 'em with me own ears. They're hammerin' away in there like a bloody symphony, not ten feet from where I stood." The men smiled grimly in the darkness.

"Where are they now? Exactly."

"Under the fault, sir," the little man replied with regret.

Chance's dark brows tightened into a frown.

"We could go in from above."

"Not without blasting."

Chance couldn't waste time on indecision. Madigan watched his mind work, with grudging admiration. McAllister was directing things as he would himself. "Murphy, you and Monahan go back for explosives," Chance was saying. "Madigan and I will sound out the rocks and determine where to set the charges, but first let's see if we can get to them by digging."

Chance looked at Jason questioningly, wondering again why this stranger would risk his life for men he didn't know. "Unless you want out, Madigan," he said. "This isn't really your problem."

The irony of the situation almost amused Jason, risking his own life in a mine he'd booby-trapped was not exactly what he'd anticipated. He'd set out to kill Chance, but failing that, perhaps something equally deadly might be achieved by his helping the man. If he left the scene at this point, his cowardice would be long talked of in Leadville; if he stayed, he'd have Chance's confidence and friendship.

"In for a penny, in for a pound," he answered.

"Mind if I ask why?"

"My reasons are my own."

The muscles in Chance's jaw set, but this was no time for argument. "Fair enough. The help is appreciated, whatever the reason for it."

Madigan nodded. They could hear the scraping sound of boots in the tunnel coming toward them as the two Irishmen returned with their burden of dynamite and tools.

The two adversaries stood for a moment in the gloom of the carbide lamps, sizing each other up—a man had to trust another to let him swing an eight-pound sledge above his head and hands. Jason smiled sardonically.

"I wouldn't be in this hole if I didn't mean to help," he prompted, reading Chance's expression, and the wary younger man nodded grudging acceptance.

"We'll spell each other with the sledge, then," he replied.

"As you wish," Madigan said equably as he picked up the heavy tool and flexed his hands around it. It was some time since his hands had labored over other than balance sheets, there would be no protective calluses, but he was no neophyte and had never feared hard labor.

All four men started to dig . . . tunneling down, stopping to listen for digging sounds on the other side, each man stripped to his trousers, bodies glistening with sweat. Chance was surprised to see the latent power in Madigan's stocky body; he was obviously no stranger to physical stress; the muscle was strong and confident, if twenty years older than Chance's. McAllister repressed the vision of Fancy in the man's arms . . . Madigan did the same with Chance.

▲ ▲ ▲

"Somebody's out there!" Hart shouted, trying to keep the excitement in his voice within bounds. The trapped men had had to cut back on their own hammering because of bad air. Far, far away, in the belly of the rock, they could hear the tapping sounds.

"Unless they got a magician with 'em, they cain't get here by diggin'," Bandana replied grimly. "Have to blast her open." He looked down pointedly at the dark water that had risen to their ankles, making life even more unbearable than it had been before. There was now nowhere to sit except in hot water, and nowhere to sleep unless sitting up. The air made every breath an effort.

Bandana settled back against the sodden rock face and squinted toward the overhanging timbers. He rose and waded to the farthest point; standing below the sagging beams, he measured them with his eye against his own height. Lower. Definitely lower than before. Pushing inward, buckling with the weight of whatever was above them, rock or water or both.

"Got a wife, McBain?" asked Kowalski, squatted near him.

Bandana smiled a little. "Never had. I expect cleanliness was never close enough to my cuticle for any woman to want me. Full-time, anyways."

"I got one. A real good one, too. And seven kids. I been tryin' to figure what she'll do without my pay if we don't get outta here."

"Got five kids myself," Johnson broke in. "Hard to think of not ever seein' 'em again."

"Cain't think like that," Bandana said; the words had sharp edges. "Got to believe you'll get out . . . despair makes dead men out of live ones." He looked around the soggy and bedraggled group. I'm probably the only man down here with nobody up there to mourn me, he thought, then angry at his own maudlin turn of mind, he spoke again.

"We're gettin' outta here, boys—you can damn well count on it." He looked once more at the sagging timber barrier and waded back to Hart. Was it his imagination or had the water gotten hotter in the last few hours? He wiped the sweat from his face where it had dripped past his bandana and sucked the sodden, filthy air into his lungs.

"You figger Chance is still out there, Hart?" he asked, knowing the answer.

"If he's alive, he's still out there," was the sure reply.

▲

"What're you up to?" Hart asked curiously. He'd been watching Bandana collecting clothing and debris and stuffing it into a makeshift cushion inside his own discarded shirt. Without the shirt, the man's shoulder wound was laid bare; ugly and jagged, it was far worse than Hart had imagined it could be, considering the strength with which McBain had wielded his pick and shovel since the accident. Yellow matter caked the wound and the skin around the edge was angry, red and puckered.

"Stuffing," Bandana replied enigmatically. "When they blast, those timbers are gonna cave. My hunch is the water's coming from that direction."

"So you're planning to hold back an underground hot spring with an old shirt?" Hart whispered, incredulous.

"Listen to me, laddie buck." Bandana's tone left no room for argument.

"There'll be no time for jawin' when that seam busts—maybe only seconds to scramble six men outta here. Every man here's got family but you and me. If there's anythin' left a' me to bury, you tuck me in beside ol' Bessie. I been missin' her sorely since she went on without me."

"Dammit, Bandana. We're getting out of here together."

Bandana didn't reply, but pulled a money belt from under his shirt. "There's a paper in here goes to Fancy," he said, and Hart knew it was the one Bandana had been working over so laboriously for the past hour. "The belt's oilcloth inside and watertight. This is real important to me, Hart, so don't fail me in what I'm askin' you to do."

Wonderingly, Hart tucked the pouch into his own money belt next to his skin; like most such repositories, it had a watertight lining and would serve as doubled protection for whatever it was that meant so much to his friend.

"I figure it'll take them out there another hour or two of hammerin' to decide dynamite's the only option," Bandana said before curling up again to sleep. "Meantime, I'm gonna catch me some shut-eye. You hear 'em stop diggin', you wake me up, understand?"

"Whatever it is you've got in mind, Bandana, count on me to help you when the time comes."

"You'll get your ass outta here with the others if you can!" Bandana snapped. "Just do like I told you to do. Fancy's gonna need someone to take care of her, and your brother ain't the man for the job."

What was there to say to that? Hart wondered; there was nothing in Bandana's soul but iron and he obviously wasn't in the mood for false optimism.

He watched the little miner sleep, clutching his absurd stuffing-bulwark against what was to come, and wondered if Fancy knew how very much the old man loved her.

▲

Chance leaned heavily on the upended pick and struggled for breath. All four men were physically spent; they weren't going to break through to the trapped miners without blasting.

"Two charges in the right position could free them," Madigan said, reading his expression.

Chance nodded. "Or bury them."

"Even so, they're better off dead quick than dying of hunger and thirst" was the pragmatic reply. "Face it, McAllister, we can't get to them in time with picks and shovels."

"The blast could kill us all," Chance said with a rising inflection, asking a consensus of the men around him.

Madigan scanned the other faces, then replied for the group. "We all accepted that risk when we volunteered." The bizarre irony of his own position struck Madigan once again; he might die here, in this disaster of his own making, or he might take something very valuable from the hole.

"I vote we blast," he said. Each man, in turn, nodded his assent.

▲

"Got somethin' to tell you, Hart," Bandana said softly, conspiratorially. The heat had grown intolerable, and the men were sprawled in varying efforts to sleep. Hart turned his body to face his friend's; Bandana looked gaunt and hollow in the eerie light, his face shiny with unhealthy sweat.

"You're a real honorable feller, Hart. And what I'm fixin' to tell you is damned important to me, so you got to promise me you'll treat it sacred and only do exactly what I tell you to do." He squinted hard at Hart's face to see if he'd agree.

Puzzled, the younger man nodded.

"I found her. Jes' like I knew I would." He stopped and drew breath. "The mother lode, Hart, Esmeralda." Hart opened his mouth to speak, but Bandana silenced him with a gesture. "I always called her Esmeralda, while I was on her trail, 'cause she seemed like some exotic woman. You know, always just out of reach . . . but the claim has another name now, it's all writ down on that paper in your pouch.

"Never said nothin' to nobody about findin' her, you understand, 'cause after we struck silver, it come clear to me that money ain't what I need in this life."

Bandana cleared his throat, more from emotion than the dank air.

"I got it in my head to give Esmeralda to Fancy. I got a hunch the day could come when old Fance might need somebody to look after her, and I might not be in the neighborhood." His voice was suspiciously husky. "I'm tellin' you about it, Hart, 'cause that paper I give you was my last will and testament."

Tears stung Hart's eyes and he quickly averted them. This strong man beside him intended to die; he didn't rail against it or waste his time on self-pity, but simply chose to order his affairs.

"If there's ever any confusion later on, about who I meant to have Esmeralda, you'll bear witness for Fancy."

"You know I will, Bandana," Hart answered him, much moved. "But you can tell her about all this yourself. Whatever happens down here, you and I are in it together."

"I've written a letter to Fancy," Bandana pressed on, ignoring Hart's statement. "It's meant for her eyes only, so you got to promise me you won't let nobody else get wind of it, *especially* not your brother."

Hart nodded, wondering if the strain had unhinged Bandana. "I'll see she gets it," he said.

"Chance ain't to see it, no matter what. I know you love yer brother, Hart, but yer not blind to his nature. He'd only squander it and what's there is for Fancy's safety." He paused, then grasped Hart's arm with fierce purpose.

"This is more important to me than anythin' in this world or the next! Understand me?"

"You can give the damned thing to her yourself, Bandana," Hart answered him sharply. "Because I'm not leaving here without you."

"Keep that belt where you cain't lose it, when the water flushes in," Bandana persisted, as if Hart hadn't spoken at all.

The old man's face was set, and Hart could see there was no point trying to make light of the mission he'd been entrusted with. He squeezed Bandana's uninjured shoulder reassuringly, and both men tried again to find a comfortable enough contortion in which to rest.

▲

The rescue party finished placing the charges. "Fire in the hole!" shouted Chance as he lit the fuses and they ran for cover. As if any of them needed a reminder.

▲

The explosion in the enclosed space deafened the rescue party and set so many forces in motion that no one later could say precisely what happened next.

Rock thundered and crumbled, water spouted in ten directions . . . a hole appeared where rock had been.

Inside the interior prison men scrambled for the newly gaping exit, as the world fell in on them, splintering timbers, jagged quartz, and water so hot welling up from somewhere within their prison, it shot them screaming toward the opening.

Bandana stood with his makeshift baffle behind him, his arms pushing upward on the falling timbers, and his own body wedged into the scalding seam that had burst with the blast. Men pushed past him toward the opening above, as Hart tried to reach his friend, against the crush of men and water. Hands from above grappled in toward hands reaching out of the steaming, swirling grave; strong men pulled strong men upward as the water rose below.

Hart fought his way through the agonizing torrent toward Bandana as hands reached down to drag him up.

"Bro!" Chance shouted against the deafening roar of water. "Bandana!"
"McBain's wedged himself in to plug the seam," Kowalski screamed as
he was yanked upward by the rescuers.

"Mother of God!" yelled Shaughnessy, hanging his head and lantern over
the side of the pit from which the men were scrambling. "Your brother's
gone after McBain."

In the seething sea of boiling water, Bandana's head, teeth, and eyes
clenched in agony could still be seen, with Hart struggling toward him;
McBain was pinned helplessly beneath the fallen timbers, yet his hands still
vied against the weight of a million pounds of fallen tunnel, as if by force of
will he could hold it back.

Chance tugged off his boots and pushed through the circle of panting,
gasping men laid out on the floor of the drift above the hole where they'd
been buried.

A viselike grip closed around him from behind. "Don't be a fool!" Madigan yelled as he wrestled with Chance to keep him from diving into the
steaming pit. "They're dead men! That's boiling water down there!"

"He's my brother, you son of a bitch!" Chance wrenched himself free of
Madigan's grip and plunged into the blackened pool.

Hart grappled with Bandana's body, but the man was wedged too tightly
—he was dead already, Hart knew it in his soul, but he had bought time for
the others with his terrible sacrifice. Despairing, lungs bursting, Hart felt
powerful arms reach around him in the swirling flood and knew they were
his brother's. He let go of Bandana's body and allowed himself to be pulled
chokingly upward toward the air.

Monahan's hands reached over the edge of the pit to pull them both to
safety, with the help of other panting men.

A thunderous roar reverberated in the tunnel, shaking more rock and
dust loose from the fragmented walls; the sound obliterated everything and
each man looked up, eyes stark with fresh terror.

"Chain reaction!" shouted Schmidt.

"Out!" Madigan screamed. "For God's sake, run for your lives!"

Chance struggled to lift the inert body of his brother, but he was weakened by the underwater battle and couldn't do it alone. Cursing, Madigan
helped him hoist the unconscious Hart and, following the retreating miners
as fast as they could, they struggled their way toward the lift ahead.

In back of them the boiling water, bubbling up from the hole they'd
blasted, surged into the tunnel and began to fill the stope behind them as
they ran.

The men scrambling onto the platform looked back and saw the water surging up behind the two who strained against the huge burden of Hart's body.

"Leave McAllister or you'll never make it!" someone shouted to the two, who dragged the body between them—the trip to the surface was dangerous enough for men who were alert, for an unconscious man it would be nearly impossible.

"I'm not leaving my brother!" Chance shouted back.

"Wait!" Monahan yelled, moving his massive body from the platform and splashing toward the three men left behind in the tunnel. With a mighty heave he picked up the dead weight and, pausing only the briefest moment to steady himself, hoisted Hart over his shoulder.

"Jesus, Mary, and Joseph!" breathed Shaughnessy in awe; a two-hundred-and-seventy-pound burden would have flattened any two men. "Fer Christ's sake, move yer asses!"

Somehow all ten men crowded onto the rickety platform and began the precarious ascent to the top, praying the ancient cable and winch would hold.

Below, the steaming water swirled and bubbled as Mother Nature reclaimed the shaft for her mountain.

77   The doctors said the men would be scarred for life by the suppurating blisters that had risen from their scalding, but Fancy, frenzied as a Fury, banished the medical men and called on every herbal remedy she knew to save them. She immersed both brothers in tubs of linseed oil and limewater, and dispatched one rider to Magda, and another to fetch Wu for consultation.

Like one possessed, she nursed the two men through the next fortnight, sleeping only when Magda bullied her into napping to keep her strength from failing. Together, the three herbalists pulled both McAllisters back to life, unscarred, except within their hearts at the irreparable loss of Bandana.

Chance recovered first, for his injuries were less severe, but Hart slipped in and out of coma for a week. He thought of his own nakedness at times, as Fancy's competent hands smoothed calendula and hypericum salves and unpronounceable Chinese unguents onto his damaged flesh, but he was far too weak to feel anything but comfort in the caress of her fingers. Was there anything we three haven't shared? he wondered somewhere in his delirium. Where does one kind of love end, and another begin? Friendship, family ties, passion, debts of honor . . . wasn't it all there, endlessly entwining them, so there was no clear line of demarcation anymore? They would die for each other . . . was there any surer test of devotion? . . . they just couldn't figure out how to live with each other. But it was all too complicated for the sick man to unravel. Sometimes the complications seemed to sort themselves out in his delirium, but the answers would fade again with consciousness—like a dream that has clarity on the moment of awakening, then dissolves against your will, so that hard as you try, you can never, ever bring it back into focus.

 78 McBain's will survived the ordeal in its oilskin pouch, and Hart knew that the time must come to give Bandana's gift to Fancy. She grieved hard for his loss. "If I had only one friend left . . ." she'd written in that letter long ago; the words had stayed in Hart's mind for he'd wished they'd been written of him.

On a morning in September, when the time had come for him to leave again, he took Fancy aside and held her hand in his own. "Bandana gave me something for you, babe," he said, and saw the glint of quick moisture glisten her dark eyes, but she simply nodded.

Fancy looked less robust now than when Hart had gotten off the stage a month before; was it the sleepless nights of nursing or the grief that had sapped her?

"There's a place we should go to, Hart. It was Bandana's favorite spot in the world, you'll see why. He called it the Rainy Day."

Fancy and Hart dismounted near the entrance to the small mine tunnel. They hadn't said a word along the trail, for they both knew they'd come to say good-bye not only to Bandana, but to each other as well.

The wounds that had existed between Fancy and Chance had been mended by his brush with death; they would try again to be man and wife. And all three who loved each other knew it would be best if Hart were not around.

The big man pointed upward silently and Fancy shaded her eyes to see an eagle sail in lazy circles above the foothills far to the east. It reminded her of Fan. Autumn haze silvered the skyline, and the sheen of mist made all that lay below seem more an inland sea than a valley. Fancy breathed in the crisp fall damp and found that the earthy scent of fallen leaves and winter moss was soothing.

"Isn't it strange, Hart? Other people go home to heal, I take to the hills. . . ."

"Maybe the wilderness is the only real home you ever had, babe," he replied.

They hitched their horses and walked to the edge of the old shaft; their footsteps crunched the apricot-colored leaves carpeting the trail. It was a soft, scuffling sound like the rustling of a small animal in a woodpile.

"I'm going to miss him so much, Hart. Even when Bandana took to the hills, I always knew I could find him if I needed to. We used to come here often just to talk about life. It wasn't that he had all the answers, you know, just that he made me feel my questions were the right ones."

Hart reached into the pocket of his buckskin jacket and silently handed her Bandana's legacy. Fancy unfolded the letter and read it through silently. When she was done, she passed it wordlessly to Hart and he could see that tears overflowed her eyes and streaked her cheeks.

"Fance, old friend," Hart read . . .

Well, I found her, just like I said I would. And now she's yours. Near as I can figure, Esmeralda's about as rich as they come, so you'll never want for bean money—those lean days that always scared you so bad are gone for good now.

There's a catch to it, though, so I'm afraid you'll have to hear me out.

You're headstrong as they come, Fance. Don't give me no arguments now, that's just the way it is. And Chance is a gambler. Put them two natures together and you got trouble.

I ain't so old I cain't see what's what, so here's my stipulation: You cain't sell the Rainy Day (that's Esmeralda's last name in case you ain't figgered it out by now) 'cause it's our special place, and you cain't give Esmeralda to Chance McAllister or any other husband who might come down the pike. Other than that, she's yours to do with as you will. But I leave you one thought to go with her.

Mining's a real clean game, Fance. You take your money outten the earth, where it never belonged to nobody else but God Almighty. So it's new, never tainted by nothing at all, till man gets hold of it and greed sets in. That's when everything changes for the worse.

Esmeralda will give you the wherewithal to get anything you want out of this life, so you got to choose what you want real careful.

I never could figger out what kind of love I had for you, Fance. Father, uncle, friend seemed possibilities. Maybe I even loved you in the same way them boys did, though I never would of said a word about that, 'cause you had enough trouble sorting out two, never mind three.

All I know is I love you an almighty lot and I want to see you happy.

Well, I guess that's all the personal part I got to say, the rest's for them lawyer fellers:

This here note is my last will and testament. I'm of sound mind, near as I kin figger. Anything I got I leave to Fancy McAllister, not to her husband. The Rainy Day claim was mine fair and square; now it's hers.

Signed: Otis McBain

P.S. Hart McAllister witnessed this here document, so anybody got a quarrel about it should see him. I trust him to do right by this testament 'cause I know for a fact he thinks about as highly of the Ten Commandments as Moses did.

Fancy looked around her, unable to speak. She saw through her tears that the trees still stood as God had planted them, the land was untrammeled by machinery, the leaf-blanket softened even the cavelike hole Bandana had dug with his own hands, and graced the rotting timbers of the entranceway with a mantle of auburn.

No wonder he'd brought her here so often, just to sit and talk; he'd planned this all along. *This here place will keep you safe and warm, darlin', if there's ever a rainy day,* he'd told her once, and she'd thought he meant it only as a refuge.

Her voice was a whisper.

"If I tell the world what's buried here, Hart, you know what will happen?"

Hart loved her so achingly in that moment, he did what he'd sworn he wouldn't do. He put his arms around her shoulders from behind and she leaned back against his chest and felt the protectiveness of his strength enfold her like a mantle.

"Barren mountainside," he answered, "trees gone to mine-timber, tailing dumps of slag draining down the mountain like an open wound."

"You've always been the one who understood it all, haven't you, Hart?" she said wistfully, but he didn't reply.

"I've got all the money I could ever need. I've got Chance back again . . . maybe that rainy day will never come."

Hart thought he could read her mind, he felt so attuned to her; or maybe it was simply that they shared the same history, so their thoughts ran together like mountain streams.

"Why not just do what Bandana said, babe . . . save her, just in case. Don't tell anyone at all."

Fancy stood very still for a while within the shelter of his arms, feeling the pounding of his heart within his great chest, feeling the safety of his love that asked nothing in return. Then she pulled away and walked as close to the edge of the mountain as she could and stretched out her arms, like one in prayer.

"I love you, Bandana!" Her voice echoed up and down the canyon between the mountains, bouncing and trailing off into the distance. "Thank you for everything!"

"Rest gently, Bandana," Hart murmured quietly beside her, the sound mingling with the lingering echoes of her cry upon the wind.

"I guess this is good-bye for us, too, isn't it, Hart?" Fancy asked, letting her eyes linger on his, an act of intimacy. She saw nothing there but love and goodness.

"I don't think there'll ever be good-bye for us, babe," he replied.

The two remounted and followed the winding trail back down the mountain.

▲

Hart did something surprising before he left Leadville; he asked his brother to liquidate his holdings in the mines and wire his share of the money to Rut Canfield's family bank in Savannah. There were certain investments he had in mind, he said, and he wanted Rut to handle his money for the foreseeable future. Hart's lack of confidence in his business ability hurt Chance, but he loved his brother too much to argue.

Hart had decided not to go to Paris to study after all. He'd made the change in plans in the mine and in the weeks of convalescence after. He was no longer immortal; life was short and every day precious. Fancy and Chance were together, and he was again the odd man out—both these revelations made college seem a pale imitation of life, more a distraction to his art than a necessity. The decision to do, instead of think, was cleansing. He would make his way southwest into Indian territory and fulfill the dream fostered by his father so many years before. He had no way of knowing how long he'd be gone.

A letter arrived shortly thereafter, telling Fancy and Chance that Hart would leave within the month to travel on the Atchison, Topeka and Santa Fe train as far as it would take him into the Arizona Territory. From there, he would travel on horseback toward the Apache Nation. Catlin had painted the Sioux; Bodmer, the Iroquois; but no one had yet chronicled the fierce Apache, and that was Hart's intent. Chance wondered out loud worriedly if it was Hart's way of committing suicide, but Fancy knew that far from wanting to die, this was Hart's way of showing them how very much he wanted to live.

IX

CANDLE IN THE WIND

·▾·▾·▾·▾·

Hart Apacheria

"A friend is one mind in
two bodies."

BANDANA McBAIN

79 The high country had begun to subside into low red sandy wasteland and risen again into barren mountains, before the melancholy ebbed in Hart.

The land south of Colorado was new to him, benevolent and strange as a moonscape. Blue-green misted mountains, with clouds lying puddled on their summits, ringed the 360 degrees of his vision; mighty mesas, chiseled out by passing glaciers in an age forgotten, stood like sentinels in deserts God had painted shades of rust and copper, mauve and tan.

Hart crossed the desert awakening to its subtle wonder, and wormed his way through canyons thick with brush or cottonwood. He drew all that he saw, and eventually the distracting pain of loss he always felt on leaving Fancy faded to an ache, and the newness of the world around him began to fire his imagination.

He had no idea where he was headed, or what he would find when he got there, and for some unfathomable reason, he didn't fear the Indians nearly as much as he should have. The few towns he passed through were full of stories of Apache raids; Geronimo's war with the army had left much of the Southwest a bloodied battlefield, but Hart had dreamed this journey too long to be deterred, and his brush with death had made him curiously bold.

He'd taken on the old ways for this trek; it was good to be dressed in buckskin again, good to be forced to rely on himself. *"Ability to stand alone is the measure of a man, son,"* his father had said, and Hart understood in his soul that this was true. He'd carefully packed art supplies in New Haven and picked up trade goods along the route, so he thought himself as well equipped as any man could be who wasn't certain where he was going. George Catlin's autobiography of his time with the Sioux and Cheyenne had become his bible; the man had lived among the Plains Indians for years and shared their rituals as well as painting them, so Hart saw no reason he couldn't do the same with the tribes that roamed the Southwest. The Apaches fascinated him more than the Hopi or Navaho, for their warrior feats were legendary, and if the army's policy was successfully carried out, the way of the warrior would soon vanish from the earth. They were the best and bravest, they deserved to be remembered.

The utter loneliness challenged him, let him listen to thoughts long drowned out by the drone of life. Self-reliance tempers a man and strips him down to the essentials of character. Just before sundown one evening, he camped on the lonesome side of an arroyo; an exotic desert plant had caught his eye and he'd dismounted to examine it and found, when he stretched his legs, that it was time to stop for the night. Listening to the quiet had become a sustaining pleasure; he began to prepare himself for another evening alone with a book by the fire, when a disquieting sound disrupted his reverie. A moan or a chant, it was sung by a human voice, but he'd never heard one so primitive, mournful, or compelling. Hart crept to the canyon's ledge to track the source.

Below him was an Indian who was neither tall nor young. Hart thought he might be Apache, by the authority written clearly in the man's aspect. His jaw was square as a lantern, grayed black hair framed a face of indeterminate age and, Hart thought, full of suffering. His lips were no more than a slash of rigid thinness and his eyes were the kind a man doesn't forget easily. Black, haunted, ancient eyes.

Commanding muscles rippled in arm, shoulder, leg, so perfected by feats of strength and endurance that Hart could see each muscle group like a page from Gray's *Anatomy*. There was a slash of yellow paint on each high cheekbone and he was naked except for a breechcloth. Some mournful ritual had so engrossed his attentions that he neither heard nor saw the artist watching him. The Indian had come to this place to grieve or mourn, Hart guessed from his expression, and, having entered into some kind of ritual trance state, to communicate with his gods.

The watcher made his way, quiet as the grave, back to his horse; he slipped a sketch pad and charcoal from his saddlebag, and crept back to his vantage point on the ledge, to sketch the man, the place, the majesty of the moment, until dusk made further work impossible. Drawings clutched in his hand, he made his way back to the horse, but in the gathering dark he stumbled over a rock and nearly fell. It was a tiny sound, just enough to tell the Indian he was there, or perhaps the ritual had ended and the man's senses had become acute again. Hunting knife in hand, he was before Hart on the trail, in the time it took the white man to pull his rifle from its saddle scabbard.

There are suspended moments in a life when a small decision changes everything forever. Some instinct took hold of Hart; instead of cocking the Winchester, he dropped it on the ground beside him and stood, arms raised before the redskin's knife. The Apache hesitated, uncertain, and Hart quickly made the Indian hand-sign for peace that his Pa had showed him when he was a boy.

Hart saw the man's eyes, cold, deadly, wary, move in that instant of indecision, from him to the sketches on the ground; he wondered if the Apache, like the Sioux, thought their souls were captured when their likeness was drawn.

Eyes fixed on the sketches and on Hart, the Indian inched forward soundlessly. Heartened at not being dead yet, the white man tried to sign again, but the redskin cut his explanation with a vicious gesture that said "Enough!" Then, without another action, he was gone, melted into the trees and crevices as if he'd never been there. It took the hair on the nape of Hart's neck several minutes to lie back down in its accustomed place.

Hart stood very still for a long moment, knowing, unequivocally, the Apache could have killed him if he'd chosen to. He thought he probably outweighed the brave by damn near a hundred pounds and topped him by a foot, but when a man faces eyes like those he sees his doom.

He slept none too well the next few nights, not out of fear but because an excited anticipation tingled his blood. A week went by, as he rode farther and farther from the white man's world; he felt certain at times that he was watched by unseen eyes, but there seemed nothing to do but travel on.

Eight days after his first encounter with the Apache, their paths crossed again, almost as if God were pointing the two men at each other. Hart had camped near a water hole and was out on foot hunting dinner, when he heard the guttural snarl of a big cat in mortal combat. The solitary Apache was rolling and tumbling on the ground, doing his damnedest to slice his hunting knife into the gut of a mountain lion who seemed near as determined to have Indian for dinner. They seemed a fairly even match to Hart, until he spied the lion's mate scrambling down the rocks for a little reinforcement. He plugged the new arrival with a neat shot from his Colt, and the sharp report of the gun startled the wrestling lion just enough to give advantage to the Indian so he could slit its throat. Two deft strokes and the female cat pumped all her remaining blood onto the sand; the Apache pushed the big predator off, and leapt easily to his feet facing his benefactor. Once again, he and Hart stood man to man, one with a still-smoking gun, the other with a knife dripping cat-gore on the desert floor. Locked in the grip of each other's eyes, the two remained for a long, breathless moment.

"If I'd wanted to kill you," Hart said quietly, hoping the Indian could speak American, "I wouldn't have shot the cat." The redman grunted agreement; he turned and knelt beside the animal carcass and commenced to skin it. He signaled to Hart that the other cat was his, and it didn't seem polite to refuse, so he set about following the Apache's example.

Heartened by this small communication, Hart tried to tell the brave why he'd come to the Arizona Territory. Using sign and some pidgin Spanish mixed in with American, he told him he was an artist, come to paint the Apache.

The Indian looked at the white man with so potent a mixture of disgust and disdain that Hart stopped speaking, realizing too late how a man who struggles daily for barest subsistence views one who has such luxury to choose his pursuits.

Hart asked to be taken to the *ranchería,* as the Apache called their villages; the brave said no. It was apparent he understood all Hart said. Hart asked if he could direct him to a village that might be more cooperative. The brave said, "Go from here." Hart turned to leave, but on a hunch he pulled a sketch he'd made earlier from his pouch, and pressed it into the Indian's hand. The brave made as though he would cast it back, but instead his dark eyes swept Hart's searchingly, then he snatched the paper from his hand and once again left him standing quite alone.

▲

Hart had painted for hours on what must have been the shore of an ancient sea, long since turned to desert. The surface stain of manganese oxide or iron had tinged the rocks around him black, while before him stretched the colorful seabed covering a thousand square miles or more, ringed comfortingly by purple mountains.

Tiny seashell fragments, worn to wisps by a thousand years of winds they should never have felt at all, had left pearlized dust at his feet, while razor ridges guarded his left, and red butte sentinels, his right. The only movement to catch his eye all afternoon was a solitary lizard, who paused for protection beneath a saguaro cactus, then darted beneath a creosote bush to enjoy the shade.

Hart shifted position to catch the swift movements of the tiny lizard, and the scorpion struck. It had crept unnoticed beneath his trouser leg as he concentrated on his painting; a sting like the piercing of a hot knife stabbed him, and he leapt up stomping and jumping, until the ugly creature dropped to the ground and scurried off. "Damn!" he shouted to the empty desert; feeling foolish and vulnerable, he began to collect his gear. The queasiness began within a minute or two. Shocked by the swiftness of the poisoning, Hart found it was becoming difficult to focus. His leg blazed with a numbing pain and began to swell and blacken. Sweat dribbled down Hart's face, and barely able to drag his poisoned leg behind him, he turned toward camp, feeling sicker with every step.

There was a snakebite kit in his saddlebag, but in his confused state, he couldn't think what the remedy was for scorpion sting. His hand trembled so, he couldn't hold the small first aid book steady enough to read, and lights like crazed fireflies danced before his vision.

Hart shook with cold long before the sun went down; with grave difficulty he wrapped himself in a blanket, using his saddle as a pillow, and collapsing onto the ground, he tried to control the shaking of his spastic limbs. He recognized the circling buzzards as he quivered on the sand; how desperate they must be to sense incapacity so quickly, he thought through his daze.

He drifted in and out of delirium, with the predatory birds a constant in his mind. Terrifying visions, funny visions, absurd visions, materialized and faded. A searing thirst made him beg for water—he heard himself. In his fantasies, it seemed to him that someone brought it to him, but the damning thirst made him sure that was a lie.

He felt his body swell and diminish, felt roasted and frozen in turn, felt madness engulf him and death tug at his sleeve.

A soft, chanting sound like the voice of the wind drifted in and out with Hart, yet when he finally awakened, the chant still sounded near at hand.

The sick man focused, or tried to. The sound ceased. A figure bent above him, a skin bag of water in his hand. The old Apache warrior grunted satisfaction, it seemed, at Hart's being alive. He dribbled a small stream of the warm liquid toward the sick man's mouth and pulled the bag away when Hart sought to swallow too much. The impassive face revealed nothing; so, too weak to fear, Hart drifted off again into unconsciousness.

▲ ▲ ▲

Hart lay, frail as a newborn, in a wickiup at the Apache *rancheria.* He was never certain how Gokhlaya—for that was his savior's name—had managed to transport him there. Two hundred and seventy pounds and six feet six inches of dead weight is not an easy burden for a man five feet five. Perhaps even in his delirium Hart had been able to sit a horse, but he had no recollection of the journey.

The wickiup was a dome-shaped dwelling made from a framework of poles joined at the top, with an overcovering of bear grass, yucca leaves, rushes, and brush. On one side was a low doorway, a skin throw stretched over it for protection and privacy. Smoke from the central firepit was a constant annoyance to the fevered guest, but aside from this the wickiup was a sound and comfortable dwelling.

Gokhlaya and a woman tended Hart in his illness. At first the sick man assumed the girl to be the Apache's wife, but this was not the case; nor was the wickiup his home, but simply a place he had commandeered for Hart's convalescence.

The need to be able to move at a moment's notice made furniture an unnecessary luxury to the Apache. Beside the wooden bed frame that raised the brush and grass on which Hart lay a foot or two above the ground, he saw a pot, a skillet, a dishpan, and a vessel in which to boil meat, soup, and *tulapai;* a *tus,* or water jug, a few bowls, grinding slabs and stones for pounding.

The girl, whose name he came to know as Destarte, labored over nutritious meals to strengthen her patient. Hart sipped only soups and gravies at first, then a wheaten bread baked in corn husks under ashes on the floor was added, and a strange concoction called *suzor* made from the crushed bean pods of the costa tree, and a meal of honey-boiled corn with a fungus called smut.

Destarte spoke as she worked, or sang softly, as a woman does with a small baby who cannot understand but needs the comfort of a human voice. Hart thought she might have been picked to nurse him because she spoke some English as well as Mexican and Apache; he found that when his strength permitted, he could communicate with her fairly well.

The Apache language was intricate and tonal; Hart had become accustomed to its strangely mellifluous cadences while only semiconscious. There seemed to be many more vowels than in English; he counted more than fifty and they glided from one tone to another to make mastery difficult. There were twenty-five or thirty consonants and so many roots or stems that once he'd figured out the system, the formation of new words became easy. He found that a very complex thought could be conveyed by a single word, just as a single line in a drawing can express enormous complexity.

Destarte told him that mescal roots and heads were collected by the women in the spring and cooked for days at a time, in pits, to create a food much prized by the tribe. Berries, cactus fruit, yucca, and piñon nuts, she said, were plentiful in season, and were also staples of the People's diet. An acorn called cherchil rendered a coffeelike drink when it had been roasted, and meat boiled, broiled, or jerked appeared in turn . . . Hart listened to her low, lyrical voice when he was too weak to talk, and later he asked so many questions that she would laugh and tell him to be still and save his strength.

Destarte was tall by Apache standards, perhaps five feet seven or eight— she had a lithe, muscular body beneath the buckskin skirt and shirt she wore. Her glistening dark hair was waist length; pulled tight back from a face coppery in color as a newly minted penny. Her name, according to Gokhlaya, meant Morning Mist.

Hart had ample time to study the girl. His eyes followed her as she busied herself about the wickiup or knelt gracefully beside him, to spoon food or medicine into her patient. Daily she would unwrap his limbs respectfully to massage them, carrying out the duty artfully and with none of the embarrassment at his nakedness that a white woman would have shown.

He saw that Destarte's face was free of lines and its planes were wider and flatter than those of the women of his own race, yet they had not the Mongolian look of the Plains Indians, and he could not guess her age. Her cheekbones were high and prominent, her dark eyes, which sought out every nuance in his condition, were intelligent and alert; and despite the animation of her eyes, there was about her a kind of serenity that comforted him and brought him peace.

Each night, in a curious ritual, Gokhlaya would visit his guest in the wickiup; he would question Destarte about her patient's condition, and as Hart gained strength, the two men would converse. Like many Apaches, Gokhlaya could speak both Mexican and American, as well as his own tongue.

"Why didn't you kill me?" Hart asked when he was finally able.

"It is no sin to kill enemies or to rob them," Gokhlaya replied with equanimity. "But if one man accepts a favor from a stranger, that stranger becomes related to the tribe, and the man must recognize his duty and let the stranger share his comforts." Hart looked puzzled.

"You killed the mountain lion," Gokhlaya responded. "You gave me the paper of enchantment." Hart realized he spoke of the portrait. "The obligation was clear." The Indian said this solemnly and left no room for further questioning.

It took more than a month for Hart to recover his strength; when he finally ventured from the wickiup for exercise, he could see that he was watched with wariness and hostility by the other braves. It was apparent Gokhlaya was held in respect, and only his sanction protected the white visitor.

Destarte told her patient that Gokhlaya was known among the People as a highly respected loner; he thought perhaps that was why both encounters in the desert had been solitary ones. Yet, with Hart, Gokhlaya was curiously forthcoming. The white man thought long and hard about that; was it that he, a stranger, and a helpless one, posed no threat to Gokhlaya, so the Apache could confide with impunity? Was it that the loneliness of the Apache's hard life had finally caught up with him and he, at last, needed a friend? Was it that like all leaders, he dared not choose a confidant from the ranks of those he led? Or was it some other bond linking the two men in the spirit world, of the sort that binds friends through different lifetimes? Destarte told Hart the Apaches believe kindred souls find each other in successive lives, just as the souls of enemies remain bound, until the debt is paid.

Whatever the genesis of the connection, Gokhlaya would arrive each night, and the two men would speak of their separate worlds, until the coals of the fire burned to embers. "I need to understand the thinking of the white-eyes," Gokhlaya said in explanation.

"And I wish to learn the way of the Apache," Hart told him in return. "I mean to record your way of life so that my people will better understand." Gokhlaya accepted this solemnly, for the tribe was worthy of respect.

Hart thought the Apache's speech quaint and slightly archaic, but powerful in its simplicity, and he loved to listen, often sketching Gokhlaya as the old man sat and unfolded the story of his life. Gokhlaya called Hart

"Firehair," and seemed not only willing to share knowledge with him, but eager to learn from him in return.

"I was born in No-doyohn Canyon, Arizona, the first moon of summer in the year the white-eyes call 1829," Gokhlaya said in the singsong rhythm of Indian oral history. Apaches tell their stories, if they choose to, at their own pace and in their own way, Hart found. The answer to a question might come to you far from the beginning of the tale, but in the telling, you could learn much beyond what you'd asked for.

"In that country which lies around the headwater of the Gila River I was reared. This range was our fatherland; among these mountains our tipis were hidden. The scattered valleys contained our fields; the boundless prairies, stretching away on every side, were our pastures; the rocky caverns were our burying places.

"I was fourth in a family of eight children—four boys and four girls. Four is a magic number to my Bedonkohe tribe and it has brought me to a special destiny.

"As a babe I rolled on the dirt floor of my father's tipi, hung in my *tsoch* at my mother's back, or suspended from the bough of a tree. I was warmed by the sun, rocked by the winds, and sheltered by the trees.

"When a child, my mother taught me the legends of our people; taught me of the sun and the sky, the moon and stars, the clouds and storms. She also taught me to kneel and pray to Usen for strength, health, wisdom, and protection. It was forbidden to pray against any person, but if we had aught against any individual we could take vengeance. Usen does not care for the petty quarrels of men." Gokhlaya spoke the Great Spirit's name with immeasurable reverence.

"My father taught me the Way of the People, and often told me of the brave deeds of our warriors, of the pleasures of the chase, and the glories of the warpath.

"With my brothers and sisters I played at hide-and-seek among the rocks and pines; sometimes we loitered in the shade of the cottonwood trees or sought the shucock, a kind of wild cherry, while our parents worked in the field.

"When we were old enough, we went to the field with our parents, not to play but to toil. When the crops were to be planted, we broke the ground with wooden hoes. We planted the corn in straight rows, the beans among the corn, and the melons and pumpkins in irregular order over the field. We cultivated these crops as there was need."

"Your childhood and mine were much the same," Hart told him with a chuckle. "My father, too, was a farmer who loved the land and respected its bounty."

"If only men could see our sameness," Gokhlaya replied, "not our differences, life would be good."

"How did you know what medicine to use to cure me of my sickness?" Hart asked, and Gokhlaya smiled a little on answering.

"The People know what herbs to use for medicine," he said. "We know how to prepare and how to give the medicine. This we were taught by Usen in the beginning; each generation has men who are skilled in healing. We know how to gather the herbs, prepare them, and administer the medicine. We know the prayers to say that make the medicine work. Usually about eight work together in making medicine, so the forms of incantations can be done well. Four attend to the incantations and four to the preparation of the herbs. But if one of the People is alone, he can do all this himself." It was easy to see the man was proud of this skill at healing, so Hart prompted him to elaborate.

"Some of us are adept in cutting out bullets, and arrowheads, with which warriors are wounded in battle. I myself have done much of this." He thought for a moment, as if to make sure he'd left nothing out, then said, "When disease and pestilence come to us, we are assembled and questioned by our leaders to find what we have done wrong, and how Usen can be satisfied. Sometimes sacrifice is necessary. Sometimes the offending one must be punished."

"What kinds of offenses might merit punishment?" Hart asked, making mental note of how he could portray this elaborate pageant on huge canvases.

"If an Apache allowed his aged parents to suffer for lack of food or shelter," Gokhlaya answered. "If he neglected or abused the sick, if he profaned our religion, or had been unfaithful, he might be banished from the tribe.

"The People have no prisons as you white men have. Instead, we send our criminals out from the tribe. Among us there is no worse punishment but death. Faithless, cruel, lazy, or cowardly members of the tribe are excluded in such a way that they cannot join any other tribe. Neither can they have any protection from our unwritten tribal laws. Sometimes these outlaw Indians band together and commit crimes that are charged against the regular tribe, but the life of any outlaw Indian is a hard one, and their bands are never very large. Besides, these bands frequently provoke the wrath of the tribe and secure their own destruction. . . ." He nodded, as if to corroborate his own statement.

"What was your own family like?" Hart prompted him, warmed by the affection with which the man reminisced.

"When I was but a small boy," Gokhlaya remembered, "my father died. He had been sick a long time. When he passed away, carefully the watchers closed his eyes, then arrayed him in his best clothes. They painted his face, wrapped a rich blanket around him, saddled his favorite horse, bore his arms in front of him, and led his horse behind. In wailing tones they repeated his deeds of valor, as they carried his body to a cave in the mountain. Then they slew his horse, and we gave away or burned all his other property, as was customary in our tribe—after which his body was deposited in the cave, his arms beside him. His grave is hidden by piles of stones. Wrapped in splendor, my father lies in seclusion, and the winds in the pines sing his requiem, for he was a great warrior." Gokhlaya paused in respect, much moved by the memory.

"Why was the horse slain and the property dispersed?" Hart asked, surprised.

"It is a tribal law most sacred. The People will not keep any property from a deceased relative. Our tribal law forbids it. Otherwise the children of one who had much property might be glad when their father dies. This would be very bad." Gokhlaya frowned for emphasis, his mouth, no more than a sliver at best, became a slash of righteousness.

"After my father's death the care of my mother came to me. She did not remarry, although according to the customs of our tribe she might have done so immediately after his death. Usually, the widow who has children remains single after her husband's death for two or three years; but the widow without children marries again immediately. After a warrior's death, his widow returns to her people and may be given away or sold by her father or brothers. My mother chose to live with me, and she never desired to marry again. . . ." He paused before continuing, and Hart felt the need to prompt him again. The Apaches were more comfortable with silences than were white men.

"Did you yourself marry?" Hart asked.

For a moment, so intense a pain suffused Gokhlaya's face that Hart regretted his question and wondered if he had transgressed some unwritten law, but after a while the Apache spoke again.

"Perhaps the greatest joy to me of my life was that after being admitted to the council of warriors I could marry the fair Alope, daughter of No-poso." Gokhlaya smiled a little, a strange, sad smile. "She was a slender, delicate girl—we had been lovers for a long time." The utter unselfconsciousness of this reply made Hart wonder if the sexual customs of this tribe might be very different from his own.

"As soon as the council granted me the privilege to marry, I went to see her father. Perhaps our love was of no interest to him; perhaps he wanted to keep Alope with him, for she was a dutiful daughter. At any rate, he asked many ponies for her, more than any man had ever been asked before. I made no reply, but in a few days appeared before his tipi with a whole herd of ponies and took with me Alope. This was all the marriage ceremony necessary in our tribe.

"Not far from my mother's tipi I made a new home. The tipi was made of buffalo hides and in it were bear robes, mountain lion hides, and other trophies of the chase, as well as my spears, bows, and arrows. Alope had many little decorations of beads and drawn work on buckskin, which she placed in our tipi. She also drew fine pictures on the walls. She was a good wife, but she was never strong.

"We followed the traditions of our fathers and were happy. Three children came to us. . . ." Gokhlaya paused at that moment and sorrow was clearly visible behind his eyes.

"We will speak more another time," he said, his voice low and husky. Abruptly, he rose and left the wickiup. Hart hobbled to the doorway and saw the Apache standing on a little rise, just outside the ring of light from the campfire. His arms were crossed in front of him, his sturdy legs were set apart, as if to withstand the force of a hurricane. His head was raised to the night sky, like that of a wolf, howling up the moon, his silhouette so still against the moon's light, he might have been a statue.

Later, after Hart had left Apacheria for the final time, he would paint Gokhlaya as he was that night, standing with all the majesty and power of a burden manly borne. Hart thought it a fine painting because it carried within it the spirit strength of a great warrior, and he was grieved when he heard that his work had been destroyed by vandals. But that was when the hatred for Indians had been stirred by the ruthless to fever pitch—and by then it was no longer simply a painting of his friend and brother Gokhlaya. For this warrior was known in the white man's world by a different name from his tribal one—long years before, the Mexicans had christened him in the heat of battle with the name he would bear through history. Geronimo.

 80 Jason Madigan had the means of staying in Leadville and Denver whenever he chose to do so, but he saw no need to outstay his welcome. Strings could be pulled from New York as well as anywhere, and plans could be set in motion when the time was right. Now that Chance had accepted his friendship and Fancy, however warily, had too, there was no need for undue haste; men like McAllister generally dug their own graves if you gave them time enough and a shovel. Meanwhile, Jason's private railroad car could transport him to his interests in Colorado whenever he wished, the telegraph

kept information at his fingertips, and his underlings did as they were told no matter which state the orders came from.

He enjoyed the time he spent in Colorado; it made him remember how much he liked the West—the entrepreneurial spirit, the hard men and the opportunities. He'd made his money in places like Leadville because he understood its mentality so viscerally; this was a world for the tough and the daring, it fit his personality like an Hermès glove.

Jason bought a house for entertaining in Denver, and built a hunting lodge outside Leadville. As long as the silver held out and Fancy continued to interest him, it made sense to provide comfortable arrangements in the area.

He'd failed to do away with his rival for Fancy's affections with his mine escapade, but he'd accomplished something better in the long run, for he'd become both a local hero and Chance's confidant. Madigan was a subtle man for all his bull-like exterior; had Chance died as he'd originally planned it, he would have taken on the status of martyr for Fancy, and it would have been nearly impossible to fight such a mythic rival's memory. As it was, Chance remained a man—one with flaws to exploit. If Jason played the game shrewdly, he could do far worse than kill Chance; he could discredit and bankrupt him, and no woman with Fancy's verve and intelligence would wish to be married to a bankrupt fool.

▲

"I've advised McAllister to put his money into certain places that might interest you," Madigan told Henderson as the two sat in Jason's library.

"You haven't made yourself an 'official partner' in any of his enterprises?" asked Henderson casually. He was a portly man, a fact he thought essential to his profession; never trust a hungry banker, he would say whenever his corpulence became a topic—weight, wealth, and power seemed to bed so comfortably together.

"Certainly not. I've made myself an advisor of sorts to McAllister . . . and a friend, of course."

"What exactly do you have in mind that might be of interest to me, Jason?"

"Nothing whatsoever, at the moment, John, as it happens. I simply want you to know I'm keeping a weather eye on things here in Leadville and Denver. McAllister has damnably good luck and he's amassing a great fortune without knowing a thing about handling it."

"So, you're helping him."

"I'm advising him."

"You wouldn't be receiving any sort of compensation for this advisory status . . . say, a commission from a bank, would you?"

Jason rolled the stem of the small glass around in his fingers for a moment before replying, and waited for the bait to be taken. "That is none of your affair," he said finally, holding Henderson's eyes with his own.

"It could be, if you were willing to steer his holdings toward my Fiduciary Bank. I would think it only proper for a man who brought in such an investor to be compensated for doing so."

Jason appeared to think this through. "Money wouldn't move me in that direction, John. But I would take it as a sensible gesture on the part of any bank I steered McAllister to, if they were to keep me abreast of certain matters, generally held confidential."

Henderson nodded; it was comforting to know he'd read the man right. "Considering your advisory capacity to Mr. McAllister, I'd say such action would be no more than expected."

Each man smiled just a trifle, content in the sure knowledge that, henceforward, both would profit from Chance's good or bad fortune. John Henderson accepted the glass Jason offered him. They had more to talk about than Chance McAllister, now that Madigan's Flume and Smelting Works was growing to be one of the biggest businesses in Leadville, to say nothing of his railroad interests, his timber rights, and his impeccable banking connections with New York and Chicago. Jason felt more than content with the way the discussion had proceeded with Henderson.

Madigan had taken the time and trouble to assess the situation between Chance and Fancy, and had come to certain conclusions. It was easy enough to understand the attraction between the two—they were much alike, too much for lasting comfort. McAllister was actually rather an interesting fellow, handsome as a matinee idol but manly for all of that—the sort who appealed to women and men alike. He was an extraordinarily gifted gambler and Jason was no slouch himself in that quarter, so his admiration was genuine. However, it was apparent that unlike himself, Chance did not know when to quit. If he won a thousand, he bet two, and he was always seduced by the flamboyant gesture; Chance had astonishing luck and he trusted it implicitly. His oratorical skills were exemplary, his memory phenomenal, and his charm undeniable, all in all, a quite formidable array of assets.

It had taken Jason a good deal of concentrated effort to understand fully the weaknesses in the man, enough to use them judiciously. His hamartias, as the Greeks would say, the fatal flaws. Madigan catalogued them once again in his mind: Chance McAllister was not ruthless by nature, a major handicap in business . . . it wasn't only luck he trusted, he trusted other men . . . he would risk everything on one flamboyant throw of the dice . . . he had a roving eye and hearty appetites . . . he did not know how to spurn a woman's advances in front of other men, without losing face . . .

he was prone to profligacy . . . he let hirelings and advisors run his businesses. Most dangerous of all, and most useful to Jason, he didn't fully understand his wife's complex nature. He had no real idea, in fact, of what an ally she could have been, so he treated her as other men treated other wives—a foolhardy error that could only cause eventual disaster.

Jason would bide his time and wait until Chance's own self-destructive tendencies played into his plans. Not forever, of course—he'd grease the skids a bit before long, but he would do so carefully, for Fancy must never suspect he bore her husband anything other than goodwill.

▲

It had taken time after the strike and the cave-in for Chance to reestablish his connections with the power brokers, but his heroics during the disaster had made him so popular with the local citizenry the pols couldn't afford to ignore him permanently. He was also a friend of Jason Madigan's, whose power seemed to reach into nearly every corner of the mining industry, so within a matter of months after Chance's recovery, all had returned to normal.

Besides, there was a staggering amount for the legislature to cope with in the burgeoning state, and Chance's popularity was a useful tool, so the party saw that his political career took an upward turn again. A new street railway was being constructed, fire companies had to be fielded and equipped, the growing number of freight companies had to be regulated, as did the constant battles among warring railroads. A water system and reservoirs were being constructed, even a light-and-power company was bringing electricity to Denver and to Leadville.

Beyond all this local fervor, there was the growing power of the Silver Alliance, which necessitated frequent trips around the state, to other silver mining territories, and to Washington. About the only area of business Chance McAllister didn't find much time for was the running of the Fancy Penny and the Last Chance. Fortunately, Jason had offered discreet suggestions to Chance on how to direct the financial empire being generated by the mine revenues, and Caz was on site to oversee day-to-day operations.

It was a great pity that Caz disliked Madigan so instinctively—the two men seemed to come to blows on nearly every major question, but at least, thanks to both their efforts, the money kept pouring out of the ground. Jason lived in New York and visited only occasionally, so Caz eventually decided that although the man's input was pernicious, it wasn't ever-present —and more important, there wasn't a damned thing he could do about it.

Besides, no matter how his profligate nature seemed to bode ill for success, Chance was winning at every throw of the dice. Ever since he and Fancy had gotten back together, Chance's good fortune had been phenomenal. It was damned hard to convince a man he was doing things wrong, when they always turned out right.

Caz would have welcomed an opportunity to talk with Hart or Bandana; he missed them sorely. He missed Chance, too, for he was accessible now only to powerful men, not to merely good ones, and Chance had been his friend, a long, long time ago.

 81

Chance, high-spirited as a young stallion, hurried Fancy with her dressing. The morning was clear, warm, and promising in Denver, where he'd brought her to stay at the elegant Windsor Hotel—the surprise he'd planned for her would make up for his mistakes of the past. They'd mended the tatters of their marriage after the mine disaster, and he'd realized, perhaps for the first time, how inextricably entwined her happiness was with his own. Nothing would ever go wrong between them again because he wouldn't let it. All Fancy'd ever really wanted was security, and this incredibly substantial surprise would give her all the security any woman could desire.

Titillated by her husband's exuberance, Fancy dressed in her newest Paris suit, fawn-colored silk with mahogany passementerie; it made her look healthy and bursting with life. She'd been so worn after nursing the boys that she knew it pleased Chance to see her hale again. The relief of knowing their love was safe again had put the color back in her cheeks; Chance was hers and the world had changed once more for the better.

Fancy tied a jaunty new bonnet under her chin, surveyed her reflection with satisfaction, and left the hotel, anticipating a splendid day.

Denver was such an exciting city, dazzling with the trappings of high society. What fun it was to leave the children and Leadville behind for a romantic rendezvous in such a showy town. Fancy ticked off the shops she intended to buy from; Joslin's, and Daniels & Fisher were first on the list. She was reborn and headlong in love.

"Tell me where we're going," she prompted excitedly, as the carriage horses pranced through the bustling thoroughfares, but Chance was brimming over with anecdotes from the political dinner he'd attended the night before, and only smiled in that teasing way he had.

The carriage stopped on Lincoln Street in front of an immense stone mansion. Standing beyond imposing gates, it was of white limestone, built in a formidable combination of Romanesque, Renaissance, and Gothic architecture; it looked as if it might endure for a thousand years.

"Chance!" Fancy pouted. "You didn't say we were going visiting. You *promised* we were going to spend the day alone together." The pouty disappointment in her voice flattered her husband. Chance tapped on the panel separating them from the driver, and Fancy, bewildered, let him lift her to the ground. The great wrought-iron gates loomed above her; beyond the gates, a flight of granite steps led to a piazza-size landing, then another longer flight extended to the entrance of the house, where an ornate crested portico was held aloft by twenty-foot white marble pillars.

"It's your present, sugar," he said, grinning, as he unlocked the gate. "So you'll never have to worry about being poor again."

Seldom at a loss for words, Fancy realized that her mouth was open but no sound had escaped it. She lifted her skirts with both hands and ran up the first flight of steps without looking back. Chance bounded up the steps to her side; unexpectedly, he scooped her into his arms and pressed her close, laughing with the pleasure of her delight. "I love you, Fancy. Nothing will ever come between us again." Then he carried her up the last few steps and into the house as if she were a bride.

Immense oval-topped windows flooded light into the entrance hall; carvings, gildings, and inlays covered the ceiling, except for an area on which clouds and firmament had been painted. Stained-glass panels atop each window spilt colors onto the polished pink marble of the foyer floor.

Fancy turned, at a loss for adequate words, and took her husband's hand in her own; like two children let loose in the most beautiful playground in the world, they walked from room to room. Sunlight bathed the pearl-gray drawing room in silvered shimmers . . . thousands of leather-bound volumes with gilded titles lined the shelves of the two-story library . . . the dining room could seat fifty comfortably . . . the oval ballroom would cast the light from its glittering chandeliers on two hundred privileged guests. The nursery was equipped to accommodate an army of children; the servants' quarters, which branched out from nursery and schoolroom, could easily domicile the huge staff needed to maintain such a dwelling.

Four parlor- and chambermaids would be required, Fancy calculated absently as she moved among the rooms. A French laundress, a linen woman for washing and ironing the towels, tablecloths, and sheets; a girl for packing and unpacking the luggage of guests and family . . . How extraordinary that she remembered how such a gracious household should be run! Six girls for scrubbing and polishing, under the guidance of a butler, preferably English. He would also oversee the four footmen and the men who would handle heavy chores. A coachman, four grooms, and stablemen would be needed. As would a chef, sous-chef, and scullions. Each family member would require a valet or personal maid; the children would need nursery staff. Fancy must have a secretary; Aurora and Blackjack would each have to have tutors and governesses . . . She felt breathless with the thrill of overwhelming abundance . . . surely even her bottomless need could be satiated by such a dwelling.

"Show me our bedroom, darling," she whispered, and they ascended the marble staircase to the bedroom floor, hand in hand. Chance smiled knowingly as he turned the scrolled golden knob and pushed back the double doors, for he'd imagined Fancy's face on seeing its splendor, from the moment he'd been shown the house. A massive four-poster stood with a puddle of sunlight spilling over it; two huge armoires, left behind by the previous owners, loomed like immense sentinels on either side of the room, but the custom-made bed, bigger than any Fancy had ever imagined, dominated the room.

She climbed the two mahogany steps to the mattress and bounced like a playful child on the resilient softness, until the expression of sheer joy on her face made Chance laugh aloud. She reached out to him and he moved to the bedside to pull her close enough to embrace.

Fancy buried her head in her husband's chest, then looked up into his face. "Make love to me, Chance. Right this minute, in this incredible bed." He chuckled softly and shook his head; it wasn't merely her joy that was seductive . . . he tugged off his coat, unbuttoned vest, shirt, and trousers, never taking his eyes from his wife's.

Fancy undid her own jacket, feeling like she owned the world. Her heart pounded madly in her chest, it might have been their first seduction.

Chance traced the flesh of her throat as he touched his lips to hers; he saw the flesh of her bare breasts respond and tighten; a smile turned up the corners of his mouth just a little, as he moved the sheer fabric aside and bent his mouth to taste them. She arched herself, stretching like a lazy cat, sucking in the exquisite feelings with every nerve ending. She kissed his face and neck, nibbled at his ear, heard him laugh with pleasure at her responsiveness. She leaned far back on the bed, expecting him to cover her body with his own, but instead his hands went around her waist, unexpectedly, and she felt herself lifted skillfully. Chance raised her body up to impale it on his risen flesh and Fancy gasped with surprise. She buried her hands in her husband's hair and pulled his mouth to her own lustily. She was his, and he was hers. They had never quarreled, injured, misunderstood each other—for they were one in this primal urgent place that they alone could find together. Never had man and woman known each other as their bodies knew . . . restive, restless, insatiable bodies, too wild for others, too irreverent and irrepressible. Her limbs entwined him, her loins extracted exquisite payment for their desires, her mind reeled and her senses with it, as she tightened herself about him, daring him to pull free as they tumbled to the bed together. This was their connection—their endless exquisite, damning

440 PAINT THE WIND

connection. Flesh to flesh, spirit to spirit, they soared and slipped and bucked and burst together into a place no one else could ever go.

"I love our house," she whispered when the final fleeting explosion of ecstasy was done.

"I love my wife," he whispered back.

Even considering the size of the mansion, the coachman waiting down below thought three hours was a very long time to take in exploration.

▲

Fancy threw herself into the business of being rich and happy again like a death-row prisoner on unexpected reprieve. She finally had a house to rival Beau Rivage and her husband was the talk of Colorado. Wherever Chance McAllister walked, eyes followed, and not just women's eyes, although there were plenty of those to contend with. Men's eyes, too, for Chance was that most envied of humans, a bona fide winner.

When he played, he won. Whether the game was business or poker, if the stakes were high, the odds were Chance was in the game and Chance was winning.

Fancy had no idea what her husband owned; although she'd tried diligently enough over the years to keep track, Chance steadfastly kept her ignorant. And now that they lived in Denver, there really wasn't time to worry about where the endless stream of money came from, as long as it kept on coming.

She had forgotten, or perhaps never really known, the price in obligations that must be paid for great wealth. She sometimes wondered if the life was changing her, as she saw it changing Chance.

Fancy suffered the endless chatter of the dressmaker and the endless pinning of her hems. The condition of a wife's wardrobe said a great deal about the state of her husband's material success, so she was on constant call for fittings and fabric selection, now Chance was in the state legislature and on every committee in Christendom. I remember when I longed so for clothes like these, I would have sold my soul to get them, she chided herself. Now I'd rather just have the time I spend standing around being pinned!

The rarefied stratum of society they inhabited in Denver and Leadville made perfection of wardrobe essential, which in turn necessitated trips to Worth in Paris, where the fashion dictator would show his collection by gaslight, on mannequins dressed only in black. It also made necessary the finding of a local dressmaker whose name was kept as secret as your age . . . and the constant parade of hatters and shoemakers and furriers who were currently wearing Fancy's patience thin.

There was the custom of making calls to be coped with, too, and that was bound in more protocol than a papal visit. Fancy ticked off the foolish rules in her mind as she waited for the dressmaker to finish whatever damn fool thing she was doing. Newly established Denverites had to wait to be called upon by the old guard, and sometimes reams of letters of introduction had to be written before you passed this first hurdle. Then you had a week in which to return the call, by appearing at the door or having your coachmen do so. If the maid said Madame would receive you, you went to the parlor, being sure to keep on your hat, veil, and gloves—a gentleman, on the other hand, left his coat with the servant but carried in his hat, cane, and gloves and then left them on floor or windowsill (never on furniture) and God help anyone who transgressed one of these absurd regulations!

On arriving in the parlor, your hostess had the option of not introducing you to any of her other guests, as they might not wish to know you. Fancy bridled at remembrance of one such humiliating moment when she'd first moved to Denver. "Fancy McAllister?" fat Mrs. Cudahy had said, looking as if she smelled week-old fish. "The dance hall girl?" How could so much derision get squeezed into three small words? "The wife of the legislator who's turning this backwater into a state!" Fancy'd responded, matching the woman's arrogance to perfection. "A former mine worker, I believe," the matron pursued. "And current millionaire," Fancy'd snapped, before she showed the old biddy a clean pair of heels.

There were still those who, despite her unconscionable wealth, referred to her derogatorily as "that actress." At least that was better than the ones who called her "that piece of baggage who had herself auctioned off in Leadville." *That* choice morsel of history refused to stay buried. A man could sleep with jackrabbits and be forgiven if he struck it rich, but a woman's past was another matter entirely.

If you arrived on other than your hostess' "at home" day, you left your card and turned down its right-hand corner, Fancy wasn't sure just why; if you were leaving town for a time, you could write *ppc (pour prendre congé)* on the bottom corner of the card. "The Elite meeting the Elect," Chance called it. At Beau Rivage one went out of one's way to be gracious to guests and to let them bask in hospitality—all this pretentious Denver protocol was just silly, time-consuming nouveau riche nonsense. *I am Fancy Deverell of Beau Rivage and I am not a beggar!*

"That's enough for today, Eleanor," Fancy said, suddenly stifled by obligation—by wifehood and motherhood and charityhood and upstanding citizenhood. She stood on the stoop outside the dressmaker's house and hungrily breathed in the crisp mountain air around her. She thought of Bandana and Jewel and their irreverence toward all sacred cows. God, how I miss being free, she thought, finally focusing on what really troubled her. I hate being nice to all those old biddies, the matrons of "The Sacred Thirty-Six" without whose sanction you were "nobody." Sacred, my eye, she thought, why it's all just mining money and intermarriage with the rich of other cities or with penniless European royalty that's put them where they are. Their money's no better or worse than mine.

No matter. She didn't care a stick about any of them. Not one of the thirty-six had the wit or wisdom of a Magda or Wes or Gitalis. At least living in Denver made her circus friends more accessible.

That's just what I need today, Fancy thought suddenly, her boredom and annoyance evaporating. I need to see *real* people. Relieved at the prospect of escaping from propriety for the afternoon, she had her coachman head toward the other end of town in search of the freedom of old, wise friends.

▲

"Uncle Jason! Uncle Jason!" Aurora shouted excitedly from the carriage window.

Jason Madigan looked up sharply from the conversation he was holding with John Arkin of the *Chronicle,* and saw the beautiful child alight from the carriage and run toward him on the dusty street as her nanny looked on disapprovingly. Her dark curls bounced and her cheeks were flushed with eager color. What an exquisite little beauty she had become.

Almost without knowing he intended to do so, Jason opened his arms to the girl and she ran into his embrace. He felt oddly flattered by her exuberance, as if he'd been singled out for some special award.

"Oh, Uncle Jason," she breathed, hugging him close. "You have absolutely *no* idea how much I've missed you! Mama told me you were here and I've been watching for you everywhere. I just knew I'd find you."

"Why that's very flattering, Aurora . . . and I must say I've missed you, too. Now that we are reacquainted, my dear, you must tell me all about yourself. Whatever has been going on in your life since last we saw each other?"

Aurora frowned. "My mother married Chance McAllister and started having babies," she said. "I barely ever see her . . . not that I care all that much."

Jason heard the crankiness in the girl's voice and wondered what had provoked it; the child had worshiped her mother, all those years ago.

"You must tell me what you *do* care about, Aurora," he prompted gently. "Now that we've found each other again, I'd like to give you a little present for old times' sake, so you must tell me what gives you pleasure."

Aurora considered the question for a long moment. "Could you come to visit me sometimes, Uncle Jason? Remember that horse you bought for me when I was little? . . . I still love to ride. Maybe you and I could ride together, like we used to."

So she still remembers me with love, he thought, warmed by the knowledge. Obviously McAllister had not captured Aurora's heart, as he had her mother's.

Jason patted the youngster's arm proprietarily. "I visit here frequently these days, my dear," he said. "I'd be honored if you would occasionally give me the pleasure of your company when I'm in town. I'll ask your mother's permission, of course, but I expect she'll grant it."

He walked her back to her carriage, as gallantly as if she were a great lady. "I shall call upon you within the week, Aurora," he promised as he bade her good-bye.

The carriage began to pull away, but Aurora stuck her head out the window impetuously.

"I've always loved you, Uncle Jason!" she blurted, then retreated into the recesses of the coach before he was obliged to reply.

Touched and thoughtful, Jason stood on the street corner for several minutes before returning to his conversation.

 82

In the year when Hart arrived in Apacheria, Gokhlaya and General Crook were playing hide-and-seek in the Sierra Madre. The Chiracahua band that the white man became part of was already thinned by warfare and wearied from the long fight with the endless stream of white soldiers and settlers who had disrupted the Apache's once orderly existence.

Despite the horror stories he'd always heard about the bloodthirsty Apaches who needlessly attacked white settlers, Hart found the reverse was closer to the truth. The discovery of gold and silver in the Southwest in the 1860s had brought a flood of prospectors into the Arizona and New Mexico Territories, which were the traditional hunting grounds and the sacred places of the Apache. The People, who knew no reason to be otherwise, were at first accepting of the white man; they believed the land to be large and bountiful enough for all to take from it what they needed, and the concept of land ownership was alien to them, as all land belonged to Usen, for the good of all men.

At first the sporadic wagon trains were merely treated with curiosity or disdain by the Apache, but as it became apparent that this endless stream of interlopers had no intention of sharing, only of taking, the People began to strike back. As hostility surfaced, and as the numbers of whites increased drastically under the protection of the army, the Apaches retaliated; ranches were pillaged, wagon trains attacked, stages were waylaid and destroyed.

Because atrocities against the Indians were considered acceptable and necessary, while similar atrocities against the white man made front-page news, soon the Apaches, who were native to this pilfered land, were treated as animals to be hunted and destroyed by any means possible. Newspapers carried items advising travelers on how to kill Indians efficiently: a mixture of brown sugar, crackers, and strychnine was one of the popular methods touted, and scalp bounties ranged from twenty-five dollars for a child's to fifty dollars for a squaw's and a hundred dollars for a warrior's, so it was no wonder that the braves of Gokhlaya's Chiracahua band looked with considerable disfavor on the warrior's white guest.

▲

Hart was definitely strong enough to walk unaided now, he thought with satisfaction as he hunkered down to crawl outside the wickiup.

Gokhlaya had introduced him to the men of the tribe; he could see they were wary and begrudging of the protection he'd been afforded, but a tightly structured environment existed in camp, rules were to be followed, taboos observed. Due to Gokhlaya's protection he was, for the moment, safe. Hart sensed he was being ridiculed, sized up, but he was not yet fluent in the Apache language, so he was spared the worst of it.

He watched the bustle in the camp and noted that most physical labor of Apache life fell to the women. They carried the heavy water *tus* and immense loads of firewood; he already knew they performed all the duties of breaking camp and moving it, for they'd done so twice since his arrival. The care of children, cooking, cleaning, making clothing and ceremonial garments was also theirs.

The men, it seemed to him, did far less. They hunted, of course, and depending upon the terrain and the season, that could be an all-consuming effort. But Hart knew from Gokhlaya that their primary function was that of warrior, so when there was no war, the Apache men spent their time in gambling or in games of skill and strength.

Gokhlaya, standing in a circle of men, noticed Hart's progress from the wickiup, and joined him as he watched a group of boys involved in an unfamiliar game.

"They are training to be warriors," Gokhlaya explained as he drew abreast. "Many restrictions are required of these novices—to become warriors they must pass numerous tests and ordeals."

So the games are not games at all, Hart thought, but training camps. "What kind of restrictions?" he asked aloud.

"A boy in training must not scratch his head except with a scratching stick, he must drink water only through a special tube. He must not be untruthful, or a coward. He must not eat or drink too much, nor have sexual intercourse more than the ordinary amount, or these things would become his nature.

"When he is on a raid, he must use the special war language and must never eat warm food."

Hart nodded, wonderingly, and thought of what fine drawings these activities would provide. "What weapons do they learn?" he asked.

"They are trained in the skillful use of bows and arrows, war clubs, knives, lances, shields, rocks, and slings. Finally, they learn of guns. They learn most of all to perfect the weapon of their own bodies, for that is the one which makes the true difference in battle. An Apache warrior is trained to run one hundred miles with one mouthful of water to sustain him. He carries the water on his tongue for the first fifty miles and then swallows it to give strength for the second fifty miles."

Hart shook his head in amused astonishment; it was little wonder the government had so much trouble subduing this tribe. What a contest of men it might have been if both sides were possessed of equal numbers and weaponry.

▲

Gokhlaya's stories of Apache training inspired Hart to set himself a daily exercise routine as soon as his body could sustain it. Each morning he would walk or run, stretch his unused muscles, and attempt to regain his strength and agility. The warriors watched his solitary efforts and joked among themselves, but Hart paid them no mind.

One morning as he emerged from his wickiup, a warrior called Blue Shirt, because of a favorite garment, beckoned the white man to join in the games that were already in progress. Hart would have thought it a comradely gesture had it come from another source; but this brave had watched him with hostility through the past weeks and it appeared, from the expression of contained humor on the faces of the other men, that he meant Hart no good.

Blue Shirt handed the white man a feather-trimmed lance and indicated with signs that Hart was to aim for the very distant target he had set up. The Kansan had no skill with the unaccustomed weapon, and Blue Shirt's smile made it clear this was a test of manhood. At a considerable disadvantage, Hart picked up the long lance warily. It was carved from the dead stalk of sotol, which had been fire-straightened and hardened, and he knew from Gokhlaya that war leaders often used lances like this one to prove their courage. He hefted the weapon and threw it far and straight, but as he had no experience of the lance's idiosyncrasies in flight, it fell short of the mark. All around him tittered, as Blue Shirt took two lances from the hand of a nearby brave and threw them in such swift and fluid movements that the first one hit the target's center precisely and the second struck so close it seemed to share the same entry point.

"Perhaps the white-eyes should hunt with the small girls," Blue Shirt declared, to the merriment of all near enough to hear the exchange. Hart noticed that the women had now gathered alongside their men, and were clapping their hands in glee. He could sense an odd exhilaration in the group and knew that if he did not redeem his manhood in some way, the disgrace would linger.

Glancing up, he saw Gokhlaya at the rear of the group frowning ominously. The Apache offered no advice or encouragement, but something in his stance told Hart that Gokhlaya's honor, too, could be forfeit by his failure; he signaled the People to wait and hastily returned to the wickiup. When he rejoined them he carried his sketch pad and charcoal.

Hart laid the art supplies on the ground and tugged his shirt off over his head; despite his recent illness, his physique was powerful and he could see the acknowledgment of his great size in the watchers' appraising eyes.

"There's one sport that's pretty much the same in any language," he called out to Blue Shirt. "Let's see what happens if we fight each other man to man."

Real excitement murmured through the onlookers—the Apaches loved few things better than a contest of manhood. They edged as close as they could to the arena. Blue Shirt grinned at Hart's response; no challenge could have pleased him more, for he was big and brawny, and cunning enough that few men in the tribe were his equal in hand-to-hand combat.

The braves who formed the circle around the men began to shout to Blue Shirt as the fight gained momentum. Wrestling and boxing, the two antagonists grappled with each other's strengths and gauged each other's weaknesses. Hart was fast for his size, but Blue Shirt was more agile and in peak condition.

The watching braves murmured at the contest's duration; these were two strong men who pitted their skills against each other. The battle increased in frenzy until, at last, the cheering crowd began to shout admiration for both combatants. Finally, Hart's formidable size and strength turned the tide in his direction, but Blue Shirt fought valiantly until he could no longer force his screaming muscles to his will. By the time the white man wrestled the Indian to the ground, locked in a hold he couldn't escape, both men's bodies were so covered with blood and dirt that except for Hart's hair, they were nearly indistinguishable.

Close to the limits of exhaustion, Hart pinned the Apache beneath his great bulk and demanded concession. "You fight like a grizzly," he managed to gasp as he made his demand.

"You fight like an Apache," Blue Shirt growled back with grudging respect.

Both men stumbled to their feet. Hart waited only long enough to catch his breath, then he picked up his paper and charcoal from the dust at the edge of the circle. With deft movements the artist sketched Blue Shirt as he'd looked with the lance, perfectly at ease and mighty in his competence. Then he sketched him as he'd looked when on the ground, bested and spent. Wordlessly, Hart handed both sketches to the waiting man, who smiled a little in acknowledgment.

A murmuring arose among the braves, and nods of acquiescence followed the pictures as they passed from hand to hand. The women peered over one another's shoulders to see what had been drawn so swiftly, and exclaimed over the accuracy of the portrayal. Hart saw the tension drain from Gokhlaya's features, replaced by a sardonic smile.

The next morning Blue Shirt awakened Hart at dawn and made it clear he wished to offer his services to train him in the use of the bow and lance. The challenge was the turning point in the white visitor's relationship with the men of the tribe; from that day forward he was permitted to test his own skills, as did the other men in the war games they used to stay in readiness for battle. The men found that while he didn't know their ways, he was no coward and had the strength of a buffalo.

To be accepted as a man by the other men of the tribe, it was obvious to Hart that he must participate in men's work. Now that he was no longer merely suffered as Gokhlaya's useless guest, he was invited to learn to hunt game with both throwing stick and hunting club. Ammunition was hard to come by and was saved for war.

Hart learned to shoe his horse with buckskin moccasins or to toughen its hooves with a mixture of deer liver and ashes; he learned to tell the passage of time by the coming of the crescent moon and to ride bareback with skills the Comanches had long ago perfected and the other tribes had emulated. Gokhlaya himself taught him the use of the lance, a formidable weapon often prepared by a medicine man, so that it possessed special power.

In the beginning, Hart told himself he learned these skills because they allowed him access to the intimate life of the tribe, which in turn would enable him to draw its rituals with passion and accuracy. But as time passed, he came to know that his connection to the People was a deeper one; he found himself falling under the spell of their simple and honorable customs. He found he wished to earn their respect.

Everything about the Apache way of life fascinated the artist and the man. The economy with which they utilized every particle they were given by Providence, the integrity of their dealings with one another, their strict adherence to the sacred laws of the tribe, which deemed lying intolerable and respect for God and one another, paramount. Nonetheless, had it not been for Destarte, Hart might never have committed himself to becoming one of them.

▲ ▲ ▲

It wasn't that Hart ever intended to fall in love with the Indian woman— the memory of Fancy still lingered. His odyssey to the Apaches had seemed a way to sublimate all thoughts of love in work and research, for what point was there in waiting forever for a love that could not be? But the long illness, coming on the heels of the mine disaster, had touched him; the cold hand of Death on a man's shoulder makes him cherish the living things of this world. As vitality returned to Hart, Destarte was there to make him remember he was alive and a man.

There was a quiet strength about her, like that of a pine tree in the forest, a stillness unruffled by the tempest that stirred the trees around her. Her skills were the sort that make life happy. Her hands on his brow were tender, yet there was strength in them; a powerful life force flowed in Destarte's veins that transfused itself to him when she was near. He took comfort from her strength and gentleness; he missed her when she wasn't nearby. With her, there would be none of the dizzying highs of life with Fancy, but there would be blessed freedom from the devastating lows as well . . . and he was lonely. Yet Hart didn't want his loneliness and his unrequited love for Fancy to be the only reasons he was drawn to Destarte; she deserved a man who loved her for herself alone.

As time went on, and his communion with the People grew, Hart felt the ties that bound him to the past fading of their own volition; almost without knowing how it happened, he had grown to be less the stranger and more the seeker in this remarkable Apache world. He struggled to justify his love for Destarte as it grew, all the time wondering why he felt the need to do so. Was it because she was an Indian, or because she was not Fancy, that he wrestled so with his growing desire? Or could it be he hesitated because she represented such a major crossroads in his journey toward the future? He could not take her for his own and then leave the tribe, when his original mission was accomplished. To win Destarte's love, he must commit himself to becoming an Apache, not merely to being their fellow traveler . . . and that was a decision demanding careful consideration. Apacheria was where Hart wanted to be for now, but what of later? If he took Destarte to wife, there could be children, and his own world spared no kindness for the half-breed progeny of such a union.

To acknowledge his growing love for Destarte was easy as breathing; to desire her nearness, to need to share his life with her seemed normal, healthy wants in the context of the tribe . . . but to make her his wife, he must plumb his own motivations beyond the shadow of a doubt, for to become Apache was a task that must be accomplished from the soul outward, and once it had been accomplished, Hart sensed there might be no going back.

▲

"Do you have a husband, Destarte?" he asked her as she prepared his evening meal in the quiet of the wickiup. She raised her head a moment from her work and looked at him.

"The man who was my husband is no more," she answered. Hart knew this was one of the Apache euphemisms for death and that except in extraordinary circumstances, no one spoke the names of the dead, who were simply called "one who is not here."

"How did you come to be my nurse?" he asked, wondering if Gokhlaya had put them together for some purpose, and she smiled.

"The one who was my husband was as a brother to Gokhlaya. When he did not return from the raid in Mexico, and I did not wish to remarry, Gokhlaya took me under his protection."

"Is this unusual?" he asked, feeling suddenly jealous of this unknown man whom she had loved enough to mourn.

Destarte let the fruit she was peeling slip down into the bowl; she sighed and sat back onto her heels as if preparing to tell a lengthy story.

"In our People, a woman has freedom to choose her husband, Firehair. Sometimes, if her man dies, a woman returns to her family. I could not do this, for my parents were both killed by the white soldiers. Gokhlaya honored my wish to remain alone for a time. My husband was a good man, I could not easily seek another."

Hart studied the lines of her face and form, her back curved gently as a willow, her honey-colored skin gleaming in the soft glow of the firepit.

"Do you hate the white men for what they did to you?" he asked softly.

"For a time there was hatred in me and that is very bad, for it eats away at the heart. But then Gokhlaya asked me to nurse you, and I saw that all white men are not murderers."

She smiled a little and averted her eyes from his. "I was afraid at first, when I saw your red beard."

Hart laughed at that. "Your men do not grow beards."

"No, it would be thought foolish for them to have hair on their faces. Each hair is plucked out that their skin may be smooth."

"If my beard frightens you, I will cut it off today," he said, smiling.

"No," she answered quickly. "I have grown to know you as you are. I would not like you to be someone else."

Destarte looked embarrassed, as if she'd said too much, and returned her careful attention to the bowl of fruit. Hart knew in that moment she felt as drawn to him as he was to her.

"You are very beautiful," he said gently, suddenly wanting to touch her soft skin and to make her understand that he restrained himself only to protect her from harm.

"Are such words spoken lightly in your world?"

"Sometimes they are. But not now."

He saw her hands begin to move again, as if she'd stopped breathing, awaiting his reply.

"There is so much I would like to say to you, Destarte, but I know so little of your customs I'm afraid that I'll blunder and offend you."

"You do not offend me, Firehair," she answered with great dignity. She raised her eyes to his, and he saw so much promise in them, it took all his restraint not to take her in his arms.

▲

The flames from the ceremonial fire flickered on the oiled bodies of the dancers as Hart sat in the circle of men beside Gokhlaya, watching the women gyrate to the rhythm of the drums and flutes. He saw Destarte detach herself from the others and move silently behind the seated men; he felt the touch of her fingers on his neck and knew she had invited him to join the dance. As he rose to do so, Gokhlaya held him back with a gesture and leaned toward him to whisper in his ear. "The woman invites you to courtship. Think carefully, Firehair. This is not merely an invitation to the dancing. . . ."

Hart lay awake for hours after the exhilaration of the ceremony, trying to fathom the future; trying to separate head and heart and loins. There wasn't any question that he wanted Destarte, more than he had any right to . . . but if he courted her and won her favor, he committed himself to stay and severed forever his last link to his own world and Fancy. Throughout the long hours of darkness he wrestled the demons of his own need and drifted off to sleep with the lingering scent of the beautiful Apache woman still in his nostrils, the feel of the satin strength of her skin making his pulse race. Oh, God, how I need to love someone who loves me back, he thought as he let sleep end the terrible confusion and soothe his heart with visions of Destarte.

When Hart woke up early the next morning he was surprised to realize he knew exactly what to do. He walked deliberately to Destarte's most frequented trail, the one along which she traveled each day to carry water. Gokhlaya had instructed him in the necessary behavior, if he chose to court her in the Apache way, so he placed a row of stones on both sides of the trail behind a tree and waited to see if she would stop there, or pass him by, unheeded, for both were her prerogatives. Hart stood in the shelter of a tree and watched the graceful movements of the woman, as she read the sign he'd left for her. Destarte lingered for a moment touching the stones, then without looking in his direction, she whispered, "I will come to you," into the air, and continued on her way.

Hart waited in his wickiup after sunset, twitchy with anticipation; he had ceased to worry about his own strange choice of future at the moment he'd gone to meet her in the woods.

Destarte made her way through the camp after sunset, knowing the other women tittered among themselves, at her madness in accepting the red-bearded stranger. She hesitated only a moment in the moonlight to calm herself, before slipping inside the wickiup, where he waited so eagerly. Her heart pounded violently against her ribs, for with this choice, she abandoned all hope of a simple, uncomplicated life and embraced an unknown future. This man she loved, whom she knew so well and so little, and whom she desired so urgently was not one of the People. Someday, he would go back to his own kind and she would not be able to follow, even though it broke her heart to see him go. She was not a fool, as the other women said, she was merely a woman who had once loved deeply and who had felt, since her husband's death, that never again would she feel alive, as she once had been. Then this strong and gentle stranger had touched her, and she had grown to know that whatever the cost, she would willingly pay it to be with him for whatever time the gods would allow.

Hart watched Destarte enter the wickiup, and was startled to see that she looked at him shyly for the first time, as if she had never tended him, or seen him naked and helpless. The shyness seemed so sweet to him that any lingering misgivings were swept away by a desire to be for her everything she needed or dreamed.

Hart reached out to her wordlessly, and she came into the shelter of his arms, where she'd longed to be. He could feel the beating of her heart behind the warmth of her breasts and bent his head to catch her lips with his own. There was passion behind the restraint of propriety, and it made the blood rise precipitously in his loins, and pulse in his head to still the phantoms of a lost love and of a world that this commitment thrust behind him forever.

Hart led Destarte toward the bed and watched wonderingly as she tugged the deerskin shirt over her head and let the soft skirt fall to the dirt floor. She stood waiting, in the dim light; her eyes met his in unselfconscious giving. Destarte's slender limbs were long and her taut body was the color of warm honey; it was nearly perfect from a life of exercise and lack of self-indulgence. She had full round breasts, so well muscled that they swayed only slightly as she bent or moved, and her waist wasn't tiny like the corseted waists he was used to, but instead it was supple and swelled into hips and buttocks that were strong and sensual.

"You are very beautiful," he said, in answer to her unspoken need to know if she pleased him. "And I love you very much." She did not reply but smiled instead, and he felt the tension drain from her body.

Hart touched her chin with his hand and tilted her face to his own; he saw so much love in her eyes, he felt washed clean by the grace of it. Destarte touched the buttons of his shirt to remind him that, he, too, should be naked, so they could learn more of this strange, wondrous choice each had made so deliberately.

Hart tugged the clothes from his body, wanting to be all that she needed. He remembered how often during his illness, he'd longed to reach for her, when she'd hovered above his naked form, soothing and comforting; now he could be the one to give and she to take. He pulled her gently to the bed beside him, and kissed her long and searchingly to still the trembling his touch provoked. Destarte lay watchful and waiting, stretched out so that the skin of breast and belly was tautened in the flickering fireglow. Hart touched her flesh with the backs of his fingers and traced his hand slowly, deliberately down the length of her, lingering at each place where he intuited her longing, learning her as he touched, and remembering. Destarte closed her eyes and abandoned herself to this stranger whose body and destiny she'd chosen to share.

How very much she'd wanted to touch more than was allowed, while he was in her care, she thought, as she felt the strength and love in him engulf her. From the time she'd begun to know his character, his body had filled her with desires she'd thought long dead. She'd watched him as he lay sleeping, and longed to caress the huge male body that promised such strength and power . . . just to imagine the force of him within her, breaking the boundaries, easing the terrible ancient ache, had driven her to wild fantasies. She wasn't wanton, merely free to love and be loved as she chose, and somehow she'd known that in Hart's arms she could find all the loving she'd craved in her long loneliness.

"Lie very still, Destarte," Hart whispered into her ear. *Belong to me, depend on me, be my love and mine alone,* was what he said to her in his heart. "Let me love you as I've imagined it. . . ." Destarte unfolded beneath him like an opening flower; she received nothing she would not willingly return, but Hart desired only to prolong her pleasure. He teased her to the brink a dozen ways, exploring her body as he'd been exploring her mind and heart. She would fill all the empty spaces in his soul, and in return he would give her all the pent-up love that had been stored so long, awaiting a recipient who would care. There would never, never come a moment when what each offered the other wouldn't be enough, and more than enough, there would never be a time when they would fail each other.

He entered her with exquisite care, as if he feared to injure her, but she raised herself to meet his thrust, hungrily, lovingly, and he knew her desire matched his own and that the strength of their love would make up for both their pasts.

"I love you," he whispered again, but she couldn't answer him, for she was lost in a place that had no words. He felt the spasms tense her body in his hands and sensing her fulfillment, he gave himself up to completion.

Afterward, as they lay entwined in each other's arms, Hart felt, more than heard, Destarte sigh.

"Are you sad?" he asked, turning her to face him so he could see the tears he knew were there.

"I am afraid."

"What are you afraid of, my Morning Mist? You must know I'll never let anything harm you."

A drop of water trickled down Destarte's cheek to the pillow.

"I am afraid you will go back to the white man's world and when you do, a part of me will go with you."

Hart touched the wet cheek with his fingers and brushed away the moisture, tenderly. "I would not have taken you to my bed, Destarte, if I intended ever to leave you . . . the Apache world is my world now."

She looked into his eyes, her own luminous in the dim light, but he could see she knew, as he did, that whatever his intention, it was inevitable he would one day go back to his own people, and she did not reply.

In the morning, when he arose, Hart saw that Destarte quickly hung his bedding out to air, before bringing him his saddled horse. He smiled inwardly at the sweet gesture for he knew from Gokhlaya that by eating what she'd prepared and mounting the pony she offered, he would accept her as his wife, just as she had accepted him as husband by hanging out his covers. He did so with a happier and more peaceful heart than he'd known in years.

83 Fancy watched Aurora pirouette before the mirror in her new dress. It was made of the softest burgundy velvet, with collar and cuffs of ecru lace. The bloomers protruding below the hem were lace trimmed, too, and thin burgundy ribbons nipped through the stitching above the deep flounce.

The child's dark hair was done up in a thousand shining ringlets, for Aurora already had her own lady's maid, as well as her nanny.

Love welled up in Fancy, as the exquisite child admired her own reflection in the glass. Aurora had been blessed with the best features of both parents—Fancy's delicate facial structure, and Chance's stature of long, lean bone and well-placed muscle. No one could see the child without being startled by her uncommon beauty, and when it came time for beaux to come calling, only the finest young men from the most prominent families would dare ply their suit for Aurora McAllister. But that, of course, was all far in the future.

"Oh, Mommy, it's absolutely gorgeous!" the child breathed, enchanted by her own reflection. "Thank you so much—you know how I love velvet."

Fancy opened her arms to catch the happy little girl in an embrace. Aurora seemed to be growing taller every day and Fancy felt sure she'd inherited McAllister stature rather than that of the diminutive Deverells.

"I know, sweetheart," she said, buoyed by Aurora's joy. "No one looks grander in velvet than you do. I declare you're growing up prettier every week, Aurora. Someday, every man you see will set his cap for you."

The little girl's attention was already back on the mirror.

"It makes my heart sing to see you so happy, darling." Watching the child evolving in the safety and plentitude of their life helped to heal Fancy's own wounds of want. If only her daughter got along better with Chance, everything would be perfect, but Aurora had never let him into her affections, and if the truth were told, Chance no longer tried to woo her; he'd been rebuffed so often.

"Nanny makes me work too hard, Mommy," Aurora said suddenly, turning from the glass. "And she's very nasty to me."

"Whatever do you mean, darling?"

"She lies about me and punishes me all the time for things I didn't do."

Fancy frowned. The nanny had impeccable credentials and letters of recommendation from families in both New York and London. She reached for her daughter's hand and drew her closer.

"Tell me what you mean, darling. Are you sure she's been unfair with you?"

Aurora sat down primly on the bed beside her mother.

"She lies about me, Mommy." The fringe of dark lashes brushed her cheek and a hint of moisture appeared behind them.

"I try my best to be good and to do my lessons perfectly, no matter how hard they are, but Miss Powell tells the other servants that I haven't done them and then she scolds me. I think she hates me."

Fancy patted her daughter's hand comfortingly. "Don't you worry, darling, I'll have a word with Miss Powell; I'm sure it's just a misunderstanding of some kind." Fancy leaned over and hugged Aurora impulsively. "You'd best take off that dress now, dear, it's much too elegant to wear on an ordinary day."

Aurora's face fell. "Please, Mommy, let me wear it for a little while at least, I'll be so careful with it. And today isn't really ordinary, because you and I are having lunch together!"

Fancy hesitated, then remembering how special the occasions had seemed when she and her mother had dined together, instead of her being consigned to the nursery, she relented.

"Very well, darling. But promise me you'll take very special care of it. That dress came all the way from New York and was very costly. Besides, it makes you look immensely grown up."

Aurora smiled sweetly at her mother as Fancy left the room. Then, humming softly, she returned to the mirror and admired herself all over again.

▲

The stern-faced nanny pursed her lips and folded her hands in front of her square figure. She had withstood the assaults of irate mothers before now and would again; she waited patiently for Fancy to finish, took a breath, and plunged ahead.

"Mrs. McAllister, I assure you I find it difficult to say the things I am about to, but it is my belief that we have a genuine problem on our hands with Aurora." The small but sturdy gray-haired figure looked as if she could handle any problem a nursery might provide.

"And what exactly do you mean by that?"

"Aurora lies, Mrs. McAllister. Almost incessantly."

"All children tell fibs, Miss Powell . . ."

"Not fibs, Mrs. McAllister. Lies. About large things and small. About events of no consequence at all. In fact, it is almost as if the child lies to keep in practice. I have never seen the like."

"I can't believe that."

"I realize it's difficult for a parent to see the flaw in such a child, Mrs.

McAllister, but I have had considerable experience in child-rearing, and it is my opinion that if you don't nip this in the bud, you'll be in for serious trouble later. And lying is not her only failing."

Fancy felt her anger surge at the woman's supercilious tone. "Precisely what other problems do you perceive?" she asked icily.

"Aurora is lazy and resents all authority. She is unresponsive to constructive criticism and pretends to change her ways while remaining recalcitrant. She is sly with other children and adults. She is not in the least intellectually inclined, but is constantly conniving and can pull the wool over one's eyes until found out." She paused for breath. "She is also cruel to those less fortunate than she."

"I've seen none of this," Fancy said hotly. "Absolutely no evidence of what you suggest."

Miss Powell looked almost smug. "That is because she lies to you and your husband most of all."

Fancy checked the fast rebuttal that sprang to her lips and tried to calm herself. It was obvious the child was right; this woman did hate Aurora for some unknown reason. No wonder her progress at lessons was so slow. Who could possibly prosper in such an atmosphere of hostility and mistrust?

"I feel that under the circumstances it would be best for you to seek employment elsewhere, Miss Powell," Fancy said evenly. "It seems apparent you are unhappy dealing with my daughter."

"Just as I expected," Miss Powell replied with a disdainful sniff. "The parents of such monsters always take the child's side."

So! thought Fancy. She has been in this situation before. Perhaps the woman treated all her young charges badly and when the parents found out . . .

"It would be best if you were to prepare to leave immediately," she said.

Miss Powell stood her ground like a small tree. "I shall go, and gladly. But you mark my words, Mrs. McAllister, the child is unnatural. There is something very wrong with her."

"There is nothing wrong with my daughter that a kind and competent nanny wouldn't cure," Fancy snapped. "I only hope that being around you hasn't already damaged Aurora in any way."

"Your daughter was damaged long before I ever arrived here, Mrs. McAllister." The nanny's tone was as cold as Fancy's. "I shall leave on the first available train."

Aurora, eavesdropping behind the double doors to her mother's sitting room, smiled with relief and walked back silently to the nursery. What fun to watch the dreary old woman pack her miserable belongings and depart. Even if her mother was so stupid she could be fooled without the slightest difficulty, knowing she was on her side was a great comfort.

▲

Blackjack was a charmer. Everybody said so. He had a face so handsome, it seemed almost beautiful instead of boyish. And he had a joyous disposition—occasionally given to petulance, if he didn't get his own way—but as that seldom happened, he had little reason to be cross.

Blackjack idolized his father, and with good reason, for Chance loved his son with single-minded passion, as if all the love he longed to give Aurora and to Fan had finally found a home. From the time he could toddle, the little boy accompanied his father wherever Chance could take him. He appeared at meetings and at the mine; he was even, according to town gossip, occasionally seen coming out of certain high-class parlour houses with his handsome father, but that might merely have been malicious gossip.

Chance bought the boy an elegant black pony, as soon as he could sit upright, and the child rode well. Indeed, Blackjack McAllister did everything with the easy confidence of a favorite.

Chance's gambling cronies were amused by the little tagalong. They gave him a deck of cards, as soon as his chubby baby fingers could fasten around them—they even showed him how to use them. Some said Blackjack used to sit by the hour, when his lessons were done, or he had conned his father into letting him escape them, just exercising his fingers . . . practicing dexterity with the deck, as his father had done so many years before.

Fancy watched her son's connection to his father with a curious mixture of pride and distress that she didn't quite understand herself. It was marvelous that Chance and Blackjack adored each other, but she wished she didn't feel so superfluous to the little boy's life. He was intelligent to the point of precocity, he had his father's astonishing memory, and he was an unconscionable charmer . . . it made no sense at all to her that something in her son made her so uneasy. She did her best to ignore her misgivings, but they were there nonetheless, and she wondered, when she let herself dwell on them, where they would lead.

"I love you so very much, Mother," Aurora said impulsively, wrapping her arms around Fancy's neck from behind. "You're so beautiful. I only hope I grow up to be exactly like you!" Fancy smiled in response at their lovely reflections in the dressing table mirror.

She was preparing to go out to a formal fund-raising dinner and Aurora had offered to do up her hair. Now that her daughter was more young lady than child, Fancy was enjoying her company in special ways.

"Judging from what I see in the mirror, my darling, you seem to be growing up to be very much like me, only far more beautiful." Aurora beamed and ran the silver-handled brush over her mother's coif one last time.

"You'd best go, Mother," she encouraged as she stood back to admire her handiwork. "It's getting late and you know how Daddy is." She laughed amusingly as she said it, and once again Fancy was filled with the hope that Aurora and Chance might reach some sort of détente. They'd come so close to never knowing each other at all. . . . They'd made a mistake by not telling the girl long ago that Chance was her real father, but the timing had just never seemed right and besides, if the word got out now, with Chance's political prominence a scandal could be disastrous. She couldn't help but wonder, though, if knowing the truth would have made Aurora any more loving toward Chance . . . not that there was any point in crying over spilled milk.

Fancy adjusted her heavy gown as she rose; the bugle beads caught the light of the lamps and fireplace and twinkled like elegant fireflies. As she picked up her evening bag, Fancy caught sight of the pile of earrings that lay on the little table in front of her. Aurora had encouraged her to try on endless pairs before the girl was satisfied with the diamonds and emeralds her mother now wore. Aurora caught the glance.

"Don't worry, Mother, I'll put them all away for you."

Fancy smiled with relief; she hated to leave jewelry lying around as temptation to the servants.

"Be very careful with them, darling. They're worth a king's ransom."

"I know, Mother—I love those jewels as much as you do, so of course I'll be good to them!"

Fancy blew a kiss to the girl, and hurriedly pulled on her elbow-length kid gloves and left the bedroom.

Aurora listened to her mother's footsteps echo down the hall, then, satisfied she was gone, seated herself at the mirror and tried on each pair of earrings in turn. The rubies were exquisite, but her mother wore them constantly, so they wouldn't do. The sapphires were breathtaking, but they were her father's newest gift and he'd be expecting her to wear them. The garnets were too old and dismal. The diamond and aquamarines would be best.

Aurora returned the other earrings to the velvet tray and slipped them into the mahogany jewel case.

The aquamarines, she dropped into the pocket of her dressing gown, and left the bedroom humming.

▲

"Chance, I've looked absolutely everywhere!" Fancy said anxiously. "My earbobs are gone. Definitely gone."

"Have you asked Aurora?" It was bad business to have a theft in your own home.

"Yes, and she said they were most definitely in the tray when she replaced it the night of the party. She's certain because she says she liked them so much, she intended to ask if she could wear them on Christmas."

Chance frowned and Fancy, looking at him, thought how the passage of years had simply made him seem all the more desirable to her, despite their ups and downs.

"Who had access to your room?"

"I'm afraid it must have been Maria, although I hated the idea of firing her. She swears she had nothing to do with it. But you know how careful I am not to let the other servants know where I keep my precious pieces."

"I'm sorry, sugar," he said, sitting down on the bed beside her, and putting his arms around her. She leaned her head back against his shoulder and let his strength be a comfort.

"I feel so dreadful about sacking Maria, Chance. She cried and pleaded and I kept thinking, what if she didn't do it?"

"Who else, then?"

Fancy took a deep breath. "You don't think Aurora could have taken them, do you?"

She felt Chance stiffen as if struck.

"No. Of course I don't think that. She knows I'd buy her anything she wants. Besides, where could she wear them? If she ever did, we'd see them. No, Fancy. That's a preposterous idea."

Fancy nodded glumly. "That's exactly the conclusion I came to, but Maria seemed so innocent . . ."

What she did not say to her husband was that other things had disappeared—a satin shift, a beaded jacket, a tortoise comb. Until now, nothing of extraordinary value. And then there was the question of the velvet dress she'd found a while ago in a ruined heap at the bottom of the dumbwaiter shaft. That hadn't been theft, of course, but it had said a good deal about Aurora's disrespect for precious things. And the girl was wasteful . . . Fancy had been poor too long ever to feel comfort with wastefulness.

"Don't worry, sugar. I'll buy you new earbobs to replace those. Aquamarines are too watery for you anyway. I like you better in bolder colors."

He reached his hand up to her face and tipped it toward him; he saw there were the finest lines at the corner of her eyes now. He thought they made her face even more interesting and bent his own to kiss away the teardrops.

"Remember that first day in Tabor's store, when I told you always to wear red or purple?"

She could tell by the husky playfulness of his voice that he wanted to make love to her. It was his way to soothe hurt, or expiate guilt or smooth troubled waters. His way, too, in times of joy or celebration. She smiled a little at the simplicity of thinking lovemaking a solution to everything, and dutifully turned her face to his to be kissed.

It wasn't such a bad way, after all, to banish the cares of the world. She felt his hands move knowingly along the back of her dress, seeking to undo the buttons. Stretching her neck this way and that to free it of the tension that had been building, Fancy arched her back and insinuated herself willingly into Chance's waiting embrace. She'd wanted to talk to him about other things tonight, but the problem of the earrings had banished everything.

It couldn't have been Aurora, she thought as she abandoned all thinking, gratefully. Aurora loves me much too much to do such a thing.

 85 Life in Denver was demanding on every level. You paid for success and money, Fancy thought, you paid with precious time, and endless energy and with never being able to show your true colors.

Chance prospered despite his strangely unconventional methods, maybe even because of them, and the more he did, the more disturbed Fancy grew that he never seemed to worry about the important details of life. He had no interest in what it took to run a household, or to train children, or to handle the unconscionable number of social obligations. Fancy found herself working harder at being the doyenne of Chance's world than she'd ever worked in business, and the work was far less fun, if more lucrative.

Not that she had any real sense of how much money they had, for the cost of their life now was too astronomical to calculate or control. Denver's life-style demanded waste as a way of proving your wealth. That seemed immoral to Fancy.

"I swear, Magda. It's just like a battle to see which rich family can squander the most money on the most damn fool show."

Fancy fretted, at the same time she strove to perform all her wifely functions perfectly.

"Don't you ever worry about anything, Chance?" she asked one night in bed. "Tell me the truth." Fancy ran her finger down her husband's side judiciously, savoring the textures of his body, knowing the response it would provoke.

"I worry . . . but I've never seen it do me a damned bit of good, so I try to keep it to a minimum." He turned to fold her in his arms; he never felt as secure as when he was in bed with a woman, and best of all when that woman was Fancy. Then all the pieces of the puzzle fit and it was easy enough to believe God had your best interests at heart.

"You've been happy here in Denver, haven't you, sugar?"

Fancy nestled in close. "It is great fun to show everybody what we're made of, I'll say that. And I do love having a beautiful house and gorgeous clothes . . . it's just that there are so many obligations for both of us now, Chance. We're always around people, never alone. It was fun for a while, all the parties and the dinners and the adulation . . . almost like being in a hit play, when everyone accepts the make-believe as real, and you feel you're on top of the world. But there's a lot about this life that troubles me, too. It seems to me about the only time you and I are ever alone now is in bed."

"All the more reason to make the best of that time, sugar," he said as he nudged her legs apart with one of his own and nuzzled her hair away from her throat. She started to say something more, but his insistent lips were on hers and she remembered how sweet it was to let him love her into forgetfulness.

"I love you, Fancy," he murmured as he moved his body over hers, the long strength of him pushing back her doubts. She knew he used lovemaking as the means of avoiding conversation, never speaking of the imbalance of their life, never looking the imperfect in the eye.

"We only learn from successes, never from failures," he'd told her once. "Failure queers the magic."

▲

Chance raked in the chips across the green-felt expanse and smiled; his expression wasn't smug or self-satisfied, merely contented.

"You son of a bitch," Jake Guthrie said, only half joking. "You got more luck than a short-tailed cat in a roomful of rockers. If I didn't think you could outshoot me, I'd be tempted to ask where the hell those kings came from."

Haw Tabor pushed back his own chair with a chuckle—and signaled the waitress for a round of drinks. "Now, Jake, you just been outclassed is all. Chance here happens to have been blessed with one of the great poker faces of our time, and uncommon good luck to go with it." Haw tended to be expansive whether he won or lost, and extremely generous to the barmaids and dealers wherever he played. "If you can't stand the heat, Jake, you know you ain't supposed to play in the kitchen."

Guthrie smiled, begrudgingly peeled off several hundred-dollar bills from a fat roll, and handed them to the girl, who scurried for chips.

"Serves me right for believing that worried look you were sporting there a while back, McAllister. I can see how you beguile the ladies and the voters with your acting ability."

Chance chuckled, taking the ribbing good-naturedly; it was the price you had to pay for having more on your plate than most men. A little envy was a good thing; too much was dangerous.

"I'm going to need more than acting ability if Fancy finds out every time I come to Leadville, I stay out all night." He glanced at his watch and thought about where to go next, home or out for a little more fun. They'd kept the Leadville house because business still brought him there frequently.

Chance had discovered certain things about himself since he'd grown rich . . . there were huge appetites that seemed to go hand in hand with power. And now that there was money to indulge those appetites, sometimes the enormity of his desires unnerved him. He wanted to be a good husband to Fancy, wanted to protect their marriage from harm, but available women were another spoil, unerringly drawn to the winner's circle, and they were damned difficult to turn away beneath the gaze of other men and against the power of his own hot blood.

Fancy was always up to her nose in obligations these days, children, society. Not that that was really the reason he sometimes strayed . . . he did it because he wanted to. It made no sense that women placed such importance on sexual fidelity anyway; it had little to do with what a man felt in his heart.

Life was damned demanding these days. It took guts and stamina to stay on top of the heap, no woman could really understand the pressures men faced in the world of their tough, strong peers. Occasional diversions kept those pressures bearable.

Chance glanced at his watch and decided to go home. He'd promised Caz a visit to the mine in the early morning and he could use the sleep.

▲

It was damned annoying that Caz kept calling him back to Leadville, on one excuse or another, Chance thought as he rode up to the Fancy Penny. There was no way he could be everywhere at once and it was good of Jason Madigan to be willing to look in on the mining operations whenever he was in Leadville. The man was an excellent engineer and a superb businessman; his ideas tended toward efficiency and cost-cutting, of course, and that never set well with a mine manager. But it was a distinct pain in the ass that Caz couldn't get along with him.

"You need to spend more time here, mate," Caz said as he passed the heavy ledger over to Chance, who had barely bothered to skim the other two journals he'd shown him.

Chance frowned. It seemed every time he came up here lately, Caz was carping about the same thing. "Look, Caz, there are only so many hours in a week. I'm on seventeen committees and I'm helping build a state out of ten thousand diverse needs . . . I can't be in Leadville any more than I am. That's why you're in charge here."

Caz pushed his bush hat down on his forehead, a gesture Chance knew well from the old days meant he was trying to keep from boiling over.

"Listen up, mate. I'm not spoilin' for a punch-up, but it's a ratbag idea to think you can run a business this big like an absentee landlord. And as to me running the damned thing—I'd be glad to, if your half-arse associate Jason Madigan would keep his mitts outta my pie. I damn near told the bloke to ram it yesterday, which I suppose is why you've graced us with your presence today. Madigan's a know-all, Chance. I'm not saying he's not smart about mining, I'm saying he's not the friend you think he is and I don't want you to come up the raw prawn in this."

Chance slammed the ledger closed and rose from his chair. Why the hell everyone tried to bog him down in the details of life, when he was made for broader concepts, was beyond him.

"I owe Madigan, Caz, and he's been helpful to me in a dozen ways since the mine disaster. You know as well as I do, he lent us the money to repair the mine when no one in town would give us the time of day, and you also know he's given me sound investment advice and he's never asked for one goddamned thing in return. He has every right in the world to keep an eye on things here for me when I'm away. Without him, we would have been out of business."

Caz stood, too, his solid bulk taut with anger. "He'll do you dirty, mate, and you're too bullheaded to watch your back. I got no proof, only instinct, but I do know the man's a fool who shelters his own assassin."

The muscles in Chance's jaw stood out like mine cable.

"You're way over the line, Caz . . . I'll let it go for now because of times past, but you're goddamned well over the line."

Chance slammed the door of the manager's shack behind him and Caz stared at the closed door for a long time, remembering the time when they had been friends.

▲ ▲ ▲

Fancy's ornate carriage looked ludicrous parked outside the small house where Magda, Wes, and Gitalis lived. Fancy could see the disdainful look on the coachman's face and was tempted to reprimand him, but as Magda stood in the doorway awaiting her, it seemed best not to draw attention to the man's contempt.

Magda opened her arms to Fancy, such an old familiar gesture, and the younger woman ran to her embrace, a child again. What a relief there always was in Magda's strength and wisdom; what blessed escape from the endless responsibilities of being Chance's wife.

"You are here for advice," Magda said as she set about making tea in the well-remembered samovar. "You are disturbed and wish for guidance."

"You've read the cards?"

Magda laughed, and in doing so seemed young again. "I've read your face. Something troubles you."

The two women sat near the kitchen window and Fancy tried to maintain her composure.

"It's Chance."

"More women?"

"Not that I know of . . . but if that ever happens and I find out, I'll leave him."

"His infidelity would be that important to you?"

"It would be that important."

"Each relationship has its own laws which cannot be transgressed," Magda told her gently. "Perhaps this is yours."

"Other women aren't what's troubling me at the moment, Magda. It's money . . . business. I don't know any way to put this gently . . . Chance is a horse's ass where money is concerned. He squanders it like water . . . stationery engraved in real gold, banquets and balls where the guests are given silver goblets as party favors . . . investments in mining properties a tenderfoot would laugh at. And gambling . . ."

"But I thought he was a brilliant gambler, Fancy. Does he not win at those games of chance?"

"He wins all the time—but it doesn't matter, Magda. It's like a sickness of some kind. If he wins a hundred, he bets two, if he wins ten thousand, he bets twenty. I have no way of knowing the true extent of his debts, but I suspect they're monumental. I've tried every way I know to reason with him, but I can see it's a kind of addiction."

Magda poured the steaming tea without speaking and let Fancy continue. Magda thought it best to let her empty herself of woes before replying.

"There's more that worries me," Fancy hurried on. "I feel disloyal even saying this out loud because I love him so. But I always feel uneasy about Chance and business . . . he never does his homework, just gets by on his charm and that incredible memory he has for details that makes it sound to people as if he knows everything. To tell you the truth, I believe he thinks men like Jason and Haw Tabor and John Henderson and the like are just not as smart as he is, because they're forever doing research and learning all there is to learn about a new venture before they leap. And there's no way on earth to convince Chance he's doing anything imperfectly, because he's so damned successful at everything he touches." She paused for breath. "Oh, Magda, I swear to heaven, I wouldn't put it past him to lose everything we own in a crap game some night, or by investing in iceboxes for Eskimos . . ." She let the thought trail off as if the subject was so overwhelming, there was no way to tell it all.

"And I take it you have not been silent on these subjects," Magda said with a slight smile. "What was the result of your advice to your husband?"

Fancy made a wry face. "We've had fights that would make Balaclava look like a fancy dress ball."

"Men seldom take kindly to their wives' advice on business," Magda replied with amusement, "most particularly if their wives are right."

"A lot of good it'll do me to be right, if I lose Chance and all our money to boot."

"Let us speak of this famous Chance of yours, child, and see if we can put your dilemma in some semblance of order. Do you love him still?"

Fancy looked genuinely startled by the question. "Yes. I still love him very much."

"As you did when you carried Aurora and you fantasized this phantom Chance, whose dreams could change the world?"

Fancy hesitated; she had never lied to Magda. "It's very different since we're married . . . he certainly isn't what I expected, if that's what you mean. But he is exciting and adventurous . . . and wonderfully irreverent, just as I imagined . . . and he does make me feel that together we could rule the world. And I love his luck, Magda—you know I never, ever felt lucky before him."

"Aha!" said Magda. "So you trust the man's luck, but you do not trust the man."

Fancy was astonished once again at Magda's uncanny knack of seeing right into her soul.

"And you hate him when he frightens you, by risking what means little to him and everything to you?"

Miserably, Fancy nodded again.

"All obstacles that are placed in our paths, child, and all great loves and hates are teachers. Nothing is haphazard in the universe, so you must begin by knowing none of what goes on between you and Chance is an accident. Instead, it is a signpost that you may read, if you use your intuition. You come to Magda for advice, and this much I will tell to you: look within your own heart for the answers you are seeking, Fancy. Look to see what you need from this man, why you chose him above all others, and what his flaws tell you of your own. Ask yourself what Chance gives you that is powerful enough to make you stay . . . and what do you give him in recompense?"

"We're incredible in bed together, Magda. The sexual desire that drew me to him all those years ago is every bit as intense now . . . maybe more so. It's the same for him, I think. We fight like gladiators and then some bizarre electric current makes us want each other more than ever, and we end up making love until we're too exhausted to fight any longer." Fancy stopped a moment. "But it doesn't change anything."

Magda pursed her lips in thought.

"Perhaps it teaches, Fancy, rather than changes. Perhaps the bonds between you were forged in another lifetime, and you simply have unfinished business with each other that is very powerful and consuming."

She let Fancy ponder that a moment before continuing.

"What of the other brother? Where does he stand in all this?"

"Why the hell would you ask that?" Fancy replied testily. "He's off somewhere painting Indians, last I heard. And besides, what has Hart to do with Chance and me?"

"You *three*—not merely two—have returned to be together in this lifetime, Fancy, this much I am permitted to tell you. You are bound by bonds so powerful their full extent is hidden even from me. Mark well my words . . . you three have chosen to fulfill your commitments to each other in this lifetime, child, and no power on earth, least of all your own willfulness, will keep you from your destiny."

The deer hunt took the braves miles from their encampment. Hunting was dangerous now, so many soldiers roamed the land that had been the Apache hunting grounds time out of mind. The scout pointed the men toward a valley more fertile than its surroundings, and divided the hunters into two large groups; Gokhlaya headed one, and Naiche, the hereditary chief of the Chiracahua, the other.

The riders fanned out into parallel ranks, so that each man was fifty yards from his neighbor, as the long lines of riders advanced toward the grazing deer. The moment the animals were in clear sight, the forward line raced ahead of the other so that a circle was formed around the unsuspecting herd. The second line shaped itself into an outer circle with such speed and agility Hart thought the entire undertaking looked as if it had been created by a great dancing master.

The Indians, silent up to the moment of closing the second circle, began to shriek and hoot and scream to terrify the trapped animals into running in all directions. Heavy-tipped hunting arrows showered into the milling herd, bringing down one deer after the next, until dozens lay dead or dying within the tightening concentric circles of braves. The entire enterprise had taken no more than twenty minutes, Hart suspected, but the meat and skins, bones and hooves, would supply the tribe for weeks or months to come. No scrap was ever wasted, even the tiniest bones were used as needles, the intestines cleaned to make a casing for pemmican that could be saved for the lean days of winter.

Gokhlaya dispatched men to fetch the women, for cleaning and dragging the kill back to camp would be their responsibility. The warriors, in high spirits, sang and talked on the return to the *ranchería,* for meat which had been scarce for months would now be plentiful. There would be skins for garments, tent coverings and decorations. Boasts would be made around the campfire in nights to come of the valor of the mighty hunters.

Hart knew by now the curious protocols that would be observed; a fortunate hunter might be forced by custom to give his kill to a less fortunate one, simply because the man asked for it—and many fine hides would go, not to the man who had killed the deer but to a quick-witted companion who begged it as a boon.

"Next time we will wear the deer mask," Gokhlaya called out, reining in next to Hart. "With these masks we can stalk them from within their midst and choose only the ones we wish to be our prey. It is best to kill the weak and leave the strong, for the good of the herd."

"I learn valuable lessons from you," Hart said.

"You teach me as well," Gokhlaya responded.

"One day perhaps you will teach me what life was like on the reservation, and why you left San Carlos before you found me. Had you never left there, you and I would not have met."

Gokhlaya frowned. "You must hope you do not learn firsthand of the reservation of the soldiers. As to our encounter . . . those who are destined to meet do so, no matter what the whims of the white soldiers may be."

Hart nodded. He'd heard stories back in Colorado, of General George Crook's relentless war against the Apaches. Everyone knew of the maverick general who dressed in buckskins and lived more like an Indian scout than a career military man, and of how he'd broken the back of the Apache nation in '72 and '73. What Hart hadn't learned back home was the truth of how the Indian agency men who took over after Crook's departure had made life so full of hardship for the Apaches that, one by one, the bands were forced to flee the reservations. Defrauded of their farms, their cattle, and even their government food rations by a ruthless ring of speculators, and harassed by a bungling and uncaring military, the tribe had escaped the San Carlos reservation and returned to the Southern Stronghold. Hart knew the Chiracahua had, in fact, been on their way to Mexico when they'd taken him in.

Gokhlaya slowed his horse to a walk, so they could talk more easily. "When the white man's wagons first came to our land, Firehair, we did not harm them for we do not own the land. No one can own the land, or the sky. All was given by Usen to be cultivated and to be shared. The People thought the white-eyes understood this truth. But they did not come to share the land with us, and soon we were pushed away from our hunting grounds and from our strongholds. Only then it was that we began to try to stop the wagons. But the soldiers came in numbers greater than the stars in the heavens and it was too late."

Hart nodded, the echo of his father's words in his head: *The Indians will be destroyed, son, and with them will go the last true Keepers of the Land.*

"Each year more was taken from us. The White Father in Washington made promises, but they were as dust in the wind. So now we fight for our manliness . . . a man who cannot hunt to feed his family is not a man. A man who cannot protect his family is not a man. We left the reservation that we could be men again."

Hart looked at the stalwart figure by his side. The Apache's eyes never wavered from the road ahead, so he could not see if there was bitterness or resignation in them.

"You cannot fight them forever, Gokhlaya. They are as many as the sands of the desert . . . if the People kill ten, one hundred will come to take their place. If you kill one hundred, one thousand will be sent. The People will be like the deer within the circle."

Gokhlaya rode in silence for a full minute before he spoke again. "I am glad you do not lie to me. If there can be truth between us, Firehair, one day there can be truth between our people."

"And if that doesn't happen in our time?"

Gokhlaya's mouth was a grim semblance of a smile. "Then, when the thousands come, we will die as men die, not as the deer within the circle." Hart and his Apache friend rode on in silence for a while. Hart no longer felt uncomfortable with long silences, for he had begun to be one with the People.

"My Power has told me that if the People die now, there will yet come a time when we will be raised up again," Gokhlaya said. "The white-eyes will not care for the land as we have done—they will kill the animals and the plants, until Grandmother Earth is nearly dead from the poisoning. Then will the white-eyes see what they have wrought, and children will be born to them who will know the way of the People. This has my Power told me of the future, Firehair, but it will be long, long from now, when you and I are one with our ancestors, and even our children and our children's children are gone from here."

"When does your Power speak to you, Gokhlaya?"

"When I am called to listen, my Power speaks . . . or when the tribe needs guidance, or when I have begged to be heard. A man must not mock his Power or call upon it unwisely."

"Did your Power come to you first when you were a boy?"

"I met my Power for the first time when I made my vision quest, as I grew to manhood. Later, when my first family was gone from me, my Power told me I was to be a medicine man and use my gifts for the tribe."

Hart knew Gokhlaya was shaman as well as warrior; he was respected as much for his wisdom and his medicine as for his courage in battle. "And you have spirit gifts that other men do not, my friend?" he asked, and Gokhlaya nodded, as if it were an ordinary question.

"My Power taught me to call up the wind, to see things that are far from me, and to change my shape so my enemies cannot find me."

Hart digested that, no longer unwilling to accept the seemingly impossible. The People believed in the world unseen; they asked dead ancestors for guidance and they cured things the white man thought incurable.

"What do you mean when you speak of changing your shape?"

"Once, when the white soldiers trapped us in a box canyon, Naiche's men and mine, I changed my warriors into stones so that the soldiers rode among us and saw us not."

Hart couldn't think of what to say to that, so he remained silent until Gokhlaya spoke again.

"The old ones and the small ones starved on the reservation. The soldiers gave to each of the People a dog tag of metal to wear about the neck. To get food, each one was forced to walk across the desert from the reservation to Fort Thomas to show the name tag. Many could not go."

"How far was it to the fort from the reservation?"

"Twenty miles. The sick, the old, the infants, the crippled, could not walk so far."

Hart shook his head in disgust; he knew from Destarte that the meat they'd been given was all too often infested with maggots, and the flour alive with weevils. Corrupt Indian agents were the norm, and with feeling running so high against the redman, there was no one to control the thieves who injured them.

The life of the Chiracahua Apache will soon vanish forever, Hart thought as he rode with the proud contingent of braves. This life of hunting, gathering, and oneness with the land will disappear and the People will be herded onto reservations, like wild horses into paddocks, and they will wither there. He was grateful he had come in time to learn their ways, for the destruction of the last true Keepers of the Land would soon be complete, and all that once had been the Apache way would be no more.

▲ ▲ ▲

"Gokhlaya's wife and children are very young for one his age," Hart said to Destarte as she finished cleaning up their evening meal and settled in to sew.

"Is it a sign of virility to have so young a wife?" He rested against the piled up animal skins, watching her work on the newly tanned deerskins.

"They are his third family," she replied.

Hart raised his eyebrows in surprise.

"What happened to the others?"

"They are gone."

"Dead, Destarte? Were they all killed, or did they die in some epidemic?"

She shook her head vigorously, to show she could say no more. Hart remembered the night when he'd first come to Apacheria, and the haunted look that had come to Gokhlaya's eyes when he'd blundered into asking about his "first" family.

It was Naiche who finally relented and told him the story of Gokhlaya's past.

"It was the time of the first treaty," Cochise's son told him reluctantly.

"The treaty that the White Father in Washington said would last forever." The broad and handsome face of Naiche creased in contempt. He was tall and imposing, standing in the shadow of the mesa beside Hart.

"We had made our camp in the Sierra Madre near a Mexican village called Kaskiyeh. It was in the year the white-eyes named fifty-seven, near the time of the spring rains. The birds chirped in the trees . . . the women and children splashed water on each other's bodies for the men were not about." Hart curbed his impatience, for he knew an Apache never told a story without first setting the scene.

"There were no guards for the *ranchería* then. The blue coats had gone from us, and we thought the camp was safe. Many warriors were hunting game; others had gone to town. Only old Noposo, the father of Alope who was the woman of Gokhlaya, remained with the women and children, for he was too old for travel.

"The daughter of Gokhlaya was four summers old—his son, two summers, a small baby, was still in his *tsoch*. When the sound of horses was heard the women thought the warriors must be returning and ran to the riverbank to greet their men.

"But then they listened again, for the sound was of horsemen who cared nothing for Grandmother Earth. They crushed things before them as they came.

"Soldiers with naked sabers were in our camp, some carried lances of iron. The children ceased to shout and play; silence descended for a moment before the screaming began.

"Alope ran to save her children, but a soldier fell upon her. She scrambled out from under him, searching frantically for her children, but the soldier pursued her and brought her down again.

"Women and children were running and shrieking; blood was splattering as at a slaughter of cattle. Her child ran toward Alope on small, fat legs. She screamed to her son to run as the wind, but the yellowleg's saber cut the head from his small shoulders and it rolled to his mother's side.

"Alope screamed and screamed for her son. She fought and kicked and scratched like a maddened wildcat at the man who threw her to the ground and covered her body with his own.

"Alope's mother-in-law snatched up the no-name baby from its *tsoch*, and tried to run away, but a hand grabbed her long hair so fiercely that her body felt it had been torn apart. The baby fell and rolled close to its mother, but she could not reach it.

"The soldier forced Alope's legs apart; she shrieked aloud, but not at her own pain. A soldier had picked up her baby and shouted to another that he would make a wager. He threw the baby high in the air and it stopped its crying. Alope saw the soldier raise the steel of his bayonet to catch the child

—she tried to close her eyes for she knew now what he intended, but she could not help but watch the tiny flailing arms and legs fall through the air.

"The laughing soldier caught the fat baby on the sharp point of his bayonet. The mother saw the astonishment, the anguish and the blood.

"The soldier disemboweled the child, and Alope shrieked out her anguish, but the soldier cut off her breasts and stuffed them in her mouth to silence her. Perhaps, she saw no more, after that."

Naiche halted in his recital. He did not look at Hart, who was so horrified by the tale he had to turn away. It would have been unseemly for one warrior to see another with tears in his eyes.

Naiche said, after a long time, "Gokhlaya found them. Later that day, his Power spoke to him. Perhaps, it told him of his Special Purpose.

"The great chief Mangas Coloradas came to him then, and told him the People must leave that place of death. Gokhlaya said he understood. On the trail, he would eat no meat and slept apart from the other warriors.

"It is said Mangas understood Gokhlaya had died with those he loved, and from that death arose a spirit so fierce, it would be remembered for all time. Where a warrior had stood, a war shaman lived . . . a spirit so powerful had come to live in him that the white-eyes will mourn his birth forever.

"Gokhlaya went up into the mountains and lived apart from the People. For one year, only Mangas visited his tipi. His chants could be heard from the mountaintop . . . they were not of this earth, but sought the gods.

"When he returned, his Power had given him certain gifts. He could sometimes see the future . . . he could free himself from bondage . . . he could call up the wind. All this have I witnessed with my own eyes."

Hart listened in rapt attention to this extraordinary recital. How was it that no newspaper, no congressman, no general, had ever spoken of the hideous wrongs that had driven Gokhlaya to such terrible vengeance? How was it no one spoke of the tragedy that had changed him into the fierce Geronimo, whom everyone called savage.

Twice later, Hart tried to paint the tale he had been told, but the sorrow he felt for his friend's great loss made him feel he intruded on sacred ground, and at last he abandoned the attempt.

▲

The year after Hart arrived, General Crook began to hound the Chiracahua again. The men painted their faces to prepare for battle and fastened the war bands of buckskin at their brows. Hart heard them joke that their scalp locks were ready for any warrior strong enough to take them, and wondered what the soldiers would think when his own red-chestnut hair was spotted among the ranks of the Apache.

From the moment the tribe had been commanded to go to war, every act took on religious significance. Gokhlaya called each object by its sacred name; horse became charger or warhorse, arrow became missile-of-death, even camping and cooking became part of the ritual.

Hart brooded over what role he was to play in the conflict. He had no desire to ride against his own kind, yet the confusion in Destarte's eyes at her husband being thought less than a man because he would not fight, made him search his heart for answers. Gokhlaya took the decision from his hands, commanding him to remain behind with the women and old men to defend the camp.

"Firehair is a novice in our ways of war," he said openly in council. "Firehair has no Power to guide him, and would be a danger to the more experienced warriors." It was an uncomfortable situation, not least of all within his own tipi; but as Hart's feelings were gravely ambivalent, in the end he was grateful to remain behind when the war parties rode out.

There was little expected of a man in camp, so Hart spent his time painting and sketching. He took out his frustrations on the sketch pad and tried to render everything he'd learned of the Apache language and customs into a dictionary and works of art. He also tried to help Destarte with her work, but she was so distressed that such help would reflect further on his manhood, she would have none of it.

▲

Destarte lay beside her husband on the rush-filled bedding, beneath the bearskin blanket she'd worked on so laboriously during the long winter nights.

"You are quiet tonight, my Destarte," Hart said slipping his arm around her shoulders. She'd seemed oddly preoccupied all evening and had answered his questions in monosyllables, which was quite unlike her. "Are you still so troubled about my not going to fight with the other braves?"

Destarte turned her body a little to nestle it into her husband's arms. "Sometimes I have been troubled about this, but not because I wanted you to go . . . only because the relief I felt at keeping you here with me was so great, I know I must be disloyal to the People. But that is not why I am quiet."

Hart smiled into the darkness. Destarte always went to such pains to be scrupulously honest with him. He wondered fleetingly how many men of any race could say the same of their wives. He waited, knowing she would tell him what troubled her in her own time.

"What would the people of Leadville think about a child who was half white and half Apache?" she asked.

"They would not be kind to such a child." Hart had wondered during the months of their marriage if Destarte might be taking measures to prevent pregnancy, for fear of such a half-breed being born to them.

"The People love all children," she said, as if thinking out loud. "But they, too, might be unkind to our son."

"But we haven't a son, my little wife," he said good-naturedly. "So you needn't worry about such things tonight."

Destarte reached for her husband's hand and placed it on her belly. "But we do have a son, my Firehair. He is so small now that no one needs to be unkind to him, yet. But one day . . ."

Hart raised himself up on one elbow and turned to her in the darkness. "Are you telling me we're going to have a baby, Destarte?"

"You are not upset with me?"

"Upset? Are you crazy? I've been afraid to ask why you weren't expecting. God knows we've given a baby every chance in this world to get started . . . how do you know it's going to be a boy?"

Destarte laughed softly, with relief. "I *feel* it is a boy. In my heart, I know he is like his father."

"A redheaded Indian," Hart said, trying the new knowledge on for size. "By God, that should set tongues wagging, shouldn't it? I love you, Morning Mist McAllister. I love you so damned much I could explode. And I love our son and I don't give a good goddamn what anybody in Leadville or Denver or Apacheria thinks about him . . . I just care about what the two people under this bearskin think."

"I, too, do not care, my husband," Destarte said. "But perhaps the child will care. I worry only that he be big and healthy and happy, for sickly babies or crybabies are sometimes killed when they are born, for the good of the tribe. Especially when there is war. . . ."

Hart put his arms around Destarte and hugged her to his broad chest, loving the sweet sense of fulfillment she always brought him, excited beyond words by the news.

"Nobody is going to kill our baby, Destarte, you can count on that. And nobody is going to be unkind to him either, so you can just put that out of your mind right now, because any man who would try to harm him would have to go through me first, and just in case you haven't noticed, I'm a pretty big feller."

Destarte looked into her husband's eyes shining with his elation, and moved her soft curves against the hard strength of his body.

"I have noticed, my husband," she said mischievously. "In truth, I noticed how big you were even before I was your wife."

"You did, did you?" Amused and happy, Hart lifted her body with ease until she lay covering him, so that her face was smiling down into his.

"Once, when you were very sick and your fever was high," she said playfully, "you were having strange dreams and your manhood grew very large and I wanted to touch it so much I had to run away from you so that I did nothing unseemly."

"I was probably dreaming of you," he said, touched and aroused by her confession.

"You fill me with joy, my husband," she whispered.

"And with other things . . ." he murmured as the warmth of her engulfed him.

▲

Naiche and Chatto, both hereditary chiefs, showed considerable benevolence toward Hart, and he found them generally willing to enlighten him with their stories of Apache history. The great leader Cochise, he learned from Naiche, had been a disciple of Mangas Coloradas, the revered chief of the five major Apache tribes, the Chiracahua, Nedni, Jicarilla, White Mountain, and Mescalero. It was clear that Mangas' memory was held in reverent esteem by all Apaches, and Hart knew he'd been captured treacherously by the white men, invited to a peace talk, taken prisoner, and beheaded. His head had been sent on tour around the country to show the bravery of the army in fighting Indians.

"If Gokhlaya is not a hereditary chief and isn't even Chiracahua, how is it that he occupies such a place of honor in the tribe?" Firehair asked, and Naiche deferred to Chatto to respond.

"Mangas was very wise," he said. "He saw in the young man, who was an orphan, unusual skills. Gokhlaya was not large in stature, yet he could beat the others at nearly every game. He was young and yet his wisdom was worthy of being listened to in the counsel of the older men. After Kaskiyeh, when Gokhlaya returned from his year of prayer and fasting, the white soldiers invited Mangas to a dinner and to bring with him the chiefs of all the tribes.

"Gokhlaya spoke and said that his Power had appeared to him in a dream and shown him the men of the Apache People, writhing on the ground and dying, although no shot had been fired. Gokhlaya counseled that the chiefs refuse the invitation, for there was treachery afoot.

"Mangas heeded the young man's warning and presented his case to the leaders. Three chose to go, Mangas, Cochise, and one other chief did not.

"The white soldiers had poisoned the stew with strychnine and all who attended the banquet died as Gokhlaya had seen it in his vision.

"After that, he was listened to."

"I can see why," Hart replied with a short laugh. God Almighty, but the whites had much to answer for—cholera-ridden blankets given to the Indians in trade, broken treaties, stolen territory, death marches . . .

"I have seen his Power with my own eyes," Naiche said. "Once, he summoned the wind to blind the soldiers' eyes with sand and once, when he was in prison, he saw the soldiers riding toward our village one hundred fifty miles away. He escaped and ran the whole way to warn us of the attack . . . some were even saved, but many were lost."

More loved ones to mourn, Hart thought. No wonder he never smiles. As to the mystical stories, he had seen too much to doubt as deeply as he once had. Two nights later he saw another example of Geronimo's Power that he couldn't ignore. A young brave named Alchise was being held in a Mexican jail and the authorities intended to hang him. Naiche, Chatto, Gokhlaya, and the braves met in council to decide how to handle the problem and while the men voted to free the boy by force, Gokhlaya offered a different solution.

"I will send word to the Mexicans that I will raise a great storm against them if Alchise is not freed," he said, and the elders agreed to the plan.

The following day word was sent to Colonel Garcia that the boy must be freed to avoid a storm that would level the jailhouse, but the weather had been clear for weeks and the captain of the guard laughed uproariously at the threat. He returned word that the skies were blue and would remain so until the boy's tongue matched their color, as it hung from his dying mouth.

Gokhlaya said nothing when he heard the reply, but went to his tipi and returned carrying his medicine pouch and an assortment of colored powders.

"May I come with you?" Hart asked as Gokhlaya gathered wood for a fire and tied it to a travois behind his pony. The old Indian nodded but didn't speak, and Hart knew by his silence that the man's Power already walked with him.

On the edge of the desert, several miles beyond the town, Gokhlaya built a fire. For more than an hour, the old shaman sat cross-legged before the pile of kindling, eyes closed, face lifted to Usen. The chant he uttered was eerie, reminding Hart of the sound that had drawn him to the Apache, long ago in the desert.

Gokhlaya poured the colored powders onto the sand beside him in glyphs Hart couldn't distinguish. Then he made an offering to the Four Sacred Directions and gathering up the sand picture, threw it into the fire. A column of dense black smoke rose and seemed to gain momentum as an odd roaring sound arose from nowhere; the smoke began to whirl and grew into a monstrous column, mingling with the desert wind, which was suddenly whipping up the sand to cyclone intensity. To Hart's astonishment, the column rose skyward, lifted itself from the fire altogether, and began to travel in the direction of the Mexican village until there could be no mistaking the cyclone's path.

Gokhlaya never ceased his chanting, which grew ever louder, nor did he look once at the cyclone he had summoned, but Hart, unnerved and fascinated, rose and grabbed his horse's reins. Mounting, he followed the cloud on its course toward Sonora.

The townspeople ran ahead of the cyclone that headed straight for the jail. He could hear the screams and see the people running; he saw, too, a bewildered Apache boy thrust unceremoniously out of the jailhouse into the street. Riding swiftly, Hart reached a hand down to the astonished boy and pulled him up behind him on the galloping horse. Hell-bent for leather, they rode beyond the outskirts of town, with the sounds of splintering wood and glass, shrieks and curses, ringing in their ears.

▲

Destarte participated in all her usual chores with an amazing strength, despite her pregnancy. Hart grew anxious about her as her time drew near, but she simply laughed at him as if he were a simpleton to worry about woman's business. He thought perhaps this bravado was expected of her by the older wives, and one night awoke to find her crying softly.

"Why do you weep, Destarte? Are you afraid?"

"My friend's child died today. The mothers cut the cord too close to the baby and death entered through his belly."

It took Hart hours to calm her enough for sleep, but it was clear to him that she worried not for her own safety, but for their baby's.

Destarte's birth pangs began while Hart was hunting far from camp; by the time he returned home he was alarmed to see his wife with her hands lashed to a tree high above her head, obviously in great pain. Hart ran from his horse to free her, cursing the fools who had treated her so cruelly. Her legs were wide apart and her face contorted by pain as he rushed to her side, but the midwives shooed him away forcefully. Destarte opened her eyes and gasped at his intrusion; he could read the confusion in her face, for it seemed to him some part of her wanted desperately to be comforted, while another strove for bravery. "I, too, am a warrior today," she gasped, her voice ragged with suffering. "I battle for our son."

The old men grabbed him by the arms and pulled him from her. "This is the way of the Apache woman," they told him. "You must stay away until the ordeal has passed, or you will shame her."

Hart paced for hours outside his wickiup, which occasioned much mirth among the men. All through the night he could see the bustle of the midwives, and several times he came close enough to see Destarte, but she looked so ravaged by her ordeal that he couldn't bear to watch.

To his astonishment and relief, Destarte herself came to him early in the morning to present his son. She was pale and trembling when he took her in his arms.

"Your child has been bathed with water warmed in the midwife's mouth, my Firehair, and he has been dried with soft moss and grasses," she said triumphantly, holding out the baby to his father.

"The sacred pollen has been sprinkled and the appropriate prayers have been said for your son. He is strong and well, my husband." Destarte's voice was tremulous with shy excitement. "He will grow to be a fine warrior . . . there is no need to fear for him now."

Hart was overwhelmed with relief, and with the heady magic of new fatherhood. Scarcely able to breathe with the excitement of the prize, Hart took the baby from his wife's arms, and tried to understand that this small life was his firstborn son. The boy's hair was straight and black as any Apache's; his features were a combination of both races that had spawned him, his skin the rosy amber of his mother, the features not quite Apache, not quite Caucasian. His perfect little arms and legs, no bigger than a plump doll's, moved constantly, and as Hart kissed the soft velvet cheek, the baby smiled toothlessly at his father.

They had lain together so many nights, feeling him kick and leap within his mother's womb, yet the miracle of his existence thrilled Hart beyond all expectation. He reveled in the perfection of fingers and toes—he unwrapped his son from his swaddling cloths so often to admire his strong body that Destarte finally ordered him to occupy himself elsewhere. So Hart began to draw the baby in every conceivable movement of head or hand, until dozens of sketches littered their tipi.

"We must name him with great care," Destarte told her husband as she bared her breast and led the baby's questing mouth to her overflowing nipple. "He will not have his true name for many years, but his baby name will have power, too."

"We will call him 'One-who-has-the-most-perfect-mother-in-the-world,' " Hart teased her, thinking the sight of the newborn boy at his mother's breast exquisite. She laughed, low and musically, for she knew now beyond doubt that her husband loved her as she loved him.

"Later, when we know his talents, we must find a name that describes them. Or perhaps a great hunter or warrior will promise our son his name."

"What will we call him now? 'He-who-has-stolen-his-mother-from-his-father's-bed?' " Hart made the small joke, but regretted it as soon as the words left his mouth, for he saw Destarte's stricken expression.

Apaches considered two or three years between children to be appropriate spacing, and any man who made his wife pregnant sooner would be considered irresponsible. There were certain herbs and plants that could be chewed as protection against pregnancy, but for a time after a baby's birth, abstinence was the unhappy necessity. He saw clearly in that instant, in Destarte's eyes, how much she, too, missed the pleasures of their love, and he scooped her and the unnamed baby into a great bear hug of happiness, and whirled them around and around until his wife forgot her worry and laughed with glee.

Paint-the-Wind was the baby name the parents settled on, for Destarte insisted that the baby's hands made the same swift movements in the air that her Firehair's did when he sketched. But in his heart of hearts, the new father christened his son Charles McAllister, after his own father . . . and wondered if one day he would see signs of his own heritage in this Apache child who was his son.

▲

"Paint the Wind," Hart wrote in his journal that night. *"Isn't that what we all must try to do? Paint our own unique colors on the ephemeral face of nature . . . and leave behind us something of value?*

"Oh, Great Spirit, before I die, let me paint at least one great color on the wind . . ."

87   Blackjack and Aurora listened restlessly to the latest nanny, Mrs. Cribbet. She was lecturing them on what was expected of a lady or a gentleman.

"What is it, Jack, that makes one a gentleman?"

"Getting born into a rich family, Mrs. Cribbet," he said with a winning smile. Aurora giggled.

"That's part of it to be sure, dear." He was such a delightful little boy, she hated to dampen his enthusiasm. "But to be a real gentleman, one must follow certain very strict rules of conduct, don't you see? These include honor, integrity, and kindness to one's inferiors. One must be generous, courteous, and not indifferent to one's dress. Can you think of any others?"

"A gentleman should be brave," Blackjack said earnestly. "And he should know about a lot of things." He'd started to say he should be a great cardplayer, but he thought that might cause trouble.

"Yes, of course he should. That's another way of saying that a gentleman should be well educated." Blackjack wrinkled his nose at that distasteful thought; education was not what he'd meant at all. Craps, poker, horses, these were the manly pursuits he'd had in mind.

"The nature of a man's occupation, his breeding, his connections, and his character are each matters of consequence," Mrs. Cribbet continued. "And perhaps most important is noblesse oblige."

"What's that?" asked Aurora, who hated her French and German lessons more than any of her other odious studies.

"It means be nice to poor people," Blackjack offered in translation; he had his father's gift of total recall.

"Oh, I always forget. But it doesn't matter anyway, because I don't have to be a gentleman!"

"Ah, but you must be a lady, Aurora. And that is a far more exacting task," said Mrs. Cribbet. "You see, a lady must share most of a gentleman's virtues, but she must possess other qualities as well."

"Like what?" Aurora asked curtly. She hated all rules, but was canny enough to know that while she might get away with a great many failings, being unladylike was not one of them.

"A lady must be cool and quiet as a sylvan pool," Mrs. Cribbet said pompously. "She must be an island of serenity for her husband and children. She must never run, nor raise her voice nor make undignified gestures with her hands. She must be decorous at all times, and must never make a show of her intelligence. And, of course, she must be pure, but that goes without saying."

Aurora nodded absently . . . what a bore it was to listen to the woman's prattle. All this nonsense about ladies and gentlemen didn't matter in the least. Everyone knew if your father owned a silver mine, you were a lady.

▲

Fancy was an early riser; she'd always loved the morning because it belonged to her alone. She and Atticus had risen with the woodland birds and he'd told her those extra hours were a gift the gods had given them, so that their day could hold more than everyone else's. The morning hours were free . . . no obligations, no visitors, no needs but her own. She tapped her pencil on the list of things that needed doing and remembered she'd promised Aurora she would have the little jewel box Chance had given her repaired. Feeling inexplicably cheery, Fancy left her own room to go to her daughter's, humming softly as she walked down the wainscoted hallway.

The jewel box lay on Aurora's dressing table, glinting prettily in the sunlight. Fancy opened the cover to empty it and the song she'd been humming died in her throat. She stared dumbly at the aquamarine earrings that lay twinkling beneath the other, childish trinkets. The missing earrings caught a glint of sun and winked up at her from the bottom of the box.

"Oh, Aurora . . ." she said aloud, as the full implication of the child's perfidy hit her. "How could you do such a dreadful thing?" Fancy saw again the tearful, injured face of the maid she'd sacked for theft and felt quite ill at the realization of the wrong she'd done the woman. Aurora was well beyond the age of reason—she knew good from bad, truth from lie—or did she?

This must be dealt with, and swiftly. She thought of turning to Chance, but instinct told her he'd be useless in such a confrontation; she must discipline Aurora herself.

Fancy left the dressing room, the earrings still clenched tightly in her fist.

▲

"I didn't take them, Mother." Aurora's gaze was steady and unblinking.

"They were in your jewel box."

"Nanny must have put them there."

"Why would Nanny steal my earrings and then not sell them, Aurora? They're worth more than she earns in a year."

Aurora's face hardened into a vindictive little knot. "She probably did it just to get me in trouble. Remember how Miss Powell was always trying to do that, too?"

Fancy's stomach tightened; the new nanny hadn't said much in the time she'd been with them, but she could tell the woman was displeased with Aurora on nearly every level.

"You're lying to me, Aurora," Fancy persevered, hating herself, wishing with all her heart that she was wrong.

She watched the angelic face dissolve into misery; tears welled up and spilled on cue.

Sweet Jesus, what an incredible actress she is, Fancy thought. How could I not have seen this in her before?

Enraged at the girl's performance and her own stupidity, Fancy slapped Aurora full in the face. The blow startled the girl for an instant, then she set up such a howl of rage and pain, Fancy was again stunned. The hatred that looked out at her from Aurora's eyes was not new; it had been freed by the slap, not caused by it. But where in God's name had such hatred come from?

"You will remain in your room for the rest of the day," Fancy shouted at her daughter over the girl's sobs. "Until I decide what punishment is appropriate to what you've done. You've not only stolen from me and lied about it, Aurora, but you've caused Maria to lose her job with your dishonesty— that young woman may not be able to feed her family because of what you've done to her. This is very, very serious."

As she turned to go, Fancy realized she had never before punished either one of her children herself; there had always been a housekeeper or nanny to reprimand them for infractions of the rules. She had no idea what an appropriate punishment would be, but whatever she decided on, she knew instinctively that it must be serious enough to fit the ugly crime, for she could see in Aurora's eyes that her distress was caused by being caught, *not* by what she'd done.

▲

Aurora flicked the whip over the pony's flank and shot out of the stable-yard like a hunter on the fox's trail. The groom yelled a warning but knew even as he did so, that the spoiled child would pay him no heed. He wondered if he should find Aurora's governess and tell her of the girl's behavior, but the poor woman had her hands full enough with the brat, so perhaps he'd best stay out of it.

"Stupid mother!" Aurora hissed over the pony's head into the wind whipping past her. "How dare you treat me like a common criminal!" She had remained in her room only long enough to be certain Fancy was out of earshot. "She doesn't even remember I'm alive except to yell at me over some trifle. She has a thousand earrings and I only took one pair."

The high-strung animal sensed the anger and fiddle-string tension in the rider and sped along the edge of the meadow. The legs that ordered him on were hostile, agitated, but they were the legs of a superb horsewoman. Despite her size, Aurora could handle her pony with the skill of a polo player.

I'll hurt you, Mother, one of these days, Aurora thought savagely in the depths of herself, and the thought gave her comfort. I'll make you pay for the way you've hurt me.

The tall, statuesque young woman stepped off the stage and adjusted her traveling suit, wrinkled from the long dusty ride. She was elegantly dressed and refined, but there was also something sensual about her that made every man on the street turn around and take a closer look. Her chestnut hair was done up in shining ringlets, under a tiny hat perched at a precarious angle. Her eyes were dark, under luxuriant brows, and her full mouth twitched, as if she had difficulty keeping it from smiling. Her skin was flawless and tawny as a Spanish dancer's; but for the indefinable duskiness of her complexion, her features might have graced the social pages of a metropolitan newspaper.

She looked around, as if taking her bearings from hearsay rather than memory. Finally she asked the man seated in front of the sheriff's office for the address that had graced a thousand letters, and set out determinedly in the direction he pointed.

She stopped, puzzled, in front of the Crown of Jewel's and glanced again at the street number over the swinging doors. How odd that her mail was being posted to a saloon. She lifted her skirts, as any well-bred young lady would, and walked over the boardwalk, through the doors and into the Crown to inquire.

Rufus spotted the unlikely arrival and called out to her, "You lookin' for somebody, miss?"

"Yes. Yes, I am. But there's been some sort of mistake, I think. I'm looking for Julia Jameson and this is the right address but . . ." The bar had quieted to a whisper.

Rufus looked to Jewel, who stood transfixed in her purple satin and black lace. There was only one person besides Ford who would call her Julia Jameson. Intense compassion was written in the black man's eyes.

Jewel thought, for one horrified instant, of fleeing, of pretending to be someone else . . . then she took a deep breath, straightened her spine, and walked across the floor to the uncertain figure.

"Welcome home, Dakota," she said as steadily as she could. "You're even more beautiful than your daddy said."

The girl's eyes widened, straining to understand who this amazing creature in the whalebone-corseted dress might be.

"Do I know you?" she asked confusedly.

"Not near as much as I hope you will, Dakota. I'm your mama."

The young woman blushed, tried to cover her embarrassment by averting her eyes. When she looked up again, her own were full of tears.

"I don't know what to say . . ." she stammered. "I thought . . . oh, I'm so sorry. I don't know what I thought. I only meant to surprise you." She put her gloved hand to her mouth, to keep in the words that sought to tumble out, then she turned and fled back onto the street.

Stricken, Jewel stood still as a pillar. Rufus thought she looked like the decoration he'd once seen on the prow of a ship.

"What you cain't duck, you might as well welcome," she said, finally, but her voice was hollow and afraid as she started for the door.

Rufus reached across the bar and grabbed Jewel's arm; he held it fast as he spoke. "A mama only one little part of what you are, Jewel. You respect yo'self out there, you heah me?"

Jewel nodded, squeezed his hand, then pushed the swinging doors aside and scanned the street for Dakota. She spotted the girl sitting incongruously on the edge of the raised boardwalk, her feet dangling like a little child's, her eyes averted and her shoulders shaking. The madam took one deep breath and crossed the dusty road to face her daughter.

"I'm real sorry you had to find out this way, Dakota. I never meant you to be ashamed, that's why I pretended like I did, through all the years. That's why I sent you east to school. But you cain't varnish the truth, I guess—it always comes out sticky. So here it is, straight and honest as I can make it. I own a saloon, and a laundry, a bathhouse and a whorehouse. Been a whore, too . . . been a lot of things in order to eat. I always tried to be decent and to tell the truth, been a good friend to some and a bad enemy to others. I guess the best you could say about me is I always loved you and wanted life to treat you different than it treated me." The girl stared fixedly at her shoes.

"And my father?" she whispered without looking up. "I guess he's not a traveling businessman?"

Jewel's hands were on her hips now, a measure of defiance in the stance; nobody, daughter or not, could be permitted to put Ford Jameson down . . . not while she drew breath.

"Your daddy is an outlaw to some, a marshal to others. Only part that counts is what he's been to you, which is real upstanding. He loves you, Dakota. He's done his best for you, even in the lean times."

The girl's body trembled and Jewel didn't know if she should try to comfort her tears. Dakota raised her fine head to look at her mother, so much merriment in her expression that Jewel was shocked. The girl threw back her head and laughed aloud, a deep, throaty sound that could have been Jewel's laugh a thousand years before.

"I'm delighted to meet you, Mama," she said through her laughter. "You have absolutely no idea how I've looked forward to this day."

Jewel felt confused and foolish. "You're not upset about finding things different from what you thought? Not embarrassed? I saw the way you looked me up and down in there . . ."

"Well, I should say I did," the girl replied with enthusiasm. "I was thinking why in the hell didn't I inherit that unbelievable body? I can see I've inherited quite a number of other things from you, Mama. Now I know why I never fit in at school . . . why I'm wilder than my ever-so-careful contemporaries. And why I want different things out of life than a proper husband and proper babies and a lifetime of boring propriety. Oh, Mama, don't you see? So many things make sense to me now that never did before this minute. I always thought you kept me in boarding schools because you just didn't want to be bothered with me. And that was the most demoralizing thing of all . . . wondering why. Now I know it hadn't anything to do with my inadequacies, and I'm so relieved I could just jump up and down right here on this glorious street corner.

"I came to find you because I want to see the world, Mama, and not the world the people at finishing school have in mind for me. I'm educated to a fare-thee-well. I can speak French and I never fail forks . . . and I can do calculus, which no self-respecting woman would ever want to admit, and if I'm not careful, I'll end up all pruned up and totally unused, and that's not what I want at all."

"What *do* you want?"

"To see the world, Mama! I want to touch, taste, feel, smell everything in it . . . to not die thinking there was something important I forgot to do. I want to find out what men are like before I get stuck married to one. I want to act and sing and dance before crowned heads, and find the source of the Nile, and maybe join the Foreign Legion . . . and just about every other mad, rebellious thing you can think of! Most of all, I want to write novels and there's absolutely no way to do that if you haven't lived. I have a splendid imagination, because it's gotten so much use over the years, but that's no substitute for experience."

Jewel smiled at the exuberance only unsullied youth can produce. "Better come back inside and have some lunch first, honey. Sounds to me like you'll need to keep your strength up." She shook her head in amusement; Fate never did let you get complacent for long.

Dakota slid to the ground, and Jewel marveled at her unstudied elegance, in some ways so much like Ford's. She could see each of them in their daughter, his dark sensuality, her own mischief, but Dakota was other things, too . . . as if the gods had added a few surprises of their own. She wondered what the taciturn and brooding new marshal of Medicine Hat would say when he heard the news that their long-lost Dakota had come home to roost, on her way to see the world.

▲

Ford felt the warmth of the young girl at his side; she held his arm proudly, lovingly. His heart swelled every time he looked at Dakota; he was relieved he wore a tin star on his chest now, so she wouldn't have to be ashamed of his profession. She'd settled in to life at the Crown, helping Rufus, helping Jewel. Wu had actually smiled when he spoke of her, she had so many Chinese virtues, he'd said enigmatically. She was industrious and honorable and she could do sums as fast as anyone he'd ever seen who did not possess an abacus.

"Have you decided what you intend to do next, Dakota?" Ford asked her. The wind blew chill off the mountains and she held fast to his arm for warmth and love.

"Part of me wants to go west to San Francisco, or Los Angeles, Daddy. I think I'd like the West better than the East, and I'm certain I could find employment there. But I'd hate to leave Mama so soon, and I wouldn't want to stay here for any length of time without working. There's a schoolteacher needed for the Leadville Consolidated School and I do love children, so I've been thinking I might apply. It's just that being a schoolmarm seems a bit of a roadblock in my desire to see the world."

Ford patted her hand as he spoke. "Could be you should stay here a while, Dakota. Get to know your mama . . . I could visit from time to time, too. Seems a shame to run off, when we three just found each other again."

"I've thought of that, too, Daddy. It's lovely to belong to someone, isn't it? Although I'm a little afraid it could be habit-forming, and then I'd never get to see all the extraordinary things I've dreamed about."

"You have a long time ahead of you to see the world, Dakota."

She cocked her head to catch his downcast gaze when she replied thoughtfully, "People get trapped in thinking that, don't they, Daddy? I expect it's why most people don't go anywhere and die knowing only the town they were born in. I couldn't bear that happening to me."

"What exactly do you think you'll find in those far-off places, Dakota?"

"Experience. Something important to write about. Heartbreak, love, adventure, tragedy, things I've never even imagined . . . I want to write books that will live after me, stories people will pull down off the shelf on a cold winter evening by the fire, the kind they'll read with tears in their eyes and then pass on to the ones they love." Her face shone with the expectation of immortality. "I've been keeping a diary since I was seven, you know. It's full to the brim with observations, but what does a girl in boarding school have to observe, really? I'm afraid I need to experience woman-things, and I'm not in the least sure I could find any real adventures here in Leadville. I envy Fancy McAllister—she's already done so many of the things on my list."

Ford knew far too much about adventures to be pleased with Dakota's plan, but he loved her too well to try to keep her dreams from coming true.

▲

"You know, Julia, she's about as interesting as anyone I've ever met." Ford lifted his chin so Jewel could fix the black string tie into a more agreeable knot.

"I quoted something obscure from Virgil today and she finished up the quote, delighted as a child that I knew it."

Jewel stood back to admire her work. "She's smart as they come, Ford . . . way beyond her mama, that's for sure. And she says the damnedest things, real insightful and funny, too. Like the other day when she told Rufus poor Augusta Tabor had the misfortune to be 'pickled up by righteousness' and that Fancy is 'bodaciously fractious.' Wu says he'll take her to San Francisco next time he goes; maybe that'll satisfy her wanderlust, for a while at least."

Ford put his arms around Jewel. "There's plenty her mama can teach her, Julia, don't forget that. In some ways, she's older than her years, but in others she's as innocent as a little girl. We'd best keep an eye on her where men are concerned, I'm afraid she'd be easy prey. Have you had a talk with her about men?"

Jewel laughed heartily. "Have I ever? That girl's as interested in the birds and the bees as she is in every blessed other thing you can think of, Ford. You would have fainted if you heard the questions she asked me, 'just as research for her journal,' she said. Would've made a rabbit blush."

Ford looked worried, as only the father of a daughter can.

"What did you tell her, Julia?"

"Every blessed thing I could think of, of course. I don't hold with innocence bein' so all-fired good—just another word for ignorance is all it is. I don't want her followin' some fancy man down the garden path 'cause she's ignorant of what he's after—so I made sure she had her facts straight. She said our discussion was 'most enlightening.' "

"No man can imagine what women say of sex to each other, Julia," Ford said with a hint of a smile. "Probably scare the bejesus out of us, if we knew."

"She said she might take the job they was offerin' at the Consolidated School, just to keep busy over the winter and earn her keep. I hope she does it, too. I don't cotton to havin' her in the saloon. It ain't the right environment for a lady."

Ford's expression softened and he pulled her in close. "You're the purest person I know, Julia," he said gently. "It could only do her good to be around you, saloon or no saloon."

"I don't know, Ford. Mebbe it is best if she moves on to somewheres she won't be tainted by our past. It's just that I hate the thought of losin' her."

"We won't lose her, Julia. Wherever she goes, she'll always be part of us. She's our immortality."

They finished dressing and walked down the stairs contentedly to the Crown at its evening revels.

89 Dakota Jameson was as beautiful as any young woman Fancy had ever seen, she decided, and it wasn't all on the outside. She was the oddest combination of practicality and zaniness; both her imagination and her tongue seemed to work overtime. Fancy invited her to visit in Denver at every opportunity, and several times made the trip to Leadville just to see the girl.

"I knew we'd be kindred souls the moment I laid eyes on you," Dakota told her. "You've lived all the adventures I've merely dreamed."

Fancy smiled and eased her horse from a trot to a walk. "My adventures took a lot out of me, Dakota, I assure you."

"Oh, but they put a great deal in, too, Fancy, didn't they? I've been trying to decide how to characterize you in my journal, but you're so complicated I hardly know where to begin. You and Mama nearly defy my imagination, and that's a real trick because I'm a mighty imaginer."

"You love your mama, don't you, Dakota?"

"Oh, yes, I do. So very much. She's a good bit larger than life, isn't she? Nearly mythic, in fact. And an awfully good person, too, don't you think? Completely at odds with people's notions about women in her somewhat dubious profession. I keep thinking of Mary Magdalene, of course—she certainly defied the popular view of goodness. Maybe it has to do with having red hair; I've always thought perhaps it's harder not to get into mischief if you have red hair. Of course, mischief doesn't seem to have anything to do with goodness, does it?"

Fancy shook her head and laughed; she'd have to remember to tell Jewel about her resemblance to Mary Magdalene. "It's a good thing you've decided to be a writer, Dakota. You'll need a place to put all those words you keep manufacturing."

Dakota laughed, and Fancy thought she saw Ford in her exotic eyes.

"I've stored up millions of them, you know . . . words and stories. All those years in boarding schools, I was so lonely that I just kept making up stories about the world and life and my parents, to keep me going. Now I can let them all out and I'm afraid there are years and years of them trying to scramble out of me all at once, so it may take me quite a while to run down. I do hope you don't mind."

"Mind? I'm so happy that you love your mother, Dakota, so happy for both of you, that you can talk to your heart's content."

"Aurora really hurts you, doesn't she, Fancy?" Dakota asked, and Fancy's happy expression changed.

"You mustn't mind my talking about personal things with you, Fancy, because we're kindred souls and because I'll only be here for a while and I'd hate to think, later, that we'd only talked about the weather and never said anything at all important to each other. I tried to find out why Aurora's so cranky at you, the other day, you know. She's got a Gordian knot of anger inside that she seems to nurture. She likes the attention she gets from being difficult and doesn't have a clue how much nicer life could be if she weren't. And she's a bit spoiled, too, I'm afraid, Fancy. I suspect it's hard to keep your perspective if you always get everything, so there's nothing left to dream of. I can't think what life would be like without my dreams! And I suspect Aurora thinks she'll never measure up to the pace you've set, Fancy, and I wish I didn't feel compelled to say this, but I'm going to because you're my friend and Mama's, too. If she can't rise up to your level of achievement, I fear she may just try to drag you down to hers—so, I do hope you'll be especially careful of her, even if she is your firstborn. I have this theory, you see, quite unproven and all, but a theory nonetheless because I've had so much time to observe human nature, that sometimes the children of our bodies are not the children of our spirits. Aurora might not even be your friend, Fancy, but that's pretty terrible to think about, and perhaps I'm wrong."

Fancy shook her head wonderingly at Dakota's perceptiveness. "My friend, Magda, would agree with you, I'm afraid. But I keep hoping you're both wrong."

"Human nature is perverse, isn't it, Fancy? Of course, sometimes life can surprise you for the good, too. All my life I wanted to know my mama and daddy, and to be sure they really loved me. I wanted to really *like* them—as people, I mean, not just love them because Fate's whim had plopped me on their doorstep. And here I am, happy as a lord, and getting ready to go off on an adventure, knowing my most special dream has come true. So maybe yours will, too."

Fancy reached over to touch the young girl's hand; she didn't trust herself to speak for her voice was suddenly full of tears.

▲

Dakota worked on her journal every day; in fact she worked conscientiously at everything she set her hand to. She helped her mother and Rufus at the Crown and she helped Wu do the books in Chinatown. She learned the intricacies of their businesses with an alacrity that startled Fancy. The girl wasn't driven as she herself was, rather it seemed she was a collector of competencies and applied herself to learning each new task with youthful verve. Dakota had told Fancy she intended to stay the winter in Leadville, before moving on.

"My journal has never been so full," Dakota said as she folded up the cash disbursement book at the laundry and passed it on to Fancy, who was shocked to see that Wu had let the financial record out of his own hands. "I used to have to make up every word in it, but now there's so much incredible reality to draw on, I swear the book looks forward to my arrival home each night, just to see what I'm going to report."

Fancy laughed. "By the time you get to writing your novel, Dakota, you'll have done so much reporting, you'll be too tired for fiction."

"No, indeed, Fancy. My stories are all alive inside me right this minute, I just haven't met them face-to-face yet. I believe they just mill around inside a writer until she's learned enough about life to give them proper voice. After all, it would be a perfect tragedy if you had the soul of a Shakespeare but only the experience of the ditchdigger to draw on."

Fancy smiled at the delightful girl who had grown so close to her heart. "I believe writing and acting have a great deal in common, Dakota. They both demand the ability to live in someone else's skin. Imagination was always my escape from a reality that needed improvement . . . yours, too, I suspect."

"Oh, yes, I'm afraid being in boarding school is dreadfully confining, and you can't help but want to be with your family, even if you know that for some reason they can't keep you. After a while, you begin to feel unworthy of being wanted, I suppose, and if you don't want to get crotchety about it, you simply have to look at things differently. I read once that rubies are the souls of lost roses, and that made all the difference for me, Fancy. I thought it was so romantic I nearly wept, and from that instant on, I knew you can *choose* how you look at the world . . . you're not just stuck looking at things like other people do. So I began to fantasize about my mama and daddy and how they adored me, but circumstances didn't permit them to keep me near, and that made things infinitely better. And now here I am, and I find that it wasn't a fantasy at all, just the unvarnished truth." Dakota's face was shining; Fancy, for no reason whatsoever, hugged the girl to her heart.

▲

The good women of Leadville did not take kindly to Dakota Jameson applying for a post as schoolteacher, but the board was finally forced to admit her credentials were impeccable, except for her parents. There was considerable discussion at the board meeting about whether the sins of the father, or mother, for that matter, could be visited upon the next generation, but in the end necessity triumphed, for school was about to open and no other qualified person had applied.

Miss Jameson had queer notions about teaching, too, the townsfolk found out quickly. "If I can't win them over with kindness and imagination, then I'd best go about my business elsewhere," Dakota said with conviction to the schoolboard's first meeting. The townsfolk thought sparing the rod a foolish whimsy, but the children of Leadville did their best to prove worthy of the pretty new teacher's trust.

The boys thought the lovely Dakota such an improvement over dowdy Mrs. Lacey and cranky Mr. Sim, that they outdid each other in scholarship to please her; the girls waited daily to see how she'd done up her hair in some new "do," and they strove to be model citizens, just to perversely prove their parents wrong.

Being a schoolmarm wasn't all Dakota had in mind for herself, but she was young and frisky, and recently enough out of school that the freedom of adulthood was heady. She put her considerable imagination to work to make lessons fun.

"We're not going to *read* plays, children," she told them. "We are going to perform them. And every single day that you've been good and done all your lessons correctly, I'm going to spend the last half hour reading aloud to you from my favorite novels." She found that the Brontës had the capacity to keep even the most obstreperous in line.

"I had no idea, Rufus, how very interesting little children can be," Dakota told him after the trail of youngsters who tended to follow her home each day had left. "Just today, little Billy Harker told me he's been studying snowflakes for some time now, and he's never found any two alike. He said, if by chance every single one is different, he thinks God is spending entirely too much time thinking up new snowflake designs, and maybe that's why the world's in such a sorry state."

Rufus grinned and tied a clean apron around his middle. "Bet you were a interestin' li'l thing when you were small, Dakota."

"I was mostly shy, Rufus, although they say I talked a blue streak from the time I opened my mouth."

"Seems like you makin' up fo' yo' daddy, child. He says only what's necessary, you say what's pretty to hear. All evens up, I expect."

"Do you think I'll get to see the world, Rufus?"

"Wouldn't surprise me none."

"Did you ever want to see it all, like I do?"

Rufus chuckled. "Seen more'n enough to suit me. You kin go see my part, too."

Dakota laughed softly. Rufus thought she had the prettiest face he'd ever laid eyes on and hoped the world would be good to her. She wore a long buckskin skirt and a knitted top that left no doubt about the litheness of her young body. She was troublingly beautiful, exotic, and, in her own way, bountiful as her mother. Men couldn't help but notice, couldn't help but want. Rufus thought there might be problems if she stayed on, and worse if she lit out on her own.

"You know I'm going to hate to leave my mama and daddy, when I go, Rufus. I admire them so."

"You do?"

"They've overcome real hardships, I think. I'd never presume to ask about them, but I expect they've seen the world, Rufus, and it didn't treat them gently. But they're good people anyway and that's admirable as all get out, don't you think? I can't help but wonder who I'll be when I've seen it all."

Rufus went about his business thinking how nice it was to be young enough to think that what the world had to offer was mostly desirable.

 Mahogany forests in Honduras, a theatre in Kansas City, mining interests in Central America, a riverbank mill in Mexico, something or other in the Yucatán, wherever the hell that was . . .

Fancy ticked off some of Chance's investments that she'd wheedled out of everyone she could—some from Jason, who seemed a more welcome visitor these days when he came to Colorado, some from Jewel, whose girls had heard pillow talk from other mine owners.

Caz couldn't tell her much, and she believed the man when he said that where the mine money went was as much a secret to him as it was to her. His instructions were to get the silver out of the ground and send the money to Chance or Jason or John Henderson at the Fiduciary Bank; after that, who could say what happened to it? Caz did volunteer that not nearly enough of it was spent on safety measures in the mine these days, or on improvements of any kind, and that disturbed Fancy most of all. Chance never paid attention to details, but he surely did care about the men. . . .

One of the new claims looked like it might be a winner, the Aussie said, but it was still too soon to say, and a great many of the recent purchases had been real clinkers. Dear Caz, Fancy thought, he'd always been such a loyal friend to us all, with never a jealous bone over the fact that we made it big and he didn't. She decided to do something nice to repay the man—maybe she could get Chance or Jason to raise his salary—of course, if she did that, it would tip them off that she was keeping tabs. She made a mental note to send a gift instead to him and his wife, Annie. It distressed her that she and Chance no longer socialized with old friends who were not on their social level. Magda, Wes, Gitalis, Wu, Jewel, Caz . . . she saw them all on her own; Chance wasn't a snob exactly, but outside of political necessity, he did only what he wanted, not what he considered a personal obligation. She forced her mind back to the problem at hand.

Surely Jason, at least, knew what he was doing, and he appeared to have provided only friendship and good counsel to Chance since the mining accident. Not that she really fully trusted him, but at least he was the one man in town who treated her as an equal. When Jason was in Leadville or Denver, he always went out of his way to be both courtly and informative; not seductive, merely gentlemanly, like an old friend from the past, which, of course, was an accurate enough description of his status, she supposed.

Fancy prepared for bed, anxious to talk to Chance about what she'd learned of his enterprises. They had so little time alone together these days, and bed was the one place where everything always went well between them; maybe she could get some satisfactory answers there.

▲ ▲ ▲

Chance tossed his trousers haphazardly onto the chaise. He's so careless of everything, she thought with the petty annoyance that enters into marriage when other, more important, things are wrong.

He hadn't backed her up when she'd punished Aurora for the theft of the earrings, and that still rankled; she'd tried to make him see the seriousness of the girl's theft, but he'd had other things on his mind, and hadn't been as shaken by the episode as she.

Naked, Chance slid into bed beside Fancy and automatically turned to take her in his arms. How like him, she thought . . . never a question of whether I want to make love, only the certainty that I'll respond. She tried to slither out of reach without really rebuffing him; she'd heard at the Geographic Society lecture that when a female whale wished to avoid a male's attentions, she simply upended herself and stuck her tail above the water until he tired of the game and left. She wished she had as eloquent a signal. Not that she didn't like to make love with Chance . . . even after all the years, she had to admit that just the sight of him entering a room could flood her with desire. But there were serious topics to discuss tonight and too often lust was Chance's means of avoiding all discussion . . . and decision . . . and responsibility . . .

Had he always been that way? Or had she only noticed it with her own growing sophistication? Or had it been that in the old days, Hart and Bandana had provided the checks and balances for Chance's improvident nature, so it was less noticeable, less irritating, and less dangerous. She wondered fleetingly where Hart was and said a prayer for his safety.

"You're relying a lot on Jason's judgment in these new investments you're making, aren't you, love?" she asked, gently moving her body away from her husband's questing hands. "I wish you'd tell me what they're all about, so I won't feel such a dunce when somebody talks to me about your newest triumphs." Maybe flattery would do the trick.

She knew that since they'd been in Denver he'd left nearly all Leadville decision making in the hands of Jason or John. Others of Leadville's rich had financial advisors, of course, but still it troubled her that Chance was so oblivious to his own role in personally controlling their holdings. On the other hand, Jason had all the business qualities Chance lacked, so maybe she was better off with this arrangement. If only she could ever *feel* Jason to be trustworthy, but in her gut she knew he was a predator. A shark always needs to feed . . . it was probably just her imagination that either she or Chance might be the prey.

Good-naturedly, Chance propped himself up on one elbow, a sensual smile playing at his lips.

"Do you really think this is the time to talk business, sugar?" he said, amused. "There's this story I've been wanting to tell you . . ."

"When *is* the time, Chance?"

"Anytime but now," he answered confidently, reaching out for her, touching just where she loved to be touched, so that Fancy felt her body respond almost against her own will. She felt the hardening of nipple, the dampening of yearning. Chance saw it, too, for he smiled and moved his hands downward, barely touching the rise and fall of ribs and taut belly, just enough to raise goose bumps of desire. Just enough . . . she thought, deeply disturbed by the intensity of her own responsiveness. Always just enough.

▲ ▲ ▲

Horace Austin Warner Tabor was expansive as all get out, Chance thought, for a man who'd placed himself smack in the eye of the hurricane with his divorce. After more than a quarter century of less than blissful marriage, Haw had left the dreary Augusta for the ebullient Baby Doe McCourt.

Fancy had greeted the news of Augusta's loss with unmitigated delight— maybe now the old battle-ax would have enough on her mind, taking care of her own business instead of other people's, she'd told Jewel with malicious pleasure. Augusta had been a leader in the movement to keep Fancy out of Leadville's polite society—as if that weren't a contradiction in terms!

The last of the countless courses was being cleared away and Fancy knew, with consummate annoyance, that any moment the women would be shooed off, so the men could talk business over their cigars and port, while she was relegated to the endless boring gossip of housewives. Fancy turned to Jason, seated next to her, determined to learn what she could before losing him to the men's conversation; he'd come to town the day before to attend this party.

"I hear the Little Pittsburgh stock is down to a dollar ninety-five a share," she said, and saw him smile indulgently at her.

"It must be trying for a woman of your intelligence to be consigned to discussing croup and diapers," he whispered back conspiratorially.

"I'd give my new lace bloomers to be a fly on the wall tonight when you men get together, so I could find out what's *really* going on around here."

"An interesting proposition, my dear, and one I'd be most pleased to take you up on, if you weren't so very married and full of propriety these days. But I do sympathize with your sensible curiosity."

"Enough to satisfy it?"

She really is one of a kind, he thought; if Chance would only use her acumen to help him make decisions, he'd be a formidable adversary.

"Word is," Jason said, his voice confidential, "that Chaffee and Moffat may have sold their own mine shares short, when they found out the Little Pittsburgh's days were numbered."

"How many shares did they short?" she asked, avid as a child.

"Fifty-one thousand, according to rumor." He was amused both by her interest and by the fact that she understood without explanation exactly what the manipulation had been. "The stock is selling at less than two dollars a share."

"God Almighty, Jason! Last January I could have bought it at thirty." Several heads, including Chance's, turned her way.

Fancy, reproved, lowered her eyes and rose with the other ladies to be sent into exile, but as she passed Jason's chair she whispered to him, "That was damned well worth my bloomers." He chuckled appreciatively, and Fancy, happy as always when she'd caused a scene, flounced off to the parlor to converse with the other ladies about the use of laudanum for bowel flux and other equally riveting topics.

▲

The Walsh library to which the men adjourned was the most lavish in Denver, which was only to be expected from the wealthiest of all Denver's elite.

Chance warmed the crystal snifter between his hands and pressed his long, lean body comfortably back into the leather wing chair near the fire. Huge logs cracked and hissed in the room's mahogany darkness; he watched a shower of snapping sparks sucked upwards by the draft. It looked to be another long-winded evening.

"Bi-metallism," Tabor was saying, "is the only sure way for the country to go. It makes no sense whatsoever to back this country's currency with gold alone. Not when the quantities mined of each metal are damned near identical." Murmurs of assent greeted this popular sally.

Jim Grant, former governor and one of the only two Democrats in the room, spoke up. "It isn't just the silver industry that's endangered here, gentlemen. Every single economic pursuit in this state is tied to mining. There's not a living soul in Colorado who doesn't depend for his bread on silver."

"Now, Jim," Tabor nudged. "No need to make a campaign speech here—you're not running for anything at the moment."

"The state'd be a damned sight better off if I were," he riposted, and everyone chuckled.

"Electioneering or no electioneering. If they wipe silver off the map, they'll just double the value of gold and gold securities and the debt securities which have to be paid in gold."

Chance thought it was time to enter the discussion; silence was always considered weakness in politics. "That's what the Silver Alliance is all about, isn't it? We've got branches set up all over the state promoting silver to everyone from senators to grannies in their rocking chairs." He rested his glass on the small satinwood table beside his chair and warmed to the discussion.

McAllister had the look of a statesman, it was said behind his back, and he was able to make voters believe in whatever he was selling. "You gentlemen seem to be forgetting one important factor," he said now all eyes were turned in his direction.

"And what exactly is that, sir?" asked Elmore Trask.

"That sensible as bi-metallism seems to us here in the midst of the silver kingdom, there are damned powerful forces back East who have just as vested an interest in gold.

"We in Colorado are the leading silver producers in America, so we can't conceive of our government walking away from silver, but it's the gold men on Wall Street who have the ears of the Washington elite. I've been to the Capitol often enough this year to know what I'm talking about."

"You're absolutely right," Jason Madigan said. "Even if we succeed in getting someone into the White House who's pro-silver, we'd damned well better not get complacent. We could lose our shirts with the stroke of a pen on the wrong bill."

Chance felt a momentary unease at the thought of silver becoming a glut on the market, but he forced the notion aside. Nonetheless, he was glad Jason had encouraged him to diversify into all those other investments, which at first had made him wary. It never paid to have all your eggs in one basket, and life at the top was proving to be very, very expensive.

Chance listened with one ear as Haw began the speech everyone expected to hear, at least once per dinner party.

▲ ▲ ▲

Dear Bro,

I've decided to keep on writing to you, even though I don't know where you've gone. It keeps you alive, I guess—I suppose it never occurred to you that I might worry about you if you took off into hostile Indian country and disappeared from the face of the earth?

It's also a means of keeping my mind clear, I think. Talking to you always kept me on the straight and narrow, bro, but I suppose you know that. There I'd be, with all my plans and dreams, running on at the mouth about how I was going to rule the world, and then you'd say some simple commonsense thing that would put me straight again . . . can't say I always appreciated the abrupt plunge into cold water, but I can see now how much I miss your honesty and goodness, Hart. I always knew, when you were around, I could run out my kite string just so far and then you'd reel me back in before I hit my head on a low flying comet.

Life's more fine than not since Fancy and I worked out our problems, bro. Aurora's a handful, though. I hate to say it about my own kin, but she's got a mean streak and an arrogance I've never seen in a McAllister. I doubt she'd give me houseroom if she had her druthers. Blackjack is so much like me as a boy he'd make you chuckle. He handles a deck like a Mississippi riverboat gambler, despite the fact that his hands are barely big enough to hold the cards—but there's more to him than that. I'll never forget the way he stood guard over his sister's coffin like a sentinel, never left her side, only a baby himself. He's the only one talks about her like she's still alive. "I guess she's up there with the eagles, now, Dad," he'll say. "She must love having wings, it was real hard for her to walk."

I'd like you to know my son, bro, I hope someday you'll have one of your own. We don't seem to have the luck with girls we do with boys, but maybe you'll change all that.

Well, I guess that's it for now. I'll just tuck this letter in the drawer with the rest and one day, when you come home, we'll get drunk together and read them all out loud and have a fine old time reminiscing.

Stay safe, bro. You mean a lot to

Your harried brother,
Chance

91 ❦ Dakota Jameson tugged at her traveling suit and wondered if she'd changed much in the year she'd been in Leadville. She felt different, more substantial, self-sufficient and all grown up. Teaching had expanded her. Living in Leadville with Jewel had added reams to her journal and the time she'd spent in Denver with Fancy had made her feel sophisticated and worldly. She wished Fancy still lived in Leadville; having her friend near at hand would have comforted Jewel, now that she was leaving. The school year had ended and it was time to go in search of material for her stories, but it was infinitely harder to part with Jewel and Ford than she'd ever dreamed it would be. If seeing the world hadn't meant so much to her for so long a time, Dakota would have gladly reconsidered. She'd found that she was a talented teacher and she'd been happier this past year in Leadville than she had ever been in her life.

Dakota placed the little toque upon her head with what conviction she could muster, and decided she was ready as she'd ever be. She tried not to think about how much she would miss the friends she'd made and the schoolchildren. . . . She'd miss Rufus and Fancy and Wu, dreadfully. Most of all she'd miss her mother and father. How on earth she'd find the courage to say good-bye to them, even for a little while, was more than she could imagine. Surely no one ever had a more interesting set of parents than she.

Dakota heard Fancy's knock at the door and opened it. Fancy hugged the girl, then stood back at arm's length to say what she had on her mind. It troubled her gravely that Dakota was leaving to face an uncertain future. "You don't have to go, you know, Dakota," she said worriedly. "Take my word for it, you can learn a lot more about life right here in Leadville than I ever would have believed. When I was your age, I ran away and I caused myself no end of troubles by doing it . . . maybe you could fall in love with some fine young man right here in town and then the two of you could go off to see the world together . . . Oh, Dakota, it's an awfully cold place out there when you're alone."

Dakota smiled at Fancy's concern and shook her head. "If I don't go now, Fancy, my courage will fail and maybe I'll never go at all—and then I'll die wondering 'what if,' and that would be so sad. Once I'm married and have children, there'll be no chance for adventure, will there? No, Fancy. Much as I hate to go, it's now or never."

"But you have such a long time to go before you die, Dakota. So much could happen for you right here in Leadville if you'll only give it a chance."

"None of us knows how long we'll last, Fancy . . . why, I could contract some dread disease tomorrow and carry memories only of St. Louis and Leadville to my grave."

Fancy laughed at the girl's fey turn of mind; she was loath to lose this young friend who had so gladdened her heart and who soothed the ache she felt about the unreachable Aurora. "That would be unthinkable, I must agree," she whispered, smiling indulgently.

Dakota, at least a head taller, hugged Fancy warmly; she took a package from the drawer of her dresser and handed it to her older friend.

"You know I've always kept a journal, Fancy, ever since I learned to write. I call it my *Journal of Dakota's Grand Journey,* because I always thought life was like a pathway through the bumptious terrain of the soul, and I wouldn't want to miss recording a single adventurous step. This trip to California will be a whole new chapter for my record, so I'm taking a brand new notebook with me, all full of clean white pages, just waiting to be inscribed. I was wondering if you'd keep volume one for me while I'm away? I'd die if anything happened to it. You see, my whole life's inscribed there, all my hopes and fears and dreams . . . all the thoughts that are mine alone in the world . . . and all the love I feel for those who mean most to me. It's the most precious thing I own."

"Of course I'll keep it for you, Dakota," Fancy said, warmed by the girl's trust. "I'll put it with my own keepsakes from childhood. My memories are sacred, too."

Jewel and Ford stood together at the Leadville railroad station, and it was easy to see they'd both cried some at the thought of this parting from their daughter. They looked solemn and only partially resigned; the look of parents who know life's hazards and wish there were a way to save their child from peril.

"I wish you didn't have to go," Jewel said, her voice suspiciously husky, as she embraced the girl and patted her back as if she were a small child.

"Hugging you is one of the nicest things can happen to a person, Mama," Dakota said, tears spilling freely down her cheeks. "I'll be back just as soon as I have something to write about and then I swear I'll never, ever leave you again."

Ford wrapped his arms around both of them.

"I want you to take this money with you, Dakota," he said huskily. "Now, I don't want any arguments, I know you saved up all your school-teaching money for the trip, but this is a gift from your mama and me."

Fancy turned her head away from the poignant scene, tears blurring her eyes, and she was startled to see Rufus running out of the Crown waving his arms and shouting something, too far away to be heard. He had his shotgun in his hand.

What happened next transpired so swiftly, no one ever after could pin it down exactly. The young man with the gun in his hand materialized out of nowhere . . . he was suddenly before them on the street, calling out Ford . . . shouting something about being faster on the draw, as he lifted the lethal revolver.

The gunfighter, always on hair-trigger alert, was distracted by his farewells and his eyes were filmed with tears. He lunged for his pistol, but had to push Jewel and Dakota away before firing. Fancy, horrified into immobility, saw the realization flood Dakota's face, saw the alien gun spit lightning, saw Dakota fling herself into the bullet's path to save her father. The velocity of the shot hurled the girl backward into Ford's body, as Rufus' shotgun blast brought the gunman down. The whole event had taken only seconds.

Blood poured out of the wound in Dakota's chest and turned the traveling suit from beige to red in seconds. Fancy, with a cry, fell to her knees in the dust beside the girl and tried to stop the overwhelming torrent with her bare hands, but there was blood everywhere, too much to stanch . . . it spurted through her fingers, pumping away the girl's life with every heartbeat.

Dakota's eyes sought Jewel's; they were the eyes of a fawn startled by the huntsman's bullet, disappointed and surprised by the perfidy of Fate. Ford fell to his knees beside his dying child, with a groan of anguish torn from the depths of his soul. He touched her trembling lips with his fingertips as if it were a kiss—Fancy thought she'd never seen so tender a gesture.

"Daddy . . . Mama . . ." the girl whispered, like the voice of the dying wind. ". . . don't want to go . . ."

"No!" Ford cried out. "No!" as if to put heaven on notice, but the light had already begun to fade from Dakota's eyes. Her mouth, which had laughed so easily, trembled and she tried to speak again, but she couldn't breathe and blood welled up and spilled from her lips . . . she looked puzzled by the betrayal.

"Oh, God . . ." Fancy sobbed helplessly, her hands were crimson to the elbows with Dakota's blood, the front of her dress was drenched with it. "Oh, please, not this joyous child . . ." But the girl's eyes stared past her into eternity and she knew Dakota had set out on a different journey from the one she'd planned.

Ford crushed the body of his daughter and the body of his sobbing Julia to his breast so savagely, Fancy felt his anguished rage tear at her like talons. She stared at her own bloodied hands, unable to think or move.

Then she threw her arms around all three she loved and they clung together on the dusty Leadville street for what seemed eternity.

Always on the run, Rufus had said a lifetime ago. *Never sleep. One day, someone faster'n you, or more ruthless or luckier . . .*

A crowd had gathered, the sheriff was shouting questions, the train had chugged into the station. Fancy knew the world was going on around them, but she could not move from the spot where she stood. This made no sense . . . this stupid, dreadful tragedy made no sense at all. She no longer railed at God, as she had in the strength of her youth, but she surely had the right to wonder at His unendurable callousness.

▲

It was a soft June day when they buried Dakota Jameson. Fancy had placed a ruby ring on the girl's finger and pinned a single rosebud to the white batiste dress, in which she would sleep through eternity. *The souls of lost roses . . .* Dakota had said. Perhaps she'd find them wherever she'd gone.

The schoolchildren gathered at the graveside, and many of their parents were with them, despite the presence of Julia's nightbirds in quiet black sateens and cottons, and Wu's large family in their curious white mourning garments. The sun clouded over just as the coffin was lowered into the ground and Fancy, numb with sorrow, thought it was a sign . . . from then on she always thought of the eighth of June as the day they buried the sunshine.

Fancy had attended to the funeral arrangements and had badgered the minister into doing his duty, however reluctant he was because of Jewel. He stood now and read the words of Christian burial over the casket that contained the earthly remains of the blithest spirit Fancy had ever known.

It occurred to her as she watched Ford standing by Jewel's side that he'd been dressed in mourning all his life, as if waiting for this moment. The two were like statues out of a Greek tragedy, Fancy thought; they had aged in the two days since their daughter's death. So, too, had she.

The minister finished his droning words; Fancy hadn't heard a single one, for she'd gone inside to her secret place, to be alone with her sorrow. She had to steel herself to look down into the hole that held the pine box, knowing Dakota was trapped inside. She wanted to tear the girl from her prison and carry her away somewhere; she wanted to shield Jewel's heart from the torment she was suffering. And Ford, sweet Jesus, just to look into Ford's haunted eyes . . .

The minister handed the shovel to Chance and he dutifully scooped earth into the casket, a dreadful final sound, then passed the shovel to each of the mourners in turn. When it came to Jewel, the sorrowful mother waved the tool away and walked close to the edge of the grave that held her only child. From underneath her cloak she pulled a tattered old book and Fancy knew at that moment it was her mother's diary, the possession Jewel held most sacred in the world. She saw there was a letter clutched in the hand that grasped the book. Jewel hesitated for a moment, then with a sigh she leaned down and let her two last gifts to her daughter fall onto the coffin—she knelt there for a time, and Fancy, watching, thought her heart would break for her friend.

Ford stood behind Jewel and helped her rise; he stared down into the ugly wounded ground as if he intended to throw himself into the hole with his child. The tension in the air around him was palpable. What must he be suffering, Fancy wondered distractedly . . . it was his death Dakota had usurped. What parent's heart could survive such a sacrifice?

Very deliberately, Ford unbuckled the gun belt that never left his body. He held the familiar leather and iron crushed in his powerful hands for a moment, as if he meant to offer them in sacrifice to a God who demanded blood payment. Then he laid the guns to rest in the grave beside the letter and the book.

A murmuring went through the graveside crowd.

"Bury them with my daughter," he said fiercely, and the pain in his voice made people look away and search their own hearts for culpability in the sins of the world. Ford took Julia's arm in his own and held it like a lifeline as the mourners filed away. When everyone else had gone, Fancy took the *Journal of Dakota's Grand Journey* from her pocket and pressed it into Jewel's trembling hands.

"She told me it was her most precious possession, Jewel. She'd want you to have it now."

Jewel looked at her friend with grief-dulled eyes.

"What's it all about?" she whispered, and Fancy knew she was asking about life, and, having no adequate answers, could only shake her head in sorrow.

That night Jewel sat for hours in the old rocking chair with the journal pressed tightly to her heart, as if to catch the echo of a soft young heartbeat one last time before it faded forever.

"I'm going to miss you so damned much . . ." she murmured once through her tears.

Finally, long after Ford had fallen into exhausted slumber, Jewel rose quietly from her chair. She stood a long while motionless, then she pressed Dakota's journal to her lips in reverent farewell, a lingering kiss of absolute devotion for the child she had loved so deeply, and known so brief a time.

She tucked the book—so small to have contained a life—into the lockbox that had guarded her mother's diary through all the long years, and wondered as she turned the key, if she'd ever have the courage to read what was written between the covers.

▲

The people of Leadville always wondered how it was that one tombstone in the little churchyard was always strewn with flowers. But Dakota loved flowers . . . so Fancy and Jewel never forgot. The inscription on the marble read:

> DAKOTA JAMESON
> BELOVED DAUGHTER OF
> FORD AND JULIA
> DEPARTED ON THE FINAL JOURNEY, JUNE 8, 1883,
> AND SORELY MISSED BY THOSE SHE LEFT BEHIND.
>
> SHE DIDN'T MEAN TO GO SO FAR . . .

92 The Apache world, which had once seemed alien, now fit Hart like a well-worn boot; there were times when his "other" life as a white man seemed to have taken place in a different incarnation. He sketched so voluminously that Destarte joked they would soon need an extra horse to carry his work from camp to camp. He'd long since learned the Apache arts of war, as well as those of peace, honing his skills with bow and lance and rifle, partly for his own pride and physical well-being, and partly because the war that occupied Gokhlaya and the others must soon be his as well. Hart listened at the counsel fires as the strategies were planned, he played the war games with the other warriors and offered advice on tactics, when he was asked to do so, and he brooded over what his place must grow to be, in this strange new world he'd chosen as his own for an indeterminate period of time.

A transformation had taken place in Hart, so subtle that he never noticed it until it was near completion, although Destarte saw his metamorphosis with loving wonder. For a long while he'd remained a white man in his heart; at least, so he thought later when he pondered the evolution of his being. Yet at some unspecified moment, the Apache way had begun to be Hart's own way . . . not an alien culture to be studied and painted and emulated, but a worthy way of life to be cherished and embraced. Was it Destarte who had worked the magic, or Charles Paint-the-Wind, whom he loved so overpoweringly? . . . Was it the simple integrity of the tribe that spoke to him so clearly, he couldn't help but respond? Or was it all these elements that wrought the change and transformed him into Firehair? He was happy in his Apache life and more fulfilled than he'd ever been; that he knew it was all coming to an end made the moments to be shared with his small family all the more precious.

General Crook had the United States government goading him to subdue the Apache once and for all, and Crook was an able soldier who understood the People more than any of his predecessors had. Because Hart knew the capacity of the military, while Gokhlaya could only guess at its strength, he knew the Apache way was in imminent danger of extinction and thought long and hard on how to fulfill his obligation to the tribe, to protect his wife and child, and finally, how to make the transition from the Apache life to the one he'd left behind.

"How did your Power first speak to you?" Hart asked Gokhlaya one evening, when the soldiers' raids had ceased, briefly. He already knew each Apache brave sought communion with his Power, in a personal vision quest at puberty; that a man's Power came to him then, and remained in his periphery to protect him both in battle and in life. It was the moment when a boy sought his Power that his life was altered, as surely as his name was changed to whatever one the Power dictated. Hart had watched the change in men when their Power spoke to them, and he had begun to desire such knowledge.

"My Power called my name once when I was a young warrior," Gokhlaya answered his friend's question. "I walked apart and fasted and called to him to come to me. I was so anxious to learn the shape of my Power. The wind lifted and swirled and there was an unnatural stillness all around. 'It is not time that you should call upon me,' my Power said sharply to me. 'I will come to you in your Shadow Body, when you have learned through many sufferings.' Then the wind rose up again and the sands of the desert lashed my face and all became darkness. I fell to the ground and slept. Many strange dreams came to me, but I had not yet the wisdom to understand their meaning.

"Then, after Kaskiyeh, when all I loved had been lost, I went to the mountaintop to mourn. There my Power spoke again and told me things of which I may not speak to any man. . . ."

Destarte bustled about the tipi tending to the meal as the two men talked; she cooked and played with Charles Paint-the-Wind, who'd grown to be a sturdy toddler, with a body that gave promise of his father's stature. Gokhlaya raised his eyes to the woman's and Hart saw a look of perfect understanding pass between them. *There are men's things to be discussed,* the look said. *You must leave.* Swift and noiseless as a shadow, she departed with her son by the hand.

Gokhlaya was silent for a moment, regarding Hart with his steady gaze; when he spoke, he sounded solemn.

"Is it that you wish to seek your own Power, Firehair?" he asked, but it was clear he already understood what the answer would be. Hart nodded, his throat curiously dry and tight. Both men knew then that the change had already happened; for the white man not only sought his Power, but he did so with awe and reverence.

"I feel that my Power is seeking me," Hart said awkwardly.

Gokhlaya nodded understanding. "That is always the best way. You must fast and clear your mind of the things of this world. You must go to the Sweat Lodge and think on your decision. If, after that, it still seems right to you to seek him, you must go alone into the desert and remain there for however long the spirit decrees. I have it in my mind that your Power will come to you."

When Destarte returned and Hart told her of the conversation, he could see in her eyes that she understood the magnitude of his decision.

Three nights later, Gokhlaya took Hart to the Sweat Lodge. The small, humped structure was made of interlaced bows and mud, covered over with a blanket; the rocks in the firepit within were heated to a glowing, sizzling red by the time the men seated themselves, and Gokhlaya began throwing water laced with sacred herbs onto the rocks, in a rhythm he alone understood. A cloud of dense steam arose in the eerie darkness and Hart, who had been fasting, felt light-headed as it seared his lungs and permeated his body inside and out. Gokhlaya had cautioned his pupil not to speak at all, but soon the sounds of the Apaches singing outside the Sweat Lodge rose with the dizzying steam, and Hart heard the rich guttural chanting of the man who shared the lodge's purification with him. The white man felt an unfolding beyond the simple relaxation of bone and muscle; a dizzying lightness of mind and body overtook him, as the tension that had filled him began to dissipate, almost against his conscious will.

After a time beyond counting, for Hart's thoughts seemed to have become fluid instead of linear, Gokhlaya motioned him to follow from the dark lodge to the riverbank beyond the village. The Apache gestured to Hart that he must bathe, and the plunge into the icy water nearly paralyzed him, but it awakened his mind to a clarity unlike any he'd ever experienced. Gokhlaya indicated that Hart must return to the Sweat Lodge alone, and remain there until he felt the urge to begin his quest for vision. Open to whatever was in store, Hart complied, and sat for what seemed an eternity in the solitary steam.

Something outside himself seemed to have control of his mind and movements, and a powerful urge possessed him to leave the lodge. He had some sense of walking past other villagers; they seemed not men but ephemeral shapes, not quite transparent, not of ordinary density; he had no desire to speak to them or be spoken to.

By the time Hart reached the open desert, he knew he was not light-headed simply from the cleansing steam, but that a kind of freedom from the restraints of matter had stolen over him. He had somehow cut all ties to the material world. He was setting out on a great and seductive journey, which he must make alone, into an unknown dimension of reality, and nothing of the earth could stop his footsteps now.

Hart sat, naked but for a breechcloth, on the desert sand; tingling, expectant, he waited for whatever was to happen.

"You will recognize it, if your Power comes to you," Gokhlaya had said. "If none comes, you will not lie. If you did that, you or one you love would die." What if no Power comes, or if it comes and destroys me? he thought, suddenly seized by irrational panic. Why had he never asked, while there was still time, if the Power could be malevolent? Terror rose and receded, fear, curiosity, exhilaration, anxiety . . . as if one after another compartment of Hart's being was explored and emptied by some mysterious process over which he had no conscious control.

Never in my life have I simply sat and waited for the unknown, he told himself, and then he felt even his thinking process drain inexorably, as if stolen by the eternal quiet. *Perhaps this is what the vigil of Death is like.* He sat and waited for a moment or eternity, until a silence more profound than any he had ever dreamed lapped at him and sucked out what was left of his will. The being that had been Hart McAllister was gone, and what was left was enveloped unresisting in the keeping of the Unknown.

Sounds began to creep into his emptiness—night sounds, wind sounds, tree whispers, rocks speaking to each other—and then something more that he couldn't name. Feathers touched Hart's cheek and he reached out to seize the bird, but none existed, although he'd felt its powerful breath and heard its shrieking cry as it grazed his face with beating wings.

A great gust whistled by him, a cyclone against which it was impossible to breathe; Hart looked around himself in panic, for he'd been admonished not to move from his spot unless his Power led him, and he saw with astonishment that not a single grain of sand or clump of sagebrush had stirred in the still desert air.

Lights danced before Hart's eyes and he felt himself sucked up violently into a vortex that carried him high, high, higher into the heavens. He saw himself deposited upon a vast plain in a Place of Infinite Light. *I am no longer alive . . . I am something else.* Four noble horses pawed the ground to North, South, East, and West and he knew they were no earthly horses, for their coats gleamed iridescence and their eyes glowed red as coals.

"Ride!" a voice commanded him, and unable to resist, Hart moved toward the buckskin horse of the East. He knew it was the voice of one of the Grandfathers of the People that had commanded him, for he'd been told of the Old Ones who guided the ways of men, from the place of Spirit, but no one could have explained the incalculable age and power in the timbre of that awesome voice, and surely no mortal had the ability to resist it.

Hart was drawn first to the buckskin; the horse was like his own dun had seemed to him long ago, when he was young. Hart was suddenly atop the incredible beast without ever having mounted; he was riding, flying through the clouds toward the eastern horizon at a speed so dizzying, he had all he could do just to cling to the magical horse's back to keep from falling like Icarus to the earth, a million miles below.

The sun was rising at the same angle as the great buckskin's path, and as horse and rider rose, so rose the dawn to suffuse the world with blinding light.

"Have courage!" commanded the voice of the Grandfather of the East. "My Power shall be with you to shed enlightenment between two worlds. Long will your vision be seen by other men." The voice ceased and the horse froze into perfect immobility, so that Hart was catapulted from his back and whirled through the vortex, to the glittering withers of the great sorrel of the South.

Into the blazing heat of the afternoon sun the steed and the seeker plunged, until Hart felt his hair and skin and beard singed by unearthly fires. His heart pounded and his eyes were blinded by the clear yellow light, as he struggled to hold his seat on the mystical beast—but a dizzying weakness sucked out his strength and he had to clutch the mane like a desperate child.

"Help me, Grandfather!" Hart screamed, and he knew as the words were formed, what a perfect act of faith it was, for in that instant he *believed* with all his being that the Grandfathers held his fate in the palms of their ancient hands.

"The colors!" the mighty voice boomed out at him. "Now must you learn the rainbow of life!" And Hart saw himself transparent, as if made of glass, with colors rising up inexorably within him. Red from the base of the spine, robust and sexual; orange at the belly, emanating creativity and will and strength. A pulsing brilliant yellow at the solar plexus, of an incandescence he could not describe, and in that saffron color was all wisdom, in all time. Soon, green suffused his heart, the green of emeralds and malachites, of jade and moss and jasper and all the grass and trees on earth . . . all mixing and pulsating with love and harmony, health and abundance.

Hart found he could ride the magic sorrel now with ease, and as the colors grew within him, so did his ecstasy. Sky blue enveloped his throat and he was exalted, inspired, filled with radiant calm. The blue became indigo as it reached his forehead, it opened a new sense of *seeing* within him and without. A mystical borderland had been passed and Hart, for the first time, knew himself, and in so knowing, tasted wisdom.

Suddenly, white-gold light burst through the top of his head with a benevolent violence . . . he felt his body vibrating as if a tuning fork had been struck far out in the universe and his energy responded to it in resonance. He knew joy and sorrow, the consciousness of all humankind; a transcendent love of all people in all time, past and future, suffused him and harmonies from a thousand generations and voices rang in his ears from the Place of All Music.

The white-gold fountain turned to rainbow, and all the colors he'd experienced were pouring out of him in a great rainbow fountain that arced the universe, as he was toppled from the sorrel and whirled through space to the back of the great black steed of the West, who caught him on his gleaming hide as if he were no weightier than a feather.

An eagle, whose wingspan was greater than the Rockies, swooped close to Hart and he knew the great bird was the Grandfather of the West, in his favorite disguise. Mythic horse and mythic bird raced through the heavens at such speed, Hart could merely cling to the hurtling stallion as time and eternity whirled by beneath the flying diamond hooves.

Below, the path of two raging torrents wheeled into view—one white, the other red as blood. The mighty rivers came to a place where they ran side by side and before Hart's astonished eyes, the white waters swelled and the red dwindled to a trickle, until the white waters overran the red completely, and as the waters mingled, the sounds of screaming, dying voices rent the universe. The cries were echoed by the soaring eagle's shriek . . . thunder cracked from his talons, and lightning forked from his glistening eyes.

"Make haste!" the Grandfather's voice cried urgently to Hart. "The time is coming and you must be ready."

Then a torrent of rain burst forth from the thunderclouds, and Hart was washed from the horse's back and hurled dripping onto the great white steed who ruled the North.

"I am the Giver of Experience," the Grandfather's voice chimed out, like all the bells that had ever rung. "I teach the Law and the Light."

Then Hart knew the rain had ceased and the Light of the Spirit had cleansed him; so breathtakingly pure was the Light that bathed him, it broke his heart to know he would never again in life see such as this.

"Behold the Circle of the People, for it is sacred," rolled the Voice and the music of the spheres wrapped round him. *I am in the Place of All Music,* he heard himself think as the voice rang out again. "It is holy and endless and all Powers shall be one Power in the People without end. They shall be scattered and go forth on the Red Road, but the Grandfathers shall walk with them in their exile, until their knowledge shall be needed, and the Earth shall call them back again to save her from destruction."

The great white stallion reared one mighty time, and Hart was flung from his back out, far out into the universe, amidst a cloud of colored stars. He felt himself floating back to earth gently as a feather on the wind, but he cried out for what was lost, like a desperate child, and as he felt himself sucked back into his physical body that lay on the desert floor, all the weight of matter and of ignorance and of darkness settled upon him, for he was no longer a Being of Light but only a man. *My name* . . . he begged, and the voice of the Grandfathers called in unison, "You are the Witness."

Hart wept for the profundity of his loss, and then he wept for what he'd gained. He sacrificed pollen to the Four Winds, as he somehow knew he must, and he stretched himself out on the desert sand, exhausted beyond all human comprehension, and waited for sleep or death, uncaring about which should find him.

When he awoke, he was no longer Matthew Hart McAllister who had been before. He was Firehair, the Witness. He was an Apache. He was a man possessed by his Power.

▲

Hart made his way back to the tribe the following day and he was conscious that the men could see clearly the change that had been wrought in him. The warriors smiled knowingly as he passed, and he could feel a bond with them that had never before existed. He longed to be able to tell Destarte of the experiences that had so transformed him, but he knew he must not, for these were men's mysteries and most sacred. It made him sad that a story of such magnitude must be kept from her whom he loved, but she seemed to understand implicitly the sacredness of what had happened.

It was shortly after Hart's Power came to him that General Crook defeated the People, and the Chiracahua were returned to the San Carlos reservation. A special sorrow wracked Hart, for he knew the moment was fast coming when he must make choices that would decide the future for his wife and child, whom he so dearly loved.

General Crook's buckskins had seen enough wear to con-form to the outlines of his body of their own accord. He was an analytical man who had earned that worst of all military epithets, "maverick," by his determination to make his own judgments, not merely follow the dictates of leaders who were, too often, wrong.

He wore the garb of a scout, not a general, because it suited him and the climate; it also afforded him access to places and information other generals would never be privy to. He'd made it his business to learn the Indian mind, when first he'd been sent to Arizona, and the more he'd fathomed, the more he'd respected his adversary. Crook was tough, as a lifetime in the cavalry makes a man; he rode like a Comanche and shot like a horse thief, but he was also fair and put great store in honor and the sacredness of his given word.

He eyed the redheaded, red-bearded giant, who towered over Geronimo, with an amused and interested stare.

"Lose your way, young feller?" he asked, squinting upward into the sun at Hart as the group assembled for surrender.

"Or found a better one," Hart replied; there was manliness about the general, he noted, and no discernible swagger. Crook nodded, accepting the answer.

"State your business, then, son, and let's see if between us we can't make peace look as attractive as war does to your friends."

Hart had been delegated to speak for the People, to avoid any trickery of language the soldiers might employ.

"Geronimo, and the chiefs of the Chiracahua and Nedni bands, wish to know your policy toward the Apache, if they agree to return to San Carlos."

Crook scratched his chin and thought a minute before replying. "I can't say as I have what you could call a policy for Apaches . . . by the way what do I call you, son?"

"I am Firehair the Witness, to the tribe," Hart replied, surprised by the man's civility. "I was born Matthew Hart McAllister."

The general raised an eyebrow and examined Hart more closely; the young man was eloquent and educated and damn near the size of a barn. He couldn't help but wonder what on earth had placed him in Apache garb, in the midst of an Apache surrender. It was obvious he was trusted by the chiefs and his Apache name suggested he'd been through vision quest, a most interesting conundrum.

"Today I speak for the People as Geronimo's representative, so perhaps my tribal name would be best."

The general smiled a little. "Firehair it is, then; can't say it isn't appropriate.

"In answer to your question, I guess I'd have to say it's always seemed to me a man is a man, red or white, and should be treated accordingly. I have orders from the President that I intend to carry out and they include getting all the bands back onto the reservation with all due haste, but I've got a thing or two to say that come from me and not from Washington.

"The simple fact is, the white settlers are crowding in all over this territory, game is going to get scarcer and the hunting grounds are going to become farmlands. It will be far better in the long run for the Apache to make up his mind to plant and to raise livestock. If they can do that, in no time they could be wealthier than the Mexicans, for the simple reason that they're more industrious.

"I have no desire whatsoever to punish any man or woman for the sins of the past. So long as the Apaches behave themselves, I'll do my damnedest to assure them of the fullest protection of the U.S. Army. But I'm telling you straight, son, if they stay on the warpath, I'll hunt them down every man, woman, and papoose, if it takes me fifty years to do it. I'm a soldier and I'll do my duty as the Lord gives me the light to see it." The general's mouth was a tight line that left no question of his intent.

"But this much I'll give you my word on, Firehair, I'll not tell one story to you and another somewhere else, I'll not make promises I can't keep and I'll play square with you, if you play square with me."

Geronimo, who had listened carefully to every word, conferred a moment with Naiche, then stepped forward.

"We will need our sacred hunting grounds."

"That I can't give you, Geronimo," Crook replied, unflinching. "Those lands have gold and farms I'm sworn to protect. The best I can offer you is arable land in the vicinity of San Carlos."

Hart glanced at his friend's consternation.

"The chiefs need time to discuss your offer, General," he said. "They've heard promises before and while they respect your word, sir, they have reason to doubt that the government will follow through on what you promise." Geronimo nodded to Naiche and the two men walked away to hold council with the other elders.

Crook lowered his voice so only Hart could hear. "You let them talk all they want, Firehair McAllister, but you know well as I do they haven't the chance of a snowball in hell unless they do as I say."

"And not much more than that, if they do, General. You and I both know General Sherman said 'the more Indians we kill this year, the less we'll have to kill next,' and his lackey Sheridan thinks the only good Indian is a dead one."

Crook pursed his lips and looked at Hart speculatively.

"Where'd you hear that, son?" Crook asked.

"At Yale, sir," Hart replied, and the general choked back a smile.

"Well, then, if you're smart enough to know all that, you're smart enough to know there isn't any fairness to life, and not a whole hell of a lot of justice either. I respect the Apache as men and warriors, but I also know their days are numbered. Do what you can, son, I can see these men are your friends."

With that the general left Hart standing in the hundred-degree desert heat, the truth of what he'd stated making his own decisions all the more difficult. The Apache had no choice but to do as the general bade them— Matthew Hart McAllister could take his wife and child and leave.

The Chiracahua and the Nedni returned to the country close to Camp Apache, near the headwaters of Turkey Creek and the White River, all part of the San Carlos Reservation. Firehair, Destarte, and Charles Paint-the-Wind went with them.

▲ ▲ ▲

"What would a woman of your kind do to show her love?" Destarte asked Hart as she patted the cheek of their sleeping son. He'd grown handsome, as well as intelligent, this young son of two worlds. Even Gokhlaya had remarked that the boy showed strength and promise far beyond his years; he was larger than the other boys, taking in everything he saw and digesting it in his own way, often startling his parents with his observations. He is the best of both of us, the young mother thought with pride; he will be a great warrior. Destarte straightened, still kneeling, and smoothed her dark silken hair back from where it had fallen forward on her face; the gesture made her look soft and vulnerable.

Hart watched, amused and in love; she asked often about white women, wanting to know everything about their skills and seductions. It pleased him because he thought it meant his wife of many summers loved him as much as he loved her.

"Nothing nearly so wonderful as what you do, my Destarte."

"I really wish to know," she pressed, not intending to be put off with flattery. "They are my rivals for your heart and I wish to know what magic they could use to lure you from me."

Hart laughed softly; when he did, the skin at the corners of his eyes wrinkled a little and his heavy eyebrows came together to form a furrow in his brow. His skin had darkened with constant exposure to the elements and his hair had burnished in the harsh sun until it gleamed with a thousand yellow glints among the deep copper.

The question of his leaving was always in her heart, he knew, especially now that they were bound on the reservation. She couldn't help but know that as a white man, Hart could have sought his freedom whenever he chose and escaped the living death of captivity. His knowledge of Apache ways now far surpassed any he'd hoped to learn, when first he'd sought out the People to render their world on canvas. He sat now in council with the other braves, and when he spoke to the white-eyes on their behalf, Destarte nearly forgot he was not one of the tribe . . . but the illusion was only momentary.

"You can go back to your world and be safe, my husband," she would say when the melancholy of reservation captivity lay heavy on her heart.

"Nowhere would be safe for me without you and Charles, Destarte," he would reply, but both knew the Indian way of life was coming to an end, and that sometime in the near future Fate might make the choice for Hart that he so assiduously avoided making for himself.

He'd long ago decided he would take his wife and child back to the white man's world with him, when the Apache way was no longer viable; but he knew, as Destarte did not, what hardships there would be for a "squaw-man's" woman, and he wished to postpone the sorrows she would face as long as possible . . . at least until their son was a little older.

Hart thought a farm might be the answer, far from prying eyes and gossiping mouths—or perhaps even Europe, where they'd be curiosities but not freaks, as they would be in Colorado. He was in no hurry to inflict what was to come on his innocent wife, or on a little boy too small to be deprived of pride in his lineage. So each day Hart taught Destarte more of the white man's language and the white man's customs; just as she had once tutored him about her world so he could survive there, so now he tutored her about his world so she could survive when the time of passage came. He had decided to remain with the People until their fate was decided by the government, for there was always the possibility that his intercession could be of help to the tribe.

▲

Hart approached both the government agents and the military when the People returned to the San Carlos Reservation. He was certain his services as intermediary could be useful to both sides, but he was treated with suspicion and derision. Any man fool enough to live with savages wasn't worth listening to, he was told point-blank by the men who counted. Crook had left the Arizona Territory and the Indian agents under the auspices of the Bureau of Indian Affairs held sway. So he simply melted back into the tribe and watched the perfidy of the government, and the outright dishonesty of the military, cataloguing every detail so that he might bear witness when the time was right. "Inequity and iniquity," he told Destarte. "One day my pictures will show the truth to any man who cares to see."

The Apaches had been promised food and money by the government, when they were captured, but Hart saw both stolen by the greedy, while a proud people was left to beg for scraps. The Apaches were promised land by the army, but it was neither the hunting grounds they needed nor the places they held sacred. They were promised dignity by their captors, but were made to feel like animals run to ground.

For nearly two years, the People and their adopted white brother tried to live as the white-eyes wanted; they raised corn and beans, wheat, pumpkins, potatoes, barley, and melons with great success, and for a time Captain Crawford, a disciple of Crook's, tried to see they were given fair trade for their produce. But by 1885, new mines had been discovered on what was once Apache land, and hundreds of new settlers came pouring in from the East to homestead. With government sanction, the corrupt politicians reneged on every promise Crook or Crawford ever made to the Apaches.

It wasn't one big conflagration that caused Gokhlaya's and Naiche's decision to bolt the reservation, Hart always thought in retrospect, but rather a thousand drops of water on the stone of their endurance. After a binge on *tizwin,* the Apache home brew that made them feel bold and manly once again, the beleaguered warriors decided to make one last break for freedom. As was the Indian way, all tribal elders met and voted; the women murmured among themselves that their husbands would rather die in battle than be turned into women, as the white men sought to do to them.

Certain Apaches elected to stay behind under the leadership of Chatto; Gokhlaya and Naiche chose to make a break for Mexico. Hart knew, as they undertook to leave the confines of the reservation, that the tribe was doomed, but he also understood their need to flee. He very nearly chose to take this moment as a sign and pack his wife and son off to the white man's world, but on the night before he intended to speak of it to Gokhlaya he had a dream that stayed him. "You are the Witness . . ." a voice reminded over and over, from the dream void. . . . "You are the Witness."

Hart woke with the words still ringing in his ears and he rose from bed knowing he could not leave until the trail of tears had been followed to its ending and the red river had been swallowed up by the white, as his vision had foretold.

▲

"Gokhlaya has told me of the shaman's journey," Hart wrote in his journal. *"In order to heal, one must have suffered illness; in order to live fully, one must have battled death and vanquished him.*

"There are plateaus along the seeker's path: Orphan, Wanderer, Warrior, Martyr, Magician; each a necessary step in the road to wisdom. What must this knowledge mean to a man? Does wisdom come like a lightning flash in the darkness? I wonder. Or does it seep into your marrow and express itself one day when you are least expecting it?

"We sat around the Medicine Circle and saw the sand painting that represents man's earthly journey.

" 'Depending on where you sit in the circle,' " Gokhlaya said, 'your perspective changes . . . until you've sat in every position, you cannot say that you have seen the grand design.'

"I wonder where on the circle I sit at this moment? And where on the wheel are those I've loved?"

 94 The decision to run Chance McAllister for governor was deliberated upon long and hard by the party. There was no question about his appeal, only about his willingness to do things the party's way. He had a damnable habit of unpredictability . . . like that time when he'd sided with the miners against the owners. Of course, the lucky bastard had come out of that particular disaster smelling like a rose. His bravery in the mine cave-in had made him a goddamn folk hero, and Madigan along with him.

Elmore Trask was a practical man, deep down where it counted; he needed a candidate with charisma and he needed one who could be led. It always depressed him that both characteristics seldom existed in the same man.

Trask put his feet up onto the leather ottoman in Madigan's study with all the pleasure of a portly man who has just finished a splendid meal, and three kinds of wine. Jason poured two snifters of cognac and handed one to Elmore before he settled into his own chair, by the fire.

"You spend a fair amount of time with McAllister," Trask began genially. "Your opinion on his candidacy would carry some weight with the boys in the back room."

Jason sipped the brandy, then moved forward in the well-worn leather, resting his elbows on his parted knees; it was the gesture of an important man about to give a judicious answer.

"I'm a bit handicapped in giving you an unbiased appraisal, Elmore, because the man's my friend, as you know. But needless to say, I owe a good deal of loyalty to the party and more to you personally."

Trask nodded sagely; he'd heard every self-serving disclaimer ever conceived of, and hadn't gotten to where he was by believing horseshit, only by recognizing its aroma.

"McAllister's a natural vote-getter," Madigan said. "Handsome, charming; says the right thing to everyone from little old ladies to presidents, excellent rhetorician. He's done fine work for the Silver Alliance . . ."

"So much for the subjects he gets A in, how about the F's?" Trask said with the smile of the worldly-wise.

Jason did his best to act as if he felt discomfited by the necessary admissions he must make; he had to bury Chance just right. He cleared his throat and took a sip of cognac—Trask thought that a nice touch.

"Gambling debts," Jason said evenly, "and his wife's questionable past are what you're expecting me to say, Elmore . . . but neither one is an insurmountable obstacle, as I see it. The biggest problem Chance presents in my opinion is his potential uncontrollability. He's a maverick at heart, and mavericks don't take orders. And he's not ruthless, not one whit. In fact, I'd say he's actually a bit of an idealist, despite his apparent pragmatism."

Praised with faint damns, thought Elmore Trask, but very potent damns. He'd have to give thought to what had been said here.

"Much as I hate to say it, he'd be a prime candidate to run in an election you don't expect to win," Jason suggested. "Like the one coming up, against the incumbent. He'd make a stronger showing than most because of his popularity, and if he lost, well . . . let's just say it would leave a clear field for someone more predictable, come the next election. Someone more along Tabor's lines, perhaps." Jason paused a moment. "Of course, you know far more about all this than I do, Elmore, I'm just thinking out loud."

"Interesting speculation, Jason. Very interesting."

"God knows it would be easy enough to find a flaw in the man's character to blame the loss on, and he has the kind of hubristic self-confidence that might make him accept the nomination, when a more judicious man would shy away." Jason would place the same thoughts in a number of influential ears in the days to come, for it was time to tighten the net around his quarry.

It was useful to find out for sure that Madigan wasn't Chance McAllister's friend. The party wouldn't wish to antagonize a contributor as generous and influential as Jason, by screwing a true friend of his, but under these circumstances . . . Elmore made a mental note to see the committee tomorrow morning, and went on to enjoy Jason's excellent hospitality.

▲

The Fancy-hunger gnawed at Jason unreasonably after he returned home from Denver. He'd thought about her all the way back—about how exquisite she was and how invigorating to talk to. She challenged him, somewhere deep down, where no woman had a right to reach; in fact, she damn near obsessed him and there seemed no way to diminish the power she wielded. It angered him and seduced him simultaneously. He didn't like not to be in control.

Perhaps it was the sense of untamability about her that was most seductive. She was elusive, never really in his grasp. She was sharp-witted and sharper-tongued, able to skewer an idea or an opponent, a most unwomanly trait he found utterly exciting. And there was still that damnable waiflike quality that evoked a protectiveness which made him feel . . . gentle. Or something like it he'd never felt before with anyone.

Challenge, obsession—strange improper words to use about a mere woman. What the hell was it about her that made him want her so insatiably, he was willing to go to such trouble to get her back?

He thundered for his secretary and the young man came scurrying.

"Get hold of Sam Southern for me."

"I don't believe I know the gentlemen, where will I find him, sir?"

"Samantha Southern is no gentlemen, Horton—she's no lady either, for that matter. She's a very high-priced whore, with a house on Lexington. See if you can get her over here for lunch . . . tell her I have a business proposition for her she won't want to turn down."

Horton left and Jason folded his hands on the desk in front of him. He'd waited far too long to get what he wanted.

▲

John Henderson managed to look lean and hungry despite corpulence and prosperity; his entire life had been spent in the pursuit of money, the management of money, and the enjoyment of money. He was well situated, as president of the Fiduciary Bank, to enjoy the fruits of his obsession as well as the company of the men who shared his passion for prosperity. He'd enjoyed the trip to New York in Madigan's private railroad car; it reinforced his old conviction that money and happiness were synonymous.

Madigan signed the papers he'd asked John to bring with him and sat back in his chair to fix the banker with the stare he reserved for recalcitrant lackeys.

"Now, John, I assume you've done all I've asked you about McAllister's loans?"

Henderson responded obliquely. "I'm far more at risk in this McAllister situation than you are, Jason, and it's beginning to make me nervous. I'm glad to have the chance to discuss this in person—I want to be certain we see eye to eye. I'm holding one hell of a lot of McAllister's notes in my bank and with my position in the mining community and my reputation in financial circles at stake, I'm running a fair-size risk, playing ball with you on this manipulation of the man's assets."

"Cut the crap, John," Madigan said with just enough irritation to make sure he was understood. "You stand to collect a goodly piece of change off everything McAllister owns because of me, as you have for quite some time, I might remind you. If you're so all-fired worried about your pristine reputation, I can just as easily steer him somewhere else. God knows, Leadville's got her share of better banks—to say nothing of Denver or New York. As a matter of fact, last time I was in Colorado, Chance said something to me about how much more convenient it would be to bank in Denver, now that they spend nearly all their time there."

"Now, you cut the horse pucky, Jason. Do you think you're talking to some half-assed stripling? You need my willingness to play along with your schemes, and my corroboration of your assessments of his holdings, and my closed mouth, just like you have since you started doing business in Leadville. He's too smart to accept your word alone—mine and the banks carry a hell of a lot of weight in Leadville.

"We made a tidy bundle shorting the Fancy Penny stock just before that mighty suspiciously timed cave-in years ago. And we both made money in what we lent him to clean up the mine and get it operational again . . . and we've made money on him damned near every day since, one way or another. We have what is known as a mutually satisfactory marriage here, just as long as the groom doesn't get greedy."

"And the bride doesn't get arrogant or stupid," Jason cut him off with a crooked smile. He'd dealt with the Hendersons of the world before. They always meant money, but they were an almighty pain in the arse to deal with just the same, and they bore constant watching for double-dealing.

"Just be certain you recommend the investments to him that I've outlined for you, John, and our partnership will continue to prosper," Jason said as he folded up the papers on his desk and prepared to dispatch the plump turkey back to Leadville. He had no real worries about Henderson; all the same, it didn't hurt to remind him from time to time who was the brains of this particular financial alliance and who was the kitchen help.

Jason poured himself a last brandy after Henderson had been seen to the door. Drawing the net tighter around his quarry was making him feel better about life than he had for some time. He'd never met a politician who couldn't be bought, or a banker with scruples . . . and Sam Southern would provide the finishing nail in Chance's coffin.

95 Chance's bid for the governorship was a resounding failure and try as he might, he could never really figure out why. The party had been behind him and the voters had seemed receptive to his ideas. . . . Not only was the defeat the single most deflating experience of his life, but by some odd quirk of fate, everything in his world seemed to change for the worse with that election, as if Lady Luck simply up and deserted him one day, for no apparent reason.

Some part of him blamed Fancy, as if all her doomsaying had queered his luck—and even though he knew it was irrational to hold her responsible for his own troubles, still she sure as hell hadn't helped any by always telling him that the way he did things was wrong.

"I think we should consolidate our holdings, Chance—sell some of the real estate and put some cash in the bank." Fancy's comment was occasioned by the newest rumor about the country going on the gold standard.

Chance didn't want to talk money with his wife, he still smarted over the election loss and he didn't need any reminders of painful reality. "Leave it alone, Fancy. I have other things on my mind."

Fancy tried to keep her temper for she knew he was hurting, deflated by his loss at the polls, worried about a lot of things he never revealed. She'd despaired of ever getting him to be honest about the serious parts of his life; when they talked, it was about socializing or about the children, and then he behaved as if Aurora was hers and Blackjack his, so that there was never any real communication.

She took a deep breath and began again. "If we sold off some of the undeveloped properties, and stopped some of our lavish entertainment, we could put a fair amount of cash away this year, Chance, just in case silver really is as shaky as everybody says. I've tried to put some figures on paper, but I don't have all the information I need."

"Dammit, Fancy, will you for once try to help me instead of interfering." Chance bristled with anger at her interminable meddling. "Don't you understand what a tightrope I walk every day? My kind of magic works only if you keep on believing. You bring me down, with your fears, and I can't work my trade when I'm down."

"But there's money being wasted, Chance. You have to stop buying until we know what's going to happen to silver. It's become like some kind of addiction for you—another worthless mine last week, another useless piece of real estate. You're scaring me to death with all this spending."

"Who the hell said what I've bought is useless, Fancy, and why in the hell do you even know about what I'm spending? Other wives don't keep track like a goddamned bookkeeper—they just say thank you when their husbands bring home the bacon, which I think you have to admit I do very well."

She tried to keep her temper from flaring and to keep the conversation focused. "It isn't just the buying, Chance, it's your way of life these days . . . you're never home, you're always out gambling . . ."

"I win a damned sight more than I lose and you damned well know it."

"Tightrope walkers sometimes fall off the wire," she said angrily; it really was demeaning to have to beg your husband for a hearing.

"Only if they lose their confidence, Fancy. And your constant pecking at me is killing mine."

Fancy bit back what she'd planned to say for she heard the truth in his words. No one worked a circus, or performed on any stage, without knowing that without confidence you were dead.

"Why can't you just love me like you used to, Fancy? I swear, when we had less, you loved me more. Don't you see how hard I'm working for you and the kids?"

"I don't think you do what you do for us, Chance. I think you'd be doing the exact same thing for your own ego, if we didn't exist."

"That's great, Fancy, just great. You have the most unerring instinct for punching holes in my balloon. I swear you're like a squaw with a Jesuit, you always know just where to set the barb, don't you? And what makes you so goddamned righteous? Can't you see I'm doing the best I can, the only way I can?"

"And can't you see there isn't any room in your world for me anymore, Chance? You've successfully managed to turn me into a housefrau and mother and I'm beginning to think that's the *last* thing on earth you really want to be married to. Where the hell do I fit into your life now? You don't share anything with me anymore, you share it all with the masses. With all those hangers on and sycophants who follow you on the circuit. With pols and gambling buddies and dinner guests and party people and all the minions who keep you from ever having to be alone with yourself or me. I need you, don't you need me anymore?"

Chance never answered, just left the room angry and hurt, but she knew some part of the soliloquy had hit home.

She was right that he wouldn't let her in close anymore, he thought morosely as he made his way up the street. But to let her in, he'd have to be honest about all that was going wrong and he didn't know how to do that . . . didn't know how to be a graceful failure. No. He'd just have to try to recoup and then make things right with Fancy. He didn't know how to do it any other way.

▲

Chance went over the ledgers yet again, as if reading them through could change the facts. It wasn't something he liked to do. He'd made a habit of never looking at bills over the years, or any of the drearier paperwork of life; when you're on top of the world, creditors seldom make nuisances of themselves.

For the most part he left the books to his managers and accountants, or to Jason or John; they were the experts, after all. Even when two of Leadville's banks had closed in '84, amid a flurry of scandals and arrests, Chance had paid relatively little attention to their demise. There'd been some serious losses for him when the banks defaulted, but Jason Madigan had been gentleman enough to help him out with a series of loans, until he could get back on an even keel. Just as he'd done right after the mining cave-in.

Chance shook his head at the strange exigencies of fate—all those years ago he'd felt nothing but anger and resentment over Fancy's relationship with the man, and yet now Jason had grown to be his major ally. The man had been a real gentleman to swallow the animosity he must have felt at losing Fancy, and to risk his life in the rescue as he had. A gentleman and a friend.

Chance closed the last ledger; the money he needed simply wasn't there—his assets weren't liquid enough to cover both the gambling debts and the bills. The gilded invitations to masked balls at the mansion, the trips and trappings for him and Fancy, the children and entourage of servants, the astronomical clothing and jewelry bills—why, Fancy's bill at Tiffany's in New York alone would have kept a small country solvent. And then, of course, there were his escalating gambling debts. He'd let himself grow reckless, as the pressures of life kept mounting, and for some unfathomable reason, his fabled good fortune persisted in its inconsistency. He'd have to keep a lower profile in certain areas, for a while, until this cash-flow problem eased—and he'd have to find a way to cut expenses.

God, how he missed Hart's counsel and his good-natured acceptance; it worried him that his brother had been gone so long. He brushed aside the idea of telling Fancy; she'd only worry and carp . . . and say she'd told him so. It might be best to wire Jason and arrange a chat with him, the next time he came to Colorado. Madigan had a seemingly endless supply of money and would understand a temporary cash-flow problem, as Fancy would not. As soon as a few of the investments he'd made in other countries began to pay off, there'd be a surplus of cash again.

Chance returned the ledger to the safe, switched off the desk lamp, and left the mine manager's office exactly as he'd found it. As he looked around the office he thought again of Hart, with a visceral sense of loss and loneliness. Hurt as Chance had been when his brother had taken his money out of the mine operation years ago, now he was glad; whatever turns his own fortune might take, at least Hart's money was protected . . . it was a fact in which he took great consolation. He really missed the big ox. He only hoped Hart was all right wherever he was; it had been a year since there'd been any word. There'd been a cryptic telegram once a year since his departure into Indian territory, just enough to say he was still out there. He was alive somewhere, of that Chance was absolutely certain . . . if his brother was in serious trouble, or dead, the sixth sense that bound them would have told him so. The odds were, Hart was somewhere in Apacheria doing just what he'd always wanted to do. How like him to assume the Apaches would let him in, without relieving him of his fine red hair in the bargain.

Chance looked around the familiar office one last time, said a silent prayer for Hart's safety . . . and then another that he wouldn't stay away much longer.

96   The flight into Mexico was grueling for an emaciated people long separated from their hunting grounds, but the mood of the refugees who fled San Carlos was exuberant with the heady thought of freedom. As the desert flatlands gave way to rolling foothills and finally to lush mountain ranges near the border, the People said among themselves that they'd come home. Even if it was only to die there, it would be better to be buried with the graves of their ancestors than to live in the white man's prison house of the spirit.

A short time after crossing to Mexico, the band made camp, and Gokhlaya came to Hart to speak of what would come. He entered the tipi of the white man who had come to be his friend, and listened for a moment to Destarte singing to her child. She had a sweet contralto voice; it always seemed to Hart like a benediction when the band made camp and Destarte sang.

"To the People," Gokhlaya said, moved by the melody, "song is the breath of the Spirit that consecrates the rest of life."

"We sing in our churches," Hart answered.

Gokhlaya smiled a little. "The white man goes to his church and he talks about God," he said. "The People go to the land and we talk *to* God."

Hart chuckled. "You are right, my friend. The Apache is far closer to the spirit world than is the white man."

Gokhlaya nodded; he looked old and wearied. "My people are few now," he said sadly. "There was a time when they covered the earth like the desert sands. Now that is but a memory. It has been given to me to know that we will soon wander far from the graves of our ancestors, my friend. I wonder, do the white-eyes think that once we have been killed they will own this land? No one can own the land, Firehair, they can but tenant it. And the white-eyes will share this stolen place with the ghosts of our dead."

"You are melancholy tonight, my friend," Hart said, wondering why Gokhlaya had come. The problems of war and flight lay heavy on the man, and Hart knew the Indian saw the handwriting on the wall as clearly as he did.

The Apache turned his powerful gaze to Hart's. "I have come for a purpose. I wish us to be brothers."

"Are we not already brothers, Gokhlaya?" Hart asked, and as he said the word, the thought of his own lost brother, whom he missed so sorely, was an ache inside him.

"You speak our tongue as one of us . . . your son is an Apache. But in your blood you are white, my friend. In a man's blood is his whole being—I would share with you my blood, for in it is what I think and feel, as it came to me from my father and from his father before him."

Deeply moved by the honor Gokhlaya did him, Hart sensed Gokhlaya wished him to do more than witness, he wanted him to carry some part of the Apache Nation back to the white man's world within him. The old warrior was too wise not to know that Hart must return to his own . . . drops from the red river in the torrent of the white, Hart thought solemnly before he spoke again.

"How can this be done?"

"The medicine man must make it so."

"It would be the greatest honor, my friend," Hart said, meaning it with all his being. Gokhlaya nodded and left the tipi to its occupants.

▲

Hart was already in bed when Destarte knelt beside him and brushed the long, straight ends of her waist-length hair across his chest. He saw that she was naked and he touched her body lovingly, wondering what it was she wanted to say or do.

"I wish to have another child, my husband," she said simply, answering the unspoken question. "It is time." Hart frowned.

He'd struggled with the constraints laid on their lovemaking by the Apache need to let three summers pass between children, but much as he wanted his wife, he thought there couldn't be a worse moment to conceive. Perhaps his reticence had made Destarte feel unloved, or unwanted . . .

He brushed back the long strands so he could see her face clearly. "I have never loved you more. But these are perilous times, my Misty One . . . to have a baby now could endanger you, while we are on the run from the soldiers, so I have held back. But it has not been because I don't desire you, my beloved—only because I fear for your safety.

"Soon the time is coming, my Destarte, when I must leave Apacheria and take you and Charles to my world—should we not wait until a safer moment to bring another child into this precarious life?"

"It is in my heart that there may not ever be a place for us in your world, my husband, even though you struggle to make one for us. I crave another child of our love, to grow beneath my heart. There is great fear in me that we may be separated by some terrible chance, and if that happens, I must have part of you to keep. . . ."

Hart sat up in the bed and pulled Destarte to a place beside him; he didn't want her to finish the frightening sentence. He took the blanket and wrapped it around both their bodies and took his wife into the shelter of his arms.

"You must know that nothing on earth could make me leave you and Charles. . . ."

"Some things are beyond even your power to change, my husband. You would not leave us willingly, yet it has come to me that we will be separated." He could see that nothing he said would dissuade her from her conviction.

"You must talk with Gokhlaya, Destarte. He is very wise and his Power will tell him to reassure you that I will never abandon you."

Destarte pushed back the blanket and raised her head so she could look into her husband's eyes.

"I have already spoken with Gokhlaya, my husband who is the Witness. He has told me to tell you to honor my need to carry your child within me."

A terrible sense of destiny crashed in upon Hart; he felt as if the earth had shifted with her words.

He pressed her back upon the bed and pushing away the encumbering coverlet, he took her body in his hands with all the recklessness denied them for so long. Far into the night he made love to her and she to him. She was wanton, as he'd never seen her, and every taste was sharpened, every sense alerted, every nerve ending electric . . . she was neither sane nor crazy, she was many women, only some of whom he knew, she was everything he needed, loved, desired, and he was the same for her. Again and again and again . . . until somewhere near morning, husband and wife, lovers, comrades, fellow wayfarers on the pathways of a world beyond their power to control, fell asleep entwined together. Each with the certain knowledge that a new life would spring from the seed of their love, and that whatever the gods had in store for them, they had wrested this one precious night from them, and it would live in memory forever.

▲

Three nights after Gokhlaya's visit, Hart, having fasted from sunrise, was led to the ceremonial circle of men by two elders of the tribe. Gokhlaya was considered a medicine man of surpassing power, and Hart could see that the shaman who would perform the ritual conferred with him. A bone-handled hunting knife had been thrust among the white-hot coals of the fire; Hart wondered what its use would be, thinking with a certain rueful amusement that he'd been an Apache long enough to know there was no place for the faint of heart in the People's ceremonies.

Solemn figures sat in ritual circle around the fire, and the flames shadow-danced on their unsmiling faces. The strength and dignity of the assemblage reminded Hart that the leaders paid honor to him and to Gokhlaya by their participation in this sacred moment. There was a turquoise-studded bowl on the ground in front of the shaman's feet as he stood in prayer.

"In a man's blood is his life-force and his honor," Gokhlaya announced to the assemblage in a resounding voice. "The essence of the man, the thoughts of his brain, the feelings of his heart, the secrets of his spirit, reside forever in the blood that flows through him." The men around the fire began a slow, even chanting to the rhythm of the drumbeat that sounded on the still night air.

The medicine man came forward and grasped both Hart and Gokhlaya by the wrists, in a grip that was strong and unyielding. He pulled the ceremonial knife from the fire and saluted the four directions reverently with it, offering incantations as he did so. He plunged the knife into the ground with great force and called upon the Earth Mother to empower it for their purpose. Then, without hesitation, he slashed the flesh of Gokhlaya's arm and the flesh of Firehair's; holding the men's hands high above their heads, he let their combined blood run unhindered into the silver bowl, and bound their wounds together with leather thongs. The muscles of the two strong arms glowed taut in the firelight, locked in friendship as stalwart as the men it bound. Then he bade the two drink the blood commingled in the silver vessel, and each did so with awe and reverence. Gokhlaya's eyes locked with those of his white brother and Hart thought he saw in them the history of the People and the courage of all brave men, in all time. We are strong men, you and I, the eyes said. Whichever of us survives will do so for us both.

"The blood is the man, the two are as one, the bond is forever," the medicine man intoned, releasing the knot that bound the two men together. He bowed ceremonially to each.

"You are my brother now," Gokhlaya said to Hart as the ritual ended. The two men embraced in the manner of warriors and Hart understood at that moment of communion that Gokhlaya knew the end was near for the People, and wished Hart not to part from him without sure knowledge of their brotherhood.

▲

". . . Greed and avarice on the part of the whites is at the bottom of nine-tenths of all our Indian troubles," Crook said, but his words fell on rapacious ears. He'd been recalled again to the troubled Indian territory for the avowed purpose of once and for all subduing the renegade Apaches. He was a soldier and had no choice but to pursue Gokhlaya and Naiche's band into the Southern Stronghold; to do so, troops poured forth from Camp Apache, Fort Bowie, and Fort Grant, to begin a deadly game of hide-and-seek.

Hart no longer needed to brood over what role he was to play in war. He was not a warrior by nature, but most men can find ferocity inside themselves when they must defend wife, children, and comrades; he told Gokhlaya that this time he would fight in the effort to establish the tribe safely in the Southern Stronghold, but that after that task had been accomplished, he would take Destarte and their children and return with them to the white man's world. Gokhlaya nodded and said that his Power had already made clear what the path of Firehair the Witness was to be, and that he accepted its wisdom.

Hart saw things in that terrible campaign of '85 and '86 that he wished could be torn from his memory. The Apaches had a reputation as the fiercest of torturers, but Hart had seen none of this practice in the years he'd spent with them. In this fearful war there was no quarter given on either side. He saw captured men bound and buried up to the neck in sand, with syrup poured on their heads so the soldier ants would eat the flesh from their living bones. He saw men tied upside down on wagon wheels, with a fire lit under their heads to roast their brains until their skulls burst. He saw prisoners with thongs of wet rawhide fastened around their heads set out in the sun, so as the rawhide dried and tightened, their brains exploded from their caved-in skulls. And, too, Hart saw Apache men, women, and children who were dear to him tortured, maimed, or killed by Mexican and American soldiers.

After a time there was no right or wrong any longer, no justice or mercy, only war and madness. His mind became obsessed with man's inhumanity to man and the devastation of the innocent ones, the women and children who were brutalized in the wake of men's wars. He recorded it all in infinite painstaking detail, by the campfire when they stopped to rest each night, never sleeping until everything he'd seen was drawn on paper, as if only by bearing witness could he justify his own continuing existence.

The Chiracahua had pursued and been pursued through '85 and well into '86. They'd headed for the Sierra Madre stronghold, which had protected the People time out of mind, only to find these fortresses were no longer sacrosanct, for Crook had employed disgruntled Apaches as scouts, as well as an Indian tracker named Tom Horn, who'd once been Geronimo's friend. These men knew the trails and waterholes, the camps and sanctuaries, as well as Gokhlaya's people did, and it soon became apparent that the canyons of Sonora would become the last grueling battleground of the Apache nation.

97 Hart took his son's hand in his own and squeezed it affectionately; he was pleased by the strength of the responsive grip. Charles Paint-the-Wind was nearly a head taller than his playfellows, broad in the shoulder and powerfully built. He was also serious beyond his years, and Hart wondered if the boy's halfbreed status made him the butt of ridicule among the other children or if this reserve was simply the child's nature. He'd seen no evidence of prejudice and attributed this both to the size and strength that were his son's legacy from the Charles McAllister he'd been named for, and to the Apaches' intense love of children that made each child a ward of every family in the tribe. Surely, no Apache parent would allow the boy to be mocked by his companions simply because of his dual heritage; respect for the dignity of the individual was inherent in the tribe's code. Later, respect as an individual of strength or wisdom or daring or spirituality must be earned in its own time.

It pleased Hart that his son took after him in stature, both because it reminded him of his father, his brother, and his own childhood, and because he knew Charles' way would be a hard one due to his mixed ancestry.

The women smiled or waved in greeting as the man and boy passed by, for they were of the People. Hart's deeds in battle were recounted by the campfire now, as were the other warriors', and since his vision quest, he was no longer an outsider. Hart measured his strides to his son's, so the smaller legs could keep up. He smiled as he looked at the sturdy little boy, with his Indian complexion and straight jet hair, and thought once again how precious his son and wife were to him, and the new baby daughter who had just been born.

"Father, why does the hunter put blue corn meal on the nose of the deer after he kills him?" the boy asked, and Hart knew the child had spotted the deer tracks by the side of the path.

"He gives honor to the deer tribe, son, and thanks the deer for his great sacrifice. He tells him that his life has been given to feed and clothe the People, and that nothing of his gift will ever be wasted. The People never take without giving back, for that is the Way. Sometimes honor is the greatest gift we have to give."

Hart saw his son looking up earnestly into his eyes, and in that instant he understood the perfect faith in his own wisdom that resided in the boy. Just as he had thought his father knew everything, so did this trusting child look to him for truth. He reached over impetuously and clasped his son to his heart.

"Why did you hug me, Father?"

"Because I love you, son, and because your questions give me a chance to tell you all I have learned that is important."

The boy smiled, satisfied by the answer, and they started down the path again.

"The Way must be followed by man as well as by animals, Charles. We must remember to take only what we need, never more than our share. And we must always remember to give thanks to the Great Spirit when we take from nature. In my other world we called Him God."

The little boy looked up with real interest. He could learn the Way from anyone, but of the white man's world only his father knew the truth.

"Why do your 'other' people try to kill us, Father?" Charles asked ingenuously.

"Because of ignorance, I think, son. Because they've been made to think the People are savages and must be hunted like the coyote or the deer."

The little boy walked in silence a moment, then spoke again. "Does that mean we are the weak ones, Father? The coyote and the deer are always taken by the hunters."

The question startled Hart with its sophistication; he thought he must take great care with his answer.

"The white men think so, Charles . . . but it is true in some ways and not in others. The white men are many and they have weapons stronger than ours, so they believe this means the People are weak. But there is much wisdom the People possess, which the white man does not . . . there is much honor and truth and courage and integrity in the People that the white man doesn't understand . . . and there is knowledge of the Earth

Mother and her children that the whites know nothing about. So, you see, in these things the People are stronger."

"But if the white man has better weapons, Father, then he can kill us, like the hunters killed the coyote and the deer."

"Are you afraid of death, Charles? A man can feel fear when there is real danger and he needn't be ashamed."

"Sometimes I'm afraid, Father," the boy answered slowly. "Mother wouldn't know how to fight the white soldiers if they tried to hurt her."

Hart felt a tightening in his chest; the boy worried about his mother, not himself.

"I will be here to protect your mother, son."

"But you go hunting, Father, and to battle. Sometimes she is alone."

"Then you must practice your skills with the bow and club, my son, so that you may be her protector when I am not in camp."

Charles Paint-the-Wind nodded solemnly, accepting this great responsibility from his father's hands. He would practice extra hard to be worthy of such an honor.

"I am strong, Father," he said with shy pride. "Not as strong as you, but I am bigger than the other boys."

"Then you must always use your strength wisely, son. When a man grows bigger than other men, he has a responsibility not to use his strength unfairly—and he must learn to be very gentle with women, Charles, for we could harm them if we're not careful."

The two walked in thoughtful silence for a while, then Charles tugged on his father's buckskin shirt to stop him.

"Can you hear the tree thoughts, Father?" he asked, listening carefully, and Hart shook his head.

"They each think different thoughts," the boy said. "The white pines laugh with the aspens and tease the little piñons . . . but the piñons are proud, because they feed the People with their nuts. Sometimes I can hear them talk to each other like Mother can."

My son is an Apache in his soul, Hart thought.

"Mother told me we have two bodies, Father. The one we can't see is made of spirit stuff. It's called your Shadow and it hears the tree thoughts."

"You're luckier than most, son. You have the wisdom of two worlds to learn from. Your mother knows things I can never know, and I know some things that would seem mysterious to her. You can have all that learning."

"Then my Shadow will grow big and strong, Father. Mother says sometimes you must be very brave to strengthen your Shadow-body. She says it's easy to choose honor on the battlefield because everyone wants to be a great warrior. But other times there isn't any glory or fun in following the Way

. . . only hard work and doing things right, even when you don't want to, but that strengthens your Shadow most of all."

Hart felt a great surge of love for both mother and child. "What else did she tell you about your Shadow-body, son?" he asked, and the little boy seemed pleased to be able to expound on such an important subject.

"Mother said you must keep your Shadow very strong, even if you have to pass the hardest tests to do it, because when your earth-body dies and you go to the Shadow World, it's all that's left of you."

Hart marveled at the precocious little boy and wondered how he could ever transpose such a spiritually open mind into the confines of the white man's constrained universe.

"Paint-the-Wind," Hart said, and the boy looked up curiously, for his father nearly always called him Charles. "Don't you ever stop seeing life like the People see it. The white man is stuck with only what his body eyes can see, and what his body ears can hear . . . most times he doesn't even know he has a spirit mind, and most times he doesn't care.

"But you have the bounty of two worlds to fill you up with wisdom, son . . . and that may make some men jealous . . . they might even make fun of you because their spirits have no Shadow. But if that happens, I want you always to remember that your daddy is so proud of you he could burst wide open, because you have the chance to be the best of two great people, son . . . and nobody in this whole wide world can take that away from you."

Charles Paint-the-Wind McAllister stood up very tall after that, as he walked by his father's side, so his Shadow would have plenty of room to grow.

▲

The journal had grown worn through the years and hardships. Hart turned the scratched leather in his hands with a kind of reverence, for it held his life between its battered covers.

Memories, in word or sketch, suspended moments that chronicle all that a man has been . . . and more. His dreams and aspirations, the secrets too mad to be entrusted to the living, left in testament to the time and place. Perhaps a child or grandchild would one day hold the journal dear, and learn from it of the man who had been Hart McAllister. He glanced at his sleeping family, opened to a page and began to write . . .

▲

"We are few and hard-pressed. I can see no way out that is not disastrous now. Yet, in many ways, it is the best of times.

"The tribe is like a single living entity, each cell a part of the whole. We

would breathe for each other if we could. Soon the tribe will be no more and the world will be less because of the loss of such love and camaraderie.

"I will miss the wind, when I go back. We have so little now, only each other and nature—so nature fills the void, each tree becomes a friend, the warmth of each sunrise a miracle, the wind is a living whisper in my soul. Civilization cannot offer such awesome communion with the Unknown . . . its comforts close our ears and eyes to God.

"I saw Geronimo ask a swarm of bees to share the flowers with us today. 'We mean you no harm,' he said, 'harm us not. We will take only what we need, little friends, we will leave the rest for you.' The bees swarmed back, so Destarte and the other women could gather the medicines they sought. Could any president or potentate command the same respect? I am changed irrevocably by what I've seen.

"We are so close to the land, we depend on its bounty, we see the place of each rock in the scheme. When my Power speaks through me, I am another man. How can I ever shut my newly opened senses away in the imprisonment of simple reason when I now know there is so much more?" Hart laid the pen aside and rested his head in his callused hands. When he again raised his eyes to the paper, they were wet with tears.

"The end is near," he wrote. *"The Witness waits."*

 98 Destarte bounced the little girlchild on her knee until the baby laughed aloud; she was an extraordinarily beautiful baby, with long straight hair as black as coal, and her eyes were a startling blue. From the moment of her birth Hart had felt drawn to those eyes, for even staring out at him from an Apache face, they were pure McAllister. What strange convoluted trick of genetics had conspired to produce that breathtaking blue-violet so like Chance's eyes, he wondered, for he'd thought that the darker genetic component always won out in such mixed parentage, and had expected his daughter's eyes to be dark as his son's.

"Sonseearay . . ." the mother whispered playfully to her baby daughter, to teach the infant what her name was. "Sonseearay is so beautiful even the birds in the trees stop singing to look at her."

The moment she said the words aloud, Destarte stopped to listen; the birds had indeed grown strangely silent for so lovely an afternoon. Instinctively, the young mother looked around her to find where her son had gone.

He was a boy of nearly five summers now, tall for his age and adventurous as the cub of a mountain lion.

"Paint-the-Wind," she called out softly, pressing the baby to her breast as she hastily gathered up all her belongings from the ground. "Charles . . ." she called, not wanting to cry too loud in case the prickling sensation that stood the hair on the back of her neck on end presaged real, not imagined danger.

Destarte could not see her son, and frightened, she ran in the direction of the woods where he and little Dahteste had been playing; she had nearly reached the edge of the clearing when a crashing sound at the far border of the trees whipped her head around. She glimpsed her son and his companion running toward her wildly, just as the blue-coated soldier swooped down on little Dahteste, yanking him off his feet and up onto his saddle.

"No!" Destarte cried, as six more horsemen broke the cover of the trees. She saw with horror that her small son had been scooped up into a soldier's grasp and that he flailed out fiercely with kicks and punches . . . she also saw the defiant look on her son's face turn to incomprehension, as a bayonet pierced his body back to front, and lifted him suddenly skyward. The little boy, who was heir to the wisdom of two worlds, stared down at the deadly steel protruding from his stomach, and tried in his agony to push it away with his hands. He did not cry out as the soldier tossed him, broken and bleeding to the ground, as heedless of the boy's suffering as if he'd been a discarded doll.

Immobilized by the thundering troops that whirled past her, and by shock, Destarte stood stock-still and clutched her blue-eyed daughter to her breast, as two-dozen soldiers raced past her down the hillside toward the unprotected camp. The men were far away and only women, children, and the aged would be available for their slaughter.

Bullets ripped Destarte's body in so many places, there was no way to count the wounds, and she buckled to her knees in the dirt. A soldier tried to tear the screaming baby from her dying arms, but Destarte clung to the child with the strength of desperation and the man had to dismount to pry the baby loose from her grip.

"Christ Almighty, Sarge," he shouted, his foot on Destarte's dying breast forcing the air from her damaged lungs. "This squaw's got a white kid with blue eyes! Must've stole it from some settlement."

"Sonseearay . . ." Destarte tried to say, her hands raised toward the man in supplication, but the blood bubbled forth from her lips, and the world around her dimmed so quickly she never felt the clothes ripped from her breasts, still overflowing with milk, nor felt the rutting man between her dying thighs. The soldier thought she might have murmured something about somebody's hair on fire, but he didn't care enough to listen to a dying squaw. He unsheathed his knife to cut off her breasts as trophies, but the milk that dribbled from them made him squeamish, so he changed his mind.

Charles Paint-the-Wind clutched his hand to his belly to hold in the slithery parts of himself that were trying to come out, and dragged himself from the edge of the woods to help his mother. He actually got as far as the bad man who was hurting her, but when he tried to stop him, the pain was so great he only hit the soldier once before darkness swallowed him. The soldier looked incredulously at the feisty child, before he cut his throat. How the hell he'd gotten so far dragging his innards behind him, he couldn't guess. Most likely these savages didn't feel pain like people did.

The raiding party returned after dark to the smoldering remains of their camp, to the dead and the dying. Hart found his wife where the soldier had left her, naked except for the blood from the bullet holes that had killed her. He saw the trail of blood and gore that marked the path his little boy had crawled, with inconceivable strength, across the clearing, in a vain attempt to protect his mother. The soldier had taken Charles McAllister's ears as a trophy of his triumph. Of his infant daughter, Hart found no trace at all.

▲

A battle rage woke in the one-time white man beyond any ferocity he'd ever imagined; he buried his family in the desert according to the custom of the People—there was no need to burn their possessions for the white soldiers had already done that. Firehair, the Witness, carved a marker after the custom of his own race, and placed it on their graves. It read

> MORNING MIST MCALLISTER, CALLED DESTARTE BY THE PEOPLE
> BELOVED WIFE OF MATTHEW HART MCALLISTER
> CHARLES MCALLISTER, CALLED PAINT-THE-WIND, BELOVED SON
> SONSEEARAY MCALLISTER, BELOVED DAUGHTER
> WHAT FOOL HAS SAID TO ME,
> "GOD HATH NO WRATH FOR THE INNOCENT"?

In his grief, Hart fasted and called upon his Power for vengeance, but instead it was Destarte who appeared to him in a ghost-vision. She stood at the fork of the white and red rivers, ravaged by an angry wind that licked the waters and churned them into bloody froth.

"You are the Witness, my husband," she called out to him in the voice of the wind. She said other things that were between man and wife alone, before she faded from his sight forever. Hart cried after her to stay, but she could not, so he sobbed silently over the graves of his wife and son, until there was nothing left within him that could feel pain any longer.

On the morning following the massacre, the braves who were left set out with Gokhlaya on the last bloody months of battle. "There is not in the history or tradition or myth of the human race," a federal judge would later write, "a campaign of such prolonged resistance against such insurmountable odds."

It seemed to Hart that the Grandfathers of the People must have ridden with the Apache on this last road of courage, for it took fifteen hundred blue coats half a year to defeat twenty-six Apache warriors and one white seeker-after-vengeance.

"Every man's hand is against us," Gokhlaya said, but Hart no longer cared if he lived or died, so it mattered not at all to him. "If we return to the reservation, we will be put in prison or killed; if we stay in Mexico, they will continue to send soldiers to fight us until we are no more."

"We will make them pay in blood," Hart replied. "And perhaps they will remember us."

Five months later, on September 4, 1886, at Skeleton Canyon in the Arizona Territory, General Miles, Crook's replacement, asked to meet with Geronimo, unarmed, to discuss a treaty; when Gokhlaya reached the parlay place, with Hart to act as his interpreter, they were surrounded and taken prisoner. Crook had resigned his post rather than be party to such treachery.

"General Miles is your friend," the army interpreter began, glancing wonderingly at the huge redheaded warrior who stood by Geronimo's side.

"I have been in need of friends," Geronimo replied sardonically. "Why has he not been with me before now?"

The soldiers laughed uproariously, for they thought the Apache's reply childlike, but Hart heard the bitter irony beneath the old warrior's words and understood what was in his brother's heart.

"Lay down your arms and come with me to Fort Bowie, and in five days you will see your families. I give you my word no harm will come to you," said the general, who was called Big Wind Double Mouth by the Apaches, but Geronimo had had experience of other generals, in other times, and knew that the long road of sorrows had merely taken another turning.

General Miles lifted a rock from the desert floor and swore an oath upon it, and Geronimo did the same, for there were no choices left to him. The two men raised their hands together to heaven and declared they would do no harm to each other nor scheme against each other's people; the oath was to bind them until the stone had crumbled into dust.

Big Wind Double Mouth made many promises he knew he would not keep; it would not be five days, but two years, before Geronimo would see his family again. And it would take a quarter century of imprisonment before the Apaches who surrendered themselves in good faith to the word of the Great White Father would be freed from the concentration camps to which he had already made plans to exile them.

So Hart learned soon enough that the proud people of the mountains and desert were to be imprisoned in Florida and Alabama, where the government devoutly hoped the heat, the damp, the inactivity, and the sorrow of betrayal would work upon them to decimate their number. They didn't know then that their beloved children would be taken from them and sent to Pennsylvania, where a third of them would die . . . and they didn't know that of the fifteen hundred Apaches Hart watched set forth into exile on that sad day in 1886, only one hundred and fifty-eight would someday be freed at Fort Sill, Oklahoma.

For that day would be twenty-seven years after the moment of Geronimo's surrender.

99   Hart's Indian odyssey was over—his wife and children, gone forever, his blood brotherhood with Geronimo but a throbbing memory . . . for the Fates had decreed that the remainder of his journey be conducted in the white man's world.

To say that his heart was broken would do a staggering injustice to his sorrow. He brooded endlessly about his sweet Destarte and their courageous son; he searched the army records for news of his daughter and begged for information from the soldiers who knew of the raid. Had she died at the hands of the ones who'd killed her mother? Or had she been stolen, because of the blue eyes and Caucasian features that might have made her seem a white child? Hart found no record of her existence, but tracked down every rumor until there were simply no more roads to follow. In his nightmares, he saw them running from the blue-coats, pierced with bullets, fading forever into a world that had vanished into nothingness . . . sometimes, in order to stay sane, he told himself Destarte's death had saved her from the ignominy of living as a white man's "squaw" in a world that could never know her value. But in truth, he saw no good at all in what had been done to her and to him, only sadness and unutterable waste.

The blue-coats, angry at this white man who had fought so valiantly beside his red brothers, tried to hold Hart prisoner of war; but he had no intention of letting the bastards who'd killed his family wreak any more havoc in his life, so he wired Rut, informing him of his plight, and Canfield pulled potent strings in Washington to have him freed. He offered one last time to act as intermediary for the captured Apaches, but as his sympathies clearly lay with the People, Hart was given a wide berth by the troopers.

▲

Gokhlaya and Hart took their final leave of each other at Bowie Station, as the great war shaman was about to be shipped out to Florida. The army band played "Auld Lang Syne," a tongue-in-cheek send-off to a hated adversary, and Hart was grateful his brother did not understand the irony. He was dressed in buckskins, for he couldn't yet bring himself to don the white man's clothes; his wounds were too fresh, and his anger at his own kind too unrelenting. He knew as he saw the vanquished Apache leader, standing in chains on the train platform, that even if they ever met again, his friend would no longer be the great warrior he had known as brother, but only a man brought low by lesser men.

Gokhlaya's hands and feet were shackled; his stern jaw and slash of mouth were set in the ancient pattern of endurance the Apaches knew so well, but his eyes were another matter—in them Hart saw no semblance of surrender.

"I have done what I had to do, my brother," the Apache said as Hart drew near him on the platform, crowded with soldiers. The white man saw that flies were buzzing around the Indian's bloody wrists, rubbed raw by his shackles, yet Gokhlaya paid them no mind. Hart, angered by the needless cruelty, stopped and picked up a handful of sand from the side of the track and dribbled it over the ugly wounds to dispel the insects. This should have been women's work, but Gokhlaya smiled a little at Hart's efforts, for he knew the man meant it as a tribute, one warrior serving another.

"So Firehair, the Witness, is Apache at the last," he said.

"It grieves me that I cannot help you, my friend." Hart spoke in the Apache tongue to avoid the greedy ears of those nearby. "My heart is heavy for your suffering and for the injustice that has been done to the People. All I can do is tell your story to the world."

"No one will listen."

"Then I will paint it, so they must see," Hart replied, angry and heartsick.

Gokhlaya's face was a mask of resignation to fate's arbitrary whims. "They will see only what they wish to see," he replied, and both men knew he spoke the truth.

Hart clasped the much smaller man in a warrior's embrace, and the milling soldiers snickered as they came to take away their prisoner. A guard took hold of each of Gokhlaya's arms and jerked him roughly out of Hart's reach; had the Indian not had Apache balance to steady him, he would have been knocked off his feet.

"Show respect for the prisoner!" a voice thundered somewhere behind Hart; he turned and saw that it was Tom Horn who'd spoken, the scout who'd breached the security of the Southern Stronghold to trap the Apaches. The men grumbled at the rebuke, for they privately hated Horn and the turncoat Apaches who had done their work for them. The soldiers nailed shut the doors and windows of the train in the 110-degree desert heat, with no water inside, so many died before they reached their exile, but Gokhlaya/Geronimo survived for many, many summers.

Hart stayed on at Fort Bowie for nearly a month and attempted to reorient himself to the white man's world. It was terribly difficult to fit in with his own kind whom he had ample reason to think of as the enemy, but he needed the time to search the army records for clues about his missing daughter. The luxuries of running water, a clean bed, a meal of more than meager war rations . . . these remnants from the past both pleased and repelled him. Firehair, né Matthew Hart McAllister, belonged in neither world, and the depth of his mourning made him give the soldiers a wide berth, for any one of them could have been the bastard who'd killed the ones he loved.

If he was ever to render on canvas all he knew of the Apaches, Hart saw he must find a place in which to work. He had no money, no clothes, and no clear sense of where he might call home; but he had pictures in his head, the like of which had never yet been painted. Somewhere far away, in a long-abandoned world, there was a fortune, a brother, and an old friend named Fancy. There seemed no way in which to reconcile his two realities . . . at least, not until he'd fulfilled his promise to Geronimo.

Hart went to the local newspaper and told them he would work as an engraver until he'd saved enough money to get to Denver; there was no need for them to know who he'd been, merely who he was now. He stayed two and a half years in Arizona, working like one possessed of a sacred mission, and trying to make an emotional and physical reentry into the world of the whites. He earned his keep, he sketched or painted what he'd seen and remembered; the dross was burned away by his passion and his pain, until only the memories and the man remained. He never asked Rut for the money that belonged to him, for he remembered Canfield's words too well: "I am precluded by my money from ever having the necessary requisite of genius," the man had said. "I can never be hungry." Hart knew he must stay hungry to paint what was in his soul; with every stroke of the brush he bore witness.

An artist knows in his heart when he has put truth on canvas; as Hart McAllister worked, he knew these were the paintings that would make him famous. There was anguish and expiation in the knowledge, for he'd painted the Apaches as they truly were, these friends of Usen, the Great Spirit . . . as men and women and children who loved and laughed and cried, who worked and learned, who lived by a code so ancient and so full of integrity that the most righteous white man would be hard-pressed to match its dictates or its decencies. He painted them as they had been in the beginning, before the yellowlegs had stolen the land they shared with the Great Spirit, when Grandfather Rock and Grandmother Earth were young and Usen had newly flung the stars aloft—and he had followed their descent into exile, at the hands of unrelenting forces they could neither comprehend nor hold back.

It was the spring of 1889 before Hart McAllister boarded the train for Leadville, like Lazarus returning from the dead. He was a vastly different man from the one who had departed there, eight long years before.

100 Allison Murdock rocked the little girl in her arms. She seldom let this gift from heaven out of her arms at all, she loved her too much and her arms had been empty too long.

Eleven years of marriage and a barren womb had made her an object of pity among her friends; even her family tended to avert their eyes from her pain, as each new child was born to her sisters and brothers.

She stared at the shining jet-black hair and wondered if it could be curled with rags when the baby grew older. Straight as a die, it looked Indian, but curled, perhaps . . . she wondered, as she had a thousand times since her husband had sent the child, what the little girl's name had been and whom she'd been stolen from. John said the child couldn't be Apache because of the strange blue-violet eyes, but Allison wasn't at all sure. The little girl almost never cried; she'd heard the Indians taught their babies that by holding their tiny noses if they fussed. The child was outstandingly beautiful, but she wasn't exactly Caucasian; something exotic shaped her face and tinged her skin a pale rosy honey.

What did it matter? Sally was hers now, and always would be. Allison ached with the love she felt for her long-awaited daughter. There was no need for anyone in this world or the next ever to know the truth of where she'd come from.

101 🌿 Madigan listened to Chance's newest tale of woe about finances with outward impassiveness. He needed to end the game that had ceased to amuse him.

"I'm sorry to have to say this to you, Chance, but you're not as good a risk as you once were."

Chance didn't have to feign surprise. "What the hell are you talking about, Jason? Are you forgetting I'm one of the richest men in Colorado?"

Jason smiled, an expression meant for a slow child. "On a certain level, that's true, Chance, but the fact is you're cash poor and that's a real problem. You own a lot of properties on paper, but they're not readily accessible. Those out-of-the-country investments, the smaller mines that haven't paid off, they've all taken a considerable toll on your liquidity." He cleared his throat. "I hate to speak of this, Chance, but I'm afraid the time has come when as a friend I just don't have a choice but to talk plainly. You gamble too heavily, you spend money like a drunken sailor, and you've speculated in a lot of areas where the risks were too damned high. . . ." He let the thought hang, for he could see he'd provoked just the effect on Chance's temper he had hoped for. McAllister, like most men, was least rational when angry.

"Look, Jason. Nearly every investment I've made in the last five years was at your suggestion."

"And most of them are excellent, long term. But you have to have cash to keep going in the meantime, Chance, and you don't seem to be able to hold on to any."

Chance said nothing, although the color rose in his face and the hint of a scowl would have gotten further if he hadn't been such a good cardplayer. "If you think all these investments you've recommended to me are so good, how would you feel about advancing me money against them?"

Madigan played poker, too. He covered his elation with a cough and a thoughtful expression. "I might be willing to mortgage some of your properties. Your shares in the Fancy Penny, for instance." Jason knew it was a foolish whimsy, but he'd always hated Chance's ownership of the only mine that bore Fancy's name.

"No," Chance responded quickly. "Not that."

"That leaves the Denver house and the other mining properties more readily available than the foreign enterprises, Chance—besides, you've already borrowed against some of the foreign investments and I can't recall now which ones." He drummed his fingers on the desktop for emphasis. "If you're looking for advice, my friend, I'd say to sell the Denver mansion and move back to Leadville. I don't think you really have any other choice under the circumstances, and frankly, I don't think Fancy gives a damn about Denver."

Chance stood his ground without fidgeting and finally nodded grudging acquiescence. Madigan admired his adversary's ability to appear calm in dire straits; it had always been a thorn in his side that he rather liked the man despite himself.

"Look here, Chance. If you'll put the mansion on the market, I'll advance you the money for it, here and now, just to help you out of a bind. I'll draw up the papers and we can sign them over at Judge Krasky's tomorrow. You know he's opened a law office here in Denver as well as in Leadville."

Chance looked up questioningly. "We've never gotten anyone other than Henderson involved in our dealings before."

"Times are more precarious now . . . all this talk of silver versus gold is forcing me to secure my holdings more carefully. You of all people know how unpredictable those boys in Washington are. They could damned well pull the rug out from under all of us. There's a real battle heating up in Congress, Chance, and some pretty powerful fortunes are backing gold. I'm not as bullish on silver as I once was, I'm afraid, and Harrison is only good for four years, or I miss my bet."

Chance didn't really want to talk silver; he had what he'd come for, but the tone of the conversation made him queasy. His immediate financial problems would be solved by the sale of the house, but now he'd have to face the hurdle of finding a way to tell Fancy she'd have to give up her home. Chance finished the conversation with Jason as hastily as civility would allow and left his office.

The house of cards will soon be down around you, Madigan thought as he stood at the window and watched the man whose wife he coveted saunter down the street. Jason watched the women's heads turn as the good-looking man walked by, tipping his hat to them, with the flourish of one who knows himself to be handsome and desirable. But Jason was no longer concerned. Rich, handsome men were dazzling to women—poor ones were a drug on the market. He himself could never set any woman's heart aflutter with good looks, but he had something far more seductive and lasting. He had power . . . and the knowledge of how to wield it . . . and the money to make it permanent. These were the ultimate seductions, for men and women alike.

▲ ▲ ▲

Fancy told Chance she couldn't be gladder to be leaving Denver for good; it was so obviously what he needed her to say. He must have been in terrible need of money to have sold the house; she'd suspected as much for quite some time. The stores where she shopped had begun to be less encouraging of her extravagances . . . a sure sign the bills were not being paid on time, and several of Denver's nastier wives had dropped snide hints that had puzzled her. Now the explanation was apparent.

Fancy swiped at her tears angrily and struggled for control after Chance left the room. She thought she'd been brave and loving toward him, in the face of her disappointment. Her acting ability had saved her in every crisis of her life; she almost smiled to herself at the thought, but she felt too awful.

What terrible arrogance made him make the same mistakes over and over? He'd rationalized about tight money and Jason's advice not being reliable. Had he forgotten entirely that she knew what business was all about, and that she damned well knew Jason Madigan?

Fancy blew her nose, dried her eyes, and stood up shakily. She struggled with two instincts: one, to delve deeper and find out the full extent of their troubles; the other, to let Chance take the consequences of his follies and carry the burden unassisted. What difference would it make, anyway, if she found out everything . . . she couldn't stop him from making blunders now any more than she ever could. It was probably best to accept his silly story and go back to Leadville like a dutiful wife—in truth, there was a great deal about going back to Leadville that appealed to her. She would be less lonely there . . . she'd have Jewel again, and Wu. In fact, she could take an active role in her own businesses, too, once she no longer was plagued by the social idiocies of Denver's rich. Life in Leadville would be far less pressured and, if she could go back to work, far more satisfying. It might be better for the children too. The extravagance of Denver was making them arrogant.

Maybe Jewel would know what to do about the fact that Chance made love to her so rarely these days. Could it be that a deflated ego became a metaphor for other deflations . . . the thought made her sad for her husband.

You don't stop loving someone because he's a fool in some things, Fancy told herself with a sigh. You don't even stop loving a man because he risks your safety, she thought, but without much conviction. You simply say he gambled and lost. I knew he was a gambler . . . whose the responsibility, then? The gambler or the one who loved the gambler?

Fancy walked to the window of the grandest house in Denver. Assess the possibilities, she told herself forcefully, striving to think. Don't let this undo you. He always pulls the chestnuts out of the fire at the last instant. At least, he has so far . . .

Three gardeners in a covey were busy pruning at the border of the broad lawn—something about them put her in mind of Beau Rivage, and the thought nearly undid her.

Oh, Chance, my dear old love . . . she said somewhere deep in her own heart. Why couldn't you be what I needed you to be?

▲

The furniture movers carted the last of the armoires down the long front steps of the mansion, grumbling as they went.

Fancy stood on the entablature, gripping the stone balustrade with both hands, her knuckles white with strain, her heart pounding in her throat. This is not important to me, she told herself sternly. I can damned well live without Denver, and the gossiping, backbiting wives of the stupid Sacred Thirty-six can just go stuff themselves. Leadville has sweeter memories for me and better friends.

Thank God Chance made certain he was away from home today. The only thing worse than doing this alone would be doing it together. The memory of the first day he'd brought her to this incredible house forced itself to the surface, and Fancy battled it down. She winced as the men set down her delicate escritoire with a thud, scraping the fragile satinwood finish on the granite walk.

"Be careful, there!" she called out to them fiercely, but they couldn't hear or else they paid no heed.

I won't let it matter to me that this house won't be mine any longer, she told herself sternly. It will be positively refreshing to be free of the burden of all those servants, all that obligatory entertaining, all that . . . all that . . . Fancy stifled a sob, reached inside the sleeve of her dress and extracted a lace handkerchief; she blew her nose to distract herself from the pain of loss.

It's my fault as much as Chance's, she said, too self-honest for obfuscation. I never needed all those Paris gowns and Russian sables . . . never needed the Aubusson carpets and the satin negligees. Well, maybe I did need the satin negligees, she corrected herself—Chance was crazy about me in those.

Resolutely, Fancy dried her tears and took one last look at the cutting garden. Oh, I'm going to miss you, she told the roses, and the peonies, the lilacs and the dogwoods. Maybe nothing I ever possessed since childhood put me as much in mind of Beau Rivage as you did. Fancy walked to the wall of exquisite roses . . . a dozen varieties graced one whole section of the garden. She bent to pick a red rose, stopped, and changed her mind. Red roses were for love. She picked a yellow rose, sniffed its heady scent and pressed the velvet moistness of its petals to her lips in a lingering kiss.

Yellow roses were for good-bye.

X

CALL UP THE WIND

▼ ▼ ▼ ▼ ▼ ▼

Leadville

"A man who was born to drown
will drown in a desert."

BANDANA McBAIN

102 Fancy, Chance, and their children trundled back to Leadville, bag and baggage, with Fate revving up her chariot, ready to take them for a ride. People speculated later on about what it was that started Chance back on his old ways. Did the debts force him to gamble, or did the gambling run up insurmountable debts? Had Fancy proved too much woman for him, or too little? The busybodies of Leadville were glad to see the Golden Couple trimmed down to size.

But Fancy was glad to be back, despite the gossip. The life they'd lived in Denver had distorted all perspective; now that they were home, Chance would be again as he'd been in the best of times. She'd behaved in an exemplary wifely manner, had taken her husband's fall from grace with courage and forgiveness—now she would go about the business of helping him regroup. The children were old enough so she could go back to work with Jewel and Wu. Surely under the circumstances, Chance would acquiesce. Life would begin again, if she had to give birth to it herself.

"Darling, I've decided the best defense is a good offense," Fancy said as she and Chance sat over breakfast coffee in the Leadville house that felt so pleasantly like home. Forty rooms had really been more than anyone needed.

He looked up inquiringly; there were slight creases about his eyes now, she could see, and the hint of frown lines in his forehead—they only added character and enhanced his good looks.

"I think we should throw a wingding of a party, Chance. The kind Leadville probably hasn't seen since we left. I'll wear that fabulous ecru gown and we'll invite everybody who counts for anything. Just in case there's any gossip about our returning home being some kind of comedown, let's show them we're still on top of the world and planning to stay there."

There's only one Fancy, Chance thought, a fact which had always both seduced him and annoyed him, about his wife.

"I'll get all the bigwigs lined up, the politicians and the mine owners. If we turn it into a charitable event of some sort, no one of consequence can possibly turn down our invitation." Fancy was already ticking off in her head the things they'd need for the party. It was a pity there wasn't a ballroom here like the one in the Denver house, but no matter, there was more than enough room to show Leadville what McAllister style was all about.

"I'll need a month to pull it off," she told him. "The fourteenth of next month is a Saturday. Let's do it then, Chance. I'll have those catty old bats and their sourpuss husbands falling all over themselves to get an invitation."

Chance left for his appointment with Caz at the mine, feeling better than he had in weeks. Fancy rose from the table, dressed in something meant to keep her spirits up, and went to tell Jewel and Wu she was coming back into the businesses.

▲

Jason gave Aurora his hand as courteously as if she'd been full grown.

"You are quite the most beautiful young lady in Leadville," he said with great authority. "I'm very flattered that you've decided to give me the pleasure of your company. You know, a lot has changed while you've been so busy growing up in Denver."

Aurora suppressed an unseemly giggle and blushed, as only a young lady of good breeding and tutoring could. She absolutely adored Uncle Jason. "When I'm grown up, I mean absolutely grown up," she corrected herself, for after all, if one could marry at fourteen, she was not far off the mark of full adulthood, "will you escort me to my first real ball?"

Jason raised his eyebrows, surprised and flattered; the child didn't miss much, he'd noticed. "I should be delighted to do so, Aurora. But in another year you'll be surrounded by so many young lotharios that I'll have to make an appointment even to see you, my dear." Aurora didn't know what lotharios were; she wasn't a very apt student—but she assumed the word had something to do with beaux and she knew he was quite right about that. There would be lines of boys at the door, just as soon as she was eligible, if only because of her wealth.

"You're my special friend, Uncle Jason. You always were the only man I ever wanted for a father. I'm going to hold you to your promise, so don't you forget."

Jason patted her hand proprietarily, touched by her admission. "I won't forget, Aurora. In fact, I'll be counting on it." He'd worked at gaining favor with both McAllister children over the years, for one day they would be his. Aurora hadn't been difficult, but currying favor with Blackjack was damned near impossible. The child was the image of his father and adored the man.

Jason tightened his grip on Aurora's arm; everything was proceeding according to plan, if slower than he'd hoped. Give a fool like McAllister enough rope and he'd oblige you by hanging himself with it, but who the hell would have thought he'd take so long in doing it? If it hadn't been important to keep Fancy in the dark about his plotting, he could have gotten rid of Chance expeditiously, long ago. Once he put the screws to the man's finances, just as he had to his political ambitions, there'd be no leg to stand on when the divorce was asked for. It had taken a considerable amount of money to sway the party; Chance was well liked and a good vote-getter, but in the end money won, as it always did. And whatever he'd spent would be repaid eventually; when he married Fancy everything she owned would come back into the kitty, not that it mattered in the least.

▲

Samantha Southern's Parlour House was elegant even by New York standards, never mind Leadville's. The girls were soft-spoken and dressed like showgirls, not whores. There were mirrors on the bedroom ceilings and the furnishings in each room suggested a different fantasy. The crap tables tended toward hushed concentration rather than noisy exuberance, and only heavy hitters sat beneath the hanging gilt lamps that illumined them.

Sam was a lanky blond, near enough to six feet tall to intimidate some men. She had an intelligent face, calculating gray eyes, and a stubborn jaw, but the ready smile and randy sense of humor softened her formidable exterior. She'd been born in Georgia, thirty-some years before, hence the surname she'd chosen for the stage, and later for the profession that was more lucrative than acting and seemed to her to require the very same skills.

She'd learned early on that men will pay a hundred dollars or even a thousand, for the same thing they could get for ten, provided the set design was right and the men were rich enough. She'd turned that knowledge into a splendid business in New York, one she was loath to leave to go to the ass-end of the world at Jason Madigan's behest. But he'd offered her damned near enough money for retirement, a nest egg of the proportion it would take her another ten years on her back to amass, so reluctantly Sam had agreed. The terms were simple enough, seduce one rich and handsome man while letting him think he was the seducer, and keep him away from his wife's bed long enough to cause a little mischief. Hell, she'd been doing that daily for years, and without the financial resources of Jason Madigan to back her up.

Sam watched Chance McAllister from the distance, assessing him. He was a magnificent specimen, that was for damned sure. Arresting eyes under manly brows, a mouth made for exploration . . . he laughed easily and well, a generous sound. She wondered why Jason wanted to bring him to heel . . . because he was handsome and successful, or merely to show he could? There was no point in speculation, there was just a job to do. Chance McAllister was all that stood between Samantha Southern and escape from the rat race.

She smiled to herself as she moved in his direction. Very few men, married as long as he, weren't vulnerable to a little flattery.

103 ❀ It had been a day of disappointments. Come to think of it, Chance realized, it had been close to a year of disappointments.

He'd put a lot of his own money into his political campaign, and all he had to show for it now was the party's half-assed thank-you; and even that didn't seem too sincere. They'd taken his loss with curious calm and he'd begun to wonder if perhaps he'd been offered up like a sacrificial lamb, for some complex political machination that his ego had kept him from seeing beforehand.

The mine production had fallen off, despite Caz's best efforts to keep the big payers active and the Last Chance and the Fancy Penny weren't alone in their decreased production; several of the mines on Fryer's Hill seemed to be petering out, too. If only his debts would do the same, Chance thought wryly.

It was hard for him to fathom how his winning streak had started to fade, but every gambler knew luck could sour on you when you least expected it, so he tried to be philosophical, and ride the losing streak through. The trouble was he didn't know how to operate except on instinct, and on his heretofore unshakable confidence in his own ability to win. The loss at the polls had somehow damaged that natural aptitude, and Lady Luck seemed reluctant to be lured back into his corner.

Chance had wanted to tell Fancy of his worries, if only to curtail her extravagances, but to do so he would have had to level with her about how overextended he was.

Chance put a custom boot up on the gold rail under the bar and downed another whiskey—at least he was having a splendid evening, considering what a lousy day it had been. He'd accepted Jason's invitation for a night of cards, hoping the evening's luck would be better than the day's.

Just the feel of the familiar pasteboards in his hand restored him; any run of luck could change in a minute, gamblers were born knowing that. How many men had given up just before the moment when the Lady started smiling again? The winning started with the first hand and showed no sign of abating, far past midnight; the relief of it made Chance feel more expansive than he had in months. He tried to focus on what Jason was talking about; he seldom drank when he gambled, but tonight he'd needed some liquid courage.

Jason folded his hand and stood up, stretching the kinks of sitting out of his back. "I'm heading over to Sam's place, care to join me?"

Chance shook his head. "Fancy'll have my hide if I get home late again."
Jason's lips formed a knowing smile. "As you wish," he said, picking up
his hat.

"On the other hand, maybe a nightcap wouldn't hurt," Chance said with
a short laugh as he fell into step. It would be good to see Sam again. Maybe
it was only pride talking, but she'd made him feel better about himself the
other night than he had in a long time.

▲

Sam sat up in bed and stretched. She'd been surprised by Chance's lovemaking—it was tender and expressive, careful of her pleasure and immensely intuitive. She could always tell a man's character by his lovemaking and this one was a decent guy and a hell of a lot of fun.

She wondered briefly what had driven him to a prostitute's bed, when he
had a wife at home like Fancy. She'd find out eventually—she always did.

Chance feigned sleep and wrestled with his conscience. He didn't really
want to two-time Fancy, didn't want to have to lie. But his confidence
needed bolstering of the kind a woman like Sam was expert at. It felt like a
long, long while since anyone had told him he was wonderful and meant it.

▲

Dear Bro,
Are you still out there, somewhere? I could really use an hour of your
time, just about now.

I've hit some bad times—not disastrous, just big disappointments. I
lost the election and suspect they never wanted me to win. I guess I let
my ego get in the way of my common sense or I sure as hell would have
seen the writing on the wall. Politics is an ugly little game when you get
right down to bedrock—a far cry from the idealistic notions we had about
it in the old days. There's damned little statesmanship and a hell of a lot
of expediency. You get caught up in the adulation and the power, but the
truth is, you're just a pawn in the game.

Then Lady Luck crapped out on me and the money sort of dried up—
not forever, I'm convinced—but it's tightened the belt for now. So we're
back home in Leadville and I can't decide if it's a comeuppance or a big
relief.

Worst thing is there's something cold grown up between Fancy and me
and I'm not sure how to fix it. I've played around a bit, bro, you know me
—and it's damned hard to know how to face her, when I feel like such a
flop in so many ways. How do we manage to complicate what should be
simple? I keep asking myself. Why is life so much harder to do right than

in our dreams? I guess I shouldn't bellyache, I've had more dreams come true than most men . . . the mine, the politics and Fancy all were pretty heady things to happen to a man. Yet here I sit melancholy as hell, missing my wife, my old friends, and the uncomplicated good times which seem like one hell of a long time ago.

Miss you, too, you big lug. I just hope to God you're safe somewhere, bro.

Your depressed-but-not-beaten brother,
Chance

 104

"Why are you here, Chance?" Samantha asked the question as she dressed.

"What do you mean? Why does any man go to a parlour house?"

She turned to him as she rolled up her stockings and gartered them. She'd had fun with Chance during the past couple of weeks and it was beginning to trouble her that she was playing him a dirty trick.

"Every man goes to a whore for a different reason, take my word for it. I just wondered what yours is." She looked up at him and waited.

Chance sat back and thought about his reply before responding; when he did the words were less flippant than she'd expected. "I'm here to keep away the dark, I guess. To find some comfort in a world grown cold and bare . . . maybe even to show my wife she doesn't pull my strings. Maybe for a lot of reasons I don't quite understand." He smiled a little; she thought it made him look young and honest.

"Why are *you* here, Sam? Anybody ever ask you that?"

"Me? I'm here because I hit a crossroads a long time ago and took the wrong turn. I ran off with a traveling man, who kept on traveling. Never could find my way back home. My daddy never forgave me and it broke my mama's heart. She died before I ever got to tell her it wasn't her fault I turned out bad. My little sister's the only one who keeps in touch—my brothers are ashamed of me. I got nieces and nephews I'll never lay eyes on. My real name's Peggy Sue Mabley from just outside of Macon, Georgia."

"Peggy Sue? You're far too elegant for a little-girl name like that. Samantha's more your style."

She shook her head. "I never could have stayed in Macon anyway, I guess. You know what they say, cain't be a midnight girl in a sundown town."

"You'd be a good person wherever you chose to hang your hat, Sam. You're wrong to think of yourself as somebody who turned out bad. I was in need of just what you had to give when you came along . . . and not just the sex, either. You've been good for me."

"My pleasure, Chance," she said, feeling more than a twinge of guilt. "But don't be too sure about me being good . . . there's a lot about me you don't know." He was too sweet a guy to lie to, and much too decent to be set up for a fall. The more she knew of Chance, the less she liked the deal she'd made with Jason—just because she was a whore didn't mean she didn't have a heart. She really hated to slip the mickey into his drink, but there just didn't seem to be any other way to make sure he'd stay the night, as Jason said he must.

▲

Fancy hummed as she bathed. The lady's maid she'd hired watched interestedly as her mistress poured nearly half a bottle of rosewater into the marble tub she soaked in. She wondered if Mr. McAllister might be expected home tonight; he seemed to have been "working late" a lot in recent weeks. The maid smirked a little. Every servant in town knew where Mr. McAllister spent his evenings and who could blame him?

Maybe he just didn't care to come home to a wife who pored over account books and ledgers all day like a common clerk. What a strange household this was, she thought with a sniff, but then, all the rich were odd. And selfish. That bottle of scent probably cost half a week's wages—didn't it have one of them foreign labels on it?

Enjoying her own nakedness, Fancy rose from the water and examined her reflection in the glass; she felt a small surge of confidence in what she saw. She would not fail to seduce her husband tonight, to make him remember how incredible they could be in bed together. She'd even try a few of the special tricks she'd gleaned from Jewel . . . things "nice" women didn't know about. If their marriage didn't get back on track, it wouldn't be because she hadn't tried.

Fancy sat on the little brocade bench in front of the dressing table, and thought about the long road they'd traveled together. Chance was still the man she wanted; there must be something she could do to give them another shot at happiness. He wasn't the only one who'd made mistakes . . . Men needed their egos massaged and she'd done precious little of that lately. Now they were home and she would recapture the magic; maybe it was a blessing in disguise that he was on the outs with the pols. It would give them more time to be together.

She'd be exquisite for Chance tonight, and seductive as hell. She'd mend whatever hurt he felt about his political failures and start all over again with the ball they'd planned for two days hence. We did it before, we can do it again, she thought spiritedly. Fancy slipped her most beautiful satin nightgown over her head and prepared for Chance's arrival home.

The minutes, filled with such anticipation, became hours . . . and the hours ticked by so slowly, Fancy thought the clock itself would drive her mad, as the evening vanished, became night and then morning.

It took a very long time before Fancy McAllister admitted to herself that her husband wasn't coming home at all.

▲

Fancy thundered into the Crown looking for Jewel, but Rufus, seeing the expression on her face, pointed wordlessly toward the kitchen.

The slamming door alerted Jewel to her visitor's presence; she looked up from the cupboard she was fishing in for a sauce pan, and knew before Fancy spoke what she was there for.

"I want the truth, Jewel. What the hell is going on with my husband since we've come back here? He never made it home at all last night!"

Jewel stopped and took a deep breath. "You sure you want the answer to that question, kid?"

"Who is she?"

"Her name's Sam Southern. She's got the fanciest new parlour house in Leadville. Scuttlebutt says she's financed by some mogul back East, nobody knows for sure who."

Jewel watched Fancy digest the news before she spoke again. "I'm real sorry, Fancy. I know how hurt you must feel, but I got to tell you, in my business you learn a lot about men, and about the only monogamous male animals I ever heard of were furbearing."

Fancy raised her hand in an imperious gesture that said she needed no pep talk. "I'm not here for advice, Jewel, just truth." She turned and left before Jewel had time to offer her a cup of coffee.

Fancy had kept the knowledge of Chance's infidelities bottled up long ago, because she'd felt responsible. But this time, he was to blame. She'd forgiven him many things over the years because she always believed he loved her, wanted her. Now she knew she didn't even have that much of him to call her own.

▲

Chance let himself into the house and found Fancy in the study, working on a deskful of paper. His head pounded and he was furious with himself for staying out all night; he must have drunk considerably more than he thought to have passed out like that.

She could barely speak, she was so angry; she didn't wait for the excuse she knew was coming. "I deluded myself that this party would change things and now we're stuck with it, Chance, but I was a just a fool about that, like I've been about a lot of other things. We don't have a marriage anymore, just a sham. I intend to go back to work full-time and make a life for myself, with or without you."

How like her to attack, rather than simply say she was mad about his not coming home, he thought with the righteousness of a guilty conscience. "I thought we settled that question years ago, Fancy. Why do you always have to go straight for the jugular?"

Oh, you great insufferable bastard, she raged internally. You great, lying, hypocritical, two-timing bastard.

"I have a right to protect myself."

"Don't you know how it makes me feel when every man in Leadville knows my wife is back running a saloon, with a whorehouse attached? I can't afford to look like a horse's ass at the moment, Fancy, and we've been through this a thousand times . . . right now, I've got other problems that are pressing on me. . . . Can't you just give me a little maneuvering room 'til I get the rest of life straightened out? Don't you want to be married to me?"

"I do want to be married to you! But I don't feel safe with you, Chance . . . you squander what's precious and you don't even know what you've done. I need to feel safe and I need to work."

"And if you can't have me and work too? Which one would you choose?"

Fancy stared at him in fury; she was not the one who'd spoiled everything. "I don't have you anyway, do I, Chance? Someone I've never even laid eyes on has that singular privilege."

Shock registered on the handsome features; he'd gotten away with so much for so long, he'd thought his indiscretions were sacrosanct. "What the hell are you talking about, Fancy?"

"I'm talking about my precious husband with such delicate sensibilities about his reputation that he can't withstand a working wife who runs a whorehouse, but he has no trouble whatsoever with having a whore for a mistress. I'm talking about the fact that I'm tired of playing second fiddle to your infidelities as well as your career . . . and just for the record, perhaps you should know that I knew about Jen in her time, and I would have known about all the others over the years, if I'd let myself. So don't even bother denying your relationship with that Southern woman. Your denial demeans both of us."

Chance looked at her in consternation.

"And while we're on the subject, Chance, let me tell you that I'm tired of a few other things too. I'm tired of being a political wife . . . I'm tired of watching you invest our money in insane projects . . . I'm tired of your careless arrogance about what's important in life. And I'm damn well tired—"

He broke in before she finished the sentence.

"Of me? Isn't that what you really mean, Fancy? Isn't that what this is all about. Who is it you really want? Jason Madigan? Odds are he'll never run out of the fortune it takes to keep you happy."

"I'm not the one who's broken our vows, Chance . . . you are."

"None of those women ever meant anything to me, Fancy. I've wanted to tell you that for a very long time . . . you're the only woman I've ever truly loved."

"That's such a lame excuse, you know. As if it's supposed to make me feel better that you left my bed for just passersby, not real commitments. I think that's even more insulting than if you'd fallen madly in love with somebody, Chance. But no. You just make love to other women to stay in practice."

He stared at her in anger and confusion. He couldn't tell her why he'd started seeing Sam, couldn't explain the fear of failure, or the loneliness.

"Please don't do this to us, Fancy. I'll make it all up to you, I swear I will. Just cut me a little slack right now, and I swear to you I'll make everything right." He reached out to touch her, but she thrust his hand away angrily.

"No!" she snapped. "Not that. Not this time." She turned abruptly and left him standing alone in the elaborate library he'd built especially for her, a very long time ago.

Fancy slammed the door to her bedroom and leaned heavily against it. When had she really lost Chance? she wondered . . . or had he ever belonged to her at all? Loss overwhelmed her and she sank down on the bed and sobbed for the stupidity of life and all the dreams it didn't fulfill. And for her own foolishness in never stopping dreaming, when she was damned well old enough to know better.

105

Chance felt the cold air snap at his face, grateful for its bite. It had always been a curse that fights between them exploded instantly into flames; he'd brooded all day about what had been said and gone up to the old cabin to clear his head and figure out what to do. She wasn't entirely in the right, but it was true that he'd betrayed her trust with Sam. Why the hell women put so much importance on a tumble in the hay was beyond him but still . . . she'd been hurt and he couldn't really blame her for fighting back. He hadn't been a perfect husband, and she'd always been vulnerable; all that bravado covered up a lot of frailty, and a lot of courage.

Odds were Fancy didn't really want a divorce, she just wanted him back as a full-time husband; it was strange how marriages seemed not to be destroyed in some great conflagration . . . rather, they just died a little, year after year, of insidious attrition. Perhaps it wasn't too late yet to turn the tide. Her temper was fierce, but like Hart's it tended to be fleeting.

He could live without Sam—he was getting too old for tomcatting anyway, it was beginning to seem more bother than it was worth. He'd turn over a new leaf and start again with Fancy, like she wanted him to. Chance was surprised at how much the thought of losing her unnerved him. The only thing to do was to brave her wrath and find some way to soothe her hurt; he'd done it before and could again.

It was late at night by the time Chance made his way back home; he stopped in the dressing room beside their bedroom, hung his coat over the corner chair, tossed his hat and gloves onto the dresser, his apology already on his lips. He turned the handle of the bedroom door.

It was locked. He jiggled the knob noisily to make sure it wasn't merely jammed, then knocked, but there was no answer, so he knocked again, louder.

"Fancy," he called. "Open the door, please. I really need to talk to you."

"Well, I don't need to talk to you," a determined voice snapped back from the other side; it didn't sound a bit sleepy.

Chance stared unhappily at the locked door as if he'd never seen one before. "Damn it, Fancy. At least let me tell you how sorry I am about all this. It's not as simple as you think and I never meant to hurt you. If you'll just open the goddamned door and listen to what I have to say, maybe you'll understand."

"Why should I? You'll only lie and make excuses for yourself."

Chance stared at the lock for a long moment, disappointment and frustration mingling; it was just this kind of miscommunication that kept them star-crossed. Whenever she wanted to be reasonable, he didn't; whenever he chose to try, she locked him out of her life. He'd be damned if he'd let her screw things up this time without a fight. He stepped back, turned his shoulder to the door, and crashed through it to the room beyond, splintering the hinges from the wall. The double-paneled door crashed noisily onto the bedroom floor.

Fancy sat up in bed and stared, astonished, at her husband.

"I won't be kept out of my wife's bedroom if I choose to be in it, Fancy. And I damned well intend to say what's on my mind."

"I don't want to hear it, Chance. I want you out of my life once and for all."

"Oh, no, you don't," he said, his voice low and dangerous.

He crossed the room in two great strides, and Fancy drew back instinctively, unsure of his intent. She scrambled from the bed, to elude this stranger to whom she'd been married so long. She ran out the door and into the hallway toward the stairs, but Chance came after her and caught her at the landing. He grabbed her arm and pulled her to him, clutching her so hard against his body that she thought he'd lose his balance and crash them both down the spiral staircase. He swung Fancy up into his arms and started back with her toward the bedroom; she struggled in his grip, but he crushed her head against his chest so roughly that she screamed. And then Chance's mouth was on her own, choking off all sound, and the kiss was unlike any there'd been for a long time . . . what lunacy was it in her that made her kiss him back with equal abandon? Chance sensed the exhilaration in this impossible, exasperating woman who had plagued his life forever, and thinking there had never been any way to communicate with her but one, he threw her onto the bed and ripped the nightgown she wore from neck to hem.

Fancy saw him tear at his own clothes, saw the look of wildness in his eyes. Never had she understood the strength in that taut body, the fierce burning strength that was bridled under urbanity and a gambler's charm. He could have killed her with his hands; the thought excited her.

He was pulling her body in to meet his thrust; she tightened and sucked in the power of him greedily, angry as he, wild as he. Chance pushed her bewildered loins past anything civilized; bullying her, swirling her out beyond space and time and sanity, he tortured the exquisite spasms from her. Fancy felt the explosion of Chance's own fulfillment crescendo with her own . . .

He lay very still beside her, their heartbeats thundering in unison. He waited for her to say she loved him, no matter what. She waited, breathlessly, for him to apologize. Neither said a word.

"God damn you, Fancy," he said finally, a strange resignation in his voice. "Why is this the only way we ever understand each other?" He rose, and Fancy saw him pull his clothes on. Why wasn't he telling her that he loved her? Why wasn't he saying aloud all the things his body had said so eloquently? She lay fearing to breathe, as she watched him turn without a word and walk through the fractured bedroom door.

"Chance!" she called after him, terribly confused. She scrambled out of bed and ran to the doorway, still clutching the bed linen to her body, still feeling the ache of him within her. "Chance, come back here!" But the only answer was the crashing sound of footsteps on the stair and the finality of the front door slammed behind him.

▲

Fancy fretted all the following day at Chance's absence and fussed at the servants and at the children. Where was he? Was it possible that what had happened between them had no meaning at all for him? She planned what she would say to him, altering her speech, as each hour ticked away and her remembered love turned gradually to anger.

Could it be that he didn't plan to attend this party she'd planned so laboriously for their triumphal return to Leadville? Could it be he intended to shame her by not even showing up? If he did that, every important household in Leadville would know the truth about the McAllisters by morning.

Where had he stayed last night? With that woman, of course. Why had he not come back when she'd called him? Hadn't he understood how much she loved him in that primitive moment of absolute surrender? Hadn't that inexplicable fire they shared reminded him, as it had her, of how much they loved each other?

All preparations for the gala were completed by late afternoon, but still no sound had been heard from Chance. He'll send flowers, she let herself hope . . . or a note asking forgiveness. Oh, please, don't let him go all day without a word . . . not after last night. For a mad instant she even thought of sending a message to Sam Southern's Parlour House, asking her husband to come home, but her pride wouldn't let her make the gesture.

▲

Fancy surveyed her reflection in the full-length glass beside the bed, and sighed. The candlelight-satin gown with its revealing decolletage and fashionable puff sleeves set off her bosom to perfection. From her tiny waist, a crinolined skirt cascaded in three deep tiers, each edged with costly ecru lace and tiny seed pearls.

Fancy had lain impatiently on the chaise for hours, with wet tea compresses on her eyes and cucumber slices on her cheeks and nose to banish the telltale swelling and redness her crying had left behind. She couldn't bear to put her body into the bed they'd shared so explosively the night before, so she had lain glum and nervous on the chaise, and tried to calm herself, while rag curlers pinched her head. The resultant mass of dark ringlets now was set off at each ear by tortoiseshell combs, to which had been fastened an intricate network of tiny pearls.

A velvet ribbon held her dance card to her wrist and a single fresh-picked gardenia nestled between her breasts. If he had the starch to come for dinner, at least she'd have the satisfaction of making him eat his heart out.

Fancy fastened the diamond drop-earrings he'd given her as a wedding gift with trembling fingers; she could titillate any man she chose, she just had never chosen to do so since she'd married Chance. When he arrived—if he arrived—she would punish him for his cruelty. Her heart pounded frantically each time she thought of him, and she had to fight back the tears that threatened her carefully made-up face.

Fancy moved among her guests with the aplomb of a seasoned performer. She smiled at the men, talked of babies with the women, and hid her seething humiliation beneath a facade of graciousness. She parried the questions about Chance's whereabouts with just the level of exasperated-but-devoted wifeliness that everyone would expect from one whose husband had been detained at business beyond the start of so important a dinner party.

Jason watched Fancy with the same astute judgment that had made him rich; when he was certain of what he was seeing, he put down the tumbler of bourbon he'd been nursing and moved confidently to her side.

"It appears you've been left to your own devices this evening, Fancy," he said with an understanding smile, not in the least patronizing. Fancy began her automatic patter about how Chance had been unavoidably detained, but checked herself as she looked into Jason's amused eyes. She hesitated, slightly embarrassed, but he rescued her.

"Perhaps, if you wouldn't think me too bold in suggesting it, I could lend a hand here, just until Chance's business is finished, of course. I'm such a close associate of your husband's, no one would think ill of us."

She regarded him with a wry smile.

"Does anyone ever put anything over on you, Jason? Truth is, I'd kill for a little help with this disaster."

He chuckled at her forthrightness. "I think such measures won't be necessary, but I would like one small boon. Would you have room for me on your dance card, Fancy? You and I once danced together a great deal, as I recall."

She felt reckless and infinitely spunkier than she had just a moment before. As a matter of fact, she damned well hoped she'd be in another man's

PAINT THE WIND 559

arms when Chance arrived . . . especially this man's. "I expect I would, Jason," she replied.

arms when Chance arrived . . . especially this man's. "I expect I would, Jason," she replied.

Madigan smiled a little and bowed, then walked off toward the knot of men who were standing near the fireplace talking politics. She heard him say something, as he joined them, about Chance having to deal with a problem at the mine; then the conversation switched to the question of the railroad's newest venture. Relaxing a little for the first time since the night before had ended in disaster, Fancy went about the business of being a hostess.

▲

Chance arrived just in time for the guests to be called to the dining table; he was dressed, as always, impeccably. Fancy had not seen the suit he was wearing before, nor the tie and boots. A knot tightened her stomach . . . he not only had somewhere else to stay, but it was someplace intimate enough that he kept extra clothes there. The realization disoriented her; she'd thought Chance's infidelities as casual and heedless as everything else he did.

"Evening, sugar," Chance greeted her smoothly. He nodded to Jason. "Sorry to be late, but some things came up and needed to be attended to."

"Seems Jason here has everything well in hand," he said, reaching to take his wife's arm from Madigan's to lead her in to dinner. But Fancy stiffened and held fast to Jason's arm, which she felt tighten as she did so.

Chance's eyebrow rose expressively; a look, half amused, half arrogant, curved his mouth and glinted in his eyes. He shrugged as if it were of no consequence, turned abruptly, and preceded them through the doorway, to take his place at the head of the table. Pointedly, he turned his charm on the lady seated to his left and Fancy, desperately wounded, shocked, and furious, needed all her acting talents to handle the remainder of her party.

Just after the last guest departed, Chance did too.

He stood for a moment outside his own front door, struggling for equilibrium, the hurt of it searing a hole in his gut . . . Fancy and Jason. Her old lover. The one man in the world powerful enough to lure her away—of course, she'd go for the money and the power; what a fool he'd been to think she'd be sitting home pining for her lost husband.

How could she not know how much he loved her? How could she not see that he'd tried to understand her needs and her moods and her endless insecurities, through all the years. This time, he had a premonition there would be no mending of the fences that separated them.

Fancy cried very quietly until there wasn't a tear left anywhere inside her. How many years had it taken for their precious love to come to this disastrous end? She hadn't been blameless in their endless dance of death . . .

but something irrevocable had happened to her heart this time. She realized, shocked by the revelation, that she no longer wanted to change Chance . . . no longer imagined she could . . . he was who he was, and not all the years or tears had changed that one iota. She just didn't want to play this dreadful, hurtful game with him any longer.

So this is the way a marriage ends for good, she thought miserably, staring out the window from her empty bedroom. It just dies of a thousand little wounds and one final big one, too fatal to be forgiven.

106   Fancy returned to work with a vengeance. Jewel and Wu saw the hurt she covered up with energy and effort; she spoke little about the dissolution of her marriage. Fancy's fortune waxed as Chance's waned and if that gave her satisfaction, no one ever knew it from her lips. She never even let on to Jewel and Rufus that she knew Chance had named his new mine "The Any Man's Fancy," a fact that occasioned considerable mirth in Leadville.

Aurora was happy to see Chance go, but Blackjack pined for his father so desperately that Fancy arranged to send him East to boarding school. Chance moved into Sam's and tried to get his luck to change; he paid more attention to his business in the three months after leaving Fancy than he had in the previous three years, but it was late in coming and there were problems to be dealt with on every hand. The two big producers were dwindling, the silver lobby in Washington was losing ground, and there were rumblings that when Harrison's term was ended, the gold standard would be adopted. Hart was gone, Bandana was gone, now Fancy, too, had left him and he felt diminished by the losses. It had been easy to consider himself a loner when there'd been no fear of loneliness. Now Chance felt alone in a way he never had before . . . alone, uneasy, and down deep, in some secret place he hadn't known about before, he felt afraid.

▲

Fancy felt caged, not freed, by Chance's departure. Aurora grew more difficult to handle by the day; she didn't want to go East to finishing school, she didn't need to work, she didn't seem to have any ambition or real interests, beyond the way she looked. Fancy tended to lose patience with the girl because she was lazy and that was one trait for which she had no frame of reference whatsoever.

Jason wanted to marry her, that was apparent. He'd been kind and helpful since the party, always available when she needed a friend, but she was thankful that divorce hadn't been spoken of, for it gave her a reason to say no to Jason's attentions without offending him.

107   Sam took the glass of champagne from Chance's hand and sat down opposite him on the plump white chaise; she'd grown fond of the man and was sorry for the unhappiness that clung to him now.

"You look like you're feeling blue as I am tonight, darlin'," she said. "Is there anything I can do to help?"

Chance leaned back on the leather couch and loosened his tie. He felt guilty being with Sam, but he felt needy, too. He'd thought of taking rooms at Billy Nye's, but there was comfort in having someone to come home to. He saw the irony in this, for when he'd had Fancy waiting for him, he'd spent considerable effort on staying away.

"Business is bad, and life seems to be all out of kilter, Sam. My brother's been gone too long, the mine production is off, I can't unload the properties fast enough to pay the bills, and Fancy is—" He stopped as if realizing it would be bad form to discuss his wife with his mistress.

"Go ahead, darlin'. I don't mind you talkin' about her. If I had to guess, I'd say you're still hung up on her."

"Why?"

"Oh, I don't know, Chance, there's just a certain look you get when she comes into your head. Like you want things to be good for her. I'd feel real honored if any man felt that way about me." She smiled to put him at ease, because she'd grown to care about him, far more than was comfortable to the role she played.

"What's got you so down in the dumps, Sam?" he countered to change the subject. He didn't like to admit even to himself how much he missed Fancy and Blackjack.

She leaned her elbow on the back of the sofa and rested her head on her hand.

"Got a baby sister outside of Macon, you know. Her name's Emma and she's about as good as they get. Churchgoin' and bighearted. She's got a husband who's a farmer and four kids, another one on the way. I got a letter from her today, Chance. Seems like Seth's took sick and they could lose the farm to the bank. Em didn't say it in so many words, but readin' between the lines, I think it's cancer he's got, because she kept talkin' about God's will and how much she loves him. I think maybe my baby sister's in real big trouble." Sam's voice was huskier than usual.

Chance's frown was full of concern. "I'm sorry, Sam. Really sorry. If money could help them keep their home, I'd be glad to lend a hand. She wouldn't have to know it came from me . . . you could send it to her."

Sam wiped her eyes and tilted her head to look carefully at the troubled man who sat across from her. "I thought you were hurtin' for money, too, Chance."

His laugh was wry. "I expect I've still got enough money tucked away somewhere to ransom a farm outside of Macon, Georgia. I'm already in debt enough so nobody'd notice a few thousand more. If it'll help your sister out, I'll get you the money tomorrow."

Samantha Southern stared very hard at Chance McAllister's face. She was never entirely sure afterward what made her make the dangerous decision she did, right then and there. But it had been a goodly while since any man wanted to do her a kindness without wanting something in return. Maybe it was that. Or maybe she'd fallen for the guy and just didn't want to see him screwed, blued, and tattooed, like Jason intended.

"I think I just might take you up on that offer, Chance," she said slowly. "And then I think I might need to ask you for enough more than that to get the hell out of Leadville."

Chance looked puzzled by the words and tone. "What are you talking about, Sam? Why would you want to leave town?"

It took less than ten minutes to tell Chance everything she knew about Jason's plans for him. She didn't even feel scared after she did it, just pleased with herself. It was a long time since she'd had a chance to do a good deed in a dirty world.

▲ ▲ ▲

The night watchman left Mr. McAllister poring over the ledgers like a man possessed. He'd never seen such concentration, scanning first the books, then the files, then every scrap of paper, like a machine digesting ore. He couldn't help but wonder what kind of slurry would result.

Just shy of sunup, Chance finished the last file. His prodigious memory had cataloged enough information to ferret out the pattern, but it would take the rest of the day to collect the proof of what that son of a bitch had done—systematically tying up his cash assets, subtly moving him away from liquidity, into a major cash-flow bind. No wonder he'd had to borrow, with Jason's helping hand the one always outstretched. It had stretched into every crevice of Chance's businesses. Christ! What kind of Machiavellian patience would make a man spend so many years bringing about another's ruin. It was a game, of course, to Madigan. Making or breaking a man's life was nothing more than a series of intellectual poker hands. Chance rubbed the sleep from his eyes and let his head rest for a minute in his hands to think.

He played poker, too, and perhaps there was still time left in the game. There was no need for anyone to know yet, what he knew . . . not until he could shuffle the deck a little.

Jesus! but he'd been stupid. Even taking into account that he'd been conned by a master, he'd still been rube enough to fall for it.

Not a single one of the foreign investments he'd made were in operation. What good were forests in Honduras if no mahogany had ever been harvested? What good were mines in Mexico if no tin or silver had ever been dredged from them? Not a single one of the mining properties in Montana or Idaho was operating at a profit. Two of the six Leadville properties were already on the market, two were out of ore, and of the big producers, the Last Chance and the Fancy Penny, more and more stock had been siphoned off to pay for the problems that abounded in other areas. The Any Man's Fancy had been jinxed from day one.

Hundreds of thousands of dollars had been spent on investments he'd never even heard of and nearly every piece of property in Leadville was mortgaged to the rafters. By the end of the night, Chance McAllister finally understood exactly what Jason's friendship had done to his life.

▲

Dear Bro,

I've had a shock today—the kind that gets you in the gut and makes the world spin out of control for a minute or two. I've been a fool, it seems, but I've made a plan to rectify that. Best not to put it on paper just yet, though.

Damned near lost Fancy for true, this time. She's been right about a lot of things, bro. In her own way, I guess she's always been my friend. A consummate pain in the ass, too, mind you, but the best friend I ever had, other than you.

Well, there's no time like the present to set things to rights, or at least try to. I guess I'll just have to teach that son of a bitch how to play poker.

Your damned fool of a brother,
Chance

"I need your help, Caz." Chance stood in the living room of Castlemaine's small frame house, feeling awkward that it had been so long since he'd been there. Caz's son Jonathan looked to be about ten years old and there were other children too.

Annie Castlemaine watched the two men stare at each other for a long moment, while her husband made up his mind.

"There's a surprise, mate," Caz said finally; his eyes sought Annie's and a barely perceptible nod of the head moved her into animation. She looked very pregnant, maybe near her time.

"We're pleased to see you, Chance," she said, her soft Irish brogue giving lilt to the simple words. "It's been a long while since you stopped by for a coal for your pipe . . . too long for friends." She didn't wait for a reply, but headed for the kitchen to put the kettle on the stove.

"No tea, luv," Caz called after her. "From the looks of the man, it's whiskey we'll be needin'."

Relieved by the welcome, Chance sat on the small couch and laid his hat on the floor beside him. Why had it never occurred to him that Caz might be in need, with his growing family and his mine manager's salary? How many other things had not occurred to him? he wondered.

"Now what's the kerfuffle, mate?" Caz asked.

"Jason's out to cut my throat."

Caz nodded.

"I need to cut his first."

"You'll need a big knife for that."

"There's a property he has his eye on over near Fryer's Hill. I want it seeded . . . very cleverly seeded, Caz—so it would fool most men, but it won't get by Madigan. I need it to look as if he's being set up, so when he finds out, he'll walk away from the property."

"And you'll buy it?"

"I'll supply the cash and you and I will be partners. There's silver in that part of the mountain . . . it's a ways down, but I'm staking my life on the fact that it's in there and I need access to some new money for a stake. If there is silver, that mine could put me back in the game."

Caz raised his eyebrows significantly and poured a whiskey for each of them.

"That's a real long shot, mate, and Madigan's sharp as a new ax. How can you be sure we can pull it off?"

"I'm not sure, Caz, not sure of anything. But I can't just lie down and let that bastard win without a fight. I've got to try something."

The two men made their plans far into the night; it wouldn't do to be careless.

When Chance rose to go, Caz followed him out into the small yard. "Does Fancy know the score, mate? There's all kinds of rumors flying around town about you and that nightbird."

"It isn't the way it looks, Caz. I've been a fool about a lot of things, including Fancy, but I mean to make it all square with her. She's tossed me out for the moment, but you know Fancy . . . she gets mad as a hornet at me, but she's fair at the end of it. She'll see I was a horse's ass, but Jason was a bastard. That'll make the difference."

"I hope so, mate. You two sure as hell lead each other a merry chase."

Chance nodded, looking uncertain. "I don't really know how to say thanks for your help—after all this time," he said huskily, and Caz shrugged.

"My pleasure, mate."

"And thanks for not saying 'I told you so.' "

Caz merely shook his head. "Don't mention it. Isn't every day I get to do a foul deed to a fine feller like Madigan." Chance mounted his horse. "And, mate . . . give my love to the sheila. But take some advice from an old friend . . . give her yours first. Old Fancy always was a pushover where you're concerned."

▲

It took Caz the better part of a week to accomplish the task he'd set himself. It was easy enough to seed a mine, bringing in rock from other digs, even blasting ore into the rock face with a shotgun; all fine, if you intended to fool a tenderfoot. But if you intended *not* to fool an expert—that was a more complex scam. If this was the only hole card Chance had, it could be a very cold game.

 108 Chance stood in John Henderson's office at closing time, too agitated to sit down; the teller at the window had refused to honor the bank draft he'd presented.

"What do you mean, you're calling in my paper?" he demanded. "There was never any time limit placed on those loans."

" 'At the bank's discretion' is what the notes say about timing," Henderson replied evenly; he'd been in banking long enough to know how to handle this kind of unpleasant situation.

"I'm very sorry, Chance, but the truth is you've mortgaged yourself far beyond the boundaries of common sense. No lending institution can carry a client who's a constant liability."

"Liability?" Chance thundered. "What in the hell are you talking about, John? You and your bank have made a bloody fortune off my investments."

"Which is precisely why we are a successful operation, Chance," Henderson countered. "We're in the business of making money, not of losing it. You can stand there and fume all day and it won't alter my decision one whit. Fact is I've instructed the tellers to freeze your accounts until a complete inventory of your assets can be made."

"Does Jason Madigan know about this?" Chance asked, bridling his fury.

Henderson pursed his lips as if deciding whether or not to speak again.

"Mr. Madigan and I discussed this action not an hour ago," he said with quiet finality.

The rage Chance felt at Madigan at that moment was so intense, he could barely contain it; he felt he would implode with the wrath that strangled him as he stood on the street outside the bank and fought for equilibrium. The cards were on the table now, there was no more time for a bluff. He sent a terse note to his enemy to meet him after the last shift broke at the Fancy Penny and impotent fury made his hand unsteady as he wrote the words.

▲ ▲ ▲

The sounds of machinery whirred in the background of the mine office and a dull yellow light from the desk lamp illumined the tidy space, and threw long shadows from the two hostile figures across the expanse of wooden floor. Chance had sent the watchman away for an hour; this was a conversation that demanded privacy.

He looked into Jason's steel-gray eyes across the room where he and Hart had spun such dreams in better days. The ghosts of lost visions resided there, and the aching sense of vanished possibilities filled his bones.

"Time for the final reckoning, Jason," he said in measured tones. "The man I thought was my friend owes me an explanation."

Madigan's expression was hard in the reflected light. "I don't think I understand precisely what you mean by that, Chance."

"Come off it, Jason. I've spent a lifetime reading men's faces over a deck of cards. I already know what you did . . . I've come to find out why.

"All these times you lent me money . . . all that sage advice on investments . . . all those mortgages. It was nothing more than an elaborate scheme to bankrupt me, wasn't it? By God, Jason, you're a patient man. It's taken you years to accomplish what you set out to do."

Jason's lips twisted into a contemptuous half smile. "You're a fool, Chance. A great, arrogant fool, who thought he could have it all without paying his dues. You always had the swagger, it was just the substance that was missing. If you want to play with the big boys, you better know the rules of the game."

Chance fought his temper back fiercely; he intended to get some answers before he killed the son of a bitch. "You're a rich man, Jason. Rich as any man in this country . . . money can't have been your motivation."

"I did no more than any other smart businessman would have done. I took advantage of a fool. You let me walk all over you because you were too self-satisfied to pay attention to what I was doing. And too involved with your public persona, your gambling, your floozies, and your endless self-satisfaction.

"Now that you're out of money, let's see how you fare with that fatal charm of yours."

"I'm not entirely out of money, Jason. It may surprise you to know that I have an interest in a new strike that looks like it has real possibilities. If there's the silver in the Down Under, and I think there is, I'll wager I can get any bank in Leadville to lend me the capital I need to tide me over."

"The Down Under? . . . You mean the claim that Australian who works for you just bought? That was salted, I found the evidence myself."

"That's right, Jason, just where I had it salted to throw you off the track. If you play cards with the big boys, you can lose your shirt."

Disconcerted by having been fooled, Jason stared at this contemptible adversary, who had more lives than an alley cat. There was no way on earth he was going to be bested by this insubstantial, arrogant fool; too much time and effort had gone into bringing him to his knees. God damn the infernal luck that always put him back on his feet! If he thought he was simply walking away from this confrontation with money in his pocket and Fancy back in his bed, he'd better think again.

"You're a loser, Chance. You'll never get that money out of the ground fast enough to save your hide. I'll see to that. You treat your businesses with as little care as you do your wife."

Chance's head came up sharply; hatred in his eyes. "My wife? There wouldn't be any jealousy tangled up in your little plot, would there, Jason? Pull the rug out from under me and see if you can swoop in and seduce my wife while I'm on my uppers."

"Your wife might welcome some attention from a man who knows how to treat her, McAllister, not one who makes her the laughingstock of Colorado with his whoring and his carelessness."

"You self-righteous son of a bitch!" Chance muttered as he lunged for Madigan. A right to the jaw sent Jason sprawling; the downed man called out sharply and three others pushed their way into the room. Chance flew at the leader, wrestling him to the ground, but the other two pinned his arms from behind. He felt a sharp blow between the shoulder blades that made his body sag against their restraining grasp. He tried to break free but a vicious kick to the kidney doubled him over . . . he was dragged upward so violently, he thought his right arm might have snapped from the force of his own weight, and he had to fight against the pain to stay conscious.

"Enough!" Madigan shouted.

"Coward!" Chance spat at him through bleeding lips. "Even now you have to hide behind other men. Is there anything at all you do in the daylight?"

Madigan's hand moved instinctively toward his holster.

"That's it, Jason," Chance taunted him, straining violently against the grip of the guards. "Why don't you shoot me right here in the dark, like you've done everything else?"

Madigan controlled himself, with great effort. "Let him up," he said gruffly.

"I say you haven't got the guts to meet me on Harrison tomorrow, you stinking coward," Chance challenged him, trying to rise to a standing position with difficulty, the pain in his right arm and kidney intense.

"Right out in front of God and everybody, Jason, I'll show you up for the skulking, back-stabbing son of a bitch you really are. Just how brave are you when you leave your hired thugs at home?"

"I'll accept your challenge, McAllister," Jason replied carefully, bridling his anger and brushing off his jacket in a studied gesture. "It will give me the greatest of pleasure to put you out of your misery once and for all. If only so your wife can find out what it's like to be married to a real man."

Chance strained against his captors, the pain in his side so severe it made the figure before him swim sickeningly in front of his eyes.

"Get him out of here!" Jason snarled at the men with dismissive contempt.

The men pushed Chance unceremoniously out the door of the mine office he and his brother had built with Bandana McBain. He had to struggle just to keep his legs, and made it to his horse only with painful effort. The two men stayed to watch him mount and head out toward the trail, just as the watchman returned to his post.

Bitter memories tumbled past each other, as Chance pushed his horse to a lope. So many signs he should have read earlier; so many dead giveaways. Fancy telling him to pay more heed . . . Bandana and Hart warning him never to let control out of his hands. Christ! He'd brought this destruction on all of them . . . that knowledge racked him far more than his injuries.

The moonlight shadowed the rocky path ahead of him, but he pushed his horse forward blindly toward home.

Where *was* home tonight? he wondered. He couldn't go to Fancy with his tail between his legs. How could he admit to her now all that he'd let happen? How could he tell her she'd lost everything she held dear in the world, for a second time?

Jason was right about one thing, Chance thought bitterly. He had been a fool.

▲

Jason dismissed the men, pulled his Winchester from its mount, and filled his pockets with cartridges. With a new silver mine at his disposal, Chance just might be able to regroup . . . Fancy might even take him back, if she learned the truth.

McAllister would never see another sunrise.

▲

Chance headed toward the house that had once been home, and toward the woman who was still his wife, even if he hadn't lived with her for three months. Tomorrow he would kill the son of a bitch who'd damned near destroyed them all—but first he'd go home and try to make Fancy understand the tangled web that bound him . . . make her know how very sorry he was for his mistakes. It was the only honorable thing to do.

Chance climbed the long, familiar staircase; he knocked tentatively at the bedroom door and waited to be invited in. He had no sure idea of what he would say.

Fancy was seated at her dressing table in a pale blue dressing gown he'd given her in the best of times, when hope was high. She turned toward him, startled by his unexpected appearance; he looked unsteady on his feet, as if he'd been drinking. She couldn't hide the quick tears that sprang to her eyes as she rose to meet him.

Chance made a move toward his wife, but she stiffened; he stopped, too vulnerable at this moment to bear the burden of overt rejection.

"I want a divorce, Chance," Fancy blurted out, needing to say it out loud, before she remembered that she loved him. "I've been intending to come find you to tell you, but I heard you were living with that woman. . . ."

"Fancy . . ." Chance began, but the word *divorce* reverberated louder than his thoughts. How could he tell her now that he'd brought them both to ruin, and then ask her to stay? How could he express all the conflicting emotions—the love and the longing to be understood, the desperate sorrow and the unutterable need for forgiveness? Too many years and too many hurts lay between them now . . . too many promises broken, hopes unfulfilled, love returned in ways that left each of them hungry and alone.

"Fancy . . . I just need you to know that I'm so damned sorry."

She turned to face him, steeling herself against the pain in his voice, and her own hurt of the last three lonely months. It had taken heartache and soul-search to reach the point where she could ask for a divorce and mean it. What did it matter that she'd always loved him—neither of them would ever change, and to remain together was like volunteering to be flayed alive.

"You've said you were sorry so many times, Chance," she said wearily. "It no longer means what it did to me when I loved you so much you could

tear my heart to shreds with your 'I'm sorry.' I don't give a damn anymore
if you're sorry or not."

The past tense of it defeated him. What was there to say to the end of
love? Even if he could cajole her out of this anger, what was there left to
offer her but humiliation and uncertainty? Without the bank behind him,
there'd be no way to work the new mine, even if there was silver in it.
Divorce. At least then she would be free to start again without having to
demean all they'd been to each other with pity.

"I wish to God you didn't feel that way, Fancy."

What's wrong with him? she thought angrily. Why won't he even fight
back? "Damn you! Chance," she blurted out, all her frustration and anger
breaking the surface. "Was what I wanted from you so damned dear you
couldn't give it to me, no matter how I begged you? Didn't you know there
was a time when I would have sold my soul just to have your love?"

He didn't rail back at her, as Fancy expected him to . . . as he always
had before. Instead he sat down wearily on the bed, pulled the buttons of his
shirt open, and leaned over to undo his shoes.

"Great God!" Fancy burst out, misunderstanding. "You surely don't
think I want you to make love to me now!"

Chance raised his dark head, as if struck. A small wry smile twisted the
corner of his mouth.

"No, Fancy. I guess that's the one thing I didn't think." He stepped out
of the trousers he was wearing and tossed them, and his shirt, onto the
chair. The sight of his familiar body made Fancy's heart ache all the more—
never had he seemed to her more noble-looking, or more desirable than in
this moment of good-bye. She saw as he bent to his boots, there was a touch
of silver that shimmered in his hair—had it been there before? The broad
shoulders were bent to pull the denim pants on over long, strong legs. There
was elegance and simple dignity in the way he bore himself.

"Chance . . ." she began desperately, but what hadn't already been said?

He looked up, searchingly, but Fancy could find no words that seemed
appropriate. He'd put on riding clothes, the oldest he owned.

"Where are you going?" she asked, her face set in a confused, tight line.
It galled her that he was returning to that whore.

"I love you, Fancy," Chance said gravely. "I've been a fool . . . but I've
always loved you." Then he crossed the room in three long strides and was
gone.

▲ ▲ ▲

The way up to the old cabin was long and arduous. Chance needed solace
after leaving his wife, needed a place to think things through before tomorrow's fight. He toyed with the idea of never going back to Leadville; of

simply riding on to somewhere over the horizon, far from Fancy and all the mistakes of the past. But he knew he wouldn't. Irresponsible, he might be in some people's eyes, but never had he been accused of cowardice. And he wanted nothing in the world so much as to kill the son of a bitch who had destroyed his world. When the fight was done, perhaps he would try to make her understand. . . .

The ground was treacherous underfoot and the way was steep, but rife with memories. There had been such hope in these hills, once, he thought glancing around him . . . this is where it all began. Maybe, if he retraced his steps, he would find his way again . . . maybe, if he rested for a while and healed the wounds, his luck would change. Tomorrow everything would look different, he told himself, in consummate weariness. First, he would take his revenge . . . then he would go to Fancy and lay the whole truth on the table and make her listen. Maybe she'd understand and forgive, if she knew the true extent of Jason's perfidy. He had been stupid, but he hadn't been wicked, as Jason had been. Even if she couldn't love him any longer, she would see the difference.

The night was inky dark on the hillside as he rode upward, but the horse knew the old familiar way. Chance let himself drift into memory. The sounds of the rider following behind him didn't reach his distracted mind until it was too late to escape.

A single rifle shot rent the mountain air. The impact of the bullet threw Chance forward in the saddle and caused the horse to bolt wildly. The wounded man tightened his legs around the cinch in a frantic effort to regain control, but the pain that stabbed upward into his belly from his groin wrenched a terrible groan from him as he teetered atop the galloping animal. The horse covered the remaining distance to the lean-to outside the old cabin in minutes; only desperation and the habit of a lifetime in the saddle kept Chance on his back during the steep climb.

Blinding pain shot through his belly as he swung his leg over the horse's rump and slid his body to the ground. The impact of landing left him stunned and breathless; he waited precious seconds until the pain-mist cleared, then he pulled the Springfield .45/70 from its scabbard, and hobbled into the pitch-black cabin that had once been home.

Almost against his will, Chance forced himself to focus on the wound in his groin, seen by the sliver of moonlight that filtered through the window. It was the kind that tended to be mortal. Cursing, he pressed his bandana hard against it in a useless effort to stanch the flow, and used his gun belt to hold the makeshift bandage into place. He'd never leave the cabin alive, not in this condition, not with an uninjured adversary outside with a rifle. Odds were he'd die here. With infinite care, grimacing against the awesome pain of movement, Chance forced himself to sit upright against the wall; with all the patience of desperation, he gathered whatever strength he had for the effort of thinking clearly.

The moonlight filtering through the window would give him sufficient light for what he must accomplish. There was little possibility that anyone other than the shootist could find him here in time. If he was to die, there was something he must do.

There had been no further sign of the assassin; perhaps in the dark the man had assumed the job to be done, or perhaps he simply waited outside for his prey to die . . . Jason wasn't the sort to dirty himself, hand to hand. He must be out there right this minute watching, Chance thought. He must be out there waiting for me to die.

With terrible effort Chance pulled from his pocket the paper and pen he'd brought with him in hopes of writing something to his wife. There was so much he wanted to tell Fancy; if only it wasn't so damned hard to find a way to say what was in his heart, he would have said it all when he'd faced her.

Slowly, laboriously, and with the last effort of his life, Chance McAllister wrote a letter to his brother, instead. He sealed it into the envelope and on it he wrote: *For Hart McAllister, when he comes home to Leadville.* He blessed his brother in his heart and prayed that somewhere, somehow, he was still alive.

Carefully he slid the letter far down inside his shirt, with the hope that whoever had shot him wouldn't stay around long enough to search his clothes. But he knew it was no trail robber who had done this deed . . . all the man outside wanted was his death. He'd already stolen everything else of value.

Chance let his weary body sink down one last time in the eerie puddle of moonlight. He closed his eyes, and thought of Hart and Fancy and Bandana one Christmas Eve long, long ago . . .

 109 The stage trip up through the mountains was both grueling and cathartic for Hart. It had been a long two years since the Apache surrender. The ghosts of his beloved dead still lived in him, but they were echoes now, and he had found a way to live with his aching memories.

He was relieved at the prospect of coming home; he needed his brother, needed to tell Chance of all that had ravaged and reworked his soul. He didn't mean to stay long; he intended to head for Paris in search of a public unbiased enough to be open to his Indian works. But first he needed to go home to find his brother.

Hart felt the buzz of tension in the town when he stepped off the train. He could sense it in the guarded greetings of old acquaintances and in the surreptitious glances of people at the depot. The big man headed for the Clarendon and checked in. The clerk read the name on the registry card and glanced up. "You any relation to the McAllister who's gonna be fightin' Mr. Madigan today?" he asked. Hart's hand snapped out across the desk so fast it was a blur; he grabbed the boy by the shirt front and got the rest of the story in record time.

There wasn't a manjack among the townsfolk who didn't know the whole tale, the boy said, or at least Mr. Madigan's version of it. Madigan and McAllister had quarreled over Mrs. McAllister—it was common knowledge she intended to leave her husband because of his philandering. Hart let the desk clerk's shirt slip from his hands; every woman who'd been waiting for years to give Fancy her comeuppance, every man who was jealous of Chance, was probably licking his chops over this disaster. Hart knew people packed a picnic lunch and took their kids to a good hanging, so a gunfight between two men of public stature could make the whole town declare a holiday.

He ditched his bags, splashed water on his face to dislodge the grit of travel, and put on his riding clothes, a terrible apprehension tightening his gut. What if he'd come home too late?

▲

Jewel Mack paced back and forth, back and forth, watching the hands on the mantel clock as if she could hold them back by force of will. Unlocking the gun rack, she pulled down a Winchester .44 and took the ammunition for it from the drawer below the rack. Fancily engraved with her initials, it delivered seventeen rounds, four more than her carbine. She'd always had a special affection for this particular rifle because Ford had given it to her.

Her own room had a better view of the street than any other spot in town. Jewel positioned herself at the window and tried to stay calm. What the hell was wrong with Fancy that she'd let things get this far out of hand?

▲

Madigan stood with the easy authority of a man who expects to win, knowing he must make this farce look authentic. He'd even gone so far as to place his men all over town, as if a gunfight were really expected. But there would be no fight today in Leadville, for Chance McAllister was already dead.

The townspeople would think McAllister had fled out of cowardice. With a little luck it would be quite a while before anyone found his body up at that deserted mine shack and when they did, time and the wolves would most likely have taken care of any evidence about how he'd met his end. If not, there was always a drifter passing through who could be blamed.

He pulled the flap of his coat back to free his gun hand, and flexed it twice convincingly over the holster. Fancy wasn't the only one in town with a flair for the theatrical.

▲ ▲ ▲

With mounting fear, Hart searched Leadville for his brother. Baffled, worried, he made his way toward the Crown; he'd remembered that Jewel's room, where he'd once painted her portrait, was the most strategically placed spot to view the fight, and there was no time to search further.

Jewel was already crouched at her window, rifle propped on the sill, when Hart slipped the lock on her door. She spun around like a professional shootist, raised wide, intelligent eyes to his, and nodded, understanding all she saw in his face. God Almighty, but he looked like a man who'd seen a lot of wear since leaving Leadville. He was lean as leather and moved pantherlike as a redskin.

She pulled the curtain aside with a meaningful nod, just as Jason's men stepped back from his side and left the man standing alone and unchallenged on the dusty street. She didn't ask what Hart intended to do, just moved out of his way so he could do it. He wondered fleetingly if she'd intended the same fate for Jason as he did, if Chance were vanquished. He glanced around and saw the woman bolt the door behind him and plant herself in front of it, as if it would take Sherman's army to move through her to where he crouched at the window ledge.

Down below on the street, Madigan waited in the full knowledge that Chance McAllister would never come.

▲

Minutes ticked by with maddening slowness; the wind blew dust and tumbleweed down the deserted street, but nothing moved beyond that.

"Something's wrong, Jewel," Hart said, his voice tense as iron.

"Something's real wrong."

"When did you see him last?"

"A day or two ago . . . but Fancy saw him last night . . . they had a big row over the divorce and her leavin' Leadville."

Hart frowned, and Jewel could see he hadn't known about the dissolution of the marriage.

"Sorry, Hart. There ain't no easy way to tell this to you. That marriage was dead as Kelsey's nuts, except for the paperwork. You know how it's always been for them two—cain't live with each other, cain't live without. Things've been real dicey, but she'd decided to leave him long before this stupid-ass fight cropped up."

Hart scanned the empty street—people were beginning to peer out of their hidey-holes. He could imagine what was being said about Chance; only the worst kind of coward would duck a gunfight.

"He's hurt or dead, Jewel," Hart said, low and strained. "Nothing else would keep Chance away. My brother's a lot of things, but coward is not one of them."

He rose from the crouch by the window and headed for the door. Jewel grabbed Hart's arm as he passed, saw the worry and the strength in his eyes, and other things she couldn't put a name to; she put her arms around him and held tight for a long moment, before letting go.

"Take care of yourself out there. If anybody got the drop on your brother, he was either damned good or damned treacherous."

Hart nodded, understanding. Next to Ford and Geronimo, Hart had never seen a better shot than Chance.

"Take this," she said suddenly, grabbing a handsome repeater from the gun rack and pushing it into his hands. "It's Ford's, the stock'll fit you." He kissed her gently on the forehead and without a word left her standing in the doorway, tears spilling down her cheeks.

▲

Hart tried the mine office first, but Caz said he hadn't seen Chance in twenty-four hours. He turned to go, but Caz pushed back his chair to follow. "Arf a mo', mate," he said, picking up a Remington from the corner. "I'll come with you. Your brother was a good friend to me, once." Hart nodded acceptance and both men mounted, with Hart riding out in the lead. Caz watched Hart ahead of him on the trail; he saw that the huge shoulders were drawn downward like a man expecting a terrible burden to be placed upon them.

They checked the area around their own mines, even the Rainy Day, before the notion of the old cabin flashed into Hart's head. Could it be that Chance would seek refuge from a crumbling world back where it all began? He said as much to Caz, and they headed up the overgrown and winding trail.

Chance's black horse stood tethered outside the old shack; his head was low and flies buzzed around the blood on his saddle. Caz caught Hart's eyes with his own, and saw the terrible understanding register. Hart ran to the cabin, the door gave way on its old hinges and creaked back with an eerie sound.

Chance McAllister lay crumpled on the floor; his handsome face was gray as dust and strong in its repose. The massive groin wound had congealed, as had the puddle beneath him, into deep burgundy.

He had come home too late. Hart sank to his knees in despair beside his brother's body and brushed the black hair back from the beloved forehead; he pressed his lips against his brother's face in farewell, but the flesh was cold and he knew the spirit had long fled. He reached beneath Chance's back and lifted him, cradling head and shoulders in loving arms, as he once had held his father long, so long ago . . . the terrible memory from the past swept through him.

Caz stood, silent as the grave, in the doorway. He saw the big man bending low over Chance, crushing the dead body in his arms, shaking with silent, racking sobs. The tears that filled his own eyes blurred the scene before Caz, and he felt compelled to turn away, for the grief within the cabin was so palpable, so private, it seemed to him even the eyes of a friend would profane it.

The minutes ticked by as Hart held the cold, still body of Chance in his arms and remembered their dreams. With infinite tenderness, he laid his brother's head to rest, cushioning it with his buckskin jacket. He saw that his hands were sticky with blood and he stared at them, unwilling to wipe it away. *Blood is thicker than water and brother's blood the thickest of them all.* He clenched his fists as if to hold this essence of his brother's life-force back from death, and clasped Chance's hand in his own one final time, but the once dextrous fingers were cold and hard as the marble on a tomb.

Hart strove to stand, staggered from the dizzying grief, then wordlessly pushed past Caz and trudged off into the woods.

Caz took a long, deep breath, struggling to control his own emotions, and entered the cabin. Reverently, he knelt beside the body. "In the name of the Father, Son, and Holy Ghost . . ." he blessed himself and prayed for the soul of this foolish, lovable man who'd been his friend.

Caz would never have noticed the letter inside Chance's shirt if he hadn't sought to compose the dead man's limbs into some semblance of repose for Hart's sake. The paper rattled, and wonderingly, Caz tugged the scribbled note free, and read what Chance had written with his dying hand.

Dear Bro,

I'm leaving this in hopes that one day you'll find it in your heart to forgive me what I've done. Truth to tell, I'm pretty sure you will, for I know you always loved me. And maybe Lady Luck owes me one last good throw of the dice for having deserted me at the end.

The gunfight I never made it to wasn't over Fancy, whatever they may tell you. It was over the fact that Jason screwed us to the wall—you, me, the mine. I guess my head for business wasn't all that good, bro. But I figure you know that, too, by now.

He planned it all . . . the cave-in, the financial ruin of the mine and me. He's got his eye on Fancy, too. Don't let him have her, bro—she's the best there is, even if I haven't always taken care of her like I should have. She always loved me, you know. She loved you, too, of course. Can't say that even seems odd to me now, that she loved us both, I mean. I'm not so poor a man I don't know a better one—I can't help but wonder what would have happened to us all if you'd been the one she chose, all those years ago. Does God laugh at us mortals do you think, bro? Or does He weep for our stupidities.

What else is there to say, I wonder. That I've been a fool—I know you'll forgive me that, you always did before. Take care of Fancy, will you . . . I know she's in better hands with you than she ever was with me. Don't be surprised if she misses me a mite, though. We were cut from the same bolt, she and me. And what a time we had of it for a while.

I don't regret much, Hart. I wish I'd been smarter and that I'd never hurt you or Fancy. But we are what we are, and I know you both loved me despite my failings. As I loved you.

Well, so long for now. I'll give your love to Mama and Daddy, when I see them. They'll be waiting for news, along about now, I expect.

Never started out on such a long trip without you before, bro—can't say I'm not a little scared. Remember that night on the mountain when we were kids? I guess I've stood on your shoulders in more ways than one over the years, haven't I, Hart? It all seems so clear to me now . . .

I want you to know one thing before I go. Through it all, you were the one I trusted. Relied on. Just this once, I'm glad I got to be reliable, too. I didn't go sniveling to Fancy with my failures and I didn't try to find you to fight my battle for me. Although, God knows, I've missed you sorely. I would have killed that bastard in a fair fight, if he hadn't bushwacked me like he did.

I love you, bro, more than I ever loved anyone in this world, I guess. Have a good life and remember me to Fancy. She'll know what I meant to say.

Chance

Caz took a long, audible breath. "God forgive me," he whispered into the silence. "I can't let him see this letter now. He'll kill the bloody bastard and swing for it."

He hastily stuffed the damning letter into his shirt and left the cabin to look for Hart.

▲

Hart and Caz brought Chance's body down off the mountain. Hart staggered up the steps of the McAllister house with his terrible burden in his arms, and Fancy met him at the door. Caz saw their eyes meet above the dead body of the man each had loved so well, and he thought that never in his life had he seen grief so palpably shared.

Fancy went nearly insane with grief and guilt; she raged and cried and blamed herself for everything . . . she refused to let anyone tend Chance's body for burial, but drove them all from the room, saying no one but she could touch her husband.

In a trance of bereavement, Fancy bathed the ghastly wound as if to punish herself for all past sins, by sharing this death in whatever way she could; she washed and dressed Chance for the undertaker, but when the man came with his funeral wagon to collect the last remains for embalming, she clung to her husband and wouldn't let him be taken away.

Jewel, Hart, and half a dozen others tried to talk sense to her, but Fancy just stared past them into space, such crazed determination on her face that they soon realized nothing they could say or do would move her.

It was Hart who thought of Magda; Hart who sent a fast rider to Denver to fetch the Gypsy woman. Late that night she arrived and found Fancy lying on the bed beside Chance, her arms around him, crying pitiably. No one, not even Hart, ever knew what Magda said to her, but whatever passed between the two women, Fancy, in a stupor of sorrow, left the room where Chance lay and Magda sent again for the undertaker, and went with him to see to his gruesome task, as she had promised Fancy she would do.

The body, prepared for burial, was returned to the McAllister home for waking. Fancy, dressed in black taffeta, her ravaged face veiled whenever anyone was near, never left her husband's casket for the three days it remained before their drawing room hearth.

Hart kept constant vigil at her side. Sometimes they spoke of the best of times, sometimes they simply sat together in heartsick silence.

Sometimes Fancy wept and Hart, too anguished to speak words of comfort, simply held her in his arms until she slept. Fancy would not leave Chance, Hart would not leave either of them. Magda, knowing more of the ties that bound the three than anyone else, guarded the door and forbade the world to interfere with the shared and terrible grief that ran its course within.

▲

The coffin with Chance's body in it made Fancy feel she would suffocate, as it stood on the hill beside the fresh-dug grave.

Closed in. Trapped! she thought, insanely. You were so restless, my love, how can they think you could ever sleep like this? How could a simple wooden box contain the body she'd loved so desperately, the body she'd made all the most hideous mistakes for. She'd loved and hated him so long, there seemed to her never to have been a time when Chance hadn't tormented her. Now he was gone but the torment still lingered.

"May a merciful and loving God give understanding of the violent manner of this man's death . . ." The minister's voice was a relentless, useless drone.

Oh, shut up, you fool! she thought savagely. There is no mercy for the likes of us. We'll go hand and hand into hell for all we've done and all the fun we've wrestled out of life. Just hold my hand wherever they send us, Chance my love, and we'll make a rollicking good time of it, won't we? She stood staring at the coffin lid and thought she might have gone mad.

People could go mad from grief; everyone knew it. Even as a child, she'd heard the servants at Beau Rivage speak in hushed voices about poor Mrs. Benton, who'd gone crazy when her husband got thrown from his horse and died in the cornfield. The woman had lived for forty years, somewhere on the upper floor of the great Benton plantation house, with servants who never abandoned her.

The casket began to be lowered on stout ropes into the ground. Fancy heard the squealing timber and the obscene scratch of earth on wood. Soon he would be beyond her reach forever, the last of Chance laid low, while the best of him still rampaged through her soul.

"No!" she cried, reaching forward, and she felt Hart's hands on either arm.

Why didn't I ever know how to make it right? Why was it only in our bed that we had it all? she longed to make him answer. I'd sell my soul to touch you one more time.

"Don't leave me, damn you!" she whispered, meaning the words for her husband, but it was Hart's voice that answered, "I'm here."

The irony of it maddened her, or was it the loss, and the noonday sun and the gaping townsfolk taking obscene delight in the fallen mighty.

Even at the end, there are three of us instead of two. Damn you for being brothers! Damn you for never being what I needed, only everything I wanted.

The casket thumped to rest, a dreadful sound. Hart, his face contorted with anguish, stepped forward and thrust aside the shovel handed him by the gravedigger. Instead, he filled his huge hands with earth and knelt at the very edge of the grave. Slowly, so slowly did he let the dirt trickle from his clenched fingers down upon the coffin that held his brother, it might have been the wind alone that had blown it there.

"Forgive me . . ." he whispered so softly that none but Fancy heard him. Then he turned and looked into her face, his own streaked with tears, and the pain that was in his eyes was fathomless and for all time.

Fancy turned her head away . . . for she loved Hart too.

110 The widowed Fancy was a different person from the Fancy who had lived apart from her husband through the past months. This parting was final, with so much left unsaid. Images crashed about her like waves against a seawall. Why had she not listened when Chance came to her that last night? Why had she let her vindictive heart drive him into the path of a gunman's bullet, just as she'd once driven him to other women? She could have saved him, if only her pride hadn't gotten in the way . . . if only she'd been kind instead of righteous . . . if only . . .

She would never have taken him back as a husband, she knew that, despite her grief. Too many bridges had been burned, too many heartaches had been etched in stone for that. They were flint and tinder together, a hopeless conflagration, and their marriage had bled to death from too many wounds, too great to stanch. But she could have saved him from this final disaster, if only she'd been more generous, and that was a terrible guilt to carry.

Fancy sent everyone away so she could cry aloud; the lingering sounds of her sorrow echoed in the stillness of the big house. Chance's lifeless body kept appearing before her vision in the fire's glow . . . the elegant long limbs she'd once caressed with skill and longing, constricted by the hours he'd lain alone, dying in the darkness. Alone and misunderstood.

"Oh, Christ, there are such ghosts alive in me, Hart," she told him in the endless hours they sat together, holding on. "Will they never be still?"

Hart was no stranger to grief. It seemed to him, sometimes, that he'd borne all possible losses now . . . that Chance had died long ago, with the others he had loved . . .

"Would you have stayed married, if he'd lived?" he asked her once.

"No. It was a danse macabre we did together. I didn't know how to make it right and neither did he."

"What would you change, if you could?"

"Oh, Hart . . . I don't know if I'd give anything back. Maybe even the mistakes of youth are better than any wisdom age brings with it. Maybe it's a sacrilege to regret even one minute of your precious life."

Hart had put his arms around her then and held her.

"Where do we go from here, I wonder," he asked, but it was two full months before she answered him.

 111 Hart and Fancy stood together near the entrance to the Rainy Day. Eight weeks had passed since Chance's funeral; Hart had ordered all his brother's affairs as best he could, and made arrangements for his trip to Europe. He thought she'd brought him there to say good-bye; she seemed troubled and oddly distant. When she finally spoke, her words were so different from what he'd expected that he had a hard time taking them in.

"If I asked you to stay with me, Hart, just for one week," Fancy said to the strong and gentle man she'd so long taken for granted, "would you do it?" Hart stared at her in confusion, trying to fathom what on earth she was really asking.

"I know it probably sounds insane to you," she said carefully. "Maybe it even does to me . . . but I wish with all my heart that you'd take me somewhere for just a little while, so we could be alone together . . . before you go. But not like we've been, Hart . . . not reliving the past anymore."

"Why in God's name would you ask that of me, Fancy?" he said, shocked by the unseemliness of it. "And what of Chance? Have you really forgotten everything so soon?"

"Chance and I burned all our bridges long ago, Hart. I loved him more than you could ever guess, but I'm afraid it's a very long time since he and I were truly married to each other."

Hart digested what she'd said and heard the ring of truth in it, even through his anger; but he was still repelled by the invitation.

"Why a week and not forever? Why any time at all?"

"Because I love you in my own way," Fancy replied, honestly. "Because I've decided to leave Leadville behind me forever, and I'd like to take some memory of us with me when I go from here. Because of all the men I've ever loved, or who've ever loved me, you've asked the least of me and given the most in return."

Hart shook his head, bitter and confused. "I don't want your charity, Fancy."

She raised her eyes to his and there was something indecipherable in them that stayed his anger. "This isn't charity, Hart. It's just all I have left to give . . . all that's left of me. I mean it as a gift, such as it is."

It was the poignancy in her voice that defeated him, he thought afterward; that and his ancient love for her.

"I've loved you a long time, Fancy. But I could hate you for this."

"I won't beg you, Hart . . . if you say no, I'll understand. We've both lost everything now. All we have left of our dreams is each other. All I'm asking of you is a week."

"One week? And what will that give us but regrets?"

"Memories. I've come to think they're the only thing that counts in life, the only thing you can rely on to be permanent. I *need* the memory of you to carry with me, Hart . . . and I need to give you a memory of me that isn't sad or angry or bitter or frustrated."

Hart's voice was so charged by emotion, it was barely recognizable. "And in that week, what are we to be to each other?"

Fancy took a deep breath, fastened her eyes on Hart's so that he felt swallowed up in the hurt he saw there. She answered fiercely, drawing out each syllable with elaborate care. "Absolutely everything," she said.

Hart turned from her and looked out toward the horizon. Jewel, too, had told him that Chance and Fancy's marriage had ended long before his brother's death . . . did that really grant him absolution for what she asked, or was it just convenient rationalization for a truly heinous act?

Whatever it was, right, wrong, or something else entirely—Hart told Fancy he would stay.

▲ ▲ ▲

Sometimes, later, it felt to Hart as if their time together encompassed eternity—other times it was no more than the briefest blink of sunlight in a dark world. Could it be true that the sun shone brighter and the air blew sweeter and the rain washed everything cleaner than it ever had before? Could it be that time could be suspended, and that only bliss could exist in the space "between," before the clock of reality began again its inexorable ticking?

For a while, Hart forgot they had never belonged to each other; for a while, he laid the ghost of Chance to rest between them . . . or perhaps they simply were as they had been on that long ago day when Fancy had come into their lives and changed them all, forever—all three together, in an embrace of surpassing intimacy.

He had the strangest feeling, somewhere between guilt and relief, that Destarte would be happy for his happiness. He had been alone for so long . . .

Hart watched Fancy as she moved, watched her as she slept, watched her as she made love to him in ways no woman, slut or virgin, ever had. And he painted her in his mind's eye as he would on canvas when she was gone, every nuance branded on his soul. She was his as he had dreamed her in the good times . . . strong as no other woman could ever be, yet so vulnerable, only he could protect and guard her.

Fancy felt Hart's love in every cell. She drank in his strength and devotion, storing up against the years ahead. She, too, had suspended time, had given herself this one moment in infinity to live without fear or guilt—for the worst would happen soon enough and she would be alone. "Do what you will to me, Destiny . . . but this one moment I demand of you in return for all I've suffered at your hand," she said aloud one night as she lay folded in Hart's arms, and he understood.

Hart was so different a lover from Chance. His lovemaking was like a force of nature. Powerful, primal as the tide and just as overwhelming. She felt washed clean in his love for it was pure—strange word for anything so lusty. When he took her to himself, she abandoned all thought or question of superiority—she was woman, he was man. They were as they were meant to be, the perfect fit of puzzle pieces, earth and sky, Adam and Eve before the Fall. There was no part of her he did not know, no tiny nuance she held back from him, as she had so often held back part of herself from Chance— in anger or in retribution. With Hart, Fancy was herself, all of herself.

"Touch me there."

"Where?"

"Everywhere. Pick a place."

"That place?"

"Oh, yes, that place. And the others."

She laughed in bed with him and they talked endlessly.

"You could get pregnant."

"I could, but I probably won't."

"In our next life we'll have children. I've envied my brother that."

"We didn't do so well with our creations, Chance and I."

"We'd do better. Your looks, my disposition."

"And exactly what's wrong with my disposition?"

"Don't be greedy. A boy should get something from his father."

"If he were half as wonderful as you are in bed, we'd have to fight the girls off with a bullwhip. . . ."

Hart covered her body with his own and the need for conversation dwindled for a while.

"What will you think about me when I've gone?" Fancy asked.

"That I wish things could have been different so we could always be together."

"Oh, no, Hart, don't you see? That's where we're so much luckier than all the rest of the world. This way, we'll never disappoint each other, never fail. Never argue, never say bitter words that can't be taken back. We'll never even grow old and have to watch our bodies fall apart and become ugly . . ."

Hart put his hand over Fancy's mouth to quiet her. "No!" he said gruffly. "Don't profane it. I'd give anything to grow old with you. I'll live without you, if I must, but you can't profane my dreams."

Fancy heard the pain behind Hart's words and was chastened by it.

She lay in bed beside him and thought about her past. Had her choices caused the holocaust of her life or had life caused her choices? Were there ever really choices at all, or do we mortals simply follow blindly where Fate leads us, deluded and without recourse?

Could it be so wrong to want, need something for yourself alone? Aurora wasn't hers, despite all the hopes she'd held for her daughter. Blackjack wasn't . . . Fancy knew he was the bone and blood of Chance, and she no more than a conduit for his entry into the world of his father. But maybe a child of love could tip the balance . . . surely anyone who belonged to Hart must be good and full of promise.

She smiled at her own insanity and tried to imagine Magda's response if she were to appear once again on her doorstep, pregnant for a second time with a McAllister child who had no father. "Imbecile! You are too old to bear a child. Aurora is nearly a woman and you must be nearing your dotage to even imagine such a thing!" But Magda would also understand.

Fancy shifted in the bed to see Hart more clearly. He was an immense presence beside her, fair skin, darkened on face and arms by the sun; freckled, too, a playful scattering. Strong, manly face, craggy and lived in, but compassionate about the eyes and full of goodness.

His bigness excited her; the heat his body exuded made her want to insinuate herself into his overpowering embrace and stay there forever. Hart raised his arm from the bed without opening his eyes and, smiling, folded Fancy in beside him, sleepily.

She should do something to protect herself from pregnancy now . . . before he touched and she responded. Before feeling obliterated thinking, and the hot hard loving force of him changed safety into something that existed only in his arms. She should . . .

Fancy sighed and snuggled warm against the rising strength of his love and opened her own body to meet it.

The rest she would leave up to God.

▲

"Where did you go just then?" Fancy asked Hart as they lay together, one night. "It's beginning to feel very lonely over here." She'd been watching him stare at the ceiling, lost in thought; she felt curious, disturbed by the distance that had arisen between them, despite the fact that they'd made love only a short while before.

His voice, when he replied, was husky, unfamiliar.

"There's something I've been wanting to tell you, Fancy . . . about my past. It's sacred to me and I never really intended to tell anyone. But now, the way things are between us . . . it just doesn't seem honest not to."

Fancy sat up in bed, chilled by his tone. She pulled the covers up over her shoulders to shut out the cold, not to cover her nakedness.

"I never think of you as the kind of man to have secrets, Hart," she said warily.

He didn't look at her when he answered. His arms were crossed beneath his head and he stared off into space, as if he'd drifted into another landscape.

"I had a wife, Fancy . . . I had two children. They meant everything in this world to me."

Fancy blinked hard. What was he saying? How could he possibly have been married without her knowledge? As realization dawned, she blurted, "Oh, my God, Hart, you had a squaw, didn't you?"

"I had a *wife*, Fancy. I loved her . . . we had a son and a daughter. I loved them too. My wife's name was Destarte."

A lump had risen in Fancy's throat; questions tumbled inside her and a queer, deep hurt wrenched her stomach. How could he have married someone else if he'd always loved her? How could he think of a squaw as a wife? He spoke her strange name with such reverence. . . .

"Where are your children?" she whispered. She felt she'd been plunged into water too deep to swim in. She wanted to know everything . . . she couldn't bear to hear another word.

"My son is dead . . . the soldiers murdered him. My daughter never was found after the raid that killed Charles and Destarte. I searched for her for a long while, but I never could find a trace. She was only a baby, Fancy . . . only a newborn baby."

The anguish in Hart's voice touched Fancy, dissipating the sense of betrayal she'd felt just a moment before. She, too, had loved and lost. Fan . . . Chance. She, too, knew the bitter sorrow of regret.

"What was she like?"

"I don't think I can talk to you about her, Fancy . . . it doesn't seem right to do that."

Fancy's heart constricted at the love she heard beneath the words. "Oh, God, Hart . . . I am jealous of her," she breathed, barely able to say it aloud. "I can't bear to think you ever loved somebody else so much. . . ." She tried to push the hurt of it down, down where it couldn't undo her. "But I'm afraid to let you keep her bottled up inside you. I can talk to you about Chance, because he belonged to you too. It isn't fair for you not to have anyone at all to talk to about your . . . about her, Hart. Maybe that's a gift I could give you . . . maybe you could share your grief with me."

Hart was so still Fancy wasn't certain he'd heard a word of what she'd said. Then suddenly he turned with a strangled sound and crushed his head into her lap. Sobs shook his huge frame as he clung to her and Fancy put her arms around him, as if he were a fevered child.

"She was so good . . ." he murmured. "So gentle and kind . . ." And then the floodgates burst and his cries were great spasms of pain and loss. Fancy felt caught up in his anguish, felt it flood her senses. There was fury underneath—frustrated, passionate rage that raked him. Christ! He had been brutalized in ways she could barely imagine.

"Hush. Hush, my love, it's all right. Please don't cry so . . ."

He gripped the bedclothes that covered her, speaking muffled secrets, baring himself of bitterness in merciless confession. Fancy bent her head over his, her long hair covering his shoulders like a veil. She soothed him as if he were a baby.

"Let it all out, love," she whispered, wanting desperately to ease his hurt. "I'll try not to be jealous or foolish . . . just please don't hide her inside your soul anymore. Please tell me . . ."

And he did. In tiny fragments, at first. And then a torrent of memories tumbling out of hidden places until, at last, he felt drained of everything, even remorse, and he fell into an exhausted slumber, his head still pressed against her flesh.

Fancy sat cradling the sleeping giant, tears obscuring the world around her, as visions of a beautiful Indian woman lying in Hart's arms called forth the worst and best within her, jealousy and compassion. "If the eyes don't see, the heart doesn't bleed," the adage said. There was so much in life she wished she'd never seen.

"I love you, Hart," Fancy whispered into the moonlit air around him, but he made no reply.

112 Their week became two, and then the better part of summer had mysteriously passed them by. Fancy brooded about what must happen next, but Hart seemed lost in their idyll and unwilling to face the fact that perfect moments end.

What was she to do with this strangely leftover life of hers? What would she make of herself when Hart had gone and she was once again alone? Who would she be then? Not the childhood Fancy, nor Jason's mistress nor Chance's wife nor Hart's love. Someone new.

"Where will you go when you leave me?" she asked as they lay together.

"To Paris. I'll paint your portraits so the whole damned world can see how much I love you. Come with me."

"What do you want from life, Hart? Has it changed for you since we were young?"

"No . . . I guess it hasn't changed at all. I still want peace of mind and a loving family. Still need to put on canvas all I've seen, learned, grown into. Need to try to set the record straight about the Apaches . . ." He put his arm around, for there were tears in her eyes that he didn't understand.

"Most off all I want to take care of you, babe. Make you happy. Have a bunch of babies that look like their mama. Maybe buy a farm . . ."

But I don't want any of that, she thought bleakly. Even if she didn't know for sure what she did want, she always knew what she didn't want. So no decisions were made and finally the waning summer days made them both restless and in need of a definitive future.

Hart took the train to Denver and came back with tickets in his pocket, hoping. He'd wired the Canfields of his plans to be in Paris by the opening of classes at Beaux-Arts in September and it seemed impossible that after all they'd shared, Fancy would stay behind.

"I've made arrangements for the trip, babe, for both of us. We could stay in New York for a few days to shake the railroad dust, then board one of those grand boats that make the crossing . . ."

Fancy broke through his nervous rush of words. "I can't go with you, Hart . . . I think you know that." She saw the tendons tighten in his neck, but his voice was steady.

"I'm going to Paris, Fancy. That's where I'm going to earn my keep. I need to get these paintings out of my head and down on canvas."

"I know that, Hart, and I understand why you can't stay with me . . ."

"In another world, Fancy, women go with their husbands . . ."

"I've done that, too, Hart. I know all about that other world. I just don't belong in it."

"What are you saying to me, Fancy?"

"I'm saying that this is my last chance to prove myself . . . to myself. Just as you need to paint your pictures, I need to find myself again. I lost me somewhere, with your brother's death, maybe even with our life together. I need to find me again before I'm lost forever . . ."

"Christ Almighty, Fancy, don't do this. Don't throw us away."

"What would I do in Paris, Hart? I don't speak the language, I couldn't perform . . ."

"You could be my wife, Fancy. I want you to marry me. I'm so much in love with you, I can't see straight. I want to spend my life with you."

"I love you, too, Hart. How could you ever doubt that after these past weeks? But I can't marry you. I thought you understood that from the start."

The color rose in Hart's face. "You're serious, aren't you? You can just walk away from me like none of this ever happened. All of this has been no more than an elaborate affair for you, Fancy, hasn't it? Everything we've had, done, shared, has meant nothing more to you than some casual fling. Son of a bitch, Fancy! I just plain don't believe you could be that calculating and cold-blooded." He paced up and down the room, too agitated to stay still. "I've held you in my arms . . . it's not possible that what you felt there was an act! Your love, your passion, they weren't casual. You can't tell me what you felt for me wasn't *real*." His fists clenched, heart pounded.

She looked genuinely stricken. "No. Of course, I don't mean that! I do love you, and every minute we've shared has replenished me, given me hope again. I only mean that I can't marry you, Hart, and give up my own identity again. Sublimated, lost . . . I just don't want to be some man's wife again. It's too soon. I need time to find out who I am now."

"Some man's wife!" he repeated, his voice choked with anger. "For Christ's sake, Fancy, is that what I am to you . . . some drifter off the street?"

"No. That isn't what you are! You're deliberately misunderstanding me."

"Who, then, Fancy? By God, who am I to you?"

She looked miserably at the furious giant and tipped her chin up, defiantly. "You're the man I'm in love with . . . the man who's given me more love and kindness than anyone I've ever known. But I cannot marry you, Hart. Not now . . . maybe not ever."

"How could I have been so fucking wrong about you, Fancy? You're nothing but a hardhearted, selfish user. You use whoever you need for whatever you want and then just walk away when you're sated, don't you?

Like a goddamned vampire." He searched her eyes and she could see there were tears blurring his.

"You used me, Fancy. And I've loved you damn near forever."

"This has nothing to do with you, Hart, don't you see? It has to do with the fact that I'm never going to marry anybody. That doesn't mean we can't be friends, does it?"

"Friends? What do you know of friendship, Fancy? As much as you do of love and commitment? I'm not interested in your friendship. It just isn't worth a damn."

▲

Fancy watched silently from the doorway as Hart packed his bag; he was too absorbed by hurt even to know she was there. As he straightened from strapping the valise, she saw him wipe his hands across his eyes. She couldn't bear the pain on his face.

"I came to tell you that I know you didn't mean those things you said about me, Hart . . . and that I never meant to hurt you."

He tried to read her face and saw only love there, ingenuous as a child's. "No."

"And to tell you that I love you more than you could ever know, and that I wish with all my heart I could be what you want me to be."

"Yes."

"And that . . . that I think I wouldn't know how to live, if I didn't believe you were my friend." Her voice was a hoarse whisper, utterly devoid of subterfuge. "Please be my friend, Hart. I couldn't bear to lose you."

Hart sighed and opened his arms to this exasperating woman he loved, with a sigh of inevitability, for he knew it was all true. He wrapped her close, resting his head on the top of hers; they clung together for a while before he spoke.

"I could no more take back my friendship from you than I could my love, babe . . . but I just can't wait around for you anymore. I guess I'm just too old for that now. I want a life, Fancy, a real life. I want a wife who'll go with me wherever I go. I need to build something real with my life. I want children to come after me, I want a home. Oh, God, if you knew how much I long for a home of my own, Fancy . . . a piece of ground I can make bloom . . . a place I can share with someone who cares about the sharing. I've been in exile, too, babe, and I want to go home. If I can't have those things with you, then maybe, just maybe, mind you, I can find them with someone else, while there's still time. But to do that I'm going to have to escape you, Fancy. And that's about the hardest task I ever looked at. I'm not so fucking noble I can live forever on the crumbs from your table, however well-meaning they are. I don't want to give my heart and soul to someone for whom it isn't enough. If that's selfish, then I'm sorry. But at least it's the bedrock truth. I'm going to do my damnedest to get over being in love with you, babe. But no matter what ever happens in this sorry world, I guess you can count on me to be your friend."

The room seemed to have grown dim around Fancy. She felt she might be drowning; what was wrong with her that what he offered wasn't enough?

"When will you go?" she whispered, standing outside his embrace.

"Today."

"Stay the night, Hart. Make love to me one last time."

He laughed, an ugly, bitter sound. "Oh, no, my very dear love. You asked for a week and I stayed a summer, and look at the trouble I've got myself into now."

"But I need you to stay with me."

Hart stared at her, searching her face. "That may be the cruelest thing you've ever said to me, Fancy, and you don't even know it." He hoisted the valise onto the floor, a gesture of finality. "There's a price for everything, isn't there, babe? I hope that what you're going after this time gives you enough in return for what you're throwing away."

He picked up the suitcase and turned toward the door.

"Hold me, Hart!" she cried out, a frightened child.

Hart stopped, but didn't turn around. "Not this time, Fancy," he replied with finality. "Not this time."

▲ ▲ ▲

Hart left again . . . reluctant, determined, and for good. His whole life had been no more than a series of escapes from Fancy; from the chaos and the need of her . . . from Chance's love for her, or his own. She was his obsession, beloved and friend—he knew that now. But she'd been right about their time together; it had been a final closing of the circle of their lives.

Before boarding the ship bound for London and then Paris, he checked on the money Rut had been investing for him. It would support him admirably while he painted. Not that money had ever really mattered to him all that much—only talent, hard work and passion dredged from experience, changed what a man was capable of creating. Hart put a large sum in an account for Fancy before he left, and wrote a note saying he'd discovered it there, a stash Chance had obviously forgotten. It would be plenty to get her started again, if she chose to keep the secret of the Rainy Day, as he hoped she would.

He stood on the quay of the great North River in New York and looked back over the busy waterway, toward what he'd left behind . . . a brother who'd been part of his soul . . . a woman who'd been the phantom of his dreams . . . a beloved Apache wife and children, who seemed to have existed in some separate incarnation. He felt spent, as if there could be little more blood payment that life could ever expect of him.

XI

I WILL MISS THE WIND

Paris and Pallas

"No good deed goes
unpunished."

BANDANA McBAIN

113 ❦ Paris was a glorious world in which to start life over; the maddest dream of an American farm boy could not have conjured such magic as awaited Hart McAllister when he arrived there.

Impressionism was beginning to happen. Truth was too naked, said the artists . . . *la condition humaine* was infinitely more interesting than the historical subjects that had excited past generations of painters. The ordinary world was still under scrutiny, but not in the gentled way of Romantics like Renoir and Cézanne. Hart found a world that had abandoned faith in myth or religion, a world that was being challenged by scientific revelation and reinvented by the all-seeing lens of the camera. Art must become *new,* the artists said among themselves . . . Hart, who had never before lived in a world of artists, couldn't believe the vitality all around him.

"The artists are now free to search out the deeper truths," Pallas told him. And what truths there were to be fathomed, and what geniuses to give them life. Hart arrived in a Paris where the urgency of Van Gogh, the intellectual geometry of Cézanne, and the passionate expressionism of Gauguin were showing the way. The farm boy from Kansas had wandered into Wonderland with Pallas Canfield to lead him through the White Queen's maze. She knew everyone; the painters and sculptors starving on the Left Bank, the crowned heads, the industrialists and robber barons who collected their work. Wherever serious art existed in Paris, so did Pallas Canfield.

She occupied a unique position, for unlike Goupil or Dusseault, she was not merely an art dealer, but rather the confidante of the artists, with whom, Hart soon realized, she did not hesitate to have affairs of the heart. She ran a salon that was frequented by the most illustrious names in Europe —all of whom sought her favor, savored her wit, and many of whom, she told him unabashedly, shared her bed.

On any given weekend at her villa in the country, one might hobnob with the Prince of Wales or the Grand Duc Alexei of the Russias. Hart was awakened one midnight by a wildly played crescendo on the piano and, having made his way sleepily to the conservatory, he'd found Debussy himself entertaining Pallas, who sat, champagne flute in hand, at the foot of the piano bench.

Not that Pallas had turned frivolous—far from it. She simply recognized genius and attracted it to her, and the geniuses recognized her too. She introduced Hart to everyone of consequence and supplied him with a French tutor.

Never had he worked harder, not even in the mines . . . there was so much to learn, such unmitigated brilliance to strive against, that every moment needed to be seized with both hands. The stars had fallen on the generation of painters and sculptors who were gathered together in the City of Light in the 1880s. If you had the barest spark of talent, it could be fanned into flame by the moment, the company, the challenge, and the dreams.

▲

Pallas Canfield was as complex as she was powerful. Hart tried often, over the years that he knew her, to fathom what a woman must feel who is out of synchrony with her time. Different from the fragile, diffident, manipulative blossoms who decorated the world she'd been born to, she must have recognized early on the force of her own lusts, not merely the sexual ones, but the hunger for power, which was just as demanding. It wasn't that she was selfish—Pallas gave freely to those who needed assistance—but she was singularly self-absorbed. It was as if from childhood on, she'd had a plan of action for herself, one that would brook no interference.

Pallas and Hart knew each other well, impresario and artist, man and woman; he never intended that they be lovers.

His first two years in Paris were fertile and purgative. Canvas after canvas lined the walls and floor of his pension to be pronounced on by Pallas' ruthless eye. "Maudlin!" she would say to devastate. "You waste yourself." Or "This one resounds with honesty. Paint what you know best, you great ninny! Do not follow what the others do. Sing your own song." Generally, she was right in her assessments, which made them all the more formidable.

For nearly two years "The Fancies" were Hart's self-indulgence and self-flagellation. He worked on them in between the other works that ravaged him, the Apache canvases. To live, he must purge himself of Fancy—must expunge her from his dreams and nightmares . . . root out the memories so inextricably tangled in his heartstrings. Pain into art, the eternal dreadful truth—in order to create, the artist must suffer . . . only what is painted in blood can satisfy an artist's hungry soul.

He would paint the bad Fancy first. Use the anger and the hurt to make her come to life in all her seductive wantonness. Avaricious, greedy, shallow, user of any who came too close for safety . . . at first he chose black, the sensuous dark of the black widow, able to seduce the male of the species, only to murder him at the height of his giving. But it was too funereal and Fancy feared funerals . . . so he painted her over in red. The color of passion, of pride, of blood. The color of desperation that clothes itself in crimson—a scarlet glory in a sensual world. He painted her as she might have been, if her lusts had not been bridled by need and she was free to be as she wished to be. It took him nearly a year to put half her soul on canvas, nearly a year to forgive enough to paint the other half.

Then he painted her in white . . . the white of sunlight on a snowcapped mountain crest, of moonbeams glistening on the face of the sea. Beautiful, vulnerable, spirited . . . the innocent child/woman of each man's most secret fantasies. As she might have been if Beau Rivage had never burned, and life was soft and safe. As she might have been if Fate was forgiving and love was forever. The compositions had lived in his mind so long, it seemed to him he'd been born for no other purpose than to paint them. He worked on "The Fancies" more to force them shrieking from his brain than to sell, he said, but the power of his love was etched on the canvas, as it always is when the passion of the artist is immense.

"Let me see 'The Fancies,' " Pallas demanded endlessly.

"No. They're mine. My purgatory."

He banned her from his studio for long periods. She suspected he neither ate nor slept when he worked on "The Fancies"; for each time he emerged he had the look of a starving child in his haunted eyes.

In those moments she could reach him once again for a time, push him into the Apache canvases, make him remember that he needed to support himself. At first, it made no sense to her that he chose to live so simply; he was a rich man who lived like a pauper.

But when she confronted him, he said, "When I'm no longer hungry, I'll no longer be able to paint." So she would leave him for a while and then return to push or pull him toward the future.

"This is growing macabre, Hart," she told him once. "You're fucking that woman every time you're alone with those despicable canvases."

"I'm fucking her out of my system," he replied, and his sardonic expression told her he would not be moved until he'd suffered out the passion.

"What a waste," she said. "There are women of flesh and blood who would welcome your embrace."

"Not yet. It isn't over for me, Pallas. I've loved two women in my life, and each one is unfinished for me still. Leave me alone and let me paint."

And so she had.

▲

Nearly two years went by before Hart let his mentor see his achievement. He had given her the Indian canvases, a huge body of work, the week before, and she had seen with disappointment that "The Fancies" were not among them.

"Are they finished?"

"Yes."

"Where are they."

"In my head and in my heart."

"Are they finished on canvas?" she said with exasperation, and he nodded imperceptibly.

"As much as they can ever be."

"I intend to sell those monsters instantaneously, just to free you from their bondage."

"No. They're not for sale. They'll never be for sale." His passion for the unknown woman turned Pallas mean.

"Oh, so you've no trouble parting with your Indian wife, but this bitch is sacrosanct?"

The rage in Hart's eyes was dangerous.

"I'll sell the Apache canvases because they're meant to teach people the truth! Destarte is part of that truth and, by God, I'd tread lightly on her memory, if I were you. I won't sell 'The Fancies' because they're nobody's business but mine."

Then, unexpectedly, a week later, he told her to come round to see them.

Pallas stood poised before the massive portraits, and tried to catch her breath. She said no single word for an interminable while and Hart, watching her, was strangled by his own emotions. Why had he relented and let her see them? Because if no one ever saw them, no one would ever know what he knew of Fancy? Or because they were the best work he would ever do?

When he could bear her silence no longer, Hart crossed the room and grasped Pallas by the shoulders; he whirled her around to face him and saw that her lower lip was caught between her teeth, like a small child's in distress, and tears were spilling down her cheeks.

"You're disappointed?" he demanded.

"I can't bear it," she whispered.

"What do you see?"

"That no one will ever love me as you have loved this woman."

Pallas put her elegant hands up to cover her eyes and began to weep, so pitiably that Hart was undone by her sadness—or perhaps by the emptiness he'd felt in his gut since the paintings were completed. He never knew afterward what made him do so, but he put his arms around the weeping woman to comfort her.

A shudder ran through Pallas at his touch and she entwined her arms unexpectedly around his neck, catching him off guard. She lifted her handsome head to Hart's and kissed him . . . intensely, passionately. No man could have mistaken the longing and the need explicit in that kiss.

And then, for no reason he could ever explain, he was kissing back, confused, stirred by her wildness—needy as she, desperate as she. Wanting to blot out the anguished memories of Fancy with another . . . to fuck her out of his system, as he had painted her out. Pallas tore at his clothes and at her own; the wantonness of it shocked him, incited him. She ripped at her own clothes as if she hated them, and naked, led him to the paisley-draped mattress on which the models posed; it was she, not Hart, who pushed them down upon it, reaching for his manhood, demanding what she wanted from him with knowing hands.

Her face was predatory, feral; despite himself, Hart felt the heat rise in his loins. This was not to be the communion of lovers but the mating of jungle beasts. This would not sully the past, for it was nothing like the past.

She had a powerful body; Hart thought fleetingly of the Winged Victory of Samothrace in the Louvre, as she pushed him back upon the bed and climbed on top of him. White marble limbs of perfect proportion to her well-muscled body; wide shoulders, breasts that would have pleased Rodin, and more fire in her loins than any wanton in Montmartre. She took possession of Hart's body as if mounting a stallion that must be taught about authority, and momentarily he was grateful to feel, not think any longer.

Her hands caressed his body, teasing, pinching, ferreting out. She was a primitive, and a sophisticate beyond his understanding; he was pushed and pulled, some savage inspiration dragging her and him in its wake. The tension she projected was so great, he feared the wrong move would push her to frenzy; she bucked like a furious animal and called his name over and over again . . . she said things he had heard no woman say before in any language.

Pallas tightened herself around his manhood at the same moment she somehow opened herself entirely; their bellies ground together and her laughter echoed in his ears. She was insane and that was fine; she would make no demands of him but those of the flesh. Her hands were raised above her head in some arcane ritual of mating, as she arched and plunged and forced Hart to the brink. Then suddenly she wrenched herself free and, sliding to the bed beside him, she pulled him on top of her and Hart, bewildered, aching for release, picked up the rhythm where she'd left it.

Pallas moaned beneath him, sounding helpless, desperate, somehow, and it evoked in Hart a flood of tenderness, different from the frenzied need that had driven him only a moment before.

Her moans became sobs . . . she called out his name . . . he sensed the breaking within her and he poured himself into her, matching her intensity.

She laughed again, triumphantly, but there were tears on her cheeks as she lay beneath him. Weary, weary, Hart dropped his body to cover hers, spent of all frenzy but the hammering of his heart. When the pounding subsided, he saw her laughing, and closed his eyes again for she was mad and this moment was mad and there was nothing left to say. She seemed refreshed; Hart felt as if he'd been trampled by a herd of longhorns. Where on earth do we go from here? he wondered, but he needn't have been concerned.

"Don't worry, Hart," Pallas said, reading him. "I never let pleasure interfere with either business or friendship."

"Ever kill anybody while you were taking your pleasure?" he asked, not knowing what to feel or think.

She smiled and sat up, lifting her hands to draw her hair up on top of her head and anchor it, mysteriously, there. There was amorality in her unselfconsciousness; nakedness flaunted was different from nakedness given as a gift, Hart thought, watching her. Yet the slope of her fine alabaster breasts and the grace of neck and arm, in the slanting north light of the studio, was tender and exquisite.

"Hold still . . ." he commanded, needing to take charge again. "Don't move at all." She did exactly as he'd said.

Hart scrambled for pad and charcoal, and did a series of quick sketches, trying to catch the elusive satisfaction of the moment.

"Will you paint me?" she asked, and he nodded yes.

A good many people tried to buy the canvas he did of her, after Hart's work had begun to fetch big prices, but Pallas never sold it.

▲ ▲ ▲

The years in Paris provided all the fulfillment Hart had ever lusted after as an artist, for the American West fired European imaginations and the integrity of Hart's knowledge made his canvases living monuments. The cognoscenti saw the truth and bought—the others merely followed suit.

Pallas guided his odyssey from obscurity to fame; a voyage of museums and galleries, of private purchases and learning how to hobnob with the rich and knowledgeable.

"Kings and princes hang your canvases in their palaces, Hart," Pallas said one day with an impresario's smug satisfaction. "Your Apache friends are renowned now because of you, what more could you wish?"

"That my renowned Apache friends had been given justice," he answered her.

XII

DANCE AGAINST THE WIND

▾ ▾ ▾ ▾ ▾ ▾

1893, New York

"Nobody ever gits too old fer
makin' mistakes."

BANDANA MCBAIN

114 *The past four years since returning to New York have been the longest of my life,* Fancy thought rebelliously, glancing at the reviews in her dressing room behind the stage. She was the grande dame of Broadway now, or so they said, nearly half a decade after Leadville. "One glittering hit after another" . . . "heights of passion" . . . "credit to her art form" . . . she read the phrases that said she was good at her craft and smiled ruefully. What was acting, after all, but a reconstruction of all the emotions you'd ever dredged from circumstance? And who better than she could know how to laugh or weep or storm heaven with useless cries?

Fancy sighed as she looked at the pictures of her children that adorned her dressing table. Aurora was older now than she herself had been when Chance and Hart had found her. She frowned at the picture, for the dark-haired beauty in the frame was so perfect on the outside, yet something unlovely seethed beneath the surface, something indefinable. She'd tried to reach Aurora, tried to coax her into revelation or even civility, but always there was the quick rebuff, the words that stung her heart and left Fancy feeling lonely and betrayed.

Blackjack's handsome face stared out at his mother from the second silver frame. Oh, God, those are Chance's eyes, Chance's laughing, fearless eyes . . . reckless, gambler's eyes. The boy was only twelve, but she knew as sure as he was his father's son that he would follow Chance's road to perdition. She'd placed him in the strictest military boarding schools she could find to fend off his improvident nature. Blood will tell, she thought, too old for fantasy. Blood always tells.

Gabriel's freckled baby face looked out from the third frame; his eyes were watchful, artist's eyes. Sweet, loving Gabriel—she'd nearly named him Matthew after his father, for who was there left in life to chide her? But some instinct told her that Matthew Hart McAllister would one day be a famous name, and that naming him after his father could cause embarrassment to them both. So she'd christened him Gabriel . . . after her mother, perhaps . . . or because it meant "gift of God." For this child had been the one headstrong act of her life that was wise.

Even Magda hadn't scolded her about this boy, who brought only joy to Fancy's heart. Each word she spoke, he listened to; nothing of her giving did he ever reject, as Aurora and Blackjack had. Not until his cooperative, intelligent nature had soothed her wounds of motherhood did Fancy fully realize the scars her other two children had left on her soul. She sighed at the thought of the long, strange road they'd traveled together. Funny, how she thought of life in stages: before Leadville, Leadville, after Leadville . . .

Jason Madigan had befriended and supported her in the years after leaving Leadville behind, and finally, reluctantly, she had married him. She didn't love Jason, but that had seemed restful in a way, love had brought her so much pain over the long haul. But it had taken nearly four years of work, motherhood, and loneliness before she'd consented to Jason's proposal.

She'd regretted the decision, almost from the first day, if the truth were told; it was such a defeat to her dreams. But she'd felt so thwarted in her attempts to reach Aurora, and marrying Jason was the one gift Aurora wanted more than any other. So she had done it to please her daughter, and out of utter weariness of spirit.

Fancy sighed again . . . she'd been a fool to send Hart away. She missed him in a thousand ways—missed his kind and gentle strength, his common sense, and his honorable spirit. She missed other things about him, too. It was hard not to remember the power of his body as he made love to her, the strength of his sexuality that had borne her along in its sweeping tide, until she forgot everything but the joy they shared so fleetingly. And she missed his loving heart. . . . How sad it was that her conscience couldn't cope with the happiness he brought her. The timing was off—too much guilt over Chance had stood between them. Perhaps she'd needed loneliness to sort out the shards of her life before she could start over.

It would be good to go home tonight, she thought, her body heavy with fatigue, and she was glad Jason was away on a business trip. Aurora had been acting very strange lately—more hostile, more volatile than ever, but with a pervasive lethargy, too, that was unusual in one so young. Perhaps she'd fallen prey to some peculiar illness, Fancy worried; the girl had never been strong in childhood. Or perhaps she simply suffered the malaise of the rich . . . no goal in life, no personal triumph to strive for. It had been a mistake to give her so much, without making her work for it—Fancy could see that now. Nothing had real value to Aurora and nothing gave her genuine pleasure.

Fancy sighed as she closed the dressing room door; she felt old and tired tonight, and the comfort of her own bed was enticing. Maybe Aurora would sit with her over a cup of hot chocolate and she would try again to reach this reluctant child, who was a woman now. How much it would mean to me, Fancy thought sadly, if my daughter could be my friend. She thought fleetingly of Dakota and had to push the memory away because of the quick, hot tears that filled her eyes.

She locked the dressing room door behind her and waved to the watchman as he let her out into the darkened street.

▲

Aurora wasn't there to greet her mother when Fancy arrived home; the servants said the girl had left orders she wasn't to be disturbed. Fancy, disappointed and weary, walked up the spiral stair of the town house alone. She opened the door to her bedroom, thinking how restorative a hot bath would feel tonight; she turned up the lamp near the doorway, and stood, too stunned to move, staring at the vandalism that lay before her.

Fragments of the ancient music box from Beau Rivage were scattered willy-nilly on the floor . . . beside its splinters lay the remains of the golden locket that had held her mother's lock of hair. All had been trampled underfoot, the delicate golden casing crushed, the fragile ringlet within, shredded on the floor. Atticus' banjo, its strings torn and useless, its neck broken and dangling at a grotesque angle, lay beside the other ruins.

Fancy's breath seemed sucked from her body; the only remnants of her "other" world lay mutilated before her, their music and memories stilled by violence. Her irreplaceable past destroyed by some ritual act of madness. What human being could do such an obscene thing to another? Who could possibly hate her this much?

Fancy stooped to touch the broken things with trembling fingers—the priceless talismans that were meant someday to bring her home. She reached for the broken locket and saw, in the midst of the carnage, a torn shred of Aurora's dress, caught in the fractured banjo's splintered wood.

Fancy lurched to her feet and made it to the gilded bathroom just in time to vomit up her anguish into the Florentine porcelain bowl. She let herself slide to the cold Carrara marble and laid her aching head on the edge of the travertine bathtub. The fragments in the bedroom were not things, they were pieces of her heart; to seek them out so selectively for destruction, Aurora had to know precisely how irreplaceable they were.

When she was finally able, Fancy stood up, splashed her face with icy water, and walked slowly down the long hallway to her daughter's room.

▲

Aurora saw her mother come in, then looked quickly away. *Oh, God, she did do it* . . . the awful truth was clear in the girl's hostile eyes.

"Why did you do such a horrible thing to me, Aurora?" Fancy asked, barely able to breathe.

The girl smiled a fraction at her mother's pain; she'd gotten her attention this time. She turned her head away from the accusing figure.

Fancy stood silhouetted in the doorway, and stared uncomprehendingly at this alien who was her firstborn. "Look at me, goddammit! I want to understand why you've betrayed me."

Aurora looked up, and her beauty in the lamplight wrenched Fancy's heart. A medley of emotions crossed the girl's face—guilt, fear, the anger of a trapped beast, the hauteur of a queen maligned.

"You betrayed me first!" she answered venomously, rising from her place.

Fancy heard the ancient hatred in the girl's words. Where had it come from?

"How did I ever harm you?" Fancy whispered, bewildered.

"Harm me? You robbed me of everything! You took my father from me before I was even born . . . then you left the only man who ever really loved me and made me feel secure. I never wanted you to marry Chance . . . all you two ever did was fight with each other."

Fancy stopped, shaken by the force of Aurora's accusation . . . could there be truth in the hurtful words?

"I was wrong to leave you without a father, Aurora. I know that now . . . but as God is my witness, I thought it was my only choice then. I thought I could make life better for us if I left than if we stayed stuck on that godforsaken mountain. . . . How can I explain to you how it tore my soul apart to make that choice?"

"I don't give a shit about your soul. Don't you know how much I hate you?"

"No! Don't say that! Aurora, please. I love you . . . more than anything . . ."

"Love me? You've *never* loved me!"

Taller than Fancy by a head, Aurora rose to her full height, all the fury of years of unrepentant hatred and envy in her eyes.

"You have everything and you left me nothing, *Mother.* I didn't ask to be born—even that was your own selfish doing. I've done nothing worse to you than you've done to me. Just think of all you've stolen from me that meant everything . . . I was simply paying you back in kind. I'm going to do anything I need to do to get what I want out of life, just like you did. And I don't give a damn who it hurts; just like you. I learned everything at your knee."

Fancy stood very still, the years flooding her like riptide . . . Aurora angry in her womb . . . Aurora wrenched into life against her will . . . Aurora of the perpetually half-empty glass, always spurning her love and her efforts, taking everything as if it were her due, giving nothing back. *She will be loved, Fancy,* Magda had said, *more than she deserves . . .*

"What have I ever done to you but love you?" Fancy whispered.

"You brought me into this rotten world. You were beautiful and talented and rich and men loved you. What did that leave for me that wouldn't always be second-best?"

She doesn't hate me for what I've done . . . she hates me for who I am.

"But you have so much more than I ever did, Aurora," she countered, incredulous and shaken. "You've never had to scratch and claw for life as I have. Every morsel I've gotten has been fought for—nothing, *nothing* ever came to me without payment in blood. I thought that what I did, I did for us both."

Aurora's eyes were cold. "Nothing you ever gave me was what I wanted. So I've decided to take what I want out of life for myself, just as ruthlessly as you've always done. I've merely copied you, Mother."

Fancy felt her anguish drain away, and anger replace it. "You ungrateful, selfish little fool . . . how can you know the sorrows of my heart? All that you've been given, that you so cavalierly dismiss as not being what you wanted—I paid the price for all I gave you in my own heart's blood!"

Fancy straightened her spine and faced this daughter who did not love her, her voice frosted crystals. "While you were learning at my knee, Aurora, it's a pity you didn't learn that copies are always inferior to the original."

She turned to go, paused, and spoke one last time with her hand poised on the doorknob.

"There are many things I've done in my life that I regret, Aurora. Never until this moment were you one of them."

▲

Where did it go so wrong? Where did all the love go? Fancy sat on the floor of her bedroom amidst the rubble, trying hopelessly to put the pieces back together, her daughter's words still echoing in her heart.

Didn't you hear me when I sang you lullabies . . . didn't you know the times I went hungry to feed you . . . didn't you feel the unselfishness when I walked the floor with you in my arms, every muscle aching from exhaustion? How can you not love me, when I've loved you so utterly?

Ain't nothin' much I seen so far about life makes me think it's fair . . . Atticus' voice whispered a response to her anguished question, and with it the last shreds of self-defense were shorn away and Fancy put her head down on the floor near her ravaged treasures, and cried. For herself . . . for Aurora . . . for all that life would never be.

She didn't hear Aurora tiptoe down the stairs and out the door, into the darkened streets of New York City.

▲

Aurora felt the opium haze enfold her—lifting, freeing, numbing. She felt the smoke snake its way into every cell, permeating brain and lung and heart, moving her inexorably into a place of blissful delusion. She was powerful. She was beautiful. She was stronger than her mother. Smarter. More desirable.

There was nothing she couldn't do, have, create . . .

But none of that was urgent now. Later, she could touch the stars and take from them anything she wanted. Much later . . .

Aurora stretched herself full-length on the opium bed; the hard wooden pillow felt downy beneath her head. Her eyes, glazed with the drug, stared with half-closed lids at nothingness.

The Chinese watched with a small twist of the mouth that could have been a smile. She was completely in his power now; her need for the drug a constant that would keep her begging on his doorstep, bringing him money, however much he asked for, by whatever means she needed.

Until she died of it.

But that could be a long way off, for Aurora McAllister was young and strong and there was much wealth for her to draw on, before the drug swept her from the heavenly haze in which she now floated, to the squalid, writhing torment of the opium addict, who would sell her body in the streets, steal from the starving, even murder to secure just one more hour of bliss.

The Chinese refilled the girl's pipe with the black tarlike substance and waited for the need to call Aurora McAllister back to him.

▲

Early in the morning, Fancy made her way to Aurora's room, uncertain of what she was looking for, but knowing there had to be an explanation for the outrage of the night before . . . some clue to the hatred and envy, some evidence of a pernicious influence that would make it understandable.

Aurora slept, peaceful as a baby, and Fancy began a systematic search of her daughter's possessions. She'd never, in all the years, rifled Aurora's things . . . privacy was important, trust was important . . . her hand closed on the opium pipe in her daughter's purse and she drew in her breath, in shock. Never once had she thought of this insane possibility.

Opium addict! The words iced her heart. Opium, lethargy, madness, death. The eternal cycle—the reason why the Chinese were so feared on the goldfields that they'd been driven out by force from town after town, for they were often the purveyors of this terrible death to desperate men, sent mad by the loneliness, the ravaging cold, and the endless, bitter disappointment.

Aurora's lethargy and sullenness made sense now. The hooded eyes, dilated pupils, unreachable spirit. The gaunt appearance, the lack of interest in what had once been passions . . . Could the temper tantrums, too, be traced to this source?

Tears ran down Fancy's cheeks and splashed on the satin dressing gown.

The drugged and sleeping girl on the bed never moved as Fancy sat beside her and laid a trembling hand on her arm and gently patted it, as she had a thousand times when Aurora was a child. I love you, Fancy whispered softly in the silence. I love you more than you could possibly imagine.

After a long while, Fancy roused herself and stood beside the bed. She picked up the folded coverlet Magda had made for Aurora in childhood, a thousand years ago, it seemed . . . for one breathless moment she held the cherished token in her hands, then she spread the blanket on her sleeping daughter and left the room.

Wu. She would get Aurora to Leadville and to Wu. He'd know what to do . . . for if he didn't, no one would.

115   The trip to Leadville with Aurora was a nightmare Fancy would never forget. The girl had screamed, ranted, and denied her addiction existed, when confronted. In fact, she'd lied so convincingly about everything that Fancy had to steel her heart to keep from believing her. She would have given everything she owned to find it was all some hideous mistake . . . she's a better actress than I am, Fancy thought more than once during the hysterical outbursts. She could fool anyone on earth.

It was Jason who hired the Pinkertons to follow the girl to Chinatown and take her into custody; he who hired the guards to travel with mother and daughter on the westbound private railroad car. Without the guards, there could have been no trip to Leadville and the ephemeral hope that Wu would possess a cure.

Jason seemed nearly as stricken by Aurora's fall from grace as Fancy was; he'd taken such pleasure in the company of Fancy's beautiful daughter, in her adoration and need of him. He consulted the best specialists in New York and was told unequivocally that opium addiction had no cure . . . that the only known treatment for an addict would consist of replacing the opium craving with laudanum, a drug that would keep the patient docile, floating in a hazy stupor, for years, until she died. He understood Fancy's unwillingness to accept such a bleak prognosis, so although he feared the trip would be futile, he hired guards to get them safely to Leadville and to Wu.

He told Fancy he would join them there, as soon as he could arrange his affairs. If Wu failed in his ministrations, and Aurora had to be institutionalized, as the doctors said would be the inevitable case, Jason knew of a hospital in the mountains north of Denver where wealthy men of his acquaintance discreetly placed their insane wives or children for safekeeping, with little probability of anyone ever knowing the sad truth. He was a realist, not a mother—he expected that before the month was out the exquisite Aurora would have left the real world behind her for good.

▲

Fancy left Aurora in the care of the Pinkertons, in a borrowed room at the Crown under Jewel's watchful eye—she couldn't bear to go to Jason's. She'd never felt she belonged in the hunting lodge; for that matter, she no longer felt she belonged in Leadville. What a sordid homecoming, she thought as she spilled out the story to Jewel and Rufus; she could see in their responsive eyes that each remembered the long-ago day when she and Aurora had come home to Leadville to start a new life there together.

"You sure Wu knows how to cure this thing?" Jewel asked. "I cain't recall ever hearin' anybody got free of opium, honey. Maybe you better keep a tight rein on those hopes of yours."

"I'm not sure of anything, Jewel, but there's nowhere else to turn. The doctors in New York will put her into a sanitorium and keep her on laudanum forever. Jewel, you know that's nothing but a living death—I can't let that happen to my daughter. There's got to be a way to save her."

"Ever see anybody cured of opium?" Rufus asked when Jewel had walked Fancy to the door and returned to the bar. Jewel shook her head dolefully.

"Me neither. She better off daid, 'steada in one of dem asylums." Jewel nodded, unable to speak, and walked upstairs to calm herself with a passage from her mother's Bible. If the Lord was Fancy's Shepherd, He sure had let one of her lambs wander off into dangerous terrain.

▲

Leadville's Chinatown had grown to be Wu's kingdom. There must be opium dens here, too, Fancy thought with a shudder; she didn't believe Wu would ever be party to them, but she knew they could not exist without his sanction. She was sure she'd heard him say once that there was a cure. . . .

Fancy waited in Wu's elaborate parlor for him to enter; the room was filled with exquisite objects, and the heady scent of incense perfumed the air. He'd grown far more prosperous over the years than she had ever imagined; Jewel had told her Wu had banking interests in the Chinatown of San Francisco, and that he'd made money on a lottery he began there, but she was startled, nonetheless, by the aura of gilded opulence that surrounded her.

Wu appeared soundlessly; he wore the robe of a Mandarin, gold threads etched flying cranes on the back and funnel sleeves, and crimson silk trimmed the neck and hem. He bowed to Fancy as in former times; she bowed, too, then ran to hug him, before blurting out her story. Wu shook his head several times during the recitation, his eyes dark with concern.

"You are aware that the way back from this addiction is steep and treacherous?" he asked carefully, when she'd finished speaking.

"Then there *is* a way back?"

The Chinese pursed his lips; his eyes betraying nothing of hope. "Sometimes . . . it is possible. Very difficult. Very painful. Without guarantee. But possible." He drew the words out slowly, as if inspecting each one. "Very bad to watch as the addicted one withdraws from the drug. Sometimes they die."

Fancy swallowed hard. "And if we don't try your way?"

"Then Aurora will inevitably perish from the drug . . . perhaps a long time from now, in her own world of oblivion." He'd offered neither condemnation nor sympathy.

"Then we have no choice but to try to save her," Fancy answered uneasily; what was it he was not saying? "Will you do this for me, Wu?"

He continued, ignoring her words. "There is more to know. This addiction is a disease of the spirit, Fancy, not the body. We may cure the symptoms, if the Gods are merciful, but the desire for the opium may remain in your daughter. If this happens, she will merely find another method to destroy herself. Most times this is what happens."

Fancy drew back. It had never occurred to her that if a means could be found to cure the addiction, Aurora would not be saved.

"All disease begins in the spirit, Fancy, and must be healed there. But opium destroys the spirit . . . eats away at it and erodes the will to remain in this world. The energy body becomes immured in etheric mucus, so that it is nearly impossible for the addict to reach the higher mind. My medicaments can mend the body, perhaps, but only Aurora can mend her own soul."

Fancy sat very still for a heartbeat.

"You will help me to try, Wu?" she asked in desperation. The old man hesitated a moment, then nodded.

"Bring her here and prepare your own spirit for the assault she will wage against you. Addiction is a disease of the backbone, too, Fancy . . . she will blame you for everything, and take no responsibility for her own actions. You may be forced to face your own demons, your own failures, your own worst terrors before we are through . . . you cannot know now what you embark upon.

"Bring the oldest clothes you own, clothes you will not want again. By one week's end, we will know if the girl will live, at the end of two we will know her resolve." He hesitated, then spoke again.

"Prepare yourself to learn, Fancy, no matter the outcome. You can be only a witness on your daughter's path . . . her choices are her own. This is the Universal Law."

He let Fancy out the door, a great sadness in his heart as he watched her retreating figure. "Destiny," Wu murmured into the gathering gloom.

▲

Aurora shrieked vitriol at her mother as she was forcibly dragged into the room Wu had prepared. It was empty of all but cushioned floor mats, big enough for a man to lie on. The windows were closed and shuttered, the door was stoutly barred.

The guards said they would stay, but Wu politely told them they would not be needed. "She's strong as a bull elephant," the older Pinkerton warned, "and meaner'n bad whiskey. You two watch your step with her."

"I will subdue her, if need be," Wu replied with equanimity, but it wasn't until Fancy saw him parry the girl's attack, in an astonishing display of physical strength and dexterity, that she understood his confidence.

Aurora alternately screamed and vomited, sweated, clawed the walls, and slept in fitful snatches. Wu made her sip a pungent liquid, when she was reasonable, and battled her to the ground, when she was not. Fancy's senses reeled from the hatred Aurora spewed forth at her—a vituperative stream of ancient injuries, hugged close through the years, hoarded for this naked moment of brutal confrontation.

Wu offered Fancy no solace in her maternal anguish.

"The gods honor you," he said once, and Fancy stared at him incredulously.

"They believe you are equal to this test."

Aurora lived through the week's ordeal; Fancy felt she had not been so ravaged by anything since the night of her daughter's birth. No one should be forced to give birth twice to the same person, she thought, and wondered at her own strange turn of mind.

Two weeks after she and Aurora entered Wu's home, Fancy gratefully led her daughter back to Jewel's, so exhausted by the ugliness of all she'd endured, so imbalanced by the weight of her own failures, that she wanted only to bathe and to sleep. At least the pain had been worth the price, for Aurora had been snatched back from death. Wu had pronounced her daughter free of the drug that had enslaved her.

A week after their return from Chinatown, the news was brought to Wu that Aurora McAllister had presented herself at the House of the Plum Blossom where opium was dispensed. She had offered a small gold ring of Fancy's in exchange for an hour of bliss.

116 Fancy let herself into the hunting lodge near midnight; she'd stayed all evening with Jewel, too disturbed by the news of Aurora's return to opium to face Jason.

It was one-thirty by the ormolu clock on the parlor mantel, and the servants had long since gone to bed. Fancy's head throbbed mercilessly; even Jewel's compassionate common sense had not been able to console her. The girl slept upstairs, her dreams doubtless drugged and deep. It was inconceivable to Fancy that after the horror of withdrawal, Aurora had again sought the drug . . . a disease of the spirit, Wu had called it, insanity of some fathomless kind was what it seemed to Fancy. *Oh, my dear, desperate child, how can I reach your spirit to save you?*

A glass of warmed milk might help her sleep, she told herself. Fancy made her way across the black-and-white-tiled floor of the foyer, toward the kitchen; tomorrow she must figure out what to do next, for Jason would press her for answers she didn't have, and no matter what he advised her, there was no way on earth she would give up on trying to save her child.

The voices startled her, Jason's and another man's in animated conversation; the sounds seemed to float somewhere just outside the kitchen window. Fancy halted near the open casement to listen—the voices drifted toward her from the French doors of Jason's study.

"I have to hand it to you, Madigan," Jason's companion was saying; the voice sounded like John Henderson's, but the man's face was obscured by shadow and she couldn't be certain.

"Who the hell else could manage to kill a woman's husband and still have her think he's her best friend."

"Watch what you're saying," Jason growled. "Fancy may come home tonight."

"Cut the crap, Jason, if she doesn't know by now, she never will. You know, I've been around you a long time and there's not much I don't know about how you operate, but it beats me how you can pull off some of the underhanded maneuvers you do and always come up smelling like a rose. Of course, you ended up with McAllister as your best friend even after you dynamited his mine, so I guess this kind of thing is just old hat for you."

Kill the woman's husband, he'd said . . . *dynamite* his mine . . . Bandana died in that mine disaster! The words thundered inside Fancy until she thought her skull would explode. She clutched the edge of the kitchen sink for support; bile poisoned her throat and made her swallow hard to keep from gagging. She listened until the two men moved inside the house again, but the first words she'd heard echoed louder than all others in her mind.

Like a sleepwalker, Fancy made her way up the servants' stairs and let herself into the guest room farthest from Jason's bedroom. If he found her, which was unlikely, she'd use the bad news about Aurora as her excuse for having hidden away. If he didn't find her, she'd simply pretend to have spent the night at Jewel's—whatever happened, she could not pass the night in his bed. She lay beneath the covers, paralyzed by the magnitude of what she'd heard. *Jason killed Chance . . . Jason killed Bandana.* She would have to find a way to avenge them both.

▲ ▲ ▲

Fancy waited for Jason to leave the house in the morning before making her presence known. She took a hasty cup of coffee and tried to organize her scattered thoughts. There had to be someone other than Henderson who knew the truth of what had happened to Chance. Aurora still slept as if dead; that would give her time to run the truth about Jason to ground. What she'd overheard wouldn't stand up in a court of law, but somewhere in Leadville, there must be evidence that would.

Caz . . . the long-forgotten name had popped into her head in the middle of the night. Caz was their friend and an honest man; he might know something useful.

Caz listened to what Fancy told him, an old sorrow in his heart. He'd always known the day would come when he must answer certain questions, but somehow he'd expected it would be Hart who would ask them. He stood up wordlessly and walked to a locked box in the center of the mantelpiece. He took a small key from his pocket and slowly inserted it into the lock, as if uncertain whether he was doing the right thing. Then he withdrew a piece of folded paper and stood with it held reverently in his hands, for quite some time, before speaking.

"I thought I did right back then . . ." he said enigmatically. His eyes came up, seeking hers for understanding. "You were so smart in some ways, you and the boys, Fancy. And so god-awful dumb in other things, after Bandana died. I thought, 'If I give Hart this letter, he'll kill the bloody bastard and hang for it.' I couldn't let that happen, you know, Fancy, he was too good a man to waste on vengeance. There's a saying where I come from . . . If you go off after revenge, first dig two graves . . . So I took it meself, I did. Never told no one about it but my Annie." Caz looked to his wife for comfort, and Fancy searched the man's face uncomprehendingly; she saw tears hovering on the woman's averted eyelashes.

"But the letter don't belong to me at the end, you see. It rightly belongs to Hart . . . and I knew someday he'd figger it all out and come to me for the answers. I never expected it would be you that'd come, Fancy, never once. Especially not after you married that bastard. . . ." Caz shook his head in consternation, an honest man trying to intuit what was the right thing to do with what he alone knew.

"I know Hart always loved you, Fancy—more than Chance, I'd say, because he was the better man. So I guess it'd be okay with him if I show you what Chance wrote before he died. Maybe I never should have taken it like I did . . . maybe they'd both want you to know the truth." Caz handed Fancy the letter and she saw how hard he fought for control.

"I took the bloody thing off Chance's body that day, you see, when we found him up there in the cabin. I just didn't want Hart to come to harm because it drove him to some terrible vengeance. He was fiercer when he came back from the Apaches, Fancy . . . I knew he'd take revenge."

With trembling fingers, Fancy unfolded the letter and read its contents. The handwriting, weak and erratic as it was, was clearly Chance's:

"Dear Bro,

I'm leaving this in hopes that one day you'll forgive me what I've done . . ."

Caz watched the changes in Fancy's face as she read the damning words all the way to the end.

". . . have a good life and remember me to Fancy. She'll know what I meant to say."

The woman's hands fell to her lap; she was unable to still their tremors, but her voice didn't falter when she spoke.

"Hart must see this letter, Caz. He has a score to settle with Jason . . . and so do I. I'll cable him today to come home to us. Keep the letter safe until he gets here, won't you? And see he reads it the instant he steps off that train."

She left Caz, unable to think clearly of anything but the fact that she was married to the man who had murdered Chance and Bandana. Her mind traveled back in time as she rode away from Caz and Annie, the scenes of her life waxing and waning like images in a nickelodeon. Bandana interred forever in the bowels of the Fancy Penny . . . Chance's blood-soaked body left to die alone in the cabin where they'd first met . . . Hart's relentless love that had withstood everything but her own good-bye. She thought of all the good people who were lost to her, and counted her own failings honestly. She had urged Atticus on beyond his strength . . . had sent Chance into the bullet's path . . . had driven Hart from her life . . . for no reason, save that she have her own way, as always. Headstrong, they'd all called her in their time, and how she had rebelled against that word . . . Now she understood.

She'd need proof to bring Jason to justice—Chance's letter would never be enough, not after all these years and not against a man with Jason's reputation. It was late in the day before she thought of suborning Henderson. There's no honor among thieves, she told herself, the banker isn't really Jason's friend, merely a greedy cohort; perhaps that greed could be turned to her own advantage. What if the man could be bribed? What if she could buy the knowledge he possessed to bring Jason down? Didn't she own a gold mine that had lain untouched through all the years? She would spend the mother lode dry if it would buy her revenge.

Fancy waited patiently in John Henderson's office. She'd thought of waiting for Hart's arrival before taking action, but even if he embarked as soon as he received her telegram, it would take weeks to cross an ocean and a continent. She couldn't conceive of living that long with Jason, knowing what he'd done.

The banker nearly choked on his cigar when Fancy made him her proposition.

"Why on earth should I help you, Fancy?" he asked, buying time to regain his composure. It had never lain easy on Henderson that Madigan had married the widow, after killing Chance. It seemed too like a Greek tragedy not to merit retribution of some sort.

"Assuming I have the information you desire, Fancy, which of course I don't affirm, why precisely should I do as you ask?"

"I am making the assumption that you acted out of avarice and not out of malice toward me or Chance, in implicating yourself in what Jason did to us, John. I'll see no charges are brought against you for complicity, and I'll pay you a king's ransom, if you'll help me bring Jason Madigan to justice."

Henderson shook his head in consternation; Fancy McAllister Madigan could be a formidable ally or adversary, and what she suggested would bear considerable thinking through. Who could tell what she really knew, and whether without his help any of it would stand up in a court of law.

"Forgive me, Fancy, if I'm naive, but it seems to me that with silver in flux, and Chance dying in financial straits, your major source of income is Jason. You can't be anywhere near as rich as he is, or of as much importance to me in future business, surely you must see that. What you're suggesting hardly makes sense to a man of 'avarice,' does it?"

Fancy gauged her audience. "Perhaps it would, John, if I told you that I own a gold mine, the likes of which hasn't been seen since Sutter's Mill, and that I'd be willing to cut you in on a percentage of its profits, if you do as I've asked."

John Henderson brooded through the afternoon and evening, weighing the possible gain against the possible losses, figuring every angle that was figurable. It was well after midnight when it occurred to him that maybe there was a way to have it all—Fancy's mine and Jason Madigan's friendship.

▲

Madigan's dapple gray pawed the ground and puffs of smoke coiled from his nostrils into the chill morning air; Henderson reined his blue roan mare in beside the gray, and looked to right and left under his wide-brimmed hat before speaking. It was the first time in all the years they'd done business together that the banker had seen Jason in other than a proper three-piece suit; he looked infinitely harder and less civilized in the foul-weather gear he now wore than in town clothes.

Henderson told his tale in an orderly, emotionless fashion; it was to Jason's credit, he thought, that he, too, remained calm, considering the content of the revelation.

"It's got to be the mine that old-timer McBain was rumored to have found," Henderson said. "I always thought it was all just prospector pipe dreams, now I'm not so sure, Jason.

"If you can lay hands on the deed and location, or if you can force her to give you power of attorney, we can thumb our noses at silver when it goes down the drain—as it most likely will before the year is out. I'll want fifty percent of whatever comes of this information, of course; that seems to me none too dear for saving your hide and discovering a gold mine for you, simultaneously." Henderson's eyes were cold as marbles.

Madigan didn't bother to reply; his mind was reeling. How the hell could Fancy have found out after all this time? And how many other people knew what Fancy did? If the gold mine really existed, he'd have to find it . . . the law would give him control of anything his wife owned, unless there'd been some stipulation to the contrary, in Bandana's will. Even so, her power of attorney would suffice, with Krasky, the local judge, on his payroll. Jason's stomach knotted at the knowledge that Fancy knew the truth— damn it to bloody hell, she would never let it rest now. She would hound him for those confounded deeds from the past and never remember all the good he'd done her. He didn't want to kill her—if she'd been anyone else in this world, his course would have been obvious, but she was Fancy, and the thought of her dead by his own hand sickened him.

Jason grunted acknowledgment of the bargain, without even bothering to dicker; if Henderson became a problem, he could be disposed of. The two men parted company and headed toward town. Jason slowed his horse deliberately to a walk and let his companion forge ahead of him. He had plenty to think about and it was the kind of thinking best done alone.

117 Jason braced himself for the onslaught of Fancy's temper and faced her squarely across the library.

"Why didn't you tell me you owned a gold mine?" he asked quietly.

Fancy breathed deeply to be certain of her control. Henderson must have betrayed her to Jason; her solar plexus tightened at the danger he'd placed her in.

"I saw no reason to mention it, Jason. I intended never to work that claim unless everything else was wiped out."

"Or you needed money to implicate me in something I didn't do," he said.

There seemed no appropriate reply, so Fancy remained silent.

Jason rose from behind the handsome walnut desk and moved in front of it; he leaned back and folded his arms. The gesture made him look bull-like and intimidating; Fancy wondered how many people had been cowed by this particular stance over the years.

"I'm afraid I shall have to ask you for power of attorney, Fancy. You can hardly expect me to allow you to go dangling this gold mine in front of every scalawag in the territory as a bounty on my life."

"John Henderson is most certainly a scalawag, but I'm surprised to hear you say so."

Jason smiled, mirthless as a rattler.

"Let's not play with words, Fancy. No one has ever admired your skillful use of the language more than I, but I'm terribly disappointed in you, and my temper is a bit short just now.

"I've had the papers drawn up for you. I'm sure you know that as my wife, any property you own belongs to me under the law, but I like to keep my affairs tidy and aboveboard and I would prefer to have your power of attorney."

Fancy's expression was full of contempt. "You might prefer to be king of England, too, Jason, but you have as much chance of that as of getting my power of attorney. And just to make things perfectly clear, the terms of the will that gave me the mine state that it can never go to my husband."

"Your power of attorney will override that."

"No, Jason. Absolutely and unequivocally no."

"I have asked you for the last time, Fancy."

"And I have told you no for the last time, Jason. I will never sign. I'll see you in hell before I'll see you get Bandana's mine."

"I can force you to do this, Fancy . . ."

"You can't force me to do diddly, you murdering bastard. You neither own nor control me; I thought you'd noticed that by now." Two sleepless nights had left her nerves on high E, and the crisis of Aurora had yet to be faced. Jason's temper, too, was stretched taut; if Fancy didn't acquiesce willingly, he'd be forced to measures he didn't wish to employ.

"I have never been stern with you, Fancy," he said, choosing his words with great care. "But you must not assume that means I'm not capable of being so. If I have to force you to sign this paper, I will do so by whatever means are at my disposal, do not mistake me in this. Silver is going under; there's no question about it anymore, just a matter of time. Within weeks or moments this country will be on the gold standard and the gold standard alone. Only a gold mine can save the men and women on this mountain, and you have no right whatsoever to let a rich vein lie dormant, when the whole of Leadville will starve to death for your selfish willfulness. Any judge in Colorado would uphold me if I have you declared incompetent."

"Why, you sanctimonious son of a bitch! Don't you dare threaten me with your judges. There must be *one* judge left in all of Christendom who isn't for sale."

His voice was deadly cold and deadly serious. "Don't count on it, Fancy. I know ten judges who'd see I have your best interest and Colorado's at heart in this. And I know ten more who could be bought with a hell of a lot less lure than the proceeds of a major gold mine."

"My best interests at heart? Really, Jason . . . did you have my best interests at heart when you murdered my husband, too?" The scorn in her voice bit through the man's control and Jason took an involuntary step toward her, then stopped himself.

"A drifter killed Chance. It's a matter of public record."

"I'm sure you purchase public record at least as easily as you purchase judges, Jason. Why don't you just tell me the whole of it, now that I know so much? Did you kill Chance so you could get the mines, or was it me you wanted? Did you shoot him yourself, or did you just dispatch a minion to do the deed, you contemptible lowlife? And how about Bandana and the Fancy Penny—do you really think I'd let Bandana's murderer lay hands on his only legacy? Why, I'd blow the whole goddamned mountain to gold dust before I'd let that happen."

Jason's face contorted with anger. "You silly autocratic little bitch. Don't you understand what you're forcing me to do? Don't you know how much I've always loved you? I could have made you happy, if you'd ever let go of your fantasy of that weakling. All Chance ever gave you was heartache and the contempt of everyone around you. I've given you love and respect and security, and you've repaid it by hiding your property and accusing me of criminal acts."

The continuing lie enraged her. "You manipulative bastard . . . I will never be your wife. I loved Chance, do you hear that, Jason? When he touched me I wanted him more than life itself . . . I feel nothing for you but loathing." Fancy tried to push past her husband, but he grabbed her wrist in a grip so hard, she cried out.

"Don't you make me do anything we'll both regret, you little fool. I can't have you threatening me or running around town making accusations . . ."

"Oh, really?" Fancy answered him with cold contempt, although she knew she was in terrible danger. *Never let a bully smell your fear . . .* "And what exactly will you do to stop me, Jason? Will you kill me too?"

Jason dropped his hands to his sides wordlessly and let Fancy pass. He stood in the doorway for a long quiet while without moving. He would do what he must to stop her from destroying him, but it infuriated him that she'd force him to harm her in any way; that was never what he'd planned. She had all the money in the world, and all the love, as long as she had him. Why could she not just love him as he loved her and let the McAllister past die the ignominious death it deserved? Chance was never any good for her —the irony of the situation was grotesque.

Jason pulled the handkerchief from his pocket and blew his nose hard; he wiped his watery eyes and took a deep breath. If he didn't want to kill her, there was only one other way he knew to stop her.

▲

Fancy packed the portmanteau, feverishly stuffing in the barest necessities. Nothing mattered but getting away from Jason, for the peril of her position now resonated about her like a live electric wire. She must get out of Leadville without delay, go to stay with Magda, until Hart arrived. She'd misread Henderson badly, she couldn't afford to make the same mistake with her husband. There was no way to know precisely what Jason would do to retaliate, but with the cat out of the bag, he would sure as hell do something fast and devastating. Fancy ticked off the list of what she must do now . . . go first to Jewel to leave a message for Hart, then seek sanctuary with Wes and Magda to plan her strategy. Surely there was a judge somewhere west of the Divide who wasn't in Jason's pocket—Wes' newspaper friends would know who was honest and who was not.

The boys were safe back East, and Aurora had refused to leave with her. "You actually want me to leave here?" Aurora had said, incredulously, when Fancy finished her breathless explanation, after the fight with Jason. "To go running off to God knows where with *you*? Haven't you figured out

yet that I can't stand the sight of you? You always do this to me, Mother.
You always try to find a way to spoil things for me, don't you. I like it here
. . . near to Chinatown." She'd smiled as if to say, I told you there were
some things you couldn't force to your will.

Fancy swung the portmanteau off the bed; she wouldn't think about Aurora now. She couldn't force the girl to come with her if she didn't want to,
and there wasn't time for coaxing. Jason cared about Aurora, odds were
she'd be in no danger from him, at least until Fancy could get help.

She looked around her for what might have been left behind, and took in
several deep breaths. She must not make any more mistakes. Letting Jason
find out how much she knew had been suicidal; God damn John Henderson
to hell for twice eternity! Fancy forced her back to straighten, patted her
hair in under the brim of her bonnet, fastened the waist of the traveling suit,
and picked up the heavy bag.

Damn! She'd taken only the most meager necessities, yet the portmanteau
was barely carryable. How insidious was this need of the material world and
all its spoils; once she could have survived on roots and herbs and the love
of Atticus.

Fancy gathered her wits, pulled on her gloves, and opened the door to the
pitch-black street . . . she gasped audibly as she looked up into the faces of
two men she'd never seen before. They stood blocking the way, with two
others behind them. Absolute terror possessed her. *Sweet Jesus, he does
mean to kill me!*

"Now you just come quietly with us, Mrs. Madigan," the one closest to
her said, as the other pulled the bag from her hand and grasped her arm
roughly. The shock of being intercepted pushed her pulse rate into frenzy
and her voice shook. "I most certainly will *not* go with you! Take your
hands off me before I call the servants!" She tried to break away, but the
second man grasped her other arm and pinned it to her side. Rage and fear
surged wildly; she tore at one man's face as she tried to wrench free. Fierce
as one of Magda's cats, she fought, screamed, kicked, gouged, until it took
all four men to drag her struggling to the waiting carriage.

Servants in night clothes stood hovering on the periphery of her vision
doing nothing, and Aurora stood motionless beside the doorway.

"Aurora!" Fancy screamed. "Aurora, run to the sheriff. Get help for me!"

"I told you she was crazy," the girl called out to the men who were
forcing her mother into the coach; then she turned and walked calmly back
into the house.

Fancy ceased to struggle, Aurora's betrayal undermining her in some
terrible way. She let the men bundle her into the cab. Aurora must have

gone to Jason . . . Jason must have warned the servants not to interfere. Where were they taking her? And what would happen when they got there? She must stay calm now. She must stay very calm indeed.

 118   The asylum stood in the shadow of the mountains, surrounded on all sides by thick woodland. It was a dismal structure of indeterminate architecture and there were bars on all the windows; the few outbuildings were similarly jail-like, but small and insignificant.

Full cognizance of the menace she faced constricted Fancy's heart with an almost physical pain. No one could possibly know where she'd been taken. The ride had lasted all night and most of the next day; she'd tried to keep track of the route, but it had been too long and circuitous. She was pulled abruptly from the cab when it halted and hustled, in a phalanx of guards, through the side door of the asylum.

Insane! Of course that was what he would attempt. A man as powerful as Jason could put a woman into an insane asylum for life, if he could get a judge and a doctor to help him. "Hysteria" was what they called it, the name stemmed from the Greek word for womb. Women became hysterical, they said irrational things, made accusations, flouted men's authority . . . and were bundled away to pay the price for these unconscionable acts of lunacy.

She must concentrate on putting one foot in front of the other until she could figure a way out of this peril . . . no judge or doctor would declare her insane . . . not even Jason could corrupt everyone in Colorado.

▲

The wardress opened the door and threw a heap of coarse gray clothing onto the bed beside Fancy. She was large and shapeless, her hair was gray and her face as square as a block of granite.

"Undress yourself, dearie," the woman said, eyeing Fancy's expensive mousseline frock, now ripped and dirtied, with malicious interest.

"When you leave," Fancy answered coolly.

The wardress laughed. "Ain't that a tickle, dearie," she said; then, frowning with immense hostility, she took an ominous step nearer and said, "Strip. Now!"

Fancy gauged the woman's size, strength, and intent, then nodded. She disrobed as decorously as possible. Stupid bitch, she thought vengefully, do you think I'll be intimidated by being seen nude by the likes of you? But the malevolent presence was frightening, and so was the sense of being trapped in a dangerous world.

"I'll need these clothes when I leave here," she said, trying not to let the livid terror she felt creep into her voice.

"That's a laugh, dearie. If you ever do get out of here, they'll take you in your asylum dress, in a straitjacket, or naked as a jaybird. No one cares a rat's ass about the likes of you." She moved toward the door.

Fancy thought quickly, assessing her options; what if her only chance might be to gain this woman's confidence?

"My name is Fancy Madigan," she said quickly. "Fancy McAllister Madigan." Surely everyone in Colorado knew that name by now.

"Sure it is, dearie. And I'm Lillie Langtry." She laughed again, as joylessly as before. "Everybody here thinks he's somebody famous. We've got two Napoleons, three Julius Caesars, and one Jesus Christ gets crucified every Friday afternoon."

"No. You don't understand! I really am Mrs. Madigan."

"That ain't what it says on your card, dearie. It says Françoise Deverell, large as life. Don't sound like no real person's name to me, mind you. But what do I care? That's what your husband put down on the paper, so that's what it is at Brookehaven."

"My husband? Is my husband here? Could I see him?"

"I don't answer no questions for inmates. But I'll tell you this much. They're just waitin' on Judge Krasky's commitment papers to get here and after that, it won't matter a pig's nostril if your husband's here or not."

Fancy stood very still after the door had closed behind the wardress; she let the panic rise and pass through her, until it was gone and only she remained.

She knew something of hospitals for the insane; most were no better than Bedlam. Pathetic lunatics crowded into concrete wards . . . filthy, hungry, beyond hope of liberation. She had once been asked to perform at a benefit for the state hospital for the insane in New York, an asylum called Bellevue. Never, never had there been a place less aptly named. She remembered what she'd seen as she toured the wards. *I will not think about that now. Later. There'll be time later to think about everything. Right now I have to find a way to get out of here.*

▲ ▲ ▲

Could there have been some narcotic in her food? Fancy wondered. She'd been feeling lethargic, light-headed, unable to gather her thoughts coherently for the past few days, and had eaten as little as possible. *I mustn't let them drug me,* she told herself resolutely, but hunger gnawed at her vitals like a mouse. If I can't eat, I won't . . . I've gone hungry before; they don't know how tough I am.

Fancy tried to maneuver her body into a more comfortable position, but ever since she'd tried to escape by the window, the day before, her wrists had been strapped to the sides of the bed. Restraints, the wardress called them. The fury and frustration of being chained like an animal made her want to flail against the straps in rage, want to scream and shriek and cry for help . . . being chained could turn anyone mad.

She heard the wardress arrive with a tray of food and turned her head toward the sound. "Time to feed you, dearie. The cook was real hurt, you ain't been clearing your plate the last few days." The huge woman lumbered in and plopped down on the bed beside Fancy, making the springs squeal beneath her excess weight. She pulled the sheet down, roughly, exposing Fancy's bare breasts; they'd taken away her clothes after the escape attempt, too, as a sign of her absolute helplessness. "Don't want to spill nothin' on your nice clean sheet, dearie," the hateful woman said, as she smiled un- pleasantly at Fancy's body.

I'll throw up if she touches me again, thought Fancy, forcing back the intense revulsion she felt toward this sadistic creature.

"I'm not very hungry, thank you," she said, trying to sound obsequious and harmless.

"Don't matter to me, dearie, if you're hungry or not," the woman replied, pushing a spoonful of food into her prisoner's mouth. The jab of the spoon cut Fancy's lip and scraped her teeth; she turned her head away and the food dribbled onto the bed. A stinging slap across the face jolted her.

"Don't play no games with me!" the wardress hissed. She grabbed the breast nearest her and squeezed it viciously. Fancy cried out in shock and pain.

"You wanna play games with me? I know other games we could play."

She raked her ragged nails across Fancy's chest in a savage swipe that made Fancy twist and buck against the chains that held her. The pent-up terror of the past days gave her strength she didn't know she had, and she began to scream. The tray of food upended, scattering its contents all over the wardress and the bedcover.

"I been waiting for you to pull something like this, dearie," the woman said, her grin malignant. "Guards!" she bellowed. "Guards! Patient out of control!" Two men in white coats burst through the door in answer to her summons.

"Get her into the tub!" the woman boomed the order at the male nurses, and the men undid the wrist restraints, overpowering Fancy's struggles as if they were mere nuisance. They yanked the naked woman to her feet so roughly, she thought they'd dislocated her shoulder. She tried to pull away and run, tried to cover herself, to protect herself from the terrible violation, but the wardress lashed out at her; a resounding slap burned across her bare buttocks.

"No!" Fancy screamed, beyond endurance. "Get away from me, you animal!" She shrieked the words over and over as they dragged her flailing body through the halls of the asylum. By the time they plunged her into the icewater-filled tub and tied her into it with a canvas covering that left only her head exposed, she was too exhausted to do anything more than sob at the pain of the freezing water—at the indignity and the hopelessness of her predicament.

She was still sobbing and freezing hours later when they fastened her into the canvas straitjacket and bundled her, unprotesting, down to the ward she would inhabit; she was so grateful for the warmth, she almost welcomed the restraining garment. Her hair was matted from having gone uncombed for days, her face was black-and-blue from her struggle, there were streaks of blood across her chest; her nose and eyes were swollen beyond recognition. Her voice was so hoarse from screaming, it was little more than a croak. By the time that Françoise Deverell was led to the gray stone room filled with other men and women in similar condition, very, very few people would have recognized Fancy McAllister Madigan.

No one will ever find me now, she told herself hopelessly, as the bleak reality of her plight enfolded her, inexorable and cold as the water in the punishment tub. No one will ever find me now.

 119   Jewel read the note Jason had sent her in reply to her query about Fancy's whereabouts, put it down on the table, thought about it, picked it up and read it once again.

Dear Jewel,
Fancy was feeling quite unwell after Aurora's troubles, and she has left Leadville with her daughter for an extended holiday. I'm sure she'll contact you upon her return.

Yours,
J. Madigan

"Bullshit!" Jewel said, fuming, as she slammed the note down again. Fancy'd never leave now, not after what Wu had told her about Aurora. Not without asking Wu's advice. Not without saying good-bye. Something real bad was happening and Jason knew all about it.

It took Jewel the better part of twenty-four hours to retrace Fancy's steps to Caz, and another twenty-four of searching before she, too, wired Hart in Europe.

Fancy disappeared. Stop. Jason playing dumb. Stop. Need you in Leadville. Stop. Get here fast. Stop. Jewel.

She also sent a wire to Ford in the Montana Territory, where he had bought a ranch after Dakota's death and was trying his hand at raising cattle. It said the same thing all their wires to each other had always said through all the years.

Come. Stop. Jewel.

Even assuming that the telegraphed messages found the two men where they were supposed to be, it could take weeks for either Ford or Hart to return to Leadville. For all she knew, Fancy could be hurt or dying—it was certain she wouldn't have gone without a fight. And where the hell was Aurora? Goddammit! She'd need a frigging mind reader to figure out what to do next. A mind reader! Of course. That was exactly what she needed now. Magda was in Denver and Denver was only eighty miles away. Jewel left the Crown to Rufus, instructed Caz to see that Hart got Chance's letter and hers the moment he arrived, and set out to find Magda to see what the Gypsy could offer in the way of help.

▲ ▲ ▲

Jewel walked down the steps to Magda's fortune-telling shop; she'd had a hard time finding it below street level. Without a clear description, a seeker could easily have missed the little room behind the glass window that was painted with a pharaoh's eye, a scarab, and a legend that read:

MADAME MAGDA
SEER TO THE CROWNED HEADS OF EUROPE
FIND THE FUTURE IN YOUR PALM, THE TAROT CARDS,
OR THE MAGIC CRYSTAL

Behind the glass door was a beaded curtain that jingled when Jewel entered the candle-lit interior that smelled of exotic incense. Magda, resplendent in her Gypsy regalia, which this night included an intricately wrapped turban of some gilded cloth, sat behind a table with a client on the opposite side. She appeared to be finishing a reading from the crystal ball, but her intelligent eyes took in every detail of Jewel's arrival.

Raising her head imperiously, the Gypsy called out, "What do you seek of Madame Magda?" Jewel presumed the theatrics were for the benefit of the customer.

"If you're so good at this sort of thing," she replied, tired from her long ride and annoyed at such damned foolishness, "you tell me." The little lady at the table gasped.

"If you had not come on such an important errand, I would send you on your way!" Magda responded, but she wasn't angry.

What the hell does she know about my errand? Jewel wondered, or was this simply more theatricality.

"Your reading is at an end, Mrs. Faye," Magda told her customer, pulling a black velvet cloth over the crystal ball with finality. "This woman's spirits are powerful ones . . . I must heed their call, for a friend is endangered."

Obediently, Mrs. Faye rose from her chair and fled to the door, while Jewel pondered what the Gypsy had said so offhandedly. "I'll be back tomorrow," the little woman called back hopefully over her shoulder as she reached the exit.

"Do that," Magda said, and Jewel could see she struggled to keep her face straight. Wind-bells tinkled prettily as the richly attired matron let herself out into the Denver night, where her carriage waited.

"She is one of the wealthiest widows in Denver," Magda murmured in explanation to Jewel, when the woman was out of earshot. "She comes here to ask her dead husband's advice on the stock market."

"Does he give her good advice?"

"Not any better than when he was alive," Magda replied. "Just because one is dead does not make one any smarter or more well-intentioned than in life." The Gypsy put out her hand to her visitor.

"You are Jewel. And you are here because of Fancy."

"How'd you know that?" Jewel asked suspiciously.

Magda only shrugged. "We will leave here and go to Wes and Gitalis. I fear this is a story we all must hear."

She pulled off the elaborate turban with obvious relief and shook her still-dark hair out from under it, threading her fingers through the tangles.

"Such a costume these fools demand! As if a Gypsy needed a hat to read the truth!" She laughed contemptuously. "In reality, prophecy is best done sky-clad."

"And that is?"

"Naked, of course. It frees the channels."

"It always freed 'em for me," Jewel responded, and Magda laughed again.

"Come, my friend," she said kindly. "I know why you are here. We will go home and speak of this trouble together."

Fancy had always sworn Magda's powers were genuine, but Jewel didn't put much store in magic; she'd never seen anything good in this life that came easy.

The house the Gypsy, Wes, and Gitalis occupied was in no way imposing, but the accumulated artifacts filling their rooms were remarkable; a jewel-encrusted Russian icon, a Chinese enameled chest with bronze hardware of intricate design, an ancient glass bowl that Magda said was Etruscan . . . the treasures were as strange and varied as the triumvirate Jewel saw before her. Wes, white-haired and handsome, frail but imposing; Gitalis, incongruously elegant for his tiny stature; Magda, mysterious and majestic. All very worried about Fancy and all exactly as the girl had described them a thousand times over the years.

Jewel took a deep breath and started in at the beginning. She spoke of Aurora's addiction and disappearance, and of the damning letter Caz had shown her.

"There is much danger afoot," said the dwarf, sounding sinister. "Why should we help you?"

"For shame, little man!" Magda snapped at him. "It is Fancy we speak of."

Gitalis smiled slyly. "I merely wished to see if you were paying attention, witch. What do I care of danger? 'He that cuts off twenty years of life cuts off so many years of fearing death.' "

"It'll take weeks for help to get here," Jewel told them. "Fancy could be dead by then. There's no way in hell she would have left Leadville walkin'— not after Aurora went back to opium. You gotta understand, we're up against a real tough customer in this Madigan feller; he's not only ruthless, he's got all the money and power in the world behind him."

" 'A man may fish with a worm that hath eat of a king,' " Gitalis replied. " 'And eat of the fish that hath fed of that worm.' " There was a great brain in that small body, Jewel could see that real clear.

"So you vote to 'memorize another Golgotha,' little man?" Wes said approvingly. "I, too, and with my whole heart. All that's needed is a plan."

"We must go to Leadville," Magda interrupted them. "Whatever of the truth is available, is there."

"You can stay at the Crown," Jewel offered eagerly. "There's plenty of room upstairs and nobody'll ask questions." She wondered even as she said it, how such a trio could possibly go anywhere without raising eyebrows.

As Jewel took her leave of them, she heard the dwarf behind her say, " 'Verily, I swear, it is better to be lowly born, and range with humble livers in content, than to be perk'd up in a glist'ring grief and wear a golden sorrow.' " She thought it meant that Fancy had reached too high for safety, and if so, she couldn't have agreed with him more.

" 'Harp not on that string, my little friend,' " Wes replied. " 'Twill be a 'good deed in a naughty world.' "

The madam smiled in the darkness as she entered the carriage she'd hired. Fancy might be down on her luck, but not when it came to friends.

▲

Magda tossed and turned on the bed she shared with Wes on the upper floor of the Crown, then sat up abruptly and moved her legs out over the side of the bed, onto the cold wooden floor beneath. She grabbed the woolen night wrapper from the chair beside the bedstand, and pulled it on over her shivering body. She must not wake Jarvis. The only hope she had of accomplishing what she must was to perform this feat alone. She opened the door to the tiny parlor that separated them from the dwarf's bedroom.

There was contact at last! Magda had seen Fancy, finally, in her dream vision, as she'd begged to do ever since she'd arrived in Leadville. For days she'd striven in vain to focus on the girl's whereabouts; she had cursed the inexactitude of her gifts, that could focus so clearly on distant places or events at one moment, and then enshroud them in impenetrable mystery, at another.

Random powers, Jarvis called them—powers that chose when to manifest and when not. Maybe she was simply getting old.

Magda passed the window and without conscious thought, checked the position of the planets in the night sky; the moon was full, she noted thankfully, the best time of all for opening the portals to other realms. She said a silent prayer for grace and lit the candles that stood beside her crystal ball.

The energy from the crystal was lighter than it had been the day before; she'd cleansed it with salt and sage, then set it in the sun to recharge. The Gypsy smiled at the ancient crystal, nestled in a ring of bronzed tigers; its energy felt benevolent and anxious for her touch.

Magda sat in her place at the table and centered her consciousness on the "third eye" in her forehead—the all-seeing eye of her astral self, the connection to the unknown and the unknowable. It blinked open in the darkness and she sighed with relief.

Reverently, the Gypsy placed her hands on the ancient orb of quartz and felt its energy move swiftly up her left arm and into her etheric self; she felt the Light course through her, surging strength to her spirit bodies and her physical being. Down the right arm, the current pulsed, then back to the crystal's endless generator. She was one with it; the crystal and Magda were in harmony with the universal life flow . . . she saw briefly, in the eye of the soul, the old Gypsy who had nurtured her gifts when she was young. Tatiana had possessed not merely a crystal ball, but a record-keeper crystal that had access to the Akashic Record, the sum total of all planetary experience.

"The crystals are a gift of the gods, Magda," the old crone had admonished. "You will pay through eternity for the way in which you use their power. Use it for the good, child, or suffer damnation through a thousand lifetimes for your arrogance."

Magda pushed the unwelcome thought away for she had stumbled gravely on the Path of Light . . . she sought to clear her mind of all unnecessary baggage. Finally, centered and in tune with the singing energy of the quartz sphere, Magda opened her eyes to perfect darkness, and no longer seeing the room around her, she let her consciousness drift outward wherever the crystal energy would take it. Probing, seeking, questing, she let the Higher Self of Magda float fearlessly into the cosmos in search of Fancy.

Cold. Dark. *Unsafe.* The focusing point within the glass began to show movement, form. Fear, so powerful it could not come from a single human, welled up within the crystal consciousness. Pain. Loneliness! Fancy was held in a fearsome place, against her will. There were others there. A place of confinement, terror—a prison, but not a jail. Sick people. Damaged people. Strange distorted mind-waves were disorienting Magda. An asylum! A place for the mad. *Of course* that is what he would do to hide her from the world! At least she was alive.

But where? Magda pushed her consciousness out, out, beyond the confining walls of the sanitarium. It took immense psychic strength to do so, for the thought-forms of the inmates were heavy with entrapment. Help me! *Help me!* she prayed to the angelic guardians. *I cannot do this alone.*

She felt her soul break free from the ensnaring boundaries; the way had been cleared for her. Air. Mountain air. Pine scent. Rock strength. A Victorian house in the mountains. A private asylum. She strove to read the name on the stone pillar at the entrance to the drive, but the mists were rising around her again and she couldn't see. She cried out, but the cry reverberated into infinity and was not answered.

Magda felt her strength recede—felt the drain of energy drag her back toward the little room and the flickering candle. *Not yet!* she pleaded, but she knew even as she did so that if she did not return to the body, the silver cord would be broken and the earth-Magda would die.

Reluctantly, she allowed herself to be sucked back into time and place. She said a prayer of gratitude for the extraordinary feat she'd been allowed to accomplish. Had she known the approximate location where Fancy was hidden, she could easily have visited her in an out-of-body state. But not knowing the locale had necessitated a quest of the whole immensity of the universe . . . the difference between finding a lost ship, knowing the latitude and longitude of its course, or having to explore all the oceans of the world before going to its rescue.

Magda laid her weary head onto the table near the crystal, and let tears of exhaustion flow down her cheeks.

"You have found her, Magda," said the quiet voice of Gitalis from the doorway. She nodded without lifting her head.

"The search has cost you dearly, has it not?" he pursued. Again the barely perceptible nod.

Gitalis moved behind the Gypsy's chair; Magda felt Gitalis' strong fingers caress her neck gently at first, moving the long, dark hair aside, then firmer and more insistent. It was very strange, for in all the years they'd known each other, the dwarf had never before touched her. She felt him knead the aching muscles, willing strength into her enervated body . . . felt him touch the pressure points that released the energy from her body's meridians . . . felt him flood her flagging consciousness with good will and the powerful strength of friendship. Wonderingly, gratefully, she allowed the proffered gift of life-force to buoy her spirit.

"She is in a madhouse, Gitalis," Magda whispered, raising her head and arching it backward toward him. He grasped it firmly in his hands. She felt the throbbing pain lessen as his iron-strong, sensitive fingers massaged and pressed and unknotted the tensed muscle and tissue with painstaking care.

"I couldn't find out exactly where," she said despondently. "I must try again when I am stronger."

"No," he answered with authority. "It is my turn now."

The exhausted woman turned questioning eyes to his; because she was seated, their eyes were at the same level. "She could not be committed to an insane asylum without legal papers," he said, gazing steadily at her. "A judge must sign such commitment forms."

"A judge in Leadville?" Magda asked, wondering why she, too, had not thought of that.

"The records will be kept at the courthouse, I think. I will find them."

"But how will you get in? Surely they'll be guarded."

Gitalis smiled, a little. It made his odd face seem endearing.

"Perhaps the gods had a purpose in making me small and agile. There are places I can travel, few others could." Dwarf, acrobat; inordinate strength in arms and shoulders . . . Magda ticked off the attributes in her mind.

"I think perhaps you are bigger than you know, my friend," she said softly, and he was surprised to see tears fill the Gypsy's eyes.

Gitalis lifted a hand to Magda's face. Gently he brushed the moisture from her cheeks. He smiled at her, an enigmatic, knowing smile, and she bent her weary head to his small chest; he put his arms around her comfortingly. She stayed there, unmoving, for a long, long while.

The record room was on the second floor of the Leadville courthouse. Gitalis, dressed in black, face darkened with grease paint from his stage makeup box, waited until the town was sleeping. He carried a scaling rope looped over his shoulders, a lockpick's tools in his pocket, a candle and two throwing knives in his belt.

120 🌿

He scrambled up the alley side of the building easily, lowered his small body to the ledge outside, and let himself into the room with relative ease. The filing cabinets were locked, so he waited for his eyes to accustom themselves to the gloom, then set to work opening drawers. It was difficult to see in the dark office; he was loath to light the candle he had brought with him, for a night watchman waited somewhere below, so instead he tried to accustom himself to the darkness.

Gitalis picked each lock deftly, and rifled the papers within each consecutive drawer, thankful for the moonlight that illumined the file room. Footsteps sounded in the hall outside and Gitalis hastily pushed the drawer back into place. There was no way for him to escape, and besides, he'd not yet found what he sought. He glanced up and saw an open transom leading to the locked office next door; heart pounding, he scaled the file cabinet near the door and scrambled through the small transom, to drop silent as a cat on the other side.

He heard the watchman open the door to the office he had burgled. Don't let me have left anything behind, he prayed, fingering the knife in his belt. If he had to kill someone here and now, the game would be up before it began.

The watchman, satisfied, moved on. Gitalis breathed easier and continued his search, but it was nearly morning when he found what he was looking for. Brookehaven Asylum, the commitment paper said. In the mountains far north of Denver.

"Oh, my poor, beautiful Fancy," he whispered into the empty room as he read the words. "What have they done to you?"

▲

Jewel checked her armament and left the keys with Rufus.

"Let me come with you," he offered, worried for her safety. "Make me sleep a whole lot easier." But she shook her head.

"Somebody's got to mind the store and tell Ford and Hart where I've gone. I'm gonna get myself a job at this Brookehaven place and keep an eye on Fancy, until reinforcements get there. Tell Ford not to worry, I'm armed and I won't do nothin' stupid. Tell him to bring his tin star and a pistol, Rufus, even though he's out of practice. Tell him Dakota would understand if he tied on a gun again to help out Fancy. And tell him to come right quick, Rufus, there's no way of tellin' what shape the kid's in by now."

The bartender nodded and Jewel headed out; she had more guts than most men and was a damned good shot with rifle or sidearm, but Rufus had a real bad feeling about her going after Fancy all alone.

121 Fancy looked around the stone ward that she shared with two dozen others, male and female; the sagging cots had ugly iron legs and mattresses too thin for more than meager rest. Mad people milled, shuffling, all around her—one pulled at her hair with clawlike fingers, another laughed dementedly and made foolish faces at her as she walked by. She felt afraid and angry and alone.

She shivered as much from cold as from anxiety—the coarse muslin she wore offered little warmth against the chill October air, but she knew enough not to complain, for things could be far worse; there were men chained in punishment cages outside, she'd been told by one of the inmates. "Be good, girlie," he'd whispered, "or they'll put you in the cage." It didn't seem possible that could be true; no one could live outdoors in a Colorado winter without protection. Or could that be just what the warders had in mind for those poor devils . . . death by natural causes, a relief to their "grief-stricken" relatives, perhaps?

Fancy forced herself to think methodically; she must steer clear of the wardress who hated her. Then she could figure out how to escape. She'd thought of seducing the young doctor who seemed less callous than the rest, but looking as she did, she couldn't rely on succeeding. If she failed and was branded "sexually overactive," she could be forced to submit to surgical removal of her womb and ovaries, or even of her clitoris. Several women on the ward had been subjected to such horrors and she couldn't risk mutilation by these conscienceless butchers.

The mind seemed to take strange turns in captivity; she found that when she faltered and needed strength just to survive, if she thought about Hart, she felt comforted.

▲

Françoise Deverell walked, head down against the cold, in a long line of patients brought outdoors for exercise. There were several small outbuildings on the grounds, each with a different purpose—one was for surgery, one for the criminally insane, one for the addicted, one for the children.

She was grateful to be permitted this exercise, for she knew she mustn't let her strength fail before the opportunity to escape presented itself. Fancy raised her dark head as they passed the punishment area, and glancing toward the addicts' house, she was shocked to glimpse her daughter. Aurora looked frail and vacant, thin as a stick; even at that distance Fancy could see the gray-blue skin of the opium addict and the unseeing eyes staring beyond the barred window of the little house. Jason had decided to leave no evidence in Leadville.

Fancy walked on breathless with this new knowledge; there was nothing to be gained but punishment by crying out to the girl, and from the look of Aurora, she would not respond. Laudanum was as deadly as its opiate sister, yet it was used as freely by physicians as if it had no side effects at all. Aurora was obviously dosed and docile; Fancy tried not to think of the girl's incarceration as divine justice. At least she knew her daughter was alive, but her presence here would complicate immeasurably her own plans for escape.

▲ ▲ ▲

Jason paced back and forth in the room to which the wardress had brought Fancy and tried not to focus on his own culpability. She looked dreadful; bruised, scratched, her abundant hair chopped short because of lice, the asylum gown hanging on a body already gaunt and bony, after only a few weeks.

"God damn it, Fancy," he said, angered by his own guilt. "Can't you see you've done all this to yourself? I would have given you anything you wanted—showered you with gifts, houses, whatever it would take to make you happy . . ."

Fancy looked at him with consummate scorn. "Why you sanctimonious hypocrite! You murdered my husband, killed my best friend, stole damned near every penny that should have been mine, and now you've kidnapped me and imprisoned me against my will in this pesthole, and you have the brass-plated balls to tell me *I'm* the one who's done wrong? Why, you're nothing but a savage in a business suit, Jason . . . a lying, cheating, murdering, no-good horse thief who dresses up his dirty deeds in highfalutin language to soothe his own degenerate conscience."

The hostile, articulate truth made Jason low and mean. "I should have killed you, Fancy. If I didn't love you, I damned well would have."

"Love me? If this is love, Jason, what on earth would you have done to me if you'd hated me?"

Jason quelled an urge to throttle this woman who had tortured his life so long, and who now presented an unsolvable problem.

"I want power of attorney from you, Fancy. Nothing more. You became unhinged because of your failure with Aurora, everyone will accept that easily enough. You are not yourself, that's plain to see. Leadville needs your mine and I'll see that the town gets it."

Fancy straightened her spine, and even in the asylum rags she looked curiously regal. "And once I've signed that paper I suppose you'll just let me walk on out of here like none of this ever happened? I'd be signing my own death warrant, Jason. Without my signature you'll have one hell of a time laying hands on my holdings—at least I'll get to enjoy your annoyance, vicariously."

"Then you'd best accept the fact that you'll never leave here alive, Fancy. Make no mistake about the seriousness of your position—there are a great many accidents that can befall a madwoman. If you were to die, everything you own would revert to me. Just remember that."

"And you just remember that I'll see you in hell before I'll sign that paper. And if any harm comes to me, Jason, as God is my witness, I will curse you with my dying breath."

Jason started to leave, then turned, frustration making him malicious. "Perhaps you'd like to know that Aurora's here with the other addicts, Fancy . . . you might not recognize her, she's so doped up on laudanum. The doctors are increasing her dosage at my suggestion, they say that if it gets much higher, she won't live beyond Christmas."

Fancy lunged at Jason across the intervening space—she clawed his face with her fingernails before he even had a chance to call for help. She cursed him and her jailers like any lunatic, and kicked one guard savagely in the groin. She broke another's nose with the heel of her hand before she was finally subdued by brute force and dragged away.

The guards beat Fancy senseless, took away her clothes, her food, and even light itself. Naked, she woke to find herself in darkness, only the padding on the walls met her frantic grope . . . bruised and filled with renewed fury, she screamed and screamed until she couldn't anymore. It wasn't pain or fear that shrieked out of her this time, only rage! Murderous rage at Jason's threatening her with Aurora's death, and at every other blackguardly act he'd committed against her, and at every folly of her own that allowed him power over her. She pounded hour after hour on the padded walls, until her hands bled from abrasion and her voice lost all power of speech.

Nearly a day and a night passed by her, until finally there was nothing left but a low, smoldering flame where an inferno had consumed her. Fancy let her body slide finally to the cold floor and lay there panting and ravaged, in the last extremity of despair, imagining only death as deliverance.

Then Atticus was somehow in the cell with her, tall and strong, the old understanding smile on his lips and strength in his hands, as he raised her up from the fetal position in which she crouched. *Are you dream or vision or memory,* she begged to know.

"Don't matter, chile," he answered her. "I'se here, ain't I? De good Lord mean to save you, He send somebody what loves you wif a helpin' hand." He said other things as well . . . and because Fancy knew that Atticus had never lied to her, she believed and survived.

 Fancy touched her hair, which hadn't been combed in
122   longer than she could remember. She had not bathed except in a small bowl of water since her incarceration began,
however long ago that had been, for time had quickly lost
all meaning at Brookehaven. She'd thought in the first week that she *would* go mad from grief, fear, anger, despair, but there was much she'd learned about herself in solitary confinement.

She'd been stupid in underestimating Jason, yet he had not killed her, as he had Chance. There was some nugget of useful knowledge in that and Fancy clung to it. He must still feel something for her . . . be it lust or love or pang of conscience, it had kept her alive so far.

A wraithlike creature wandered by her, silent, ghastly, toothless. In the beginning Fancy had feared the mad ones, cast adrift by those who should have loved them, then she'd grown to understand and care for them.

This was not the state asylum to which she had been brought, but a private place, where people could be made to disappear if their relatives paid the tariff. She'd learned to play many roles in the weeks since her arrival, placating subservience with the guards and wardresses, madness with the mad, nurse to the helpless. What if this is all there is ever to be for me? she asked herself sometimes. . . . What if no one ever finds me here?

After the horrible scene with Jason, Fancy had ceased to hope that he would relent and grant her freedom, but perhaps as long as she kept her wits about her and didn't sign his power of attorney, she could stay alive long enough to make a plan for escape.

She no longer tried to convince the doctors of her identity; many people here thought they were someone else. Napoleon, Galileo, Christ, a Virgin Mary or two. A Fancy Madigan would cause the doctors no second thought. *"Who you be is inside you, Fancy,"* Atticus had said. *"Nothin' dey do to you kin change dat."*

She found that she'd learned to pray to God, not merely to chide him, as she'd done all her life. *Are you listening, God, I could use some help down here? Help me stay alive . . . help me understand.* But not only that . . . not only for herself.

The ragged woman who sat on the edge of the cot next to Fancy's rocked her empty arms in front of her, and crooned to the dead baby who had perished at her breast the month before she'd been committed by her husband, seven years ago . . . Fancy prayed for her.

The ancient blind woman who paced a small square of floor endlessly back and forth, because the chain that held her reached only so far . . . she prayed for her.

The demented boy, with the misshapen face and limbs who had once been sane, until his parents had locked him in the root cellar for fourteen years because of his deformities . . . for him, she prayed most of all. How he must have railed against the darkness. How he must have shrieked and screamed to heaven to free him from the torment of captivity . . . and then become mute, in the face of odds beyond the capacity of the mind to accept. Now he was docile. Ever since the last shred of hope had died in his heart, the boy had been a model patient. His fate seemed a grotesque, misshapen image of her own. She, too, was docile now. But she wasn't beaten—not by a long shot.

▲

Fancy rose from the cot and fastened her asylum gown about her. She didn't hate it as vengefully now as she had, she was too grateful for its scant warmth. Others at the sanitarium were far worse off than she. She'd learned compassion and endurance here, an end to false pride and a thankfulness for the smallest crumb from God's table.

She stood in the early morning dark and looked around the ward full of little iron cots and tried to decide who would need her most today. Perhaps the old woman who'd been sent here by her son so he could steal her money. Or the young man with the amputated leg that wouldn't heal. She thought she might have convinced the young doctor who liked her that a poultice of comfrey and marigold would do more good than the evil-smelling salves the staff kept slathering on the putrid wound.

Then she would see to the seventeen-year-old girl who sat and stared into space, from dawn to dusk. Fancy could never look at her without seeing Aurora. This girl harmed no one, but lived in some fathomless darkness where life could not harm her either. Was that the limbo that Aurora sought through opium? And if so, what terrible sorrow had brought her daughter to such despair? What had she herself done or not done to cause Aurora to lose faith in life?

There were many she could help today; if only the doctors would let her use her own vast knowledge of healing herbs to help the sick and injured ones here . . . the poor desperate mad ones, who no longer repelled her. In helping them she had found a measure of salvation.

The young fair-haired doctor with the golden beard stood in the doorway and watched Françoise move from bed to bed, comforting here, smiling there, soothing everywhere she went. She had begun to sing, a beautiful, intricate melody in some minor key. The doctor paused to listen—what an unexpectedly beautiful voice she had, surely not that of an amateur. He shook his head in sadness; how much more unfair it always seemed to him when the gifted ones were mad—the beautiful, the intelligent, the talented. Somehow madness was easier to bear in the misshapen and ugly—then at least you could tell yourself they were simply an example of nature gone awry. But when you looked at one like Françoise . . . why, it made you question God's wisdom.

He shook his head sadly again, and went about his rounds.

XIII

INTO THE STORM

▼▼▼▼▼▼

The Chips Are Down

"The Lord tends
to wait 'til the last minute . . . maybe
He means to strengthen our trust."

BANDANA McBAIN

123 Hart felt he'd grown old somewhere between Apacheria and Paris. He wasn't sure where or when it was he'd lost the last vestiges of youth; perhaps when Destarte, Charles, and Sonseearay had perished, perhaps when Chance had died, perhaps when he'd accepted Fancy's farewell. He was now a man who understood life's finite limitations; he supposed that meant he'd come of age.

He'd achieved more fame than he'd ever dreamed possible and he was wealthier than any man needed to be, in his estimation. The money he'd left behind with Rut had grown in the man's competent care, and the money he'd earned from his paintings in Europe would guarantee he could live the life of his choosing. If there were only someone with whom to share such a comfortable life, Hart would have bought a farm and settled down; he longed for the stability of the kind of love his parents had shared, and wondered if he must finally settle for less, in order to find some measure of peace.

Hart wanted to go home, even before the telegrams arrived that made the trip imperative. It was as if one day he awoke in the midst of his opulent life, and all the gold of it had turned to dross. Surely enough years had passed by, so that all old scores were settled, old flames were embers; there was no longer any reason to remain in exile. He felt a longing for the familiar, for the world in which he'd been formed.

Pallas understood. All artists are given the latitude for mad acts by their impresarios, and Hart had surely used up less than his quota in their lengthy relationship.

The year was 1893. Hart was forty-four years of age. Fancy needed him and he was going home.

Jewel slipped the nurse's gown over her head and tugged it into place. The cold metal from the pistol pressed painfully into the flesh of her right breast, but she smiled with satisfaction at her reflection in the looking glass.

"There ain't another set of tits in Christendom could hide a forty-five, two derringers, and a hunting knife," she said aloud to her reflection. She forced her unruly hair under the linen nurse's coif. Satisfied with the results, Jewel tossed the nurse's cloak over her shoulder and set out to do what she intended.

▲ ▲ ▲

The attendant who answered the asylum door stared at Jewel for a moment, then let her enter behind him. Jewel looked around the bleak interior with repugnance; Fancy had sure as hell gotten herself into a pickle this time. A small amount of investigation had turned up the fact that such hospitals as these were always shorthanded, few nurses wanted to work asylums and fewer still a place as isolated as Brookehaven.

"Letters of introduction for Dr. Endicott," Jewel said, offering the skillful forgeries Gitalis had provided from Herc's printing press; the little guy really had a storehouse full of talents. It seemed Gitalis not only knew something about near anything you named, but he had a real knack for a few things that would have made him a superb cat burglar. She wondered where and why he'd learned all he knew of thievery.

"I've heard there's work here . . . I've been at Barnesdale three years, but my husband's lungs brought us up here to the mountains . . ." She let the story trail off when she spoke to Dr. Endicott, trying to seem self-effacing, earnest, and in need of work, and the pay was so lousy she couldn't imagine why he'd turn down anyone foolish enough to take it.

The interview was easier than she thought; help must be real hard to come by. The big attendant named Jeb brought her from the doctor's office to a small room on the far side of the main house.

"We always search people coming in from the outside," he said. "Doc says I should search you real good." His eyes couldn't help themselves, and focused on the bosom so many men had found inviting.

Jewel smiled knowingly and fixed his eyes with her own.

"You can search me if you think you're man enough, buster. But you touch these tits before I want 'em touched, and I'll geld you where you stand."

"What with?"

"My teeth, if I have to. Nobody touches the tits without my leave. If I want 'em touched I can get real friendly; if not, you proceed at your own risk."

The attendant shook his head; he could see it wouldn't be a good idea to force this one to disrobe; she looked right feisty. He'd learned long ago that nurses who handled the insane knew how to defend themselves. Later, after he got to know her some, she'd be more agreeable; it was mighty lonesome up here on the mountain.

"Yeah, well just don't go tellin' the doc I let you get away with nothin', okay?" he said, trying to make friends with the owner of the breasts.

Jewel chuckled, her good humor restored. "Sure, Jeb, sure. You and me will get to know each other real well later on. I'm friendly enough when I got me a pal, and I make friends real easy."

The man walked off and Jewel peeked surreptitiously down the corridor before taking a deep breath and shifting the armament that was biting painfully into soft flesh. Once she had a room of her own she could ease the firearms out of her corset and start to breathe again.

As she walked out into the hallway following Jeb's retreating figure, she saw a woman inmate shuffle by. The dress she wore was threadbare and pocketless. If Fancy wore the same, how the hell would she be able to slip her a weapon? Oh, well, Jewel supposed she'd just deal with that when the time came.

▲

Jewel was working in the asylum nearly a week before she located Fancy and figured out how to gain access to the ward she inhabited without arousing undue suspicion. She also found Aurora, but, in truth, the girl's plight didn't trouble her. She'd never liked Fancy's daughter all that much; Aurora had been spoiled and arrogant from the time she'd met her, and she'd never seen her lift one finger to help her mother, a sin Jewel considered nearly unforgivable.

She had been nervous through the first day at her new job, fearing that her lack of medical knowledge would alert someone to her impersonation, so she'd tucked one derringer into her corset and another into her garter before reporting for duty. But it soon became apparent that what was required of her was no more than common sense; nurses at Brookehaven were keepers, not healers, and none displayed any great medical know-how. Jewel did her best to ingratiate herself with the wardress, the guards, and the doctors, and used her spare time to case the facilities in anticipation of Ford's arrival.

Christ Almighty, but the kid looked grim, she thought when she finally spotted Fancy. Shockingly thin and that hair! Lordy, what would Hart say when he saw her? Or Ford, for that matter. They'd tear off Jason's *cojones* when they saw what he'd done to Fancy.

Jewel committed the layout of the sanitarium to memory, the Victorian mansion, the four outbuildings and their parklike setting. Beyond the borders of the manicured lawn lay forest, thick pine woods, and rocky ledge, not unlike the area around the Gulch, easily manageable on horseback during the good months, Jewel calculated; but now that there was frost and the threat of snow, the terrain would pose major problems for anyone on foot. She prayed Hart and Ford would bring extra horses, provisions, and warm clothes for Fancy. It wouldn't be all that hard to break out, once the men arrived; security was more lax than it would have been if the asylum's location hadn't been so god-awful isolated.

Jewel made a ritual show of her daily hike into the woods, which she said was essential exercise for good health. Thank God for the voluminous nurse's cloak that could hide whatever she'd been able to steal each day. Three old blankets, a canteen, needle and thread, a ragged pair of gardener's gloves, a length of rope, a roll of bandage . . . whatever might be useful to survival found its way out to the hollowed tree trunk, where Jewel had stashed her hunting knife, her purloined treasures, and the items she'd secreted in the false bottom of her suitcase. A Colt .45 for Fancy, extra ammunition. It wasn't for nothing that she'd spent a lifetime with Ford Jameson. All her hoarded items were cached in a string bag and covered over with dead leaves; she felt fairly certain no one had tracked her, the lawn ringing the sanitarium provided little cover until you reached the edge of the woods, so she would have spotted anyone following. God forbid she and Fancy might have to beat a retreat without reinforcements—but if that happened, the bag of supplies would give them at least a fighting chance in the wilderness.

125 It was a worried Caz who met Hart at the Denver train station, with all the information he'd been given by Jewel and with the letter he'd safe-kept so long. Hart stood on the train platform, staring at the scrap of paper that was his last link with the brother he'd loved so dearly. Caz stood beside him, just as he had on that terrible day, five years before.

Dear Bro,
 I'm leaving this in hopes that one day you'll find it in your heart to forgive me what I've done . . .

Hart read and reread the words, barely able to see through the tears that filled his eyes.

When he put the letter into his pocket, he knew certain things: that he would kill Jason Madigan was as sure as the sunrise, but first he must rescue Fancy from wherever the son of a bitch had stashed her. He listened intently to Caz's hoarded information, and the two men beat a hasty path to Leadville.

It was a month since Jewel had sent her cable—far too long for safety, but long enough for Ford Jameson to have arrived from Montana. The two old friends made plans to follow Jewel.

▲

Wes and Gitalis paced the small familiar parlor at the Crown; Magda watched their agitation. Hart and Ford were planning to go after Fancy, Jewel was already doing her part to save the girl; it was plain to see it didn't set well with these two men that they would be forced to idleness in Leadville, while the drama unfolded somewhere else.

"He deserves to die," Gitalis muttered. "The law must go after him."

"The law!" Jarvis spat contemptuously. "The law will do nothing to anyone as powerful as Jason Madigan . . . if we want him destroyed, we must handle it ourselves."

"And get hanged in the bargain," Magda interjected. "How lacking in subtlety you men are tonight. That man must be discredited. Shamed. So that his powerful friends are no longer friends. There are other ways than guns to destroy a man like Madigan . . . and there are other evil men involved in this . . . the judge who signed the papers of commitment, that man Henderson at the bank. If you go after the louse, you cannot forget to destroy the nits as well. Remember, he's far from home in Leadville, he doesn't have the reinforcements here that he would have in New York."

Wes and Gitalis stared at Magda, then at each other. The scam was born in that instant; they hadn't worked a thousand carnies without learning the intellectual potential of a truly great sting. And what a lark it would be to put their time to good use until Hart returned with Fancy.

"One last great role, Gitalis," Jarvis said excitedly. "The two of us, against the Philistines."

"I shall bring my slingshot, good my lord. Let Goliath look to his brow."

"Such a role I have in mind, my Magda. The greatest of my life."

"If you can withstand the strain . . ." The Gypsy let the thought end there.

"To act again? For such a chance as that, I would sell my soul, not merely my body."

She looked into his eyes a moment longer, then nodded. "Do as you must," she said.

"And you, my friend? Will you risk all for friendship?" asked Wes, looking fondly at the dwarf.

" 'Let the end try the man,' " Gitalis replied.

Well into the night the three old professionals planned their sting.

▲

Jarvis St. John, personal representative of the Earl of Stonehaven, has arrived in Denver from London, to consummate certain mining investments in this area. Mr. St. John declined to comment on the exact nature of his mission, except to say that the earl has intentions of becoming a "major power in the mining enterprises of Leadville, during the coming months."

Wes Jarvis smiled at the copy of the article he'd had placed in a prominent spot in the prestigious *Rocky Mountain News.* He'd had to call in an old marker to do so, but that was surely what markers were for. He glanced one final time at his own reflection in the mahogany-framed mirror. One of the best makeup jobs I've ever done, he told himself appreciatively. The regimental mustache . . . the precise white of his still-generous mane of hair . . . the Mephistophelian eyebrows to enhance his own more benevolent ones . . . the impeccable clothes from a British tailor of his acquaintance. The gold-headed walking stick, the spectacles, and, of course, what nature had already provided—a venerable and authoritative age. Himself, but not himself.

The accent would pose no problem; he'd proclaimed the Bard's work for a lifetime. He had met Madigan once fleetingly, years ago in Denver, but because Jarvis could be of no use to Jason, the man had paid him little mind. Madigan would not remember him.

Wes felt the rising adrenaline that always presaged great performances; the color had returned to his cheeks, the spring to his step. He took one last look at Jarvis St. John in the mirror and closed the door behind him.

There were three pigeons who must be brought home to roost, by virtue of his and Gitalis' acting skills. John Henderson at the bank, Judge Krasky at the courthouse, Jason Madigan at the Madigan Mine office. He ran through what he knew of each, for the hundredth time. Smart, self-protective, ruthless . . . all these traits were clearly written in the men's countenances, but they were not the key to the sting. What he counted on most of all was the fact that each would also sell out his mother for a price.

Divide and conquer. Together the three men wielded formidable power, but separate, they were just three greedy bastards, each vulnerable in some specific way. What delicious irony to let each one turn the screw on the other; quite Shakespearean, really, he thought as he let himself out into the morning sun of Leadville.

▲

"Mr. Henderson," Jarvis began, letting the mantle of his new identity settle over him with the delicious comfort of an old pro doing what he did best. "I'm told you are a practical man." He handed an impressive vellum business card to the banker, proclaiming his identity as the earl's representative. It was clear Henderson had seen the newspaper article as well.

Henderson nodded and offered a cigar to the consortium's representative, which the man declined. The banker, like everyone else in Leadville, was intrigued by the story in the Denver paper. Why should the English be interested . . . and why now, when Leadville's very existence was threatened by the possible demise of silver? What did the earl know that the Leadville silver barons didn't?

"It has come to our attention that you and a certain Jason Madigan have done a good deal of business together," Jarvis began. "Some of it of a nature you would just as soon keep private."

Henderson scrutinized the Englishman more closely. "What exactly are you getting at, Mr. St. John?"

Jarvis smiled disarmingly, warming to his new identity. "Only that the consortium I represent has a potentially lucrative proposition for you to consider, but we do not wish Mr. Madigan included in it on any level. I need to be assured that you are a free agent, and that if we deal with you, you won't feel pressed to share our information with Mr. Madigan."

"And why is that?" asked Henderson.

"It appears there is a modicum of bad blood between the earl and your Mr. Madigan—a leftover from some dealings on the Comstock. The stipulation about his exclusion from our negotiations was made most clear to me." Jarvis relaxed into his chair and watched Henderson's mind work. Greed versus caution, loyalty to Madigan did not enter in at all. How fortuitous it was that Fancy had once told Magda of the row Madigan had recounted with the titled head of a British mining empire.

"I'm a free agent, Mr. St. John," Henderson said after a time. "I give you my word on that. Whatever you tell me will remain in this room."

Jarvis nodded pleasantly; he reminded himself of how long Fancy's confidential message to Henderson had remained confidential.

"Then I may be frank with you . . . our geologists have discovered gold in Leadville, Mr. Henderson. Quite a lot of gold, really. When silver fails, we will be in a position to change the complexion of business in this area and we intend to do so. If you join us, you will reap rewards beyond your grandest dreams."

"Gold?" Henderson replied. First Fancy had conjured a gold mine in Leadville, now St. John did the same . . . if it was true, perhaps the demise of silver needn't mean the demise of the Gulch. "What do you want from me in return?" he asked.

"Your absolute loyalty, your silence, and an investment of two hundred and fifty thousand dollars, in cash, to assure us of your seriousness of purpose. You do have that much ready cash, I suppose?"

"I do," Henderson replied with more confidence than he felt. He'd have to dip into the bank's cash reserves to come up with such a sum. Under other circumstances, he'd go to Madigan, but that would be out of the question now.

"And what would our partnership consist of, precisely?" Henderson asked.

"We would mine the metal, and we'd use your bank as the central repository for our funds. We would, of course, bring in other businesses—smelters, refineries, stores to supply the laborers, I'm sure you're well aware of how many ancillary enterprises we could share . . ." He let the thought fade off, in the sure knowledge that Henderson was already counting his profits.

"If you wish to participate in this enterprise, Mr. Henderson, I'll bring the proper papers around to you, and all you'll need do is see that your share of the cash is here. I intend to be on my way back to London before the week is out," Jarvis said as he rose to go, sure the fish had taken the bait. "So, I'm afraid, I'll need your answer within twenty-four hours."

"You may have it now, and needless to say, my answer is affirmative."

"I believe you'll find this a decision that will change your entire life," the elegant visitor said amiably, thinking what a delightful understatement that really was.

126 Jewel, in her starched nurse's uniform, followed the doctor meekly on his rounds. She'd been assigned to a ward on the south side of the house, far from Fancy's, but one of the other nurses had come down with a fever and Jewel had jumped at the chance to volunteer for North III.

As she entered the locked ward, she saw Fancy bending over an old woman who appeared nearly comatose; Jewel had to force herself to pay attention to what the doctor was saying.

Fancy tucked in the covers around her charge, and turned toward the doctor and nurse's murmured conversation. Her startled eyes locked with Jewel's before she averted them, fighting for calm.

Jewel made no effort to speak with her friend, for there was no chance of privacy, but the mere fact of her appearance at Brookehaven was message enough for Fancy: Be ready when the moment of rescue comes.

▲

"The consortium is convinced of the existence of gold in these mountains, Mr. Madigan," Jarvis St. John began, after seating himself comfortably in Jason's office. "We have, in fact, staked three separate claims in this area." He smiled benevolently enough, but it was a shark's smile, predatory, waiting to feed. Jason recognized a man who played the power game, not for the sake of money but for the sake of the game.

"My consortium is prepared to open negotiations with you, as regards the future of our operation here."

Jason raised an eyebrow and put on his best stern-but-interested face. "The earl was never an admirer of mine. Why on earth would he want to do business with me?"

"He doesn't," Jarvis replied, tersely. "In fact, he can't abide you personally, Mr. Madigan. But you see, the stakes here are rather monumental and the earl is a practical man. The longer it takes us to get into operation, the more money we lose. You own the best flume and smelters, and you control quite a number of enterprises that could make our job easier and swifter. And you are quite ruthless—you see, Mr. Madigan, the earl does remember you from other days. Ruthlessness can be such a useful tool in the right hands, such a time-saver." Jarvis smiled again; he thought he made quite a chilling job of it.

Jason did not reply.

"My purpose here is twofold, Mr. Madigan. First, to lay claim to the right properties, and second, to consolidate our position in Leadville. Once silver crashes, and I assure you it will do so momentarily, we must know there is sufficient wealth here in gold to make this place worth our while." He waited for that to sink in.

"When the crash comes, we will buy up every silver property we can, and using our considerable resources, we will dredge out of those useless silver mines enough iron and molybdenum to make them a sensible investment for us. Meantime, we will be mining gold . . . and, of course, silver won't stay dead forever, just long enough to bury Leadville, if we don't step in to resuscitate her."

"You still haven't told me why you're taking me into your confidence."

Jarvis smiled to acknowledge Jason's shrewdness in noticing the oversight.

"My dear fellow, you have just the credentials we're seeking. You own a flume and a smelter which will be worthless to you when silver goes down the drain, but immeasurably useful to us for getting into business with all possible haste. You know the ins and outs of Leadville, and you are heartless enough to foreclose on your desperate neighbors." He made these sound like most agreeable traits. "With our money and technology, we can convert your operation to gold processing in a month. Without us, it will take you six months to begin operation, and then only on the assumption that you, too, know the location of gold, as we now do. In those six months, you and we could take a lot of gold out of this otherwise tawdry little mountain."

"You're far from home, Mr. St. John," Madigan began his counterassault. "I own the timbering you'll need to work your claims, the flume you'll need to move the timber, the equipment you'll use to process and a goodly portion of the railroad on which you'll ship. I can make life infinitely easier, and less costly, or . . . I can make life tough and expensive. It appears to me there are bargaining chips on both sides of the table."

"There are ways to circumvent any obstacles you could throw into our path . . ." Jarvis parried.

"True enough. But they take time and time costs money."

"Let's not be petty, Mr. Madigan. Let's take the broader view, shall we? When silver falls, we can be of great benefit to each other . . . our interests and yours will be identical. The Sherman Silver Purchase Act will be repealed momentarily, Mr. Madigan. I suppose I needn't tell you that the earl has highly placed friends in Washington, who will know what the congressional vote will be on the silver question, somewhat before the rest of the world does." He paused just long enough to be sure Jason knew what bait was being dangled . . . if any man knew the outcome of the vote before the stock exchange did, he could make a fortune shorting silver.

"When the bottom falls out of silver, Leadville will vanish from the financial face of the earth, unless there's enough gold here to keep the town and all its more lucrative businesses thriving."

"I have more than a passing interest in what you propose," Jason said carefully, and Jarvis nodded.

"I expect you do, Mr. Madigan. Your silver mines will soon be worthless, but the rest of your little empire could save us time and trouble."

Jarvis left Madigan's office and Jason prepared a telegram to New York to ask the Pinkertons to check out Jarvis St. John's credentials in London.

▲

"I thought you'd laid down your guns for good, Ford," Hart said, watching the man tie down the rawhide thong on his thigh with a practiced precision.

Ford straightened, pulled the six-shooter from the holster, and opened the action to fill the cylinder with cartridges.

"Julia needs me," he said simply. "Dakota would understand." He spun the cylinder, clicked it into place and holstered the gun, then raised his unrelenting eyes to Hart's. "Anyone harms either one of our women answers to me."

"Madigan's mine," Hart said steadily. Ford did not reply.

The street was windswept as Hart McAllister strode toward the saloon where Madigan's boys said their employer had gone. Puffs of ghostwood rolled down Harrison, pushed by the stiff breeze, but Hart, single-minded in his purpose, never saw them at all. The rage tightening his belly was cold and purposeful; there wasn't time now for the revenge he intended, and he sure as hell couldn't find Fancy if he had a posse on his trail; but that didn't mean he couldn't put Madigan on notice that his days were numbered.

Jason, impeccably tailored and smelling of lavender from the barber shop, had a whiskey halfway to his mouth when Hart's shadow darkened the doorway of the saloon. He looked up questioningly, a smile of welcome dying on his lips at the sight of the huge man's face.

"What have you done with Fancy, you cowardly son of a bitch?" Hart demanded, his voice deep and clear; all other voices in the bar ceased.

Madigan's eyes narrowed. "I don't have any idea what you're talking about, McAllister. But whatever it is you'd best do it in a different tone of voice, and you'd best reconsider your choice of words."

"You've got her stashed somewhere, Madigan," Hart said in the sudden quiet of the saloon. "I'm going to find her and you'd better pray that I find her alive. Then I'm coming back for you."

"See here . . ." Madigan began indignantly, but Hart's words sliced through them viciously.

"You killed my brother and Bandana McBain. You kidnapped Fancy. I'm here to tell you, Madigan, there's no place far enough in God's world but I'll be waiting for you."

It took a moment for Madigan to recover his poise; by the time he did, Hart's back was already to him on its way through the swinging doors.

"You heard him . . . that was a threat, by God! Everyone here heard that!" Jason called to the unmoving men around him. But even the syco-phants averted their eyes to their drinks or boots, for they'd seen the truth in Hart McAllister's face and no man had a right to interfere with ven-geance.

Ford Jameson sat his restive horse just outside the saloon, holding the reins of Hart's mount. He hadn't tried to stop Hart from throwing down the gauntlet to Madigan, a man had to do what he had to do in these matters, but just in case Jason thought of plugging him in the back on his way out the swinging doors, Ford was there.

"Shee-it!" the old-timer who decorated the saloon's steps called up to the shootist, as Hart pushed back the doors and made for the street. "Hope that big feller knows what he's got hisself into. That Madigan's a damned fine shot."

"Don't lose sleep, old man," Ford said as Hart mounted. "I taught the boy myself, and Geronimo finished his education." He wasn't given to loose talk, but it wouldn't hurt to put Jason on the defensive end of nervous.

The two men turned their horses' heads toward the north at a determined pace; they had a long ride ahead of them.

▲ ▲ ▲

Jason checked his trail gear and pulled the cinch tighter on the dapple gray. Things were getting out of hand. With McAllister back and Ford Jameson with him, they'd be relentless in their search for Fancy, and if they found her, the game was up.

He loaded rifle shells into the pocket of his parka. Much as he regretted it, Fancy would have to die. He'd been a fool to keep her alive once she knew, but love makes a man do incomprehensible things. He regretted the day he'd ever laid eyes on her.

Jason had already dispatched two men to bring her back from Brookehaven; they were not bright men and not woodsmen. He would trail them without their knowledge, and catch them unprepared; one shot from a high-powered rifle would put an end to Fancy and all the torment she'd caused him, and no one would be any the wiser about how she'd met her end. It was regrettable, but absolutely essential now that she die before Hart get to her; the two men he'd sent to fetch her would come back to report the accident, not track her unknown assailant.

Jason checked the sight on the Winchester, slipped it into the saddle scabbard, and pulled the scarf up over his ears. The trail in front of him looked as bleak and hard as his mood.

▲

"They're coming for the Deverell woman," Jeb said over dinner. The help ate together at long wooden tables in the kitchen, and Jewel had used mealtime to make friends, a relatively easy task in the isolated environment. Everyone welcomed news from the outside and Jewel had spent a lifetime winning people over with entertaining anecdotes. Her heart lurched at Jeb's words, but she stayed calm enough to ask, "How come?"

"Who knows. Doc Endicott just got word from her husband that he's sending people here Saturday, to move her somewheres else for her health." He was utterly disinterested in the movement of patients.

This was only Thursday, Jewel thought with relief; she'd have to make her move before Saturday, with or without Ford's help. She'd had her eye on Jeb since day one as part of her contingency plan; he'd been there the longest of all the guards, held the keys to all wards, and never looked at her above the neck.

"Kinda lonesome up here, ain't it?" She smiled up at him as they left the dining room. He was big as a prizefighter and she thought he might have been one, for his face was scarred and oddly puffy in places, as if from repeated beatings.

Jeb smiled knowingly; the nurses always came around, once the isolation got to them. His bed had seldom lacked for company since he'd been at the asylum.

"I could maybe do somethin' about that," he offered magnanimously. "Like maybe a little visit after hours."

Jewel smiled seductively and groaned inwardly—she could tell this big cluck would be a real pain in the ass in bed. Not that there was very much choice, and it would hardly be the first bozo she'd bedded for a purpose, although it had been quite a while now since she'd slept with anyone she didn't want. Tonight she'd set the scene, tomorrow night she'd get Fancy out of this hellhole.

127 Gitalis knocked at the door of Nellie's room in the parlour house on West State Street. Rufus had told him the name of the girl whose life Fancy had saved so many years before; she'd prospered since then, and had her own house now. She'd been sick for a while after Fancy helped her out of the fix she was in, but that had been years ago, and she was doing just fine these days and was possessed of a very loyal clientele.

Nellie received her small visitor with curiosity; not that she'd reject a dwarf, but Gitalis was a surprising sight, all dandied up in a custom-made suit and boots that would have fit an eight-year-old. She was dressed in a night wrapper and had rags tied in her hair to curl it, for the hour was early and her trade was a late one.

"Can I do something for you?" she asked, interested.

"I have no doubt you could do a great deal for me, *cara mia*," Gitalis said gallantly. "But what I require at this moment is merely conversation, and a favor for a mutual friend." Nellie, looking quizzical, ushered him in and closed the door; every guy had a different way of getting around to what he wanted, but this was the first time she'd ever had a customer request conversation.

"Fancy McAllister Madigan is in trouble," Gitalis began as he seated himself in Nellie's parlor. "She needs a favor, and Rufus has told me you are in her debt. I've come here in hopes of securing your promise of a special kind of favor that requires the services of one in your particular profession."

Nelly shifted uncomfortably in her chair. "What kind of trouble is she in? And why not ask Jewel? I can't get mixed up with the law, you know—a working girl has trouble enough steering clear of the sheriff."

"The trouble Mrs. Madigan is in, dear girl, is the kind that could kill her. Just as your trouble could have killed you, if I understand the story correctly. And Jewel is unfortunately out of town, at the moment."

"Okay, I'll listen, but I ain't promisin' nothin'."

"If you hear me out and you don't wish to help me, all I ask is your word that you'll hold your tongue about what's been said here. You could kill her if you betray us, Nellie, and that would be poor payment indeed for one who saved your life. Will you agree to this stipulation?" Nellie nodded again.

"If Jewel were here, she'd handle this end of things—as it stands, time is of the utmost importance and we seek to topple titans, so the stakes are very high. Mrs. Madigan is being held against her will by her husband, with Judge Krasky's complicity."

Nellie's eyes grew wide. "Jason Madigan and Horace Krasky! Why the hell should I buck anybody that big? Either one of 'em could squash me like a bug. I've worked hard for what I got, and I ain't throwin' it away to even up an old debt."

"If we squash them first, they cannot harm you, Nellie. If there's trouble with the law, Mrs. Madigan will pay your way out of it. She will also see to it that you are amply rewarded financially for your troubles. As to why you should extend yourself . . . I thought that was clear. It is a matter of conscience."

Nellie laughed out loud. "You know, you're a cute little feller—it ain't everybody thinks whores got consciences."

Gitalis outlined the plot, no words wasted; by the time he left Nellie, he had extracted a promise of her help. He walked the distance back to the Crown thinking you never know in this life where a single favor might lead, you just never know at all.

128 Jeb appeared at Jewel's door right on time, Friday evening at 10:00 p.m.; the sanitarium was still as death, all doors locked, inmates and keepers retired to their beds. Never in all his years of fornication had he spent a night like the previous one with the new nurse. Sweet Jesus, she knew tricks that could turn a man inside out—he felt the color rise with just the thought of what she'd done to him.

He let himself into her room and enveloped Jewel in a bear hug that knocked the breath from her.

"Slow down there, sugar," she admonished with an appropriately lascivious grin. "I got great plans for us tonight." She pulled out a fifth of forbidden whiskey, and poured two tumblerfuls; the bottle of laudanum she'd pilfered would assure her amorous friend of a good night's rest, once a few drops found their way into his drink, but she'd save that for later, after she'd exhausted him with a few of her more spectacular feats. Jewel couldn't afford to make her move until after midnight, when everyone was sleeping soundly. If there were to be pursuers, they had best be groggy ones. At least with Jeb out of the way, there would be no cohesive leadership, for he was the unquestioned head of Brookehaven's security force.

Jewel saw the ring of keys attached to the belt Jeb was happily unhitching. She groaned at the sight of his risen organ, he was hung like a buffalo and judging from last night's exercise, she'd be sore for a week. She smiled seductively and went about her business with the cool competence of an inspired professional.

▲

Jeb snored a little; he'd consumed enough sedative to sleep through New Year's, Jewel thought with disgust, as she dressed in as many layers of clothing as she owned, packed all she'd need, tucked her pistols and throwing knife wherever she could fit them, and moved out stealthily into the corridor, the precious keys to every door at Brookehaven in her pocket.

The darkened house creaked beneath her tread; she cursed silently and held her breath, but no one appeared, so she continued on her way. It took precious seconds to find the right key for the ward that housed Fancy. Thank God no guard was set on the locked wards at night, the only security to be worried about was outside the building, and one lone nurse sat nodding sleepily at her desk inside the ward. Locked doors and the fact that Jeb's room was next to the front door had made Dr. Endicott confident no escape would go unthwarted. It was unlikely anyone would risk escape at this time of year anyway; there was snow on the mountain, and without provisions or warm clothing, survival would be nearly impossible.

Jewel knocked on the window to attract the nurse's attention; the woman looked puzzled at why anyone should appear there past midnight, but opened the door to her colleague nonetheless. Her eyes widened in disbelief as she saw the .45 Jewel pointed at her stomach with one hand as she made the sign for silence with the other. Wordlessly the woman obeyed and Jewel motioned her back to the chair she'd just vacated. Jewel tied the woman into a straitjacket, feeling pleased by the justice of the act, and gagged her with bandages before making her way down the row of cots to Fancy.

"We're gettin' out," Jewel whispered urgently, her hand on Fancy's bony shoulder. "Jason's comin' for you and we ain't got much time."

Fancy nodded, her heart thudding in her chest; wordlessly she pulled on her clothes and the sweater Jewel handed her, and followed the woman stealthily out the door of the ward.

The nurse thought of trying to attract the attention of one of the sleeping inmates, but some self-protective instinct stopped her. What if all the lunatics awoke to find her helpless? What if they decided to take their revenge on one helpless nurse, who represented all that they'd suffered at Brookehaven? Wisely, she held her peace and watched the clock on the wall that would mark the time until change of shift. This promised to be a very long night.

▲

Jewel unlocked the room where the yardworkers kept their heavy outer garments; boots, woolen sweaters, and animal-skin coats filled the narrow closet. Fancy threw her arms around Jewel, clinging for a moment. "We ain't got time for wastin' on sentiment, kid. Put on every stitch you can—I had to make my move without reinforcements. We're on our own from here on out, and it's damned cold out there."

Fancy dressed herself hastily and pulled an extra coat and scarf from the rack. "Aurora's here," she said breathlessly. Jewel's head came up, an expression of extreme distaste on her face.

"Yeah. Kinda makes you think maybe there really is justice in the world, after all."

Fancy looked steadily at her friend. "I can't leave without her, Jewel."

"Jesus Christ, Fancy, are you off your rocker? The kid's a dope fiend."

"I can't leave her."

"You'll kill us all."

Fancy shook her head emphatically. "I've got to take her with me, Jewel . . . she's mine and she could die here if I don't. I can't trust Jason to keep her alive. I know exactly where they've got her stashed. Just let me make a try for her and if I'm not back in ten minutes, you leave without me. I can't ask you to risk yourself any more than you already have."

"In a pig's patootie, I'll leave without you! God damn it, Fancy, I come here to get you out of this hole, and I intend to do it, if I have to take you back across my saddle. I don't give a flying rat's ass about that useless brat of yours, but I sure as hell intend to get you out of here."

Jewel held out the key ring to her in the darkness; Fancy stuffed it into her pocket, as Jewel pressed the Colt revolver into her hand. Automatically, Fancy spun the cylinder and saw that it packed five cartridges, the hammer resting on an empty chamber; she stuffed it into her belt with conviction.

"Let's get the little bastard," the redhead said, pulling a woolen hat down over her curls as Fancy yanked her out the door and into the icy night.

▲

The two women extricated Aurora from the small house with little trouble; all the patients were so drugged, no one had ever required guarding at night, beyond the locked door and the barred windows and a nurse as easily overpowered as the one on Fancy's ward. Aurora was so full of laudanum that Fancy had to help her dress.

Jewel eyed Aurora with disapproval. "You look like shit after a shower of rain," she said as they bundled her through the door of the small outbuilding and headed toward the high wall with the single gate that stood between them and freedom. Two guards with sidearms patrolled the wall, Jewel said, but they would not be expecting trouble. There might be a third at the gatehouse.

Aurora's hair looked as if badgers had nested in it. The circles beneath her eyes were the color of mud, her skin like putty; she was gaunt where she'd been rounded, and skeletal where she'd been slim, but she followed them clumsily and without expression.

The two guards who tended the gate in the winter had only once been called upon to thwart an escape after dark, and that had been seven years ago. Most nights they snoozed in shifts between rounds, or played cards; this night, one dozed while the other patrolled the perimeter of the sprawling property. The resounding crunch of Jewel's gun butt on the head of the nodding man made him sleep even sounder. She trussed him quickly with stolen bandage, and gagged his mouth. Fancy sighed with relief, and reached for the gate keys, but a deep male voice broke the stillness behind her.

The guard stood silhouetted in the doorway, a .44/40 pointed at the escapees, a self-satisfied grin on his face. He was big and brawny with soulless eyes.

"Put those guns down nice and easy," he said, and Jewel, her heart pounding violently, complied. Fancy held her ground and the guard frowned at the defiant look on the younger woman's face.

"I said give me the gun," he barked, so forcefully that the glass shook in the little guardhouse and Jewel wondered what on earth Fancy had in her mind. She looked as if she had no intention of letting go of her gun. As she watched, an expression of utter defeat began to suffuse Fancy's face, her lower lip trembled as if she might cry. Her voice, when she spoke, was as frightened as a child's.

"You don't know how horrible it is back there," she faltered. "I'd do anything you want, absolutely anything . . . I mean, we both would— wouldn't we, Jewel? If you'd just let us go." Fancy kept talking, her mind at fever pitch. She didn't know for certain if she could pull it off; she was weak from hunger and inactivity and her heart was pounding so she could barely breathe.

What in the hell is she up to? Jewel thought; she ain't gonna sweet-talk that hulk into letting us go.

"Turn the gun around real slow and hand it to me by the barrel," the guard growled, and suddenly Jewel knew exactly what her friend intended.

Crestfallen and teary, Fancy seemed to tremble as she offered the .45, butt-end toward him, to the armed man who stood so menacingly before her. Put slightly off guard by her performance he lowered his rifle and reached out to grasp the .45.

The Roadagent's Spin happened so fast, even Jewel barely saw the gun twirl around Fancy's index finger and come to rest in firing position, with her finger firmly on the trigger. She slammed the hammer back, and the Colt spat fire once, in the ice-still night. The guard slid wordlessly to the floor, his rifle still clutched in his hand, and a look of consummate astonishment on his dying face.

"Sonuva*bitch!*" Jewel breathed as she grabbed the keys and kicked the body out of her way efficiently. "Ford sure would be proud of you! They'll be after us now and the law with them."

"No choice," Fancy answered huskily, knowing how close she'd come to being dead. Jewel nodded her assent; looking right and left, the fugitives, dragging Aurora behind them, ran for the cover of the woods, as lights began to flicker on in every window of the asylum.

All three women reached the cover of the trees, hearts racing and steam clouds puffing from their nostrils at every breath. They halted long enough to retrieve the bag of provisions from the place where Jewel had hidden it, then pushed on into the woods despite the darkness. There was already one man dead behind them, and the more miles they could put between themselves and their pursuers before morning, the better their chance of survival. Traveling in pitch-black wilderness was neither safe nor smart, but it would take the asylum people time to figure out the full extent of what had happened, and those precious minutes were the only thing in their favor. All other aces were in the wrong hand.

The moon was a crescent sliver and Fancy tried to calm herself enough to find communion with the darkened woods around her. She'd never killed a man, the memory of his startled dying eyes kept trying to surface. She couldn't think of that now, couldn't think of anything but the spiritual connection she needed with these woods, to keep them alive in alien terrain. She must force her ears to hear what others wouldn't, force her eyes to see the invisible. *Oh, Atticus, I need you now,* she breathed into the frigid air as she took her bearings from the stars and pointed in the direction they must go.

It wasn't until morning, when the drug had long worn thin, that both Fancy and Jewel could see what a serious problem they had on their hands in Aurora. In the dawning light, the girl raised hooded eyes to Jewel and then to Fancy. She looked ravaged from the drug's withdrawal, but Jewel could see the virulence of the hatred she bore her mother. She wondered if Fancy saw it, too; if so, by God, she must be bleeding inside. Hatred or no hatred, the kid would have to shape up, or she could damned well be left behind. Jewel had no intention of getting killed or captured because of Aurora's grievances against her mother.

Jewel jerked her head sharply in the girl's direction, then turned toward Fancy. She was winded from the relentless pace Fancy had set them through the awful night, and angry enough at Aurora to want to set ground rules.

"Listen, Fancy. I've gone along with you about draggin' Aurora with us, but it's my life, too, at stake here, and I got to know what exactly you want us to do with her. She don't look to me like she's got our good at heart . . . and I wouldn't trust her any farther than I could throw Rufus."

Fancy had seen the naked hatred, too, and with no energy to spare at the moment for other than survival, had decided to ignore it. "I've got to get her back to Wu, Jewel, he's the only possible hope, and I'd like to give her a fighting chance. But I know you're right that we can't trust her worth a damn—she's gone back to the drug already—I'm afraid she'll do anything she has to, to get it again."

Jewel grunted. She knew better than Fancy the degradation to which an opium addict could stoop—pinch your poke or cut your throat, whichever was more convenient.

Jewel moved in close to the surly Aurora and stood facing her in the dim light of spreading dawn. Hands on hips, fingers of her right hand half fastened on her piece, Jewel said very clearly, "Now you listen to me, kid, and understand real good what I'm tellin' you, 'cause there's a couple or three things we'd better get straight before you get any older. Fancy loves you—I don't. Whatever stupid-ass quarrel you think you got with your mama, just you understand this one thing from Jewel. You hurt her, or even *try* to, while I'm around, and I'll send you straight to hell myself. And if you should be damned fool enough to try to get the drop on me, you'll be lookin' at this mountain from the underside, faster'n you can say 'Rest in Peace.' I'm older than you and I'm a damned sight tougher, so you give me any crap and I'll see you make a real good breakfast for the wolves."

"Jewel!" Fancy cried out.

"Shut up, Fancy! This here's between me and the kid. I ain't takin' her with us unless she's tied up, and I ain't trustin' her far as my hind foot." Jewel snatched a piece of rope vengefully from her pack and looped it around Aurora's unresistant wrists, tying knots that wouldn't easily come loose. *She has the eyes of a rattlesnake,* she thought, yanking the rope taut instinctively—*she'll kill us if she can.*

Fancy saw Aurora assess Jewel's intent and, deciding there was no point at all in trying to con this woman, relax back into her bonds.

"You got the option of goin' back to the asylum if you want to, or of comin' with us of your own volition. We got a mountain to climb and we cain't afford to leave no trail behind us. We got work to do to stay alive, so if you come with us, I'll untie your hands when it's time to do your share, but that's it until I think I can trust you—if I ever do, which is real unlikely."

Aurora's head snapped up. "You can't be serious! I'm not walking over any mountain . . . we're a hundred miles from nowhere and I feel rotten."

"You got a great eye for distance, kid. If you're stayin', now's the time to say so; those men behind us'll find you soon enough. If you're coming with us, quit bellyachin' and start walkin'."

Aurora glared at Jewel, but the older woman was already in motion. Reluctantly, the girl straggled after her, and Fancy lagged behind to obscure their tracks.

▲

"How far do you think we are from home?" Fancy asked, her eye squinting up at the sun's position.

"Could be a week or so walkin' . . . more, if the weather kicks up or grumpy here slows us down." Jewel nodded in Aurora's direction; the girl had sulked and dragged behind, until they'd had to attach a rope to her waist to force her to keep up the pace.

"Maybe she's sick," Fancy said uneasily.

Jewel harumphed. "Maybe she's lazy and would like them guys that are followin' us to catch up."

Aurora stared at the two women with unmitigated loathing; at first she'd decided to go with them because she'd thought anything was better than that stinking rathole of a sanitarium. But what they expected of her now was insufferable—her feet hurt and her hands were rubbed raw from unaccustomed work, she was freezing cold, and so far all they'd eaten was hardtack and stale biscuits. Her mother had said they couldn't spare ammunition for hunting, and they couldn't stop long enough to set a snare; Aurora's stomach grumbled, and it never occurred to her for a moment that Jewel and Fancy might be hungry, too.

The next night, they made a shelter by scraping together boughs and ground debris for protection from the bitter cold.

"The smaller the shelter, the less energy it will take to keep us warm enough to stay alive," Fancy told Aurora as she dragged a long, fallen pine limb to the center of the clearing and began to weave branches into the framework for a mound-shaped dwelling. The size was just large enough to fit the three women with no room to spare. "We can last three days without water, and weeks without food, but we won't make it through another night without shelter," she said grimly.

"For God's sake, just build us a fire!" Aurora demanded. "I'm damned near frozen solid." But Jewel shook her head emphatically.

"We don't know yet how far behind us they are, Aurora. We cain't afford to show 'em our whereabouts with smoke, it's too damned open here. We ain't got nothin' to cook anyway."

"If we cram enough debris into this framework I'm making, we can insulate ourselves enough to get by without a fire tonight," Fancy added, breathing hard from the exertion of fighting the unruly branches. "You'd better start helping me . . . the only thing between us and this mountain once night falls will be whatever we manage to stuff into this shelter. Believe me, we wouldn't be the first three who ever froze to death in a situation like this."

"That way's east," Jewel said, taking her bearings from the dying light. "Face the entrance that way, Fancy, so at least we'll catch the first rays of sun in the morning. The wind will be at our backs."

The three fugitives huddled together for warmth and finished their dried food allotment from Jewel's stolen supply, in silence. In response to Aurora's constant whine, Fancy had built a tiny tipi-shaped fire that gave off barely any smoke, but they had to take turns huddling over it with a blanket over their heads, and Aurora, unskilled in such an awkward effort, couldn't manage to keep her balance.

"We'll need meat to keep up our strength, you know," Jewel said, finally. "In this weather, we won't last a week without animal flesh." Fancy nodded wearily; the effort of building the shelter in the worsening cold had drained her.

"We cain't risk giving away our position with a shot, but I been thinkin', kid . . . Ford taught me how to use a bow and a spear, years ago. If we could make one or the other, I could maybe catch us somethin' worthwhile for dinner. If I could bring down a slow deer or even a rabbit, we'd have meat and an extra pelt for warmth."

Fancy looked up, with more animation. "I could try to make a throwing stick or a slingshot, Jewel. I used to be pretty good with rabbits and squirrels. If we can figure out where the animal runs are and what they're eating, we can feed ourselves."

So, for the next three nights, wherever they camped, the two women worked on fashioning a throwing spear, slingshot, and rudimentary bow, a difficult task with fingers stiffened by the cold. Aurora watched the labor with disdain, until Jewel managed to bring down a small doe with her invention and Fancy contributed a snowshoe hare to their larder. The women dressed the meat gleefully, hiding the wastes from their pursuers and cutting the meat they would carry with them into strips. They saved the sinew to use in fashioning a sapling bow, and took the rest to roast over a small fire, built in a cave to hide their smoke.

"At least we'll die on a full stomach," Jewel said, her mouth watering over the aroma of venison; she'd tried hard to ignore her hunger, but her strength had ebbed and Fancy, in her already weakened condition, had needed meat desperately, although she hadn't complained.

Aurora watched the surprising skill with which her mother dressed the meat and prepared the meal; just one more thing she was good at, one more talent to crow about . . . not that these skills were any Aurora would ever want to possess. Fancy tried to show the girl how to skin the carcass and clean the meat, but Aurora said disgustedly that she never, ever intended to do such a revolting task, so there was no real point in learning how.

Jewel and Fancy knew they were being closely followed. Brookehaven couldn't face Jason without having mounted a party to trail the missing inmates, and Jeb was probably murderous in his embarrassment. Worse yet, if the asylum's security staff was incompetent, Jason's boys were not, so if they had joined the pursuers sometime on Saturday, the odds against the fugitives had worsened considerably. Fancy took pains to cover their trail, but the intermittent snow flurries worked against her, and if the men had a good tracker with them . . . she couldn't afford to think about that now.

Nourishing food and a decent night's rest in the warmth of a real fire and the safety of a cave were their foremost needs tonight; if they didn't stay strong, they'd never make it out of the treacherous wilderness. The men were mounted, they were on foot. The men had serious armament—they had only the guns and ammunition they'd stolen from the guards at Brookehaven, and the weapons Jewel had stashed. Cunning and desperation were their only allies now, Fancy thought as she roasted the meat on a spit —but when your life and freedom hangs in the balance, maybe they tend to tip the scales in your favor.

"This is just like old times for you, ain't it, kid?" Jewel asked as they sat huddled by the welcome fire, after the first real meal they'd had in days. "I mean, with Atticus and all."

Fancy smiled with memory. "It was a hell of a lot warmer in the woods we traveled through, Jewel, most times, anyway. He was really an amazing man, I see that now. He took such good care of us." If Atticus were here right now, she felt certain he'd know how to handle Aurora. A disease of the spirit, Wu had said, a disease the girl was obviously still riddled with; but Atticus could have healed her. Fancy sighed to think that for all her wealth and worldly wisdom, she was still so much less than Atticus had been.

"Ford and me spent some time in the wilderness, too, you know," Jewel said, sitting back against the rock wall, bundled up in her blanket. "That's how I know how to hunt with a bow and fish with a string and a stick, and such. Bandana was with us, part of the time—we was on the run from somewheres—cain't think now just why. Anyways, Bandana—we called him Otis back then—he used to sing for us every night around the fire. It kept us from the lonelies, I guess, all that music, and all the yarns we spun for one another." Jewel let her eyes wander toward Aurora.

"Cain't live without friends, you know," she called over to the silent girl. "A lot of lovin' and a lot of learnin' comes from friends." Aurora didn't answer.

That was when Fancy started to sing; she didn't know why, exactly, except it seemed the right thing to do. She sang and Jewel sang, the sounds echoing and reechoing in the cave's hollow interior; they laughed and reminisced until the fire had burned down, feeling strangely replete. Aurora told herself she was bored by their stupid behavior; what was wrong with them that they could have such a good time out here stranded on some stinking mountain, half starved and half frozen, with hostile men closing in on their trail? But after a while she realized she would have liked to participate, if she'd only known how. But she didn't want to give them the satisfaction of asking, so instead she went to sleep, the sounds of the women's incomprehensible laughter still ringing in her ears.

▲

"I thought I told you to keep them boots dry," Jewel thundered at Aurora's stupidity. The girl just smirked; she'd let her boots get soaked on purpose to slow them down. She was tired of taking orders, tired of this horrid trek; it would be better to go back to the asylum than to put up with this misery any longer. At least at Brookehaven she'd have the comfort of the laudanum, which was nearly as good as opium.

"I guess we'll just have to wait until they dry out," Aurora said loftily.

"Oh, no, we won't," Fancy spoke out quite clearly, thinking of a pair of wet shoes long ago. "I'm afraid we can't do that, Aurora; we can't afford to lose the time that would take."

Aurora's cursing, as she sloshed along in the wet boots, did Jewel's heart good—the kid had a real inventive repertoire.

▲

That night, Fancy saw Aurora sobbing silently over her badly blistered feet. Fancy untied the girl's bonds and looked at the swollen skin and open sores from walking all day in the wet leather.

"Would you like me to help you?" she asked her daughter carefully. "I know of a remedy we might be able to find around here that could soothe those blisters."

Aurora looked up and nodded; she didn't seem hostile for a change, just miserable.

"Why did you do this to me?" she asked in the voice of a hurt child.

"I didn't," Fancy answered softly. Her heart ached for the girl's pain and for her lack of understanding. "You made your own choice, Aurora. I just didn't save you from the consequences this time."

Fancy got up to leave.

"Don't go," Aurora said hastily. "I'd like to know what I could do to fix my feet—I don't see how I'll even keep up with you tomorrow."

Fancy nodded; it took all her self-restraint not to be more sympathetic. She found some willow bark after considerable searching and showed Aurora how to boil it into a decoction. The remedy would kill the pain, she knew, and help speed healing.

"You ain't given up on her yet, have you?" Jewel whispered to Fancy later, when Aurora was finally asleep.

Fancy shook her head. "I have to hope, Jewel. I learned from living in the wilderness, maybe she can, too."

"Just don't get your hopes up too high, honey. You learned because you had a heart to learn with, Fancy. I ain't seen no indication Aurora ever thinks of anybody but herself." Jewel patted her friend on the shoulder comfortingly.

Fancy turned her face toward her in the fireglow.

"You've been some good friend to me, Jewel. Saving me years ago from those men, risking your life for me . . . stuck out here next to nowhere, freezing cold, no way home but the hard way."

Jewel snorted and rearranged her limbs seeking comfort on the frozen ground. "Wouldn't have missed it for the world, kid. It ain't everybody gets to do the things your friends get called on to do." Fancy took the chiding good-naturedly and settled her own body in to rest.

129 Judge Horace Krasky grinned as only a rich man with three nubile young ladies, about a third of his age each, on his arm could. Nellie had chosen her two accomplices from the newest crop of girls; they were green enough so they didn't ask too many questions, just as long as they got well paid.

"You run a lovely sporting house, Nellie," he said, patting the woman affectionately on the rump. "It's always good to keep the competition lively in your line of work."

Nellie snuggled in close to the judge, and hoped she'd decided rightly. That fast-talkin' little dwarf said what they were up to would cook Krasky's goose for fair—if it didn't, she would be unemployed, and the little feller would have a lot to answer for. It was a good thing she'd gotten a promise in writing that she'd be paid what they'd promised if the plot blew up in their faces.

Nellie, Evelyn, and Mariah, hand in hand, led Horace Krasky up the stairs to the room that had been especially prepared for him. He'd consumed enough of Nellie's whiskey to make the ladies fearful he might pass out before being able to make good on all the amorous promises he'd lavished on them during the lengthy evening.

"Goddamnedest pretty women!" he slurred as they led him to the bed and tugged playfully at his trousers. The good judge spent a fair amount of time in Leadville's whorehouses, all of it unpaid for because of his position in the legal scheme of things. There was nothing he liked better, after a long day on the bench, than a bottle of bourbon and a romp with a willing bride of the multitude, or two, if luck provided such an opportunity.

Revived by the spirit of merriment he sensed in the girls, and by the bouncing breasts Evelyn had freed from the restraint of her corset, Krasky, who felt randier than he had thought possible at the foot of the stair, lurched in the direction of those enticing playthings. All three ladies were quite naked now except for some strategically placed black lace garters and stockings.

"Oh, Judge!" Nellie giggled provocatively. "I'll bet you can't catch me!"

"I'll bet I can," he mumbled as he clambered across the bed.

When he finally caught the girls, in a welter of scrambled limbs and certain unmentionable parts, it made quite a picture.

At least that's what Herc Monroe thought when he photographed it from the doorway of the closet, where Gitalis had helped him install his new camera. Maybe the judge would like a copy of it to use on his campaign poster next time an election year came due. Herc wanted to ask the judge if he'd like a few extra prints to scatter around town, but the man was in too much shock, and far too busy trying to pull his pants on, for lucid conversation.

▲

Wes Jarvis and Gitalis had a busy day following the judge's indiscretion. Wes told the bank auditors about a $250,000 shortfall he thought they might find in their cash deposits, and turned over to them in proof the money Henderson had given him. Gitalis was busy distributing a certain photograph of Horace Krasky, *en flagrante,* to the newspaper office and to as many of Krasky's political opponents as he could find.

Jarvis filed a complaint, via circuit rider, with the federal judge in Denver, charging Madigan with Chance's murder. Gitalis witnessed an affidavit signed by Jonathan "Caz" Castelmaine stating all he knew about Chance McAllister's death, and both men filed a complaint with Sheriff Harley, stating that they knew for a fact that Fancy McAllister Madigan and her daughter Aurora had been abducted against their will for the purpose of foul play.

When the day was done, the two old actors had a feeling that by the time Congress finally voted the repeal of the Sherman Silver Purchase Act, Henderson, Krasky, and Madigan might have more to worry about than selling short their silver stock.

130 🌿 As they trudged in a zigzag pattern across the mountain, Fancy tried to instill some lesson from the past into Aurora. The girl was not an enthusiastic pupil.

They stole a horse from a small isolated camp they passed by. Fancy and Jewel decided to take only one of the two animals corralled there so the family wouldn't be left stranded.

"Take them both," Aurora urged, angry that they'd be so stupid—two horses could carry all three of them.

"These people are poor," Fancy snapped in exasperation. "And far from help. They'd be in terrible trouble if we left them no horse at all. As it is, we'll have to find a way to repay them if we get out of here."

So nobody rode, but having the horse meant they no longer had to carry all their possessions on their backs, and that was a considerable relief. Fancy walked behind the animal and covered his tracks religiously.

Jewel listened to Fancy's efforts to teach Aurora and even pitched in from time to time, but from what she could see the lessons mostly fell on deaf ears.

"You ever pray, Aurora?" she asked unexpectedly one day.

"No, I don't believe in God."

Fancy's heart sank at this fresh evidence of her failure as a mother; her own relationship with the Almighty might be shaky and unorthodox, but it was a relationship, nonetheless.

"Well, you should, you know. Got to exercise your soul, just like your body. Got to say thanks once in a while for what you've got, too. I pray all the time."

"But you're a whore," Aurora said viciously.

"So was Mary Magdalene," Jewel replied, thinking of Dakota with love.

▲

The long trek in freezing temperatures was sapping their strength; Fancy and Jewel each could see the toll the hardships were taking in the other. Their fingers had been scraped raw from wrestling recalcitrant brush and branches into shelter, and while the animal meat they'd managed to procure assuaged their hunger, it provided severely unbalanced nourishment. They were always thirsty, and each morning, now, they awoke feeling stiffer and colder than the day before.

The men were getting close, Fancy could feel it with all six senses. If they caught up, there was no telling what would happen to any of them; the imminent danger made her feel bold about her daughter.

"I've decided now's the time to finish this fight between us, Aurora, once and for all," she said stonily as they settled in for the night, weary and footsore. "There's nothing left to lose that I can see, and those men are closing in, so God only knows how much more time we've got together." At least she knew her daughter's head was clear of opiates now, so perhaps some part of what they said to each other would sink in. If not, at least she'd know she'd tried the best she could.

"That's just fine with me," Aurora responded, her tone matching Fancy's. "I have a lot I've wanted to say to you for a very long time." Fancy eyed her daughter's haughty expression with resignation and replied, "Be my guest."

Aurora looked quickly at Jewel, then back at her mother. Jewel seemed intent on whatever busywork she was up to, and Fancy seemed willing to listen. Aurora was feeling mean from discomfort and welcomed the chance to attack; she'd been storing up her weapons for enough years to have an overflowing arsenal.

"First and foremost, you don't know how to be a mother . . . and you never did," she said acidly. "I wanted a mother like the other children had, soft and homey, and always there when I needed her to be. You were always too busy getting famous or being taken out by rich men to even know I existed."

Fancy sat down wearily, but said nothing, so Aurora gathered momentum.

"I wanted a father, too, in case you didn't notice. Not some stinking lie you made up to cover the tracks of your fornication. Did you know, I used to make up stories to tell the other kids in school about where my father was, and why he never came home to visit. He was always off somewhere, on some exciting adventure, in some new country. . . . After a while, nobody believed me anymore."

Aurora looked to her mother to see her response, but Fancy was sitting with her knees drawn up and arms around them, her chin resting on her folded arms. She didn't seem inclined to reply, so the girl continued.

"I was never first on your priority list, you know. Never once in all those years you were so busy making a name for yourself. And Christ! How I hated all those adoring men of yours. Except for Jason, of course. He was good to me. But then you left him to go to Leadville, the second worst place God ever made."

"What's the first?" Fancy asked, curiously.

"Where we are now!" Aurora snapped without hesitation, and Fancy nearly smiled. Jewel, listening, turned her head away to keep from laughter. The kid should only know some of the hellholes she'd been in, if she thought Leadville was lousy . . .

"Then you married that idiot Chance, and started having babies and giving dinner parties and going to balls every night, and then there was nothing left for me at all. And I was empty inside and nothing ever felt good or made me happy . . . and I was so damned bored! And I wanted to hurt you like you'd always hurt me . . ." Aurora's voice had turned small and nasty. "So I made some fast friends, and I found out about what opium could do to make life better. The rest you know, I guess . . . except for how good it feels to smoke a pipe, how free and happy and full of hope it makes me . . . when I'm high on opium I feel I can do anything I want to!" She said the last of it defiantly, trying to elicit an angry response.

So this is Aurora's truth, thought Fancy. It was not so impossible to understand. Distorted, some of it. Unfair in part. But honest, at least, and clearly stated. And not all of it unwarranted.

"Is that it?" she asked finally; she'd heard a good deal of this shrieked at her when they'd been at Wu's. Obviously, it still festered. "Are there any other things you hate me for?" Aurora, emptied of ammunition, shook her head sullenly.

It was all so clear . . . and so very, very sad. Fancy wondered if Aurora's world would ever encompass anyone's pain but her own. She took in a long, slow breath and exhaled, straightening her spine as she did so; she would be no less honest in return than her daughter had been.

"I'm truly sorry, Aurora," she said, her voice low and uncertain of how to say what she meant to. "I'm sorrier than I could ever say, for all the things I've done wrong for you, in this life. I'm sure you don't believe how much sorrow I feel for your obvious pain . . . and how much I wish things might have been different between us. And I guess you'll never know how very much I longed for us to be friends, or how much a loss it is to me that now we can never be. But all that notwithstanding, I owe you no less honesty than you've given me." She paused a moment, to quiet her own heart.

"Life is more complicated than you yet know, Aurora. And infinitely harder. When I was about the same age you are now, I fell in love with a man—a dazzling, handsome gambler, who didn't know or really care that he held my future in his hands. When I became pregnant, I ran away from him, for a lot of reasons I doubt you could understand . . . sometimes I don't understand them all that well myself. But one thing I can tell you in absolute honesty, that it never once occurred to me then, that I would harm you by leaving him. Perhaps that was selfishness on my part, or maybe just youth and inexperience, but in some weird way I thought by doing what I did, I was saving us both from poverty, and from the fate of the other poor women and children I'd seen in mining camps, living and dying with nothing . . . nothing to hope for but a hard life and an early grave. You were so much part of me then, how could I ever have imagined that what was right for me wouldn't be right for you?" Fancy looked to her daughter for understanding, but saw only hostile bewilderment.

"That was stupid of me, I suppose. I guess you'd have to say I've done a lot of stupid things in my time . . . a lot of headstrong things." She paused again, wondering why she had never thought until now how badly her choices had injured Aurora. "The man I loved and ran away from was Chance McAllister."

"Chance was my *real* father?" Aurora asked, obviously shaken by the news.

"Chance was your real father."

Both mother and daughter remained silent for a long time after that. Finally, Fancy spoke again.

"I had talent and ambition, Aurora. I'd been rich and I'd been poor, and rich was infinitely better. Safer . . . I always longed to feel safe." The wistful note in Fancy's voice made Aurora look at her mother wonderingly; it was not the voice of one who knows all. It was the voice of frailty like her own.

"I never felt I could really trust anybody to get for me what I needed, so I went after it all myself. I wanted to be the best mother and the best actress —later on I even wanted to be the best wife." Fancy smiled ruefully. "Someday maybe you'll understand how very hard it is to do all those full-time jobs." Fancy stopped a moment, then plunged on; Aurora began to speak, but her mother stopped her with a gesture.

"There's more, Aurora . . . more that I want you to know before we finish with each other. I've heard all you've said to me—the list of my own failings is a longer one than I knew, but I've listened and I guess I understand now what your quarrel is with me, and I even think parts of it are fair. I've told you I'm sorry for having hurt you, and that's entirely true . . . I am sorrier for that than for any of the other mistakes of my life.

"But I think you should hear something else besides my apology, tonight, inasmuch as one or both of us may be dead tomorrow. I think you should hear who I am and what I feel, because you are not the only one here who has been hurt by life . . . that, my dear and angry daughter, is just what life is all about. You do the best you can with it, and you learn from the hurt more than you ever learn from the happiness, and when you get as old as I am now, you try to face with some semblance of honesty what choices you've made, and you find to your dismay that some were right and some were very wrong. But you damned well have to have the guts to live with that knowledge without sniveling.

"So, I want you to know that in my heart, I don't feel guilty and I do *not* apologize to you or to anyone on this earth for the choices I've made, because I've paid the price for every one of them in spades. I can live with my failures, Aurora—even my failure in motherhood, which is a very hard admission for me to make, much harder than you know. I've paid for every mistake I've ever made, most times in blood. But I never meant for you to pay for them . . . and that's the part I regret."

With that, Fancy stood up and walked away, fighting memory and tears; Aurora watch her mother's retreating figure, looking slightly dazed by all that had been said.

"The likes of that conversation ain't been heard lately," Jewel said with a low whistle, as Fancy reached her. "Nought but blood and bone left, once you scrape off that much meat." Fancy simply nodded and brushed away her tears, angry at them; she had a lot of thinking to do tonight and more than a few wounds to lick before morning.

"She's not all wrong, Jewel," she answered, finally.

"And you ain't all there, if you take all the blame for that selfish little twit. Aurora made her own choices, just like the rest of us. If you're so willing to own up to your own faults, Fancy, then you damn well better let Aurora own up to hers." Jewel grunted and reorganized her blanket for sleep; the ground was cold and hard and she was bone-weary.

"You know, kid," Jewel said after a moment or two. "I was listenin' to what you two said to each other, eavesdropped on every blessed word of it, like it was my sworn duty to hear it all. It kinda made me wish I could ever once have told my mama what was wrong in my life and have her understand like you tried to do, just now. I really loved my mama, more'n anybody . . . but I never once got the chance to do what you two did tonight. I cain't help but wonder if maybe everything coulda been different in my life, if my mama'd ever known the truth."

"I love you, too, Jewel," Fancy said wearily as she stared into the dwindling fire; she needed time to think it all through and to renew herself. She had been sapped by the soul-search, and if she didn't recoup her strength, she would endanger them all. The grim possibility that by tomorrow night they could be captured or dead was very real, but at the moment it was hard to concentrate on anything but her wounds of the heart.

131 🌿 The clatter of many horses roused the women from uncomfortable sleep, and Jewel spoke rapidly as she scrambled everything she could find far into the cave; it was the third time since they'd set out that they'd found a hideout that allowed more cover and security than the open woods. "Sounds like they called out the goddamned militia to track us."

"Might as well fight them here as anywhere," Fancy answered gravely, when she returned from reconnaisance. The pursuers were not far below them on the mountain. "We have the cave to hide our things, and we're on higher ground than they are. We could use the advantage a surprise attack would give us—they'll be on top of us in less than an hour, and we can't outrun them."

"We ain't got much ammunition to hold off a posse," Jewel answered, emptying her pockets of cartridges. "Thirty rounds between us for the .45's, fifty or so for the peashooters." She grimaced at the tiny derringers. "They ain't no use at all unless you're close enough to count the hairs in a man's nose."

"We've got the cartridge belts from the hospital guards, too," Fancy reminded her, "and we've each got knives."

"Sure, but that's a real tough way to kill a man and you ain't big enough to risk gettin' in close." She expelled a breath expressively. "But, if it does come to that, kid, and it might, let me tell you how it's done. You go in low under the ribs and push up toward the heart for all you're worth, or you go for that big artery in the neck, from behind. Ford showed me how, years ago." Fancy nodded.

"If it comes to hand-to-hand, you knee 'em in the balls; don't kick, or he'll catch your foot and send you flyin'. You can ram your fingers into a man's eyes or up his nose and disable him, too, but for Christ's sake, if you go that route, do it for all you're worth, or you'll just make him meaner. The palm of your hand can break a man's nose easy—I know 'cause I've done it more 'n once—and sometimes that can buy you time to get away."

Fancy nodded at the grim instructions and checked her pistols with an expert's touch, before stowing them into the holster she'd stolen from Brookehaven. "Every bullet has to count, Jewel," she said as she stuck the knife into her belt with the other armament.

Aurora watched the two older women with incredulous fascination; they were actually going to make a fight of it, against armed men.

"You two are insane!" she called out, meaning it. "You can't win against odds like these."

"Not if we don't try," Jewel replied laconically, shoving her own pistols into her belt and moving silently toward the covering pines. The dust cloud on the winding trail below revealed the men who hunted them.

Six men had been sent to bring them back, three of Jeb's boys, Jeb himself, and the two of Jason's men who'd been sent to collect Fancy. Three women, unarmed, couldn't put up much of a battle, it had seemed to the pursuers when they'd set out. The wonder was that the escapees had survived ten days on foot already, and had covered their trail so professionally. It had been damned hard to track them in this rocky terrain; if it hadn't been for the patches of snow, they might have disappeared altogether. Those three might be crazy, but they sure as hell weren't stupid.

Jeb intended to make the redheaded bitch pay for the embarrassment she'd caused him—he had to bring back the other two alive, according to Doc Endicott, but nobody gave a shit what happened to the redhead, and he would see to it she died hard for making him a laughingstock.

Fancy and Jewel had hidden their packs, and the horse, far back in the cave with Aurora, making their last-minute tactical plans. They hugged each other hard and wordlessly, then each woman positioned herself on a different side of the trail, high up on the rock ledge, and waited for the riders to round the last bend below.

Jewel picked off the straggler of the six, as the men headed up the trail toward the hideaway. He fell from his horse and was dragged a few feet before the animal scrambled, riderless, for safety. There was a Winchester, Fancy noted, still in the animal's saddle scabbard; if she could double back later, she might be able to grab it. The other men dismounted instantly and fanned out, as Jeb shouted orders. Fancy could see by their movements that two were skilled woodsmen, three were not.

Jeb headed stealthily in the direction Jewel had gone; Fancy moved toward higher ground. A bullet whizzed by so close, it ripped her coat. She dropped to her knees and returned fire—the man who'd sent the shot her way wasn't expecting the bullet that winged him; he backed off into the trees clutching his shoulder. Fancy wondered, fleetingly, if the pursuers had been instructed to bring their prisoners back alive, or if that was left to the discretion of the men.

Jewel grunted hard somewhere below Fancy's position; the sounds of a scuffle and curses rent the morning. Fancy crept forward far enough to see that Jeb had Jewel in a hammerlock; she was struggling wildly to break free but the man was far too powerful. Obviously Jewel, at least, was deemed dispensable. She'd been caught from behind and hadn't a prayer of freeing herself. Fancy gauged the plausibility of the difficult shot from where she was positioned—if she tried and failed, Jewel would die from the bullet, before strangulation. She centered herself and aimed, squeezing off the potent round. Fancy felt the gun roll back in her hand, saw Jeb drop his hold on Jewel and sink to the ground, an expression of incredulity on his ugly face. No matter where you hit a man with a .45 slug, it brings him down, Ford had said and he'd been right.

Jewel gasped for breath like a fish on a riverbank, then tugged Jeb's revolver free of his pants before running for cover.

Fancy saw a glint of sunlight bounce off a nickel-plated barrel; she fired at the spot almost without thinking, and knew by the crackling sound of breaking branches that a body had rolled away through the underbrush. How badly the man was wounded she couldn't tell, but now there were three wounded or dead that she knew of, and two against three was a damned sight more negotiable than two against six. She flattened herself against the rock and tried to intuit where Jewel might have gone.

Gunfire spat to the left of her and Fancy scrambled out of the way for cover; she spotted the man on the ridge just as he drew a bead on her. Jewel's bullet caught him full in the chest, as he squeezed off a round that skittered uselessly into the trees.

"Are there three down?" Fancy gasped breathlessly as she reached Jewel's side.

"Four," Jewel answered grimly. "Stuck one with my huntin' knife." Fancy's eyes widened in admiration.

"Their two best men are still on their feet," Jewel said worriedly.

"So are ours," Fancy replied. Not waiting for a response, she slid off into the boulder-strewn bracken; Jewel smiled at her pluck and moved in the direction of the road. Fancy was right, of course, the odds were better now, but there was damned little ammo left.

Jewel made her way stealthily toward the best cover she could spy, wishing with all her heart that Ford and Hart would appear just about now, like the cavalry always did in storybooks. She saw the gunman disengage himself from the cover of the trunk of an ancient pine, too late to protect herself. She fired, but despairing, heard the hammer of her pistol fall on an empty chamber. Shit! Ford would kill her if he knew she hadn't counted her shots, only a rank amateur—

The man's slug caught Jewel full in the chest before she could turn to flee. Her arms flew out like a crucifixion, but the impact of the bullet spun her around and crashed her violently to the ground. Fancy saw the woman fall and shot her friend's assailant where he stood over Jewel's crumpled form.

Her brain raced—a diversion—that's what she needed, and fast. Frantically, Fancy doubled back to the cave and freed the horse that was hidden there. Maybe she could distract the remaining man's attention long enough to get to Jewel . . . she slapped wildly at the horse's flank and the riderless animal tore through the trees to the trail, crashing undergrowth noisily as it ran.

"One of them's getting away!" a voice shouted angrily, and Fancy fired toward the shout, but missed. She heard someone mount laboriously; someone she'd counted out must only have been wounded; she heard the man light out after the runaway horse. The diversionary tactic wouldn't give her much time, maybe just long enough to drag Jewel back to the cave, provided she wasn't already dead. Fancy shuddered at the awful possibility, just as Aurora slipped up behind her; Fancy had made the decision to leave the girl untied; if the two women were killed, Aurora would have to be free to defend herself as best she could.

"Mother," Aurora whispered urgently. "I know where the other man is." She tugged Fancy toward the spot where he was visible, his back turned toward them, red with blood from a shoulder wound; he was scouring the ridge for prey or accomplices. Aurora watched her mother brace herself for the shot, close her eyes a moment as if in prayer, then plug him with one of the last two rounds she possessed for the .45.

Breathlessly, the woman and girl dragged Jewel toward the sheltering rocks, then Fancy doubled back to cover the shattered undergrowth. She prayed, as she did so, that the last remaining tracker would choose to go back to Brookehaven to report the expedition's failure, not return to storm their hideaway. When she reached the cave and slipped in through the covering of tree limbs and leaves they'd constructed, she found Aurora kneeling over Jewel's body, pressing a torn piece of her shirt to the bloody wound.

▲

The bullet hole was deep and jagged—Fancy examined the ugly wound gently as she could, but she heard the deep intake of breath and the soft curse as Jewel, returning to consciousness, fought for control of the pain that had followed the initial numbness.

"Fuck, shit, piss, and corruption! I can't believe the little bastard brought me down." Jewel's whisper was hoarse with hurt and fear, beneath the bravado.

"The lead's still in there, Jewel. You know I can't leave it there to fester."

Jewel took that in, sighed, and nodded. Both women knew what it meant to remove a bullet this far from help or antiseptics.

Fancy pulled the blanket up over the wounded woman, then walked to where Aurora watched. She ran her fingers through her hair to push it back from her dirt-smudged face and as she did so, Aurora read the terrible tension in her mother's gesture and saw the blood running down her arm, where a bullet had grazed her.

"He'll come back for us, won't he?" the girl asked.

"Yes. But if we're lucky, he'll go back to Brookehaven, or at least to the nearest town, for reinforcements first. That'll buy us some time." Aurora nodded.

"I'll have to get the bullet out of Jewel's chest right away, Aurora. It's close to her lung, if it stays in there she'll die for sure."

"But if we stay here, they'll find us! He knows where we are now."

Fancy looked steadily at her daughter, too weary and heartsick to argue the point.

"I'll have to find some herbs, roots . . . something for the pain, something for infection," she said, holding Aurora's gaze with her own. The girl's eyes were clearer now, more focused than they'd been, and the pupils were the right size. "Will you help me?"

Aurora scanned her mother's face, saw the fatigue and anxiety there, but it was something else that stayed the quick reply that rose to her lips. This had been a request, not a demand, for help.

"I'll try to, Mother," she said, her voice low and softer than before, uncertain but willing. Fancy nodded acceptance of her answer.

"Do you remember any of the herbal lore I taught you, years ago?"

Aurora shook her head uncertainly and Fancy noticed for the first time that she had combed her hair and plaited it into a semblance of normalcy.

"We'll need white willow bark for the bleeding and inflammation, even poplar would do. If we can lay our hands on some oak galls, we might be able to keep the tissues from weeping too badly . . . the bark will work, if we can't find anything better for the swelling." She tried to force her mind to function, but there was so little available in the cold, flowers were long dead, roots hard to dig in the frozen ground. "Thistle or goldenroot for the lung, or ironwood," she said aloud, then seeing the girl's ignorance of all she catalogued, she shook her head in exasperation.

"I know they're not easy to find now in winter, but there aren't many possibilities this time of year. You stay with her while I search, and for God's sake, Aurora, keep the pressure on that bandage."

The girl moved forward and Fancy saw Jewel strive to ease the derringer from her belt. Fancy knew Jewel thought to protect herself from Aurora's possible treachery, but there were no choices left; without the right remedies, Jewel had no chance whatsoever. Fancy took a deep breath and would not let herself think that Jewel could die.

▲

The makeshift surgeon thrust the knife among the red-hot coals of the fire, and put the two decoctions aside. She'd pulled Jewel as far back into the cave as possible, and had baffled the entrance with branches and leaves to dissipate the signs of the fire, but the air was thick with smoke and it made her eyes water. Their borrowed horse had doubled back from his wild run and nosed at the brush-cover; he could easily have led the survivor of the pursuit party back to their lair. She thought the odds were the wounded man would have ridden in search of reinforcements, rather than risk another sortie. She motioned Aurora to tether the animal inside the dark rock hiding place close by them; it would be nothing but the grace of God if he hadn't already betrayed their whereabouts. The paste of chewed winter leaves and spiderwebs would have to do, to stop the bleeding—there was no mugwort to be found, at least not quickly enough.

The white willow bark would help with the lung inflammation, and the wild ginger could fight infection, but the real crisis would come with the surgery she prepared for. It was too late in the season to find yarrow, to help with the blood clotting. How deeply entangled in muscle and ligament was that bullet? And how close to the lung? Fancy breathed deeply and tried to force her consciousness to obedience, as Magda would have done. She'd scrubbed her hands in the water from their canteen until her skin had turned raw, and she'd splashed them with her disinfecting decoction and would again before attempting surgery. Now only the skills she'd learned from Atticus and her own courage would sustain her. But what in God's name would sustain Jewel? The pain alone could kill her.

Fancy tore a piece of flannel from Jewel's bloomers and fashioned it into a roll to place between the woman's teeth. If Jewel cried out, she could alert the searchers; Fancy saw her friend's pain-bleared eyes follow every movement; there was real fear in them and absolute understanding.

Fancy knelt beside her and brushed the sweat-soaked hair back from her brow with her shirt sleeve, so as not to contaminate her hands. She saw Aurora watching but paid the girl no mind.

"I'm going to have to cut to get at it," Fancy whispered, leaning in close. "I'll try to be fast, Jewel, but I won't be able to do much about the pain . . . I couldn't find anything out there that could ease it for you." She stroked the deadly pale cheek, as she spoke the last of it, then plunged on. "I can't let myself get distracted, Jewel, or I'm liable not to get the damned thing out." Fancy paused, holding back tears.

Jewel nodded, her face gray from pain and blood loss. "I know what you're up against, kid," she whispered, coughing. "I'll do my best to keep quiet." Fancy took Jewel's hand in her own and held it to her cheek. What an incredible friend this woman had been through thick and thin—wise and funny, always allowing Fancy her faults without rancor, always there at the end of it, to cheer and encourage.

"Oh, Jewel, I'm so damned sorry!" she said, swiping at her eyes with her sleeve, afraid to soil her cleansed hands by touching her own tears.

Jewel would have grinned if she'd been able. "I love you, too, kid. Don't you go blamin' yourself if I don't make it—cain't do no more than your best in this world, Fancy, like I always told you . . ." She coughed again and stopped, breathless; the talking had drained her, but there was more she needed to say. Gripping Fancy's hand hard she whispered, "You tell Ford I love him and thanks for everything. Tell him I've gone on ahead to meet Dakota. And one thing more, kid . . . don't let them bury me in Boot Hill. I want a proper grave like the churchgoers get. My mama was real religious about stuff like that."

Fancy nodded, choked with tears. She didn't hear Aurora steal away to unhitch the horse and mount it, only the sound of hoofbeats in the eerie stillness of the cave roused her to stare at the retreating horse and rider. Both women knew the girl never even stopped to replace the brush-cover Fancy had so laboriously put in place to shield them.

Jewel's eyes locked with Fancy's, but instead of "I told you so," Fancy saw only compassion there. She kissed Jewel's cheek, hugged her gingerly, and placed the cleanest cloths she had around the wound. Then she cleansed her own hands one last time and prayed for courage for them both.

Fancy mentally calculated the time before she pulled the glowing knife from the coals. It wouldn't take Aurora long to find their pursuer and alert him to the whereabouts of the cave—she shuddered in revulsion at yet another betrayal, and at her own infinite capacity for being an idiot.

She placed the flannel between Jewel's teeth without a word, and then, praying silently to any god who would listen, sliced the damaged flesh above the wound and plunged her bare hand in after the bullet.

Jewel groaned at the hideous intrusion and Fancy felt every muscle in the woman's body tense in desperate agony. Her own fingers slid through slithery blood and tissue, to the bullet lodged in rubbery muscle; blood welled around her knuckles, obscuring sight, and her heart pounded so savagely, she feared she might pass out. *"Your hands have eyes, child,"* Atticus had said. *"You kin see with 'em if'n you need to."* Fancy shut her eyes tight and "saw" with her fingers. Jewel groaned and writhed beneath her, as she grasped the battered lead and pulled for all she was worth. The lump of flattened bullet tore loose in her hand so hard she nearly lost her balance; a shriek of agony was ripped from Jewel.

"I've got it!" Fancy shouted in triumph, but Jewel had mercifully fainted. Hurriedly, Fancy sutured the gaping wound with the needle and thread Jewel had stolen from the asylum; she bathed the whole area in the diffusion she'd made, then pressed the spiderweb concoction and dried poplar-leaves poultice into place.

"Sleep, Jewel, sleep. Stay unconscious just a little while longer." Pressing the bandages she'd made from their clothing down onto the incision with all the strength she could muster, and hoping she had damaged no artery in her efforts, Fancy let herself breathe again with the relief of completion. Sweat dripped into her eyes, but she couldn't move her hands from the pressure bandage even for an instant, and all she could do was try to wipe her sweat-soaked face awkwardly on the shoulder of her shirt.

Hoofbeats sounded on the trail beyond the cave and Fancy's head snapped up in the direction of the noise, but she couldn't leave her task to hide. She moved in closer to protect Jewel's body with her own, never slackening her grip on the pressure point. She eyed with conviction the position of the knife she'd used for the surgery. She would not let them take her back alive to Brookehaven; better to die here on God's clean mountain than to return to living death. And if they tried to kill her, she'd damn well take someone with her on the trip to eternity.

The horse sounds slowed to a walk and Fancy heard the crash of shredding leaves and twigs as the rider broke the sanctuary of the cave, crunching stones beneath the horse's hooves.

Fancy, back straight as a young tree, heart pounding fiercely in her throat, hands still pressed to the life-giving bandage, heard her daughter's voice pierce the smoky darkness.

"I came back, Mother," Aurora said softly. "I couldn't leave you."

Hart and Ford found them less than two hours later. The sounds of gunfire had drawn them to the women.

XIV

RAINBOW WIND

▼▼▼▼▼▼

Final Reckonings

"Life ain't in holdin' a good hand, but in
playin' a poor one well."

BANDANA MCBAIN

Jason scanned the horizon and drank the last swallow of coffee. Steam rose around the tin cup and warmed his face in the frigid air.

He'd followed the trail the guards must take to return Fancy to Leadville, and finding nothing, had proceeded to Brookehaven. That idiot Endicott had made enough excuses for three fools, but the end was the same—Jewel had freed Fancy and Aurora, and all three women had taken to the freezing woods on foot. Fancy could handle herself in the wilderness, probably Jewel could, too. The man had said warm clothing had been stolen, and guns. Resourcefulness was one of the traits he'd liked best in Fancy in other days . . . at least Aurora would slow them down. He regretted now the choice he'd made of men: Bill and Pete would be useless as trackers.

Resolutely Jason broke camp, scattered the remains of the fire, and headed toward the route he intuited Fancy would take. He wondered if the telegram to London had produced any response yet about St. John. There'd be time to investigate the man's credentials after Fancy was disposed of.

The sounds of distant gunshots echoed on the still morning air; Jason stood up and listened sharply. They were southeast of him and halfway up the neighboring mountain, not more than a few hours' ride. He grunted with satisfaction. With any luck the men would have already accomplished what he needed.

▲

Hart rigged a travois, Apache style, behind Ford's horse to carry Jewel. Made of two long poles with a blanket slung between them, it was the only possible means of getting her out of the woods, but it was uncertain if the unwieldy device could navigate the tricky mountain trail.

"I can ride ahead for help," Aurora offered. Hart and Fancy exchanged glances.

"Jewel's life may depend on you," the man said uncertainly. "Can you handle it?"

"About the only thing on earth I do well is ride," Aurora answered. "Give me a chance." She was already packing her gear into the saddlebags.

"There's a ranch about eight miles south of here, Aurora. You can get there long before nightfall. Ask for a wagon and find out if there's a doctor closer than Leadville." The girl nodded and mounted, looking up at the leaden sky.

"Snow," she said, and Hart nodded without answering. "I'll do my best," she whispered. Then she was gone.

Fancy tucked the blankets around Jewel's nearly comatose body as the first light flakes floated out of the sky—she turned abruptly to find something with which to protect Jewel's face from the coming storm. The movement saved her life. The unexpected rifle shot caught Fancy on the arm and spun her around.

Ford and Hart both dove for their rifles and returned fire in the direction the shot had come from.

"It's only a flesh wound," Fancy shouted, stuffing her kerchief into her jacket to stanch the blood. "Don't worry about me. Just get the bastard. It has to be Jason."

Hart and Ford exchanged glances. "You take the women, Ford. You've got to get Jewel to a doctor fast. Jason's mine to deal with."

Ford didn't argue. "Can you travel?" he whispered urgently to Fancy.

"You bet I can."

Hart was already in the saddle and moving into the trees.

▲ ▲ ▲

The night was moonlit, cold and brittle. Jason had managed to elude his tracker through the darkening afternoon. Snow had created delicate traceries on branches and it lay in scattered patches, but there wasn't enough of it on the ground to assure footprints. Hart would have thought such a night lovely under other circumstances; tonight his only interest was in how much light the moon would provide for tracking.

The Apaches make no war after nightfall, for fear the souls of the dead would be damned to endless wandering. He didn't think such a fate too good for Jason Madigan.

The man had angled up through the timber; snapped twigs, torn bark and grass, churned-up loam all marked the trail. The landscape had quickly roughened into ridges and ravines, so the track provided excellent cover. Jason counted on the changing terrain above them and the dark; it would be hard to track in the craggy boulders, loose spurs, and rock face. Hart could see by Jason's spoor, he was showing no signs of panic and he had a woodsman's instincts, despite his city heritage.

Hart took a deep breath and watched the mist clouds steam around his nose and mouth. How easily he could repossess the mantle of the Apache . . . effortlessly . . . second skin, second nature. But something more than that possessed him—the spirit of the predator that heightens the senses and blocks out all that is irrelevant to the chase. Only Jason and the mountain existed for Hart now; he was once again Firehair, and his Power stalked his quarry at his side.

The air was ice crystal; Hart felt his horse energized by the brutal cold. The sorrel pranced and snorted as he made his way upward, but he never missed his footing once. This horse had guts and intelligence and seemed to sense the energy of the quest; perhaps he, too, was a predator. Whatever the reason, he carried Hart up a scrambling, panting bluff and once, when the rotten granite under his feet split and crumbled, he plunged to solid footing before the pathway could dissolve out from under them. Hart felt the wildness in that horse and the survival instinct, and trusted him to do what he must.

They were into the trees again and still climbing, when a shot zinged by so close to Hart, it singed his sheepskin. He slid from the sorrel and looped the reins around a branch, relieved to see that the rifle shot hadn't spooked the animal.

The area was pockmarked with caves and abandoned mine tunnels—like as not Jason would hole up in one and try to wait Hart out until first light. It didn't matter to Hart how Jason played the chase; this man had killed his brother and Bandana, and tried to kill Fancy . . . he wouldn't live to see another dawn. Hart's eyes were accustomed to the darkness now, and his senses alert as they hadn't been since Apacheria. He intuited, more than saw, the snapped twig, the broken thread, the twisted sapling, the spent cartridge. He saw his quarry peer stealthily from the mouth of the cave; the moonlight caught the sweat-sheen on Madigan's forehead despite the cold.

"Why'd you do it, Jason?" Hart called out; Jason fired at the spot where the voice had been, but Hart was no longer there.

"I don't answer to you, McAllister!"

"This the way you tracked my brother, Jason? This the way you kept him pinned in that old cabin 'til you were sure he'd bled to death?"

"You're out of your mind!"

"Just like Fancy, Jason? Is that why you put her in that lunatic asylum?" He edged closer.

"It's all over, Jason. You haven't any more chance than my brother did."

"Nothing's over yet, McAllister!"

"Fancy's free. She'll bear witness against you, Jason . . . your confederates won't save you this time. If you know any prayers, say them."

Hart heard the man scuffle back a little, farther into the cave. He lobbed a few rounds in to push him back, then with rifle cradled in his arms, Indian fashion, he dove across the intervening space and landed, rolling, amidst a clatter of rifle spit. Hart still clutched the Henry as he scrambled to his feet inside the blackened tunnel where Jason waited.

He heard his prey move backward into blackness; Hart had to grasp the rock face in order to follow; the ground beneath his feet was slush and frozen mud. Hart moved into the hostile blackness that was shattered by a burst of gunfire. He returned the fire, hardly realizing he'd pulled the trigger, and heard a gasp of pain reward his efforts.

Madigan was moving again, this time erratically; there was a crashing sound, a scream, and the scrabble of rockslide. Hart gauged the probability of a trap.

"For Christ's sake, help me, McAllister!" Jason screamed out, his voice echoing in emptiness; there was genuine terror in the sound, for the first time.

Hart picked his way with extreme caution toward the voice, his eyes barely able to discern a dangling shape in the pitch-black tunnel. Jason hung by a handhold over a hole in the cave floor, his legs flailing desperately into eerie endless space. There was no gun in the man's hand that Hart could see; he must have dropped it down the shaft when he stumbled.

Hart reached a hand to the struggling man and hauled him, scrambling, up over the edge of the pit.

"Don't mistake me, Madigan," he said roughly. "I don't want this hole to kill you. I intend to do that myself."

Hart pushed Jason toward the moonlight.

"Are you planning to shoot me in the back?" Jason asked, a sneer in his voice, as he was propelled along the dark passage with none too gentle shoves.

"That's your style, Madigan, not mine."

They emerged into the clearing and Jason turned to face his captor. "I want to know why you did it," Hart said, each word harsh and unmistakable.

Madigan's expression was pinched.

"Because I loved her . . . because I was obsessed with her. You, of all men, should understand."

"I understand the love. Not the murder."

"I'm a rich man, McAllister. I'll make it worth your while if you let me go."

"Don't be a fool, Madigan. You killed my brother and Bandana. You tried to kill Fancy."

Fear was rising in Jason; there was something inexorable in Hart's even tone.

"You've got a reputation for being an honorable man, McAllister. You're not a savage like those redskins you lived with. You can't just shoot me in cold blood."

Hart raised the barrel of his Colt and pointed it at the center of Madigan's chest; he looked steadily into the eyes of the man who had wrought such evil in the lives of those he loved.

"There's nothing cold-blooded about vengeance, Madigan," he said.

Then he pulled the trigger. The shot blew Jason's body backward into the rocks, before it crumpled on the frozen ground.

Hart stood for a long while staring at the dead man and thinking about Chance. "I have vanquished your enemy, my brother," he called out, his voice husky with his grief. He hoped Chance would hear him in the Shadow World. "I have brought him to you, according to the custom of the People."

Visions of his brother flickered in his mind; he saw him as he'd been in their youth, untrammeled by life's harsh lessons. Too blessed and too cursed, he was, Hart thought in sorrowful understanding. He never judged me at all, as I did him . . . just loved me . . . no questions asked, no changes wished for.

After a time, Hart stretched out his arms in an attitude of prayer, and anyone seeing him would have thought one lone Apache had somehow escaped the army's justice. Except, perhaps, for the tears that coursed silently down his cheeks.

"For Chance McAllister!" he shouted to the Old Ones, who kept the record of all men's souls.

"For Bandana McBain!" He called the roll so the spirits would know he kept his promises.

"For Fancy!" The words rumbled down the mountainside like thunder.

Hart mounted up and sat his horse, motionless as death itself, lost in the bittersweet memory of better days. His heart within him was leaden as the slate-gray boulders of the frozen gorge below. He felt empty and alone.

A sound began to gather in his ears that he didn't recognize at once . . . an eerie rhythmic cadence rising from the very stones around him. *"Only the earth lives forever . . . only the stars live forever . . ."* it reminded him, as if the Grandfathers gathered round him on the trail. The Apache Death Chant . . . the warrior's farewell.

Hart lingered a moment longer, reluctant to leave this ground where the shade of his brother seemed to hover just beyond his reach. Finally, he turned his horse's head and began to retrace the path by which he'd reached this place of vengeance. His horse's hooves on the rocky ground echoed the ancient chanting in the relentless quiet of the night. *"Only the earth lives forever . . . only the stars live forever."*

133 🌷 Fancy sat at Jewel's bedside and held the hand of her friend; it was limp and fevered. The trip from their camp had torn loose the sutures she'd stitched so frantically in the cave; the doctor said the internal bleeding had been massive before he'd been able to perform proper surgery, and infection had set in.

Fancy rose as Ford entered, intending to leave him alone with the woman he loved, but he motioned her to stay. His eyes asked silently if there had been an improvement, and Fancy's own filled with tears, as she shook her head no.

"I've done all I know to do," she said miserably. "If it hadn't been for me . . ."

"She'd have died before we found you. Julia made her own choice to go after you, Fancy. Accept the gift, don't spoil it with guilt."

"I've had a lot of time to think, Ford. Hart, Jewel, you . . . you've always been there for me.

"I've been willful and headstrong. . . . People used to tell me that, and I thought they were mean and spiteful, but I've lived long enough to see they were right. I never meant to be a bad person, Ford, only to survive in a world too big and cold and hard for me. After a while I got so caught up in trying to get back what I thought God owed me, I lost track of all that Atticus ever taught me."

Ford had taken his place at Jewel's side, he held her hand in his own, but Fancy could see he was listening carefully.

"I forced everything to my will . . . and everybody. Chance did me wrong, sure enough, but maybe I was so all-fired busy getting him to understand me, I never listened long enough to understand him. I used Jason and he, in turn, used me. I loved Hart a lot longer than I knew, and then, when I could have given him happiness in return for all he'd given me, I panicked and sent him packing."

She saw the tenderness and understanding in Ford's somber eyes, but he didn't refute any of what she'd said.

"You know, when I was a little girl, I listened to every word Atticus told me, but if I didn't like the sound of it I just said to myself, 'I'll prove him wrong, I'll show him I know better!' Then I got to that terrible asylum, and if it hadn't been for what Atticus had instilled in me, I wouldn't be alive now . . . and I sure as hell wouldn't be sane."

"What comes next for you, Fancy?"

"I don't really know, Ford. Hart's made a fine life without me and I have no right to interfere with whatever peace he's found. I guess I'll see what I can do about getting the children raised, try to get to know Aurora, if she'll let me . . . I'd like to do something to help those poor people left behind at Brookehaven, too.

"I guess I just wanted you to know that I've learned the things I should always have known, and I wish to God I could tell that to Jewel."

Ford's voice was gentle. "I think that's called growing up, Fancy. And I expect Jewel would think you're being a mite hard on yourself . . . making mistakes is a real human failing. I never knew Jewel to hold humanity against anybody, least of all the ones she loves."

"Oh, Ford. What will you do if she doesn't make it?" The man with the saddest eyes in the world held the fevered hand in both of his and raised it to his lips; he placed his chin on the hands that held Julia's.

"I went to the preacher today to see about a grave in hallowed ground for Julia . . . she always wanted that, being religious like she was. He told me no Christian burying place would take the likes of her." A terrible ferocity underlay the quiet words.

"How very Christian of him," Fancy said bitterly. She sat stone-still for a minute, then stood up, as if she'd made up her mind about something major.

"Then we just can't let her die, can we?" she said. Before Ford could answer, she was gone.

Ford Jameson laid his head on Julia's breast and cried for only the second time in his life.

▲

Magda listened to Fancy's story with alarm; Jewel sounded so gravely ill, she might well be beyond their reach.

"Death is a transformation, Fancy," she said carefully. "A process that goes through stages before the separation of soul and body are complete." She could see clearly the guilt that Fancy carried and the love she bore Jewel. "Once the seed atoms which connect spirit and matter have been reabsorbed by the Oversoul, no one on this side of the Veil can halt the transformation. If she is as ill as you say, child, what you ask may be impossible. It would take immense strength and fortitude even to try to call her back."

"But I'll help you, Magda," Fancy pleaded, swiping at her tears. "Maybe Wu will, too. Please say you'll try to save her—I'll never forgive myself if Jewel dies because of me. And think of Ford . . . oh, Magda, he'll have no one left in this whole damned world to love."

Magda glanced at Wes, and his compassionate smile gave her courage. "If we are to wage battle for her life, we will require four healers," she said thoughtfully. "Four stalwart souls can generate a great deal of energy—you and Wu and I will need one more person who is willing to storm heaven on Jewel's behalf. But I must warn you, Fancy, this task will require courage and brutal self-honesty—one cannot seek to do God's work with a sullied soul." She turned her gaze upon the dwarf, who watched them from the far corner of the room.

"Will you help us, old friend?" she asked him gently; her eyes seemed to grip Gitalis, so that he felt transparent beneath her gaze. "Understand that to do so you must confess your most secret sins to your God and beg of Him forgiveness."

Gitalis stared at Magda, wondering greatly that she should have chosen him for such an effort. Could it be she knew how desperately he needed absolution?

"I am a sinful man, Magda," he said quietly. "But who knows my imperfections better than you, unless it be God? I will do my best for you, if you show me the way."

The three friends collected Wu from Chinatown, and headed for the doctor's office, praying they were not already too late.

▲

The room where Jewel lay seemed silent as the grave; the color of her skin matched the muslin sheet that covered her.

"If you have an object you hold sacred, place it in your hand," Magda told the three would-be healers. "We must connect our souls to the Unseen with unshakable intensity." Self-consciously, Gitalis tugged a silver rosary from his pocket and Wu brought forth a small gold amulet from beneath his robe. Fancy searched her mind for something she might hold, but she had no such talisman.

"I have nothing sacred to bring, Magda," she said worriedly, and the Gypsy handed her a clear quartz crystal from the pouch she always carried at her belt.

"Your friendship is the sacred gift you bring, Fancy," Magda said reassuringly—she moved swiftly to the table on which Jewel lay near death.

Magda examined the festering wound with the gravity of a practiced physician; it was easy to read in her face that Jewel was in terrible danger. The Gypsy stood for a moment above the body of the injured woman, eyes closed, sensing with her hands and intuition. . . . She spoke to the doctor in measured tones.

"Dr. Philmore, I must ask you not to interfere with what we strive to accomplish this night. I believe you already know there is little more that a mortal doctor can do here. We must petition the Great Physician for this woman's life."

The doctor shook his silvery head in firm agreement. "I wouldn't give you a plug nickel for her chances, as things stand now. If you've got some miracle up your sleeve, madame, you just go about your business with my blessing. I hope I never get so old I cain't learn somethin' new."

Magda nodded her acknowledgment and turned to the small worried band of helpers, hovering nearby.

"My friends," she said gently. "We seek to call Jewel back from a journey of transformation. You must understand that she may not wish to return with us . . . if this is so, you must find the courage to send her forth in love. All healing is God's work . . . we wish only to act as channels for His infinite mercy—but to do this we must be as pure as we are able, within the boundaries of our own human frailty.

"I ask each of you to search your own soul with unflinching honesty. Whatever blemishes you find there, you must purge without compunction if you wish to save her. This honesty will be your sacrifice to lay before the Throne . . . you need not speak your confessions aloud, but you must ask forgiveness nonetheless, with your whole strength and with your unstinting intent."

Gitalis stepped forward and knelt reverently beside the sheet-draped table.

"I will say the words aloud," he said resolutely. "I wish to make certain heaven hears my confession." He took a long, deep breath and spoke again.

"I killed my father," he said. "It was very long ago."

Startled eyes turned toward the dwarf's stricken face.

"He hated me because my small stature demeaned him. He tormented my mother because of her failure to produce the proper heir to his fortune.

"I studied night and day, in an effort to please him and to protect her from his wrath. I learned eight languages, but none spoke to his granite heart. I rode like a centaur, I fenced, I learned marksmanship. I honed my intellect as if by doing so I could debate him into loving me . . . force him to logic or ethic or morality. Instead, he struck me from his will.

"I went to bid my mother farewell and found her at the madman's feet, bloodied and beaten.

"He screamed unholy things at me . . . called me names I shall carry to my grave. We grappled and he pulled a sword from a display of arms near the bed and cut me to the bone . . . but in the end I was the better swordsman, for his hatred had driven me to excellence."

"Your father chose his own death, Gitalis," Magda said firmly. "We all choose our own death."

"We all do not have a son to help us do the deed," he replied sardonically. "I beg forgiveness for my sin with my whole heart."

Wu raised his eyes to each of the members of the group in turn, as if deciding . . . the only sound in the hushed room seemed that of Jewel's labored breathing.

"Long ago," he said finally, "in another lifetime . . . I escaped a hideous death by leaving my comrades behind me to die in my stead. Perhaps it was their destiny to die . . . but their cries are shrill and unrelenting in my dreams, and I fear I must carry my own cowardice and their torment to the seat of Judgment."

Fancy could see that there were tears glistening in his dark eyes, before he averted them.

She stepped forward uncertainly and clasped Jewel's hand tightly in her own; her voice wavered with emotion as she spoke her ancient secrets.

"I pushed Atticus to go on when he was too old to travel," she said humbly. "I didn't listen when Chance came to me for understanding . . . I forced Hart away, when I could have made him happy with my love. I hurt Aurora without even knowing how much she suffered." She shut her eyes and took a breath, then hurried on.

"I got Jewel into this mess . . . if she gets out of it, I swear I'll never do another headstrong, selfish thing 'til the day I die."

Magda made an arcane sign with her hands as she, too, stepped forward to Jewel's side.

"My sins are legion," she said, gravely. "But arrogance and lust must lead the list. Forgive me, Father . . . forgive me, Mother. Give me the strength to deliver this kind woman back to those who love her enough to humble themselves before You . . . they sacrifice their pride to help a friend. I ask this boon not as a priestess, but as the humblest supplicant before Your Eternal Throne."

The words seemed to echo in the ears of those assembled—Fancy saw Ford and Hart had entered the small room and wondered how much they'd heard.

Magda waited for Fancy to finish, then stepped forward to speak.

"Jewel's energy system has been disrupted by the bullet wound and her heart chakra ebbs life-force," she said. "We must share our strength with Jewel to keep her soul from leaving the body—we must lend her our life force for whatever time it takes to call her back. I will attempt to channel healing to the wound, but while I work, you must give of yourselves, more than you know you can give. If we are successful, her body's own resources will take charge and she will remain on this side of the Veil."

Magda instructed Wu to clasp Jewel's feet, with his thumbs pressed to the center of each sole, and she positioned Fancy and Gitalis on either side of their patient, with their hands on a spot just above her hipbones. The Gypsy then moved her own strong hands to the top of Jewel's head, and as she did so a current of electric energy seemed to radiate from her touch.

Fancy caught Gitalis' eyes across Jewel's body, for the flesh that had been cold beneath her hands had suddenly begun to pulsate with some unseen force. She could see by his astonished expression that he, too, could feel the energy surging from Magda to Jewel; it seemed to have filled each of them with a quivering fire . . . each face around the table was alive with an unaccustomed light.

Magda leaned forward and placed her face close to Jewel's heart—Fancy could see she held a crystal in each hand. An indescribable sound arose in the Gypsy's throat, a shriek, a keen, a note of such intensive clarity, it was unlike any the watchers had ever heard from a human throat.

"She recharges the heart with its own eternal sound," Wu murmured as Magda raised herself, and all could see by her rapt expression that she was in a healing trance of some profound kind. She placed one hand beneath Jewel's back and laid the other one atop the ugly chest wound. All three around the table felt a surge of energy so staggering, they could barely keep their hands in place; the electricity pulsed and sizzled around them like ice-cold fire. Jewel's body on the table bounced and jerked between Magda's unrelenting hands, and Fancy felt afraid. She thought her knees would buckle with the effort to stay upright, but she held on doggedly and prayed for all she was worth.

Deep into the night, the four kept their shared vigil, exhaustion lapping at their reserves. Each prayed within his own soul for mercy, and Fancy knew in her heart that Jewel was not the only one whom Magda intended to be healed before morning. She marveled at the Gypsy's stamina, for she seemed to be pouring forth enough energy to power the whole of Leadville.

It was nearly dawn when Jewel opened her eyes and tried hard to focus on the group around her. The deadly pallor of her skin had been replaced by the faintest flush of color, and the inflammation around the terrible wound had somehow been transmuted to a healthier hue.

"I had a dream . . ." she murmured thickly. "There was a Light . . . Dakota touched my hand . . ." Fancy saw Magda close her eyes and lift her face to heaven and she knew the Gypsy thanked her gods.

"Jewel wasn't the only one of us who needed to be healed, was she, Magda?" Fancy whispered as she saw her return to more normal consciousness; she seemed weary but at peace.

"We are all pilgrims, Fancy," Magda replied gently. "When we strive to help a fellow wayfarer on the Path, we touch God's outstretched hand. By giving we receive . . . it is the Law."

When Magda had released them from their places and Ford had taken up the vigil at Jewel's bedside, Wu instructed the doctor in what herbs he must use to continue the healing they had begun. Fancy felt dizzy with fatigue and wonder—and strangely at peace.

"Doctors got no business bein' positive about livin' or dyin, I guess," Doc Philmore said with a smile. "Guess we ought to know more about miracles than anybody."

"This was not a miracle, Doctor," Magda answered him. "This was merely the manifest power of love."

"Well, now, I'd say love's about the biggest miracle of all, wouldn't you?" he replied.

 The letter from the War Office was waiting for Hart when he returned to Leadville. It had followed him to Europe and across country and had taken two years to catch up with him.

Dear Mr. McAllister,

It has come to my attention that a soldier under General Miles' command at Fort Henry removed a girl-child from the Apache encampment, thinking she was white.

I have been told that after the surrender, you moved heaven and earth to find such a child and so I feel duty bound to let you know of this development. One of my troopers made a statement on his deathbed that leads me to believe this may be the child you sought.

If you are still interested, contact me at this address. There are many wrongs I cannot right in this infernal war, but perhaps this is one that can be rectified.

There is always more than one witness, Firehair.

George Crook
General, United States Army

Hart reread the letter for the dozenth time, folded it back in his pocket, and watched the world speed by outside the train window.

She was alive, and with her the knowledge that some part of Destarte hadn't perished; some evidence of the love they'd shared still lived. This child of his heart and loins was living in Pennsylvania. Hart checked his watch, for the City of Brotherly Love was only minutes away.

Odds were the man who'd taken Sonseearay was the one who had killed

Destarte and Charles. Ancient anger tightened Hart's stomach and flushed his brain with adrenaline. His daughter had lived eight years with a murdering bastard, but today would put an end to that.

He glanced at the big beribboned box on the seat beside him. He'd bought every pretty article he could find that would clothe Sonseearay in the beauty she deserved. What would she be like, this lost angel who had never for an instant been out of his heart or mind? Some instinct had kept him from giving up hope; some part of him had known she was alive, somewhere, alive and waiting for him to find her and bring her home.

The train pulled into Philadelphia station and Hart hurried to find a cab.

▲

"Sally, darling, give Mama your hand." Allison Murdock smiled as her daughter's fingers clasped her own. It's so hard on the child since I'm bedridden, she thought, but the eight-year-old never complained. Every day when school was done, she sat with her mother and recounted the day's events, or read her stories from *Copeland's Treasury for Booklovers*. Allison had taught her to read and write at three years of age and the precocious child read voraciously and with great sophistication.

"It's so beautiful out today, my darling, why don't you play with your little friends, instead of staying here with me? You must get lonely for children sitting here every day."

Sally looked reproachfully at her mother; she would never leave her all alone in the bed she hadn't left for over a year now, especially not today. The hours she spent reading to her were some of her happiest; they recited poetry and sometimes sang songs or played games. Mostly they were just together—that was the important part. If the worst happened, and God summoned her sweet mother away forever, as the minister said He might, she would always have these shared times to remember. Or if Mr. McAllister really forced her to leave with him . . . No! She couldn't even think about that unbearable possibility. She must be brave for her mother's sake.

Allison laid her blond head back against the pillows and wondered if she would ever again be well. She let her frail hand rest in Sally's on the counterpane; the pallor of the older one made sharp contrast to the tawny perfection of the younger. God had been so good to her in sending this beloved child, she only prayed she would live long enough to see her raised to womanhood. Already her beauty was noticed by the others, some with envy, some who merely praised God's perfect handiwork. A fine man like her John was what she wished for Sally when she was grown. He'd had so much to cope with since her illness and he'd done so lovingly and without complaint.

Sally smiled reassuringly at her fragile mother. "You're going to get better soon, Mama. You'll see. You know I can see things other people can't."

"Hush, darling. You mustn't say things like that. People might misunderstand."

"But you understand, Mama. You always understand." Sally picked up volume four and turned to the place she'd left off yesterday. The sound of children's laughter outside caught her attention for a wistful moment. Then she began to read aloud page eighteen hundred and thirty-two. They had started a year ago, at page one.

The mother and child had cried for days, ever since the terrible letter had arrived from the War Office, but today they'd made a pact that each must be courageous for the other's sake. Allison Murdock could not let herself think about the horror of what this day could hold in store for them. . . .

 135 Hart hammered on the Murdock door, emotions jostling each other for position in his mind. The blood hammered just as hard in his chest as his fist did on the door. He'd waited eight hungry years for this moment.

A man with the bearing of a career soldier answered the knock. He was strongly built and Hart had to push down the rage that flooded him at the thought of Destarte in his grip, of Charles at the end of his saber.

"Lieutenant Murdock?" he said with forced control.

"You're McAllister," the man responded. "I remember you." Hart quelled the urge to throttle him where he stood. He, too, remembered the fort and the pleading for information, the stone wall of silence, and the grief. . . .

"Where is she?" he demanded; the muscles knotted in his neck stood out like ropes on a mast.

"Upstairs. My wife is an invalid. I'd appreciate it if you'd go gently on her, McAllister. She loves the child. I'm afraid this could kill her."

The man's voice nearly broke and he cleared his throat. Hart thought he looked haunted, as well he should.

Hart climbed the stairs; at the top, a door stood open to a sunlit room. An ethereal-looking woman lay delicate as glass, on the high bed. An eight-year-old, straight and supple as a sapling, stood at her side like a sentinel. Protective, stalwart, unmoving. The mother and child had clasped their hands together on the bed in a knot so tight, it trembled.

"I would have known you anywhere," Hart said huskily to his daughter. "Do you know who I am?"

The little girl's feet were parted, her stance not defiant but firmly planted as an oak.

"You're the man who wants to take me away from my mommy and daddy," she answered, her voice just tremulous enough to betray her fear. She held fast to the hand that linked her to the past. "If I don't go with you, my daddy will have to go to jail."

Hart closed his eyes against the pain, before he spoke in a voice so strained, it was nearly unrecognizable.

"Do you know why?" he asked.

Oh God, those are Chance's eyes in Destarte's face, he thought, ravaged by the child's unblinking gaze.

"My daddy saved me from being killed by the Indians, but he wasn't supposed to."

Hart had to wait for the clamor in his chest to quiet; when he spoke again his voice was gentle.

"Could you leave us alone for a few minutes, sweetheart? Your daddy and I have things to say to each other." Sally looked at her mother for permission, then nodded and slipped from the room. He noticed that she made no sound when she moved.

Allison Murdock's bright eyes had never left Hart's face for an instant; she seemed to be studying him intently. "John, dear, why don't you take Mr. McAllister out into the hallway and speak with him for a moment. Then I'd like to do the same." The man nodded, his jaw set as stone. He walked into the hallway with Hart and closed the door behind them. It was easy to see the love he bore the woman on the bed.

"I'm sorry, McAllister. So damned sorry . . ."

Hart made a contemptuous sound. "That you murdered my wife and son and stole my daughter? How do you apologize to a man for that?"

"She was just a squaw, dammit, how could I have known? She wasn't a Christian—"

"And you are? You fine upstanding Christian who gutted my son and raped my wife as she was dying?"

"Jesus, McAllister, it was a war, she was only an Indian! I didn't know."

"She was my wife, you bastard." Hart's voice was unrelenting. "I loved her more than my own life and I've waited eight long years to avenge myself on you, you sanctimonious son of a bitch."

Murdock's eyes were bloodshot with the strain, his breath ragged.

"I thought the baby was white, as God is my witness, I did! I thought she'd been stolen from some settlement."

"Bullshit, Murdock. You knew I was at the fort looking for her. You saw me there, I remember you."

"But that was later, McAllister! Don't you see, by then I'd already sent her home to my wife. She was so happy to have that baby . . . we'd been married so long without any kids and she was so desperate for one. It was like God had sent this baby to me for Allison. She's the best wife a man ever had . . . I couldn't take Sally away from her, don't you see, I loved her too much to break her heart?" The truth rang in the man's voice and Hart had to cling to his hatred, wrap himself in it, because this pathetic creature was only a man, not a monster as he'd always seen him in his nightmares. He'd done what a thousand others would have—a monstrous deed by an ordinary man—and Hart felt robbed even of his vengeance. He left the man in the hall and let himself back into the bedroom where Mrs. Murdock lay upon the bed.

"You poor man," she whispered, seeing his ravaged face. "I've been trying to hate you for what you are doing to Sally. But I can see your anguish so clearly in your eyes."

She paused, as if the effort to speak had drained her, and she closed her eyes a moment; Hart thought it was as if a light had gone out in the world. She had lovely, intelligent eyes and they seemed the only part of her still fully alive.

"It's important that you and I understand each other, Mr. McAllister, and there's so little time . . . I love Sally more than you could possibly dream. She is the only perfect thing that's ever happened to me and I'm grateful she was mine for even a little while." Silver tears welled in her eyes, but she didn't allow them freedom.

"She's so good and gentle, Mr. McAllister, that she sacrifices herself for me, now that I'm sick. Taking care of me, taking care of the house with John away so much. I know you're a rich and famous man and you wouldn't have searched so long for your child if you weren't a good one." She lay very quietly for a moment, looking like translucent porcelain. "I had planned to beg you . . ." she whispered, and then was still.

"You must promise me you'll take good care of her, Mr. McAllister. Not just by giving her things, but by teaching her and giving of yourself. She's very intelligent and strong, but she's so loving that she does what's best for others, not herself. And she's a little fey . . . I don't know how to say this to you, but she seems to know some events before they happen and she feels connected to every living thing in a way ordinary people just can't understand."

Hart could hear the love in every word the woman spoke, love and understanding. There are some women born to be mothers, endowed with the right gifts for the calling. This woman would give up her child to a better life, because she loved her more than she loved herself.

"I'd like to talk with my daughter, Mrs. Murdock," he said wearily. "The

Apaches believe that children belong to the whole tribe . . . I can see you've been a foster mother my Destarte would have approved of."

Allison Murdock searched his eyes, then spoke quite tenderly.

"You poor man. You've lost too much, haven't you? Far too much already." He could only nod, uncertain of his own voice.

"What did you and your wife call Sally?" she pleaded as he was about to leave. The father didn't turn around to answer, even the memory of her name broke his heart.

"We called her Sonseearay," he said, his hand on the brass knob.

"It suits her, Mr. McAllister. There's more Indian in Sally than you know."

Hart took the dark-haired child and led her outdoors. The leaf carpet was thick and apricot-colored beneath their feet.

"Are you afraid of me?" he asked, and she looked up to answer, for he towered above her.

"I'm afraid you'll take me away from my mother."

"You love her very much, don't you?" he asked with a sigh.

"I love her and she needs me. She's very sick."

Hart nodded and squeezed the small honey-colored hand. "It's real good to be needed, isn't it, sweetheart."

"Why do you call me that?"

He had to look away, for tears blurred his sight. "Because long ago, in another world . . . there was a little girl named Sonseearay I loved very much. I called her sweetheart."

Sally raised her eyes to his, great searching eyes that seemed to see inside him. "I'm sorry you're so sad, Mr. McAllister. I wish you didn't have to be so sad." He noted she hadn't once pleaded to be left behind, although it was apparent that was what she wanted. There was strength and stoicism in her that he recognized, but she was no longer his; the realization wrenched at Hart's soul. She was someone else's child now and Destarte was well and truly gone forever, and the tiny fragment of their love that he had thought salvaged was only an illusion.

Hart sat down heavily on the park bench, not knowing what to do, the quiet child beside him. He put his head in his hands; to face the loss of her a second time was more than he could bear. Or perhaps she was already lost in the white man's world that bore no trace of the sensibilities she'd been born to. He felt bereft and heartsick.

"Do you hear them talking, Mr. McAllister?" the small voice asked suddenly, trying to distract him from his grief.

"Hear who, sweetheart?"

"The trees. The oak is so much kinder than the elm." The big man thought his heart might have ceased to beat in his chest. He looked searchingly into the shining eyes that were watching his in such innocence.

"I hear them," he answered, tears running down his weathered cheeks. "Your brother taught me how to listen before you were even born." Hart took the beautiful child into his arms then and clasped her so close, she could barely breathe. It wasn't all lost, not the best of them . . . because she was alive and she was wonderful. In her, the red and white rivers flowed and only the Great Spirit knew her destiny.

Hart tried to regain his composure before letting her go.

"Would you write to me sometimes, sweetheart?" he asked. "Maybe later, you could come visit me and we could be . . . friends."

"I knew you wouldn't take me away," she said with great seriousness. "The sycamore told me you aren't mean at all." She smiled at him, and in that smile they all lived again. Chance, Destarte, Charles. Hart clasped the perfect little fingers and brought them to his lips.

"Someday, Sally, I'll tell you about Sonseearay, and her mommy, and about a little boy who talked to trees. And maybe then you'll understand why you know things other people don't."

Hand in hand, father and daughter walked back to the Murdock house. It was a white house with a porch swing, on a tree-lined street; a perfectly fine house for a little girl to grow up in, he thought, as he kissed his child goodbye.

"Until we meet again, Sonseearay . . . Sally," he whispered into her long, straight hair as he held her to his heart.

He walked, with a heavy tread, up the stairs to the sickroom once again. John Murdock's arms were around his wife's thin shoulders, the visitor could see that both were crying. The man's protectiveness of his sick wife touched Hart, it was a good trait in a man.

He cleared his throat to alert them to his presence, and to gain control of his own voice.

"Take care of her for me, Mrs. Murdock, will you? She loves you very much. I brought a box of clothes with me—I'd like Sally to have them, if it's agreeable with you."

The woman's eyes seemed large in the shrunken face. "Then she isn't yours, Mr. McAllister?"

Hart smiled a little. "She's mine all right, and her mother's . . . but I can see she's yours too. I'd like to stay in touch, Mrs. Murdock. No one ever knows what the future holds, and I'd be grateful if I could be there, should she ever need me.

"I guess you've noticed that her soul isn't all white . . . someday she might need me to help her understand what's Indian in her nature."

Husband and wife threw their arms around each other in relief. Murdock rose from the bed and held out his hand to Hart; his eyes were red-rimmed and his voice unsteady. "I don't know how to thank you, McAllister. There just aren't any words that could say what's in my heart . . ."

"See that you take damned good care of her, Murdock . . . I'm not doing this for you. I'm doing it for Sally and your wife. You'll answer to me if any harm comes to her, do you understand me?"

Murdock squared his shoulders, a military gesture.

"That's as it should be, McAllister. Whatever your reasons, I'm grateful."

"We'll consider her fostered to your care, for now. I'll see to her having a proper birth certificate in her right name, that much I'll expect you to agree to. That, and my right to see her from time to time. I'll send money for her keep, and I'll pay for her schooling. Any child who could read and write at three like Mrs. Murdock said in her letter should have every chance for an education. There are universities that take women now—if Sally's got a mind to go to one of them." He cast about in his mind for any detail he'd left uncared for.

"Mr. McAllister . . ." Mrs. Murdock's voice was soft as spring rain. "Whatever terrible wrong was done you, you have my word, we'll make it right with Sally. I'm no Indian, Mr. McAllister, but I understand that child's soul, too. Nothing I ever do will interfere with the good she got from both her parents. You have my word on that."

Hart caught her eyes with his own and she felt the suffering she saw in the man tug at her heart.

"God's ways are mysterious, Mrs. Murdock, but here is where He sent her and it might be He knew what He was doing." He reached out for the woman's hand and she clasped his with surprising strength.

"I see her in you, Mr. McAllister," she said. "Someday, perhaps, she will, too."

Hart stood for a moment outside the small frame house and watched his daughter playing in the leaves, through tear-blind eyes. He had dreamed of bringing home a daughter, not a memory. She turned and smiled, waving at him.

"I love you, Sonseearay," he said softly into the sunlit silence. "I will always love you." Then, because he loved so much, he turned and forced himself to walk away.

136 Hart brooded hard over the loss of his daughter and Fancy watched him worriedly, trying to decide if what she considered doing would help or hurt. Gabriel was the last of her secrets, and it was time Hart knew the truth—he had a son, as well as a daughter, perhaps the knowledge of one could assuage the pain of the other. She sent for the boy soon after Hart returned from Philadelphia and tried to decide how best to break the news.

Hart dismounted behind Fancy's house and was walking toward the porch when he spotted the redheaded child. The sturdy little boy was sitting near the stable, busy and not particularly well dressed, he was without benefit of any adult supervision that Hart could see. The child had dark red hair of the kind favored by Titian, and enough freckles for three youngsters. Hart paid the boy little mind, assuming him to be the son of one of the hired hands. But, then, as he drew near, he saw that he was drawing a picture and felt a strange ache rise up in him for his own son, who had been not much younger than this boy, when he died.

"Not a bad likeness," Hart said amiably, looking at the half-done drawing of the horse. "But he could use a little meat on his bones."

The child looked up, serious as a senator, and regarded the huge man like a general on an inspection tour.

"I'm Gabriel," he said, as if that should mean something special to Hart. So this was Fancy's youngest, he thought, taking a closer look. The boy was nothing like his brother or sister, but there was something familiar about him nonetheless.

"My name's Matthew," Hart said, "although nobody ever calls me that."

"I know," the boy replied, and he returned to his work. "They call you Hart. Mama told me all about you, and I saw your picture."

Hart smiled at the stocky child, built big for his age. "Care to have me show you an easy way to draw that pony?" he asked him.

"No, thanks, I can do it." Gabriel went right on with his work; his matter-of-fact confidence made Hart laugh out loud, but the youngster never flinched.

"I like a man with a mind of his own," Hart told him, and turned to leave, when the boy spoke again.

"Jewel says I look just like you."

That was the instant Hart knew, not before. The age, the hair, the sketch . . . the quirky movement of the head, so like a little boy who lay buried in the desert. It could have been genetics and some common ancestor coming out in both of them, but it wasn't, and Hart knew it sure as God made little green apples.

He felt that sudden sharp focus in the gut, as only happens when the truth hits you squarely, when you're least expecting it.

He stood very still, barely able to breathe; what he felt was entirely too complicated to name. Relief that all the children of his seed weren't lost to him . . . hurt that Fancy'd never let on . . . joy that some tangible evidence of their love existed in the world. And *anger*. But at whom? he wondered. At her, for tangling them all so inextricably in this strange web? At destiny, or himself, or all of them?

Gabriel's eyes followed Hart as he mounted the steps of the house, not in an overly curious fashion, just watchful . . . as artists' eyes are meant to be.

Hart made his way to the parlor to find Fancy, moisture clouding his vision.

"Gabriel is my son, isn't he, Fancy?" he demanded when he found her.

"Yes, Hart. Gabriel is yours."

"Why in God's name didn't you let me know you'd gotten caught?"

"I wasn't caught. I wanted him. He's very like you, just as I hoped."

Hart frowned, in great confusion. "Are you trying to tell me that you did love me, back then? That you wanted to have my child?"

Fancy straightened her back and looked directly into his troubled eyes. "I loved you then, and every day of my life since then," she said quietly. "I love you now."

Hart stood very still, trying to connect with this incomprehensible truth. "You know, Fancy, I've spent my whole life running away from you. From not wanting to compete with Chance for you . . . from your own pigheadedness . . . from my own heart. To Yale, to the Apaches, to Europe.

"I've spent twenty years loving you and leaving you . . . and longing for what we could have had together, and wishing you loved me as I loved you. I think maybe I'm not going to do that anymore . . . not going to let you choose wrong one more time. I think you're going to marry me today if I have to tie you to my saddle to get you to a preacher."

Fancy smiled at the man who'd loved her so long a time. "It might be a little more romantic as proposals go, if you at least say you love me, too," she answered, but all he did was smile and shake his head as she walked into his waiting arms.

They were married that night at the Crown of Jewel's, which seemed the only appropriate place for such an important social event.

137 ❦ The avenue of oaks and elms stretched corridor-like in front of them. Spanish moss trailed wisps of lace, breezes rustled the leaves above the trotting horses and the stately carriage. Fancy leaned against the seat, tilted her head far backward, so she could look up through the lacy filigree that formed a canopy above, just as she had a thousand times when she was small. She felt a compulsion to loose her hair and feel the soft bayou breeze ruffle through it. Hart saw there were tears on her cheeks, enough to wash away the bitterness and longing . . . enough for what was lost and what the years had given in its stead.

He glanced sideways at Fancy's gesture and smiled. "You look like a little girl doing that, babe. How are you holding up?" He had tracked down Armand Deverell through the Canfields—he was the last of her kin and the last of her unfinished business.

Fancy smiled up at her husband and straightened herself into a more dignified posture. "I'm scared to death, I suppose. It's hard to come home after thirty years of wanting to. I don't know what to expect of Armand . . . and these old bayous keep whispering Atticus' name to me."

Hart squeezed his wife's hand reassuringly; it was best to face the phantoms of the past that plagued the heart, but it was god-awful hard, sometimes.

Fancy breathed in the air that was fragrant with memory. The need to get back Beau Rivage had pulsed inside her so long, she couldn't remember a time when it wasn't there.

Coming home. Oh Atticus, I'm finally coming home!

The avenue of trees parted and the shell of Beau Rivage materialized on its hill; the unexpected reality made Fancy gasp. "My God, Hart, it's just exactly as I left it that dreadful night. They haven't rebuilt a stick of it."

The blackening from the fire had been washed away by three decades of rain; the crumbling, ravaged timbers were overrun by the encroaching bayou inexorably taking back its own. Creepers trailed up chimneys, ivy obscured the tattered edges, pungent honeysuckle wafted on the summer air, and wisterias had grown wild so long that they'd become twisted trees, heavy-laden with white and purple blossoms. Bees buzzed unmolested and Fancy could see again in her mind's eye the pickaninnies with their fans and swatters, keeping the insects from the plantation's inhabitants, oh, so very long ago . . .

Hart watched his wife's eyes sweep the landscape searchingly; he could see how hard she fought for composure. As they neared the ruined house, Hart and Fancy saw two men and their horses standing nervously near what had once been the verandah of Beau Rivage. They were elegantly dressed and their mounts were excellent animals.

"Oh, Hart," Fancy whispered as she realized that the middle-aged man before her was her brother Armand. The last time she'd seen him he'd been nineteen, resplendent in his Confederate uniform . . . "Can we have grown old, too?"

Armand Deverell was of just above medium height, dark-haired and slender, but with the slightest paunch, to betray the good life. He was dressed in the latest riding gear, his polished boots gleamed in the sun, his jodhpurs and hacking jacket were perfectly tailored to enhance his stature. There was a trace of her father in Armand's manner, Fancy thought, but more of her mother's forebears in his arrogant expression.

Without thinking, she raised her arms and held them out to her brother, but instead of doing the same, Armand Deverell cleared his throat, looked hastily at his companion, then walked toward Hart and Fancy with exaggerated dignity. He put his arms around his sister in greeting, but there was no warmth whatsoever in the gesture.

"Fancy, darlin', I can't tell you how shocked I was to find out you were alive." Odd choice of words, Fancy thought as she breathed again; that must explain his restraint. She checked her own desire to hug him, to ask a thousand questions . . .

"We never knew what happened to you, Fancy. When I got back from the war everything was gone. Mama and Papa dead. There were crazy rumors about you going off with some old slave, but of course I never gave any credence to that."

"But surely you must have looked for me, Armand." Fancy let the question hang in the soft air, her voice low and puzzled.

The man averted his eyes as he answered. "I can't say I ever did, darlin', what with the war and all. It was nearly a year later, you see, when I left my regiment, it hardly seemed you could still be alive by then . . ."

Fancy listened carefully to her brother's discomfort.

"Later, Armand, after I was famous, didn't you ever think the Fancy Deverell who was written about in all the newspapers might be your little sister?"

There was a hint of irony in her voice, and Armand shuffled his well-shod feet. "I don't really have any knowledge of theatricals, Fancy. I expect I was so distressed to hear you were a performer, I just didn't know what to do."

Hart's eyes followed the interchange with grim fascination; he could feel the storm gathering in Fancy and wondered if this dandified twit had any idea what he was up against.

"Perhaps your delicate sensibilities might have been suspended long enough to inquire whether I wanted my share of Papa's inheritance," she said evenly.

Armand's eyes closed slightly in calculation, the false smile faded. "If it's money you're after, I've brought my attorney, Mr. Cadwallader, with me to discuss terms. Considering the life you've led, I can't believe you have the starch to come back chasing Papa's money after all these years . . . not that there's very much left, God knows. With Beau Rivage destroyed and the Yankees in power, I've had to make my way by my wits . . ."

"That must have put you at a considerable disadvantage," Hart interjected before Fancy spoke again with studied contempt.

"Money? Armand. Why, I have money to throw at the birds. What I want from you is justice, my dear brother."

"A fine word coming from a notorious scarlet woman like yourself, my darlin' sister. Oh, yes, I admit I've made it my business to find out all there is to know about you and your infamous past, Fancy. Marriages, illegitimate children, madhouses . . . auctioning off your body like a common nigger gal. Or maybe you learned all that from Atticus. It *was* Atticus you ran off with, wasn't it, Fancy? Just like they all said and I wouldn't believe. I can't imagine how Mama and Papa must be spinning in their graves over what you turned out to be."

"I ought to crush you in my two hands like the despicable slug you are," Hart said, but Fancy stepped in front of him.

"Every word you've said about me is true—the things I've had to do to survive would probably turn your lily-livered carcass green, Armand. But let me tell you something about Atticus—you aren't fit to wipe his boots. There isn't anything he ever taught me I couldn't take with me in pride on Judgment Day. I'm *proud* to have known him . . . proud to have called him my friend."

Armand opened his mouth to respond, but Fancy cut him off.

"I know what Papa's will was like, well as you do, Armand, and I don't need any shyster lawyer to tell me my rights. Half of everything Mama and Papa had was mine—however much it was, or is. And do spare me your sob story about the Yankees . . . it doesn't appear you've spent one plug nickel on repairing Beau Rivage.

"Which brings me to why I'm here, dear brother. It may interest you to know I have more money than God Almighty, so rest assured that isn't what I want from you."

"Not with silver down the drain, you haven't," Armand countered; Fancy could see he'd done his homework. The Sherman Silver Purchase Act had been repealed the previous year.

"Not silver, Armand . . . it's gold I'm talking about. Enough to pave the heavenly highways. Which is simply my way of telling you I want only one thing from my inheritance—the land we're standing on."

"Beau Rivage? Whyever would you want this place? It's been worthless since the war. The house is gutted, you can't work the land without slaves . . ."

Fancy looked at her brother with consummate repugnance. She'd been wrong; he didn't look like her mother or father at all.

"I want the land where Mama and Papa are buried. I want the land I was born on. My husband's a farmer; he'll know what to do to make it work." Fancy smiled up at Hart and he nodded acknowledgment; this was her show, he wouldn't interfere unless she needed help.

Armand's lawyer cleared his throat and took a step forward.

"Now you see here, Miss Deverell . . ."

"Mrs. McAllister."

"Mrs. McAllister, then. You must understand, this land is very valuable. Mr. Deverell wouldn't consider parting with it except under certain very specific conditions. As his lawyer—"

Hart cleared his throat forcefully and interrupted. "Now let's just cut this charming little do-si-do short, Mr. Cadwallader, and get to the meat of this parlay. My wife wants Beau Rivage. It's less than her fair share, but she's willing to settle for it. What *I* want is for my wife to have what she wants. We have at our disposal enough money and enough lawyers to keep my less than generous brother-in-law in litigation for the next thousand years or so.

"Now, out West where I come from we don't take kindly to men who rob women and children of their birthright—and we tend to be real direct in how we deal with them. But in deference to my wife's kinship to that selfish, self-important, squirrel-faced little varmint over there, I'm willing to consider more peaceable means of getting what I want. But let me leave you in no doubt whatsoever, Mr. Cadwallader, that get what I want, I will."

Armand Deverell and his lawyer exchanged meaningful glances before Mr. Cadwallader recovered his speech.

"My client will give thought to what you've said, Mr. McAllister."

"I expect that would be sensible."

The two men mounted their horses and prepared to go; but Armand turned his horse skillfully and moved him in so close beside Fancy, she could feel the breath from the horse's nostrils.

"I can see every word I've heard about you is true," he said with lofty contempt, "you're nothing but a slut and an opportunist."

Fancy raised her hand to stop Hart's instantaneous movement toward the man.

"Better that than a sniveling coward who hides behind his lawyer's skirts to do a dirty deed. If you make me fight you, Armand, rest assured you'll lose. You just aren't up to my standard."

Armand steadied his horse with a violent tug on the reins. "If you were a man, by God, I'd challenge you for that."

"I wouldn't be too swift to do that either, Deverell," Hart said, half amused. "The lady could trim that dainty little mustache of yours right nicely with a forty-five."

Armand wheeled his horse around and Cadwallader followed suit. Fancy and Hart watched the pair canter down the avenue of untended trees and disappear from view.

Concerned for his wife, Hart put his arms around her from behind and turned her to face him, expecting tears. But Fancy was smiling, the cat-that-ate-the-canary smile he knew so well.

"Selfish, self-important, squirrel-faced little varmint indeed!" she said. "You really are a fine judge of men, Mr. McAllister."

"Never anything but a surprise, are you, Fancy?" Hart said, as she took his hand in her own and walked him over the land that had lived in her memory for an exiled lifetime.

"Are you really a farmer?" she asked as they surveyed the fertile bottom-land, long gone to nature, but magnificent in its savage lushness. Hart bent to scoop a handful of the rich alluvial soil and let the blackness trickle through his fingers. He spoke without looking up at her.

"Can't help but remember what my daddy fought against in that hard Kansas land, Fancy. With soil like this he could have planted the Garden of Paradise."

"Chance always said you were just like your daddy." She touched his shoulder with her hand and thought about how very much she loved him.

Hart looked up, squinting against the sun or tears, she wasn't sure which.

"God, but I miss him!" he said from his heart, and she knew he spoke of Chance. "I miss him damn near all the time."

"I miss him, too," she answered. They were both past jealousy or anger; time had brought forgiveness and left in its wake only memories of the good that had been among them all.

"Love takes you down some real strange highways, doesn't it, babe?" Hart asked, and she knew that every one of them lived in him, as they did in her.

When had it been that she'd discovered that life was nothing more than a learning process? Sometimes tragic, sometimes gold with glory . . . a road with many turnings, each with its own gift of hard-won wisdom.

Hart had brought her home to where she'd always longed to be, but now she knew it wasn't the destination that counted, only the road that led there.

That its endless twists and turns, its obstacles and roadblocks, its occasional inexpressible beauty, and its ceaseless wonder were the gifts in themselves.

Would it end here where it all began? Or was this simply another cross-roads and a new beginning?

"I love you, Matthew Hart McAllister," Fancy said with all the fervor of her passionate nature. "I think I might be getting the hang of this."

"Of what?"

"Of life, Hart. I might be getting the hang of what it is God wants from me."

And so she was.

From the Journal of
Matthew Hart McAllister

Hart raised his head from where he'd rested it, on his big gnarled hands. His glance lingered for a while on a tiny music box, glued together from fragments, and a map made of oilcloth that was framed behind it on the wall. He picked up his pen a final time.

"So there it is," he wrote definitively on the last page of the lengthy manuscript. "Their story . . . and mine."

Some of it I'm proud of, some not. Some I'm going to have to answer for at God's great Judgment Seat, but I'm willing to take my chances that He'll understand. I had two fine gifts in this life—one for painting and one for taking care of Fancy—so if that was what He had in mind for me, I intend to tell Him with a real clear conscience, I tried my best on both scores.

Blackjack has relived his father's life, but in shoddier times. He was wild-catting for oil in Louisiana, last time I heard. Aurora lives in England now, the wife of an earl or a duke, I don't remember which. She and Fancy maintained a fragile peace with each other through the years. Sally is a lawyer who spends her time fighting for Indian rights and Gabriel paints pictures that would make the angels sing . . . they're both the kind of people who make you feel real good about the human race. Wu and Jewel went off to San Francisco and started a successful bank there for the Chinese commu- nity. They say Wu died as rich as any Mandarin in China. Ford never touched a gun again, far as I know—they made a moving picture out in Hollywood about his life, but they got most all the facts wrong. He and Jewel finally got to stay together and made a damned good life as upstanding citizens. Destarte and Charles Paint-the-Wind's bones lie bleaching some- where on the desert's unrelenting vastness . . . and I remain.

So there isn't any "fair," I've lived to learn. But there is truth . . . and occasional justice. And, believe you me, there is love.

Now, some might think that Fancy didn't love me in the same way she loved Chance . . . nor maybe even the same way I loved her. But she loved me real well in those twenty-odd years we lived together as man and wife, and that was a hell of a lot more good than comes to most men in any single lifetime. Whatever you may think about the story I've just told, you must have noticed she was one of a kind.

We bought back Beau Rivage and restored it to near its former loveliness. We brought Atticus' broken banjo and Chance's body there for burial, after we'd decided to make our home in Louisiana. And Jewel's, too, years later, to lie in hallowed ground. Fancy sleeps beside them now, beneath her great stone angel, these five years past. Which is why I guess I decided to try to write this memoir.

Fancy and Chance . . . Chance and Fancy . . . There isn't a day that goes by they aren't in my thoughts, those two I loved best—and it seems to me their story should be told before the last of us is gone.

I guess you might say the world has turned round a time or two since Fancy and Atticus set out together to find their destinies, and my brother and I left Kansas. The rustlers are gone now . . . or they rustle on Wall Street or on the London Stock Exchange. The gunslingers win or lose in more elegant crapshoots than in the old days. The Sante Fe Trail is covered with macadam and the cows are shipped to market on trains that were only a gleam in someone's eye when I was a boy.

But if you're real quiet and you close your eyes a little, just around sun-down on a certain Colorado mountaintop, by God, you'd swear Bandana McBain was out there playing that banged-up banjo of his, and old Jewel had her soiled doves spiffying up for the evening's fun.

And Fancy. Well, I like to think she's riding on ahead . . . she always did lead a man a merry chase. And I'm like some old desperado waiting for the last train out, anxious to be on my way to meet her.

I can almost see her, yonder on the trail; her dark hair flying out like a mustang's mane, her untamed laughter riding the wind like an eagle; fearless she is and free at last.

She'll be trying to make me believe she doesn't want me catching up, of course, but she'll be leaving sign along the trail for me just the same, like she always did, in hopes I'll pay no mind to her headstrong foolishness.

When I get to where she's camped in the Spirit World, I expect she'll toss back her head and look at me, the way she used to. "You took your own sweet time in getting here, Hart McAllister!" she'll say to me with mischief in her voice, and then we'll set a spell and let the night air still the woods around us. I'll hold her in my arms so she feels real safe, and she'll tell me stories in the glow of the campfire like the ones old Atticus told to her when she was just a little girl.

And we'll talk about them all . . . and maybe figure where the rendezvous will be. The Apaches say the Great Spirit will show you the Way over there like he never did in this life, and I can tell you for certain, the Indians know a heap more about such things than the rest of us. I've got a hunch He has a real stable home in mind for Fancy there—she never meant to be so reckless—life just never let her be too peaceable, until she married me.

Then again, I might just arrive and find she's staked out a claim or two on those Streets of Gold . . . she could be damned unpredictable.

The Indians call memory the haunting of the heart . . . they're right about that too. If ever a heart was haunted by remembrance, it was mine.

"The Fancies" hang now in the Louvre in Paris, but I kept up painting those pictures of her that I used to do each year, even after she was gone— every year another, same as if she was with me. Never would sell them, either, although I did let the Metropolitan borrow them last spring for an exhibition. I expect the one I'm doing now may be the last I need to do from memory.

You know, sometimes I talk to her aloud while I paint, in case she's over there listening and wondering if I'll be there to catch her, should she falter.

"Won't be long now, babe," I tell her.

But I know she knows.

AUTHOR'S
NOTE

So much of what we know of the West is the story of men's adventures . . . yet women won the West as much as they . . . women worked, loved, laughed, cried, fought, died, too, a truth that seems to have been somewhat lost to history despite the fact that these westward-bound women helped create life, and sometimes they helped create legends.

There isn't a single act of Fancy's, Jewel's, or Magda's lives that couldn't have been accomplished by some woman, in those turbulent and exacting early days of America, when only the most outrageous facts were true. My tale and everyone in it, with the exception of those noted at the beginning of this book, is entirely fictitious, but the spirit is factual.

The story of Geronimo's first family's massacre follows the tale as told by Forrest Carter in *Watch for Me on the Mountain*. Needless to say, as the victor writes the history of all wars, the white man's historical memory differs somewhat from Mr. Carter's. But inasmuch as Forrest Carter was a full-blood Cherokee and a hereditary storyteller to his tribe, my instincts tell me that his rendition is probably closest to the truth of any available. I would wholeheartedly recommend his books to anyone who feels a desire to learn more about Native Americans, their kinship with the earth and the unseen world around us. It was from him I learned of the talking trees.

Several passages in which Geronimo tells his life story to Hart were taken nearly verbatim from Geronimo's verbal autobiography, *Geronimo, His Own Story,* as I thought this extraordinary Apache deserved a hearing in his own words. Geronimo's ability to alter weather was documented in the diaries of white soldiers as well as in the folktales of the Apaches, but I was unable to find an eyewitness account of what rituals he used in performing this feat, so I've followed the methodology as outlined in *Rolling Thunder* by Doug Boyd, who witnessed Rolling Thunder, a modern-day medicine man, invoke a cyclone to free a jailed boy. I am indebted to Arnold Elliott's *Blood Brother* for the ritual of blood brotherhood, which is a men's mystery, and not spoken of freely with women, but which was practiced in much the way I've portrayed it in many tribal cultures around the world.

My belief that an honorable white man and an honorable Apache leader could have had the kind of friendship described in my story is based on the fact that Cochise, the great Chiracahua leader, called on his deathbed for his friend, the Indian agent Tom Jeffords, and on the fact that Elbys Hugar, the great-granddaughter of Cochise, verified the closeness of this friendship for me.

There were no Chinese in Leadville, although the tale of Wu could have happened in many other mining regions of the time. There are no hot springs under Leadville, although the disaster I've described could have happened at other mining districts. I've slightly altered the exact dates of Tony Pastor's theatre opening and Geronimo's incarceration and war with the white man, in deference to the needs of my story.

Otherwise it could have happened exactly this way. And, who knows? Perhaps, it did . . .

Cathy Cash Spellman
Westport, Connecticut